Rio '71

BLOOD OF EMPIRES
Trilogy - Volume I
A NOVEL

D1522669

JOHN LAWRENCE BURKS

John Burks

xulon PRESS

JOHN 5:39

www.xulonpress.com

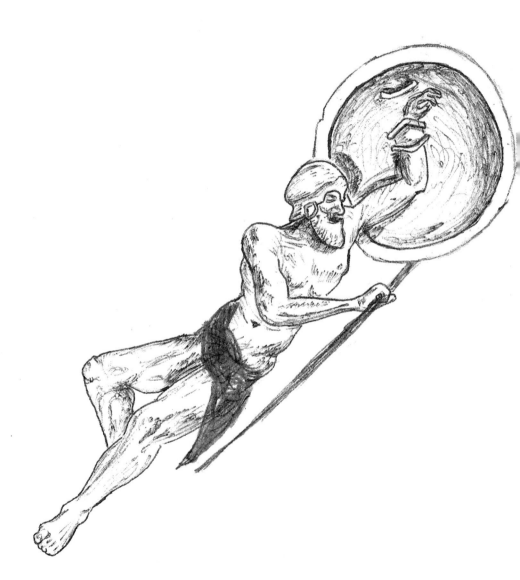

PROLOGUE

Rome – Sunset on the 1st day of September (the 9th month as adopted by Julius Caesar's Julian Calendar and the 2nd year of Rome's Adoptive Emperor, Marcus Ulpius Traianus Trajan. Sixty-seven years since the crucifixion of Jesus of Nazareth. (100 AD)

"Every man is the architect of his own future."   Sallust, Roman Historian

Midnight is approaching in a few hours. Once it arrives, I will turn 91 years of age; and the 130th Actium Era commences. I sit here in Rome in a city jail with bars at the top of my cell looking out at the street level of the *Forum Romanum*. A Praetorian Guard is standing watch outside the iron door, and I count two more guarding out in the street near my window. Sitting with me in my cell is my faithful scribe quickly penning my words onto papyrus. Tonight is the last night of my life in this world; and I have only tonight and part of tomorrow to dictate my experiences from age 10 until 24 when I experienced the most momentous day in history: the crushing of heaven's greatest treasure, the crucifixion of Jesus of Nazareth.

I hope that this story will be finished before I am tabled for execution in the *Amphitheatrum Flavium/Colosseum* sometime in the afternoon break period of combat shows where many spectators leave for the bathhouses for a swim or a late meal. My Roman name is Venustus Vetallus, but my friends called me Venu.

I will begin my story on this date, 81 years ago, with the onset of my 10th birthdate. It was also the commencement of the 50th Actium Era, the most excellent holiday in the Roman Empire. The Actium Era is the date of the

Battle of Actium, the adopted date for the end of the Roman Republic and the birth of the Empire.

Just a note to the reader, I will tell all that I remember from the eyes of a 90-year-old man, not a 10-year-old boy. It is true that I was not an average child at age 10 but one with a very inquisitive mind. I still remember all the smallest of details. Before we begin, please remember that entire day of the 50th Actium is still rooted deeply in the recesses of my mind stored away in its own locked-away chamber complete with fiendish mosaic floors and hideous murals on the walls. Yes, it is essential to understand at age 10 I did not have the vocabulary to express all that I will share now at the end of my life. Therefore, my words and descriptions that I will be dictating to my scribe are not those of a child but of a seasoned adult.

I would like to start with the moment I woke up on that day long ago, but I shall first begin in the middle of that day before my morning awakening in my room when my *mater* touched me and whispered for me to arise.

Oddly enough, I wish to start with the unbearable heat of that day. Near the middle of that day, the air was scalding hot. By noontime the temperature reached its highest intensity once the sun was standing straight above the city of Rome. Without a doubt, it was the most unbearable concentration of deep humid *estrus* (or heat) I have ever experienced in my long 90 years.

Rome – Noon on the 2nd day of September (the 9th month as adopted by Julius Caesar's Julian Calendar) in the 5th year of Emperor Tiberius and 50 years after the Battle of Actium.   *(September 2, 19 AD)*

There are seven problems with Rome: no reverence; no obedience; no sobriety; no cleanness in all human affairs; no sacred rite of marriage; no honor to parents; and no respect for elders.   Flavius Josephus

It was now the middle of the day; and the sun was bearing down like a giant, iron blast furnace making everything incredibly hot. Even the heat from the pavement stones was penetrating through my leather sandals into the soles of my feet. My legs ached from hours of running, and I shook from exhaustion like a sheet of papyrus desiccating in the wind. The only relief came from my wet tunic, which was quickly drying in the scorching, hellish temperature. I began moving my feet towards the *Statilius Taurus Amphitheater,* seeking only shade. This was the largest and first stone-wood amphitheater in Rome, built in the center of the *Campus Martius* one year after the Battle of Actium and now showing its age.

Once I reached the *Statilius Taurus,* I felt strangely alone, even with people walking and standing around this somewhat ugly but intimidating, lofty structure. I entered one of the arched tunnels that ran under the many tiers of seats, funneling down to ground level where the arena stood. Tens of thousands of spectators were crowded into every available space not even noticing the extreme heat, but instead they were all entranced upon what was happening on the sand-covered arena.

I was not supposed to be there, according to my *mater's* mandate; but I needed to know if my father was inside watching the games. I also needed shade. If I found any inside this monstrosity, I could have easily remained hidden for the rest of the day among the crowd of 50,000 spectators watching pairs of gladiators trying to kill one another. Once inside, I discovered the arena floor was actually situated a little below the street level, perhaps by 10 feet. There were many stairs and tunnels to traverse to whatever upper levels one found comfortable. The amphitheater was overflowing with spectators and voyeurs leaving no space available except standing room only. I was able to squeeze to a rail at the lowest level of the arena, and my eyes witnessed two men battling on the sand. This was my first experience of such a sight. As I watched, my stomach felt tight; and my chest began pounding. Sensing that what I was experiencing was wrong, I knew the better choice would be to turn around and leave; but I did not.

Instead of leaving what I knew to be forbidden to me, I moved my eyes up the tiers of seats towards the top of the amphitheater. It was then I realized this structure looked like an enormous open conduit, narrowing down to the red-colored sand that mockingly masked each spot where a man had died this morning after his life's fluids had drained from their horrible wounds. If the red-colored powder sand were designed to hide the marks of bloody deaths, then two realities jumped out of my inquisitive mind. First, men had been fighting each other for many hours before I had arrived. Second, the arena became a metaphor for all the struggles we all fight throughout our lives. The red-colored sand symbolized, in one simple picture, all the little tricks our minds play by throwing up a myriad of fallacies, which help us hide from the truth. Is it not true that at times we all deceive ourselves on purpose? Almost moment by moment, our minds trick us from concerning ourselves with the horrors that are always staring at us. Do we not camouflage all painful thoughts such as the idea we are all going to die someday and what can we expect after death?

The only shade I saw was an awning called a *velarium.* It flapped in the breeze over the seating on the far side of the cone-shaped construction, where the patricians, senators, and even Emperor Tiberius sat. Seated with the emperor in his own private box, situated slightly above the floor of the arena, were two men and a woman in regal foreign robes. Above them in the senatorial section were many women dressed in the finest garments Rome had to offer. I found my eyes riveted to the sovereign of Rome although I had never seen him before this moment. I could not believe I was actually looking at Emperor Tiberius sitting amid senators, distinguished guests, and all the other wealthy Romans, all situated in their own personal sections appearing as nothing more than a mass of insincere sycophants. With my eyes staring at Tiberius, I saw a contradiction to what I expected. On one hand, the emperor looked illustrious and somewhat distinguished; but on the flip side of the coin, he appeared utterly ridiculous. The very nature of what I saw was nothing but pure antipode (or opposition) to what he should have been. His personal features were in such contrast to his clothing and setting, I would have laughed if I had not been so hot and tired. It is best to say Tiberius did not match his pomp and circumstances. His bright purple robes and golden crown did not hide what anyone could see on closer inspection. The ruler of the Roman Empire appeared gaunt, angry, and unhappy. He was round-shouldered, thin-lipped, and slouching in his elevated, white-marble chair. His hair was gray and sparse beneath a polished golden spiked crown, which intended to make him appear as if rays of light were shining from his head. The spiked crown was part of the emperor-divinity-cult that had started in Rome with Julius Caesar.

In retrospect, I realized that Tiberius was unable to hide the scabs on his face along with several open and draining sores. His face alone was disconcerting, to say the least. It seemed hard to believe people took him seriously as a living avatar. He looked more like a diseased corpse under a god's curse rather than a happy, healthy deity. Yet, many explained this away because he did not have Caesar's blood coursing through his veins; an arranged adoption provided him with Augustus's legal inheritance. This was the only weakness in his emperor divinity claim. On top of this shame, Tiberius long ago wed Augustus's daughter in order to provide some sense of legitimacy to Augustus's bloodline. However, anyone who had Julius Caesar's blood streaming in his veins could possibly topple Tiberius. This obscure detail is vital to my starting this story on my tenth birthday, all because of my father's stratagems to acquire the throne for himself, which led needlessly to the murder of my mother only a few hours earlier and many other innocents who were cheated of life in this world with an early departure.

My eyes went back down to the floor of the red-sand arena. What pulled my eyes away from the emperor was a sound of pain that whimpered its way up to me, which seemed to stir the hot air around my head. The moans were coming from a dark-skinned Nubian. His frightened pain had pulled thousands of eyes upon him; but instead of sympathy or empathy, the spectators seemed to relish against him with a cruel, feverish excitement. Circling the wounded Nubian was a light-skinned Barbarian. The pallid and colorless Barbarian had to be Marius, Rome's most famous gladiator. He was much shorter than I had imagined. His bare arms and legs showed pronounced muscular strength as well as many purple and white, worm-looking scars. Besides slowly stalking around the Nubian, Marius would systematically strike out with a sword thrust towards the dark-skinned warrior. There was blood already covering the Nubian's right arm, which must have led to the first cry of pain that stirred the crowd's attention. Thousands cheered again when Marius lunged with a deeper thrust at his opponent with his short, double-edged sword. The black man's three-pronged, razor-sharp, bronze-tipped trident quickly blocked the sword with a downward thrust. When the Nubian stepped back while throwing a net full of iron fish hooks towards Marius's head, the crowd hissed against the wounded black man's efforts to beat their champion. With a quick sidestep, Marius ducked the deadly trap; and the net landed in a useless heap on the red sand. Now the crowd went wild with ecstatic cheers, which went silent in my mind as everything appeared in a blur. Marius began to execute his signature move. With lightning swiftness, Marius faked his hips one way and then charged off the other foot towards the black gladiator, driving his shoulder into his opponent's legs. Both men went down in a pile of flesh, sweat, and red dust. Those who were not standing rose to their feet and screamed with an ear-shattering thunder when Marius used his diving momentum to reverse his crash into a graceful backflip, landing on his feet behind the downed Nubian. During the flip, Marius's sword struck backward like a striking snake and slashed open the black gladiator's left calf as he was trying to rise from his knees. I learned a great lesson at that moment. Always go forward in a fight, and never allow your opponent to force you into a position of only protecting yourself. In the future, I would fight Marius at least four times; and I believe I am the only living person who ever bested this great gladiator, only because I knew his one and only tactic – hit hard and fast. To win, I used his own tactic against him, without his ever knowing I watched him at the age of ten. I should explain that, on this day, I was just a boy; and Marius, a man, although in reality, he was perhaps eight years older. On this blistering day, there was no idea in my head that I would become just as lethal as this legendary gladiator.

Marius held up his arms showing the spectators his super awe-like qualities. His barbaric behavior was ruthless and merciless. I grieved for the injured combatant. His trauma and suffering became mine, and tears began to stream down my cheeks. The black net-man got to his feet very slowly and could only hop on his one good leg using his trident as a crutch. I took my eyes off his pain and counted the many dark spots on the red sand. Before I had counted 50 blood spots, my nose detected the scent of sweet flowers, which seemed strange and out of place. I looked for the flowers but instead noticed a single long pipe with many nozzles stretching around the arena just below the top stone wall; the pipe was spraying an invisible perfume mist around the entire amphitheater. I concluded this was intended to block the odor of blood and other unpleasant stinks emitted during each death struggle. Across the arena in a somewhat hidden pit was a woman in blue playing a water organ. There were others in this orchestra pit just under the emperor's box. Accompanying her were a couple of flutists; several men playing horns, drums, pan pipes, and cymbals; and a young boy with a lyre – all playing heart-throbbing music to match the action of the gladiators. The crowd's behavior had taken on a shared and fanatical state driven by the evil excitement of watching the death of other humans all accompanied by music. I began to hate what I was experiencing and remembered my mother's warning: "Mark my words; you will never be the same if you attend a gladiator fight." She was right with her wisdom, which I had not heeded. Now, at my ancient age, I realized she only wanted to protect me against this iniquitous form of malignant ghoulishness.

I glanced across the spotted arena into the senatorial section. I wondered what I would be doing right now if my father had not sent me back to the villa this morning. With this thought in my mind, I spotted my father for the first time as he stood a few rows above the private box of the emperor. He was screaming for the death of the Nubian with the same chant of the thousands that rocked every level above the fighting ring. In an extraordinary moment, something struck me as out of place. I looked for Lentulus, my father's faithful bodyguard; but he was not to be seen. However, little did I know at the time, although Lentulus was missing, all of my future enemies were present, including Marius the gladiator.

Ironically, three of my future adversaries were sitting together in Tiberius's box, just below my father. One was a woman of spectacular beauty who I later learned was Herodias, the new wife of Herod Antipas, the Tetrarch of Galilee and Peraea in *Palestina*. The second nemesis was her husband, Herod Antipas; and the third was Antipas's bodyguard, a man just named Saben. Much will be said about these three later, but for now it is essential to understand that Herod Antipas had only one ambition in life. His ultimate desire was to become King of the Jews just as his father Herod the Great had been. The title he envisioned for himself had been vacant for 23 years ever since the death of his father, Herod the Great. I would later learn that Herod Antipas just that morning had scandalously stolen Herodias from his half-brother Philip, the Philip who lived in Rome. Herodias divorced Philip to marry her brother-in-law and uncle, Herod Antipas, which occurred just before the games had commenced this morning. Being the personal guest of Tiberius was a wedding gift from the Emperor of Rome. After Herod the Great had departed this world, Herod Antipas's half-brother, Philip of Rome, did not receive any province to rule. All he received was a large sum of coins; and Philip decided to live in Rome, where he held the coveted prize of Roman citizenship. He had only been married to his niece for a short time. Unfortunate for him, his half-brother made a visit to Rome a few years earlier; and just this morning that unscrupulous brother pilfered Philip's wife for himself. Apparently, the rich and powerful lived by different rules than the rest of Rome's citizens. I still remember Herod Antipas sitting smugly in the imperial box with his beautiful niece-wife Herodias, who herself was the granddaughter of Herod the Great. She was remarkably attractive on the outside, but I would later learn this only masked her inner corruption. She was a contradiction to most who knew her; and in my assessment, this woman was rotten to the core, more morally diseased than her new husband-uncle sitting next to her; and that is not saying much for her. This woman, in a little over a decade from this day, would be the primary influence that resulted in the beheading of a holy man called John the Baptist, perhaps one of history's most remarkable men to walk this earth. There are many other despicable deeds she engaged in, which I will wait to reveal later when appropriate. Herod's brother and now ex-husband to Herodias, Philip of Rome, apparently was not present on this day and never became an enemy to me. Actually, I never laid eyes on Philip of Rome; and I am not able to comment on his character in any manner.

The last of my future antagonists was sitting above the imperial box, only one row above my father and a little to his left. There, looking rather bored, was a little boy about my age. He was not standing and cheering for Marius the Gladiator but looking somewhat jaded and not interested in anything. He was a handsome fellow wearing a senatorial tunic like mine and did not look at all like the person he turned out to be in just a few years. Little did I know this boy would grow up to become one of the most treacherous humans to threaten my life, causing me more misery other than what my father's wife Claudia had perpetrated against me earlier this morning. Yet, this little boy sitting above my father did not appear to be the insidious person he was to become. On this sweltering *diurnal* of days, he seemed to be innocent, disengaged, and completely harmless.

Still, at the rail of the arena, my gaze dropped upon my *patra*; and I tried to understand his betrayal to my mother and me. I thought he had to be drugged out of his senses when I noticed him lifting the skin of wine and gall to his mouth as an ear-shattering roar washed over the stadium. Looking back towards the sand-covered arena, I witnessed Marius plunging his short double-edged sword into the wounded fighter's chest. This image caused my strength to give, and I fell to my knees. What took only a fraction of a second seemed to last much longer as my mind tried to process all that I had witnessed. The people in mass were jumping and lifting hands in cheers for Marius. I fought to get up so I would not be crushed. Instead, I was knocked down twice while people rushed to the rail to see the final moments of the mortally wounded gladiator. The dying gladiator dropped his trident-crutch and placed both his hands over his eyes. It was common knowledge by all Romans that Julius Caesar and Pompey the Great both covered their heads with their robes while they were being assassinated. Perhaps it was to hide the horrid moment of their own fear of death from the eyes of those who had struck the killing blow and to any other onlookers. I heard a sad *trepidus* (or fearful cry) uttered by the Nubian and then a second thrust-thud of Marius's sword to his victim's left thigh, just below his groin. The crowd of thousands lapsed into an ecstatic scream as they witnessed the Nubian's death cry.

All I wanted to do was escape. I began pushing through the crowd towards the tunnel that led back to the outside world. I placed my hands to my ears to shut out the piercing screams while I moved and weaved around the slow-moving bodies. I was unable to tolerate anymore and sought only the light at the end of the tunnel. I ran; but before reaching the exit, I blindly collided into an *amphora* that was as tall as I; it was filled with red wine, and we both crashed to the ground in the arched entrance. The huge clay bottle exploded violently under me, and the liquid gushed like my very own life-blood through the tunnel forcing back the crowd crushing in from the street. I got to my feet with my tunic stained red. The angry wine-seller knocked me onto the wet concrete floor. Suddenly a blow came from nowhere hitting me on the side of the head. I rolled away to avoid the seller's kicks and slaps and ran into the street receiving a few more blows from some of the spectators splashed by the wine.

I finally escaped from the forum area to a fountain. It was at this fountain that I thought my life was to end. From behind me, an invisible hand grasped the neck of my tunic. The unknown grip held me tightly, trapping me.

A READING GIVEN AT THE GREAT LIBRARY OF ALEXANDRIA BY EPAPHRODITUS

The following lecture was given in the year of the four emperors. During this year of civil war, a great fire broke out on in Rome on Capitoline Hill, destroying much of Rome's archives. Due to this loss, the scholars of Alexandria's Great Library requisitioned anyone with past knowledge to recreate the history of Rome. 69 AD

ONLY ONE SUN RULES THE DAY – NOT TWO THE ORIGINS OF AN OUTLAW RELIGION

From birth, we live out a mystery called life filled with every facet of experience imaginable. It is only when we come near the end of this life that we actually understand although we comprehend dimly, like a cloud of white-hot smoke dissipating on a breezy day.

At the beginning of life, we soon learn each day slowly ebbs and flows like the tides with our asking only one question: "What will this day give me?" Once we leave the innocence of childhood, our rational will and responsibilities change our views of this life. The most significant change is when we realize each day blurs into another leaving us to ponder, "What will I do with this day?" From that point forward, life becomes a long series of choices and tasks that seldom entirely end. One thing we try not to think about is the last day we must all face – death. We push aside that idea, the thought of our own demise; yet, it always looms on the horizon of our existence and experiences.

Before the coming of that final day, how do we explain all the myriad of events that happen to us each and every day? Our moment-by-moment decisions, whether they be minor or major, construct our quality of being. Still, in our humanity, we must face three poignant questions: First, where did we come from? Second, what are we supposed to do? Finally, what is next? It may appear we unconsciously suppress these questions with the many "things" we do to avoid answering. By not addressing these three queries, we risk the barrenness of a busy life. All the seemingly minor deeds, whether good or bad, swirl around and ultimately shape who we are. Therefore, the collections of all we think or do brand us like galactic slaves. The prospect of a divine, final evaluation of our beliefs and acts, whether it be praise or condemnation, is sobering and makes every aspect of our lives genuinely meaningful. The notion of judgment gives meaning and direction to our hearts and minds; yet, that idea cannot be seen except through the eyes of faith. At the twilight of our years, if we reach that far, we finally consider, "Where have the days gone?" Facts plus faith equal knowledge. Correct facts plus correct faith equal truth. Life is that simple and that hard. When the puzzle before us is finally put together without force and what we see makes flawless sense, then we know we have discovered the elusive answer to life. Many centuries ago Alexander the Invincible from Macedonia, the greatest general to have ever lived, was chronicled to have devised the uncomplicated statement, "Only one sun rules the day – not two." Almost four hundred years after Alexander's death, this verity erupted into the greatest spiritual battle that determined who would indeed rule eternity. The outcome changed and influenced humankind, on earth and in the heavens forever. Never was a battle more fiercely waged. It started on a beautiful spring Passover Day in Judaea when the Roman Empire was introduced to a man who did not repudiate the claim made by others that he was a king. Rome initially decided that this so-called king was not a threat to Rome, believing he was nothing but a sun-dried Jew spouting words no one could understand. When it was revealed that he was in the lineage of the Judean kings from the distant past, way beyond the memory of anyone living, it became painfully evident that this apparently harmless king was indeed a future threat to Rome just like the Jewish leaders who clamored for his death believed. The only logical and diplomatic solution for Rome was to keep status quo with the Jewish leaders. Rome felt its only option was to crucify this humble man on a wooden cross. Outside the northern walls of Jerusalem, a few hours after sunrise, a crucifixion occurred on a knob of a hill called Calvarius in Latin. Rome carried out this cruel act of punishment, allowing this perplexing and enigmatic Jew to die wearing only a derisive and scornful cap of thorns upon his gory and scourged head. A titulus nailed over this crown of mockery proclaimed his pseudo crime in Latin, Greek, and Aramaic: **Jesus of Nazareth, King of the Jews.**

"INTRODUCTIO"

I witnessed two empires in their infancy both born in blood: one spilling; the other, shedding. This is my account of how, as a child becoming a young man, I inadvertently befell this cataclysmic collision of two kingdoms. My heart's desire had always been to record this extraordinary and unique tale of my life and how I witnessed these two empires eventually clashing in the ancient city of Jerusalem, paradoxically known as the City of Peace. My most extraordinary tale begins on my tenth birthday, the second day of September, ironically the same date tomorrow when I am slated by Rome to die, making it my 91st birthday.

There is plenty of oil in the lamp on a small table in my cell located in the city of my birth, Rome. My scribe sits across from me in the eerie glow of torches out beyond the iron bars of my Roman cell. My scribe is only a few years younger than I, and I wonder if I should be penning this story myself. Resting next to his stool are many rolls of papyrus, an ink device called a gimbal, several alabaster bottles of Indian ink, and many pens to complete this monumental task.

I shall start at the end. Tomorrow I die at the Colosseum. I will die in a monument to killing, which was ironically financed by looted gold and treasure taken out of the ashes of the Jewish Temple in Jerusalem, which was utterly destroyed by Roman soldiers under General Titus, who himself would later become Emperor and High Priest of Rome. Little did the Romans understand thirty-seven plus years after the death of the man on the cross that they had actually lost this celestial war. On the day the Roman General Titus watched in horror, little did he know a prophecy given by the prophet

Daniel was being fulfilled as his disobedient troops destroyed the Temple on the 9th day of the Jewish month of Ab. This villainous date now stands as the exact day, 624 years earlier, when the Babylonian Nebuchadnezzar destroyed the Jews' first temple.

As I begin my story, I want to set the record straight before I am executed in a few short hours. My own crimes as a citizen of Rome are enormous and dark. I should state that I deserve to die tomorrow, according to Rome's laws. However, I will die not for the crimes that I have committed against my fellow man or the Empire but because of the man I will not disavow – the Promised Redeemer, who died naked on that cross in Jerusalem, now 67 years ago.

Two things are important to understand about my tenth 10th birthday, the day this tale starts. One, it was the first time I learned of the Promised Redeemer. Second, that day was the day that changed the way I viewed life. It was the last day I awoke thinking like a child. Before that day ended, I would never ask again, "What will this day give me?" It was also my final day as a pampered and privileged Roman child – not that I became a man that day, but my childhood was forever crushed. What led to my loss of innocence on that day was the terminal hours of my mother's life. To say, "A day is what happens after your plans are made," might be the defining maxim in describing the start of this story because my quondam concern that morning was to go with my father somewhere special for my birthday celebration. How the next hours ended was a dramatic contrast to how they started.

JOHN LAWRENCE BURKS

BOOK I

WHERE DID WE COME FROM?

PART ONE

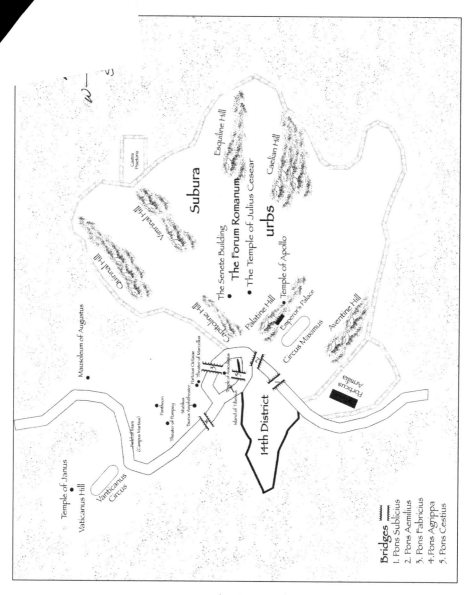

ROME (19 - 33 A. D.)

CHAPTER ONE

Rome – Villa of Gaius Metallus Crassus. Six hours earlier, just after sunrise, on the 2nd day of September (the 9th month as adopted by Julius Caesar's Julian Calendar) in the 5th year of Tiberius Claudius Nero, or just Emperor Tiberius, 50 years after the Battle of Actium.   *(September 2, 19 AD)*

When I was a child I spoke as a child, I understood as a child, I thought as a child: but when I became a man, I put away childish things.Saul of Tarsus

O n the morning of my tenth birthday my *mater* referred to me as her Little Soldier. Hardly did I know this was going to be my last morning waking up in this room listening to the far-off cock crowing somewhere in the dark valleys of Rome. After the crowing had stopped, I would drift back to sleep until the darkness was slowly replaced by the incoming light from the eastern sky. After my mother had told me to rise and called me by her view of me in the future, I vividly remember my mother's gentle touch and soothing words that brought me out of my dream world to what most would agree is the material world. At the start of that day, it first appeared like any other, except beyond the physical reality I still vividly remember feeling a static presence in the air – a crisp energy giving off an unusual quality. These feelings proved to be truthful heralds of what was to come before this day ended.

My tenth birthday began almost prophetically after a violent night storm hammered the Imperial City. The disturbance had taken most of the nocturnal period to pass; but before daybreak, the storm was over, and the sky was now a bright and brilliant blue. I lived in my own small room in my father's extensive villa located on Equestrian Hill, the adjacent hill to the Palatine, where all the emperors lived and played. Between the two hills lie the *Urbs* and the *Forum Romanum* where Julius Caesar's temple stands and the Senate meets. Most Romans think this is where the center of the world prevails. I awoke to a gentle kiss on my forehead completely unsuspecting the horrendous trauma that was about to occur. I later learned my mother was aware of some of the inauspicious events planned but certainly not of her death. I still believe my mother's murder was a spontaneous mishap perpetrated by my father's legal wife, Claudia Pulchra. All the evidence points to my father's innocence in the death of my mother, for I believe he planned to sell her to a wealthy merchant friend who lived in the city of Ephesus, across the Great Sea. Claudia Pulchra was the instigator behind the vicious events that were to unfold on what started as a beautiful and not-so-hot morning.

After my mother kissed my forehead, she whispered, "Up and about, my Little Soldier. Today is your birthday." Her words sounded like a confirmed fact that was as solid as the stones that held up the Circus Maximus. All I could focus on was she had called me "her little soldier." A term of endearment that she had never used before, but a prophetic statement, nonetheless. The feel of her hand on my shoulder was as gentle as a hand arranging a bouquet of flowers. With a second kiss, a second soft touch, and her soothing voice, she coaxed me from my sleep. "Little One, wake up. You have a busy day ahead of you," she recited with a smile.

I was still a child at this time, but the ensuing events aged my perceptions way beyond my years. Honestly, my childhood ended that day; and adulthood came upon me like a horrific nightmare from the deepest pits of Hades. Over the years I have reviewed the last few moments with my mother on that morning, and I still can smell her freshly washed hair and feel her smooth skin against my forehead as she kissed me from my sleep. Perhaps people glorify their loved ones beyond reality after they have departed this life. I do not think this is the case with my beloved and kind *mater*.

Once I rubbed my eyes, I smiled up at her. At that innocent age, I experienced a wonder to life as the moments of a new day unrolled like a scroll into fresh discoveries of incomprehensible and awe-inspiring things. Now, 81 years later as an old man, I awake with painful memories wishing I could find not just more time to sleep but the ability to even slumber. At my old age, my thoughts invade each day like wild animals wanting to devour me. There are just so many things to be accomplished, but my time and energy are running out like the last sands through an hourglass. Time seems different now that I am looking back and not forward. In some ways it is like crossing the Alps; the mountains look one way going up and quite another when you gaze back to where you have been. Being alive seems to pass more quickly as you get older. I always imagined that, when I was old, my days would be dull and pedestrian; yet, I could not have been more mistaken. They are just more arduous, and time is like water passing through my hands.

"Hurry and dress," said Arena, a name I never used; I only called her *Mater*. She had a striking comeliness about her on the surface as well as from within. Now that I am an old man, I remember her beauty was beyond any woman, something I did not really see or understand as a small boy. She had hair the color of honey, skin of silk, and eyes of creamy blue like the sky near the horizon on a cloudless summer day after a night of rain. Although she wore the ordinary robes of a slave, she never appeared as one. Her form was delicate and always radiating a beautiful smile. As a child, I did not correctly understand her status in my father's home. Perhaps I did not want to. I realized that she was a slave, but I did not realize that she was more of a mistress to my wealthy senatorial father. She worked as a house slave but at times served as one of many concubines my father kept at each of his many villas scattered throughout the lands of the *Mare Internum* (or the Mediterranean Sea), the area known only as the inner boundary of the Lake Empire.

There are three ways to become a slave in the Roman Empire: those born into slavery, captives taken in military campaigns, and people unfortunate enough not able to pay their debts. Born, captured, or sold, these three conditions describe over half the population of Rome and her vast Empire. My mother fell into the third category, a victim of her father's indebtedness to his taxes. She had been born free but into poverty in the Macedonian city of Philippi. On the outskirts of this town was the famed site of the battle between the armies of Octavius and the old retired soldiers of Pompey, gathered by Brutus and Cassius after Caius Julius Caesar was assassinated. Brutus and Cassius wanted to defend their savage act of murdering a dictator at the *Theater of Pompey*. Their justification was Caesar had become a threat to the Republic. Sixty senators, a little over a half century before I was born, had supposedly planned to plunge daggers into Caesar's body when, in actuality, only half that number participated in the nefarious deed. This act in the *Theater of Pompey* in Rome set the stage for two long, bloody civil wars. In the end, the Republic died; and the Empire was born under the control of a young Gaius Octavius, the son of Caesar's niece, who changed his birth name to Augustus Caesar. The new dictator took control of Rome's government as Eternal Consul; and the slain martyr, Julius Caesar, was deified. Caesar's subsequent lineages were now the bloodline of gods. This is why Octavius had ordered the son of Caesar and Cleopatra slain after Actium, to prevent Caesar's son growing up and claiming a grander divinity above someone just being a grandnephew.

How my father acquired my mother as a slave I never really knew. All I ever learned was that my father was a young military tribune, had been garrisoned at Philippi, and served Rome's legions about thirty-four solar years after the Battle of Philippi. My mother was purchased in Philippi as a child, sold by her father to pay his imperial taxes for that year and some bottles of wine. For a slave, life under the Republic was no different than it was under the Empire. It was servitude and drudgery no matter what system controlled the world. Slavery was an unsavory institution that treated humans as animals. Since my mother was a slave, I, too, was a slave at birth. That status changed after my father redeemed me by adoption shortly after I was born. My father was a Roman Senator and the master of my mother. He was perhaps the richest man in the world besides Caesar or Augustus. Ironically, I was the product of this union: the son of a lowly, powerless slave and a Roman Senator of unimaginable wealth and power. This was both my blessing and my curse; but, ultimately, it was my mother's situation as a slave that provided my identity and eventual freedom. In the end, the strange legacy of my life would be how the lineage of being a slave actually liberated me and gave me true life.

My father brought my mother to Rome to be groomed as a future concubine after his time with the legions ended; and 20 years later, I was born. During that interval Gaius Vetallus Crassus launched his career in business and took his place as a senator, an honor assured him at birth. My father wiped away my stain of bastardy by officially adopting me, freeing me from slavery and ultimately giving me the Senatorial birthright, even though my mother had never been considered his official wife. In the same way, Julius Caesar adopted his grandnephew Octavius, who had become Rome's first emperor. Octavius had likewise adopted his third wife's son from a previous marriage. That son was now Emperor Tiberius. Through adoption, Augustus gave the young boy the right to become the next emperor and god after Augustus died. The adoption of Tiberius also placed him as part of the Julian Dynasty, even though Tiberius was not from Augustus's loins. For me, there was no limit to my future as my father's eldest legitimate and biological son. Little did I know at the start of my tenth birthday that my adoption was in actuality a curse. It was the bloodline of Claudia Pulchra that made all the difference between my half-brother and me. This half-sibling was Julius Vetallus Varus, who was born a year earlier to my father's legal wife, Claudia Pulchra Vetallus Varus. When Julius became of age, my career as a senator would have already been launched;

so I considered that I had no fears regarding this infant. The only person I feared at the age of ten was Claudia Pulchra, especially concerning my mother. I was to discover many years later that Claudia had married my father on the anniversary of the 48ᵗʰ Actium, and that is when everything began to change such as the quiet disappearance of my father's house mistresses. In my innocence, I believed my mother had protection because I was my father's eldest son. However, today I see my folly just as clearly as I see my faithful scribe writing these very words I am dictating in my gloomy underground jail cell.

As I woke up but still in my bed, my mother now said to me, "Your father is waiting in the atrium near the *vestibulum*. He is taking you with him today." Her gentle voice and loving smile gave me great peace and hope for the future. I dismissed her apparent sadness. She must have sensed there was going to be a disruption; and my father and Claudia would be at the center of this figurative, encroaching storm. I noticed she also seemed distracted, staring at some invisible landscape that only she could behold. I remembered each detail of her in my room as if it happened just an hour ago. It was in its own manner a particularly significant day, one that I never forgot. It was the last day of my youth, forever etched on the tablets of my heart as well as my mind. I can still sense the smells, the temperature, and the start of a heated dampness in the air. I believe great trauma imprints our memories, much as a painting forever captures its moment in time. Those memories are like the hardening of molten tin and copper in terra-cotta molds, transforming the two soft metals into a new, harder man-made metal called bronze. I can vividly recall the new tunic my mother held in her hands for me to wear. It had a fresh, clean smell and was snowy-white with a broad purple stripe running from the neck to the hem, the same type of tunic all senators wore beneath their white wool and purple-edged togas. I had never worn such a splendid tunic. I was hesitant about putting it on, for only senators could wear the purple. Imperial sumptuary laws governed the types of clothes one could or could not wear. Only someone with Roman citizenship could wear a toga, which was highly coveted by non-citizens and a symbol that even controlled entrance into all imperial amphitheaters, circuses, and bathhouses. Violations of this rule made by the Senate resulted in severe punishments of various types, including crucifixion.

"Your father wants you to wear this tunic since you will be with him today for the first time in public," said Arena sensing my hesitation.

"Do you know where *Pater* is taking me this morning?"

"Let your father show you off, and he will be very proud of you," my mother replied apparently evading my question; perhaps she did not know our destination.

Senator Gaius Vetallus was clearly the wealthiest and most notorious nobleman in the Roman world. Many called him Crassus, named after the richest man who had ever lived in Rome and who died fighting the Surean clan of the Parthians at the Battle of Carrhae on the far side of the Euphrates River. My father had inherited a vast fortune from his father and used it to purchase his way to the top of the economic world by shrewd investments and financial manipulations. He controlled shipping companies throughout the Empire as well as most of the slave trading at Delos, an ancient slave market island, located in the center of the Aegean Sea. All slaves according to imperial protocol had to pass through Delos, and this was the Greek origin of the word for a slave: *doulos*. My father received a portion from each human soul destined for a life of servitude or *servire*. Each *doulos's* soul sold at Delos provided Gaius Vetallus a life of opulent splendor, unfathomable luxury, and unlimited access to power. At the age of ten, I never thoroughly comprehended the tragedy of exploitation that came from the unsavory institution of human degradation. It would become painfully apparent after I became an adult.

My father also controlled most of the copper mining pits and foundries in Iberia, the tin trade in Asia, and almost all the gold veins beyond Cyrenaica. He also owned and managed the largest grain *latifundium* (or plantation) extending from Rome to Brundisium that stood on both sides between the spine of the Apennines and the Appian Way. He bought, sold, and deposited commodities and personal lives as some men taste cured olives and old wines. Many Romans openly declared that my father had been assigned a tutelary deity at birth that enabled him to survive any attack or wrong decision made. This was based on an old Roman belief of the *genius* or *jinni* spirit that some people received at birth, guiding them throughout their lives. Multiple companies and businesses bore the name **Vetallus**, making it a well-known name throughout the entire Roman world. His colossal fortune, along with his personal driving force in the Roman Senate, assured his place as one of the most powerful and feared men in the Roman Empire, just a few steps behind the most powerful man on earth, the Emperor himself. My father's unbridled ambition to gain control of the world set my course for the rest of my life. I later learned, no matter how peculiar this may sound, I was the only obstacle, even at the young age of ten, to my father's final and ultimate goal.

Sitting on the cold flagstones of my bedroom, I placed my new ornate and somewhat ostentatious sandals on my feet and worked the unique white leather laces. Once the white leather sandals were tightly secured, I noticed my mother had been staring at me without her usual smile. She appeared troubled about something.

"I will ask *Pater* if you can come," I said in a child's way of trying to help her cope with whatever was her apparent distress.

"That is impossible. Your father believes little boys must grow up and leave their mothers. Remember to show yourself a well-disciplined son."

"I will be good, but where is he taking me? Do you know?"

My question caused a strange look in her eyes, almost like a passing cloud that briefly blocks the sun. She squatted down to look directly into my eyes, and I could smell her perfume-scented breath mixed with her clean hair as she clutched my hands in hers. With a hushed whisper, she said, "Venustus, I have something that is critical for you to learn; and you must never forget, even when you don't believe."

I sensed my mother's deep passion for telling me something important, and I became somewhat frightened. I had seen this look only once before when she scolded me for stealing fruit from a neighbor's tree. Yet, this apparently was not a scolding, even though her eyes had become very dark and her countenance seemed agitated.

"Venustus, can you hear me?" she whispered.

"Yes, *Mater*, what is it you want to do?" I asked, also in a whisper.

"Not me. It is what I want you to do, my son," she implored while tilting her head as the sorrow on her face intensified. "I learned something as a little girl, and it is something that has sustained me all these years. Someone is coming into the world to correct all that is wrong, a person you must trust; and I want you to follow him when he comes. I know this is hard to believe; but the gods of the Greeks, Romans, Egyptians, and even the Barbarians are false. Do you hear me? Also, the Vestal Virgins, who serve Vesta, are spurious and not real. Julius Caesar is not a god, even though you have seen his temple in the *Forum*. There is no Janus, Jupiter, Venus, Minerva, or any other god or goddess. Sol from the East is also false. They are all fake and false imaginations of men's minds."

I had no idea what she was talking about, but I acted as if I understood. Silently I nodded my head to indicate that this little secret was our own conspiracy.

My mother glanced towards the door before continuing. "This long-awaited one is alive and lives in the faraway land of Judaea or perhaps *Aigyptos* or as Rome calls Egypt. I have been hearing stories about him since before I was purchased as a slave and brought to Rome by your father. The Jews call him the Redeemer-Messiah, the Anointed One. When you find him, you will discover the greatest treasure in this world. Even if you do not understand what I am saying today, you will later. Never forget. You must promise me to never forget."

I told her, "Yes." When my answer did not seem to satisfy her, I added, "I will go and find him." She smiled and appeared relieved by the mere fact I had faith in what she was telling me.

"There is something else I want you to do."

"What, *Mater*?"

"I want you to regard others as more important than yourself, all the days of your life. Do you understand, Venustus?"

She rarely called me by my given name unless she was angry. She typically called me Venu, like my friends called me. I nodded again, although I was not sure I knew what she was saying. Then she folded me into her arms. I remained a little stiff because I was now at an age when little boys should start becoming men and mothers should not hug them. She understood and wiped her tears with her tunic sleeve as she stood. After a few moments, she seemed to regain her composure and asked me to repeat what she had just said. In a small voice, I repeated what I remembered; and she tutored me with her proverb until I had it memorized. "Regard others as more important than yourself. Regard others as more important than yourself. Regard others as more important than yourself."

"Venustus, this is the greatest gift of wisdom I possess. Please remember it when you think of me. When you find the Teacher, he will tell you all you need to know. I have prayed to the one and only true God that you will find this holy instructor, and I believe you will."

Suddenly I felt I understood her strange behavior, and a deep despondency gripped my heart. I thought that my mother was being disposed of or removed in some way because of Claudia Pulchra Vetallus Varus and that I would not see her again. This was not the first time a slave woman disappeared mysteriously because of this vile woman. This kind of thing had repeated itself almost a dozen times in the last few months. As I have already stated, since my mother was only a slave to my father, her status as a mistress could change at any time. I wanted to ask her about this, but she put her finger to her lips to be silent. She stood cocking her head, listening to something that only she seemed to hear. When she felt we were safe, my mother took her hand from her lips and reached into a pocket from the inside of her slave tunic. From this hidden spot, she brought forth a heavy, round fig cake that fit in the palm of her right hand. "Here is your breakfast. Now you must hurry, and always remember I love you."

I was about to ask her if she was going away when a high-pitched, somewhat forged voice came from the doorway. "Yes, hurry! Your father is waiting!" spewed Claudia Pulchra, who was now leaning on the doorframe where my room opened out into the atrium garden. She was acting as if she had been there all the time listening to our entire intimate conversation. "Do you want him to be angry with you?"

Claudia was considered one of the highest-bred women in Rome with a haunting beauty to match. Yet, in my eyes, her beauty could not be seen. What the world saw was hidden by my knowledge of her heart, almost as if thick Chinese silk conceals a woman's curved figure. Today, Claudia was wearing a mint-green diaphanous *stola* made from the thinnest of Egyptian flax. A silk *palla* of the same color draped like a cape over her shoulders and wrapped around the front concealing what the *stola* did not. High on her head, she wore a massive red wig, ornately plaited and curled. She moved into the room almost in a movement that looked like she was sliding. When she was within a few paces away from my mother, she stopped. Claudia was quite thin like my mother, even though largeness and even obesity were the preferred figures for patrician women in Rome. To be a hefty woman declared openly you were patently and obscenely wealthy. Claudia did not fit the mold in the elaborate amphitheater of norms; but she asserted her power and wealth by the way she walked, dressed, and behaved. As a child, I heard many house slaves behind her back calling her a slang name that was a reference to a female canine. Not wanting to anger my father, I immediately took the fig cake from my mother's hand and began to leave.

"I will see you tonight, my little soldier," said Arena in a soft voice.

I was going to respond; but, instead, Claudia Pulchra's voice boomed in a vicious tone. "Don't lie to the boy! Tell him the truth! Tell him that *Mater* has been sold to a wealthy merchant who lives in Anatolia and that you depart today at noon!"

Arena lifted her hands to her face and began weeping while Claudia released a high-pitched laugh, throwing back her red curls in the process. I froze in shock watching both women in the extremes of emotions. It had to be true. Claudia was getting rid of my mother, and my heart dropped like a rock off a bridge. The scene before me was particularly painful to watch. Here was my *mater* being tortured and humiliated by a few sharpened words from this revolting woman. I felt only contempt towards Claudia, sensing how she enjoyed injuring my *mater*. This perfumed and painted woman seemed enveloped by a thick and dark, repugnant dreadfulness that steered her iniquitous power. A raging anger began rising up within me; yet, my age restrained me. In a sense, I felt powerless in the face of this hideous force. All I could do was hurt her with my words. "You are what all the slaves call you!"

"And what would that be?"

I said the slang word; and my mother scolded me at once by saying, "Venustus, shame on you. Is that thinking of others as more important than yourself?"

I tilted my head almost to the floor and said, "No!" Now I had injured my mother instead of Claudia. "I will deal with all the slaves for that bit of information you little, wet runt! Even if I have to kill every slave in this *domus*, and you will be the cause."

All I had at my disposal was my position; and I pointed my finger at her and cried, "No! You will not get away with this! I am going to tell *Pater*! He will not let this happen! If I were older, you would not treat my *mater* this way in front of me!"

There, I had said it. Claudia responded by grabbing her sides and laughed as if she were at the theater watching one of old Menander's hilarious comedies. When she had expended her explosive show of mirth, she looked at me with a snarl and hissed, "You are nothing but a *mater's* boy! The runt of a dead-end litter." After that declaration, Claudia glanced over at my mother, who was still shaking in her grief. In a quiet but hideous tone, Claudia said, "And I will deal with *Mater* later!" With that threat delivered, Claudia laughed and twirled with her nose in the air and sauntered out the door leaving only the view of the garden behind her. I just stared at the flowering plants, focused on nothing, while a crippling fog drifted through my mind. This numbing mist mysteriously removed the pain in my fractured heart and mind. Something was flowing through my body that was sturdy and durable enough to calm anything that always foiled great shock and that I would later experience many times, especially as a soldier in hand-to-hand combat. In the future, I would learn to accept shock as a halcyon that enabled me to accomplish what others in the same situations could not. "*Manage your fear*" became one of my mottoes for survival. Nevertheless, this morning, still only a child, I did not know what to do because this fear was a strange sensation I had never experienced to such a degree.

Turning towards my mother, I noticed she had stopped her weeping and sadly looked down at me. I wanted to comfort her, but hugging my mother would only mean Claudia was right about me being effeminate in some way.

Instead, I said, "I will speak with *Pater*. You are not going to this faraway land. Claudia just likes to hurt you and me. She hates us, and I do not know why."

"There is a reason for everything. Treasure my words, my son; and this applies to Claudia as well. Remember; think of others as more important than yourself. Calling people names and thinking of them as inferior is the sign of a weak mind and spirit."

I shook my head no, for I could not understand the contradiction of my mother's words: forgive Claudia even though she was a depraved and wicked demon. I did not respond to my *mater* as I began the process of hardening my heart. She was wrong about this selfless creed. I turned and left my room not knowing it would be almost ten long years before I would return to this very place that I called my only safe sanctuary. I did not say, "I love you, *Mater*." Nor did I kiss my mother goodbye. Instead, I marched out of my room as I imagined a hardened, heartless soldier would act. This was how I envisioned myself in the future, and only then would I not fear the likes of Claudia. As I left, I could hear my mother's grief washing over her again. Exactly 81 years later to the precise date, I now wish I could go back and say those four little words – "I love you, *Mater*."

A READING GIVEN AT THE GREAT LIBRARY OF ALEXANDRIA BY EPAPHRODITUS

This lecture was given in the year of the four emperors or the Year of the Four Legates. Soon after Emperor Nero committed suicide, a new civil war began in the Roman Empire, actually the first civil war since the Republic. That last civil war ended after the Battle of Actium, which ushered an end of the Republic and the birth of the Empire.

In the year of the Four Legates, Legate Galba (governor of Hispania) took the throne for seven months after the death of Nero, the last of the Julio-Claudian Dynasty. Galba was executed in the Roman Forum at the base of Capitoline Hill by members of his Praetorian Guard. On that very day, the Roman Senate proclaimed Legate Otho with the name Augustus. During the next three months, Germanium legions proclaimed their governor, Legate Vitellius, as emperor. Vitellius sent half of his army to march on Rome and defeated Legate Otho at the Battle of Bedriacum. Otho committed suicide after he had realized his forces had been defeated. During all of this turmoil, the troops of Syria and Judaea proclaimed their Legate, General Vespasian, as emperor. General Vespasian had been fighting in the Great Jewish Revolt for over two years when his troops proclaimed Vespasian as the next emperor. In response to this declaration, Vespasian relocated his new throne to Alexandria while preparing to send forces taken from Syria and Judaea to secure his bid for the throne in Rome.

Before the Syrian and Judaean troops could be sent, Danubian legions loyal to Vespasian fought Legate Vitellius's legions at the Battle of Cremona. With a victory in this battle and the demise of Emperor Vitellius at this sight, Vespasian was able to return to Rome and end the civil wars.

During this turbulent year of internal fighting, a great fire broke out in Rome and consumed all the significant structures on Capitoline Hill, which destroyed much of Rome's archives. Due to this loss, the scholars and librarians of Alexandria's Great Library requisitioned anyone with past knowledge to recreate the history of Rome and its Empire. Many scholars and others delivered many lectures on the afternoons of the seventh day of each week for about a year after the great fire. A generous fee of 25 denarii was paid to anyone who provided information that could replace any history of Rome. I decided to supplement my financial situation at this time by contributing several lectures. I have chosen a few excerpts from my lecture readings to coincide with this story. 69 AD

THE IMPORTANCE OF THE BATTLE OF ACTIUM AS A MARKER FOR THE END OF THE ROMAN REPUBLIC

Actian Games were instituted by Augustus in honor of the historic battle against the fleet and troops of the Queen of Egypt, Cleopatra, and her Roman lover, Mark Antony. This engagement took place on the western waters north of the Greek city of Patra. This battle anniversary, established by Augustus, marked the birth of the Roman Empire. The Battle of Actium to me was very important, indeed. It marked my passing of years of age since the engagement of Actium occurred exactly 50 years before my birth. Therefore, not only to me but the Battle of Actium is one of the significant markers of time for the Roman Empire. Augustus, the father of the Julio-Claudian Dynasty and first emperor, established Olympic-type sporting events called the Actian Games in honor of this historic action.

The Actian "era" constituted a date on some imperial coins with the battle as year one along with the number of years an emperor had been ruling, giving a double date on such coins. Therefore, a coin minted in the year of my tenth birth date would be 50/5: 50 years since Actium and 5 since Emperor Tiberius became emperor: Tiberius being the next emperor after the death of Augustus Caesar. I should note that some senators tried to substitute Humanus for Augustus. The designation of Augustus was carried over by Tiberius, who chose to abide by the decree issued by the first Augustus that the Augustus title be used by future rulers from his bloodline, including Tiberius, an adopted son. Tiberius being adopted did not have one drop of Augustus's blood flowing in his veins. The godhood deception occurred when Livia, the third wife of Augustus, was given the title of Augusta. It should also be noted that Augustus always stated publicly that he was not Augustus but only the Senatus Consulta. This trickery was almost laughable if it were not true. Augustus wanted the people and the Senate to believe he was just a consultant to the 300 ruling senators and not a theocratic dictator. The truth is Augustus Caesar was assuming all three major institutional realms onto himself: family, government, and religion. This gave him ultimate power: Father of Rome; Consultant of the State; and High Priest or Pontifex Maximus, head of the Roman religion. In his lifetime, many altars and temples would be built to him throughout the Empire. He and his descendants now were controlling everything visible and trying to convince the world they had also tamed the invisible.

Octavius, the victor at Actium, returned to Rome following the suicide of Marcus Antonius (Mark Antony) and later Egypt's Cleopatra VII. (Cleopatra never used the number *VII* in her lifetime but was assigned this number by Roman historians.) *After Octavius's triumphal entry into Rome, Octavius took his seat as consul for life as head of the Julio-Claudian Dynasty. The Roman Senate granted Octavius the change of name and title he demanded: Augustus Caesar. Augustus is an ancient Latin baby name, meaning venerable one or majestic. This was chosen by Octavius to show his humbleness as Rome's new dictator. It is important to understand that Octavius desired the title Augustus over the Senate's alternative: Romulus. Octavius disliked the title of Rome's first king, Romulus, only because this man murdered his brother before he became Rome's first king. Rome's historical records originally recorded that seven kings came and went before the emergence of the Republic of Rome, SPQR, replaced the early monarchy with yearly elections of two Consuls from the body of the Senate. The Senate arose from those wealthy ones who controlled the salt trade at the fording of the Tiber and wished for oligarchy rule over a monarchy.*

Today, Actium marks the end of the Republic and the rise of the Empire. The term 'augustus' was used at first, only in a religious context, morphing into a new and higher meaning: Holy Father Forever. Later Octavius united Augustus with Caesar, and the deception was now complete. Julius Caesar was now seen as a martyr who only wanted to be dictator for life. And over time, all martyrs are easily perceived as gods; therefore, what was wrong with a god ruling for life? This was a straightforward and ingenious way Octavius wanted to communicate to all Romans their first emperor was more than human. When he later assumed the claim, "divi filius" or "god's son" or "son of god," the spiritual hoax was complete. One month after Augustus Caesar's death, five years after my birth, the Senate indeed officially decreed the first Roman Emperor, Gaius Julius Caesar, among the gods of the State.

In conclusion, the 50th anniversary since Actium became a defining day for me as a child living in Rome only because of something that happened on that day that I will never forget. This personal heartbreak, which befell me, transpired because of this insidious lie of divine emperor worship.

CHAPTER TWO

Rome – The 50th Anniversary of Actium, shortly after sunrise. *(September 2, 19 AD)*

For what shall it profit a man, if he shall gain the whole world, and lose his own soul?

Marcus of Jerusalem

I rounded the corner of the *peristyle* garden near the front of the spacious atrium hall, also called the *vestibulum*. I stopped in this colonnaded porch area near a rose-colored pillar and began looking for my father. Not seeing him at first, I found myself distracted and drawn to the misty clouds of steam beginning to rise gently from the many damp flowerbeds and pools of water left standing from the night storm. Heat from the rising sun was evaporating this water up into the first heaven. I remember thinking the sun on this morning must have been steadily climbing for the past hour, and it was going to be a scorching *diurnal* of a day. The temperature, which always affected the air, water, and the human body, would not be a problem to this flowering creation of my father, due to the ground being saturated with rain during the night. This magnificent conservatory contained many plants and trees alien to the native soil of Rome. Shiploads of dirt from various lands along with plants and trees had taken years to collect and ship to the wharves of Rome. From the docks on the Tiber River, everything ended its journey at this spectacular three-story villa located on Equestrian Hill. This horticultural wonder was separated from the principal dwelling on its two long sides by a *peristyle* of double matching, rose-colored Ionic-styled support columns, which held up a sloping cedar roof. Protecting the rear of the garden was a high wall opposite the atrium facing towards the west side of the villa. The west side wall stood on the edge of the property line near a winding lane that went past this villa to the other massive *domii* of wealthy Romans and connected down below Equestrian Hill to the road that led to the heart of the city called the Urbs. Mosaic walkways and statues plundered, or "liberated" as my father liked to brag, from Greece, Asia, and Africa decorated the park-like garden as well as the many rooms and hallways in the villa. The residences my father owned, scattered around the Empire, could not compare with the one on Equestrian Hill. This was the grandest and most talked about by Romans and even kings. The atrium and *vestibulum* buttressed up against a paved patio by a single row of rose-red marble Ionic columns, which held up a high 30-foot roof of cedar timbers and sandstone blocks. The magnificent plantings in the garden occupied an area perhaps 60 feet wide and 200 feet long. My father had designed this atrium and garden years before I was born.

The grand garden-park was the hub of the villa, with one long side reaching up three stories. The atrium and *vestibulum* located at the east end of the *domus* were my father's favorite rooms. He would take most of his meals in the atrium, and the *vestibulum* is where he held his lavish weekly parties. Every minute detail of the garden and atrium had been considered. For instance, all the garden chairs and benches stood three steps below the atrium and faced east to prevent the glaring afternoon sun from blinding guests who were being enthralled by an extraordinary performance of gladiators, or the reading of a poem or book by some famous author, or perhaps a tragedy by Euripides or a Menander-style comedy. If necessary, slaves could quickly raise a tarp *velarium* to cover the patio when rains threatened the lavish parties and exotic exhibitions being staged by my father and Claudia for their rich and powerful friends. On other occasions, usually during the winter months, the indoor *triclinium* (or simple dining hall) was used. The *triclinium* was not far from the atrium. Every wall in this extravagant room exhibited exotic statues and red-hued, tempera-type murals, hand-painted by the Empire's most gifted artisans. My *mater* had forbidden me to enter the *triclinium* because two of the four walls contained pornographic depictions of men and women in various orgy-type activities. I only went into the *triclinium* once at age nine; the wall paintings made me feel sick, and I never entered that room again. It was fortunate for me that children were never allowed to eat with adults in my father's *domus*.

Whenever the weather allowed, the atrium was the preferred location for most weekly gatherings. Slaves were well-trained in transferring high eating couch-beds from the *triclinium* into the *vestibulum* part of the atrium. The dining beds always faced inwards towards tall tables, always positioned into a U-shape configuration. This particular arrangement was the standard array throughout the Empire. This open square plan allowed slaves to enter the middle area with food and drink and also allowed the guests, when slaves were not blocking their view, to delightfully gaze in a drunken stupor out into the vast array of impressive plants, flowers, and trees, which stretched out for more than two hundred feet beyond the patio. After a long meal, the guests would step down the three steps to the patio to find a seat on one of the dozen or so stone benches and chairs, arranged in a semi-circle, facing the *vestibulum*. Many slaves would scurry around setting up a backdrop for that night's entertainment while the guest stretched on their way to the patio or disappeared to the *vomitorium*. When everything was ready, the sun was usually setting, providing unique illumination for whoever were the performers up on the atrium stage. The seated guests out on the patio now had the perfect *locus* to view whatever was planned for their entertainment.

Still standing next to the rose-colored pillar on this early morning, I moved my eyes up and scrutinized the floating clouds in the creamy blue sky. When I heard laughter, I looked away and spotted my father leaning with both hands against a rose-colored column on the far outer edge of the atrium. Mayus Lentulus, who was the captain of my father's bodyguards, stood behind him, draping his master's white toga with its broad purple edging over his left shoulder. Once the folds were in place, my father started tucking the loose section of the white garment with its wide purple edge into the belt of his tunic. My tunic this morning was an exact copy of my father's tunic, which he sported under his senatorial toga. Besides the tunic, there were no similarities between his dress and mine. My *patra* wore not white sandals but the traditional red sandals of a senator, along with two iron rings of a patrician, one on each middle finger. White-dyed wool was the standard material for Roman togas; but on a scorching day as this, men wore a lighter cotton toga. Today, my father wore a cotton toga made from an unusual plant that was cultivated in the Indus River area, far beyond the eastern edges of the Empire. Mayus Lentulus wore a more common Egyptian cotton toga. This toga was a much shorter version of my father's, minus the purple edging. Lentulus's short toga was the simple uniform of all Praetorian Guards inside the walled city of Rome. Apparently, Tiberius did not want all his soldiers looking like soldiers with armor and helmets and such.

My father and Mayus Lentulus were laughing with great mirth. With a tooth-missing grin, Lentulus glanced briefly at me. He rarely had anything nice to say to me and at times made me feel like one of the household slaves rather than the eldest son of the wealthiest man in the Empire. Mayus Lentulus, a ruthless man with many visible war scars, had previously been a legionary in Liberia before serving the mandatory allotted 16 years as a Praetorian Guard in Rome for Augustus. After the death of Augustus, Lentulus began serving as captain of my father's personal bodyguards, which included 70 ex-soldiers, all who were employed to guard this villa as well as my father. The 70 were divided into three groups that worked in an eight-hour rotation pattern, starting with the rising of the sun. There were thousands of other ex-soldiers and mercenaries under Lentulus's command, but they were all located around the Empire. These professional men all protected my father's businesses, mines, villas, ships, slave operations, and a vast number of properties. I once heard a drunken guest say that my father controlled more than a legion of soldiers. At the time I did not think this was any kind of a threat to Tiberius, who had 25 legions managing the peace throughout the entire Empire. Still, if that drunken man had been correct, 6,000 men attacking the capital city could easily defeat all the Praetorian Guards and topple Tiberius before one legion could be recalled from the closest frontier to save his throne.

Along with his personal mercenary army of 70 in Rome, my father was allotted a dozen *lictors* to accompany him wherever he went. This was because my father held the elected title of *Magistrate Praetor*. Roman law allowed all *Magistrate Praetors 12 lictors*. A *lictor* was a carryover from the Republic. Besides their function as bodyguards, *lictors* were symbols of power. Each *lictor* wore a white priestly tunic, and each carried a *fascis*. The *fascis* was a hefty bundle of birch rods bound by red leather thongs to a single one-sided, iron-headed ax, secured in the center of the birch sticks. The head of the ax was visible at the top of the birch bundle. The bundle of rods was called the "right of force" or *fascis*. During the early years of the Empire, those opposed to the new dictatorship of Augustus called themselves Radical Republicans; and they coined the word "*fascism*" from *fascis* to describe the rule of Augustus. By the time Augustus had fully entrenched himself with ultimate power up on Palatine Hill, the term *fascism* explains what the Radical Republicans had perceived as an attack on Roman liberty. Today, from what I have seen in my long life by all the Julio-Claudian rulers and those who came after, has since given the Radical Republicans a solid leg to stand on by using the word "*fascism*" to describe the Empire. Just in my lifetime, I have seen the Roman Empire morph into a centralized, autocratic, militaristic governmental system, which deceptively allowed private ownership of property to hide what the Empire had become. What became routine to all under the yoke of Roman rule was the understanding that the state controlled all the main financial systems. This control was easily enforced because the government minted all silver and gold coins. Whoever manipulates the repository of all monies has all power. I would later learn that any government that tells the owners of property what to produce, what prices can be set, and how to handle their profits is truly a *fascist* state. This was the creature Rome had become, and this *fascist* political philosophy was justified only because Rome convinced its population that Rome graciously served the poor, free workers, and the elderly. Even the voiceless slave population could be thrown into this mix of twisted thinking. The truth is Rome practiced a brutal form of radical state control of the economy and its subjects. The only freedom for the private owners of property in the Empire was the granted freedom to seek pleasure with their profits. Therefore, the poor and the old were trapped by the state-controlled pleasure facilities, all designed to distract the free citizenship from caring that this oppressive state controlled everything else, including their lives.

The *lictors* accompanied any Roman possessing *imperium magistrate* power. *Magistrates* with *imperium* power actually had the right to have any person, by word or flick of the wrist, put to death by a *lictor*. Typically, this was not the custom concerning a Roman citizen. Roman citizens had the right to a legal trial before receiving a death sentence. Beheading was the standard form of death for a citizen, and crucifixion was reserved for non-citizens. If a citizen named his *patroni,* then a trial was not necessary. In the case of someone naming his *patroni*, the Roman possessing *imperium magistrate* power would deal directly with the *patroni*. For now, I will explain the *patroni* system later, if I do not forget. Yet, it should be understood that, if a citizen had no *patroni* (or rich client) to support him, a trial would usually be quick; and the accused found himself either innocent or swiftly beheaded. Rome did not have many lingering for years in jail cells or prisons. Justice, or a form of it, was quick and brutal. My father's position as a m*agistrate praetor* gave him the right to have half the number of *lictors* as the emperor. My father, who had 12 *lictors* assigned to him, rarely had more than 4 with him, at any one time. Twenty-four *lictors* were the maximum anyone could have, and that only applied to the emperor. Thus, Tiberius maintained this number; but he rarely had more than four with him at any public event. I believe this may have been the reason my father allowed only four *lictors* to travel with him, only to prevent the appearance he was not upstaging the emperor. The number of Praetorian Guards was a different matter. Hundreds might surround Tiberius in the streets of Rome, if he ventured out beyond Palatine

Hill and the Imperial Palaces, which was rare, despite his presence today at the *Amphitheater of Statilius Taurus.*

After retired Praetorian Lentulus had glanced at me showing his toothless grin, I realized I did not know his age. Perhaps he was in his mid-forties. He was shorter than most grown men, structured like a bull with a thick, brawny neck. There was not an ounce of fat on his sinewy but muscled body; and his skin stretched over his muscles giving the appearance of a bag of huge, bulging olives. He kept his physique under strict discipline. Even though Lentulus was famous for his gluttony and laxity in morals, especially at my father's weekly parties, he always ended the evenings with a visit to the *vomitorium.* A *vomitorium* was a place found only in the homes of the wealthiest and most powerful men of Rome. I first read about a *vomitorium* in a scroll during my daily studies at Senator Carnalus's home. The scroll I read suggested the first *vomitorium* appeared in the city of Pompeii in the late Republic period. The city Pompeii was located in southern *Italia.* Pompeii was initially an old Samnite settlement that still stood adjacent to the monster volcano of Mount Vesuvius. Pompeii and Herculaneum were two of the most significant Roman cities south of Rome and, yet, still had more of a Greek influence rather than Roman. Both cities were slowly becoming Roman copies of the capital on the Tiber similar to Capua or Brundisium, two other large, Romanized towns in southern *Italia.* My understanding from my studies was Capua and Brundisium were extensions to Rome because of the oldest all-weather road named the Appian Way. The Appian Way highway built under the supervision of an ancient Roman censor and engineer named Appius Claudius had been standing as a lifeline of *Italia* for over three hundred years. This road had been built during the Samnite Wars to provide a quick way to move Rome's armies to meet any threat. Since Pompeii and Herculaneum were far beyond the famed Appian Way, there was a disconnect to Rome and the rest of *Italia.* To reach Pompeii and Herculaneum, it would be easier to travel there by sea. Still, the history of the *vomitorium* traces back to Pompeii.

I also guess that the *symposium,* an ancient Grecian practice, most likely came to Rome via the ancient Greek colonial cities in southern *Italia* and *Sicilia.* The *symposium* was the favorite activity of well-to-do Greeks centuries ago throughout most of the 400-plus city-states during the time before and after Pericles, the great Athenian *strategos,* who was the force behind the building of the *Parthenon.* The practice of *symposium* was simple. A small number of men would gather at someone's home on a rotating basis. Each host was expected to provide a lavish dinner party. After the dinner had concluded, all servants and women removed themselves, leaving only the male guests alone in the eating room with a huge vat of wine. For the rest of the evening and often until dawn, the men occupied themselves in deep philosophical and dialectical debates while sipping wine. Plato's dialogues provide an excellent description of how the *symposiums* functioned.

Most Romans I know these days usually fall asleep while reading any of Plato's dialogues, which shows one significant difference between the two cultures. The *symposium* became a co-opted and altered activity to accommodate Roman taste. For instance, the opposite sex in Rome was not encouraged to leave after eating; nor did anyone wish to engage in philosophical discourse. At a Roman dinner party, guests would rather tear someone down in order to build themselves up; and this type of chatter and prattle went on and on instead of any intellectual discussions. The *symposium*, therefore, morphed into the *orgia* or "party of ecstasy," a Roman invention. No longer did only men spend hours bantering ideas like the Greeks; but they, instead, delighted in the pleasure of eating multiple courses of food and delicacies provided by the host. What may have been only an hour for the Greeks now took many hours for the Romans. A guest wishing to eat all that was before him had no choice but to make assorted visits to the *vomitorium*. Sometimes the Romans would begin an eating *orgia* at noon and end the next day in the early hours near sunrise.

The *vomitorium* was a simple room with a birdbath washstand and a trough of water flowing near the side of the chamber. A guest used a feather down the throat to initiate vomiting. Most of the food and drink of the day entered the water that flowed along the floor channel that continually circulated under the floor and finally ended up dumping into the sewers that crisscrossed under the streets of Rome. The birdbath basin was there to splash one's hands and dampen the face and mouth. A slave would be present holding towels for the guest to wipe their hands and face or to hold up a bronze mirror, especially for females to examine their hair and makeup. Elaborate terracotta and lead pipes snaked from only the wealthiest Romans' villas into river-like channels running deep under the streets in the different valleys of Rome. These street water cavities were so large a slave could navigate easily by walking on a ledge underground with a torch to discover any blockage that needed attention. Round stone covers in the paved streets above allowed entry into these sewage warrens. The circle was the chosen design for the stone lids, which led into the sewers, since a circular cover could never fall down into the sewers below as long as the opening lip was slightly smaller than the round stone manhole cover. SPQR appeared as the state brand, carved into the manhole covers to proclaim Rome was still a Republic and not an oligarchy or even a dictatorship. "*Senatus Populusque Romanus*" or "the Senate and the People of Rome" was the origin of the acronym SPQR. This four-letter mark was the only carryover from the Republic into the Empire. Eventually, all these underground sewage rivers came together and emptied at different intervals into the Tiber River that meandered around the Imperial city. Many centuries of sewage dumping into the Tiber soon fouled the river beyond any human use, and the river on hot days smelled putrid with a significant amount of green moss growing from the bank out into the deeper waters. Pollution was the apparent condition of this once-grand, slow-moving river; and on any hot day, the rotten sewage smell prevented many from wishing to use the few bridges that crossed the river to the other side. Ancient city leaders of the Republic and still today have had to construct dozens of aqueducts from the mountain lakes in the Apennines to convey fresh water to a population of a million strong. Now at the dawn of the Empire, the city had perhaps ten times the water for its present population's daily needs. Thus, all the excess water flowed abundantly into fountains and bathhouses and helped keep the gigantic sewers flushed with gallons pouring non-stop out of the sewers into the Tiber.

Since I am on the subject of Rome, I should explain the religions that composed Rome's identity. Religion dictates man's values, morals, and ethics. These beliefs were at the center of each man's or woman's decision making. Since life is nothing more than one decision after another, one begins to understand the importance of religion. Early on at the time of the Republic, Rome co-opted the Greeks once again. Zeus became Jupiter, Dionysus became Bacchus, and Aphrodite became Venus, and so forth. All the Greek gods and goddesses morphed into the Roman deities along with their morals, values, and ethics or lack of them since most Romans were guided by these adoptive gods' activities. Therefore, the gods of Greece entertained themselves on Mount Olympus with the *symposium;* and the Romans turned this pastime into an eating *orgia,* which slowly transformed into *orgies.* Romans sincerely believed all the gods bestowed blessings to all the eating, drinking, and other activities that any Roman citizen could bring to his wildest imaginations down upon and around the Seven Hills.

One of the greatest partakers of this activity was Mayus Lentulus. The only difference between him and other corpulent Romans Lentulus would awaken after my father's weekly orgies and devote the next morning to strenuous exercise, which ended with running four complete laps around the track of the Circus Maximus to sweat out the poisons. He would then bathe and lounge in one of the public bathhouses near Palatine Hill, using the steam and heat rooms before plunging into a cold lap pool called the *frigidarium* for a hard swim. This practice was how he maintained his physical shape and healthy muscles into middle age.

"Where is that boy of mine?" asked my father between his jovial, bawdy laughs with Lentulus.

"He is coming," said Lentulus, pointing at me with his chin.

My father glanced over to where Lentulus had indicated my presence. "We haven't all day!" he yelled. This loud but straightforward rebuke coming from my father clearly communicated his impatience towards me after I was spotted. A chill ran up my spine, maybe because my *patra* seemed aloof or even angry whenever I was around him. Maybe it was a false perception on my part, but I felt like he held no emotions at all towards me. He pulled his gaze back to the red column he had been leaning against and slapped his right palm loudly against the smooth stone as if releasing some kind of rage or giving a signal to some heavenly god that he was angry with me. Precisely at that very moment of the sound of a slap on stone, the top of the orb of the sun came streaming in over the red roof tiles, illuminating the atrium and half of the garden. Looking back at that moment in time, I realized how wondrous, yet peculiar, it all appeared. Beams of light stood out painting the dust particles floating in the air and bits of water vapor drifting above the pools of rain on the pavement paths out in the garden. Like most pleasures, it did not last; and I forced my attention back to my father. I noticed he was feeling the hilt of a gladius with the hand that had just struck the pillar. I clearly saw the ornate silver-embossed knob that stood out at the end of the ivory handhold. His hand absently caressed the gladius hand portion, and he lifted the entire sword just a little to make sure it was not sticking, before pulling his toga back to hide it. I thought the sword was out of place, for I had never seen him carrying one. Typically, I only remember him with a dagger called a *cultellus* concealed under his toga. Why was he carrying a cumbersome and clumsy sword this morning? I dismissed this observation when my father looked out towards the far side of the garden. Screened by the pillar where I was still standing, I noticed my father staring at Claudia, who was gliding towards him and Lentulus from out in the lush greenery. I was hoping the Ionic, blood-colored pillar shielded me from her sight. My father smiled broadly as Claudia approached them using one of the many stone pathways. She suddenly stopped in front of the atrium steps, in the area where the marble benches stood as sentinels of debasement. She stared at her husband with a fake diminutive smile and dropped her green silk *palla* from her shoulders, allowing the sun's illumination to envelop her slender but curvy shape.

"Good morning, my goddess; you look like Venus herself!" exclaimed Gaius with an even wider grin than when laughing with Lentulus. Claudia did not return the greeting but instead lifted the *palla* back into place as if she were just adjusting its drape. Taking the three marble steps into the atrium, I noticed one foot moving exactly in front of the other. This must have been her trick to appear as if gliding instead of walking. Moving in this way and offsetting her movement after every third step, she reminded me of a snake shifting stealthily through a forest. She stopped just inches from my father and Mayus Lentulus. I heard her say expeditiously to the two men with a clear tone of ultimatum, "Neither of you is to weaken today concerning our plans, especially regarding Venustus."

I strained with my utmost concentration to hear the rest of her exact words. "This morning it is to be done," she hissed very plainly and factually. "If you do not eliminate Venustus today, he will be the one to destroy all our plans and hopes! You will spend all your energies pursuing him if you fail! May the *ensi* of Ur hear and prevent this prophecy from failure! Even Isis herself will hear and also mark my words this very day!"

I understood her final statement to be some kind of ancient Egyptian or Sumerian incantation. Claudia was a dabbler, if not an outright devotee, of the dark arts of many mystery religions coming to Rome from faraway, even beyond the Empire. My Jewish slave friend Eli told me that Claudia owned a scroll called the *Atharva Veda*, an old collection of incantations initially written about one thousand five hundred years ago in Sanskrit by the light-skinned Aryans before they crossed the Hindu Kush Mountains, passing over the same location Alexander the Macedonian used when he entered the land of the Hindus. Today this route through the Hindu Kush Mountains is known as the Khyber Pass. Besides the valley of Megiddo in Judaea, this is perhaps the second most contested battle sight in human history. These light-skinned Aryans conquered the dark-skinned, docile Dravidian farmers down on the Indus River Valley, using bows, swords, and chariots. These cities without walls did not have a chance except submitting to the Aryans and their nature gods, along with the teachings of the Vedas.

Now I was frightened, for I distinctly heard what Claudia had said about me. My eyes widened when my father waved his hand towards me to show Claudia I had been listening. Claudia Pulchra's head pivoted slowly as some kind of slithering creature hanging from a branch. When our eyes met, she opened her mouth saying some sort of witchcraft curse only she understood.

She then turned her gaze back to my father and spoke as if she did not care if I overheard.

"He is one of the key persons to die this day," she said very clearly and distinctly as if she were talking in front of a stupid slave. Then looking back to me to ensure I was included in this conversation, she finished her statement an octave higher: "Perhaps above anyone else!"

After this iniquitous prediction, Claudia gave me a surprisingly sweet smile, accompanied with a quick wink that vanished as fast as it appeared. She turned back to her husband, and the smile was gone; I also noticed he lowered his head almost in a pose of sycophantic obsequiousness. With his head bowed, she moved up on her tiptoes and kissed him on the forehead. After a quick peck, Claudia said nothing more and exited from the atrium, passing through the *vestibulum* into a hallway leading to the main house and her private chambers located on the third level of one of the wings near the front of the villa.

Gaius watched her saunter away and then slapped the pillar again with the heel of his hand. "That woman is too much for me to handle. I love her one moment and hate her the next. Old Janus must be playing the game of confusion with me; or maybe she is his wife, deceitful Hora, sent to intricate my mind."

"Ole' Hora, I doubt," replied Lentulus. "The former perhaps; yet, she is more to the liking of Venus as you first declared."

"She is no goddess, but she does have the blood of Caesar running through her veins; so maybe she is," retorted Gaius. "Yes, on second consideration, having the blood of Caesar does make her a goddess. This is why I married her and had a son with her. Now my son Julius is the real avatar in this drama."

"And that is what this is all about," Lentulus responded in agreement with my father.

"Exactly!" confirmed my father.

I noticed a twisted grin on Mayus Lentulus's clean-shaven face. I found myself frozen as I listened and memorized every word. Had I been a fly on the wall, I would expect a rolled-up papyrus whacking me or a slave's rage cleaning an insignificant speck of dirt off the wall.

"Well, Lentulus, a bloody day this shall be; and Rome will never be the same after it. Rome will witness a day that is even more decisive than when Caesar fell dead at the feet of Brutus and the other Republican fools. Even the day when Dictator Lucius Cornelius Sulla posted a list of 1,000 names to be murdered here in Rome will not be like today. And if we are successful, you shall be Praetorian *Prefect* in the near future."

"No!" answered Lentulus with downcast eyes. "I will never live to see your dream completed, but I will be your strong arm until the hand of Jupiter prevents me. Besides, I believe Sulla had massacred over eight thousand before he was able to declare himself dictator."

"Oh? Have you been listening to that bag of wind Valerius Maximus lecturing about Rome's history at the bathhouse, or have you just been playing with your oracle bones again?"

"The bones say I will die at the hands of Jupiter before all of this is finished," commented a sorrowful Lentulus. "Yet, still many years in the future. I believe I will be dead before I reach my 60th year. Besides, Valerius Maximus is an impressive and entertaining scholar."

"He is a windbag, but you are free to listen to whomever on your own time. Now, if your bones tell you Jupiter will be behind your death, then should I expect you to be struck down by a lightning bolt? Now tell me, have you ever in your life seen anyone hit by the flashing of light from the first heaven?" Expecting Lentulus not to answer him, my father placed his right hand on his bodyguard's shoulder. It had to be a form of a mock jester as I watched my father remove his hand from Lentulus's shoulder almost instantly looking away and up towards the track of the sun, trying to gauge the time. Turning his head back towards me, he motioned with the same hand to come. "Well, boy, do not stand there like a slave; get over here!"

I found myself running to him. My age only allowed obedience; it did not demand to understand.

"Why are you slack in meeting me this morning?" Gaius asked in a reproving tone. "If you had been on time, all of this embarrassment could have been avoided."

I felt now was the time to speak to my father even though he was blaming me for his troubles. "Claudia told me *Mater* has been sold to a merchant from faraway and leaves today. Is this true?" I searched his face for any sign to authenticate the veracity of what I had just declared, but to my surprise I saw nothing. All I noticed was a slight tightening of his mouth and a slow wagging of his head, which indicated to me that he did not believe this was happening.

"Oh, in the names of Jupiter and Janus, these two gods have cursed me with Claudia. You heard what she just said; that woman is out of her mind making all kinds of damnable and monstrous threats."

Then he changed completely from seriousness to flippancy with a felicitous intonation in his voice. "Now, my boy, I assure you there is nothing to worry about. Your mother is going nowhere. Claudia is just trying to upset her. You know – or will know someday – how women are," he said with a little laugh. "They are just a bunch of wild Egyptian cats fighting because of jealousy."

"What I overheard is not true?"

"True? There is not a shred of truth in what that woman says. I tell you now that this is going to stop. I will have a word with Claudia tonight; and, if it ever happens again, I will have her severely reproved. Now have you used the *lavo* this morning?"

"No, *Pater*, why do you ask?"

"Well, look at you bouncing around from foot to foot. Do you have bugs under your tunic? Hurry, and meet me out front; and make it quick, or we will be late."

My father was correct, I had not emptied my bladder since I awoke and decided to run to the *vomitorium*, which was closer to the atrium than the *lavo* (or lavatory) I was supposed to use. There were several *lavos* in the villa, but as a child I was only allowed to use the one near the back wall. No one had instructed me about not using the *vomitorium* as a *lavo*. In my innocence, I was not sure what purpose the *vomitorium* served, except for me to do my business. Besides, I never saw anyone using it during the daytime. Reaching the infamous room, to my surprise there was an old slave on his hands and knees cleaning the mosaic floor, paying close attention to each colored stone that he wiped with a rag. I said cheerfully, "Good morning," to the old man trying to practice my mother's edict; but, not being accustomed to a salutation from the master's son, the elderly slave instead appeared startled. He nervously replied something in a foreign tongue and then hung his head in what looked like shame. I said nothing more as I did my business into the moving water flowing in its channel and then hurried to the front of the villa.

Standing on the pavement near the fountain that occupied the center of the circular stone entranceway to the *ostium* (or double, heavy, wooden doors) to the villa was a gold-and-silver litter with white silk curtains. There were four *lictors* today holding their *fasces*. They were standing in front of the litter, so I assumed they were going to lead the way. The sun was pouring forth its late-summer strength, and the air was growing hot and oppressive. I noticed whiffs of more heat fog wafting over the walls that encompassed the villa. Lentulus held back the silk curtains while my father stood beside him waving for me to hurry. My *pater* climbed in after I scurried aboard, and he sat opposite me resting his left elbow on a silk cushion. The silver palanquin rose smoothly up to the shoulders of eight black, muscular, identically clad litter-bearers; and off we went. Like floating on a cloud, we drifted down the narrow lane much like the heated mist leaving Esquiline Hill; and before long we had entered the bowels of Rome known as the *Urbs*. In a short time, I saw a crowded sea of bodies swarming the narrow streets and heard a slave with large lungs shouting in front of the *lictors* yelling, "Make way for *Magistrate Praetor* Vetallus! Make way for Senator Vetallus! Make way for *Magistrate Praetor* Vetallus!"

Sweat was beginning to drip from my forehead; and I wiped it with the back of my hand before I asked, "*Pater*, where are we going?"

His mood improved as the palanquin forced a path through the crowd like a ship plowing the waves. What I understood later was he was drinking something that did more than improve his mood and had nothing to do with the swaying ride above the heads of the people in the streets. He kept lifting a swollen wineskin and drinking deeply from what I presumed was wine. He lingered a moment over each gulp feeling the effects. Before answering my question, which I had been asking all morning, he took an extra-long gulp. His gaze finally fell on me; and I knew he was, at last, going to reveal our destination. "Well, boy, today you are going to see the better things in life – the things that make it worth living! You will soon wonder how anyone can bear to live without experiencing these pure pleasures."

I did not understand. Why did my father's words make me feel uneasy and almost physically sick? Maybe I was becoming ill due to the gentle swaying of the litter. Truth spoken, I did not know what he was saying. Perhaps it was my age, which prevented me from thinking abstractly. What are true pleasures? I began to panic after feeling a strange pain in my chest. It was a racing pain making a rapid patter that was similar to a well-trained pair of horses pulling a chariot. The pounding was deep inside my chest, and I physically pushed two fingers onto the left side of my chest hoping to stop the pounding. The scrutiny of my father gazing at me demanded a response. I wanted to change the subject and escape this discomforting conflict. Unfortunately, I had to respond to something. All I could come up with was a familiar antiphon sung responsively by some of our Greek slaves at sunrise to Apollo. I copied the sound and words with a Greek twang so my father would understand its origin. "What are you talking over? The sun always rises." I have always tried to use words and wit to protect myself from the harshness of all the sobering realities that confront us each day. In the years to come, I developed quite a caustic wit and ability to alter the direction of any conversation. I found that words sometimes could be as powerful as a sword or a sharp knife. Used like quick darts to the target, words could defuse a strained situation or, on the other hand, escalate the inevitable.

Gaius Vetallus began to laugh at my nine little words as if he had heard the funniest joke imaginable. Instead of delight, I felt embarrassed because of my immaturity in what I feared my father was eluding concerning our destination. I felt something rising up to my cheeks maybe due to my trepidation of where we might be going. Now I became worried I might throw up. My life, up to this time, was quite sheltered from the outside world of my father's business deals and his weekly parties. Each day for the past four years, unless it was a religious or civil holiday, I spent most of my time doing schoolwork at Senator Carnalus's villa on Quirillian Hill. A well-respected schoolmaster known as a *didace* from Greece tutored the Senator's son Decimus and me in the Socratic Method. Questions and answers, issues and solutions, all day long from a backless stool had become my lot in life. The only name I knew for my *didace* was Zeno.

Zeno would ask, "Why is the sky blue?"

I would answer as quickly and correctly to the best of my understanding. "The sky is blue because of the firmament between us and the sun. The sky is in the first heaven, and the sun is in the second heaven. Beyond all of what our eyes can see at night is the third heaven."

"What color is the first firmament at night?"

"At night it is void appearing like the color black unless the lesser light rules."

"There is no such color as black!" Zeno would snap.

"It is the illusion of blackness because of the absence of light. Perhaps the light of the sun is diffused by clouds or the shadow of the earth upon the moon. Just when the lesser lights do shine, a bluish tint becomes the color our eyes detect."

This was constant and dangerous if I did not quickly have a reasonable answer because Zeno never spared the rod. A slave known as a *pedagogue* escorted me to the senator's large *domus* each morning. The elderly *pedagogue* would wait all day at the senator's villa and escort me home near dusk. This had been my safe routine and would be for another ten years or until I entered the legions to serve my allotted time as a military tribune. I was beginning to dislike my educational experiences because Zeno never laughed, and I perceived him slightly sadistic hating little rich boys. A day would not go by without at least one strike on the hands by a wooden stick for either being slow with my abacus or giving an inadequate answer to his endless, dialectical questions, or worst, his inductive questions that required a logical guess between several options. I preferred the dialectical questions only because there was just one correct answer based upon several established propositions.

"Without pain, there is no knowledge" was an old Persian mantra adopted by Zeno. The way Zeno used it I felt that maybe he thought he was the origin of this maxim; however, he was the source of the pain. "To learn is hard work, and work involves pain. Learn to accept pain, and knowledge will be yours. It is something no one can take from you." Since everyone's thoughts seem somewhat eclectic, I doubt these were Zeno's original ideas.

The litter halted amid the social traffic jamming the narrow street between the blocks of multi-level *insula* housing, wherein hundreds of apartments for the poor and working class of the city lived. My father turned and asked, "Are you, or are you not going to tell me? Let me put it this way. What is the greatest excitement you have had in your life?"

I flinched involuntarily as though I was sitting before Zeno and he was about to strike me for not answering quickly enough. I was still feeling ill, and the odor of human excrement from the alleys complicated my condition.

"Well, what is it?" he asked again with a slightly irritated expression.

I speculated that my father was possibly taking me to some sex show at the *Theater of Marcellus* or maybe one at *Pompey's Theater*. Lately, Greek tragedies at the famous *Marcellus Theater* that could seat 15,000 with a capacity of another 5,000 standing were becoming unpopular. I had learned from my friend Decimus that attendance was waning and that people were growing bored with these productions. Only if the plot called for murder or patent sex would people flock to these performances to watch some unbeknownst slave actually killed on stage during the death scene or other unspeakable live acts. Another reason for low attendance, according to Decimus, was due to a new form of entertainment called "Burlesque" that was drawing people away from the so-called slow-developing plots of the tedious Greek plays. These burlesque shows moved with the constant speed of short acts, one after another, usually around bevies of young girls and well-endowed women running around on stage disrobing to loud scores performed by huge orchestras that were in pits concealed in front of the stage. My only source of information was from Decimus, my only boyhood friend other than the slave Eli, whom I considered my best friend even though he was a Jewish slave of my own age in my father's household. I considered him my best friend because we played together at nights and on days I did not go to school due to some high Roman holiday. Today was such an occasion, the anniversary of Actium, 50 years past. I would rather have been with Eli today, but I was also proud to be with my father for the first time outside the walls of his villa.

I did not consider Decimus as my best friend – because he was the son of Senator Carnalus and was two years older than I. He did not look older because he was small in build and looked to be my age. The truth was he was older mentally and socially. His father had already taken him to two of these burlesque shows and one tragedy with an actual death scene. I feared this was now my introduction to such affairs. My father had been promoting these types of shows hoping a new, healthy wave of Epicureanism would sweep the city of its ancient Stoicism.

Epicureanism, my father's choice of philosophy, was diametrically opposed to Stoicism. I heard my father many times decry at his parties that Stoics were the scourge of the Empire; and, only when Epicureanism reigned supreme, would there be peace and joy in the world. He would then release a loud belch and pass wind in the most indecent way provoking all attending guests into laughs and howls. At night I would sometimes hide in the garden with Eli and listen to the conversations of my father and Claudia's visitors when they ate in the atrium. My mother always found us before the parties turned riotous and led me to my room for sleep. Eli also went to his room when my mother found us, and neither of us ever viewed these parties before they grew into the orgy state. I was always deep in sleep and never understood the answer to my curiosity about such things.

To answer my father's question truthfully, I would have to say I found pleasure in the love freely given to me from my mother and the stories she would tell of Homer's epic poems before falling asleep. I knew he would laugh at my answer and then call me a *mater's* boy. That shameful epithet would embarrass me, and I felt I was at the crossroads of my young life sitting in the somewhat comfortable litter moving through the hordes of the unwashed. I could not make sense of the philosophical contradictions I was experiencing from my father, Zeno, and even my own mother. Each person's voice was speaking to my mind at the same time, "Seek pleasure, and embrace selfishness." "Accept pain, and seek knowledge." "Love others above yourself." I could not go down all three roads at the same time and be faithful to each tenet.

Under Roman law or *dominium*, the father was the patriarch of the house and even had the authority to have his children put to death if he received permission from only one of his neighboring patriarchs. The *patria potestas* that began in early Rome and was still the practice today gave the head male of a home complete rights over his wife and children including death. It was a brutal system; yet, very few children actually died at the hands of their father, and I never heard of any wives killed by their husbands. This system did keep children respectful and obedient to their fathers. I knew of only one example where a father actually took his son out into the street calling his neighbors to watch as he declared his teenage son rebellious without hope. The boy stood paralyzed when the father thrust an old gladius into his stomach and left him wallowing in his own blood as the father locked his door behind him. I did not witness this event, but Zeno and others repeated it many times as an object lesson. I should say many in Rome were masters of lies but not old Zeno, who had a reputation for telling only the truth and not gossiping. Therefore, I believed this story.

My father looked at me differently this early morning in the litter he placed his hand on my left knee and said, "Venustus, you are a good boy; but it's time to ripen and experience the better things in life."

"But are not the things you speak of called the evil things in life?" I blurted out without consideration.

Gaius looked me hard in the eyes and then turned away very coldly and uttered, "That is your mother talking!" What he meant by this I was not sure but would later understand. "No! They are not evil to those who are brave enough to try them. Nothing is evil; and, if you go around judging things good and bad, you will never be happy. That Stoic teacher of yours is also a poison, and this is going to change today. Remember my words."

"I am sorry, *Pater*; I guess I am confused."

"That you are, but it isn't your fault." He quickly smiled and slapped the wineskin. "Now, take wine, for example. You drink the right amount, and you feel good. Drink too much wine, and you become sick. Therefore, drinking wine is not evil unless too much consumption causes your body to reject the wine in sickness. Now that might be the body rejecting the wine or maybe Bacchus controlling his influence over you; I do not know. Nevertheless, what god tells us what is right or wrong other than that Jewish god *Jah* or *Yahw* or however his name is pronounced?" For a few moments, my father retreated into deep thought while I looked into his vacant eyes. When his gaze refocused on me, he spoke about what was in his heart. "Those Jews, now that is a group of people the world could do without! Do not mistake my words on this as well. Those Jews will all be put to the sword or crucified before I am finished."

I began to fear I would soon become like him if I did not sit under the teaching of Zeno. I then started thinking about Eli, my playmate. Why would my father want Eli dead, or maybe he did not know Eli was a Jew? A long silence again ensued after my father's attack on the Jews and their mysterious god. I was very ignorant about the subject of god or gods; the entire subject frightened me because talk of the gods always included the topic of death. My father was now even more deeply distracted in his thoughts, and I noticed he began pulling back the curtains to get some air circulating in the litter. We started to travel again as the crowd moved out of the street. Apparently, we had stopped because a fight had broken out in the roadway between two men. Citizens wearing white togas finally pulled them apart, but they were still yelling threats to one another and swinging their fists.

"*Pater*, I will try anything you want me to," I said in what I now perceive was a feeble attempt to gain his love.

He closed the curtains and with a strange grin reached for his wineskin. "Here, drink some of this," he offered. I did not know if he was testing me, but my mother did tell me to be obedient. I took the wine and raised the skin to my mouth, for I was thirsty not having had any liquids since I had awakened. I lifted the skin in the same fashion copying my father, and the liquid tasted different from anything that I had ever consumed. A bitter almond taste rose up followed by a burning, sharp sweetness; but I decided people did not drink wine for the taste but more so for the ethanol that was a byproduct of the crushed grapes mixed with yeast and allowed to ferment. At least that was how Zeno explained it. A warm feeling struck me at once as it hit my stomach, and a firm jolt tingled up my spine shooting to my head. A glow replaced the first lurch, and I decided I liked the feeling. The previous sickness had vanished miraculously; and I desired another mouthful, which I took. Maybe my father was right; he did know about life, especially the things that were exciting and different. Besides, if I were not here with him, I would be having my hands beat by Zeno at Senator Carnalus's villa. Moreover, from what my father had just declared, I might be free of Zeno for good.

"Be careful. That is expensive wine mingled with gall."

"Gall? What is gall?" I asked.

"Gall is the nectar of the gods! It is the juice of the most brilliant red opium poppy grown faraway in the valleys of Asia near the famed Khyber Pass. Rome has to pay a hefty price for the milky juice of these flowers that grow far beyond the Empire but are worth every *denarius*. Gall allows your faculties to perceive things much clearer. It is a prerequisite before one goes to the arena to watch the gladiators fight. The gall will tweak the action in slower motion, and colors will become brighter such as the redness of blood."

I sat back realizing that it was already working. My senses were becoming numbed, yet heightened. It was a state of mind I never knew existed, and everything was new and exciting. The colors out in the drab street that I could see through the slits in the curtains came alive with new vividness as if time had halted and we had all the space in the world to watch every movement around us. People appeared like scripted actors unaware they were performing only for my pleasure. Life was a living stage, and I was a spectator in the middle of the action. I had fallen in love with the effects of gall, a curse that would plague me for many years. I recognized a new hunger for food and remembered the fruitcake my mother had given me that I had placed in a pocket in my tunic. I retrieved it; and it, too, tasted delicious when before it was very bland.

"Where are we going? For if we just stay here, I am happy," I said, realizing that I did not slur my words.

"The gods be blessed! You have spoken volumes of wisdom that Epicurus himself could not have uttered from his own garden." Now I was miffed. What did I say that sounded profound? "To answer your question, we are going to the *Amphitheater of Statilius Taurus* to watch the game of the year. One hundred and twenty gladiators will all fight to their death, minus one, all in honor of the 50th Anniversary of the Battle of Actium."

"We are going to watch a gladiatorial fight?" I asked in astonishment. Mother abhorred gladiatorial games, and they were much worse than sex shows according to my mother. Arena had warned me many times to never view a gladiatorial match, for I would become addicted to the lust of blood and would never be the same again. Why was she against something that had her name attached to it? I began to wonder if this was the drug talking to my head. I then wondered why a gladiatorial game had never entered my mind as to the place my father was taking me.

My father raised his left hand in delight. "Not just a gladiatorial fight, but a 120-men match-off. Two men, usually a Samnite and a Thracian, begin to battle until one is dead with no exceptions."

As I have already said, the southern Roman city of Pompeii had been a Samnite settlement before becoming Roman. I thought of the Roman general Quintus Fabius Maximus Verrucosus who fought the young Carthaginian General Hannibal during the second Punic Wars. Maximus earned the name *Cunctator* or "the delayer" because of his delaying tactics against the Carthaginians. From that period in Roman history, such a delaying policy became a *Fabian*. I wondered if a Samnite gladiator was famous for his delay tactics. I felt various topics from my studies under Zeno symmetrically crossing my mind; perhaps it was the effect of the gall. I grew quiet while thinking of General Maximus's descendant, who was also a Roman general several hundred years ago when he defeated the Etruscans, the Samnites, and their allies at the Battle of Sentinum. The rush of more concepts and learned facts at the foot of Zeno made me understand they had deeper roots than I realized. I began to miss my teacher and felt like crying. Would I ever get to see him again?

"The winner fights a new challenger until someone is killed and so on until the last man is standing." My father's words had interrupted my thoughts and saved me from the embarrassment of weeping in front of him. "Moreover, if the last man lives, he receives the wooden sword from Tiberius, which means he has obtained his freedom and a title of honor. Now you will see *laquearius*, *retiarius*, *provocator*, and *murmillo* gladiators all showing their best skills, all taught from the best schools trained by the best *lanista* teachers."

"I have heard of the wooden sword. Did not the Barbarian gladiator named Marius receive the wooden sword twice?"

"Yet, he remains a gladiator because he loves the fame along with the thrill of danger. You know of Gladiator Marius? I am impressed. Well, he is the most famous fighter to have ever lived. I am surprised at you! Yes, he will fight today; and, if he survives, he will be the greatest of all arena warriors."

"Marius will be fighting?" I asked before realizing my father had already answered that question. I was lost in the odds of his survival, which had to be astronomical.

"You will be a witness of history, all on your tenth birthday and the 50th anniversary of the Battle of Actium. Something you can tell your grandchildren."

My chest swelled at my father's words, for he was being nice to me instead of ignoring or shaming me with his words. The litter stopped once again, and now I felt the sensation of dropping. The litter was now stationary on the ground. My father got out first while a deep dread flooded over me like a rogue wave on a windy day hitting a reef at Ostia, the port city, and dockyards of Rome. Being in this drugged condition, could I even walk? I grabbed the wineskin and drank a quick mouthful hoping this would calm me banishing that dark sensation of falling over my own feet.

"Yes, bring the skin; and hurry along, Venustus," said my father as he stepped away from the litter.

Once out into the sunlight, I found my legs without any problem. I actually felt light as a feather but remained motionless with the skin of gall cradled in my arms. I marveled at the vast wood-and-stone amphitheater that stood in the old floodplain of Rome, just outside her 32-foot walls, out on the ancient field where her legions used to gather before they marched out to defend the city during the years of the Republic. Currently, under edicts of the Empire, no legionaries in *Italia*, let alone in the city, could legally wear their uniforms openly. Only Pretorian Guards in their unique, short nonmilitary-looking tunic-togas could carry swords and do the Emperor's bidding. This modern law and custom of no soldiers in *Italia* except the Pretorian Guards caused great divisiveness between these two groups of warriors. Combine this dissension with the fact that a Pretorian Guard had all the luxury of living in Rome, was paid much more than a legionary, and served only 16 years instead of 20; and jealousy fomented. Legionaries found themselves in harsh conditions fighting bloody battles and receiving only a *denarius* a day. A Pretorian could expect double the wage; a warm, comfortable bed; and no risk of dying in a fierce battle against determined enemies on the edge of the Empire. Due to this conflict, there were many rumors of violence floating around the city. Retired soldiers visiting or living in Rome would secretly murder a Praetorian Guard if one were found wandering alone on a dark street at night. Usually, a dead Praetorian would be dumped down one of the thousands of circular manholes falling into the vast sewer warrens, which emptied out into the Tiber. Jealousy, envy, and anger over a blatantly unfair disparity between legionaries and Praetorians were most likely the cause of this common trend that killed perhaps a hundred or more Pretorian Guards yearly. Being aware of the danger, most Guards never moved around the city alone, especially at night. The companion system became mandatory; yet, fights between ex-legionaries and Praetorians in broad daylight broke out in taverns, street markets, bathhouses, and even in the stands of gladiatorial and chariot venues.

The Amphitheater of Statilius Taurus was the first stone amphitheater in Rome. As I have already stated, it was built during the rule of Augustus by his good friend and lieutenant general, Statilius Taurus. If it had not been for the invention of Roman concrete, this type of construction would not have been possible. The word concrete most likely originated from the Latin *concretio*, which means growing together or congealing a matter. Perhaps *concretus* is the Latin etymology of this word, which means to compact or condense to produce something new. Whatever, the Romans knew that placing horsehair to the mix prevented cracking and adding blood made concrete more frost-resistant. Builders purchased the bodies of all dead gladiators just for their vermilion-cerise life fluids. Building contractors collected excess blood from the temple sacrifices along with dead horses from the chariot races in the city. On any given day, dozens of chariot horses were either put down from injuries sustained during races or perished during the seven-mile circuit run from either exhaustion or crashes. After the dead animals had been gathered, each one was first shaved for its hair; then blood was collected by opening the large veins and arteries. The horse flesh was later sold in meat markets for the poor, and the rest was boiled down for glue.

Concrete may have been Rome's most significant discovery because concrete could be molded into different shapes, which then allowed builders to use the arch and keystone concept, enabling the construction of vast vaulted rooms that boggled the imagination, even for the engineers. Thinking about concrete, I turned my head and spotted the *Pantheon* at the far end of the large forum, in which I found myself standing. Marcus Vipsanius Agrippa's *Pantheon* was the largest, un-reinforced, stable, concrete domed structure in the world that would stand for thousands of years. My teacher Zeno told Decimus and me that fist-size, hollow terracotta balls had been placed into the concrete mix making the fabricated stone lighter, which also prevented the weight of the solid domed ceiling from caving in by its own mass. In the *Pantheon's* structure, a circle at the top of the dome served in the same fashion a keystone did to an arch: all the strength of the structure pivoted around and down from the circle evenly. Concrete was truly one of Rome's major contributions to humanity, leaving the world with all her monstrosities and monuments. This unique, man-made, manufactured rock material was only a mixture of sand, lime, volcanic ash, and water. Using the right portions of each, the wet mix soon turned into a stable aggregate when dried. It could even desiccate underwater into a molded stone that should last until the world ends.

Once again, I had learned all of this from my teacher Zeno, a brilliant man but rude to little boys. I could not believe this was what was occupying my mind in my drugged state as I stood next to the litter holding the wine-gall skin. I turned my attention to a sizeable stone-and-concrete aqueduct near the amphitheater, superimposing its shadow upon the multi-levels of the circular side of the amphitheater that loomed before me. Stretching my head up and up the straight wall of the amphitheater, I marveled at the size of this monstrosity. Looking up even higher, I shifted my eyes to the sky; and I was astounded by how blue it was and how dark and puffy the clouds seemed as they skirted over the city. I lowered my gaze to all the people around me and was caught up in the excitement of all those entering the many arched entrances and tunnels. For the first time in my life, I believed that maybe this *megalopolis* called Rome was the center of the universe and this was the eternal city. I turned to tell my father that I was going to have a grand day with him, but he was busy speaking with a corpulent man wearing red sandals and a purple-bordered toga. He, too, had to be a senator because of the two iron rings on his middle fingers, just like my father had. I counted two more *lictors* conversing with my father's four.

As the two senators were engaged in what looked like a serious conversation, I could hear the shouts inside the theater yelling, "Strike him! Slay him! Burn him!" Then a strange hush came from the amphitheater, but it was only a few seconds before a massive roar rose like a mountain wind rushing down a steep valley whistling through the pines. Apparently, a contest inside had concluded leaving a victor along with a victim. I found myself turning back to my father hoping he would hurry and finish so we would not miss the next fight. It was at this point my father's four *lictors* all turned and walked together towards the city wall, which we passed through when we entered into Mars Field.

Not long after the four *lictors* had departed, the obese senator headed towards one of the amphitheater's entrances. When my *pater* turned to me, I was stunned to see an ashen pale over his visage. He slammed a fist into his left palm and then felt for the gladius hidden under his toga. Satisfied that it was there, he erratically walked towards me and reached for the wineskin. Snatching it as an eagle would a fish from some lake, my father quickly lifted it to his mouth for a long swill. After the long gulp, he barked orders to the litter bearers and Lentulus before addressing me.

"Bad news, Venustus. My plans have been dipped in black dye. Something has gone awry. Now listen carefully. I want you to return to the villa and find your mother. Tell her to accompany you back here as swiftly as possible in this litter. Do not allow Claudia to see you. Do you understand, boy? Do not let Claudia see a hair on your head, or I will have heavy wages to pay if she does. Now hurry back in the litter, and remember this is a life-or-death situation. I hoax you not!"

"But, *Pater,* what do we do when we return? How will we find you?"

"Do not fret; I will find you. Just come back to this very location, and wait with your *mater*. I am going with Lentulus to Senator Carnalus's home. That senator who was just here informed me that Senator Carnalus, your friend Decimus, and your teacher are all dead. A group of assassins murdered the senator, his son, and your *didace* early this morning. Lentulus and I are going to see for ourselves, but I will be back here before you return."

A SHORT READING GIVEN AT THE GREAT LIBRARY OF ALEXANDRIA BY EPAPHRODITUS

Given during the year of the four emperors.   *69 AD*

THE IMPORTANCE OF STATILIUS AND AGRIPPA AS FOUNDERS OF THE EMPIRE

Titus Statilius Taurus had paid for the building of an enormous amphitheater that stood not far from the Pantheon on the Field of Mars. The Amphitheater of Statilius Taurus was not only the largest amphitheater in the world at this time, but also the most massive structure standing in Rome at the start of the Empire. Taurus was Augustus's greatest admiral/general after Marcus Vipsanius Agrippa, and both men were acknowledged for their combined victory at sea and land off the coast of Actium precisely 100 years earlier. Statilius Taurus commanded the land army at Actium while Agrippa led the ramming attack ships at sea. More than any others, these two men molded Rome's first emperor, the boy Octavius, into Augustus.

Both men also put their mark on Rome and its new empire since that pivotal battle. Taurus was later known for his amphitheater. Agrippa also marked himself as a genius architect with the construction of his theater where Julius Caesar was murdered and the Pantheon, a temple dedicated to the dozen zodiac constellation gods who purportedly controlled the 12 sections of the heavens from east to west and north to south. The Pantheon's dome ceiling has an open circle at the top that allows sunlight to pour in during the day giving illumination to the 12 niches holding the 12 bronze deities. In addition, Marcus Agrippa built the first great public bathhouse in Rome along with the Julia and Virgo Aqueducts. After the completion of the two aqueducts, the new abundance of water allowed Rome to flush many sewers plugged for hundreds of years. The Tiber, now a flowing cesspool, polluted over the centuries due to ignorance and the convenience of emptying drains into this main artery flowing next to the world's largest city. Ever since the river that flowed past Rome had become the most massive sewer-conduit in the world, fresh water had been a problem for the city fathers for hundreds of years. The only source of clean, fresh water had to come to Rome by lead pipes and arched bridges stretching from mountain lakes and streams located miles away in the center of Italia. Had Rome not contaminated its own water source, there would have been no need to build a dozen or so costly aqueducts that required hundreds of slaves for its daily maintenance. These aqueducts became the first major drain on the economy of Rome that slowly led to the inflationary practices of minting coins to keep up the expenses of massive armies and infrastructure that continually added to overhead costs.

THE RISE OF THE CAESAR CULT

The obvious conclusion was if Julius Caesar was, a god in death along with Augustus Caesar, then Tiberius Caesar must also be a god in life. With thousands of years of Egyptian history testifying to the mythology of the pharaohs being both physical kings and spiritual gods rolled into one, the notion seemed the perfect myth for Rome. Even the Egyptian queen, Cleopatra VII, had a huge stone relief carved in Upper Egypt depicting her holding Julius Caesar's child in the same fashion as 3,000 years of sculptures and reliefs showing the goddess and her son, Isis and Horus. The image was apparent; Cleopatra was portraying herself as the goddess Isis and Caesar's infant son as the god Horus. Since the god Osiris and father of Horus was murdered with a dagger and cut into pieces before being thrown into the Nile by Seth, the evil brother of Osiris, so was Julius Caesar cut down by knives of angry senators in Rome. This idea of a mother-child cult along with the father being murdered was present in almost every society from the beginning of time and can be attested to by statues of bronze or stone along with written records from before the Kingdom of Chin, the Hindu people, and all the Barbarians living to the west, east, and north of Rome.

Years ago Julius Caesar tried to introduce into Roman society his pseudo-queen, Cleopatra VII, as the Egyptian goddess Isis. I believe this was the start of a blasphemy of human worship in Rome when Caesar erected a golden, naked statue of Cleopatra in the temple to Venus during her two-year visit to Rome with her younger brother-husband along with her young son sired by Julius Caesar. She stayed at Calpurnia, Caesar's legal wife's villa outside of Rome just a short walk to reach the walls of the eternal city. When Caesar allowed this arrangement at his wife's villa, it set the future standard of behavior regarding mistresses for all Roman nobles in the Empire. Once Augustus came to power, the Cleopatra-Venus golden statue disappeared forever; but, ironically, Rome became the mother-goddess mistress of the world.

Today Caius Julius Caesar's ashes are resting in a small yet consequential temple in the unique and strategic location of the Forum Romanum standing next to the circular temple of the Vestals. According to ancient Roman traditions, human remains were never to be entombed inside the walls of the Seven Hills. Julius Caesar became the first human buried within the city in his own Greek-style temple. This act was perhaps the most decisive move to destroy the Republic and create the new emperor-god cult. Clearly the elevation of Julius Caesar to god status after his assassination made it entirely logical to believe the god bloodline ran through the then mere teenager Octavius, grandnephew of Caesar, who would eventually be elevated to divi filius or a god living with humans. The only person Octavius knew who stood in his way to godhood was Caesarion, the son of Cleopatra and Julius Caesar. Just three years before the Battle of Actium, Cleopatra, the queen mother of Caesarion, had him anointed with the title "King of Kings." After the battle of Actium, Octavius ordered the young boy, who was just a few years younger than Octavius, executed. I might add none of the other children by Cleopatra suffered this fate. These were the children of Marcus Antonius (Mark Antony), and all were given to Octavius's sister and ex-wife of Mark Antony to be raised under Augustus's watchful eye. Octavius needed a title to battle a now-dead King of Kings; and he did it by changing his name to this baby name, Augustus, yet a name of magnificence combined with the nickname of a now-dead god, Caesar. This was undeniable proof of the orchestration of the human-god cult now present in Rome, the worship of Augustus Caesar.

Thus, with Ptolemy Caesar (Caesarion) dead, Octavius knew of no one who could claim divinity from Julius Caesar. Augustus's final act to show his diabolical intent was his arrangement after his own death. Augustus was to be buried in a grand mausoleum built on the Field of Mars but outside the walls of the city near the Tiber River. He commissioned the manufacturing of a mountainous tomb for all to see. In my lifetime, no other human was interred within the walls of Rome – just Julius Caesar. Whoever could prove a connection to Caesar's bloodline could claim to be the next human-god.

Three thousand years of Egyptian might, eight hundred years of Greek learning, and two thousand years of Jewish moral influence all came crashing to an end once Octavius became Augustus. The Roman Empire was born with Augustus allowing the worship of anything except the truth. The new norms were the practice of eating, drinking, and entertainment all involving sex and death orgies. What had once been considered evil was now good and what was good, now became evil. Augustus, as his reign dragged out, first tried to stem the floodgates of the immorality and the loss of morals that occurred throughout the Empire. The Emperor's own family became victims of a valueless and moral collapse due to the tolerance of all religions except the one that followed the risen Jesus of Nazareth that began in Judaea after Legate Pontius Pilate ordered the execution of this teacher outside Jerusalem on a cross now stretching out 36 years ago.

Debauchery and wanton depravity could not be stopped even in the household of Augustus Ceasar. Nothing changed even after Augustus sent his only daughter and later his granddaughter to be lonely exiles on deserted islands as an example to all of the crime of sensuality. Their public punishment for their infidelities and other deceitful sins, which had become known by all in Rome, did nothing to deter Rome's ethical illness. In some unspeakable way, the scandalous behavior of all classes in Rome spread like a transmittable disease.

It is vital to remember Julius Caesar had no sons other than the bastard son of Cleopatra, whom she anointed as the "King of Kings" in her homeland of Egypt. Caesar's daughter Julia became the wife of Pompey, the general who conquered Palestina for Rome and who was later murdered in Egypt by Cleopatra's younger brother-husband. Caesar's daughter Julia had since died in childbirth. After Julia's untimely death, she was honored by being entombed in a splendid tomb in the Campus Martius. The Field of Rome was initially considered the outskirts of the central metropolis of the Seven Hills but not contained within the original 12-foot-thick, 32-foot-high red-brick walls that encompassed the Seven Hills of Rome. I can never overexpress the construction of a temple for Caesar's remains being allowed inside the walled city of Seven Hills still standing today in the Forum Romanum within sight of the Roman Senate Building. This temple-tomb made Julius Caesar the only human to have a sepulcher in the city limits of the Eternal City. As I have already alluded, this was the start of Caesar worship; and the idea that a god could become a human and live with us mere mortals is not a new conception. What was new for Romans was this idea of a holy bloodline running from the loins of Caesar. Even if it were an indirect bloodline, Octavius was destined to become a son of god, all because he was from Caesar's bloodline, a son of Julius Caesar's niece.

Before Caesar's daughter Julia married Pompey, she bore a daughter from an earlier marriage; her name was Atia Caesaris. Atia was the mother of Octavius; and his sister Octavia was the mother of Marcellus, the name of the great theater on the Tiber. Once Augustus became emperor, it was widely spread in the streets and halls of Rome that Atia had given birth to a male child by the god Apollo. Here is another virgin born story built on top of Octavius being the grandnephew of the god Julius Caesar. Octavius was 18 years old and away at school when he learned of the death of his granduncle, Julius Caesar. It would be later determined by the reading of Caesar's will that the late dictator had made Octavius his chief heir. Once again, this is how the teenager Octavius, adopted as a son by Julius Caesar, became the first emperor of Rome, today known as Augustus Caesar. It would take a few years and the secret and not-so-secret deaths of many people for this to finally materialize.

First came Caesar's assassination at the hands of radical Republican Senators; after those assassins were dead, then came the murder of Ptolemy Caesar in Egypt,

Cleopatra's son whom she dubbed the King of Kings. Ptolemy Caesar, according to Antony, was the biological heir of Caesar. Therefore, Caesarion, the name used by the people of illustrious Alexandria, indeed had Caesar's blood and the blood of the goddess of Isis running through his veins. If it came to a showdown between a grandnephew and the direct bloodline of Caesarion, Octavius would surely lose. Given enough time, Rome would consider a living bastard son of Caesar as a legitimate god over a distant nephew. Had Octavius not ordered the bastard god's death, history may have gone an entirely different direction, perhaps making Alexandria the world capital instead of Rome. It must have made perfect sense to Octavius to have this "King of Kings" murdered, for here was the only threat to Octavius that would prevent him from becoming a god. I should note that no other child of Cleopatra was killed by Octavius. Ironically, Augustus's sister Octavia, the mother of Marcellus, raised all of Cleopatra's children sired by Antony along with Octavia's own children through Antony and previous husbands.

Like Alexander the Great, the namesake of this cherished city, once said, "Only one sun rules the day – not two." Two years before Caesar's assassination, Octavius was a teenager when he was secretly but officially adopted by Caesar as his son. The people of Rome were not shocked when Caesar's will was presented to the populace, and they learned that Octavius was going to become their future emperor-god. Since Caesar was officially recognized as a god by the Roman Senate, just two years after his assassination, Octavius, now age 21, was declared at the same time divi filius or "god's son" or "son of god." The people of Rome accepted this without protest since Octavius at age 17 had ridden with his granduncle in the lead triumph chariot through the streets of Rome in Caesar's last triumph.

Another biting datum to ponder is to remember that Caesarion was murdered at the same age as Octavius when he rode in Caesar's chariot at the last great triumph. Ironically, it was precisely 17 years after the death of Julius Caesar when Octavius returned to Rome to become emperor of the New Empire. According to tradition, a slave had to ride in the chariot at all triumphs and continually whisper in the ear of the exalted one, "You are only a man. You are only a man." Maybe Caesar and Octavius were not listening. Two years after the triumph, Caesar was assassinated and the Vestal Virgins produced Caesar's most recent will to be made public. After the people of Rome had learned of Julius Caesar's wishes, the people of Rome accepted Octavius as Gaius Julius Caesar Octavianus, the grandson of Caesar's sister Julia and son of Julia's daughter Atia, as Julius Caesar's adopted son. From that day forward, Octavius was the sole proprietor of Caesar's title and fortune. It took 17 years before Octavius could return to Rome for his own triumph ride through Rome and up Capitoline Hill.

In those 17 years, Octavius defeated the second triple triumvirate, which he was part of at the start. He then had to defeat Marcus Antonius (Mark Antony) and the Ptolemaic Greek Queen, Cleopatra VII, and to murder Caesarion, Caesar's bastard son with the Queen of Egypt, the very mother who was depicted in gold at the Temple of Venus in the center of Rome.

Soon after Octavius's return to Rome and with all his enemies subdued, Octavius declared, "The Republic restored." Then hypocritically Octavius demanded a new name for himself, that being Augustus Caesar. Here was the smoke in the eyes of Rome: the day Octavius declared the Republic restored is the day it died. It was also the day the Empire rose in its place with the son of Apollo now living on Palatine Hill.

It should be noted that the only temple to a god allowed to stand on Palatine Hill is to Apollo, the god of light. No one disputed that Augustus was Rome's new god, especially since no one knew of any other bloodline that could interfere with Augustus Caesar's claim to the throne. The myth had already been sown declaring the bloodline that ran through Caesar and Augustus came through a miraculous birth by a virgin mother seeded by the god Apollo. If anyone has any doubts to what I am saying, there still is only one temple standing on Palatine Hill. Travel there, and see for yourself that this lonely shrine is none other than the temple to Apollo.

After Augustus firmly held the reins of Rome including the Empire, he needed to show the people who was going to be the next pseudo-god. While his generals of Actium were building grand public and religious monstrosities, Augustus began to construct next to the bank of the Tiber one of the most magnificent theaters in the world, the Theater of Marcellus. This was an obvious move to show that Augustus thought Marcellus would be an excellent emperor; thus, the name Marcellus Theater. The theater was named after Augustus's sister's son, who mysteriously died before his 20th birthday, long before the theater was completed.

If there were foul play involved in Marcellus's death, the only person with a motive would be Augustus's wife, Livia Drusilla, also known as Julia Augusta, her name after she was adopted into the Julian family once she married Augustus. She was the only one to gain from the strange death of Marcellus other than Agrippa, who was on the island of Lesbos when the boy died. Let the reader understand, when Livia married Augustus, she brought to the marriage the small child Tiberius. It is also important to remember this little boy was the son from her previous husband from whom Augustus had stolen Livia. At the wedding ceremony between Livia and Augustus, Livia was heavy with another son, Nero Claudia Drusus, also by her former husband. After Marcellus and Agrippa both had died of a strange sickness, it was accepted by all in Rome that

Drusus would follow Augustus as the next emperor. The reason for this belief was quite simple. The fame Drusus had obtained while leading Rome's legions in Gaul and Germania, is without dispute. In a foreign land, Drusus fought in single combat with three different Barbarian chieftains and killed all three. Drusus was the last general since Alexander the Great to actually participate in a battle. Yet, Alexander never engaged in single combat with any king or general. Fighting in a gladiatorial bout, not once but three times was something people only read about in ancient tales. Yet, here before the people of Rome was a new hero named Drusus.

Shortly after Tiberius joined his younger brother Drusus near the Rhine River as a co-legate, Tiberius found Drusus convalescing from a horse-fall injury. This event happened about two years after Tiberius had wed Julia. It was not long after this visit by Tiberius when Drusus died from some strange illness, which had nothing to do with his horse-fall injuries. Since Tiberius was present on the frontier when his younger brother died, people began to wonder. Many in Rome speculated that Tiberius might have poisoned his little brother with the help of his mother Livia. Why would a woman kill her son over another? This question answers why Livia remained untouched by any scandalous rumor. Yet, how does anyone explain the sudden and unexpected death of the healthy Drusus? Here was a champion who would have cemented the Caesar Cult for all time. There would never be anyone popular with the people, the soldiers of the legions, and even Augustus as Drusus.

It would only be many years later when the Livia rumor and accusations came forward. It was not until those with long memories reflected upon the many unusual connections between Livia and strange deaths of other possible successors to the throne of Rome. Perhaps someday Livia might be revealed as a cold-blooded murderer of her own litter. She may have even poisoned her husband in his old age in the name of gaining sovereign control of the Empire with her son Tiberius.

It should be stated that it was under the rule of Augustus Caesar and two years after the death of Nero Claudia Drusus, the younger brother of Tiberius, that the virgin birth of the one called the Nazarene occurred in the little town of Bethlehem in Judaea. I will later explain that it was in this same year of the Nazarene's birth that Herod the Great murdered one of his own sons. Now, may I add that Augustus died mysteriously a month short of his 77th birthday? I had personally talked to some slaves who were alive on Palatine Hill when Augustus was old; they told me Augustus feared his wife was going to poison him. Augustus actually grew his own food and very carefully watched its preparations. These slaves said to me that the only way Livia could have successfully poisoned her husband was by injecting his fruit trees, the fruit of which he would pick himself and eat. No one that I have talked to has suggested that Livia was observed doing *such a thing, but that is what I was told. After Marcellus, Agrippa, and Drusus were removed from the board of life, people of Rome quietly speculated; but they felt helpless with what was happening on Palatine Hill. Was Livia really that ambitious? I am sure there were many questions after Agrippa married Augustus's only daughter Julia and so soon after Marcellus's death. Agrippa was 43 when he wed Julia, and she bore him many children in the next nine years before Agrippa passed away from a long, strange illness. As I have already stated, he was buried along with Marcellus in the mausoleum of the god Augustus. But it should be understood that there was a spread of about eleven years between the deaths of Marcellus and Agrippa; people tend to forget that both men are entombed together.*

CHAPTER THREE

Rome – Middle of the morning on the 50th Anniversary of Actium. (September 2, 19 AD)

"We women are the most unfortunate creatures."   Euripides' Mede

Lentulus stood stoically next to my father pointing to the litter. I obeyed by getting into the ornate silk-and-wood carrier while Lentulus tied the curtains shut on both sides, which gave me the feeling of being trapped like a bird in a cage. Sitting back on a silk cushion, I felt myself slipping into a state of paralyzing fear. I believed it to be fear only because this was the first time in my short life I knew of anyone or anything that had died. At my present juncture of age, I am not sure I had even seen a dead bird or rodent, let alone a deceased person. Ironically, only moments prior I wanted to go watch people kill each other; but that was before I learned the fate of Zeno and Decimus. The intoxication that had filled my head just a flick of time ago as I stood before the giant amphitheater with the aqueduct shadow over-laying its side quickly vanished like an invisible vapor. Punishment replaced my aberrant thoughts, and a horrible dread loomed over me like a vulture circling its dying prey.

The litter jerked violently up and began moving like a rocking ship in a storm. The litter bearers were now jogging because they had orders to get me to my father's villa straightway. The air inside the closed palanquin became oppressive, almost like the fervent heat in a foundry. My avarice thoughts and desires of wanting to find enjoyment in men killing one another, only for entertainment, was now sickening me. This discipline of dread I was currently experiencing in the litter was overwhelming and incomprehensible. How the gods worked with such speed in punishing me befuddled my mind. Why did my friend and teacher have to die along with Senator Carnalus? According to my childish conclusions, I was the cause of everything.

Tonight sitting in a Roman jail 80 years later dictating this story, I need to digress to once again explain myself at age ten. Most of the ideas I am now ascribing to myself are coming from a man who is a few hours from turning age 91. To be honest and accurate, it took many decades of returning vicariously to that day and reviewing each event repeatedly before I was able to grasp all my thoughts and reactions. Nevertheless, what I am describing now were my exact thoughts as a child on that day but now in the voice of an old man. Obviously, I did not even have the vocabulary at that age to express what I am describing now; for that took years of trying to attribute a sense of understanding and ascribe thoughtful words to all the events on that Actium holiday. Now, at the end of my life at age 91, you could ask me what I had for breakfast yesterday; and I might not remember. But on that day at age ten, I do remember tasting a fabulous fruitcake while I was with my father in the litter. I also remember everything else about that day in vivid colors. This must be one of the mysteries of life. The past is profoundly frozen with clarity, but the near past is lost in a murkiness of fog. I also need to say that today I totally reject my childish conclusions of any idea that some powerful god of Rome was the cause of the state of my mind that morning in the swift-moving litter racing through the streets of Rome. Assigning self-blame was also an incorrect conclusion. Childhood is just that, childish and irrational, especially when it comes to tragedy. Nevertheless, I am recording my mentality of that morning after many years of self-examination; and I am just trying to be truthful even if there is no logical reason why I would have such cognitive conclusions such as self-blame and judgments from the gods as being attributed to my actions. Nevertheless, I believed I was the cause of everything. I thought the gods were angry with me, and I questioned what it would take to appease them. Shame washed over me like an avalanche of snow rushing down a steep mountain. For the first time in my life, I questioned, "Was every thought and deed being recorded? Did everyone have to pay the price for all his or her wrong deeds and evil thoughts?" I would later learn that we do have to answer for every thought, word, and action on the Day of Judgment, and sometimes before that day. If we suffer before the Day of Judgment, this is much better than suffering after that final day. Today I believe there will be a *Book of Works* opened on the Judgment Day but there will also be another book that is much more important to have your name in. That would be the *Book of Life*.

66

At times, we certifiably do reap what we sow; yet, it usually takes time for the crop of transgressions to bear its ugly fruit. I did not think of the thousands inside that killing building not being punished in the same fashion I was. Had I observed that thought, then why was I being singled out above all of them? I had not even gone inside at that point; yet, why would I be guiltier than they?

Riding in the swift-moving litter, my body was profusely secreting fluids from my forehead. As I was resting on the silk cushions, my body began to slip into a state where it started to shiver and tremble uncontrollably. I did not know nor understand at that age the dangers associated with fear and shock. Now I noticed sweat pouring like a river flowing down my sides from under my arms. I had never perspired from there before, and this worried me. Was there something physically wrong with me? Was it the gall and wine trying to escape my body? My plague compounded itself when my chest began to ache from the heavy pounding from within my body, and I pressed once again with my fingers hard against my ribs in an attempt to stop the inner pain. I flattened out on the silk cushions and lifted my feet above my head to help my physical discomfort. Little did I know this was the correct thing to do. I began to feel slightly better when everything turned figuratively and literally over.

Something out in the street had caused the eight men carrying the litter, to make an abrupt halt, and I heard strange yelling from outside the litter. Once the litter had stopped, I peeked out the bottom of the tied curtains to get air and to see what was happening. To my surprise, two men were running towards the litter from a side alley, each holding an unsheathed gladius. These double-edged swords were just like my father's: the length of a man's forearm with an ivory handle attached to a large ball pummel. Both men looked malicious but familiar. Their blades were wet and red as if recently dipped in paint, but their white homespun tunics gave them away. Both men's garments were splattered with fresh blood. They both looked like they had escaped the arena during a gladiator battle.

The two men advanced toward the silver-and-gold palanquin. One man had his eyes locked onto mine as I was peering from under the silk curtain. I just stared back trying to understand. The other man vanished out of view as he quickly cut in front of the stopped litter carriers. The other advancing man was still holding my eyes with his before he reached out with his left arm to grab me. It was then I moved away from the extending hand. He missed his opportunity, and the man in front apparently stabbed one of the litter bearers because I heard a sickening swish and thump sound along with a gurgling scream that followed. The right corner of the palanquin went down forcing the man's hand up and away from grabbing my tunic while I tried to roll away to the other side of my birdcage. The litter whipped up and flipped over tumbling over several times. Somewhere in this callus event, I found myself outside the litter lying in a gutter next to a right-angled, elevated walkway of paving stones. Out of the corner of my left eye, I saw the litter bearers using their poles to protect themselves. Now I understood why the palanquin went flying up and away as it did. These poor slaves were just trying to save themselves from two killers. My paralysis was completely gone when I gained my feet. One of the killers noticed me and turned towards where I was now standing. I quickly turned and ran down the street jammed with people. Ducking and weaving through the crowd seemed to work, for the screaming of witnesses at the sight of the litter crash started to fade away. Still, I could hear someone pursuing me. I turned a corner and quickly grabbed a woman's hand who had her back to me. She seemed startled, but I tried to smile up at her acting as if she were my mother. The man with the sword ran past us, perhaps confused by the ruse of a little boy holding a woman's hand. After the man had passed, I released the sweet lady's hand and reversed my direction, turning down a side street, still twisting and turning through the sea of people as only a little boy can. I kept turning my shoulders and driving between men and women who pressed this crowded city in a constant, chaotic melee. I ran and ran until I was only a short distance from the lane that wound up to my father's villa. Finally, I stopped to gain some breath. Heaving for air, I bent down with my hands on my knees and noticed I was soaking wet from sweat. Looking back from where I had come, I saw no pursuing man. I straightened and continued up the hill as fast as my feet could run. On reaching the circle entrance to my father's villa with the enormous fountain in the middle, I fell upon the water, gulping the sweet liquid like a dog.

"Hello, Venu," said a familiar voice.

I looked up; and there stood Eli, my little Jewish friend, smiling broadly hoping that maybe we could play. "Eli, my mother, do you know where she is?" I asked in a choking yelp almost like the squeaking sound of a young, startled puppy.

"Yes, follow me," he said with a strange excitement such as he would when I came up with a new game to play. He led me through the unbolted *ostium* through to the *vestibulum* after passing the *sacrarium*, the room where the household gods stood on stone pedestals. We also passed the *tablinum*, the central office of my father. Eli stopped once we reached the back of the *vestibulum*, and Eli pointed out beyond the vast atrium to the grand garden that stood on the two sides of the *peristylium*, which stretched out beyond the patio and the stone seats. She was out into the garden. I slowly walked into the atrium where my father and Lentulus had been waiting for me earlier. Out in the flower section was my mother quietly sitting on a stone bench. She was wearing a blue-and-white embroidered *himaton* made from expensive Dravidian cotton.

At first, I did not recognize her; for I had never seen my *mater* out of her simple slave garments. Why was she dressed as a wealthy matron of the villa? She was also wearing a light-blue silk sash wrapped around her waist; and on her feet, she wore a pair of white sandals similar to mine. Her hairstyle was also different. It looked as if it must have taken lots of time to style it since I last saw her. A blue strip of matching Dravidian cotton held her towering blond hair in place. The back, which I could see from where I stood, was quite attractive and was also held together with a silver clasp-looking comb. Resting on the stone bench next to her was a modest white cotton bag with a drawstring at the top. It looked as if she were waiting to go on a trip. Did my father lie to me, and had Claudia told the truth? I told Eli to hide at the side of the *peristylium* because danger was coming. He must have sensed my seriousness, for he did as I instructed. I waited until he slipped into a side *cubicula diuna*, which was similar to my small bedroom. I then tried to move soundlessly down the three steps onto the mosaic patio. Both sides of the garden had hundreds of identical blood-red columns stretching out and growing smaller as each line of pillars looked like they were pointing to some invisible vanishing point. It was almost as if I were having an intense, irrational dream when I locked my eyes onto my mother. Adding to the nightmare came a fiendish voice cutting me to the core. It was none other than Claudia Pulchra Vetallus Varus. My only salvation was she had not spotted me. I quickly dropped into a squatted position next to a stone chair on the patio.

"Arena, my dearest! Sorry you have to leave us!" mocked Claudia in a pretend voice. She had approached my mother from the far side of the garden. "But at least you don't have to die like your son!"

My mother jumped up holding her cotton bag, and she looked abnormally statuesque as Claudia's words washed over her. "Yes, your feeble, effeminate little boy Venustus is most probably already dead! His loving father set the trap himself by sending him back here alone in the palanquin into the hands of my two lovers, Janius and Jamus. You know them – my two loyal litter bearers. Yes, they are waiting for him in the streets below as we speak."

I could not believe I heard this open confession. Did my father order my death, or did he not? I wanted to judge him as innocent. At the amphitheater, he sounded genuine and, indeed, planned to save my mother and me. Yet,

Claudia knew of it and was serendipitously using her servile litter bearers to execute me in the streets of Rome. How could this be happening? Claudia lapsed into a sadistic, raging fit of laughter. Then the most astounding thing happened. Arena stemmed her grief as she lowered her right hand into the cotton bag; and out came an old, rusty-looking dagger with a yellow bone handle. Claudia did not seem to notice while she laughed exposing her milky white neck with each cackle. Using that opportune moment, my quiet-natured mother executed a vicious slash with the old knife across Claudia's throat spitting out the words: "You stinking demon witch of Isis! You are nothing but an underworld wretch!"

A surprised Claudia screamed as she flew back gripping her throat with both hands. After she had taken several steps away from my mother, she lifted her hands to see how much blood should have been gushing from her throat – but there was no blood. Later in life, I would learn that cutting someone's throat, even in that fashion with a sharp knife, is almost impossible due to all the muscles and other sinewy tendons in the neck. It is better to drive a blade from the side just below the ear; and once the blade is buried in the neck, either push or pull the sharp side out forward. Nevertheless, my mother did not know this; nor did I at this time in my life. Claudia kept her eyes locked on her clean hands and placed them once again to her throat and looked to see if she was bleeding. I noticed only a horrible, long red welt on Claudia's throat. I knew at once as well as my mother that the rusty knife was old and dull and had not even cut the skin. Claudia, now moving with cat-like speed, attacked with her fingernails slashing at Arena's beautiful face. My dear mother was pushed back onto the stone bench and absently dropped the dagger when she flew backward off the bench. After my mother's fall, she tried her best to get away from this fiend who was going for her face with her blade-like nails. Whatever fear I had up until now was gone. All I wanted to do was rescue my mother. I sprinted out into the garden grabbing Claudia's left arm from behind her. Claudia looked surprised to see me alive after she had turned to see who was holding her arm. She just stood staring at me while my mother was able to gain her feet. I just froze and watched Claudia's crazy eyes widen before she slapped me squarely in the face with her open right hand. I went flying to the ground onto my back feeling my head bounce off the stone walking path. Shooting stars interfered with my sight, but I felt no pain.

"You are alive!" declared my mother with great relief. Hearing my mother's voice, I tried to get back to my feet despite my vision problem. I could not stand for long but, instead, tumbled over into some flowers from the dizziness swimming in my head; yet, I was determined to save my mother. I quickly crawled towards Claudia who was now looking back towards my mother. I sank my teeth into her left ankle. She shrieked in pain before she kicked me in the head with her other foot. I went back again into the same flower bed of oriental flowers rolling like a leather ball.

"Run, Venustus! Save yourself!" screamed my mother standing not close enough for me to rescue her. I was now entangled in the long stems of unique flowers and watched what happened next in horror. With unexpected speed, Claudia scampered around the bench my mother had been sitting on before Claudia had appeared. Bending over, she retrieved the old, rusty dagger. I wanted to stand but couldn't. In Claudia's right hand was my mother's dull knife, which oddly looked like a Minotaur's claw. In one swift leap, Claudia plunged the knife-claw in a downward plunge deep into my *mater's* chest. It happened so fast; had I blinked, I would have missed it. My sweet mother let out her last gasp of air, while Claudia executed a quarter turn with her hand and then pulled the rusty weapon from my *mater's* chest. Time ripped like a giant tree just axed; and slowly but magnificently my mother fell towards earth like a majestic, falling cypress. Her lifeless body slumped onto a bed of purple and pink flowers. Of course, my *mater* was more than a giant tree to me; but I knew she would never rise again because of the barbaric act of unimaginable evil, which toppled my *mater* forever in this life. Claudia slowly turned her gaze towards me while I only stared at my mother, who looked strangely serene and beautiful. There was a unique peacefulness about her as she rested on her pyre of flowers. Once I lifted my eyes to Claudia, there she was standing over me heaving for breath with my mother's rusty *pugio* still clutched in her hand. Instead of attacking me, Claudia appeared distracted by something. Looking back toward the atrium, she absently patted her head with her left hand. A look of horror rose up into her eyes, and her head moved back and forth searching for something lost. I finally realized it was her missing wig. Irrationally, we both looked around for the wig. I spotted it first; resting in a bed of flowers, it seemed like a small, slain animal. When I pointed to it, Claudia smiled at her fake hair but left it as she turned her gaze back to me. I noticed her green Egyptian linen garment was torn at the bodice, which she was now holding together with her knife hand.

"Now you're next, you little *mimus* tick!" gasped Claudia between heaving breaths. When she switched her left hand to the torn bodice freeing her knife hand, I knew I had to escape; or I, too, would soon be dead. I rolled to my feet wondering why she called me a "farce" arthropod. I let it go and started sprinting through the garden heading for the far wall. As I ran, I could hear

Claudia rushing behind; but not surprisingly, I was much quicker. One sudden look back showed me why. Her long, torn garment was the cause of her slowness. I turned my focus back towards the back wall. It was rushing towards me, and I knew it would take all my agility to jump and hook my fingertips on top of the high wall. Miraculously, I did it with such skill that it surprised me. With my fingers on the top edge, my feet were running up the wall that had to be twice my height. I pulled and ran at the same time. Once at the top, I reached for the back part of the wall pulling myself up to the upper portion with all my strength. This white-brick plastered wall had always scared me because it was an encompassing barrier in my life. This mid-morning it inexplicably became the opposite. It was the first lesson of my new life, an experience that I would not understand for many years into the future: any obstacle will not stand in my way and will become a barrier to someone else. As I lay lengthwise at the top of the wall, I took a big gulp of air and wiped the sweat from my face with the sleeve of my pseudo-senatorial tunic. Down below me was Claudia running towards the wall with her garment held up in her left hand as she was flashing milky-white thighs. She must have stopped somewhere in the garden and ripped off the lower portion of her *stola* to allow her to run faster. This extra moment had given me all the time I needed to scale the wall. In her right hand was the rusty dagger with my mother's blood dripping down onto her fingers and wrist. I quickly glanced over to where my mother was. I could see her small, stately body lying statue-like among purple and pink flowers with her honey-colored hair covering her bloody face. This picture would never fade from the gallery of my mind – horrible mental baggage I would carry with me for the rest of my life.

When Claudia reached the wall, she lunged with her left hand trying to grab me. I waited until the last moment and kicked out with my sandaled foot towards the grabbing hand. There was a noticeable sound similar to a small tree branch breaking as her middle finger snapped back. She gave out a horrid scream, dropped the knife from her right hand, and grasped her injured finger with the now-knifeless hand. I saw that her middle finger was pointing backward at an abnormal angle, and I felt a warm glow fill me.

The instant she looked up at me, a string of curses in the name of Isis flew out of her mouth. When she finished, I declared in a loud voice that surprised even me, "I will return someday and kill you in the same way you murdered my mother!" With that declaration of childish bravado, I spat in her face, rolled off the backside of the wall, and found myself outside my father's villa. I ran down the road from behind the wall until I reached the narrow street that wound up the hill to the many expensive dwellings of the oldest and wealthiest patricians of Rome.

Following the lane back down into the city, I finally found myself next to a red-bricked wall of a bread bakery. I was gasping for air as I looked towards the lane leading up to Esquiline Hill and wondering what to do next. My mind felt like a ship lost at sea, all due to thick darkness. Evil had come to visit my heart and would become my friend for many years to come. I did not define it as revenge; but, in the moment of hate, I did spit in Claudia's face, which somehow opened a dark door of shame while other indescribable feelings started rushing to control the very center of my being. I now had only one purpose in life: to carry out my threat against Claudia. Nothing else mattered. As I was fomenting that decision, I realized I had been weeping torrents of tears with each gasp of air. I do not remember how long I leaned against the wall of the bakery; but my mouth repeatedly uttered, "I love you, *Mater*; I love you. I am sorry I did not save you. Please forgive me." I knew she could not hear me; but I kept whispering this mantra, similar to that of a Hindu *yogi* sitting cross-legged on a street corner in Rome mumbling something over and over and over again as his hand worked beads to count the number of times he said whatever he was speaking in his foreign tongue. After I had stopped my weeping, I used my tunic sleeve to blow my nose and wipe away the tears that stained my face.

"There he is! Do not let him escape!"

Looking up, I recognized the same two men, Janius and Jamus, Claudia's litter bearers, both holding Roman swords. They too seemed out of breath and sweating profusely. There was also something different about them. They both were splattered head to toe in much more blood than had been on their clothing when they attacked the litter earlier. Blood dripped from their tunics, hair, arms, and sword handles. The men appeared to have participated in some kind of blood baptism. My knees at first began to knock together in fear of my own demise; but, as they started to rush forward, I regained control. Like a scared dog, I instinctively turned towards flight. Moving down the now-empty street, I realized I was only a boy and could not outrun grown men. There were no pedestrians to run between, and I wondered why all the people in this street earlier had vanished. My mind raced for a solution of escape after dismissing the thought of the empty street. When I realized my only option, I darted into the nearest alley that I knew was knee-deep in human sewage cast there from the windows above on both sides of the alley. Without any running water in the ten-story apartments above, the residents each morning emptied their hundreds of chamber pots out their windows. This was why the *Urbs* smelled worse than the Tiber, especially on hot, humid days like today. I was hoping these knee-deep, filthy alleys would dissuade the men from following as I lifted my feet high after each splash in the brown-and-black sewage that splattered up into my tear-stained eyes.

I do not know how long I ran through the putrid back alleys; but, when I stopped, there was no one behind me. The sun was high in the sky but now hidden by dark, black, rain-laden clouds, which produced a stifling humidity that felt like a wet, hellish heat-breath. Such oppression made it hard to even run or breathe. It was now the noon hour of the day, and never had I been this hot and uncomfortable. I dismissed my condition happy that my plan had worked. I was still alive, and the two assassins were gone. I assumed that the two killers did not want to follow me through the sewage and that many hours must have passed since my flight began. Walking out of the alley, I found myself looking at a crowded and noisy forum. To my utter surprise, there standing before me was the *Amphitheater of Statilius Taurus*. My mind could not even comprehend that I was at the very same amphitheater my father and I were at earlier this morning. Here I was back in the *Campus Martius*, and just knowing where I was provided me some distant comfort. Finding a wall behind a fruit seller's stand, I slid down hugging my knees to my soiled chest staring absently out towards the monstrous amphitheater. The stone-and-wood structure seemed to be alive even though I knew it was inanimate.

It was not long before an old, portly fruit vendor noticed my smell and yelled, "You, boy! Get up from there! You stink like dung!"

I looked away from him heaving like a blown horse after a chariot race in the Circus Maximus. Decimus and I would go and watch the grooms on holidays when we did not have our lessons with Zeno. After each race, these young boys would start by toweling down the sleek, gigantic beasts after they were unleashed from their leather chariot leads. The exhausted steeds would stand quivering even after buckets of cold water were thrown over them, and the water and sweat were scraped away with long bronze *strigilii*. Their blood-red nostrils would be open like two caves on a rock wall. Veins would be sticking out like ropes on their heads and necks. Thinking about these tired horses, I began to shake uncontrollably. I realized a violent mental disturbance was starting to take a toll on my mind and body. Looking down at my own hands and arms, I noticed my own veins protruding like those of chariot horses after a grueling race. Was I slipping into a pit of thick darkness, which could lead to my death? Above all this, the fruit seller was still yelling; and the roar from the amphitheater filled the background noises as my mind only remembered my mother lying on her bed of flowers. In my young mind, I just could not accept she was dead. The thought that it was only this morning she was breathing and alive would not leave me alone. It is strange how the mind never rests but, becomes confused at times of high stress. I could only compare my state to chariots screaming at breakneck speeds only to crash into one another at the first hairpin turn on the track of the Circus Maximus. Everything in my inner and outer being was racing towards a violent crash just like the chariots at the first corner causing unspeakable pain and weeping from horses and drivers alike.

I felt something strike my head. I looked down at what hit me and noticed a rotten pomegranate resting in the dust next to me. Glancing up at the fat fruit seller, I saw that he was holding a second pomegranate to throw at me. "What do you want to do – drive my customers away? Go wash yourself at the public latrines!" He barked in a low tone now that he had my attention. I realized he was determined not to dirty his foot by kicking a demented, sewage-covered little boy. It was strange that the smell did not bother me; yet, I was the one covered in the brown-and-black stuff.

"I have no money to pay entry," I replied in a timid voice hoping he would leave me be. The unyielding stare of the fruit dealer persisted until he cursed some minor god and reached into his red, faded robes and pulled something from an inner pocket.

"Now go before I throw more rotten fruit at you, you little scab!" He hissed in disgust while tossing a small bronze coin into the dirt next to me while pointing with his other hand towards a public latrine. I picked up the tiny coin off the ground and left my hiding place.

Crossing the vast area between the buildings and the amphitheater, I noticed the shadow of the aqueduct was missing from where it was this morning. My mind dismissed the lost shadow as quickly as I had registered its absence. I began looking for Claudia's two bloodied killers, perceiving they might be more important than missing shadows. Why did they not follow me into the alleys? They both were soiled from blood and sweat, so what was the problem with sewage? I would never learn the answer.

The public toilet was located across the open forum from the amphitheater. Looking down toward my hand, I found myself staring at the little coin. This was the very first coin I had ever held in my hand. I almost did not give it to the old, wizened female *lavo* administrator who sat on a tall, three-legged stool near the door. It may seem unusual, but I never needed any kind of money until that moment. It was an effort to give it away to the wrinkled woman who stiffened her nose in an upward motion at my odor of sewage.

I ignored her after giving up the coin and entered. Inside the large, open rectangular lavatory, I was surprised to find it crowded. Men were standing around engaged in various levels of conversations or in doing their private business. There were a couple of women standing and talking to a smaller group of men. I worked my way around the crowded white-marbled room to the back corner. Once there I noticed everyone quickly moved away from me. I just stood there not wanting to disrobe in front of all these people, but they must have been trying to get away from me because of my smell. Looking down at the water running in a long, narrow open receptacle in front of the many white marble seats that surrounded the room, I realized how thirsty I was. I almost dropped to my knees to lap up the badly needed refreshment when someone came into the public *lavo* yelling, "Everyone, hear me! Gladiator Marius has entered the arena!" A cheer went up, and the room emptied of everyone except me. I was astonished at my great fortune. I could now disrobe and clean my tunic in the floor trough in private, without embarrassment.

I decided not to drink the water from the floor of the lavatory, correctly thinking it might make me ill, but did disrobe. Going to my hands and knees, I began washing my tunic in the slow-flowing water. After I had gotten all the mess I could out of my tunic, I started using the moving water to clean my arms and legs, as well as the rest of my naked body. Again, I returned to rinsing my senatorial tunic, repeatedly slapping it on the stone floor to beat out as much filth and water as I could. I had once watched old women washing clothes at the Tiber, and they beat their clothes against rocks in the same way I was slapping my tunic against the floor and the edge of a marble *lavo* seat. When I felt my tunic was as clean as it was going to get, I realized it would be permanently stained a gray color with the purple border looking much darker than it had been. No longer was the beautiful purple color present. I finally wrung it out the best I could and slipped it back on before anyone returned to the *lavo*. The wet material was actually refreshing against my tired body, and I knew it would dry quickly in this heat.

Next, I returned to my knees and began washing my previously white sandals; and my mind returned to my room this morning when my mother handed them to me. I started to heave with great sobs as I stopped and leaned against a marble stool with its rounded slit on top and front-side. With my head resting against a marble armrest, which was carved into a jumping dolphin, I sobbed and sobbed. During this heavy heaving of emotion, I decided the entire world was an illusion filled with a sickness of evil and hate. My very father and wicked Claudia had arranged for the only good people

I knew to die. My mother, my friend Decimus, and Zeno were gone forever. The death of Zeno did not affect me as much as the deaths of my *mater* and Decimus. I concluded I did not like Zeno very much; yet, I am sure he meant well when he used a *ferula* to strike my hands and on rare occasions a *scutia* to whip me. Fear and loneliness swirled around my mind. I needed to leave the lavatory or senselessness would overtake me; and for some reason, I did not want it to happen in such a place, not that it really mattered where someone lost all sanity.

At which point an old man entered the *lavo*, I decided it was time to leave. Back outside the public building, I looked up and down the wide-open area that circled the amphitheater. I was looking for any sign of Claudia's litter bearers. I spotted, over to my right, a fountain where some slave women were fetching water in clay pots. I again realized my incredible thirst. Moving towards the fountain, I discovered something wrong with my legs. With each step, my legs were cramping, especially in the back calves. I had to stop several times and point my toes up towards my head to relieve the excruciating pain. I felt like an old man and not a ten-year-old boy as I hobbled toward the public fountain. Once there I put my head into the pool of refreshingly cold water. After I had pulled my head out of the water, I began gulping until I remembered the horse grooms at the Circus Maximus always warning each other from allowing their soapy and lathered creatures from drinking too much after a race. Evidently it was bad for them, and I pulled away from the water thinking it might be dangerous if I filled my belly with too much since I had been running in this heat through the alleys. Standing next to the fountain I realized that I had gained valuable lessons when Decimus and I had spent hours on Roman holidays around the paddocks of the Circus Maximus watching the horse grooms. The stable boys would walk the horses for hours after a race only allowing their horses short drinks at a time. Now I understood why the grooms walked their exhausted creatures for a good hour or more after a long race before putting them back into a stall. Seemingly, there must be a similarity between humans and horses since a horse could cramp up and then injure itself by casting in its stall. Perhaps I just needed to leave the fountain and walk around to prevent cramping. I did not know if humans were like horses, but the principle seemed sound. I put my head back under the water not to drink but to wash my hair with my hands. When I removed my head out of the fountain the second time, the slave women watching me were incensed. I assumed they were afraid to say anything seeing my soiled senatorial stripe on my tunic, but a woman in a simple garb and wearing the red bonnet of a freedwoman was not intimidated.

"You, filthy little rich boy, what manners you are lacking! Our drinking water comes out of this fountain, and here you are sticking your dirty patrician head in it!"

I apologized profusely believing she was going to tell my mother, and I left hoping for no more attention. Quickly walking away with my head down, I did not realize until I was across the forum area the folly of my fear of the freedwoman telling my mother. I leaned against what I realized was the *Statilius Taurus Amphitheater*. All I wanted to do now was hide in a crowd of people, and here was the perfect place. A large percentage of Romans at this very moment were inside this very amphitheater watching its latest hero slaughtering other living humans. Claudia's litter bearers would not think a small boy would conceal himself in a crowd watching a gladiatorial game.

To my amazement, I found the games were free to Roman citizens. This seemed inappropriate to me since the public latrine cost a small coin, which was not much; but still, it seemed almost like a parable of the insanity of the times. Zeno had once instructed Decimus and me on the ills of the Roman government, which started with imperial encouragement of the wealthy to help subsidize, along with the state treasury, the different spectacles being displayed almost daily somewhere in the capital city. These events were designed to keep the unemployed masses happy and free from rioting. "Bread and Circuses!" This became the chant of those in the Empire who could make it to Rome and somehow acquired citizenship. This unique retirement plan for any citizen started as a necessity several hundred years ago shortly after the Second Punic War began. From what I had learned from my history lessons, Hannibal, the Carthaginian general, who had crossed the Alps to the southwest, was not strong enough to take the walled city of Rome. This young general was able to defeat any army thrown at him in open combat, but he was not strong enough to place the capital city in a long siege. Hannibal started with an army of 100,000 men. This number was whittled down to a quarter of its original size by the time it reached the walled city. Hannibal's only option was to take his depleted army away from the city of Rome and inflict as much injury and harm upon all of *Italia*. This he did for the next 16 years. The farmers of *Italia* during those dark years fled to the walled protection of Rome, and many did not return to their farms after the war ended. A decade or more of dependency on free food given to them by the state during the crisis was something they could and would not give up. The newly dependent people living in Rome realized they could threaten to riot and burn the city to the ground if they did not get what they wanted. City leaders had no other choice than to continue the practice of bread and circuses. This had been going on for more than three centuries. Today the children of the children, of the children, of the children, are permanently born and raised to be sustained by the state. At the present Rome is allowing this inherent weakness to perpetuate where half its capital population lives off the largess of the government. As long as there are other lands for the Romans to conquer, then taxes can be placed on the newly vanquished people to continue this vile practice. The subjected people of the occupied provinces, along with anyone with citizenship who chooses to work, pay heavy taxes, which in turn supported the rabble of Rome. Only the patrician class was exempt from taxation, and this is where the hook was placed when Rome needed help in sustaining a daily dose of entertainment to slacken the masses thirst for something to occupy their time. The alternative to the wealthy was to suffer the destruction of their opulent villas up on the hills around the lower slums when and if the bored masses looked for an outlet for their boredom. Thus, free admittance to the amphitheater on this 50th Actium celebration holiday, as well as any other day, was customary.

Zeno had explained to Decimus and me about an incredibly strange belief of the leaders of Rome, that being the majority of the members of the ruling senators believed in the free, unlimited minting of coins. Augustus and Tiberius both clearly understood the pitfalls of such a practice of having too much coinage floating around in people's moneybags; yet, it continued. Too much minting of coins and the value of an individual coin would undoubtedly drop causing extreme price increases on all goods and services. Maybe it is like eating too much honey: a man will become sick, and it may even harm his body. A little is good; too much is bad. I believe this principle fits with the creation of coins and other forms of monies. However, the majority of the ruling aristocrats of the Senate foolishly did not understand the problem. Their thinking was only based upon several questions. First, why not mint as much as the state wished? Second, what harm could come of this practice? Third, as long as the coins were made of precious metals, would there not be value in whatever was minted by the Empire? Therefore, the Roman Senate and other leaders did not consider any harmful economic consequences would befall them in extensive mining and unlimited minting of coins. The minting of coins was pushed to the side as the most prominent issue loomed over the leaders of Rome: what to do with the shiftless mass of rabble living in Rome. Could the Senate stop this dependency on the state without unleashing violence on the city? Almost half of the people residing in the Imperial city indulged their *ennui* of depravity to the extreme. Additionally, the remaining half million who were slaves also lived in the capital city; and they lived better than most of the freed citizenry, even when the freedman was living on the assistance from the Empire. The only difference was the slaves were not allowed to attend any of the free entertainment. It would not be until years later in my life that I totally understood this corrupt system of state benefits for all citizens in Rome and why it was unjust and laden with a cesspool of unfair practices. On the day my mother died, I had no understanding about the inflationary damage of unrestrained coin creation, caused by the power classes, which was directed and allowed by a small minority of those controlling the Empire who held onto an obscene amount of the world's wealth. It is ironic that the richest of all of the Roman people was my father, Vetallus Crassus.

All I could comprehend on this blistering day as I entered the *Statilius Taurus Amphitheater* was why there was no need to pay for entrance? Evidently on this day, nothing made sense to me. My only thought at that moment was it seemed strange that it cost money to use a toilet but not to enter a gladiatorial game. That was the mystery occupying my mind as I walked stiffly through the throat of a tunnel leading inside this structure of death. Even decades later it still brawls me a bit when I ponder the irony of it.

A READING GIVEN AT THE GREAT LIBRARY OF ALEXANDRIA BY EPAPHRODITUS

Given in the year of the four emperors.   *69 AD*

SLAVERY AND CRUCIFIXION IN

THE ROMAN EMPIRE

The highest aspiration for tens of millions living in the Roman Empire is citizenship. There were only three avenues to citizenship: first, being born a citizen; second, earning it after serving 20 years in the legions; third, purchasing citizenship by making an astronomical payment to Rome's treasury. Once Roman citizenship became a reality, a person received imperial security concerning legal issues such as being shielded from torture and death by crucifixion. Crucifixion was the most feared form of execution imaginable, worse than burning, strangulation, or drowning. The Romans made crucifixion their trademark in subduing and dominating their provinces far and wide. The leaders of Carthage were commonly believed to be the first who practiced this savage form of execution, but I have read about this practice as far back as the first rule of the Babylonians. I would not be surprised if it is discovered in the ancient records of Egypt. Rome tries to present itself as the origin of all things when, in truth, Rome is the world's greatest embezzler of ideas in history. Very few original thoughts come out of Rome unless the notion has to do with war, an art in which they excel. The only people to successfully defeat the Romans in combat were the Parthians, who discovered a weakness in Rome's military strategies. This weak point I will hopefully describe in a future lecture.

Some forty years before the Battle of Actium, over one hundred thousand runaway slaves under the leadership of Gladiator Spartacus battled Roman armies in Italia for three years until two Roman armies trapped the gladiator's army in Southern Italia. About six thousand of Spartacus's army survived the final contest near Mount Vesuvius. Marcus Licinius Crassus was the general of one Roman army and the origin of my senator father's nickname, Gaius Vetallus Crassus. Anyway, General Crassus ordered that all the males be crucified along the Appian Way from Capua, the city where the Spartacus revolt began, reaching to the gates of Rome. It must have been a terrifying sight and a powerful object lesson to anyone thinking of defying Roman law or authority anywhere the legions marched. These crosses remained in place along the Appian Way for years with the remains of the decaying slaves crucified. Just

81

a note, the number of miles from Capua to Rome, divided by 6,000 condemned men, would probably work out to be about 50 crosses for every mile; and that should be about one cross every 100 feet.

After the death of Herod the Great in Palestina, a Roman general named Varus crucified more than two thousand Jews to stem the revolt to break away from the Roman occupation of their nation. Varus was one of the most hated individuals in Palestina for many years because of this act; and his wife was none other than Claudia Pulchra Vetallus Varus, my father's once legal wife and slayer of my mother.

Back to the subject of crucifixion, an average healthy male could survive up to two days and nights hanging from a cross with only iron nails driven into his feet and outstretched hands on a crossbeam or patibulum. After two days, exhaustion and muscle spasms would generally overtake the victim. The cruelty in crucifixion is more of an object lesson for society over being a death sentence. I was once told by a Roman diplomat that he estimated about one thousand individuals were crucified in the Empire yearly. What is it that brings about death when you are crucified? The answer is what keeps us alive: the air we breathe. Crucifixion is a slow process of suffocation and poisoning from our own air. When crucified, a person has to push up with his nailed feet to breathe out or exhale his breath. To take in air, a crucified victim must shift his weight to his outstretched hands and not his feet. This process is repeated for each breath. To exhale, the victim must push up, straightening the body higher than when hanging just from the hands. To breathe in is the opposite process. Two days was usually the limit to someone's strength before surrendering to exhaustion and expiration. When there was no more strength to push up by the feet, the nailed sufferer would slowly drown in his own poisonous air that could not be expelled. The usual signs of being near death were when a man's chest began to swell out and the lower extremities began to distend. Not to be coy, I believe being a witness to a crucifixion caused more suffering to the observer than to the victims. Watching the muscle spasms the twitching and violent bashing of the head back and forth is very torturous besides observing the up and down movement just to breathe. This might explain why even hardened soldiers conducting these types of executions drank significant amounts of wine and gall during the long wait. Please do not misunderstand: I would rather be forced to watch a crucifixion over being nailed to a cross for two days. But let it be known: only a sick individual would enjoy watching such suffering of his fellow human.

Even Julius Caesar apparently broke after witnessing several men being crucified. As a young man in his 20s, Caesar had been kidnapped at sea by pirates when he was returning to Rome from his schooling in the city of Rhodes.

After 40 days, his wealthy family finally ransomed him; and Julius immediately hired a ship, along with mercenaries, which he led to capture the men who had abducted him. Once the pirates were captured, they were delivered to Pergamum, the closest city under Roman jurisdiction in Asia Minor. The ruling Roman magistrate ordered all of the pirates to be crucified; but, while they had been hanging from crosses for only a short time, Julius Caesar slit their throats. Some say he showed mercy towards those who were sentenced to crucifixion because he had become friends with some of them during the 40 days as a captive, or he could not stand to watch the torture and intervened. I can empathize with the latter, but the former explanation is understandable as well.

Thus, one could assume that citizenship removed the greatest fear any human would encounter at the end of his life: crucifixion. A woman has less freedom in the Empire than a male, but a woman never had to fear crucifixion. The most hideous and despicable crucifixion I personally witnessed was just a stone's throw away from the northern walls of Jerusalem in the 19th year of Tiberius. It was the execution of the man from Judaea, the one who challenged not only the Roman Empire but also the whole world's belief system. Had he been a citizen of Rome, he would still have been put to death but most likely by beheading, the most common form of capital punishment for citizens.

Roman citizenship not only gave legal protection, but it gave males the right to wear a toga; and that guaranteed free bread and access to mass entertainment, along with unrestricted access to any bathhouse in the capital city. This was an immeasurable goal for retirement, and even slaves dreamed of hoarding enough money if they became freedmen just so they could purchase citizenship in their old age.

A final note about citizenship in the Roman Empire: Only Roman citizens are allowed to wear a toga. No toga, no free entrance to the Circus Maximus or any other pleasure facility in Rome. A person without citizenship caught dressed in a toga in the city of Rome was ordered by anyone with imperium power to be crucified.

CHAPTER FOUR

Rome ~ Afternoon on the 2nd day of September (the 9th month as adopted by Julius Caesar's Julian Calendar) in the 5th year of Tiberius Claudius Nero or Emperor Tiberius and 50 years after the Battle of Actium.   (September 2, 19 AD)

"The naked ones" (Argos)
"Wearers of sheep-skins" (Sicyon)
"Dusty feet" (Epidaurus)
"Wearers of dog-skinned helmets" (Corinth)
                    — Slang terms for the inferior ones or slaves

Before I entered the amphitheater wearing my rinsed tunic and while I was leaning against the wall of this house of death, my eyes located the spot where my father told me to return with my mother. I did not go to that place but surveyed it from a distance. No one was there waiting, and I concluded I would be safer in the crowd of the amphitheater. How wrong I was. Nevertheless, I did enter and saw what I saw. In all fairness, it would have been better had I jumped overboard a ship during a violent storm and at night. I exited the amphitheater after my great distress from what I witnessed at the hands of Gladiator Marius. Once I was away from the *Statilius Taurus Amphitheater*, I ran towards the only familiar spot, the fountain. There at the same font I had washed my hair earlier, the mysterious hand grabbed me like the talons of an eagle snatching a fish from a lake; and I surrendered like a defeated slave. However, it was not to my demise. It became one of my great surprises in life when I discovered the hand was to my rescue and not my death.

"Venustus! Stop it; it is I – your didace!"

I could not believe my ears. I ceased my struggle and turned as the hand loosened its hold. To my great delight, I beheld my old schoolmaster Zeno, who was one of those slaves who desperately longed for Roman citizenship.

"You're alive!" I blurted out in great astonishment. "I was told you were dead! But you can't be; you're here!"

I would have babbled forever had Zeno not done something he had never done before; he hugged me. My babbling turned to blubbering; but I was only thinking of myself, which my mother had warned me from doing. Had I been thinking of Zeno, I would have realized his dream of gaining Roman citizenship was forever lost. His coveted goal had just flown away at the very moment he placed his hand on my neck and did not shove my head under water. Indeed I was surprised that Zeno was not dead, but at that moment, I did not think of his lost chance for a toga and citizenship. Yet, it was hard to think of someone else at that young age, especially after just escaping two assassins and the nightmare of the amphitheater and now experiencing the hand on my neck, which I first perceived was to my death. Naturally, when I discovered it was Zeno's hand that held my tunic from behind, trapping me only for my survival, how could anyone express anything but amazed surprise? Before I knew who was holding me, I tried to escape as a captured bird might; but the hand held tight. I wanted to let out a scream; but I knew I was alone in the world, and no one would have come to my aid. Innately, I decided to submit to the inevitable and finally relaxed as a strange peace of acceptance came upon me as I waited for the deathblow I was sure would come next. I felt separated from my body while my short life began flashing before me. I am confident I could be excused for thinking only of myself in that tragic moment, and at times I still do. It would be years later that I understood the exact price Zeno paid to save me. He actually was sacrificing himself, like the true Stoic that he was. I could not even vaguely understand his dilemma that hot summer day at the amphitheater forum fountain, but today it is plain to see the great love this man had for me although as a child I did not understand his teaching methods and even disliked him. Truth be told, all Zeno had to do on that boiling day was turn me over to my father, and he would have received Roman citizenship on the spot as well as freedom for his efforts. I had misjudged this old man in my childish mind but wish to honor him now as I speak of his selflessness.

With my head buried in Zeno's robes and tears pouring from my eyes, all the bad things I felt about Zeno vanished. My weeping seemed to go on forever, but I am sure it stopped as soon as my old schoolmaster released me. When Zeno squatted down to be at eye level with me, in my heart, I forgave Zeno for all the beatings he had given me.

"Venustus, listen to me; your life is in grave danger. We must go somewhere safe to talk."

I agreed, and my *dadace* herded me away from the forum near the *Statilius Taurus Amphitheater*. We walked at an average pace, actually entering back into the city, passing through one of the massive open gates. It was strange to my mind that I did not remember passing out of the city earlier when escaping by using the sewage alleyways. Somehow, I evidently passed through this or some other gate that morning. Life is like that. If you do not define something, you really do not actually see it. In many ways, life is nothing but a series of identifying all the things that surround you. A foreigner coming to Rome for the first time sometimes sees more in the city than a little boy who had lived there for ten years. The *Statilius Taurus Amphitheater* was actually outside the city, which was where the *Campus Martius* or the Field of Mars was located.

When Zeno and I arrived at the back of the massive *Theater of Marcellus* and the *Porticus Octaviae*, both adjacent to the Tiber River, only then did I begin to understand where I was. Zeno pointed to a short bridge. We together crossed over this old stone bridge, holding our noses to the smell of the river. This bridge was known as the *Pons Fabricius;* and it led to a small island in the bend of the river dedicated to Aesculapius, the god of medicine and healing. A modest, reddish-brown sandstone temple stood near the center of the island; and I remember thinking, considering my mental state, if there were a shrine I needed to visit, this was beyond appropriate. Only a handful of people could be seen walking around the island. The people I noticed seemed to be in prayer. They were congregated around the steps of the temple to the god of healing. Maybe they were praying for help. Those walking around the area of the temple seemed to be in a suspension of consciousness, perhaps hoping for a dream or word that would tell them what to do. The shrine island was also the hope of many old and ill slaves who were left there by their masters to die. Most of the isle resembled an unkempt park with bushes and trees around the water's edge. It may have been maintained better in the past; but still, the grass areas looked like inviting places to relax as the river slowly flowed on its way to Ostia, the dockyard of Rome. As long as the wind was blowing in the right direction, the Tiber's foul stench was not as acute; and it was at these moments this island in the Tiber was the perfect place to enjoy and contemplate about life. I never understood the atmosphere of gardens to provide such mental activities.

Walking past the not-very-impressive temple, I could hear the death rattle of an old slave alone in his last hours of life on one of the four steps to the central platform. Cripples hobbled along on homemade crutches, the lame lay on stretchers, and the blind sat so still they almost looked invisible. Zeno guided me with a steady hand on my shoulder to a private area at the far end of the tiny island covered with thick, untamed-looking bushes. I was still in a state of confusion over the revelation that Zeno was not dead. After both of us had sat on the grassy ground between a large bush and the river that was flowing away from us, Zeno looked at me as he had never before. Then came his first words since the fountain: "Listen carefully, and answer a few questions before I tell you anything."

I nodded my compliance.

"First, I need to know when and why your father sent you back to your home this morning. I also need to know exactly what he mentioned before he sent you."

I had no idea how he knew all this about my morning, but I placed my full trust in him. All I wanted to do was please him more than I could ever imagine. "We had just arrived at the amphitheater, and I had stepped out of the litter. An obese man, wearing a senator's toga, came up to my father. They talked for a brief moment; and, after the large-bellied man had gone, my father told me that assassins had murdered Senator Carnalus, Decimus, and you. My *patra* instructed me to return to his villa by way of the litter, fetch my mother, and return to the amphitheater. This was all to be accomplished without his wife's knowledge."

"You speak of Claudia Pulchra?"

With the wag of my head and eyes cast down, I acknowledged yes to his question, feeling a sharp pain in my soul by just hearing that horrible woman's name.

Zeno was quiet for a long moment and then asked another question. "Can you remember what time it was when your father sent you back to Esquiline Hill?" Zeno had affectionately placed his hands on my shoulders to emphasize the importance of my answer.

"I do not remember, except I think the games in the arena had just begun."

"How do you know the games had just begun?" he queried with a pale face and those large, penetrating eyes focused on my lips.

"I remember waiting for my father and the fat senator. I recall that the crowd from inside the amphitheater was yelling, "Burn him; slay him. The shadow of the aqueduct near the amphitheater will also give me the correct time if you think it is that important."

Zeno's eyes lit up, and color rushed back to his face. He released my shoulders and clapped his hands. "Good! Good! That means it was too early for him to have known."

I did not comprehend Zeno's delight, even though he did not ask about the shadow of the aqueduct.

"Listen, Venustus; both our lives are in grave danger, especially yours. This morning four men entered Senator Carnalus's home by force. They first stabbed the door slave with long military-looking swords and then proceeded to the senator's bedchambers where he was struck down with the same swords. Two men found Decimus and the senator's Greek bookkeeper, whom I am assuming they mistook for me. Decimus and the bookkeeper, like rats in a grain galley, were hacked to death. I was outside at the time talking to the head gardener when we heard the very same chants you described coming from the amphitheater down inside Mars Field. It was at that exact moment I also heard the screams of Decimus from inside the house. As the gardener and I reached the front of the villa, we froze behind a tree when the four intruders exited the *domus* carrying bloodied swords; the men sported white tunics with the blood of my master and his only son clearly splattered on them. I recognized them at once as Claudia Pulchra's litter bearers. I instructed the gardener to follow them at a safe distance and to report to me as soon as he found something."

On hearing this account, I was shocked at this revelation and wondered why only two men attacked me in the streets of the *Urbs* when Zeno saw four. I buried these thoughts saying nothing but listened to my teacher.

"I entered the house with caution, stepping over Plutus the doorkeeper, and finding three more dead bodies and a few frightened slaves who were hiding. I ordered the house slaves to come out – that it was now safe. I instructed several to cover my master, his son, the bookkeeper, and Plutus with bedding sheets. Before all the bodies were covered, your father arrived by himself without his bodyguard or *lictors*, which is very unlike him since he is a *magistrate praetor* with *imperium* power. Your father looked surprised to see me and asked what had happened as we both stood next to old Plutus's uncovered body. A slave was holding a sheet to cover Plutus, but I indicated with a hand jester to wait. It seemed peculiar that the sight of Plutus did not disturb your father. I dismissed the thought since, as a *praetor* and earlier in his life as a military tribune, he would have seen much blood on the battlefield, in the arena, and at executions. I told him I did not know anything and asked why he happened to visit this morning. I did not think he was looking for you since you said yesterday that you would be with your father on this day, it being your birthday and a great Roman holiday. I inquired about you, and he said that you had become sick and that he sent you home. Your father said he was here to see if Senator Carnalus wanted to join him instead at the Actium celebration at the great wood-and-stone amphitheater in *Campus Martius*. It was at this time he asked me a bizarre question. He asked if I or anyone else knew the mother of Decimus. Your father apparently suspected that I might know, but I acted as dumb as a mule and did not give him an answer. You see, Venu, my master was never married; yet, he had a son. The question is who is the mother of your friend and classmate Decimus?"

"Who is Decimus's mother?" I asked in my confusion from all I had just learned.

"Never mind that for now. We have very little time left to talk. First, let me finish telling you what happened with your father. He said someone needed to notify the Praetorian Guards since they functioned as city police besides guarding Tiberius. I told him that I would be glad to report the crimes, and he accepted without hesitation. Before he left, your father informed me that, if I needed him, he would be returning to the games to forget this heinous incident. He left, and it was a wait; but before long the gardener returned. He had your Jewish slave friend from your father's villa with him, the boy named Eli."

"My friend Eli?" I asked, trying to understand.

Zeno shook his head twice with his eyes closed in what looked like frustration before continuing. "The gardener reported that he followed the four until the group split up into pairs. One pair went into the city, but he followed the other two to a wine shop. After a few cups of wine, they left and ventured back to your father's villa. He said he waited in some bushes for a short while watching the two sitting near the fountain. Finally, the other two came up the hill and joined the first two sitting near the front of your father's villa. A couple of your father's soldier guards at the entrance followed the four into the house."

"Did they still have blood on their tunics?" I asked in my child's mind, still thinking about my friend's blood on their white tunics.

"I am assuming the blood was still on their tunics. Now allow me to finish," he said in frustration at my childish question. "All four entered the dwelling together, and it was not long before Eli ran out the front entrance with his face looking white as a surrender flag. The gardener ran to grab the fleeing boy, who mumbled incoherently about what was happening inside. The gardener and Eli then quickly returned to report to me. By the time Eli was calm enough to speak with me, he had explained how your mother and Claudia began fighting in the garden. I understand you were not able to save your *mater* but did bite that witch hard on the ankle and broke her finger on your escape over the back wall." It was the first time I had ever seen Zeno smile. I noticed he was missing a couple of teeth near the top left side of his mouth. I almost started to laugh at this new revelation but kept quiet like I did each day under his instructions. Still, I had a question I needed to ask.

"I broke her finger?" I asked before remembering I kicked her from the wall.

"Yes, and Eli stated it was then that the four men, all holding swords, entered the garden from the front of the villa. Eli was still hiding because you had told him there was danger coming. The four litter bearers found Claudia in the garden clutching her hand, and she ordered the four to kill all the slaves in the villa. Yes, she ordered the litter bearers to kill everyone, male, female, and child. Eli told me he heard her say, 'Kill them all as if they are sheep for the slaughter! They will all die for what they have called me behind my back!'"

"What about the other guards or *lictors* present in my father's home?"

"I do not have an answer to that question. Perhaps they are all busy killing others in the city. I am sure many stand in the way of Claudia and your father's plans. Eli did not stay long enough to see all the results of the slaughter. When he saw an opportunity, he ran."

I was now in complete disbelief thinking of the cooks, housekeepers, or whatever they may be; there had to be at least three hundred slaves in the villa. "All of the house slaves were killed?" I uttered in a whine of disbelief.

"Eli told me most of the slaves just stood frozen like statues and died where they stood. The shock of what they were witnessing rendered them helpless to Claudia's killers. Eli, however, was able to exit the villa as fast as he could without anyone seeing him. When the gardener and Eli arrived, I ordered the gardener to hide Eli in a storage room in the senator's *domus;* and I quickly came looking for you before your father or Claudia's litter bearers found you first. And thank Mercury and his winged heels that I did."

I was still trying to grasp all that I was hearing, but it all seemed too grotesque to comprehend. I had no one to trust except Zeno, and I put my life into his hands. When he asked me to disrobe, I gave him my tunic with the now-darkened line running down the center, along with my sandals and the small gold signet ring that aligned me to the Vetallus clan. Like a newborn lamb going to the slaughter, I found myself completely naked. Zeno instructed me to hide in a wild bush behind where we had been sitting and not to leave my cover until he returned. I nodded and crawled into the bush.

I then hugged my knees to my bare chest trying to hide my privates. I could hear Zeno leaving with all my only possessions, and I lowered my head in sorrow and shame. The humidity in the air grew in its intensity, and it was stifling. Bugs were landing and biting me from my feet to my face; and after the wind had shifted, the river began to smell like the sewer it was. I had no idea how long I was to sit naked in the bushes. Lamenting silently, with tears streaming down my face, I could not comprehend all the pain I had experienced because of Claudia and my father's betrayal. The long afternoon's heat increased until the clouds broke, and a torrent of rain fell soaking me to the bone. Now I was sitting in mud, and I wept openly allowing the showers to muffle my wails. After the rains had ceased, I tried to be quiet again. The ground began to bake after the sun peaked out of the clouds, causing steam to rise just as it had this morning in my father's garden before all this entire dreadfulness started.

Only a few sick and elderly individuals slowly passed my bush. They had no idea a scared, naked little boy was hiding in the mud. I tried to focus my mind on the soothing sounds of the Tiber and not on the distant roars from the amphitheater that was just across the river and a couple of stone throws away from the *Porticus Octaviae*, a structure adjacent to the *Theater of Marcellus*. The *Porticus Octaviae* complex had been built by Augustus in the name of his sister Octavia. The portico had a central colonnaded walkway between the temples Jupiter Stator and Juno Regina. In the rear portion was a library built in the name of Octavia's dead son, Marcellus. In the distance, I distinctly heard the name of the gladiator being repeatedly chanted. His name floated on the wind over the *Porticus Octaviae* and *Theater of Marcellus*. It was the incantation of Gladiator Marius. Just as the humidity had gone from bad to oppressive, the nightmare of the amphitheater would not leave me alone.

A few hours before sunset, when I almost gave up all hope, Zeno returned. In his hands were a bundle of clothes and some food. Standing behind Zeno, with his head down was Eli, my Jewish slave friend. We both smiled awkwardly at one another, but I did not want to embrace him since I did not have on any clothes. After I had crawled out of the bush, I slipped on a tunic that must have been Decimus's and a pair of old and worn sandals. I ate an entire barley loaf and washed it down with some red wine in a skin, much like the skin from which I drank earlier with my father. I realized that this loaf of peasant bread was the beginning of a new existence; and no longer would I ever again enjoy honey cakes, peacock brains, or flamingo tongues. My life of wealth and extravagance was over.

"We must be going now," declared Zeno after I ate my last bit of bread. We left the island in the middle of the Tiber by recrossing the *Pons Fabricius* and entered once again into Rome. We turned right: and on our left stood the *Theater of Marcellus*, perhaps the last major construction project in the closing years of the Roman Republic and the start of the Empire. The theater was named after Emperor Augustus's nephew Marcellus, who died mysteriously before his 20th birthday and before the completion of the theater. Soon after the young man's death, Agrippa, Augustus's longtime friend and general, returned to Rome from the isle of Lesbos. Apparently, Agrippa was supposed to have been in Syria, where he had initially been ordered to go, but returned to Rome before reaching his goal after hearing of the boy's death. Two years after his surprise return, Agrippa married Marcellus's widow Julia, the only offspring of Augustus. Julia was 18 years old when she wed Agrippa. At that time, there were scathing rumors about the mysterious death of her cousin-husband of only two years. Now the widow Julia was marrying a man twice her age. The marriage appeared to mimic that of Julius Caesar's sister Julia marrying a much older Pompey the Great. Whatever designs Agrippa had for his future as the next emperor ended nine years after his marriage to Julia when he died of a mysterious sickness. Surprisingly, Marcellus and Agrippa were both interred on Mars Field in the *Mausoleum of Augustus*, and both were then declared to be gods.

Agrippa, the builder of the *Pantheon* and winner of Actium, was good friends with Herod the Great, King of the Jews in *Palestina*. In the land of *Palestina*, Marcus Vipsanius Agrippa provided many reforms for the Jews and some building projects, which caused the local population to appreciate him. I know of no other Roman besides Agrippa whom the Jews liked. Perhaps this was one reason Agrippa was not worried about returning to Syria after he learned of the death of Marcellus. I think Agrippa had knowledge that Herod the Great ruled with a heavy hand in the region of *Palestina*, the province south of Syria; and Agrippa most likely knew Herod would interpose his mercenary army into Syria if the need arose.

After the death of Agrippa, Julia was once again being forced to marry for political reasons. This time her father pushed her into marrying Tiberius, the eldest son of Augustus's third wife, Livia. Augustus had stolen Livia from her previous husband; and she brought her toddler, Tiberius Claudius Nero, who was named after the man Livia divorced to marry Augustus. The way Tiberius became the next emperor is very strange, especially when one considers his name and that he had no direct bloodline to Julius Caesar or Augustus. All

Tiberius had was a declaration of a royal bloodline after he married Julia and because Livia, his mother, was declared to be divine by order of Augustus.

It should be noted, on that late evening when Zeno, Eli, and I walked past the *Theater of Marcellus*, I was just ten years old and was too young to understand any of the intricacies I have just described. What I do remember was the sun beginning to set in the west and the three of us were slowly moving past the *Theater of Marcellus,* a concrete monstrosity, sheathed in white travertine marble. I distinctly remember looking at the white stones that were slowly turning into an angry orange color. All I knew that sad evening was that the *Theater of Marcellus* was named after the first husband of Julia. I had trouble understanding how Marcellus was the son of Augustus's sister Octavia, which made Julia and Marcellus cousins. I would later meet Herod Antipas, Tetrarch of Galilee in *Palestina*, who was married to Herodias, who was also his niece. Herod Antipas and Augustus had stolen their final wives from other men. The only difference was Herodias was first married to an uncle, the half-brother of Herod Antipas. Herodias had brought her daughter Salome into the marriage with Antipas, just as Livia brought Tiberius and his younger brother Drusus. Perhaps people with power live under different rules; yet. I have learned there is a substantial cost to what any of us do in this life. Queen Cleopatra VII was first married to her younger brother before giving birth to Caesar's bastard. Instead of divorcing her brother, Cleopatra had Caesar's troops kill her brother-husband and throw his body into the Nile. Cleopatra committed suicide at age 39, not an old age. What has a person gained if they capture the whole world but lose their soul?

Walking past the *Theater of Marcellus* after we left the island in the Tiber, we could not see the *Porticus Octaviae*, also built by Augustus in the name of Octavia, his sister. The massive theater hid the famous *portico* from our sight. A year earlier Zeno had explained the history of these two monumental buildings, standing near the Tiber, to Decimus and me. We were on one of our weekly walking outings. I believe Zeno thought of himself like Socrates, who commonly wandered around Athens with his disciples, discussing whatever. I doubt most Romans even know these two buildings, standing near the bend of the river, are named after mother and son who were connected to the first emperor, Augustus Caesar. Now that I think of it, I never spoke to anyone who even openly stated the possibility that Livia may have had a hand in the death of Marcellus. I believe she may have but will include a lecture I gave in Alexandria on this topic, which my scribe will find and later incorporate it with this manuscript.

Today, on the 50th anniversary of Actium, hundreds of people were brutally murdered under the same suspicious circumstances that played out in the many years before the Empire began. Once again, these strange deaths were all for the same reason: Rome killed its own on the premise of who was going to be the next god to control the world. Now, a fundamental question had to be asked: who honestly had the bloodline of Caesar running through their veins? The problem with Tiberius was whether he actually came through a pure bloodline of Caesar. If he didn't, this could open the door for someone to undermine his claim to the throne of Rome.

To repeat, at the age of 10, I did not know any of this information concerning bloodlines. I did look over to Zeno and surmised that he must have known some of what my father and Claudia were doing on this day, but he was not sharing any of this with two little boys. What I was soon to learn was the plans orchestrated by Claudia and my father was apparently driven by bloodlines to Caesar. This is why I, as the eldest son to Gaius Vetallus Crassus, was required to be dispatched like an unwanted bug. Why else would Claudia have told my father in my hearing this morning that I was the key person to die? If my father failed, Claudia feared, I would be the "fly in the ointment" for the rest of their lives. This was Claudia's prophecy that did come to pass; yet, sin does bring disgrace no matter how intricate our plans are to hide and twist the vile justifications we perpetuate.

When Zeno, Eli, and I walked past the *Pons Aemilius* and then the *Pons Sublicius*, the oldest bridge in Rome, we could still hear the chants and screams from the *Amphitheater of Statilius Taurus* behind us in the *Campus Martius*. Ironically, the *Amphitheater of Statilius Taurus* is located not far from the *Theater of Pompey*, where Julius Caesar was slain, also in the *Campus Martius*. Even though the screams and noises from the amphitheater were reaching a feverish pitch, it seemed obscene to me that tens of thousands crammed behind the amphitheater's stone-and-wood walls were worshipping their famed gladiator. It was easy to hear the name "Marius! Marius! Marius!" being repeated like a Hindu *mantra*. We kept moving until the sun began to fade behind us as well as the commotion from the amphitheater.

Beyond the oldest bridge in Rome stood the white-marbled Circus Maximus and all the Imperial palaces standing guard, high up on Palatine Hill. Following the flow of the Tiber River, we reached the *Porticus Aemilia*, the massive market warehouse in the *Forum Boarium,* where the *Monopteros* or the little round temple of *Hercules Victor* stands. This long and multi-storied warehouse, *Porticus Aemilia*, was originally started 200 years ago by a *censor* named Marcus Fulvius Nobilior but was finished by a wealthy friend, Marcus Aemilius Lepidus, after Fulvius's untimely death. Over the years the Aemilius clan maintained the *Porticus Aemilia*, formerly called the *Basilica Fulvia* before the Aemilia clan changed its name. I share this history to show who actually controls the wealth and power of Rome: those who survive the longest. Plebeians can endure a long time, but only patricians with money and longevity are the controllers of Rome. My father always said, "It is the middleman who makes all the money, not the Persian peasant making a carpet out in the mountains beyond Susa nor the store owner selling the same carpet in his beautifully stocked showroom in Rome. The intermediary or middleman is the one who buys the carpet from the Persians and gets it to Rome. Therefore, those who own the caravans, ships, and warehouses are the wealthy rulers of the Empire."

I believed my father up to a point, but the Emperor appears to most of the 50 million living in the Empire to be the final authority regarding matters of life and death along with minting money and levying taxes. Those issues matter to most citizens, the freedmen and people of the provinces, who make up over half of the population of the Empire. As I have already stated, the other half of the population were slaves; and their opinions did not matter.

It should also be observed that most those living in the Empire when Augustus became emperor, understood that Augustus arranged his dictator position to appear as if the senate was in control and passing all the laws. Augustus made it seem as if he were only the law enforcer, but that was far from the truth. If Augustus learned anything as a teenager under the tutelage of Julius Caesar, it was not to move and make changes too quickly. Gently boil the water, and the turnips taste better than if cooked via a quick boil. The truth about worldly power is that it is always in the hands of the one who has the most gold. On this day of the 50th Actium era, my father, Gaius Vetallus Crassus, controlled more gold than the Emperor himself; but it was invisible to anyone looking. My father's pride and vanity wanted the world and history to know that he was the one indirectly pulling the strings, not Tiberius. That was his mistake, and Claudia was right when she said I was the most important person above everyone else to die this day. I was the key to their failure on this hot, humid day in Rome, which was now closing with the sun retreating towards Ostia. Little did I know the killings were going to continue even after the sunset.

But still, my father's dreams, along with Claudia's, flowed down the leaded pipes to the Tiber, along with all the other unspeakable things they had done, all because I did not die on this day. My father was truly the "Ghost of Rome" as some called him from behind his back, but the move to have me killed was perhaps his greatest mistake if he wanted to come out of the shadows. Without my knowledge at this time, my father was going to spend a great deal of his fortune trying to find and kill me. This one weak link in his chain became his downfall just as Claudia had spoken this morning. Walking towards the east of Rome at this late hour, I still did not know whether my father knew about Claudia's litter bearers waiting for me in the streets of the *Urbs*. Yet, how did Claudia know where and when to send her litter bearers to find and kill me if my father was not involved?

Now passing by the colossal warehouse *Porticus Aemilia*, I thought again concerning my father and wondered about his adage of the intermediary being the real winners of history. This one building stood tall between the Tiber and near Aventine Hill in the *Forum Boarium* around the edge of the city. Behind *Porticus Aemilia* were many smaller warehouses, one after another. Surely, everything that came by boat from Ostia and the rest of the known world entered Rome right here. If I were a general of a vast army, this would be my first target. If one wanted to make Rome suffer in an unmeasurable way, one should burn this section of Rome first, which would cut off the head of pleasure. The god of leisure and bliss would cease to exist, and Rome would be crippled into utter chaos. Even as a child of ten, I could see this was the most significant weakness of the entire Empire. Too bad the slave Spartacus and the Carthaginian general Hannibal did not understand what I was looking at, or they would have achieved their goals and changed history.

Dismissing these thoughts of destroying Rome, I asked Zeno where we were going; and he told Eli and me that we were walking to Ostia. I thought to myself that it would be easier to take a barge down the river but held my tongue, realizing that maybe doing so was not safe.

Once we reached the *Porta Trigemina*, we exited through the Servian Wall as we left Rome and walked on the grandest thoroughfare of the Empire, *Via Ostiensis*. After passing through the Ostian Gate, I looked back at the 400-year-old wall that stood over 30 feet high and realized it had protected Rome from many attacks, most notably Hannibal and even the army of 100,000 slaves led by Spartacus. This was the first time in my short life I had physically left Rome. Inexplicably, this was exciting; and it helped to keep my mind off my mother's death. We were now on our way to Ostia, the Emporium of the Empire. I calculated that it would take us close to six hours of steady walking to reach Ostia. If Eli and I had been older and Zeno younger, we could have made the trip in under four hours.

The first things I noticed as we left the walled city were miles and miles of wagons filled with goods. They all had been loaded up in Ostia and were waiting for the signal to enter the city. Only wheeled vehicles were allowed into Rome at night, but the signal depended on what was happening in the streets. Even if it were dark, there still might be a quarter of the city walking the streets after leaving different theaters, race tracks, or amphitheaters. Only when most of the thoroughfares were free of human traffic would the Praetorians guarding the city's 16 gates allow any wagons to enter the almost five square miles girded behind walls. Next to the waiting line of wheeled vehicles stretching out on both sides of the broad and well-maintained road were thousands of tombs. Romans believe in honoring their dead by grand monuments; yet, monuments were a luxury only for the very wealthy. The poor had to bury their loved ones underground in miles upon miles of multi-leveled tunnels called catacombs, which honeycombed outside the gates surrounding Rome. Burying the deceased outside the walls of all Roman cities was believed to protect the living. Most pagan armies trying to take a town were, in fact, afraid to trample over the dead. There was also the belief that the spirits of the dead would haunt the living soldiers if they did disturb their resting spots and the city where they once lived. Tombs and catacomb warrens were familiar sights along all roads leaving or entering any town or *polis* of the Empire, not just Rome. Superstitions, along with strong walls, protected many cities of the Empire for many years.

When the sun finally slipped completely down in the west, we continued walking the now-empty *Via Ostiensis*, which skirted along the outer bank of the Tiber. The *Via Ostiensis* was straight, and the Tiber turned and twisted gently like a snake slithering towards the sea. It was precisely a six-hour trek by the time we three reached the outskirts of Ostia. A waxing moon had risen during the last three hours of our walk and had made it bright enough for our feet, now that all the storm clouds had moved away. I would have to say this was the most extended hike in my life up to that time, and I realized I did it without any complaining. Eli, on the other hand, wanted to rest every few miles, which we did for only a few minutes. Zeno kept us moving for our own safety.

Once we reached the coastal city of Ostia, I found that the sprawling seaport of Rome was alive with activity even though it was almost midnight. Torches and oil lamps licked the big, red-bricked warehouses and buildings, standing everywhere in the city. I realized there were other worlds outside my own little experiences in Rome. Here was a town that never rested because all the commerce was coming from every corner of the water Empire of Rome. Dozens of ships maneuvered up against concrete moors or were being pulled out by smaller push crafts manned by slaves using long oars. Sea galleys, grain barges, and military triremes rocked gently at their moors and docks or anchored out in the calm sea of the pseudo-artificial harbor stretching out beyond the front of Ostia. There were large and small ships of every design, from every destination one could name.

Zeno led Eli and me to a darkened alley near the wharves and settled us behind a stack of rain-soaked bags of grain, wet from either the rain last night or the afternoon showers. There was a slight fermenting stink in the alley as loose, crushed grain seeds were beginning to turn into a gaseous-smelling ethanol.

Zeno squatted down to our level and said, "I want you boys to stay here, and I will return within an hour. Do not leave this alley," he ordered in his stern teacher voice. We both nodded in a submissive agreement.

After he had walked away with a slight limp, we both watched an old yellow alley cat rubbing himself against a dark reddish brick wall. The cat later came up to us and wanted us to rub his ears and stroke his back. When he was satisfied, he moved on; and we sat in silence. Out in front, at the entrance of the alley, we could see, tied up to a concrete moor, a single ship rocking gently in the ebb of the tide as well from the wakes from other vessels passing by. The heat of the day was now gone, and a chill had taken its place. I put on an old mantle that had belonged to Decimus, which I found in a red bag I had carried from Rome. Eli did likewise with a wool cloak that was in his bag, and we both sat in silence in the shadows of the night's umbra that was mixed with an orange tinge, thrashing the alley walls into a gloomy glow from lamps and torches, out on the wharves, which provided us a little glimmering light where we sat behind the grain bags.

When I looked over the top of the bags, I could not see any activity on the ship in front of us; and we could clearly see a few people periodically walking past the alley on the public street illuminated by the lights of torches and lamps. I had never been up this late at night, and everything was new and exciting. I never knew people lived in the darkness of night when most slept. After what seemed like over an hour of just sitting and not talking in the dark shadows behind the grain sacks, a man stepped into the alley and called out to someone down the street. "Over here, come on!" My stomach dropped, and my heart came to a halt as I instantly recognized the familiar voice. It was clearly that of my father, Gaius Vetallus. How did he find me? I thought my short life was over. Then Mayus Lentulus entered the alley after my father beckoned again. Eli recognized the two men as well and pulled at my cloak forcing me further back into the shadows behind the grain sacks. There was no place to run, and we both held our breath hoping for some form of rescue.

"What is going on, Gaius?" a third man asked who entered into the semi-darkness of the alley. "What games are you up to? I have waited half a day and night for you, and now you call me into this putrid alley!"

With abundant relief, I concluded my father did not know we were behind the grain bags. Now the question was why was one of the richest men in Rome here in a smelly, darkened alley of Ostia in the middle of the night? If there were any suspicions about my father's innocence, those thoughts vanished in what I witnessed next.

"Sorry, Flavius," spoke my father with lighthearted levity. "Something has come up, and my plans have changed."

"Where is Arena and what about the boy?" asked Flavius refusing to be consoled.

"My hands are bound. Arena and Venustus are both dead, and I cannot send you home empty-handed."

"What?" Flavius said in confusion. "How?"

"You see, that has always been your problem, old friend. You would have wanted to know the truth, and that would have caused me only more difficulties."

"Gaius, why are you talking in the past tense?"

"I'm sorry, old friend"; and Eli and I heard a loud thud and a groan of air coming from the mouth of Flavius. I peered around the grain bags in time to see Lentulus withdraw a long dagger from Flavius's lower back. In great revulsion I saw my father pull his gladius from under his robes and quickly thrust his own weapon into the heavy man's stomach, making a sickening thud as the sword cut into his old friend's belly fat through his robes. With a flick of his wrist, he eviscerated the man's bowels. Flavius fell to his knees with his eyes wide open and mouth ajar, holding onto my father's blade with bloody hands. When the body crumpled back onto the alley pavement, my father told Lentulus to open Flavius's throat with his razor-sharp *pugio*. "We must take no chances," he hissed.

I pulled back behind the bags and froze in fright after Lentulus and my father left the alley. We could hear a slight gurgling noise as the dying man's blood pumped from his wounds. Silent tears began to roll down my cheeks as I realized the true nature of my father. If he could do this to his old friend, he could do it to his own son. Eli and I sat frozen when we heard the voice of a little girl looking for her father.

"*Patros*, where are you, *Patros*? Are you in there, *Patros*? The waiter said you came over here."

I found myself standing; and with unusual agility, I immediately went towards the little girl, who looked to be a few years older than I was. The girl let out a cry when I grabbed an arm and pulled her back into the darkness. I did not want this slight female to discover her father and suffer what I had experienced this day. When she began to cry again for help, I cupped my hand over her mouth; and Eli helped me pull her back to our hiding place as she tried to get away from us.

"We're not going to hurt you," said Eli in Latin; but the girl did not seem to understand. I repeated the same in Greek since that was the tongue she had used when she cried out for her father. She finally realized we meant no harm, and I pulled my hand slowly away from her mouth.

"Who are you, and where is *Patros*?" demanded the frightened girl.

"Is your father, a large man dressed in a purple robe?" I asked hesitantly.

"Yes, where is he?"

"Your father is over there," I said pointing around the bags to a dark shadow on the ground just inside the alley. The little girl's eyes had now adjusted to the darkness; she saw her father's massive body lying on his side with his knees bent in. She began to choke on her gasps of horror and disbelief. I took the tiny creature into my arms, for she was quite petite. While she cried, Zeno returned not seeing the body of the girl's father until he tripped over the dead Flavius and fell face first onto the pavement.

"What in the name of the gods is this?" he clamored as he noticed blood on his hands and the edge of his robe.

"Go and help him. Explain what happened," I ordered Eli as I still held the crying girl. Zeno looked extremely agitated when he learned about my father's presence at Ostia but gathered the boldness he needed declaring that we needed a new hiding place. Like a mother hen, he clucked and led us like little chicks out into the street. He found an empty warehouse that loomed at the end of a long pier. We entered, and all settled in behind some wooden crates in the back of the old dilapidated, wood-slatted warehouse.

"There isn't much time, and I need to give final instructions before you two boys go," said Zeno looking at both Eli and me. We, three children, were huddled together on the wooden floor around the aged sage while he sat upon a wooden box. "I'm going to stay in Rome for various reasons, which I do not have time to tell; but I will try to join you later, Venu," he said with a kind and caring gaze upon me. This was the second time he had used this name of endearment, pronouncing it with a long "e."

"Venu, I have obtained passage for you on an empty grain ship that is headed past the Hellespont for the Roman colonies north of Bithynia and

Pontus across the Euxine Sea. However, you will disembark at Piraeus, the port city of Athens. Once there you will find Athens no more than an hour's walk from Piraeus. You must go to the Acropolis, which is the highest hill in the city of Athens. Find the Temple Athena Nike, a small temple located on the right as you climb the stairs leading up to the top of the Acropolis. Ask for a certain priest named Hector. He owes me a great favor and will watch over you until I arrive later."

After Zeno had put his hand gently on my head to reassure me, he shifted his gaze upon Eli. "You, faithful friend of Venu, will be leaving for *Palestina* where you will have to locate your uncle who you told me owns a pottery shop in Jerusalem." Eli nodded and said he knew right where it was in relation to the Temple of Yahweh.

Zeno's eyes next rested upon the little girl, who stiffened at his gaze, trying to hold back a new torrent of tears. "You, little one, will stay with me; and we will find your home and mother."

"But my mother is dead, and my home is in Asia at the city of Ephesus."

"Somehow, I will get you home. I am sure some relatives will take care of you."

"There is no one now that my father is dead," and the tears broke again. Zeno reached down and held her as he had held me earlier at the fountain. She had a long cry, and then finally the convulsions stopped.

"Now, now! Everything will be taken care of, and you must not worry. First, I will escort Eli to his ship, which leaves first. Venu, you stay here with..." and we all realized no one knew the little girl's name.

"Messina; I am named after a city-state in the Peloponnese, where my father was born." She had pronounced her name as "My-see-nah," with a short "a" after the "n" sound.

"Yes, the arch-enemy of ancient Sparta," replied Zeno. "A proud people, the Messenians. You must now wear your name proudly."

Turning his gaze upon Eli, he said, "Are you ready little one? Say goodbye to your friend, and we will go find your ship bound for Joppa."

I hugged Eli thinking we would never see each other again; and he whispered, "*Philos,* Venu; *shalom.*" I repeated the phrase feeling awkward as I had never said such a thing, even to my mother. Now I desperately longed for a second chance to say to my mother, "I love you, or *philos Mater*; peace be upon you."

"Venu, you tend Messina; and I will be back shortly."

I looked over at the tiny girl through the flicker of torchlight coming in through the open slats of the wooden walls. I could see that Messina was quite attractive. She had long, dark auburn hair with flecks of gold and red that matched the freckles on her tiny nose; and she possessed the most beautiful, translucent blue eyes. I spoke first. "My name is Venustus, which means son of Venus."

"That old man called you Venu. Is that short for Venustus?"

"Yes, you may call me Venu if you wish."

"Venu is nice, but I do not like Venustus; it sounds like a pagan name."

"I am not aware of what you mean," I said looking down at this little imp with disdain and pain.

"I'm sorry," she quickly said realizing her words had wounded me. "I'm a Jewess. You see my mother was Jewish but not my father. According to the Hebrew culture, if your mother is Jewish, that makes you a Jew. If it were the other way around, I would be a pagan like you; unless, of course, I converted from paganism."

"My mother was Greek and my father... well, he is Roman." I looked away realizing Zeno and Eli were gone. I wondered when they had left. I must have been distracted by this little girl's cuteness.

"My father was also Greek," she said smiling for the first time; and she was beyond cute. She was actually beautiful beyond anything that I had ever seen. She had little dimples when she smiled, and her straight white teeth tugged at my soul. My heart began to race as I felt a closeness to her, something I had never felt before. "In Greek, your name would be Epaphroditus, son of Aphrodite."

"Yes, but no one has ever called me by that name," I said, amazed at her volubility, especially for a girl. "I am sorry; I, too, will be leaving you. What I mean is you seem to be a nice person, and I would like to have you as a friend," I struggled to say.

"We are friends or can be," she said sensing my inner feelings and trying to reciprocate.

"I do not think we will ever see each other again after tonight," I uttered with exact injury and hurt in my voice.

With a quizzical look, Messina again smiled the most radiant smile and then moved her head to mine and kissed me on the mouth. It was something spontaneous and probably something that happened because of the trauma we both were going through, at least that was how I perceived it.

"What was that for?" I asked with embarrassment.

"For what you did for me back in the alley. You were very brave and kind. You were selfless in protecting me from the horror of seeing my father... well, you know."

I reached for her hand and lowered my eyes as I said, "My mother, only a few hours ago, was also murdered. I can tell you, in a few hours, a hurt will come upon you like a wall falling and trapping you under it. I do know exactly what you are feeling. To make it even worse, the man who was behind my mother's death was also the one who killed your father. That man is my father. I will return to Rome someday when I am older and avenge both their deaths. I will do this to vindicate your father and my mother. I will then look for you until the end of my days. I will not kiss another girl until you tell me there is no hope for us." Why I said all this, I had no idea. My own words even surprised me as much as they seemed to startle Messina.

"What?" she said almost disbelieving my words. "Are you making this up just to comfort me?"

"No, but I wish I were." I took my hand away and stood looking elsewhere hoping Zeno would soon return and end my embarrassment by taking me away.

"This evil man who murdered my *patros* is your father?"

I did not want to be attacked by her in her pain; so after I nodded yes, I walked away to the warehouse door. I peered out looking for Zeno's return or any sign of my father or Lentulus. Had I spotted my father at that moment, I fantasized finding a sharp weapon, running up to him, and impaling him in the back. I banished the thought realizing it was foolish and looked back into the warehouse. I noticed in the flickering light that Messina's tear-stained face was fixed on mine. She was not angry; but, instead, she appeared peaceful. Something was uniting our hearts as we both looked from a distance at one another. Our spirits became intertwined that night as one. Something deep within us was growing, and we both sensed its tug. Maybe it was *kismet* as the Egyptians like to say, or maybe it was because we each had experienced the death of a parent on the same day. I felt bonded for life, and it was something unspoken that we both felt and knew. It did not matter that we were just children; this bond was real and everlasting. Everything I had confessed was true. I would not look at another woman until I found Messina again to learn how she felt about me.

A READING GIVEN AT THE GREAT LIBRARY OF ALEXANDRIA BY EPAPHRODITUS

Given during the year of the four emperors.   *69 AD*

TIBERIUS AND HIS MOTHER LIVIA

Over the years, I have heard many stories concerning Tiberius and his mother Livia. I will share what I believe to be reliable testimony from first-hand sources. I will not explore but only mention the early deaths of Caesar Augustus's daughter, Julia's two sons, Gaius and Lucius, whom she had with Marcus Vipsanius Agrippa, the great general of Augustus and Battle of Actium fame. Livia had raised both boys before they died mysteriously at the ages of 24 and 19, respectively. It should be understood that Augustus planned to groom the two grandchildren to be his successors, but death changes everything.

Apparently, in Livia's mind, Tiberius was to become the next emperor after her emperor-husband died. Perhaps this was planned long before the deaths of Marcellus and Agrippa. I do know Tiberius was forced to divorce his previous wife, Vipsania Agrippina, whom he apparently loved, to marry into the god-bloodline of Augustus, that being Julia, the only daughter of Augustus. However, I have good sources that have told me Tiberius had no choice in his divorce and new marriage to Julia. When Tiberius did become emperor, the bloodline joke was that Julia was not living with Tiberius and passed away because of malnutrition (due to her exile) just a few months after the Senate made Tiberius emperor. The truth was that Tiberius had no bloodline connection whatsoever to the god Caesar or Apollo. After the arranged marriage to Julia, Tiberius secretly visited on many occasions the woman he was forced to divorce. Due to this and other reasons, Julia quickly became estranged from Tiberius; and the disenchantment only grew worse as the years passed.

Marriage to a disillusioned wife apparently was not a problem to most Romans as long as the illusion of happiness remained in place. After Augustus had died, Tiberius became the next emperor of the Empire. Tiberius's bloodline, in the minds of most Romans, was not openly questioned because he had been married to Julia, the daughter of the god-emperor, with Caesar's blood in her veins. Augustus had officially adopted Tiberius as his lawful son, and Tiberius's mother Livia was also declared a goddess by Augustus while Tiberius was still a child. Most Romans could care less about bloodlines; however, ancestry is far-reaching to Roman aristocrats, especially the dozen or so clans that filled the ranks of the Senate. The only son Tiberius fathered had been with his first wife.

The boy's name was Drusus Caesar; and he died by poison about four years after the 54th anniversary of Actium, the ninth year of Tiberius Caesar.

It was in the Statilius Taurus Amphitheater four years before Drusus's death when I personally first saw Tiberius. I was just a young boy of ten when I saw him sitting in his box near the edge of the arena wall. My first impression of Tiberius was that he looked like a sick man; and if he were a god, he was a pseudo-god, based on his outer appearance. The only legitimate way to see Tiberius as a god was to view Livia, his mother, a goddess, which Augustus had arranged when Tiberius was just a child.

No one was surprised when Julia rebelled against all of this chicanery just a few years into her marriage with Tiberius. Once Julia's defiance became public knowledge, Augustus, unfortunately, was the last to learn the truth concerning his only daughter. After Augustus had heard that his daughter was a woman of many affairs with numerous noblemen, he had no choice except to have her banished from Rome. I assume Augustus lost all hope at this point concerning his worldly kingdom he had created by many murders-including the public death of Caesar's son with Cleopatra. When Julia died just a few months after her father's death, she was not allowed to be buried with Augustus in his mountain mausoleum along the Tiber on the far edge of Campus Martius.

After Augustus had become emperor of Rome, two events seemed to have broken his will to live. These events do not include the mysterious circumstances of the deaths of Marcellus; Agrippa, Drusus; and later the sons of Agrippa: Gaius, and Lucius, all who were being groomed to succeed Augustus on the throne of the Empire. It was the death of the latter two boys that finally broke Augustus. He and Livia were raising the boys on Palatine Hill after their father's mysterious departure from this world. It wasn't until after all the strange untimely deaths of all these previous individuals that Augustus desired Tiberius to assume his throne, an adopted son Augustus never liked.

Actually, when Augustus learned of Julia's licentious extramarital behavior, this might have been the first blow to his heart. Augustus seemed to have actually loved his only daughter. This revelation occurred about nine years after Julia's marriage to Livia's son Tiberius. Two years after the wedding of Tiberius and Julia, the younger brother of Tiberius died. This brother was named Drusus; and three years after the death of Drusus, Augustus became enraged when Tiberius abandoned Rome and his wife. Augustus knew nothing of his daughter's Epicurean-liberal lifestyle, but Tiberius did. It was four long years later before Augustus learned of Julia's behavior and understood the reason why Tiberius retired from Rome. It was at this point Augustus warmed back up to Livia's oldest surviving son, which prompted Tiberius to return to Rome and

Palatine Hill.

Therefore, what became of Julia was the first crushing blow to Augustus. His only daughter had openly for years flaunted Augustus's Family Value Program called the lex Iulia de adulteriis. This Augustinian edict was a program designed to curb the apparent moral decline that was sweeping the capital and even the Empire. These reforms made adultery a public crime. Julia's adultery and violation of her father's moral law left her father with no other option other than to banish Julia to the barren island Pandateria. To complicate this curse upon the house of Augustus, Julia's daughter, who was sired by Agrippa and who was also named Julia, took up her mother's practices of immoral sexual behavior and later found herself in exile by Augustus to the island of Trimerus in the Mare Adriatieum located ironically just north of the location of the Battle of Actium.

I should note that many of these misfortunate tragedies were happening around Augustus in a somewhat overlapping time period. For example, Lucius died four years after Julia's banishment to Pandateria; and Gaius died two years after his brother Lucius's death. Shortly after Lucius's death, Tiberius returned to Rome from his own self-exile at Rhodes. Not long after the death of Gaius, Augustus adopted Tiberius and made him his heir. Both Gaius and Lucius died from some kind of strange, mysterious sickness possibly due to poisoning. What was also strange to many observers was that Livia took Julia's two boys to raise because their mother was on a solitary island. What may have been unfortunate for the two lads was that Augustus wanted them to succeed him. Perhaps Livia did not wish that succession to occur.

The second massive blow to Augustus occurred about eleven years after the banishment of Julia nearly five years after Gaius's death. This last event must have been like a war-club crack to the top of Augustus's head. This event was when Germanic Barbarians destroyed the three legions under Augustus's legate to the Rhine, Publius Quinctilius Varus. The entire northern army was lost in Germania, a disaster ranking just below the defeat at Carrhae by Crassus during the Republic at the time of the First Triumvirate. I would later learn Claudia Vetallus, the architect of the murderous attack upon me when I was sent by my father in his litter to fetch my mother, was first married to this very same legate. As strange as it might sound, Varus and Claudia were husband and wife before she married my father a few years after Varus took his own life near the Rhine River.

JOHN LAWRENCE BURKS

WHAT ARE WE SUPPOSED TO DO NOW?

PART TWO

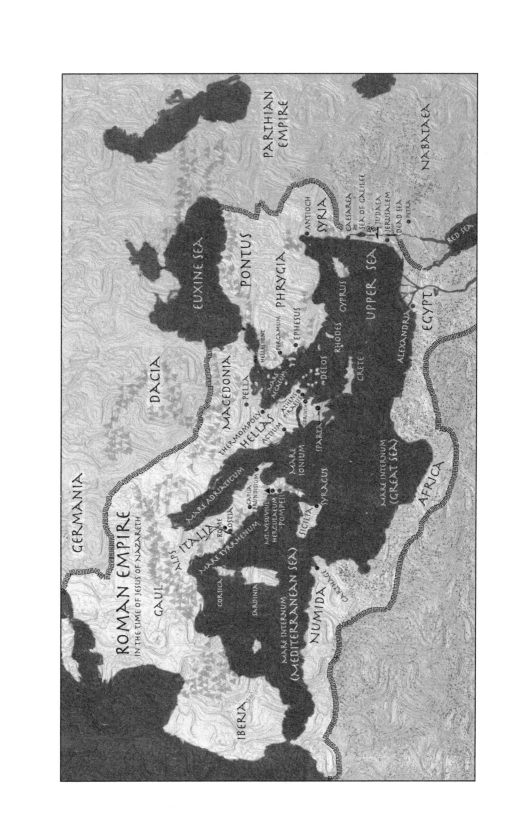

ROMAN EMPIRE
IN THE TIME OF JESUS OF NAZARETH

GERMANIA

GAUL

IBERIA

ITALIA
ALPS
ROME
OSTIA
CORSICA
SARDINIA
MARE TYRRHENUM
MT. VESUVIUS
HERCULANEUM
POMPEII
CAPUA
BRUNDISIUM
MARE ADRIATICUM

MARE INTERNUM
(MEDITERRANEAN SEA)

NUMIDA
CARTHAGO

SICILIA
SYRACUS

MARE IONIUM

DACIA

MACEDONIA
PELLA
THERMOPYLE
HELLAS
ACTIUM
ATHENS
PIRAEUS
CORINTH
SPARTA
MARE AEGEUM
DELOS
HELLESPONT

EUXINE SEA

PONTUS

PHRYGIA
PERGAMUM
EPHESUS

RHODES
CRETE
CYPRUS

MARE INTERNUM
(GREAT SEA)

UPPER SEA

ALEXANDRIA

AFRICA

EGYPT

PARTHIAN
EMPIRE

ANTIOCH
SYRIA
CAESAREA
SEA OF GALILEE
JUDAEA
JERUSALEM
DEAD SEA
PETRA

NABATAEA

RED SEA

CHAPTER FIVE

Ostia – After midnight on the 3rd day of September (the 9th month as adopted by Julius Caesar's Julian Calendar) in the 5th year of Emperor Tiberius and 50 years after the Battle of Actium. *(September 3, 19 AD)*

Fear God and keep his commandments, for this is the whole duty of man. For God will bring every deed into judgment, including every hidden thing whether it is good or evil. Solomon, Son of David and Ancient King of Israel

It was not long before I spotted Zeno down near the end of the wharf looking a little anxious as he hobbled towards the warehouse carrying a bag at his side. After seeing me standing at the half-opened door, he waved me back inside. Once he was again inside, he ordered me to sit next to Messina on the floor as Zeno placed himself back upon the same box he sat on earlier. He gulped a large mouthful of wine from a skin bottle he had extracted from a large, red woolen bag, the one I had carried from Rome. He must have had the red bag with him when he left with Eli. Watching Zeno drink, Messina must have known I was a bit stressed. There was a quizzical look on her face as she stared at me from where she sat. I guessed I must have had a perplexed look on my face, but I did not even remember Zeno taking the red bag with him when he took Eli to his ship. Nor did I remember a wine bottle in the bag when we walked from Rome. As I looked at the bag on the ground between Zeno's feet, there seemed to be other items in it that were not in it earlier.

After Zeno had cleaned his mouth with the sleeve of his cloak, he tightened the cork stopper into the mouth of the animal-skin bottle. "The rest of this wine is for you, Venu." I then watched him reach over and pull several objects out of his large white bag he had carried from Rome. Once everything was in the red bag that he wanted there, he said, "Make the wine last along with the few loaves of barley bread and fruit I purchased for your trip. I do not know how many days it will take; it all depends on the winds. There is also some money in the bag for extra food when the ship puts into port along the way. Now, remember where I told you to go and whom to ask for once you arrive at your final destination."

I nodded that I remembered.

"Good! Now there are also two scrolls in leather containers in your red bag," he said patting the red woolen bag that rested at his feet. "One is for the priest you will find, and it is only for his eyes. It has a single wax seal on it. The other one is only for your eyes, and do not ever let the priest know that you have it. This is for his as well as your own protection. Find somewhere to hide it that will be dry and safe; and, when I join you later, I will tell you what to do with it. Now, are you ready?"

"Yes," I answered trying to sound brave; but my bravado did not seem convincing even to me.

"Say goodbye to Messina, and then we will be off," said Zeno taking the red woolen bag with him, leaving his white wool bag sitting on the wooden floor next to Messina.

When Zeno stood, it was with obvious pain in his knees and other joints. He moved somewhat stiffly to the warehouse door. While he ambled away, I turned to Messina; and she leaned over kissing me on the lips once again. Her act of affection surprised me; for no one had ever kissed me there before, not even my mother. This time I detected the taste of green olives on her breath. I wanted to touch her shoulder or arm, but I did not. I did not resist her kiss, but I was surprised. She had the sweetest but also the saddest look in her blue eyes as her head leaned a little to her right as she said goodbye after she kissed me. I do not remember saying anything like, "I hope to see you again one day" or even "goodbye." In one way, it was strange not to say goodbye; but it was not necessary to say anything because it was as if we both had already discerned that we would see each other again. What she did say next was without words. Her eyes locked on mine as if she were speaking to my spirit. I had never experienced someone reaching down to my heart with just his or her eyes; and, in a strange way, it felt good. From that day forward, when I would feel an internal storm brewing, I would remember her translucent, azure eyes and that slanted look and smile. It was as if I understood every unspoken word she revealed with her eyes. When I conjured it back, everything always became calm. For the rest of my life, that one moment lingered upon my spirit, sometimes for hours.

From the entrance to the warehouse, Zeno told Messina not to leave for any reason. I could recognize that she was scared, but I informed her that Zeno was a virtuous and honest man and someone not to fear. Her smile returned. It was the same beautiful, beaming show of two deep dimples and straight white teeth. I remember thinking my teeth were not that white or that straight, and I began questioning why she liked me. Another oddity was our age. I was a good two years younger than she was, if not more. Why would an older girl like a younger boy? Those were my last memories of her at that age; and I wished I were an artist, for I would have loved to capture her sitting on that old and dirty wooden floor. I would have carved or painted a fresco of that scene on a plaster wall that would have stood for centuries in some basilica or library, revealing that exquisite smile in the torchlight from outside the slats striking her perfectly.

Outside the warehouse, I obediently followed Zeno along the wharf. Walking next to him I asked, "Why did you take my clothes and leave me naked in that bush?"

A satisfied smile came to his face when he said, "I took them to the amphitheater and found your father in the senatorial section behind the emperor's box, where you told me I would find him." That was very odd because I did not remember telling him about my father sitting above Emperor Tiberius. "I handed the folded pile to your father and said your clothes were found on the *Fabricius* Bridge where witnesses saw you disrobe before jumping into the Tiber to kill yourself. I told your father I gave a report at the *Castra Praetoria*, the Praetorian Guard camp that Tiberius had built on the outskirts of the city. Augustus had kept his elite bodyguard army miles outside of Rome, but that changed once Tiberius became emperor." Zeno mused with a funny crook to his mouth, which he often did, taking a few moments to think about something only he knew. "Well, anyway, I told your father I was giving a report at Praetorian headquarters regarding the killing of Senator Carnalus when a soldier carried in your clothes. I recognized the Vetallus ring and asked for the items to take to the family. Your father faked tears in his eyes when I told him this tale, and he gave me his moneybag full of silver coins for being so thoughtful. By the way, those same coins bought your passage to Athens and Eli's to Joppa; and what remains are in this red woolen bag, still inside your father's leather moneybag. Use them wisely."

There seemed to be some dark emotions welling up in Zeno as he handed me the red woolen bag full of food, scrolls, and silver coins. He stopped next to an old grain ship tied to a cement block. It must have been getting closer to morning; for the air was cooler now, and the darkness was much deeper.

"Hurry up, down there! We cannot wait any longer! The tide is almost out!" yelled the sea captain from over the rail of his ship. He then instructed his crew to drop the sail from the mainmast and throw in the ropes.

Zeno knelt to one knee to talk eye to eye. "Remember the priest's name is Hector; and he can be found at the Temple Athena Nike located on the Acropolis, which is the highest hill in the center of Athens. There are many temples on top including the one Pericles had constructed while a strategos or leading general at great expense using money from the Delian Lague hundreds of years ago for the goddess Athena. You will have no trouble finding the small temple you will be looking for. It is the first building on your right as you climb the double stairs into the temple complex of the Acropolis, for there is only one way up to the top. It is the smallest of all the temples up on top. The one scroll is for Hector and the second for you. Yours is the one with Senator Carnalus's seal, and it is for you to keep and guard. Remember it is vital for your survival, and its contents explain why everything happened the way it did today."

"Move it, boy! In the name of Neptune, move it!" called out the ship captain again.

Zeno stood and shook compliance to the burly man with his hand and then asked me if I had any questions. Of course, I had questions; but how do you ask when the ship is soon moving away, and I had to get on it?

"Now, Venu, I want you always to study and remember that, if you take revenge, you will be hunted and followed the rest of your life. Forget about all that has happened today as everyone thinks you are dead. Trust me; they will forget about you, and you may have a second chance at a healthy and peaceful life. Remember what I am trying to say; please forget it all for your mother's sake. Forget all of this. That is what Arena would want you to do."

I was stunned and was not sure I agreed with all that Zeno was saying. The captain ordered the plank leading up to the ship pulled aboard. I clutched the red woolen bag close to my side and did not answer Zeno yes or no. I just felt the need to get on that ship, or I would break down and weep again as I had done earlier in the large bush on the island in the Tiber River. Turning with the red bag in my hands, I ran for the boarding plank. I jumped as it was sliding up onto the ship. Once aboard the small grain galley, I stood at the railing lifting a single finger as a goodbye wave to Zeno. He had a sad look as he must have known I would not listen to his admonition and forget this day.

The main, dirty-looking, square hemp sail caught the warm night breeze; and the moon, hanging low in the south, painted everything a bluish color. As the ship pulled away from the dock by the aid of a small trireme, the breeze seemed to increase its intensity; and the ship slipped quietly out to the open sea once the trireme released its towline. If it were not for the dark wound upon my heart, I would have been thrilled beyond belief to be on my own, sailing out to a new adventure. Nevertheless, to be brutally honest, I was too young to know anything beyond my nose. I had turned ten only a few hours earlier; but in other ways, I had aged 30 more years before it ended. Yet, I still had one more surprise that night to comprehend; and actually, I would not understand all its entire implications until years later.

I used the edge of Decimus's cloak to wipe away the last tear while I vowed to never cry again. I made this promise to the warm breeze, for I did not believe any god was worthy to trust with such a serious matter. In addition, in my childish mind, I thought the creator of all things was in the breeze. I wanted to believe in Messina and my mother's god, but I had no knowledge of this deity; so I stuck with the wind. Ostia was now becoming a distant twinkle of lights from torches and lanterns while I remember making this vow, a pledge that became very hazardous and damaging to my future emotions. Little did I know I was going to become a cold and hard-hearted person for many years. It all started that night when I made a promise to the breeze to never cry again.

"You, boy; are you talking to yourself, or are you praying?" asked the ship captain, who had come up behind me as I was blankly looking out towards Ostia.

"I was just praying," I replied sheepishly.

"If it is praying, good Ole' Neptune hears all prayers out here. When you are done, you can find a place to sleep either here on the deck or down below," spoke the burly sea captain although not so gruffly as he was earlier; maybe he had witnessed me wiping away my tears and thought I was mumbling to Neptune. He patted me on the head and then said, "Do not worry, boy. I will keep an eye on you, and no one will bother you on this voyage. You have my word on that promise as a true mariner and a devoted servant of Neptune." He turned and walked away swaying in an unusual side-to-side gait. I watched him until my hands began to shake with fatigue. The red woolen bag fell from my shaking hands, and then my legs started to rattle like my hands. I tried to wish them to stop, but they would not.

"Here, little man, try this," said a gentle-looking, middle-aged man holding a wineskin. I realized I was incredibly thirsty, so I took the skin and lifted it to my mouth taking a huge gulp. To my surprise, it tasted similar to the almond taste of my father's wine and gall from the litter. A familiar warm glow reached down my throat and went through my arms and legs. Once the heat hit my lower extremities, the shaking stopped.

"Never fails when you need it," said the man. "Now pick up your bag, and I will show you below. Down a steep wooden gangway, an enormous crowd of people, mostly men, were drinking by lamplight from skins and clay jugs. I made the assumption they all were excited by the start of a new journey, but I could not have been further from the truth.

"To Marius!" yelled a fat, bald man from the front of the crowd.

"Yes, to Marius, the greatest gladiator ever to live!" bellowed another.

I turned to the man who had led me below and asked why all the praise for this Marius. The answer to my question was the last surprise of that fateful day, which started with my mother's gentle touch and now ended with this astonishing news.

"Well, little man, Gladiator Marius won the wooden sword for the third time. He beat the unbeatable odds and has removed himself from the prisons of Rome to become one of the richest and most famous men in all the Empire."

"By Mars he did!" said another. "All by just spilling the blood of others!"

"Almost like a priest sacrificing at his temple!" laughed someone else.

"What a profound image," stated another. "The amphitheater is the true temple of Rome, and all of Rome worships this new god of entertainment."

Everyone, but I, began to laugh at the last man's statement. All the men below deck found this thought hilarious and worthy of boisterous merriment.

Another reveler croaked, "I did not realize how religious we Romans have become!"

"Do not put me in your mix; I'm a Greek," snickered someone in the back with apparent mirth. The laughter was deafening again, and I could not believe hearing such blasphemy. If religion is a gateway to one's soul and spirit, then what revelation was this to a ten-year-old boy? How many men must have died at Marius's hands? At least forty I calculated and all defeated, one at a time, by that short brick of a man. I left the drinking passengers and went forward. I found a small hole near the front of the ship between stacks of empty grain bags. I used one empty bag for a pillow covering up with Decimus's cloak; I fell into a deep, death-like sleep that lasted well into the next day.

When I awoke, I was not sure what time it was; but once on deck, I noticed the sun was high in the sky. What woke me was the swishing of the waves against the sides of the ship, a rhythmic sound that was very pleasing and relaxing. The sound carried throughout the ship that seemed apparently empty, except for passengers. I later learned that not much cargo left Rome except people. On the other hand, all vessels going to Rome were burdened with items from every corner of the Empire and beyond. Rome was a consumer of pleasure and not a dispenser of products. The only things Rome gave back were soldiers, diplomats, businessmen, and gold and silver to buy whatever Rome wanted. Humans in the Empire were even for sale: peoples's talents, their minds, their beauty, their strength, their souls, and even their blood. Most ships that departed Ostia left empty only to return repeatedly laden with whatever treasures imaginable – even cages of wild and exotic animals for the arenas to become a bloody massacre for public entertainment.

I roamed the ship with the red woolen bag in hand. Some of the passengers started joking about the boy with the red bag. Nevertheless, the ship captain, true to his word, warned those joking to leave me, as well as the bag, alone. Without his protection, who knows what would have happened to my person or my red bag.

After a few hours of roaming the ship, I finally gathered my nerve to open the scroll that Zeno said was meant for my eyes only. I picked a quiet time when most of the passengers and crew were napping or resting away from the hot sun that was baking even the deck boards, which were too hot to walk on with bare feet.

Down I went into my hiding spot between the empty grain bags. It was there that I finally pulled out the leather scroll case meant for my eyes only and broke the seal, which displayed Senator Carnalus's ring imprint pressed into the red wax. A cold sweat broke out on my forehead, and my heart began to race in my chest just as it had yesterday when I was returning to the villa in my father's litter just before the two bloody men attacked. I unrolled a beautiful parchment sheet that was made from the finest sheepskin I had ever seen. There was enough light coming in through an open hatch cover from above, allowing me to read this scroll.

Gaius Cracus Carnalus, Senator of the Roman Senate, has dictated and signed this document in order for it to be read in case of my death and also upon the death of my son Decimus and/or my slave Zeno, who is my son's schoolmaster. Claudia Pulchra

Vetallus Varus has threatened all of our lives. Her motives for the threats stem back to her family heritage.

Claudia's lineage places her as the grandniece of the Princeps Augustus Caesar; thus, she is a member of the Julio-Claudian family. She was first married to Publius Quinctilius Varus and bore him two daughters. Her husband Varus had been proconsul of Africa and legate of Syria during the time of the death of Herod the Great. Soon after the death of Herod, unrest broke out; and Varus marched south to brutally put down the insurgents by allegedly crucifying about 2,000 Jews in Judaea. About fifteen years later, Varus was appointed by Augustus as legate of the Rhine, where he killed himself after the three legions under his command were destroyed in the Saltus Teutoburgiensis, a dense forest near the Rhine River. Augustus never forgave Varus for losing his three eagles, and this was Augustus's only northern Barbarian policy failure.

I was a close friend of Varus since the time I served under him as an officer in Africa. I took his widow, Claudia Varus, into my home after her husband's death because of the shame that was leveled against her by Rome; and I only wanted to protect her. One year after the death of her husband, Claudia bore me a son out of wedlock. I felt obligated to care for her and our son. Claudia refused to lawfully marry me. The son by Claudia and me is Decimus Carnalus Clamentus, whom I have since adopted and am presently grooming for the throne as a future Caesar since the blood of Augustus flows in his veins through his mother.

After eight years of living in my home, Claudia abandoned her son and me to legally marry my good friend, Senator Gaius Vetallus Crassus. She has, at this writing, bore Senator Vetallus a son named Julius Vetallus Varus Caesar Augustus, who is now two months old at the drafting of these words.

Not one soul knows about the lineage of Decimus except his Greek schoolmaster Zeno, who will become an ex-slave at the point of my death. All who have power in Rome know the lineage of Julius Vetallus Augustus but not that of my son, Decimus

Carnalus Clamentus. The birth records are held in the Temple of the Vestal Virgins if there is any dispute in what I am declaring in this scroll.

This is an official document to be used as proof of the truth in case any acts of crime are committed concerning me, my son, or my trusted slave Zeno. Knowing Claudia Varus as I do, she is capable of murder to pave the way for her son with Senator Vetallus to become the future emperor-god, which rightfully should go to my son Decimus.

The date today is the first day of the month Sextilis, 49 years after the battle of Actium, the 5th year of the reign of Tiberius Caesar. (July 1, 19 A.D.)

I could not believe what I had just read. I reread the scroll many times before I rolled it up and placed it back into the leather tube. Now I understood the motives of Claudia and my father. Everything was being arranged for my half-brother, Julius Augustus, to someday assume the throne of Rome. As a ten-year-old, I had no idea about bloodlines and their significance; but, certainly, at age ten I did understand the murderous ramifications. It would be years later when I read about Livia, Augustus's wife, who may have arranged the death of other successors to the throne to get her son Tiberius on it. It was then that I understood how either Decimus or my half-brother Julius had a better bloodline claim to be emperor-god of Rome over Tiberius. However, I could not understand why so many people had to be murdered, besides those killed by Gladiator Marius. There was no telling how many more innocent people were going to perish before Julius was old enough to become emperor, including the emperor himself. I began to harbor a burning desire against my father and Claudia, and someday I would punish them for their evil deeds. I secretly made this my life's purpose, even though I was ashamed of myself when I first confessed it after reading the scroll. Zeno understood me better than I knew myself. He had warned me against using my dead mother's memory to stop this business of revenge. He was aware that revenge was a vile industry; yet, I comprehended nothing about its consequences. I also did not understand what my crime was that I had to die, but I tried to remember Claudia's words to my father: "If you fail in your task to kill Venustus, then you will spend your future and fortune hunting him down." I was confident those were her exact words. However, I was having a hard time remembering.

Maybe because yesterday was so painful, I was now trying to bury it faraway. Yet, yesterday was never going to stay hidden. I decided to square this injustice and fulfill my vow to Claudia to the same degree I made my promise to the wind to never cry again. I began to mumble silently to the dead air in the bowels of the empty grain ship that I would return someday to Rome and kill Claudia and my father.

I pushed my cloak and bag of food to the side of my spot between the grain sacks; and in my anger, I fought back the tears, remembering never to ever cry again. I did not know it at the time, but I was walking down the dark path of hardening my heart. I closed my eyes and finally fell asleep after I rolled up in a ball on top of the empty grain bags.

It was dark when I awoke, and my tunic was drenched in sweat. A fire was burning in my body, and I could not muster any strength to stand. All I could do was fall back to sleep. The next thing I remembered was finding myself on a cot in the sea captain's quarters. It was a small room with shelves and scrolls, along with some bound books. Zeno had told me once, "Only a rich man can afford bound books, so do not covet them over scrolls." He had explained that scrolls were made of inexpensive papyrus. Books, on the other hand, were made from very costly animal vellum.

The story of how the first books came to be was due to a competition many hundreds of years previously when two mighty kings both wanted to build the world's greatest library. One was in Egypt at Alexandria; and the other, in Asia Minor in the city of Pergamum. The King of Egypt, Ptolemy II, passed a ruling that no papyrus would be allowed to leave Egypt since that was the medium for all written material at that time. Papyrus came from a swamp plant that grew only in the delta region at the mouth of the Nile. Slaves and peasants harvested the stalks, split each one apart, and laid them out to dry in a square-weave fashion. Once dried, the long sheets were cut to size and rolled onto a wooden spool. These sheets of paper were forever known as Papyrus, named after the swamp plant from where they originated. Egypt was the only land that grew the papyrus plant and, therefore, held a monopoly of this inexpensive material. When Ptolemy discovered the plans of Eumenes, son of Attalus, the King of Pergamum, he refused to have any rivals to the Great Library of Alexandria. Ptolemy declined to export any papyrus outside of Egypt, no matter the loss of unspeakable revenue. The angry king of Pergamum, learning of this embargo on papyrus, began to work on a plan to solve his problem. Finally, someone in his kingdom discovered the art of taking animal skins, usually sheep, and turning them into a new medium for writing. This new material was called vellum or parchment. Due to the enormous cost of vellum, both sides were inked; and the sheets were too short to roll up like papyrus. Soon a new system was discovered. The two-sided pages were cut and bound together, creating *biblios* or books. People found that it was more convenient to read a book because the reader did not have to unwind and rewind a scroll to find an individual passage; just flip a few pages, and there it was. The few books I had seen and read under Zeno's supervision were a great treat; and I, too, preferred books to scrolls. When Zeno recognized at once I preferred books over scrolls, it was then that he warned me.

From the cot in the sea captain's quarters, I began to smile when I saw the bound books. The next thought was why I was in this cabin? My final thought, where was my red bag containing the two vellum scrolls and my money? A profound relief came to me when I spotted the red bag on the floor next to my head. I felt it, and all seemed to be there. It was at this time when an old woman entered the room and discovered me awake. She told me I had become seriously ill with a fever, and I learned that the captain was true to his word to watch over me. He had found this kind woman on board to care for me. She had placed cold towels on my forehead and bathed my body with cold water until the fever broke. Now she brought me soup and mothered me as a cat would her sick kitten. She explained to me I had been in a delirium for almost a week. It had taken another week before I felt my usual self. The day my convalescence ended, ironically, was my last day at sea. Around the middle of the day on the final day aboard the grain galley, I was at the bow of the ship getting some fresh air while holding my red bag. The sea captain came beside me and put his hand on my shoulder in a fatherly manner.

"Well, my boy, you missed most of this voyage. For a while, I was worried that you would not make it and that we would have to wrap you in a hemp sail, weight it, and drop you to the fish. But Ole' Neptune gave you grace; that is for sure."

"Thank you for your help," was all I could say as I did not believe in Neptune and did not know what "grace" meant. It was a nice-sounding word, and I would try to find out what it did mean. Oddly, the day I discovered its meaning was some days after I watched a man die on a Roman cross outside Jerusalem; and that one little word changed my life. From that day forward, I understood its meaning, and "grace" became one of my favorite words.

The old captain ruffled my hair and said, "Nothing to thank me for, boy. Ole' Neptune will bless me plenty."

"When will we reach Athens?" I asked, trying to change the subject, which was a habit of mine.

Taking the hint, he took his hand off my head and pointed out towards the fall of land on the horizon. "Up ahead is Piraeus, the port city of Athens. Athens is about four miles beyond Piraeus. That is where you are going, is it not?"

"Yes, sir," I said trying to be polite for all the kindness he had shown me.

"Look carefully, and you can see the white marble temples up on the Acropolis. Do you see them, boy?"

I was trying to see the Acropolis until I realized it was more to the right of where I was looking. "Yes, there it is!" I exclaimed with genuine excitement.

"Do you see the Acropolis now, boy?"

"Yes, sir, it looks like a diamond in a setting of gold."

"Well put, boy! Well, put! That is where you are going. Is it not?"

"Yes, sir," I said again, not sure how much information I should divulge.

"That old fellow who paid your passage told me to make sure you were pointed in the right direction once we landed in Piraeus. He did slip me a silver coin with the emperor's image on it for my troubles, so do not worry. When we land, I will walk you to the road that has the long walls, which will take you to Athens. I will make sure you get there. First, we will dock in the harbor Kanthatos, which is to the north of the city. There are two smaller ports on the southern side, Munichia and Zea. Those two in ancient days were the great military bases of the Delian League or, indeed, the Athenian League. Do you know your ancient history?"

"A little, but mostly about the Punic Wars and Alexander's conquests. I have also read about the famous Persian Wars, as well of those of Caesar's engagements in Gaul; Pompey's wars against Spartacus; and Pompey against the pirate fleets. I tried reading Marcus Vipsanius Agrippa's biography but found it hard to understand and somewhat dull."

"You sound like a smart lad. Well, the city at which we dock is where the word '*pirate*' comes from. Long before the days when Pompey cleaned out all the pirates roaming the seas, sailors from Piraeus sailed and raided shipping and even coastal cities, enslaving their entire populations. With the natural harbors here at Piraeus, it was almost impossible for any city-state to attack Piraeus's fleets. But do not worry boy; the people of Piraeus are quite gentle these days, even though there are still a few pirate groups working the islands up north, but nothing for you to fret over."

"What is at the military harbors today?" I asked thinking of possible places to explore in the future.

"Well, there are still the remains of the ship sheds at Zea. Many years ago there were hundreds of ramming triremes kept in their own private sheds that circled the entire harbor. Yes, you can still see some of the old remains. The Romans hold some of their military ships at the smaller port of Munichia. Go there someday, and you will see what the ship sheds used to look like. The Romans copy everything the Greeks did: their ships, roads, sewers, aqueducts – all that made Rome great; and what it is today came mostly from the ancient Greeks. But, to be fair, I should say the Romans have made superior improvements on what they copy. Romans are not a creative lot, but they are great engineers and efficient diplomats, even though they rule with a heavy hand," he said with a good-natured laugh.

Once the ship docked, the galley captain was true to his word and escorted me personally to the Long Walls Road. I fell in with a crowd of people walking that late afternoon towards Athens. I carried the red bag with its contents, happy to be alive. All my good fortunes during my sea trip were because of the kindness of a couple of gruff old men and an elderly woman. It was during that late afternoon I decided to be kind to children when I grew old. A good practice I might say. I can now honestly say I aspired to that goal. To be fair to Zeno, he did show me another side of my *didace*.

Walking with the crowd, I discovered I could not keep up because of my weakness. It did not matter, for I found myself alone and whistling slightly as I walked between the two long walls bordering on both sides of the road all the way to Athens. The Athenians eventually rebuilt the original Long Walls, razed by Sparta after the Peloponnesian Wars hundreds of years ago. The long walls were a defensive system that tied Athens to the sea in case of a long siege. Perhaps they still might serve as they did long ago, but this time they would benefit the Roman Empire.

The walk had taken over an hour before I reached the outskirts of Athens. After passing through the Piraeus Gate, I discovered the city was different from Rome in that it was smaller and much older looking, which made sense since Athens was a significant capital when Rome was only a mud hole in a swampy piece of land at the fords of the Tiber hundreds of years ago.

I followed the only street that pointed towards the Acropolis, which rose dramatically in the center of the city. The *Parthenon*, temple of Athena, goddess patron of Athens, was the most spectacular of all the magnificent temples atop the Acropolis. Once I reached the base of the high, flat-topped rocky plateau, I found the steepest and longest marbled staircase I had ever seen – bigger and longer than any in Rome. As I climbed, I counted close to a hundred steps to the entrance of the temple complex. At the top of the stair-ramp stood a six-columned building resembling a temple but was only an elaborate entrance to the Acropolis called the *Propylaea*. Just before the

Propylaea to the extreme right was a small gate that led to another temple, minuscule when compared with all the other structures. Actually, it was a small and simple edifice on the Acropolis and the one I was looking for. The little structure I would later learn was dedicated to Nike, goddess of victory; in Rome, this same goddess was known as Victoria.

By the time I climbed the steps, especially huge for a young boy, I was breathless. I thought only old people got this way when climbing steps. Nevertheless, considering I walked all the way from Piraeus and I had not had much activity since my fever passed, I assumed this was normal. The sun was just setting in the west, casting a pink hue on all the snowy white marble structures. It was truly a magnificent sight. I felt famished; but my bread, fruits, and the wineskin were missing from my red woolen bag. All I could find in the bag were the two scrolls, Decimus's cloak, and the bag of coins. The wax seal on the one scroll for Zeno's priest-friend had not been tampered with, but the other could have been read by anyone during my sickness. Nevertheless, it did not matter; for there was nothing I could do about it. I still had it so I could give it to Zeno when he arrived. I smiled to myself knowing I was now at the end of my journey, and I had reached my destination.

I passed through the small gate in front of the temple of Athena Nike. It was an Ionic building with ancient shields attached to the outer walls. It looked like these shields had been hanging up there for almost a half millennium. Up above the balustrade were relief carvings of women and animals. The women had such thin material pressed close to their bodies that the carvings were, in effect, nude. I turned away, embarrassed by the images in the last light of day. I mounted the four steps leading to the entrance and slowly passed into the sanctuary. Inside I found a man lying in the middle of the floor. He was either sleeping or praying. Not wanting to bother him, I left the sanctuary to sit outside until the man was finished or woke up. Perhaps he knew who Hector was. I did not have to wait long before the worshiper emerged from the temple. I stood and asked if he knew the priest of this temple named Hector.

"Nike be declared, I am Hector. Why do you ask, little boy?"

I said nothing but instead reached into the red woolen bag and withdrew the scroll case meant for his eyes only. He opened it and read it by the remaining light of the sun. His lips moved silently as he read; and, when he was finished, he looked down at me. I could see a kind smile cross his face. He then patted me on the head, much like the ship captain had done the first night on the grain galley, as well as a few hours ago.

"Zeno is a good friend. I will take care of you until Zeno arrives or until you want to leave, whatever comes first. Now you must be hungry. No?"

"Yes, sir, I am starved."

Showing a grand smile, he put his arm around my shoulders; and we walked down the long staircase and down a street to a small, humble, three-room stone house near the bottom of the Acropolis. This was to be my home and sanctuary for the next ten years.

CHAPTER SIX

Athens – From the 5th year to the 15th year of Emperor Tiberius Claudius Nero. (19 AD–29 AD)

Friendship is a single soul dwelling in two bodies. – The roots of education are bitter, but the fruit is sweet. – Education is an ornament in prosperity and a refuge in adversity.   Aristotle of Athens

The next nine-and-a-half years in Athens passed like a peaceful dream. There were times of hard work as I grew into a man; yet, it did feel like an antecedent period of delightful conditioning. In these formative years, I had the total support and moral guidance given by Hector, my surrogate father. Today as I look back as an old man of 90 years, I mostly remember those days being surrounded by the joy of discovery and learning. For the first two years after arriving at Hector's home, I became his little helper at the temple of Athena Nike and doing other odd jobs that he performed. To supplement his income, Hector was the caretaker of several buildings in the *Agora,* including my favorite, the *Painted Stoa*. Every morning before sunrise, Hector and I went to the *Athenian Forum* or, as it was called in those days, the *Agora*; and there we swept the floors of several government buildings as well as the *Painted Stoa*. The *Agora* was located between the Acropolis and before one reached the Piraeus Gate. On my first day after entering the Piraeus Gate, I passed through the *Athenian Forum* without knowing what it was except a place with beautiful, ancient buildings surrounded by wide-open, grassy park-like areas with many ancient structures interspaced between the groves of olive trees and large, open gathering areas. After a few weeks, Hector put me in charge of personally cleaning the floor and steps of the *Painted Stoa*.

The *Painted Stoa* was a unique structure. It was a traditional Greek design, ringed on the outside with Doric pillars with an inner row of Ionic columns that supported the massive, single-beamed cantilever roof. The four exterior walls were encased with shields captured in ancient battles along with large oil paintings on wooden panels hanging beneath the large, round shields. These paintings were depictions of many famous battles from Greece's history, painted by three of Athens' most celebrated artists at the time. The *Painted Stoa* was built sometime after the Persian Wars against Xerxes, King of Persia, or perhaps during the Age of Pericles. This stoa was quite old by the time I became its caretaker. It was initially built to be a memorial to the victory over the Persians, who finally were driven out of Greece after burning Athens to the ground. I had four favorite paintings: the battles of Marathon, Thermopylae, Plataea, and the sea engagement off the island Salamis. All these major military engagements were written about by Herodotus and occurred during the Persian Wars. Out of the four battles, I loved the painting depicting the Battle of Marathon. It was incredibly detailed with the Persians drowning in the mud of a swampy area near the sea. One early fall day I hiked all day to the battle site on the beach of Marathon. I spent a night sleeping on the hard ground and walked back to Athens the next day but not before I located the famous monument that marked the spot the slain Marathon Fighters were cremated. All 192 names were still visible from the carved stone monument. I could not find the swamp where the Persians died in the mud, which must have dried up in the last four hundred plus years. After digging around before I left, I found a bronze, Persian socked spearhead. I never told anyone about this find until now. I kept it in the red woolen bag that contained the leather scroll tube with the Carnalus Scroll given to me by Zeno. I would love to tell the story of how this Persian spearhead saved me but, unfortunately, I do not think I will be able to share that story; for it occurred after the events relating to this work, which I am dictating to my faithful scribe. All I can say now is the Persian spearhead saved my life years later in *Britannia* in the Battle of Watling Street. This occurred after the Barbarian Queen of the Iceni tribe, Boudica, led over 100,000 Iceni and Trinovantes against Londinium, burning and destroying this Roman city to the ground.

At the *Painted Stoa*, there were also other battle scenes that were quite respectable, such as the one between Athens and Sparta, the Trojan War as described in the Iliad by Homer, and Theseus's War with the Amazons. The *Painted Stoa* was a favorite meeting place on the northern edge of the *Agora*, standing next to the Panathenaic Way, the major road leading up to the Acropolis. The *Painted Stoa's* location was nearly the perfect spot in Athens. With the Acropolis looming up in the center of the city, this mini mountain provided protection from high winds that frequently came from the direction of the sea in all the months except winter. During the cold months of winter, northern winds blowing towards the *Painted Stoa* were not as deflected by the Acropolis. In the summer the sun was low enough to shine in and illuminate all the exquisite details of all my favorite paintings, and in the winter the high position of the sun kept the *Stoa* in shadows and ironically cool but not cold. On most of the hottest days of the year, the *Painted Stoa* was almost pleasant, maybe due to the old, tall cedar trees surrounding its east, west, and northern exteriors.

Approximately two years after my arrival in Athens, Zeno had not appeared; nor did any message from him arrive. On the night of the celebration of my 12th birthday was when Hector made a chilling declaration. After our meal that evening, Hector said with unquestionable assurance, "Zeno must be dead."

"What! Why do you believe this?" I asked, almost dazed by his blatant announcement.

"I will show you his letter you delivered to me when we first met at the Athena Nike two years ago." Getting up from the simple wooden table that occupied the center of Hector's main room in his stone house, he went to a wall of shelves that covered the entire back wall. Here is where Hector kept his prized collection of scrolls and a few expensively bound books. This mini library was at least four times the size of the sea captain's collection from the grain-galley. Over the years, I ravenously consumed all his books, especially the mathematical works of Euclid and the histories written by Herodotus and Thucydides. However, it was Hippocrates' writings on medicine that especially captivated me. I studied his techniques on wounds to the head, fractures, and joints along with surgery. Reading Hippocrates inspired me to become a physician. I would dream of following great armies and caring for wounded soldiers. I developed a theory that many combat deaths sustained after battles were due to a lack of good surgeons near battlefields. Years later my theory turned out to be true. Too many soldiers lost their lives to simple wounds that were not correctly cared for after a battle. By the time I reached middle age, I had tried my best to correct this problem and was known by both Barbarians and the Roman legions as a decent surgeon of sorts.

On that dark night of my 12th birthday celebration, everything changed after Hector declared Zeno dead. With the leather scroll tube from the top shelf in his hand, he pulled out the single sheet of vellum. He handed it to me and said, "Here, read this, my son." Hector had used the term "son" as he had been doing since I arrived, and he had treated me as his only beloved child from day one.

I took the sheet and read it aloud, which is the custom I learned from Hector when reading. The theory of reading aloud was considered the best way to correctly pronounce words and supposedly increase retention. Most people who could read in Athens did mumble to themselves when reading. Nevertheless, reading aloud was discouraged in public places such as libraries or in the many *stoas* at the *Agora,* where people gathered to converse with one another and did not want someone muttering to themselves.

Zeno, a servant to my dearest friend, Hector. The boy standing before you is Venustus Vetallus, the son of the well-known Senator Gaius Vetallus Crassus. A great task now awaits you. I am asking and hoping you will be able to watch and care for this young lad until I reach Athens sometime next summer. I have been his tutor the last four years. He has a remarkable mind and is well behaved. I am sure you will find him to be a complaisant child. If necessary, do beat him; for children are like dogs: the more you beat them, the more they love you.

Here is the situation, my friend: Senator Vetallus and Claudia Pulchra (old Varus's wife and mistress to my master, Senator Carnalus, and now the wife of Senator Vetallus) tried to have Venustus murdered as well as me. This plot failed; but my master, my master's only son, and his bookkeeper along with Venustus's mother were not so fortunately protected by the Fates. I am both thankful but sorrowed at this malevolent set of circumstances. I now have my freedom as the result of one of my master's dying declarations, but this is of little comfort. I am hoping to liquidate some of my master's assets and join you and Venustus in Athens within the year. I only hope Vetallus will wait before his next attempt on my life.

The whereabouts of Venustus is not known by anyone except you and two small children. One of the children, a little girl of 12, lost her father by Senator Vetallus's own hand only moments ago as I write to you from Ostia. The other child is a Jewish slave boy about Venustus's age, who is from the Vetallus's household and was a witness to the killing of many slaves at the Vetallus villa this very morning. He also witnessed the brutal murder of Venustus's mother by Claudia Pulchra. I have just sent the Jewish slave boy to his uncle aboard a ship bound for Judaea. I have not decided what to do with the little girl at this time. Senator Vetallus believes that Venustus is dead and will not be looking for him. Please take care of him, my friend. May the gods be with you, especially Victoria, since you serve Nike and she stands in the hand of Athena in the Great Parthenon up on the Acropolis. May knowledge and wisdom dwell with you always. Until next summer.

Zeno: Your faithful friend always, on the night of the 50ᵗʰ anniversary of Actium.

"I see why you believe Zeno is dead," was my only comment. My mind also pondered the knowledge that Messina was two years older than I was, but it did not seem to matter; for I concluded I would never see her again despite my childish feelings in the warehouse in Ostia. My heart still tugged at the reading of her age. The only other thought was why had Hector never laid a hand on me in the past two years. Was Zeno correct about his maxim of beating children? I never asked Hector, but there must be some truth to sparing the rod and spoiling the child. Yet, too much beating or extremely harsh chastisement can injure the spirit of a child. Raising boys, I later learned, is an arduous task, to say the least.

"I know it is hard to accept, but do not worry. I am going to educate you and raise you as my own son."

"How did you and Zeno know each other?" I asked as I handed back the scroll and he returned the vellum back into the leather tube. Watching him, I tried to remember when Zeno asked Messina her age. This event must have occurred after she had cried into Zeno's shoulder and he asked her silently after she had finished. This was the only time Zeno could have learned her age, for I was always with her and him; and this question would have been something I would have remembered.

"I knew Zeno as a student years ago at the Lyceum, and that is where you are going. I have saved up enough money for you to enter as a student; and, since I am an alumnus, you should not have any problem being accepted. If you like the school, you can take the summer months off and work on the fishing boats out of Piraeus to earn enough for the next year. What do you say?"

It sounded like a lot of work, but seeing the joy in Hector's eyes made me say "yes" with conviction.

Within a week after my reading of the Zeno scroll, I was enrolled at the ancient school of Aristotle, still known as and called the Lyceum. The new school year always began one week after the Actium celebrations and ended late spring, one week before the start of Vestalia, a festival for married women who took gifts of food to the Vestal Virgins; and only women were allowed to make sacrifices at the Vesta Temple in Rome. Once the school year ended, I would have a good three months to work on some fishing boat to collect the fees for the next year. The Lyceum had been in existence for over three hundred fifty years. It was located north of the city wall, only a half-hour walk from Hector's house. Here I continued my education in basic reading, writing, and mathematics along with a few hundred boys, some from wealthy families as faraway as Rome. The boys not from Athens typically stayed with other wealthy and influentially connected families from Rome. A very few had to rent a room somewhere in Athens for the school year. School days lasted from just after daybreak to about an hour before dusk. For my protection from the boys from Rome, Hector changed my name to Eunus. This name was the name of a famous slave who led a revolt against Rome in *Sicilia* 60 years before the infamous Spartacus slave revolt in *Italia*. Just like Spartacus, Eunus had defeated several Roman armies with his freed and runaway slave army. Eunus was finally defeated and captured by the *consul* Publius Rupilius and later died in captivity. Hector said it was a fitting name, considering I had been the son of the wealthiest man in the world, much like Rupilius, and now was living lower than many slaves, such as Eunus. Since my mother had been a slave, I was proud to carry the name Eunus. Going to the prestigious Lyceum did not seem to me to be the life of a slave; yet, I understood and appreciated Hector's reasoning for selecting this famous slave's name.

At the Lyceum, all the students were divided by age and ability. I was one of the youngest but brightest of the older boys. This was due, I am sure, to the private tutelage of Zeno. All of us, no matter what age, sat on small wooden stools; and we all used a wooden-framed wax writing tablet. Each boy owned and always carried a metal stylus for writing, which had a sharp tip at one end and a flat head at the other for rubbing out the wax and starting over. On special occasions, we were allowed to use papyrus and a reed pen dipped into black ink. We were never allowed to use expensive vellum.

By my third year at this school-gymnasium-museum, I was introduced to music. I never did master any instruments but worked hard at both the lyre and the pan flute, to no avail. History, philosophy, and rhetoric were also added to my curriculum by age 14. My greatest joy was the museum portion of the Lyceum. How it became a museum is a fascinating story. The story was told to me that Aristotle, the formerly distinguished philosopher and the Father of Logic, was the school's founder; and he rented an old gymnasium that was outside the old walls north of the city. When the Lyceum first opened, it was not yet a museum. Years before Aristotle had started the Lyceum, he had been a student at Plato's school called the Academy, located on the opposite side of Athens. It, too, had been a gymnasium at one time. Aristotle had been a student for about eighteen years up until Plato passed away at a friend's wedding at the ripe age of 80.

I do not mean to break this narrative, but I just heard the city crier call out the time. Based on the city water clock, it is now midnight. I am currently 91 years old, and it is the start of the 131st Actium celebration. After I just stopped talking to listen to the crier, my scribe stopped writing and asked me if I was beyond ripe – just a little humor from my secretary as he transcribes my spoken words during this dark night in my prison cell here in Rome.

Before I finish my story about the Academy and Lyceum, it should be noted that both schools still exist today. The Academy and Lyceum both have been rival schools in Athens, and both had been standing for more than three hundred fifty years. Students come from every corner of the Roman Empire. Now back to the story of the Lyceum. After Plato's death, Aristotle became disappointed with the direction the Academy was headed under the leadership of older students and some teachers. In great disillusionment, Aristotle left Athens in search of all the things he had learned. A dozen years later Aristotle returned with a wife, something Plato never had; but Aristotle was disappointed. It looked like the Academy was still under the control of the same incompetent hands, so he started his own school at an abandoned gymnasium on the other side of town and called it the Lyceum.

During the interim of his return to Athens, Aristotle worked as a private tutor as well as traveled throughout what is now the Roman Empire. One of his pupils was from the north of Greece, that being Macedonia. At the city of Pella, King of Macedonia, Phillip II, hired Aristotle to tutor his eldest son, Alexander. This was the very Alexander who would later become Alexander the Invincible or referred to after his death by the Romans as Alexander the Great. This famous ex-student began to conquer the Persian Empire at the young age of 20. Once Persia fell to Alexander, Aristotle's ex-student crossed the Khyber Pass through the Hindu Kush Mountains leading his small army with him into the Indus Valley. It was in this vast plain during the long summer months when the rains started, which are known as the monsoons. For over two months, there was extreme heat accompanied by constant rains that sometimes reached the shoulders of their horses. It was then Alexander's troops, who had never lost a battle, finally had enough and mutinied. Alexander had no other viable option except to return home. However, his plan was to establish a capital city for his new empire; but it was not going to be located at Pella, Macedonia. Alexander had decided on making Babylon on the Euphrates his eternal capital. I am sure this decision was not difficult since Babylon was the grandest city he had ever witnessed with all of its ancient history, architectural grandeur, and 70-foot walls, making it more spectacular than the mud-and-stone hovels of Pella. From Babylon, Alexander dismissed his old army and began rebuilding a new, younger force. He retained his old generals and began the arduous job of training a new army, mostly made up of Greek mercenaries. He planned to attack Arabia and Africa, including the Carthaginians. From there he was going to sail to the southern tip of *Italia* and conquer the Greek city-states that had colonized this area centuries earlier. Later he was going to move north up the boot of *Italia* and attack the Etruscans, which would have included the Latins, living in the mud and brick city of Rome. Alexander believed Babylon would always remain the capital of the world; but, unfortunately, Alexander never lived to see his future dreams completed before he died prematurely. At the age of 32, Alexander mysteriously became ill in the ancient but still opulent palace of King Nebuchadnezzar, which overlooked the Euphrates River. Less than a week later, Alexander died but not before he had requested his generals to burn his body like the Hindus and throw his ashes into the Euphrates River. Instead, his generals had his body embalmed. The story of how the body reached Alexandria, Egypt, is another long story; but that is where he ended his long journey in death. It was the boyhood friend, General Ptolemy, who ended up with the corpse of a dead god.

Soon after Alexander's death, rumors arrived in Athens claiming to be factual that Aristotle had somehow arranged Alexander's death by supplying the poison that did him in. This assertion was based on Aristotle seeking revenge over the senseless murder of Aristotle's nephew by Alexander at one of his drunken parties out beyond Susa and Persepolis. Aristotle's nephew had been following Alexander's army as a historian. The following story was told to me by a respected teacher at the Lyceum: "One evening, during a drinking party on the plains of Persia somewhere beyond Persepolis, a drunken Alexander proclaimed he was the Son of Zeus and demanded that all his officers bow to him. He had been calling himself the son of Zeus, ever since he visited an Egyptian priest out in the desert when his army was in Egypt. Many refused to bow to Alexander, including Aristotle's nephew. In a drunken rage, Alexander grabbed a spear and impaled the nephew in front of all his soldiers."

This was not the first time Alexander while in a drunken rage murdered. It was common knowledge in Alexander's day that the Macedonian general-king believed he was divine. He also openly claimed to be virgin born by Zeus, who physically impregnated his human mother Olympias via a snake. Olympias was a known Bacchus and snake worshiper and, hearing of her son's boasts back in Pella, quickly admitted to his unique birth. She even claimed that the Temple of Ephesus, where the sex goddess Diana or Artemis to the Ephesians was worshiped, burned to the ground on the day of his birth – as proof of his divinity. Apparently, Alexander was not doubtful and believed he was an avatar of Zeus. The visit to the priest out in a desert oasis in Egypt had apparently solidified Alexander's thinking that he was the son of Amon, as declared by the Egyptian priest, whom Alexander understood to be none other than the Greek god Zeus. After this event, Alexander starting minting thousands of silver coins with his image, which included horns of divinity coming out of the side of his head. This outlandish claim of Alexander actually resulted in Aristotle's self-banishment from Athens when Aristotle became fearful for his own safety since he had been Alexander's private tutor when Alexander was a young prince of Macedonia. Aristotle left his beloved school when he learned that many city leaders were asking questions at Mars Hill and down in the *Agora*: "What ideas did Aristotle plant into this young, malleable mind, who is now conquering the world?"

I was sitting through a long-winded lecture when this very same teacher at the Lyceum went on to say, "Once the report of the murder of Aristotle's nephew was known and when most of the scrolls stolen from Athens by Xerxes 150 years earlier arrived in Athens, the citizens asked for Aristotle's return." The same instructor stated with authority that, after the stolen library was safe, only then did an inebriated Alexander give permission to his troops to burn Persepolis to the ground. Susa was the administrative capital, and Persepolis was the elegant ceremonial center of the Persian Empire. "Once the library returned to Athens, the city fathers apparently felt sorry for their old philosopher's loss of his nephew and were no longer blaming him for Alexander's erratic conduct, including other spectacular crimes of murder and blasphemy."

Whether this story was true or not, it did feed into my decision to seek revenge against my father and Claudia. If Aristotle possibly had a hand in the death of Alexander to square the tables for the death of his nephew, then so could I. Truth be told, I today tend to believe it was not Aristotle but his generals who plotted against Alexander. I have personally read an abundance of evidence to show that most of Alexander's generals agreed in Babylon that Alexander had gone mad with power. I believe the evidence leans heavily towards Alexander's generals conspiring against him using poison during a funeral feast at Babylon in Nebuchadnezzar's Palace. The poisoning transpired at the start of a funeral feast for Alexander's lover, Hephaestion. The only ancient records I could find indicated Alexander suffered from the symptoms of blackberries of the belladonna plant shortly after the funeral feast for Hephaestion began. The justification for his murder was because Alexander was suspected of killing his lover and general, Hephaestion. It was almost a repeat of Aristotle's nephew when he, too, refused to kneel before Alexander during a drinking party in Darius III's imperial tabernacle captured after the Battle of Issus. This monster tent was carried all the way from the Battle of Issus to the Indus River. Each evening this gigantic royal banquet tent that could comfortably fit hundreds was erected. It was reported that Alexander drank himself into a blackout state each night during these drunken parties. The next morning following Alexander's blackout in Darius's throne room tent, he called for his friend; Alexander did not remember he had murdered Hephaestion the night before. Due to the hostile circumstances out in the mountains where the red poppies grow that produce the milky white fluid for gall, west of the Hindu Kush Mountains, Alexander decided to wait to have his lover's funeral dinner once his army returned to his new capital. When Alexander became sick at the Hephaestion memorial feast in Babylon, only trusted surviving generals were present. Many records from several generals' diaries suggest Alexander died of ethanol poisoning. This is like waving a white flag to lure an army into a trap because I could never find any record of Alexander vomiting during the days he was sick after the feast and before death. The physician Hippocrates wrote that vomiting always, always, always accompanies ethanol poisoning. No record of vomiting, no ethanol poisoning. Therefore, I lean towards one or more of his generals doing the revolting deed, much like many senators in Rome murdered Caesar for almost the same crime, that of claiming to be a god and guilty of committing murder upon their own friends.

Whatever killed Alexander, this famous general still had admiration for his old teacher. Due to this unique relationship, Alexander continually shipped looted treasure for almost a decade of warfare in the East, sending it all to Aristotle in Athens. Animal skins, preserved flora, rock samples, manuscripts, artifacts, and much more came to the Lyceum. The little school on the outskirts of Athens soon became a repository of many ancient and unusual objects. Thus, it became a museum. The word "museum" comes from the Greek word "muses," the nine goddesses of Zeus, who were responsible for the inspiration of poetry, music, and dance along with most of man's other intellectual activities. The collection of rare artifacts in one location is now the definition of a museum. To my knowledge, the Lyceum was the world's first museum; but never was this unique collection ever open to the public such as museums that can be visited today in Alexandria, Pergamum, Rhodes, Rome, and Antioch. While I was a student there were times the school sold an artifact to another city only to generate funds for expenses and repairs.

As a student of the Lyceum, there were still thousands of precious objects filling several storerooms at the Lyceum. Besides dried flowers, animal skins, rocks, and historical items, Alexander also sent many ancient manuscripts in their original script. Some books were in *Sanskrit* and even *Pali*, the tongue of Siddhartha Gautama from India, who was called the Buddha or *Tathagata*. There were other writings on wired bamboo pages, written in a beautiful calligraphy of pictograms from the land of Chin. When I told Hector about these precious items, he suggested to the headmaster of the Lyceum, if my tuition were lowered, I would compile lists of all the things packed away and forgotten in the many storage rooms. My fees were cut in half, and I was extremely fortunate beyond paying a lower tuition for just touching such ancient artifacts and to dream of all these articles from the past. In a three-year time, I had all the items listed in their own categories and a map of their location in the storage rooms.

As I have already stated, both the Lyceum and the Academy were originally gymnasiums; and both structures looked the same. Both were built in a square fashion with four long wings enclosing a vast, secluded exercise courtyard in the center. It was in this *tripedalis* that I gained my most valuable education, how to fight and kill. How this came to fruit is an interesting story. Physical education at the Lyceum occupied every afternoon out in this sand-covered courtyard. Greeks believed that exercising the body was just as important as mental gymnastics. Each afternoon in the interior courtyard students devoted themselves to the Greek sports of throwing the discus and the javelin; running; jumping; and my favorites, boxing and wrestling. As I grew older, sword and knife fighting were added to my curriculum. All exercise was performed in the Greek style, which was in the nude. Given that traditions are hard to change, all training at any gymnasium in the Roman world was conducted in the nude. This rule I did not like. Exercising naked reminded me of that day in the bush next to the Tiber River and all the shame I had to endure on that fateful day. Consequently, without telling anyone why, I politely refused and implored the leaders of the school to allow me to exercise wearing a simple loincloth or as written in *Sanskrit,* a *dhoti.* A great debate ensued: could or should the rule be changed? The Greek word *gymnos* means nude, and *gymnos* was the central argument for the continuation of this ancient tradition as made by students and teachers alike. The argument was as old as the practice of exercising in the nude. To change a tradition is synonymous to blasphemy. For individual sensibilities to win over a tradition, which stretched back hundreds of years, just was not tolerated, let alone discussed. I did not recognize nor care about the havoc I had brought to the Lyceum. However, in a most mysterious way, I prevailed in the end, thanks to Hector's behind-the-scenes help and influence. I believe Hector had privately made the argument of personal liberty and sensitivity, which helped override an outdated tradition. I never forgot his many debates and arguments that I used myself many decades later when I ran into a fight over the power of traditions, which clearly needed to be done away with. There were also several substantial donors to the school, whom Hector persuaded to pull their funds if the rule of nudity was not dropped. In the end, I won. Out of it all, I learned a valuable lesson. Anything and any person can change no matter the force of habit, influence, or long-standing custom. The truth is the highest power over lies and false traditions. We do live in a world of darkness that can be changed with light, which can drive out the moral wrongs and iniquitous habits we humans perpetuate without knowing why. One thing I have learned in my long life is a long-standing evil is one of the hardest stones to move.

At first, being the only one in a loincloth, I was treated poorly and mocked by the other boys. Nevertheless, my strength and ability to stand my ground changed many attitudes. After a few months, other boys began wearing the simple *dhoti* covering to show solidarity with me. By the time I left the Lyceum, those who exercised in the nude were in the minority.

All boys, naked or not, were required to rub olive oil over their bodies before each afternoon session. Dust and sand were thrown over our own oily bodies, which made a pseudo-second skin. This technique helped to protect against the heat of the sun and during the winter from the cold. It was incredible how this method worked, and it did save my life up in the snowy regions of *Germania* years later. We exercised no matter the weather; it could be pouring rain or blistering hot, and still we were not allowed shelter.

I remember one distinct vicious thunderstorm; a lightning bolt hit the only one tree in the courtyard. Fortunately, no one perished; but all of us boys were knocked flat to the ground from the impact on the tree. I thought from that day on, if anyone could harness this power, it would change the world as we knew it. A few years later I would witness a bolt of lightning directly hit a man, and the result was hard to describe. I will give details of this event later. On the topic of death, I should mention several boys at the Lyceum came down with severe chills and one did die after exercising in the nude one frigid winter afternoon. After the boy's demise, the teachers just commented that the fates were thinning out the weak. I felt this was a ridiculous conclusion but held my tongue.

After every afternoon workout, we boys went to the washroom and sat in hot water provided by slaves, who poured it over our heads from pitchers as we sat in clay hipbaths. I should state that I never saw a female slave at the Lyceum, only males. It is odd that I never thought about this until now. While in the tubs, we would rub and scrape off the sweat, oil, and mud with a small, curved bronze *strigilii*. It worked just like the larger ones that were used on the chariot horses bathed by the grooms at the Circus Maximus or other circus racetracks in the city of Rome. As I have already stated, Decimus and I had spent many hours watching the grooms on holidays in Rome along with the one rest day a week. On those days we were free from our studies from Zeno. I would later learn about the weekly rest day that always fell on the seventh day of each week. It was due to the Jewish immigrants residing in Rome who refused to work on what they called their Sabbath rest. Rome eventually lost this "tradition fight" with the Jews of Rome because the fourth command handed down by Moses forbid any work to be performed on *Dies Saturni* or what the Jews called the seventh day of the week. The reasoning behind this rule was to honor the Jewish God, who rested on the seventh day from creation. However, it was not a major fight; most Romans looked for any reason to have a day off from any work and to be able to spend more time attending the theaters, amphitheaters, or chariot races. I would say Rome has at least one hundred and fifty holidays each solar year, including all the *Dies Saturni*, where no one works in the capital city except slaves who performed duties at eating establishments and bathhouses along with gladiators and grooms.

After a hot, soapy bath in a hipbath, a slave would give each of us a good scraping. It actually felt terrific when a skilled slave used the *strigilii*. The Greek washrooms, I believe, must have been the inspiration for the Roman bathhouses. The Romans evidently improved upon the Greek model, just

136

like the galley ship captain had proclaimed. A Roman bathhouse was a massive building, or even buildings, with hot and cold pools for swimming or soaking. There were steam rooms, warm rooms, and other amenities for the creature comforts of the human body such as small libraries, lecture halls, and even small shopping stores. The one main difference was in Rome: both men and women bathed and swam together in the nude. Sometimes both men and women strolled together into the lecture halls, libraries, and stores stark naked. That, again, was always a problem with my sensibilities; but this practice was only seen in Rome. All the bathhouses in the other major cities of the Empire segregated men and women to particular times of the day when the two sexes could use the facilities separately. This latter practice was more to my liking even though I rarely would use these habitations of immorality unless I could be alone.

Every afternoon after our exercise routines boys 16 or over remained in the courtyard where Grillius, the famous Spartan *paidotribes*, trained them for an additional hour each day. Grillius, whose name fit his personality, was an old, stern exercise teacher or *paidotribes,* who taught all the individual gymnastics and other physical activities. Grillius was originally from the ancient city-state of Sparta and had been a mercenary for many years before coming to work at the Lyceum. He was persistent and harsh and was a dour, old trainer who did not laugh or believe in any boyish foolery. Our training was always severe and stringent.

When I reached 16, I was overjoyed that I was finally going to learn the art of combat. My promised threat to Claudia was still smoldering in my heart, but I lacked training in the art of war to successfully carry it out. One week after my 16th birthday and the start of a new school year, I stayed after gymnastics with the other boys of my age to learn the art of war. This was the beginning of my fifth year at the Lyceum. From late spring until the end of the summer, the Lyceum was closed. Each academic year began one week after my birthday. On my first day in my fifth year, I stood proudly in line with the older boys for training in the use of the gladius and the longer *xiphos*. The *xiphos* was a double-edged, single-handed sword used by the ancient Greek armies after their spears were of no use. The Spanish gladius, also a double-edged sword, was shorter and heavier. The gladius was the primary weapon of the Roman legions and was made of iron compared with the weaker metal of the *xiphos*, which was bronze. At first we used a wooden version of these two swords, and our courtyard must have resembled a gladiatorial training school or *ludus*. We also became skilled in the 10-foot spear called a *doru*. This was the ancient Greek hoplites' primary weapon in the phalanx. We learned to fight as a team using the *doru*, stabbing and slashing from a distance, but as a moving unit, running at the sound of a trumpet or particular flute notes. We also trained with the 21-foot *sarissa*, designed by Philip II, King of Macedonia and biological father of Alexander the Great. This incredibly long spear had to be handled using two hands, not just one hand like the shorter *doru*. A neck strap was attached to the top edge of a shield, which enabled the soldier to maneuver a shield that was only connected to a man's left forearm. The *sarissa* was an unusually long weapon and combined with the shield neck strap required many hours to learn how to use both shield and spear in tandem when fighting. The left hand was in front of the right when holding the heavy-weighted shoe at the end or butt of the *sarissa*, which gave it a counterbalance. We trained in charging; and, once the enemy was engaged, the right hand did the thrusting, using an underhanded motion while the shielded left arm provided protection from any oncoming bronze-tipped spears. In a phalanx attack, the first 5 rows of men holding long pikes or *sarissas* were level in a charge with the remaining 11 rows of men slanting their *sarissas* up and forward to deflect hurled stones and arrows. The appearance of the phalanx attack was like a forest of trees. This new tactic of war, designed by Philip II, was extremely problematic to master; but, once it became second nature, it was an unbeatable force when fighting with hundreds of men against thousands. No one knew how to defeat the fighting phalanx until the creation of the Roman cohort system, first used against a relative of Alexander through his mother's side, a king and one of histories greatest generals, Pyrrhus, King of Epirus. Three hundred years ago in southern *Italia,* King Pyrrhus won several major battles using the fighting phalanx against Rome. Due to the fact, King Pyrrhus lost almost three out of four soldiers in the first two of three major battles against Rome, but still won the battles, thus giving the world the axiom: "Pyrrhic victory." When Alexander was age 18, Philip was assassinated by one of his own bodyguards; and Alexander became king in Philip's stead. From that day forward, the fighting phalanx was Alexander's secret weapon against the forces of the last Persian king, Darius III.

Boxing, wrestling, and equestrian skills were also part of our training during my fifth year at the Lyceum. This extra hour each afternoon became the highlight of my year. I lived and breathed for each new lesson I learned from our Spartan *paidotribes*. By the end of my fifth year, most of us boys became skilled with the weapons we trained with. Now we were allowed to engage in many mock fights, using shields and sometimes real swords. We also fought with whips, nets, and trident spears, just like gladiators in the arenas dotting the Empire. I never wished to become skilled with a trident spear, thinking it was an inferior weapon because of my experience at age ten watching the Nubian at the *Statilius Taurus Amphitheater* perish at the end of a gladius wielded by Gladiator Marius. During these mock matches, many received scars that the students carried proudly for the rest of their lives. I personally did not see it that way, especially after having received a long, white, ugly scar on the top of my right forearm, which I sustained in one of those bouts.

Besides our learning combat skills, Grillius began teaching us boys military tactics, such as how Alexander's "fighting phalanx" worked versus the Roman cohort. These lessons became precious to me years later and saved my life on many occasions when fighting with the Roman legions in the Barbarian lands of *Hispania*, *Germania*, and *Britannia*. I can still remember many times during my long life whispering a silent "thank you" to the austere Grillius in the purple-scarlet Spartan cloak after one of his well-taught tactics saved my life. I can still picture him ambling with a peculiar limp and all of his long, white scars on his legs and arms and one mark crossing his face. That one particular facial injury, traveling from his left eyebrow to his right cheek, made him appear beyond fierce. He was really a no-nonsense warrior we all admired and secretly wanted to emulate.

Two weeks after my 19th birthday, shortly after the start of my final year at the Lyceum, an incident occurred involving Grillius that changed my life dramatically. It was the start of my eighth year as a student. The school year always began one week after the Actium celebration, which allowed most students to celebrate this great Augustinian holiday and still arrive close to the start date. At the commencement of each school session in September, I always became a little depressed due to the memory of my mother's death. One week after school started, my spells of miasma left to never return around any future Actium holiday or birthday. It was several weeks after the 59th Actium that I acquired a new, unique friendship that helped to heal the hole in my heart regarding my missing mother. It all began in the training yard of the Lyceum. After my extra hour of sword training, I returned to the empty *tripedalis* after my bath and scraping were completed. I had forgotten my flask of oil, which I had left in the exercise yard. There it was near the half-dead tree, the one hit by lightning years earlier. After I had picked it up, I noticed a body slumped over in a corner. It was Grillius, the old Spartan. As I approached him, I noticed he was sweating profusely; and his skin looked very pale. He was facing down with his head in the sand. I saw dust moving with each labored breath, which meant he had not died from whatever ailed him. After feeling his forehead, I concluded he must have a high fever; for his head was burning to my touch. I tried to awaken him, to no avail. I then reached behind his arms and dragged him into a storage room where many of the artifacts I had cataloged were stored. I made a bed of rags and straw and stayed with him until way past sunset. He still did not respond, and I had tried all the tricks the old woman used on me in the galley when I had a similar debilitating fever. Not knowing where he lived, which I assumed was somewhere in the city, I hunted up a handcart and used that to transport Grillius to Hector's house. Hector proved to be an excellent medical clinician along with his other skills. Within a couple of days, Grillius had pulled out of whatever had overtaken him and was up and back to normal.

Two days after Grillius had returned to the Lyceum, he asked me to see him in the courtyard after my bath. I found him standing near the back corner where I had located him face down in the sand a few days earlier. Grillius was pacing back and forth like a caged lion but one wearing a purple-scarlet Spartan cloak and unique knee-high military boots. He always wore his hair long and tied in a tail that reached almost to his waist. Only the Spartan Corps of *hippies,* or bodyguards of ancient Spartan kings, were allowed to wear their hair long like Grillius. In the ancient Classical period, there were only 300 *hippies* out of the 9,000 Spartan status-quo soldiers. Only an elite soldier between the ages of 20 to 30 was invited to become a *hippie.* These 300 particular soldiers guarded the warrior king, not the second or civil king, who stayed behind in Sparta when the 9,000 *hoplites* marched off to battle. *Hoplites* were soldiers between the ages of 20 to 60, and all males in Sparta were soldiers. I assumed Grillius must have been a *hippie* at one time in his youth, even though Sparta was no longer the power city-state it once was. He most likely wore his hair long in his youth; and, since only the elite guards were the only Spartans allowed to grow their hair long, it must have been his badge of honor. For most of my life, I would also grow my hair long; but it was for other reasons, which I shall share later. On that late afternoon, when Grillius saw me walking towards him, he turned and approached with his head lowered in the form of humility.

"Eunus, I not so good with words like you boys. But what I want to say is I appreciate you and your father, what did me; and I feel indebted."

"No, *paidotribes,* I would have done the same for a stray dog, not that I think of you like a dog. Actually, I love dogs when most do not." Many religions believed messengers from the gods would not come to someone if this animal lived in or near his or her home. I still think this belief is off the edge, and I have had many dogs as companions in my life. I cannot think of any other creature that God has made that shows more unconditional love and can teach us, humans, a thing or two about loyalty. Dogs actually show much more affection to a person than a well-trained horse shows. I rank horses just above cats in the arena of loyalty to their masters.

"Dog or not, I still have decided to give something you would most likely never learn; and it will be something you will need later in life."

"What would that be, *paidotribes*?"

"You may call me by my given name when we are alone, for I now consider you a friend and not just a student. Call me Grillius."

"Yes, sir."

"No, call me Grillius."

"Yes, Grillius."

"But only when alone when no other boys around. Understood?"

I nodded politely that I did. Grillius now looked me square in the eyes with much seriousness. "Excellent; now, what I am going to teach, only you, are all the skills that I have not taught the other boys. You may in the future find yourself in a knotted situation when you will need to defend yourself with your hands or possible only a knife. I will teach you the art of killing another man in a matter of seconds. These skills will possibly save your life. I will first teach you *pankration*, a brutal form of ancient fighting with no rules. This was once an event at the Olympic Games held every *quadrennium,* or fourth years at Olympus."

I did not know what to say but felt it was important to Grillius that I learn all of these arts of warfare and fighting. Besides, these things might help me with my future plans for my father and Claudia. "When will you teach me these things?" I asked trying not to show any excitement.

"You will come see me right here in the courtyard after your bath each late afternoon. We will start when all the other boys and teachers have gone for the day. We will work on something different each late evening. It will not take much time except you will need to practice each maneuver and stratagem on your own. No one is to know about this, even Hector. Also, none of the other boys or teachers are to know; or I will lose my job if this information is known."

"I will be discreet," I answered him; and, over the next year, I learned a new artfulness of devastation that made me quite proficient in the skill of defending myself and killing any dangerous opponent. Each day I learned something new, which I had no idea existed. I discovered dozens of different ways to eliminate another man with just my bare hands or a sharp object, such as an unassuming metal stylus we boys used for writing on our wax tablets. My hands, knees, feet, and elbows all became lethal weapons. Even my teeth, I learned, were serious weapons as a last resort. I developed these new techniques with long hours of practice. At first, I had to master *pankration*. This was the event at the ancient Olympics that combined boxing, wrestling, kicking, and strangling. I had to learn how to twist when trapped in a position that seemed inescapable. Grillius insisted that I be proficient in the "ladder-grip" hold, which was a move no man could escape. This grasp was when you attacked your opponent from the back and looped your legs around your foe's stomach placing your hands under his arms and clasping your fingers together up behind the nape of your adversary's head. In the Olympics, this one sport was the most dangerous if one did not count chariot racing. The only rules in *pankration* were no biting or gouging the eyes; otherwise, everything else was permissible. One could kick his opponent in the head, break fingers, or twist a foot out of its socket; and all neck holds were allowed.

Grillius taught me every conceivable move in *pankration* and then added more from the fighting arts from the Far East that he learned while serving as a mercenary when he was a young man fighting in the Gupta region near the Ganga River. Around this northern river in the subcontinent of Asia, the Great Horse Rule people ruled. They were called the Gupta rulers, and Grillius served as a guard for several *rajas* or warlords. The Great Horse Rule originated where each *raja* allowed a great stallion to run free for one year. In the spring of each following year, each *raja* would lead armies against his neighbors if his horse had entered into their land any time during the previous year. Attendants and spies watched each animal and reported back if the horse, indeed, crossed any boundary that would lead to the next year's war. After working around the Ganga River, Grillius traveled into the Han Dynasty region as well as the Four Island Kingdom of *Nippon* located beyond the Yellow River far to the north across the sea. In those faraway islands, Grillius learned many other skills of fighting and forms of combat. Grillius was an expert with a bow but preferred his sword and the knife for close-up work when fighting. I was taught the skillfulness of archery and the art of making bows and wooden arrows along with feather fletching. I never really could master the bow to make myself a master archer but was good enough to hit a man from 50 yards. Perhaps this was because Grillius did not like this weapon and felt it was a coward's defense.

The belief systems in these faraway lands were very puzzling to me as explained by Grillius. He often called the Indus and Ganga River region the land of *maya* or illusion. *Maya* was the logic of the religions on this far edge of the world, a region of relativism with no absolutes. *Maya* teaches that all we see, touch, smell, hear, and taste is not real since everything of substance is only an illusion. The goal in life is to escape out of this *maya* world and enter into *nothingness*, which is real. After listening to Grillius, I felt everything in the West was turned on its head in the minds of the East. The question is will the West and East ever agree with the logic of *maya,* compared with Aristotle's logic of inductive and deductive reasoning. *Neti, neti,* or as this Sanskrit word teaches, "Yes, but no, but yes, but no."

Since Grillius never could fully speak the language of the Gupta people, he grew frustrated with the little he did understand. "Transmigration of the soul after death and doing good deeds to wash away bad *karma* with *darhma* (or good behavior) does not make sense," he said over and over to me. "I especially do not understand why all *karma* could not be erased at death and why excess bad *karma* traveled with one's *atman* into the next life after death. The teachers or priests of this land, called *yogis,* taught that a human did not have a soul or spirit; but, instead, both the human soul and spirit were combined into what they described as a man's *atman.* Meditating to shut out pain and suffering to more quickly reach *moksa,* the state of escape from this life to get to nothingness, is nothing more than mind-numbing."

Grillius also spoke of the idea of *yin* and *yang,* practiced in the Kingdom of the Han, combined with the *middle way* from the followers of a teacher called Buddha. Grillius observed that the idea of balance was the one similar principle between these two divided societies. "All the people living on the Hindu and Ganga Rivers and the Han people living between the Pearl and Yellow Rivers and including the clans living on the four islands all shared this idea of the *yin-yang* or *middle way.* Balance in one's life was essential to good health, and this makes sense to me," commented Grillius on one late evening after my extra training. "Good *karma* does produce good actions. Bad *karma* does produce bad deeds. These are the only ideas of the land of relativism that make some sense. But the idea that life is not real but more on the order of a dream or an illusion is crazy thinking."

"What do you believe to be truth, Grillius?" I asked since we were on this subject.

"What we do in this world in the few years we have to be alive does echo into eternity. I believe we have only one life to live, and our decisions in this life determine our eternity. I feel in my heart that all men live forever in some kind of state, and the decisions we make here and now somehow determine each person's eternity; and that is why what we do clearly reverberates into eternity. I believe we humans will all live forever in some form after death but not through *samsara* (or transmigration of the *atman*) into another life in this world. Being trapped in another body with all your memories erased sounds like a cruel joke to me or something very evil. Surely, this idea of reincarnation and *maya* have to be a lie from the Evil One. What I believe in more than anything is there surely has to be an invisible Evil One."

Here was a man who possessed more wisdom than all my Lyceum teachers put together. By just looking at Grillius, no one would see this side of him. The old idiom comes to mind: you should not judge a man by his clothes. A warrior could be a philosopher, and here was the proof standing before me. "What else can you say on this subject, Grillius?"

After rubbing his trimmed beard, he looked up to the sky and started sharing the root thoughts of his heart. I wondered if he had ever voiced these ideas before now. "What philosophy or religion in this world is correct? Well, this is the quest of all humans. This is what I have learned in all my travels. Only one idea is correct, and all others are deceptions of the truth. Know the truth, and it will be obvious to spot the lie."

I stood shocked to my core, for here was truth in its purest form. We are alive to question and seek the one truth. This truth, according to my mother, was to find a long-awaited one, who she believed is alive today in the land of Egypt or *Palestina*. I decided to make this my quest and search for this teacher once I was finished with Claudia and my father. Today I can see back in my school days revenge was my guiding purpose. I believed I had mastered the art of war and fighting, all to fill my lust for vengeance. Therefore, all these different philosophies and religions Grillius spoke about I mostly ignored. My fundamental goal was to become quick and agile. My focus was to enhance all these different fighting skills and concentrate on the various exercises Grillius taught me. However, I can say today I learned much more from Grillius over just being able to defend myself.

One cold evening Grillius explained about the tallest mountains in the world, a band of mountains much higher than the Alps. These peaks were located to the north of the Ganga River. The tops of these mountains were above the ability for a human to even breathe and blocked any direct land route for anyone trying to reach the Kingdom of Guptas to that of the Hans. He told me, when he wanted to see the land of the Hans, he had to board a strange type of ship to get there. It was the largest vessel he had ever seen, bigger than a 3,000-ton grain galley sailing the *Mare Interum*. He found this multi-masted ship at the mouth of the Ganga River, which he boarded and sailed to the Land of Chin. After weeks at sea, the vessel finally reached the Pearl River, another massive river that any ship could sail up for hundreds of miles. Grillius explained that the ship after a few more weeks ended its journey on the Yellow River. Grillius said it was correctly named because the water was of the color of the soil and clay found in this region. It was near the Yellow River that Grillius discovered a book entitled *Art of War*, by Sun Tzu. "It took over a month to find someone who could read it to me in Greek. It was not a long book, and I enjoyed what it had to say."

Grillius also learned all about "black eggs" and the "star" throwing weapons. In this land, Grillius noticed a green stone called jade that was carved into many beautiful shapes and worn as jewelry. "These people believed this stone had magical powers but not as much power that comes from the dead spirits of their dearly departed, old people. All the old living people were treated almost as if they were gods."

I smiled and said, "I would travel there when I am old and allow these people to take care of me." Grillius did not smile but agreed with my plan in mock seriousness. I looked at Grillius with one eye closed wondering if he were serious. When I realized he was pulling my leg, we both had a good double-up laugh. This was the first time I ever witnessed Grillius openly laugh. During his time of hilarity, I noticed he was missing a top eye tooth, and the rest of his teeth were somewhat destitute.

Grillius told me there was only one prominent philosophy in the Han Empire, which was started hundreds of years ago from a man the Romans called Confucius. Grillius said this one man was a mere teacher; and after he had died, his disciples not only worshiped at his grave but wrote down his maxims into a book called the *Analects*. He told me there was a copy of this book in the Lyceum library, which he brought back with him and donated it to the school. I said I had seen this book and was surprised to discover a second copy of this same book, but it had been translated into Greek. It was called the "Collection of 500" or the *Analects* in Greek. Grillius seemed astonished when I told him I had read this book. He actually wanted me to tell him what it said. I shared a couple of maxims with him, and he smiled and said he wanted to hear more on another day. I told him I would memorize a couple of lines a day and share them with him in the evenings during training. Grillius seemed very pleased with this idea.

Later that year after our special classes, Grillius mentioned the teachings he learned in the land of Chin about a man who lived at the exact same time as Confucius but in the land of the Hindus. This man was called the Buddha, which translates from the *Sanskrit* texts as "the man who woke up." The *Pali Texts,* the language of Buddha, only called him *Tathagata,* "he who came, went, and came back." Grillius explained that the Buddha lived and taught around the Ganga River in the Gupta region at the same time Confucius resided and imparted his ideas south of the Yellow River, which meant both men never met nor learned of each other's beliefs. There were some similar ideas between them, like *the middle way* and *yin-yang*, but mostly there were significant differences between each teacher's doctrines.

"They both died around the same time around the year the Greeks were fighting the Persians in the great battles of Thermopylae and Salamis. The man named Confucius was called in his land *Chiu Kung* or *Kung Fu Tzu*. I believe the origin of his name in Latin, Confucius, came from a misunderstanding of his title, *Kung Fu Tzu* or Kung the Master. In the land of Chin, the last name was the first name, and the first name was the last or family name. You see, *Kung* was his first name with the added title *Fu Tzu*, which meant *the master*. His title was first translated into Greek as *Confucios*. Many years later, *Confucios* was changed by the Latins into Confucius."

In the months I trained with Grillius, I did share many quotes from the *Analects*. Grillius and I both felt like Confucius was teaching men to become more sensitive or almost womanly in their actions. Grillius said this meant a man should be more *yin*-like and not *yang*. After I was much older, I changed my view on many of his adages. I would later learn that truth is truth, no matter who says it, and for a man to be sensitive does not mean he is feminine. Today I would say there are some excellent teachings found in the *Analects*, and there is wisdom if men acted in a more sensitive way over being just a beast with no understanding.

Grillius taught me about silk and *kaolin* pottery. *Kaolin* was a very fine white clay that the Chin people used to make delicate cups and plates. "In Rome, these pottery dishes are called *Bone China* because, when they broke, the insides looked like the color of bones."

"Tell me about silk."

"It is a cloth from the Land of Chin. This unique material is made of the strands of a worm. These strands are woven together, and the result is a wonderful material and the strongest material in this world. Since this *kaolin* pottery and silk was coveted by the wealthy patricians of Rome, trade routes sprang up and were established by different Barbarians groups stretching between the Roman Empire and the Hans. There are many roads to travel in the north of the great mountains between the land of Chin and the Hindus. When I returned to Greece from the land of Chin, I followed one of these trade routes. I hired on as a guard for a huge caravan of camels that had two humps. We went north of the tallest mountains but soon were crossing huge deserts and other mountainous regions. The convoy was transporting all kinds of items. There was jade as well as ivory carvings. I was told that the

Barbarians call these roads the Silk Routes. As far as the Han Dynasty knew, the local people were just buying the Han Dynasty goods for themselves. Little did they know their products were being transported to the streets and shops of Rome. All these intermediary Barbarian groups are the ones growing rich by carrying bolts of silk, cases of *kaolin*, ivory, jade, individual spices, and *pharma* products (or drugs)."

I wanted to tell Grillius I already knew all about this from my father in Rome, except even he didn't understand that the Hans were not aware their goods were being sold in Rome. I decided not to tell Grillius of my real father in Rome and leave the idea that Hector was my real *patra*. I remember changing the subject from the Silk Routes to the people living on the Four Islands. "Tell me about these strange tribes on the islands beyond Chin."

Grillius explained to me that the people of the Four Islands were different in looks and build from those in Chin. These island people worshiped many gods, but their principal deity was the creator who was the sun. This goddess was named *Amaterasu*. Nevertheless, the *Amaterasu* people did share many similar ideas and archetypes from the land of Chin such as their dress and building techniques. Grillius told me that some people were very hairy, and then there were others with very little hair on their bodies. Everybody was dusky in color and had dark hair but a little wavier than those in Chin. Both people had the same kind of dark eyes without lids or did have lids, but their eyes looked slanted. "I tell you now no man or woman did I see with almond-shaped eyes like here in Greece or this part of the world. In the land of the Four Islands, the teachings of Buddha from the Ganga River were well known and practiced by many. Ancestor worship was also strong. Apparently, a powerful king in the Hindu River area called Asoka years after the visit from Alexander the Great's invasion of the Indus or Hindu River region tried to unite all of the sub-continent of Asia under his rule. Hundreds of thousands were killed, and much more than that were moved to other parts of his growing kingdom. Right when King Asoka was about to finish uniting the tip of this land to his empire, a Buddhist priest introduced the king to the teachings of Buddha. King Asoka converted; and since killing any living thing was forbidden by *Noble Truth* number four of the *Four Noble Truths*, Asoka stopped his war. The tip region is known as the Chola Kingdom still, trades with Rome, and was never conquered by Asoka. After Asoka's conversion to the teachings of Buddha, he put all his energy into building 84,000 Buddhist *stupas* (or temples) with a Buddha bone inside each temple or *stupa*. Asoka also dispatched hundreds of Buddhist priests to every corner of the world to spread what he believed was the only *Way*. Every priest who went West returned with no results. The Greeks, Persians, Egyptians, and others laughed at the idea of *atman* and *maya* as well as the goal of life is to *moksha* into *Brahman* (or nothingness). Salvation to Buddha was to escape self and suffering. I am sure Epicurus and Buddha would have had fun sharing their ideas with one another."

Grillius went on to explain the goal to reach Nirvana or *nothingness*; and then I understood why Buddha's teachings would not appeal to Epicurus, the Father of Epicureanism. I learned that the *middle way* of Buddha was very popular in the land of Chin and the Four Islands. To this day, there are many followers of the Buddha in these localities according to Grillius, but strangely enough very few follow Buddha in what used to be the Kingdom of Asoka.

"Hindu priests rose up after Asoka's death and physically killed or drove out the followers of Buddha from their land of the Ganga River. Understand the Buddhist had nothing to do with Asoka and his killings before he converted, but the Hindu religion suffered a great deal under Asoka."

"Therefore, the Buddhist became the target of reprisals after the death of Asoka?"

"Correct. Since the Buddhist would not kill his enemies, Noble Truth number four, many submitted to death or escaped to the north. Death to a Buddhist was considered an excellent release of this illusion or *maya* and his *atman* could now travel to *nothingness* or come back as something or someone else."

"What about the people on the Four Islands? What are their ideas of Buddha?" I asked.

"Besides accepting ideas of Buddha, the people of the Four Islands still hold onto their original religious concepts. They called themselves *Nippon* (or Sun Origin) people. They believed their goddess, *Amaterasu*, created the Four Islands as the holy land. These people actually think of themselves as half-human and half-divine. Their word for divine is *kami*. Since they believed they are part *kami* and part human, they have minimal contact with outsiders."

Grillius went on explaining that the *Nippon* people saw Grillius on the level of a horse or dog, saying he was just human. They felt they were superior because they are all part *kami* and part human. What Grillius did discover that was exceptional was that *Nippon* (or Sun Origin) people were the makers of the best and strongest swords ever crafted. "They heated and folded the thin, long iron blades seven times. Each fold required placing the iron sword into ovens filled with wood that had hardened after many burnings. This combination of the heat and the burnt wood formed a metal they called *steel*.

It was lighter than iron; and these long, thin *steel* swords could cut through an iron sword such as a gladius."

Grillius said he even witnessed a *Nippon* sword cut through an iron helmet as if it were made of lard. The sword makers would brag on how many men their swords could cut through in one swipe. Some said their swords could cut through up to seven men. Grillius told me he would have purchased one of these swords, but just one sword's price was more than buying two good slaves. "I guess I will never own one," he said almost sadly, reminiscing his younger days in these mystical islands of *Nippon.*

Near the end of my eighth year at the Lyceum, Grillius told me I was ready. "You, Eunus, are one of the most gifted warriors I have ever witnessed." He went on to say that very few, if any, in the Roman world knew the fighting tricks I now knew including most veteran soldiers of Rome or other lands the many Barbarians to the north of *Italia.* Now at the age of 91 in my cell in Rome, I can safely say Grillius was correct in what he told me at age 19. On that day Grillius made this declaration concerning my fighting skills, I remember thinking that, if Grillius and I ever fought in a battle together, we would be invincible. Little did I know that we would fight together, and my notions proved to be true.

Besides learning all that I did from Grillius, I taught myself a particular skill that Grillius knew nothing about. In my private time in the mornings after I cleaned the *Painted Stoa* while it was still dark, I practiced the art of knife throwing. Once I discovered my ability to throw a well-balanced knife overhand, side-armed, or underhand from up to 25 feet and place it on a target as small as a man's eye, I knew this would be my secret weapon. This ability to throw knives was something I had never witnessed before or since. It was all a matter of practice, concentration, and the flick of my wrist. Every morning in a cedar grove near the *Painted Stoa,* I would practice. I kept a wooden target inside the vacant interior of the famed building. On rainy days, I actually practiced inside the empty area of the *Painted Stoa* with the illumination of a palm lamp. Inside was about 25 feet, and that was why I became skilled at that distance. I actually started practicing at the age of 16, shortly after sword training was added to my Lyceum curriculum. I had been thinking about using throwing knives whenever I contemplated my promise given to Claudia. No one showed me how to throw a dagger; I just figured it out for myself. In the grove of cedar trees or inside the building, I would throw using various positions until both my arms grew numb. Throwing a dagger became like breathing, something I could do in my sleep; and this art saved my life on numerous occasions.

Two final things that need explaining are black eggs and throwing stars. Grillius first showed me how to make a black egg. The process required a good-sized duck egg preferably. A hardening lacquer is then painted onto the outer shell making it appear as a black rock once it dries. Grillius showed me what to mix together to make the black hardening solution. He told me it was close to the ingredients used by the Egyptians when they wrapped mummies after a person died. After the egg's shell had been thoroughly dried after several days in the sun, the insides were then removed by cutting a small hole at one end and sucking out the innards. Crushed glass smashed to a fine powder would then be inserted into the empty space; and then the duck egg was repainted, especially the hole at the top. The idea was to be able to throw or use a sling to deliver a black egg into someone's face, which would hopefully explode and temporarily or sometimes permanently blind the person with a cloud of glass in his eyes. The Han army used these eggs when its enemies began using face shields to protect against arrows, but the glass still entered the eyes when a black egg struck a face shield.

The star daggers, or throwing stars, were merely a dagger that was the size of a man's hand with at least six points circling a flat metal surface. The star dagger in the palm of a man's hand looked like a spiked wheel. It was best to throw it underhanded when one was only a few steps away from an attacker, instructed Grillius. Flicking it required only a little practice; and, even though one most likely would not kill his opponent, the dagger always stuck without much skill because it had six points in a circle. Just the thumb and pointing fingers were needed to deliver into an enemy. The star and egg were weapons of surprise, which gave a slight edge of disruption before the attacker closed in using a heavier, lethal weapon.

Besides fighting, Grillius taught me the anatomy of the human body. Many hours at the darkest time of night were used in this strange business. Grillius knew an evening worker at a dead-house near the *Dipylon Gate*. This man allowed Grillius to cut into dead corpses that no one claimed. A couple bodies a month showed up at the dead-house that were found dead on the streets of Athens or at some *pharma*-den. Whenever an unclaimed body turned up, Grillius would get the word and then tell me to meet him at the *Dipylon Gate* at such an hour and before the body was burned outside the city walls. For a small fee, the night worker at this dead-house would leave us alone for several hours where we would spend the time under lamplight cutting into the interior of the human body. Grillius was a master at dissecting cadavers, and this fascinated me more than anything I learned from any of my other teachers at the Lyceum. To look inside a human body and understand how it works is a miracle in itself. This was when I began to believe in a Creator of infinite intelligence. Only an immense, vast entity, with ultimate power, could design such delicate organs that at times could withstand considerable trauma and still live and, yet, could also cease to function with the slightest touch at a weak spot. The key, according to Grillius, was to know all the weak points of the human anatomy. He showed me under lamplight all the vulnerable places of the human body on these night visits to the dead-house. Altogether, we visited the dead-house a dozen nights during that school year, I learned to understand the anatomy of a human that was crucial in comprehending how to kill or wound someone with just one hit or even a pinch of a nerve. This became a colossal fountain of knowledge for me. Not only was it a fascinating experience in how to destroy a living body, but it also provided insight in how to repair a wound or correct different bodily ailments. This new understanding of the human body became an overwhelming insight into life. I believe it was at this time I was certain I wanted not only to become a physician but a surgeon as well.

CHAPTER SEVEN

Athens ~ Mercury Day in the month of Junius (named after the goddess Juno or June) in the 15th year of Tiberius and only three months away from the 60th anniversary of the Battle of Actium.   *(29 AD)*

"Have a good breakfast, men; for we dine in Hades!"   The words of Leonidas, the Spartan king, on the third and

last morning of the Battle of Thermopylae, as recorded by Herodotus.

had been living in Athens for over nine years. Arriving at age 10, I was now 19. In a few months, I would turn 20; but today was the completion of my eighth year at the Lyceum. It was a rainy, overcast spring day when my stay in Athens came to an end. When I awoke to the patter of rain on Hector's roof of his three-room stone house, it was still dark and today; was final exam day at the Lyceum. All I was thinking about was my examinations that determined whether I would move to the next level of my education. If I passed all my examinations today, I would be eligible to become a teacher after the next period of three years. Hector appeared more nervous than I. He seemed to be extremely nervous when I came out of my room as I rubbed my face to wake up. Hector was hobbling around the hearth trying to fix some breakfast. He already had my lunch prepared in a bag for me to take to school. It seemed to be a typical morning, except for Hector's injury. He had been having an epidemic of accidents and troubles in the last few days. Recently a severe rash had appeared on his left arm, which would not go away. I remember looking at it before we retired to bed; and it seemed to be getting worse with a deeper, ugly red color from his wrist to his elbow. It almost looked like some strange plague that I hoped was not contagious. A further distress was an accident he had that previous evening. After I had examined his rash, Hector had been searching for something in the dark and came back from outside with a skinned shin and a broken toe. He said he tripped on some boards that had been placed out near the road where they should not have been. The foot this morning was black, blue, and quite swollen. I felt sorry for his condition and offered to clean the temple Athena Nike this evening so he would not have to climb all those stairs. Usually, on any rainy morning, there was no need to clean any of the buildings in the *Agora*. I felt the rain today was a gift from the Fates because I needed extra time for my studies. Before I had finished eating my morning meal, Hector joined me at the wooden table.

"I agree to stay here all day and rest my body. How do you feel about your coming exams?"

"My last orals will be over philosophy, and then I go to gymnasium out in the *tripedalis*. Afterward, I can run into the city and up the stairs to the Acropolis before the sun sets and sweep out Nike." Nike was the little temple to the right of the stairs where I first met Hector almost a *deka* ago. "How does that sound?" I asked with a smile and the most pleasant display of my teeth that I could manage after a sound sleep. I am sure he knew my heart was not in doing his work, for I could see it in his eyes. The fire in the hearth clearly revealed Hector's sad-looking face.

"Tell you what; I don't think I could climb all those stairs today. After your visit with Grillius, you go to Nike; and it will help me a great deal."

"I will do Nike for you. It is not a problem. Besides, I will not be tired since neither of us is going to the *Agora* this morning. I know you want me to become a teacher at the Lyceum, and I could use the extra time to study for my orals."

"Eunus, I know teaching may not be your top desire; but spending your time at the Lyceum would give you a most pleasant life and a safe haven to hide from the scrutiny of detection."

"That would only be if my father from Rome discovered I am not dead."

"If he knew, trust me, we would have known about it sometime in the past nine years."

I agreed with Hector; but I wanted secretly to become a physician and not just a medical practitioner but someone who specialized in battle surgery. Someone needed to learn how to save people without just cutting open a vein to take away some mysterious whatever. The art of bleeding sick patients seemed ridiculous to me and actually speeded up the death process. I wanted to be someone who knew how to cut open a living person and fix whatever problem he or she was suffering.

Hector hobbled over and patted me on the head, just like the sea captain did years ago when I first put my eyes on Athens from the deck of the grain galley. "Just go to Nike after your exams, and that will be splendid; but, if you fail any exam today, I will never forgive myself."

"I will do just fine, *Baba* Hector. I had started calling Hector *Baba* after I read the word in a Sanskrit text a few years back when trying to read a Veda. I discovered the word just meant "The Old Learned One." Hector only accepted my using it because he knew it meant father in Arabic and was close to the Hebrew word *Abba*, which also meant father. I never told him what it meant in Sanskrit. "Just remember to bring a pot of water with you when you go up on the Acropolis. There will be a sacrifice at noon on the altar to the Unknown God, and it's my lot to clean up."

"That will be no problem, but I will not be able to get to Nike until sunset." Hector nodded his head absently while his right hand went to scratching at his rash. "It will be a couple of hours before sunrise, and I have a lot of studying to do. I will leave shortly and study at the Lyceum library."

It was not long before I was ready to leave. I had on my old, ratty gray cloak and matching felt hat. At the door, Hector handed me the cloth bag of food to sustain me until dark tonight.

"*Baba*, take care of yourself today," I said before closing the door. Thinking of Hector as my father felt good even though I used the Sanskrit word for *old learned one*. Once I left the simple stone house, I began thinking maybe I would enjoy being a teacher. I started entertaining this idea from a different perspective for the first time. Then the idea came to me that maybe I could replace Grillius when he retired. With that thought, I wondered if Hector would approve of my not being an academic instructor as he imagined.

The day went as expected as dozens of instructors threw questions upon questions at me. I felt confident concerning my oral and written answers to all the questions. The only surprise was my last assessment, which was my final exam out in the *tripdedalis*. When I went to meet Grillius in the courtyard, I was surprised to see no one out on the sand-covered area except Grillius. He was waiting for me near the tree that had been struck by lightning.

"Eunus, I have nothing more to teach you." It was quite strange as if Grillius knew something that I did not. He acted as if I were going to leave him and never return to the Lyceum. I began to feel guilty because I wanted his job in a few years. Maybe he did not wish to retire until he died, and he looked quite healthy for a man his age.

"Are you sure, Grillius?" I asked once the surprise from what he said left.

"I told you; I have shown you every trick I know. You are now a dangerous young man. You might think not, but you are. I want you to remember your skills, but never try to impress anyone with what you know. Just know what you possess, and you will always have the advantage. Do you understand?"

"Not really, Master Grillius." I had stopped calling him *paidotribes* when we were alone as he wished. Only when we were with other students did I call Grillius *paidotribes*. This was the first time I had called him Master. It had been close to nine months of extensive training under Grillius's tutelage, and I wanted to honor him. Calling him Master was my way of showing respect to this unusual man, who had become like a father to me, just behind Hector. Grillius just gave me a peculiar look after I said, "Master" before his given name. It was then I realized Grillius had improved on his syntactical speaking over the year with me in the courtyard. He was not leaving out personal pronouns and making all the little mistakes that peasants did. It was true: people judge one another by the way they speak. Sad to say, Grillius nine months ago, was judged by me to be somewhat ignorant only because he constantly butchered the standard *Koine* Greek. Today I could see how ignorant it was of me to think such thoughts. Here was a man who knew medical skills and fighting techniques beyond any human I would ever know. Now that his speech had improved, I felt like I had given him something back for all that he gave me. I wondered if he knew proper syntax all along and just let everyone think he was just a dumb Spartan. I wanted to believe the former conclusion, maybe because of my own vanity.

A short word about the *Koine* or common Greek. Every tongue of man tends to become corrupted as the time passes. Shortcuts are developed to make the language more convenient or conventional. What was known as Classical Greek was no longer in use by even scholars at the Lyceum or the Academy. The only time Classical Greek was used was when these scholars read anything from the old Greek philosophers such as Pythagoras, Socrates, Plato, Aristotle, Epicurus, and the Stoics. Presently only the common or *Koine* Greek had supplanted the more elegant and precise classical language employed by the likes of Hesiod and Homer. Before my private tutoring, Grillius spoke like a country peasant who apparently was never taught how to converse intelligently. If I were right, I wanted to smile internally knowing the influence I had had on Grillius's speech. From this day forth, Grillius would not be judged for being a stupid Spartan warrior, but people would show more respect to him after they conversed with him. However, because of his being a Spartan and somewhat laconic as most Spartans seem to be, many might not hear his improved speech.

"I am sorry, *paidotribes;* I will call you only Grillius after this day. From now on I will see you as my equal; but in my heart you will always be Master Grillius, my special *paidotribes.*"

"Splendid, my lad; now you are dismissed, and there will be no more need to meet me secretly after gymnasium if you return next school year. However, if you require advice or have a question, I will always be here. Now remember to practice what you know, and you will never lose the advantage. These skills are like the edge of a sword; they need constant oiling and sharpening to keep them ready. Thucydides said long ago, 'The strong do what they can, and the weak suffer what they must.' Let this be your motto."

"Yes, Grillius," I said absently touching the scar that I received foolishly in one of the school's sword fight tournaments exactly one year ago with another student named Demos Treverorum. This had just happened a few months before my private training began. Because of Grillius and my training that mistake, which led to my injury, would never happen again. Demos was the son of a wealthy and influential Roman senator. He was devious and arrogant. I always wondered what role Demos would have played in my life had things gone differently back in Rome when I turned ten. I still remembered him as the little boy in the amphitheater sitting behind my father the day Marius won the wooden sword for the third time. As strange as it may appear, Demos was the little boy of the same age, who remained sitting and seemed bored with what was happening down on the red sand.

Grillius broke my thoughts by giving me his arm to grip. It was a soldier's salutation, where both men grasped the entire lower arm up to the elbow. When he pulled his hand away, I did not understand what he meant by this rare show of affection. Was it a warning or a farewell? This I did not know, but I always took it as a sign of equality.

By the time I reached the top of the Acropolis with a pot of water for the altar to the Unknown God, the sun was just setting over the mountains in the west. The *Mare Aegaeum* to the east was catching the last rays on the white caps as the winds blew towards the land. I could see dozens of small fishing boats coming in with their square sails, and I recalled the many summers that I worked as a fisherman out of Phaleron. Tomorrow at this time I would be back in one of those boats, bone tired with rope burns on my hands.

Phaleron was a small fishing town a little northeast of Piraeus and was actually closer to Athens than Piraeus. It was the perfect place for the summer winds to blow the small boats out in the morning; and just as predictable, the evening winds would blow them back before dark. The sun now looked the color of hot iron coming out of the coals right before it was beaten with a hammer and then immersed in water. The snow-white marble of the temples and western walls of the Acropolis buildings appeared a soft pinkish-orange in its illumination from the setting sun, but the rest of Athens down below the high Acropolis was now falling into an ugly grayness. I did not have much time or light left, so I hurried with the cleaning of the white marble altar that stood all alone in the center of the Acropolis not far from the Parthenon. Carved below on its front in the lower quarter were the Greek words TO AN UNKNOWN GOD. The ancient Greeks were covering all the angles by building temples and altars to every god imaginable, and here was an altar to a god that was apparently missed. I guess it is true: we do not have all knowledge and never will, and this shrine acknowledged that fact in an honest way. I said to myself that I would find this Unknown God and worship him. His simple stone platform was the only sane, rational, and sensible declaration on this hill of religion.

Using an old rag and the water from the clay pot, I cleaned up the dried blood from the lamb or whatever had been offered earlier this afternoon. The meat from the sacrifice had long been taken or sold in the meat market down in the city. Only the dried blood and burnt bones of the small animal remained on top. After waving away all the flies, I began to scrub on my hands and knees. Afterward, with the bones and ash in the clay pot along with the rag, I made my way to the southern end of the Acropolis to complete my duties at the temple where I had first met Hector almost ten years earlier. The evening was now getting much darker, and my eyes were adjusting; so I did not look directly at where I was heading. Grillius taught me the trick of seeing in insufficient light by using what he called the "vision of edges." It meant looking askance at objects, which, in turn, made the images easier to see in the dark until your eyes had adjusted to the lack of light.

When I turned the corner in the small courtyard of the little temple of Athena Nike, a quarter-moon began to rise from between Phaleron and Piraeus, providing some needed light. At that very moment of the rising of a crescent or sliver moon, I saw a most peculiar sight. Sitting on the steps leaning against the closest pillar to the entrance was an old man. His appearance marked him as a man from the desert lands of Judaea or Egypt. He did not look dangerous but definitely out of place sitting at the front door of a pagan temple. He appeared to be about Hector's age, which put him past his 60th year. How was I to treat this old stranger who was sitting in front of a pagan temple? One of my instructors had said during my orals this morning, "To have sympathy and pity, along with sorrow for others, is to have the noblest *pathos*, which connects one to the reality of the divine."

My reply at the time was to repeat my mother's last request: "One must always regard others as more important than one's self."

The instructor stopped his steady pacing for a moment digesting my words, and a broad smile slowly formed on his sour-looking face. Then he replied in a delighted manner, "Excellent! An arrow fired straight into the center of the target!"

That would be my answer to this situation. Treat this foreigner as Hector treated me almost ten years earlier. "Can I help you, sir?" I asked with kindness in my voice that even surprised me.

"Oh, yes. I need to find a lad about your age," answered the man in Greek salted with Aramaic but garbled in some foreign accent. As he tried to stand at my approach, I could see he was stiff with age.

"What is his name?"

"Venustus Vetallus, but he might answer to Venu."

There it was. My old name had just been spoken. I had discarded the name Venustus almost a decade ago, a name my ear had not heard since I was a child. Who was this man who was looking for Venustus Vetallus? Might he be a spy working for my father?

"Why do you look for this lad?"

"Would this person be you by chance?" asked this stranger, but the question was not meant in malice.

"Who are you, and who sent you on this mission?"

In the rising moonlight, I saw a gentle face behind the wild, graying whiskers. His eyes crinkled at the corners. There seemed to be a bright fire peering out from those calm, dark eyes as he realized I was Venustus and his task was at an end. "Yes, it is you; Eli described you very well. I am Anab, the uncle of Eli; and, Praise be to Yahweh, I have found you."

"I know Eli. How is he?" I asked hoping this was not a trap.

The old Jew stepped towards me with much difficulty and placed his right hand on my shoulder as I moved towards him. When his hand touched me, a great sadness washed over his face. "That is why I am here. It was perhaps nine or ten years ago that Eli arrived in Jerusalem. He was scared and hungry. He told me about you and all that he had witnessed in your father's home back in Rome. Over the years he spoke of you frequently and implored me to seek you out if anything ever happened to him, anything unusual that is." Anab lowered his head; then after a pause, he continued. "I never paid much attention to his fears and never dreamed anything would happen to him. But then the soldiers and those two hard men came to my pottery shop and destroyed everything. They told me my punishment would be later because I had harbored a fugitive from Rome. I was knocked to the floor and kicked by the short, burly one, the one besmeared with scars. When I came to my senses, all I could see was Eli being dragged out into the street with his hands tied behind his back. I was frantic until I remembered Eli's words, which were ringing in my head. 'In the case of trouble, seek out Venustus, who lives in Athens. Go to the Acropolis, and wait for him at the temple Athena Nike.' It has been a long trip for many days, and I have been here since last night. You are actually the first person to approach me since I slept over there." His long, bony finger pointed to the back of the temple platform.

"When did they take Eli away? How many days ago?" I asked as Anab slumped down on the bottom step of the temple. Eli's life was in great danger as well as mine, and the resurgence of all the feelings along with fears that had long vanished came marching back to visit.

"Oh, Venustus, you must help Eli."

"Yes, I will. Nevertheless, you must help me. What day did they take Eli away? How long ago?"

"I'm not sure what day it was, but I left Jerusalem that very hour and hired a man to drive me in his cart to Joppa. I booked passage on the first ship to Greece, and now I am here. I did not waste a moment's time."

"Very good, then no time has been lost. Tell me; did Eli say anything while the soldiers and the two men were arresting him? Anything could be significant."

"He did recognize one of the two men who were not soldiers. Yes, he knew the stout, bear-looking man, now that I think about it. I believe he called him, Lentulus. Yes, now I remember; his name was Lentulus. What does this mean? Can you do anything?"

I looked out towards the eastern darkness, and I felt my heart speeding up and the muscles in my jaw tightening.

"What does all this mean?" implored Anab once again.

Looking back to Eli's uncle, I put my hand reassuringly on his shoulder, much like the sea captain had done to me years earlier. "If this Lentulus is who I think he is, then Eli is on his way to Rome."

"Then you believe he is alive?" asked Anab, who feared the worst.

"I will be honest with you; Eli is still alive as long as he tells no one where I am. Once he reveals my whereabouts, he will die as surely as the sun has just set. Eli witnessed my mother's death along with the slaughter of my father's household slaves about ten years ago. His tongue will be silenced one way or another but only after he talks."

"Oh, Creator of the *Cosmos*, I came here to nothing!" cried Anab throwing up his arms. "I need to pray. Which way is it towards Jerusalem? I need to pray facing the Great Temple of Yahweh."

"You will need to pray for sure," I said. "But you did not come for nothing. I will go to Rome and try to save him."

Anab turned his head with a questioning look on his face. "Tell me what you know," begged Anab as he dropped to his knees in front of the steeped platform of the Temple of Nike in prostration or perhaps exhaustion.

Not wanting a man on his knees before me, I found myself sitting down on the lower step where he had been a moment ago. "Please get off your knees, and sit with me; and I will tell you."

Anab quieted down and pulled himself together before he sat with me. I looked to my right, out towards the rising moon, gathering my thoughts much like a bird pulling a worm from the ground. When I was ready, I began. "There was a man in Rome named Zeno, who sent Eli to you and sent me here. He never arrived here as promised. He most likely was captured by my father and revealed Eli's whereabouts since I am the one my father really wants. This Zeno must have revealed that I was alive and told where he sent Eli. Now, I will go to Rome and exchange myself for Eli or rescue him."

"I don't understand. Why would Eli be going to Rome?"

"I am only guessing; but that is where my father is, and he is the one who wants to find me. If he wanted Eli dead, he would have been *vetoed* at your pottery shop."

"*Vetoed*? What do you mean?"

"It's a Latin word meaning 'I forbid.' But *veto* is also slang that the boys use at the school I attend. It is a euphemism. To *veto* means to take someone's life. The two men would have just *vetoed* Eli as well as you had they wanted him dead. I am surprised they did not *veto* you in your pottery shop, or perhaps someone followed you here. Nothing would surprise me."

"No one followed me, I am sure of that. I was very careful, except..."

"Except what?"

"There was this agreeable Roman soldier on the ship, but he was already on the vessel when I arrived at Joppa. I believe no one followed me."

I did not necessarily believe him, and I found myself looking around for any movement in the shadows. Anab became reluctant to talk as I looked around and tried to put the pieces together in my mind. Then it all came into focus. "My father must have found Zeno and tortured him to find Eli. He also must know I am alive but does not know where I am. I'm just guessing; but, if Eli is his only link to me, then Eli is alive and is on his way to Rome."

"Oh, I hope and pray you are right and Eli is alive."

"Yes, let us hope for the best, but prepare for the worst. Now come with me, and we will work up a plan to rescue Eli."

"Before we go, could you answer one question?"

"What is your question?"

"I have been here at this temple all day. Inside there is a stone statue of a goddess I presume is Nike, but she does not have any wings. Why is that? I always pictured Nike or Victoria with wings."

"Hundreds of years ago the Athenians did not want this goddess to leave Athens. Her wings were chopped off to keep her here to protect this city. The pagan mind thinks in strange ways."

"You are not a pagan?" he asked kindly.

"Spiritually, I am lost; but just today I decided to follow the Unknown God that has an altar here on this plateau. Before that, I just prayed to the wind."

Anab just smiled and said we should go. I led this old Jew out of the temple complex of the Acropolis and down the long staircase to Hector's stone abode. After I had explained who Anab was, Hector welcomed him like a long-lost brother. They instantly became close friends. Hector dished up three bowls of steaming-hot lamb stew, and we all sat on simple stools at the wooden table in the center of Hector's living quarters.

After the dishes had been cleared away, Hector stood and laid out the facts. "Well, there is only one option. My son who came to me almost ten years ago as Venustus will return to Rome as Venustus." His eyes sparkled with a father's love as he looked across the table at me in the light of the few oil lamps resting on the table and the few embers glowing in the hearth. "Yes, Eunus, you must return to Rome as Venustus on the fastest transport and somehow find Eli and help him. You are not to exchange your life for his, for that will only lead to both of your deaths. Rescue is your only option. All that Grillius has taught you will aid you in this task."

Hector must have seen my look of surprise as he revealed his knowledge concerning Grillius and my secret training after school. Hector sat next to me after he spoke and put his arm around my shoulders and looked me in the eyes. "I am the one who asked Grillius to teach you his unique arts after the fever incident nine months ago. Grillius wanted to pay me, and I proposed something more valuable than money. Yes, I knew all along but asked Grillius not to reveal that I knew about the special classes after school."

161

This was indeed a day of surprises, and I was having trouble absorbing all the new revelations. Grillius just today had ended my lessons, which Hector had secretly arranged; and now I happened upon Anab at the very spot I met Hector, which seemed like a different lifetime ago. Now I was to travel back to Rome as Venustus and rescue my slave friend, Eli.

"Now, when you get back to Rome, you must also learn of the fate of my dear friend Zeno," said Hector. "If you are successful in rescuing Eli, you both must not return to Athens until it is safe. I will arrange a secure system of communication. Nevertheless, you must get on the military bireme, which leaves from Piraeus every Thor or Jupiter Day for Rome, a weekly military dispatch ship manned by over two hundred slaves who row the entire time it takes to get to the wharves of Rome. This imperial bireme is perhaps the fastest ship on the seas. Tomorrow is Jupiter Day, and it leaves from the main naval harbor of Zea at dawn. There is no faster way to Rome, but it will cost a pretty price."

"Wait here," I directed as I pushed away from the wooden table and went to my bedroom, which was really the storage room of the house. Once inside, I used a small palm lamp that had been my reading light for many years; and I went to a cornerstone at the base of the floor. I grabbed a rusty, old knife that I used to cut wicks and now used to dig out the plaster that I had made to look like cement mortar. After pulling out the cornerstone, I reached into the hole and pulled out the leather Carnalus scroll case inside the old, red woolen bag, which also held the Persian socket spearhead and the remaining silver coins Zeno had given me that night in Ostia. I put back the Carnalus scroll and the spear tip and replaced the stone. After mixing a little saliva with the plaster, I was able to patch the cornerstone to look like it had before I opened it. After cleaning my hands, I returned to the main room with the red bag and leather purse. I then poured out all the coins onto the table asking Hector if these were enough.

"May the gods be praised!" cried out Hector.

"No! No," said Anab. "May the only true Creator of the Universe be praised!"

"Oh, I forgot I now have a new Jewish friend," blurted out Hector with real joy and delight in his voice. "We are going to have fun after Venustus leaves! Yes, may this one God of the Jews be blessed; and these coins are more than enough," he said looking at me with great affection. "Now, Venustus, where did you get these old coins?"

"They were given to me by Zeno, and I saved them for passage back to Rome someday to square the score with my father and Claudia."

I had never talked about revenge to anyone, and Hector looked a little shocked at my declaration. The old priest's face had a hurt look as he searched for the right words. Finally, Anab held up his hand to speak. "Venustus, you are so young; and now you have chosen to go up against giants."

Anab reached over and touched Hector's left arm as if understanding his concern. It was then I noticed the red rash was no longer on his arm. It had been there when I arrived with Anab but now was gone. Anab smiled up at me forcing my eyes off Hector's healed arm. "God will be with Venustus. He reminds me of David going against Goliath."

I was only half listening because I was still wondering about Hector's missing rash. Had there been a miracle in this humble house?

"I'm sorry. I know nothing of your people's history," confessed Hector. "I consider myself a scholar and historian of all religions and men except the Hebrew people."

"You have never read our Scriptures, even the Septuagint, which is in Greek?"

Hector shook his head in what looked like embarrassed shame, and then a smile came to his beaming face. "You, my new friend, can share all your history and stories with me. But first, tell us about this David character."

Anab smiled and moved his hand away from Hector's left arm and placed his palms together in what looked like a pose of prayer. The gesture looked just like what he had done right before he ate and Anab asked again what direction was Jerusalem. After a few moments of silence, Anab began his story. "Over a thousand years ago, David was first a shepherd boy in the Judaean hills; and then he became a great king with his capital in Jerusalem. The Holy Scriptures say that one of David's future sons will become the True Shepherd, the Righteous Ruler of the world, the Anointed One we Jews call the Messiah. When he comes, peace, rest, and truth will reign."

"This is fascinating. I never heard about these oracles!" declared Hector.

"Well, that is what the prophecies declare," continued Anab. "When David was merely a humble shepherd boy, he was perhaps about the same age of Venustus. There was in the land at that time a giant of a man named Goliath living among the Philistines. This beast of a man was the champion of the Philistines, a Gentile people who lived down near the lower coastal region along the Great Sea. The Romans now refer to my land by this long, dead name of these people who humiliated us Jews for so many years. That name is *Palestina*, the land of the Philistines, a name of derision and disrespect."

"This is information I never knew," confessed Hector with delight in his voice.

"Well, anyway, David was only visiting his older brothers at the battlefield by request of his father. You see, this was before he became king; and his brothers were soldiers in Israel, and Israel was at war with the Philistines. It was then that David heard the giant cursing the God of Israel and making the challenge for anyone in Israel to a gladiatorial contest. Since no one volunteered, David the shepherd boy stepped forward. Mysteriously, the king at that time, named Saul, allowed David to be Israel's contender. With only five stones and his shepherd's sling, David went out to meet the heavily armored Goliath, who was perhaps twice the size of any average man. David said he came in the power of Yahweh, the God of the Universe. The two then engaged, and David put only one stone into his shepherd's sling. With only several swings around his head, David let the rock fly. It sank deep into Goliath's forehead ending the contest before it started." After Anab had finished his story, he reached across the table, placed his hands on mine, and declared, "I believe my God will take Venustus to the Giants of Rome and give him success over those who have captured my Eli."

I was enraptured by this remarkable story. I felt a connection to this hero David. Grillius always taught that the one who made the first strike in a fight usually won, and that is exactly what David had done with his sling. He must have been quite gifted and wise.

"So this David later became a philosopher-king?" asked Hector. "And will his lineage bring another philosopher-king, this Messiah?"

"Oh, yes! I suppose you could call him that," exclaimed Anab as he released my hands. I had never experienced a man who touched another with his hands. It was a nice feeling, but something I never was able to fully appreciate. After this night, I never experienced this from another man in such a fashion as I did on this night. However, I can think of only one other man who used his hands to communicate something deeper and as powerful as his mouth. "And this Messiah will come from the lineage of David; yet, the prophecies say he will be virgin born."

"When will this happen?" I found myself asking.

"Well, my new Gentile friend, perhaps he is alive today in my homeland. There is a man who lives out in the desert baptizing people in the Jordan River. Before I left Joppa, I heard some saying the man in the Jordan Valley who baptizes with water might be the promised son of David. Even the kind soldier on the ship said as much. Some of our religious leaders were sending men to ask him who he claimed to be before I left to come here. I believe they said his name was John, and he is from the house of David through his mother. I understand this desert preacher's father was a Levite and a priest at the Temple in Jerusalem. The only problem is I don't believe he is virgin born," explained Anab as he looked almost affectionately at my *Baba*.

Hector lowered his eyes in what looked like shame. Conceivably Hector wanted to believe in this Jewish god, and I suspected Hector did not believe in Nike or even the other gods or goddesses of the Greeks. His work over the years had only become a job of convenience. I was guessing that Hector was experiencing a burning from within by just listening to this unpretentious clay thrower.

I decided to break this spell and asked, "Not to interrupt and change the subject, but how am I going to get on this bireme in the morning?"

Hector looked up at me with a smile. "I would go with you and talk to the commander of the naval harbor of Zea," said Hector. With his right hand, he picked up one gold coin in the pile of seven silver coins. "This one coin will get you to Rome; but on second thought, I do not think I can make it to Zea with my broken toe. So, instead, I will write a short letter; for the naval commander owes me a favor; and, with all these remaining silver coins, you will have no problem once you arrive in Rome. You will have enough for a few days to buy food; and somehow you will find means to return here with your old friend, the nephew of Anab."

After a few hours of sleep, I had said my goodbyes to Anab and Hector. With the one gold coin, the silver, Hector's letter, several apples, cakes, and a wineskin all stuffed into the old, red wool bag, I left the good years behind. From the foot of the Acropolis, I walked through the semi-dark streets of Athens toward the Piraeus Gate and the Long Walls Road. However, before leaving Athens, I stopped at the *Painted Stoa* in the *Agora* and retrieved a few items from the interior room that contained my wooden target. I picked up my two matching bronze throwing knives; three palm-sized six-pointed throwing stars; and one black egg, cushioned in straw, resting in a little wooden box. I also exchanged my old sandals for a new pair of sturdy military-type boots I had been saving for a day just like this. The boots were exact copies of Grillius's Spartan military boots. I also exchanged my ratty, gray cloak for a new scarlet-purple *chlamys* that was also exactly like the one Grillius always wore. The cloak, falling to my ankles, completely covered my short, tan-colored tunic or *chiton*; and I hoped Grillius didn't see me now, or he would think I was copying his look without earning the right to be a Spartan. In my own justification, I had taken on a part of Grillius; and I was emulating him by wearing the sandal-boots and the scarlet-purple cloak of a young Spartan warrior. I told myself that I was paying honor to Grillius by dressing like him. Before leaving Hector's stone house, I had asked Hector to make contact with Grillius and tell him why I had to leave Athens. When I mentioned Grillius, there was a grand smile on Hector's face. He said Grillius would become our plan of communication; and he instructed me to send any letters to Grillius at the Lyceum, and Grillius would forward them to Hector. If any of my letters were traced to Grillius, Hector concluded, Grillius was capable of taking care of himself.

When I left Hector's home, my surrogate father followed me out into the empty street. Hector had not said anything about my plans for revenge but, instead, had hugged me for the first time since I arrived. After he released me, he had one final word. "My son Eunus-Venu, you have studied the wisdom of the Greeks; and you know the lustful and power-maddened mind of the Romans; but you and I have not mastered the Jewish spirit. If we are to find the true God, perhaps it will be there. I suspect the Jews are worshipping what we Greeks call the Unknown God. Also, this new Jewish visitor I believe was sent to us by this God. You would agree that Anab is convinced his God is the greatest of all the gods. In all my life, I have never witnessed such sincere conviction in any man. And to think Anab is a simple clay man tells me this God of the Jews is the actual Creator of all things." It was after Hector's oration that he showed me his arm. He told me the rash left the moment Anab touched it. I clearly remembered the incident right after I had voiced my desire for revenge upon my father and Claudia. "You see; this is a sign that Anab knows what he is talking about."

"Or this God is trying to show you the truth," I said, only to comfort my *Baba*. I told Hector not to worry; and, after I had grasped his healed arm in an affectionate hold, I told him I loved him as my true father. "I promise you, if I find the answer to life, I will come and tell you."

He moved his head in agreement; and before he waved me on my way, he said, "I would like that, but I believe I found it. When Anab entered our home this night, it was like he was destined to arrive right at that moment. I do not know how to explain it other than what I just stated."

Changing the subject but only slightly, I asked, "Do you think Anab even knows the rash left?"

"I believe his God was showing me a miracle and a sign. I do not believe Anab knows how his God used him."

I smiled showing Hector I agreed with his conclusion. I did not know how to show love to Hector and all he had done for me. I knew I could not cry since I had not shed a tear since my tenth birthday. I tried to smile and hoped he understood what I was thinking before turning to begin my new journey.

Right when I was ready to leave the *Painted Stoa,* a homeless man came up to me from the shadows of the direction of the cedar grove, which surprised me. "Tell me the truth. You are the Roman who knows how to throw knives?" asked the smelly, harmless-looking man.

"Why do you ask?" was all I said wondering why the question, especially when I looked more Greek than Roman.

"You have the spirit of a Roman. My father years ago taught me to be aware of Romans. He taught me to tell a Roman just by the way he walked with his nose up in the air. You have that air about you. I sleep over there in the trees. For many years now I have been awakened by your throwing daggers into a board you set up over there." He pointed to the exact point where I did practice throwing my knives. "You are a splendid thrower, I might add. I think people would pay money to watch you throw knives. Maybe you could get a woman slave to stand against a tree, and you throw knives at her missing every time," he said with a silly grin.

"Do you not like Romans?" I asked, learning that I needed to change my walk and not lift my head when I walked. Grillius had taught me to keep my head up and aware at all times, but maybe it made me look like an arrogant Roman.

"My father hated the Romans. He especially hated General Sulla. About a hundred years ago, Sulla entered this city hunting for Mithridates' generals along with any Athenians supporting Mithridates and his troops from Macedonia and Pontus. You are too young to remember Mithridates, the king of Pontus; but my father told me this entire marketplace called the *Agora* was filled with blood up to your knees. I am homeless because my family lost everything in those days. I grew up a poor freeman but with no money or skills. General Sulla stopped the killing only because of the *Painted Stoa.* The massacre ended here because the Roman general was in love with the classical Greek culture, especially the paintings hanging on the walls of this building, where I sleep when it rains. If there is no rain, I sleep over there under all the stars."

"To help you have some peace, I am going to Rome today; and I will try to set the record straight for you and your family's loss." The man flashed a lopsided smile possible because he was not right in the head. I tried to be kind to him and gave him one of my silver coins hoping it might give relief to the burdens in his life. I had no idea of the value of this coin at this time, but it was a very generous gift. I then left the smiling vagrant, the *Agora,* and Athens. Meeting this man was a strange occurrence as I considered all the years of coming to the *Agora* early each morning and never seeing him in this spot before this dark morning. Was it some kind of warning or omen?

Was I being counseled in some spiritual way about a massacre that was about to occur in Rome and I would be in the center of the chaos? I had no idea; and after a while, I put it out of my mind. In many ways, I can now see it as a strange warning of what I was to become: a person who would shed blood but still would stop if it meant destroying something unique like the paintings on the walls of the *Painted Stoa.*

By the time I reached the outskirts of Piraeus, the dawn was slowly making its entrance on what looked to be a bright and beautiful day. When I found the ship-sheds of Zea, the sun was finally coming up in the east. The ancient foundations of sheds from the days of the Delian League could clearly be seen in the circular harbor of Zea. The Roman government had rebuilt a dozen sheds for its own small battle fleet of triremes, but the port was only a small glimpse of the glory this military harbor must have been hundreds of years in the past. Once I found the commander who was indebted to Hector, I humbly produced the gold coin and added four silver coins along with Hector's letter. He was still a little sleepy; but after reading the letter and taking the coins, he waved for his adjutant to escort me to the docks. Rocking in the small harbor at the end of a concrete pier was a long but slim dispatch bireme that was getting ready to leave with the morning winds that I knew so well as an angler. On the deck were a few military men in long, red cloaks along with a few Roman civilian diplomats in white wool togas. There was even one wearing a toga with the purple stripe and red sandals of a senator; I planned to stay faraway from his presence. Sailors were readying a huge blood-red sail with the imperial eagle stitched into its center with gold thread. Below deck, hundreds of slaves could be seen through the many air slits on the top decking. The slaves were all stripped naked, and I was sure they were all chained to one other. As I boarded the long, narrow vessel using a simple gangplank, I could smell the sweat and stink of the slaves that wafted up through the air slits. Once the ship was on its way, I was sure the smell would depart with the wind. There were no private quarters on this fast-moving vessel, and the few passengers had to make due on the main upper deck. Near the bow was a tarp stretched to protect the few passengers should it rain. There were a few military folding stools apparently for the diplomats and the one senator. I noticed three soldiers sitting on the deck with their knees bent up to their chins covered for warmth with their red cloaks.

Commands were shouted out as the ship dropped the gangplank and the slaves pushed out their oars through the pole holes on the sides of the vessel. When the bireme was far enough away from the pier, a long line of double rows of oars stretched out from both sides, parallel to the water. At the sound of a timing drum down below deck, the two hundred oars expertly dipped and pulled through the sea as the red sail dropped and billowed out when it filled with a gust of wind making a loud pop sound. Using wind and human power, the long, slender craft moved with incredible speed through the small, round harbor and out into the open sea. I had never traveled at such speed in my life even when I learned how to ride horses at the Lyceum and would gallop as fast as a horse would go. This ride on the bireme was an experience that I found exciting beyond description. As we passed other ships, barges, and small fishing boats, it appeared as if they were just standing still in the blue-green sea.

The morning sky was now turning a milky blue as the other passengers lay down near the bow to rest since most had been up early to catch the bireme. I was not tired maybe because of the excitement of my new adventure, and I stayed at the back of the ship looking towards Piraeus. After a bit of searching, I moved my gaze up and over towards the majestic Acropolis with its white temples illuminated from the side of the sea. I remembered this same view from when I first arrived by the grain galley almost ten years earlier. It was the start of fall when I came, and now it was the beginning of spring as I was leaving. The city of Athens clustered around her slopes with most of the people living on the east side. I remember reading the works of Hippocrates, and he had discovered that the eastern aspect of the Acropolis was the healthiest spot in which to live. Thinking about his observations, I realized it was true; the winds from the sea in the afternoons blew away any odors, and in the morning the sun would strike there first warming this side of the city as the sun came up each morning.

When my mind wandered back to when I first arrived in Piraeus and I was on the deck with the kind but gruff galley captain, it seemed like yesterday. The sea was an emerald-blue on that late afternoon, and the captain was reciting the history of Athens. "Hundreds of years ago it was the great capital of Attica. Two great archons – Draco, who issued laws written in blood, and Solon, who gave the city-state a constitution – are two men you must read about and learn from."

He also pointed out the island of Salamis, which the bireme was approaching to our left or port; and the sea captain demanded that I learn about the great victory of the Greeks over the Persian fleets out in those waters. He told me to study about the Golden Age of Athens when Pericles ruled. "Also, do not neglect the Peloponnesian Wars; and learn from Athens' mistakes, which twisted her great democracy. Beware of a liberal form of government even under democracy. When values become twisted, even the voting population who rule themselves move into strange waters. Remember, it was just a few years after the Peloponnesian War when Athens condemned Socrates to death. The people believed their government when they were told that Aristotle was corrupting his young students and despising the gods. Oh, might I point out that one of those students he was to have corrupted was Plato. Someday you will see and understand the folly of men even when all the citizens vote and are free. There definitely is something wicked about the hearts of men even in a democracy."

As I looked out towards old Attica, I smiled to myself realizing I had accomplished all that the galley captain had requested. I had studied everything he suggested and much more; yet, now I wondered whether Socrates, Plato, Aristotle, and all the Stoics who came later understood what Hector was now discovering, since our visit from Eli's uncle. Hector had no faith in the gods of the Acropolis, and his influence had corrupted me. I was just like Hector, now looking elsewhere for truth. Even if the Unknown God was the true god, this issue of just one god was a very deadly and dangerous business as Socrates discovered before he drank the poisonous hemlock. "It is a hazardous thing to be right when the government is wrong," according to an old adage. "You can be right, or you can be happy. Therefore, be happy; and keep your mouth shut" – something I could never do.

My mind kept returning to the old sea captain. I remember him telling me he had run away from home as a boy and had become a seaman. The galley captain said he regretted that decision. Then he said something bizarre that I never forgot. "Now, boy, you should be obedient to your parents; and, when you return to Rome, do as they say." Apparently, he knew nothing of what transpired in Rome. However, here I was finally returning to Rome; and I was far from being obedient to my father but, instead, was contemplating his removal by *vetoing* him from this world.

JOHN LAWRENCE BURKS

RETURN TO ROME:
RESCUE, REVENGE, & REVIVAL

PART THREE

CHAPTER EIGHT

Piraeus to Rome – The month of Junius (the goddess Juno or June) in the 15th year of Tiberius and 59 years after the Battle of Actium in the year of the 201st Olympiad. (29 AD)

"Stare."
"Not how many, but where."
many, but where is the enemy.

The most famous Spartan proverb of all.
To a Spartan, it was not important how
Plutarch

Piraeus was now fading into the distance; and my hands were resting on the starboard rail near the stern of the bireme when I absently looked down to the scar on the top of my right arm the one Grillius had grasped the day before. It was long and white and ran from the top of my hand along the length of my arm, almost to the elbow. I could now see Demos Treverorum in my mind's eye, and his arrogant smile lit a fire deep in my stomach that joined the other smoldering embers for Claudia and my father. The story of how he cut me is worth telling because of the events that were about to engulf me.

I received the wound and almost lost my life one year ago at the Lyceum. It happened during the last week of school in my seventh year, just before the summer recess began after our yearly exams. It was three months before my private training with Grillius started. At the end of each school year, all the boys from distant cities and lands went back to their homes and parents. A week before finals, Grillius always held a sword tournament to celebrate the end of spring. We boys called this event the *Munera* or Gladiatorial Games. This year, Grillius asked me not to participate because it might reveal my secret lessons. I had stayed away and had no knowledge of how the Lyceum

Gladiatorial Games went. Therefore, last year was my final *Munera*. Weeks before my infamous *Munera,* many of the boys began pretending to be famous gladiators. Demos Treverorum demanded the name Marius and said he alone had the right to use it because he had witnessed the gladiator's famous last match that earned the fighter the wooden sword for the third and final time. Little did anyone know I, too, was a witness to the same *lanista* or contest at the *Statilius Taurus Amphitheater.* Demos, as I already stated, was the son of an influential senator from Rome; and I did not want him to know I also was from Rome. Demos had dark, flowing hair that he was very proud of; and he grew it long going against the style of Rome and even Greece for boys our age. Only older men in Greece wore their hair long, past their shoulders, such as Grillius, who actually wore his to his waist but always tied it in a single braid resembling a horse's tail. During our gymnasium sessions, Demos always tied his hair up into a topknot much like the warriors and holy men from around the Indus River or, as the ancient Persians used to call it, the Hindu River. Grillius later told me that elite soldiers from the faraway land known as *Serica* or Chin wore topknots. He said even the Nippons (that sun-origin land of the Four Islands) had famous heroes who also wore topknots. Grillius never told the boys how to wear their hair; but he said to me privately that he believed Demos, wearing a topknot, was strutting around like a rooster. "Demos does not deserve the honor of a topknot."

It was at that time of my first *Munera* when Grillius told me to watch my back when around Deva, which was Grillius's nickname for Demos. He gave many nicknames to the students, which most of us did not understand. I later discovered Grillius's word *deva* was an ancient Sanskrit word. Sanskrit was now a dead language but could be read and understood if you were a scholar of the land on the other side of the Khyber Pass up past the Hindu Kush Mountains. The Sanskrit meaning for *deva* was an evil spirit or fallen god. I shared this knowledge with no one keeping it as a hidden joke on Demos since all the boys had no idea what it meant. I just happened to stumble upon it when cataloging an ancient Sanskrit *Veda* sent by Alexander the Great when he was in the Indus Valley. I asked the only instructor at the Lyceum who knew some Sanskrit for its meaning. He did not know but told me about a scholar-teacher at the Academy. This rival school, located across the city and beyond the walls to the southwest, was the primary school Plato had started a few decades before the Lyceum began. I skipped classes one day and walked to this school to find this teacher. When I found him, I learned the meaning. The word originally meant an *evil one* or *demon*.

On the afternoon of the tournament, all the older boys in the gymnasium at the Lyceum gathered in the *palaestra* (or courtyard-*tripedalis*) with Grillius who threw lots to see against whom we would be matched. I drew Demos, and I was a little concerned since he was by far the best swordsman of the school. Once our contest began, I discovered I was holding my own against Demos; and, when he lost his temper, the advantage was mine. Demos kept circling around thrusting with just brute strength, and I successfully blocked each thrust with my bronze Greek sword or *xiphos*. Each block led Demos to invoke an evil incantation against me using the name of every god of the Roman pantheon I had heard and some names I had not.

We only had an allotted time for each match that was determined by a simple water clock. Grillius decided who was the winner based on points unless someone was disarmed or fell. Finally, Grillius blew the wooden whistle that always hung around his neck on a leather thong signaling the end of our match. Over the years, there had been a few accidents; and some boys had been cut but not seriously until Demos attacked me that afternoon after the whistle. Once Grillius declared me the winner by points, I dropped my guard; and Demos took the opportunity and swung a free blow across my sword arm. One of the cutting sides of his two-edged *xiphos* opened up my forearm from wrist to elbow. All I remember was a burning sensation; I quickly looked at the source of this burning and saw only a white bone in my arm before the blood began to gush. Before Demos could do any more serious damage to me, Grillius knocked Demos to the *agogeo palastra* by hitting him across the side of his head with his cedar walking staff, which he always had with him.

That evening after Grillius had sewn up my arm in the bathhouse, he said that Deva was an evil, rotten boy. I told Grillius I had discovered that *"deva"* meant *"demon"* in Sanskrit. He asked me not to blabber it all over the school. However, Grillius smiled for one of the few times I had ever seen him do this. I told him it would be our own secret, and he laughed again and patted me on the head. He then said I had learned two valuable lessons today.

"What might those lessons be?" I asked.

"Well, first, to never let down your guard; and the second, I will let you figure out on your own."

"May I have a hint on the second lesson?"

Grillius smiled for a second rare moment and then said, "It is the greatest proverb of a Spartan warrior. But it applies to the mouth as well as the eyes."

It was many years before I figured out the proverb concerning the second lesson even though it was evident this lesson had something to do with my eyes as a weapon in more ways than just seeing. However, at the Lyceum, I was keeping quiet for reasons other than what Grillius thought. Thanks to Grillius's expert surgical skills, my arm healed without any permanent damage to my fingers or hand movements. All I was left with was an ugly reminder of the incident along with the knowledge to never take your eyes off your opponent and keep your mouth shut. Had any other surgeon worked on my arm that day, I believe I would never have had the use of my right hand, let alone keeping the arm from amputation due to infection. I later learned Grillius was more intimate with human anatomy than any human I had ever known. He could have been a famous surgeon if he had chosen to be. I learned his skill as a surgeon after he repaired my arm and the nights at the dead-house doing dissections of human bodies.

If my relationship with Demos was icy before the incident, afterward the relationship grew into a mountain glacier. To be honestly fair, I was not close to any of the boys for two reasons. First, I never wanted to reveal my identity; and second, I did not have the time to cultivate a friendship with anyone. I was the only student I knew who had to pay his own way and had to work every free moment outside of his studies to help supplement what I had to pay. During the school year, I worked in the *Agora* in the mornings and the Acropolis in the evenings doing domestic duties with Hector. In the summer, I spent three long months working out of Phaleron as a fisherman on small fishing boats. I learned rigging, net mending, spearing, and hauling in nets along with cleaning fish. The days were long and exhausting. I developed mostly superficial relationships with these older anglers, and the only friends I had were Hector and Grillius. The boys of my age at the Lyceum were superficial interactions hinging on shallow, insincere associations. I considered my books and scrolls my real friends, which took me away on many vicarious adventures. I was a "lone wolf," and I grew to like it that way. If anyone criticized me to my face or even behind my back, it cut me to the bone even though I made it appear that nothing cut through my outer armor. When it came to females, I knew nothing other than the two kisses from Messina inside the warehouse of Ostia.

That summer after Demos's cowardly act, I had to forgo being a fisherman due to the time I needed to heal my arm. I spent that last summer reading as much as I could in the Lyceum library. Some teachers called me Aristotle, for Aristotle's nickname at Plato's school was *The Reader*. I paid for the next year from the silver coins hidden in my room in Hector's house the coins in the leather bag given to me by Zeno, who received them from my father in the *Statilius Taurus Amphitheater* after reporting I was dead. When I did count all the coins after I had reached Athens, I discovered it was a vast amount to an average person in the Roman Empire. I did not reveal to Hector I had any money, nor did I tell him the truth about the fees for the following year at the Lyceum. When Hector asked about my tuition for my last school year, I falsely explained I earned the fees from odd jobs that summer when actually I was spending all my time reading from morning to evening at the Lyceum or in the shade of the *Painted Stoa*. That summer of my 18th year became the best summer of my life; and it was all due to the evil act of Demos, the *Deva*. I checked my remaining coins at the rail of the bireme and counted only two more silver denarii with Augustus's image in my father's old moneybag. This was going to get me to my father's villa but not much further.

Another reason I distrusted Demos and tried to keep my distance was his constant bragging about his father being a Roman senator meaning Demos was above the rest of us boys socially. If he only knew who my father was, Demos would have shut his mouth. When he first came to the school, he was 14 years old, the same age as I, but started two years after I had already attended the Lyceum. Most of my classes were with older boys, and Demos was only present at the afternoon gymnasium yard. He was not gifted intellectually but more so physically. A few months after he arrived, I will never forget a particular incident. It occurred after gymnasium one winter day when we were sitting in the terracotta hipbaths scraping oil and dirt off our bodies after discus training. He looked over to me after he entered the room and said, "So you are the one who is a 'goody-goody' and won't exercise in the nude."

He was very proud of his body and paraded naked in the *palaestra* as well as in the bathhouse showing off his muscular physique and his man-hair where other boys of 14 were lacking. When he got into his own tub, he asked whether anyone wanted to hear about Marius winning the wooden sword since Demos was an eyewitness when he was ten years old. All the boys loved his telling of this tale, but this was the first time I heard it from his lips. After he had finished his embellished story, he drifted into the other spectacular account of the murders on that day involving Senator Carnalus and the household slaves of Senator Vetallus up on Esquiline Hill. Speaking dramatically from his hipbath, Demos said, "First, everyone suspected Senator Vetallus had something to do with the killings until, of course, everyone realized that no one would kill over three hundred of his own slaves. Besides, there was great empathy for Senator Vetallus when it was revealed that his eldest son had committed suicide off the *Aemilius Bridge*."

Clearly, Demos was embellishing again; for I was supposed to have jumped off the *Pons Fabricius,* not the *Pons Aemilius.* Demos told all the students, "I remember all these events because I was with my father on that

Actium celebration watching the famous *Munera* in the senatorial section above Tiberius's box when an old slave brought the clothes and ring of Vetallus's son to Senator Vetallus, who was sitting below me. Senator Vetallus wept openly at the news of his son Venustus committing this cowardly act of suicide. Why this weak-spirited son jumped is beyond me, and I surely would not cry openly over such shame to my family or its name. Then a rumor began to spread about a year later that this Venustus was not dead but in hiding somewhere. Maybe he is among us in these hipbaths, for he would be about our age," he said with great seriousness and then broke into deep laughter.

The entire room of twenty or so boys also fell into hilarious laughter including me, as I joined in for my own protection. It was extremely problematic trying to laugh when I was chilled by the memory of the bored little boy sitting behind my father in the amphitheater and now realizing it was Demos. After the revelation in the washroom, I knew the time would come when my identity would be exposed. I was unnerved for a long time after that event; and I purposely stayed away from Demos until a year ago when, at the sword match, Demos cheated and cut my forearm to the bone.

On this early morn at the starboard rail near the stern of the swift-moving bireme, I was still staring at my long, still red, worm-looking scar given to me by Demos. I realized this ugly scar was always going to be an unforgettable mark. I also grasped the fact it was precisely one year ago since Demos put this ugly blemish on the top of my arm. I found myself wondering whether my life had not been altered by returning to my father's villa on that day of the Actium Games. Would I have become as arrogant as Demos had I attended the games as planned with my father? It was an interesting but an insane thought, and the answer was almost too disturbing to contemplate. I also wondered if Demos and I would have met on that day and started a friendship. These were truly my thoughts when I heard the arrogant voice of Demos from behind me just at the moment I was reminiscing about the 50th Actium Games. I could not believe it at first, for it all seemed like a phantasm. I slowly turned, and there was the very person I had been thinking about and wondering whether I would have been just like him or even his friend.

"Is that you, Grillius Junior?" came the mocking words of Demos with an insipid sneer plastered across his patrician face. He was wearing a white tunic with the senatorial purple stripe running down the center, just like the one I had on my last day in Rome. I was surprised to see him only in a short tunic and not also wearing a coveted toga. After the age of 15, a Roman male was considered a man and was allowed to wear the toga. At a special ceremony called the *toga virilis,* a boy-to-be-man put on his first toga.

Starting after the start of his second year at the Lyceum, Demos was always wearing a senatorial toga with the wide purple borders. Maybe because of the morning heat, he was only wearing a senatorial tunic. Once I looked past his insipid, fiendish grin, I quickly noticed his long hair had been cut short in the Roman style accompanied by a purple ribbon that matched the tunic stripe. The ribbon was tied around his head giving him the appearance of a Greek athlete. I removed my gray, felt flop hat or *petasos,* which had a wide brim; and I allowed it to drop from my hand onto the deck. I had adopted the *petasos* after the long hours as a fisherman to keep the sun from baking my face day after day during the long, hot summer months. Now I did not want the brim to obscure any quick movements made by Demos as Grillius had warned. I found myself just staring at him with no hint of what was on my mind, the second lesson Grillius alluded to when he finished sewing up my arm.

"Well, are you young Grillius or what wearing that purple cloak and those boots? Oh, except Grillius would never wear that flower hat," he said laughing and thinking he had just made a high joke.

"What are you? A Roman Senator or a Greek sprinter?" I finally asked in a flat tone in my Greek, which did not require any inflections simply because of the Greek vowels that delimited any need for intonation compared with all the other ancient languages in the world that lacked vowels.

"Oh, very clever," he said with both hands behind his back, which he had that way since I turned around and dropped my felt hat.

"What do you want?" I said, very controlled with a low, non-threatening voice.

"With that rig on, who do you think you are? Could it be your idol is that old, blood-eating, wind-blowing bag from the Lyceum's *palastra*?" mocked Demos now using his customary villainous laugh that typically led to a brawl with another student he had decided to bully.

The only advantage I had was Demos stood before me alone. This was very rare since he was one of the most popular boys at the Lyceum even though he insulted everyone and skillfully played one boy off another. Yet, foolishly here he was trying to provoke me without his group of bullies. I quickly looked to my right and noticed several Praetorian Guards standing around the fat Senator near the stern of the bireme. Maybe Demos thought they were his new bully gang and would come and save him if things went ugly.

"If you are referring to our *paidotribes*, I do honor him by wearing the Spartan scarlet," I said more as a challenge than as an explanation. My right hand touched the hilt of one of my throwing knives I had tied to my girdle under the cloak. I could have it out in the blink of an eye if it were needed, so my bravado began to rise.

"No offense, Eunus! How is your sword arm? Can I see the scar you have hidden under your Spartan cloak? I guess ole' Wind Bag saved you this year from my sword when he mysteriously canceled your appearance at last week's *munera lanista*. You should have seen me; I was the school champion."

Was this a trick to bring my right arm out from under the cloak without the knife? On the other hand, should I bring it out with the knife in hand? If I had not dropped my hat, I could have used it to hide the knife in my left hand. No, showing him my dagger might reveal that I was possibly afraid. I decided there was no harm in showing him the scar; and, hopefully, he would back away from this dangerous game. I slowly brought forth my right arm without the dagger for his inspection.

Demos's eyes brightened remembering that day. "Looks impressive; and you will never forget your friend Demos, will you?"

I casually put my arm back into my cloak and said, "I will not remember Deva as a friend but for the feral coward he is." After I had spoken, I stared him straight in the eyes but made the mistake of provoking him before I was ready. He jerked his arms from behind his back; in his right hand was the most magnificent, bejeweled dagger that I had ever seen. It looked like a ceremonial knife only a king would own. The price of the oversized blade was worth easily a hundred golden *aurei*, which could have paid all my years of education at the Lyceum including a dozen other students' tuitions and fees.

"You like my *cultellus*? It was a gift from my father for my 20th birthday and my appointment as a Roman tribune to the legions. Are you yet 20? No matter, if not, you will likely be soon; and perhaps you will join the legions as a spearman, and I will be your commander. Then who is going to be the coward?" hissed Demos as he waved his *cultellus* up towards my throat. "Do you see my father up forward in the senatorial toga and the Praetorian officers with him in their long red cloaks? You will not humiliate me in any way by revealing I went to school with such a peasant as you, Fisherman. Did anyone ever tell you that you always stunk of fish? Did they, Grillius Junior? That is why you never had any friends. And you always have fish breath; is that because all you kiss are fish?"

"Did you cut your hair for Senator *Pater*, or did he order you to cut it?" I asked grinning to gain the second that I needed to disarm this arrogant whelp. When he smiled back at me, I made my move. My empty right hand flew up grabbing Demos by his knife hand, and my thumb quickly pressed his thumb inward from the handle of the dagger. It was a move Grillius practiced and practiced with me repeatedly. With my left hand, I readily took the *cultellus* from his weakened grip. Now with the curved blade in my left hand, I released the pressure off Demos's thumb and rotated my grip around to his wrist; and with my thumb now pushing in on the top of his hand, I forced his hand to bend inward with his fingers touching the underside of his arm. He let out what sounded like a girlish wail before going to his knees before me. With him on his knees, I did a half twist of his arm, which rolled him over to his back as he wailed like a sacrificed pig. Out of the corner of my eye, I saw the corpulent senator and Praetorians all look over at me at the moment I flicked the dagger out over the railing into the sea. It did not make much of a splash, but the effect was electrifying and more powerful than a huge wave crashing over the bow of this ship in a mighty storm.

"Release my son!" Yelled the senator as he began to try to run forward with the three military men in their long, red cloaks, all toting short swords from richly ornate scabbards and straps. I did as I was commanded and slowly placed both hands back into my scarlet-purple cloak and felt for the hilts of my throwing daggers. I could kill two before they reached me, but then I would have to go into my red bag to retrieve a third weapon; and they would be on top of me by then. My only chance was to make this a battle of words, something Grillius frequently warned me against.

"Never tongue lash; only stare," was his constant admonition. I generally took his adage as a laconic idiosyncrasy of all Spartans, most of whom could not form a sentence if their lives demanded it. Yet, Grillius drilled other warnings that were not as laconic. "Blood and iron determine the events of history, not long-winded speeches. And never use your hands if there is a weapon around that can be utilized. Remember just about anything can be turned into a lethal weapon. There is no sense in hurting your knuckles or breaking your wrist when a good, strong board is within reach."

"What did you do to my son?" snarled the senator after he reached his son's side. Demos was now getting back to his feet with the aid of one of the soldiers. The senator must have been in his early 50s with gray, thinning hair; wrinkles around the eyes; and much flesh around his jowls and throat giving him the appearance that he had two or three chins. His face was scarlet red, and I wondered if he was going to have a heart problem due to his short run from the bow to the stern of the bireme. The other three were in their early 30s and very fit looking. Everyone had their hands on the hilts of their short swords except the one helping Demos, but all swords were still in their sheaths. If any had pulled their swords, I am not sure what I might have done with my daggers now in my right and left hands under my cloak.

"Father, he threw my *cultellus* into the sea! Did you see that?" Demos whined like a little boy who just lost his pet puppy.

"What *cultellus*?" asked the senator.

"The one you gave me yesterday for completing my studies at the Lyceum and for reaching my 20th year."

"Into the sea? That was what I saw him flipping into the ocean?" roared the senator looking at me in a red rage. "That *cultellus* cost more than the price of two good house slaves or a team of chariot horses! Are you demented, young man? I will demand payment or your life!"

There was the threat. Should I go into action and strike first? I still decided to use words; and, if that did not work, there would be blood and iron all over this deck in a few moments.

"Your son held it on me, and I acted only in self-defense by disarming him."

"Not true!" cried Demos, who now moved next to his father still rubbing his wrist. "I was just showing Eunus my gift. He became jealous and threw it out into the sea."

"This peasant, the mercenary boy, is a classmate of yours?" the senator said to his son, not really wanting an answer. He then turned his three chins towards me and demanded in a powerful and imperious voice, "And what is your business on this royal vessel?"

"What you ask, according to the Father of Logic, is a loaded question. But I will answer both. First of all, I am a classmate of your son; and second, my business is personal."

"Nothing is personal when a senator from Rome asks a question while on Imperial property! And if need be, these soldiers will chain you down below as a galley slave where you will remain for the rest of your living days!"

I noticed Demos smirking and the three soldiers moving out for position. My options were fading fast. As a fisherman, I had learned to swim. I could easily jump over the rail and make it to land. Nevertheless, I would not get to Rome and save Eli. Besides, jumping would only delay my recapture and could cost Eli his life. If I fought, what then? There were other soldiers and sailors on the ship, and I would eventually be overpowered. Then there was the killing of a Roman senator along with his son, which would be an incredibly serious matter. I decided to play my most expensive token in this game of life and death – my name.

"My apologies for the loss of the dagger, and my father will compensate you for its loss once I get to Rome."

"Are you joking, peasant boy?" cried out the fat senator. "And who might be your father?"

"You know him very well, for I now remember you at his Frigg Day villa orgies. Besides, were you not speaking with my father outside of the arena on the 50th Actium Games on the morning before Marius won the wooden sword for the third time?"

"Oh? And you then are a Roman citizen, which means you cannot be sentenced to the galley bench?"

"You are correct on both accounts."

Demos now smirked with open laughter. The senator quickly glared at Demos, which promptly silenced his spoiled-rotten son. Turning his hooded gaze back towards me, the senator knew I was going to throw the dice once again. Depending on what he said next determined whether it was talk or fight. I knew what Grillius would do, and I prepared my mind for the latter. "Who is this illustrious father of yours, young man?"

I had hesitated only a moment before I played my most valuable voucher and threw the dice one last time. "Senator Gaius Vetallus Crassus." I could almost hear Grillius moan at my choice; but I had to get to Rome to save Eli, not die or end up in chains.

"What?" laughed Demos's father with complete disbelief. "Gaius has only one son named Julius, who is much younger than you by perhaps ten years."

"Very true. I have a younger brother named Julius; and his mother is Claudia Pulchra, the ex-wife of General Varus, the very same Varus who committed suicide for losing three eagles belonging to Augustus."

"Hold it. You could not be," said Demos with a look of horror crossing his face as he figured out my identity.

"Could not be who?" demanded Demos's father, now somewhat befuddled.

Demos looked at me and then at his father. "He is Venustus, the son that supposedly jumped off the *Aemilius* Bridge the day Gladiator Marius won the wooden sword for the last time almost ten years ago."

"No! That son is dead. He killed himself on that day," said Senator Treverorum.

"Your son is correct, senator. I am Venustus Vetallus, and I am very much alive. And it was supposedly the *Pons Fabricius*, not the *Aemilius*," I said correcting Demos with a smile.

"Can you prove you are the son of Vetallus?" asked the corpulent senator, even though his look now revealed he was beginning to believe my identity.

I, too, was now confident that this Roman was the fat senator at the amphitheater talking to my father when Claudia's litter bearers were murdering Decimus, right before I was sent home into the trap in the streets of the *Urbs*. I realized I had walked into a dangerous game where killing the senator and his son would not solve my problems. Now I knew I had made the correct choice to fight with words and not iron or bronze. This was the first time I realized a name and a few words could be a powerful weapon. Here was a weakness in Grillius's arsenal. "Lentulus is my father's bodyguard, and perhaps you want directions to the *vomitorium* from my father's atrium up on Esquiline Hill," I said with slight sarcasm.

"How do you get to the *vomitorium* from the atrium?" he asked still trying to believe.

"First, you must pass by the wall with the mosaic of the battle of Jhelum River with Alexander and King Porus of the Punjab facing each other in the heat of battle. Alexander is on his black warhorse Bucephalus, and King Porus is sitting on a white elephant. Evidently this mosaic was commissioned in memory of history's most famous horse. Did not old "Ox-head" die after this battle?"

"And why was Alexander's horse named Bucephalus or 'Ox-head'?" queried the plump senator before me. Now I knew I did not have to kill him and his evil son.

"Was not that the brand on his left shoulder?"

"I read it was on his haunches," stated Demos now regaining his pride back.

"Plutarch writes that the horse dealer Philoneicus was selling horses of Thessalian stock. Still, today all horses from Thessaly have their brands on their left front quarters. Why would that be any different 300 years ago?"

Senator Treverorum looked confused as he turned to his son and asked, "How in the name of Amon does he know all this? Did you ever tell him what Senator Vetallus's villa looks like?"

Demos started to stutter, the first time I had ever seen this out of him. Finally, he got ahold of his tongue. "He has never left Greece in all the years I have been at the Lyceum; and, no, I have never told him what Senator Vetallus's *domus* looks like even though I have only been there once with you, Father."

Looking back at me, the rotund senator said, "Perhaps you are who you say. Does your father know you are alive?"

"He knows. But he is not expecting me, for I am going to surprise him once I reach Rome. Afterward, I will ask him to replace your son's dagger; and I will deliver the price personally within one day of my return to Rome."

"Very well, son of Vetallus. For if you are telling the truth, I would not want to put enmity between our two families. I will expect your visit at my villa, which is on Quirinal Hill, within 24 hours after our ship docks. However, if you fail to show up or if you are lying, I will have these men along with others hunt you down," he said waving towards the men in the red cloaks and two others who had joined the Praetorians who looked to be *lictors*. "And you will pay one way or another. Do you understand?"

"Fair enough, senator. I will return the cost of the dagger, or you can send your *thags* after me." I smiled insincerely towards the serious-looking soldiers, calculating they had no idea what a *thag* was.

"Oh, one last thing. Do not come near my son for the rest of this voyage," said the senator as Demos looked a little embarrassed since he now was placed into the coward's position.

"I can take care of myself, *Pater*. Look at his right arm, and see the scar I put on it during a *munera* with the *xiphos* out on the Academy's *palastra* a year ago."

"I will gladly stay away from all of you," I said without removing my arm with the scar from under my cloak.

"Let's go!" barked the obese senator sounding more like an emperor's mastiff dog.

"No, look at the scar first," whined Demos.

"I said, let's go!" surfaced the hard words again from the rotund senator. Demos now glared at me trying to give me his final insult. The father changed the tone to a certain extent when he dismissed himself by attempting to be polite before he turned and walked away, or perhaps he wanted to show correct social conduct to a senator's son. Demos, on the other hand, was still looking at me with a look worthy of the name Grillius had given him. After his squinty stare accompanied with pursed lips and apparently thinking this look would scare me and signal this was not over, Demos slowly turned to join the group at the bow of the ship. I watched until all seven sat under the tarp either on the small, wooden camp chairs or the deck boards. What was strange was how they all had their backs to me except one curious-looking Praetorian.

For the rest of the voyage, the Treverorum party stayed away from me at the stern of the bireme; and I remained away from them at the bow.

About five hours after the incident with Demos, the ship reached a spot north of the city-state of Corinth; and waiting on shore was a gang of 500 slaves. As soon as the ship beached itself, the slaves attached ropes and placed rolling logs under the keel. For the next four miles, the slaves expertly pulled the long bireme across the land to the Saronic Gulf, which opened out into *Mare Ionium* and *Mare Adriaticum*. Dozens of Roman soldiers guarded the slave gang carefully while they performed a well-practiced operation. After everyone including the galley slaves had disembarked the trireme, the group of

500 began portaging the bireme. With hundreds pulling on ropes, four men teams ran in orderly perfection carrying long rolling logs on their shoulders, jogging along the starboard side of the ship, and placing the logs under the bow to act as wheels in the same fashion the ancient Egyptians transported massive stones for the pyramids. Once the logs were set correctly, the four men teams ran back to the stern on the port side to fetch another log freed by the vessel's forward movement. There was only one ten-minute break when the 500 slaves fell down on and around the wide, all-weather road that was paved with massive, flat stones to help support the weight of a heavy ship being transferred over the Isthmus. This ingenious operation apparently was designed to cut our time in route to *Italia* by at least 185 nautical miles. I later learned this road was first constructed by Julius Caesar and later improved upon by Tiberius. The name of this broad roadway was called the *Diolkos* as it was pronounced in Greek.

The galley slaves went unguarded after they disembarked. I wondered why until I realized no one would get very far if anyone tried to escape. Only a few older ones walked alongside the bireme whereas the majority jogged ahead to the Saronic Gulf. Seeing these men in daylight and off the ship was a shocking sight. A third of them were completely naked, and the rest wore only rags or just a *dhoti*. Obviously being in cramped quarters inside the bireme did not allow much leg movement. Jogging was something many of the slaves evidently wanted to do, or perhaps they just wanted to get to the other side and sleep until it was time to go back to work. Whatever, watching these sinewy men jogging away was odd to watch because of the way they looked. Here were men of different ages, skeletal in appearance, but all with enormous muscles in their thighs, calves, arms, and shoulders. It was like watching a migration movement of some kind of subhuman forms from another mysterious continent. Aside from the oversized muscles, all of them looked underfed and on the edge of death due to malnutrition. When I reached the end of my walk, I noticed the horde of galley slaves had eaten a hot meal of what smelled like cooked lam;, and those who were finished stretched out on the ground sleeping. I began to think that maybe I was the one on this trip starving and underfed. It looked like a small detachment of Roman soldiers were in charge of providing the cooked food. From a distance, I watched the Treverorum group partake in the lamb dinner. To repeat, I felt like the one starving even though I did have some food in my red bag, packed quickly by Hector; but I could have used a hot meal of lamb.

When the ship was back in the water, it was not long before we were passing Patras, the last coastal town on the Peloponnese side of Greece. From there it would be a quick shot to reach the bottom of *Italia*. Once we passed under the mainland, we would turn northwest and move between *Sicilia* and *Italia*. Traveling at the speed the bireme was moving, I calculated that what was left of this day and the coming night would put us near *Sicilia*. When I asked an old sailor when he thought we would arrive in Rome, he said the longest should put us in by the morning of Saturn Day. With this information, I figured it would take the next entire day and night to reach Ostia before the bireme ran up the Tiber to Rome. Just thinking of how fast this ship was moving, compared with the weeks it would normally take any other vessel leaving Athens for Rome, was beyond incredible. I now started wondering if it were even possible to reach Rome before Lentulus got there with Eli. Only time would tell.

Hundreds of years ago, during Sparta's expansion period, 9,000 *hoplite* soldiers could hold and defend the narrow piece of land that connected the Peloponnese to the Greek mainland of Attica. With Spartan soldiers stretching out over four miles long, it would be impossible for an invading army to pass by land into the Peloponnesian portion of Greece. Therefore, the city-states of Peloponnesia, all controlled by the one city-state of Sparta, were all safe except by sea invasion on their flanks.

Before we began crossing the *Mare Ionium,* I became friendly with the oarsman-pilot who handled the two steering oars, one on each side of the stern. A wooden handle was attached to each rudder-oar allowing one man to guide the ship by using both hands. It was a tricky job steering the ship in a straight line but not a problem on a calm day, which we were experiencing. I relieved the thin-looking helmsman of 30-something a few hours after it got dark. I told the pilot I had been a fisherman for the past six years and knew how to handle a rudder. He was aware that I had been watching him work for most of the day, so he gave me the handles. I could not sleep very well as the bireme skimmed at an incredible speed, and I could not shake the thought that Demos might sneak up in the dark and slit my throat. The commander of the vessel, an old gruff Roman mariner, would have been the pilot's replacement shortly after I took over the rudders; but after he had watched me a bit, he said I could take his shift.

"With the sky free of any overcast, navigation should not be a problem. Just keep a sharp eye out for the islands up ahead that can be seen by the crescent moon and starlight."

The old commander informed me of what islands to steer towards and then went back to sleep near the mast. Island navigation worked for a while as I kept my eyes on the landmarks. When one island moved away, I had to quickly find the next marker until it faded off to either the starboard or port side. Both the pilot and commander forgot to wake up, and I just let them sleep. Not knowing what islands to steer against, I started using the stars as my reference guide. I just kept the Pole Star to my right shoulder using the Dog's Tail constellation as a pointer. The seven bright stars at the top end of the dog looked to me like a ladle more than what the old seamen out of Piraeus called a plow or a wagon. If one looked beyond the top rear edge of the wagon or when looking at a plow or scoop, it was the top front lip, which always pointed to the Pole Star. It was a comforting feeling watching this bright constellation of a dog or, as some sailors call it, a bear circle around the only star in the second heaven that never moved. I just kept this unmovable star to my right shoulder and did not worry a great deal about unreliable shadowy islands out on the horizon. Why the captain allowed a 19-year-old passenger, who looked like a young Spartan mercenary, to assume such responsibility on an Imperial vessel was a mystery to me. But I did enjoy the trust. I was sure they both thought I must be a mercenary besides being a fisherman in the way I handled the Senator's son yesterday morning.

Just when the sky started to lighten but the stars were still visible, both the helmsman and the ship commander awoke realizing they had forgotten to relieve me. The ship captain was agitated at first until he realized I had kept on target without his long litany of islands to steer against. When both men saw the familiar shoreline of southern *Italia* far out in front of us, both were amazed at how I got the bireme here and considerably ahead of schedule. I just smiled and gave the two handles of the double steering oars to the helmsman before I rolled up in my cloak to get some needed sleep. I now felt comfortable thinking both the helmsman and commander would warn me if anyone approached me for harm.

When my morning nap was over, I sat up realizing we were now heading into the north. The helmsman commented to me that we had just passed between the three-mile-wide straight between *Sicilia* and *Italia*. I shared some of my bread and wine with the helmsman. By the time I put away the wineskin, the helmsman had pointed out Herculaneum. It was a sprawling coastal city up ahead on the coast with Pompeii a little behind it. The dormant volcano of Mount Vesuvius was the dominant point to steer against now that the sun was coming up. There were a few puffy clouds up around the conical peak of this majestic mountain. I noticed the southern edge of clouds hanging around its top were a dark red color. Looking towards the east, I realized the sun was obstructed by a thick bank of clouds that stretched to the southwest. I immediately recognized the ominous sign. Just like the clouds up above

Mount Vesuvius, everything in the east spreading to the south and onward to the west were painted in the darkest red color I had ever see. It was nothing short of an ugly, angry sky, all painted a fiery hue and a warning to any sailor of a coming storm.

Both the helmsman and commander commented on the red sky when they noticed where I was looking. All seamen tend to worry about the weather. To get my mind off the fiery sky in the south, the helmsman pointed out the island of Capri up ahead off to our port side. It was jutting out from the point that protected Herculaneum and Pompeii. He said that was where Emperor Tiberius was living these days and not in Rome. The pilot became talkative maybe because he was worried about the coming storm. What he was telling me sounded appalling but true. Tiberius apparently had become entirely depraved while living on this island of lechery. The helmsman then proclaimed with assured factuality that Tiberius possessed on this little island, the world's most extensive pornographic library. "Tiberius also has little slave children trained in the art of erotic behavior."

After I had looked at the helmsmen to see if he were fooling with me, I realized he was dead serious. "I kid you not. Tiberius daily swims in pools with these little children, some not yet off their mother's milk. You can only guess at what evil things he does in these pools for his pleasure." The tall, skinny sailor also said, "Each afternoon criminals are brought to Capri from Rome..."

"And Tiberius always finds them guilty," said the Roman commander who apparently walked up to us and was overhearing our conversation. "The sentence always entails a quick trip off the balcony of one of his high-cliff porches."

"He throws people off his high porch each day?" I asked to make sure I heard correctly.

The sea commander made a sad jester with his tongue before he answered. "Ostensibly this is a daily activity."

"But he does not personally do the throwing," said the pilot with a squeaky little laugh. "He has soldiers do it while he gives an assessment concerning the victims on how well they screamed and dropped to the rocks below. You ask anyone in Rome about these horrible stories, and you will find them circulating the Imperial city on a daily basis."

The sea commander said, "You can ask tonight in any tavern to see if we are not telling the truth."

"We will be in Rome tonight? Isn't that sooner than expected?" I asked trying to prepare myself for why I was on this fast-moving ship.

"Because of your straight steering last night and if this coming storm is at our back, we will be in a little after the sun has set tonight," answered the commander. "And concerning Tiberius, if you do ask anyone about Capri, you will discover our dear emperor's popularity is not as high as his Capri porches."

I was shocked, to say the least, at this last comment; but the helmsman gave out a squawky, seabird-like laugh.

The commander in his newly revealed humor slapped his helmsman on the shoulder and said, "This is why I call my beloved steersman Seagull. Not only does he laugh like one; but all he does is squawk, eat, and lift his tunic continuously to relieve himself. The helmsman launched into his bird-like laugh at his commander's joke to the point I thought he might choke.

When both men finally composed themselves, I asked, "Who is running Rome if Tiberius is out on his pleasure island?"

It was the sea commander who answered. "A few powerful senators like the one you tangled with yesterday morning. However, Sejanus, the Praetorian *Prefect*, holds the real power of Rome and the Empire. Rome is not a safe place these days because of Sejanus; therefore, you better be careful from what I hear."

"What do you hear?" I asked.

The skinny steersman who answered. "Some of the sailors overheard that the senator up front is plotting something nasty for you after you set foot in Rome. What it is I have no idea, but you better keep a sharp eye."

"It would really help me if you could get some specific details, and I will give you a silver *denarius* for your efforts."

The helmsman looked to his superior who made a jester for him to take me up on my offer. Seagull smiled, and the ship captain turned and walked over to check on the ropes holding the sail. "Well, Seagull, are you going to earn a silver *denarius* or not?"

Before he could answer, I took hold of the rudder-oars and instructed Seagull to go forward and snoop around to see what he could learn. Within an hour, he was back and reported to me that, as soon as we reached Rome, one of the soldiers with the senator was going to follow me and kill me if I did not go to a particular villa on some hill. I told him it had to be Esquiline Hill, and I felt it was worth a silver *denarius* to know this. I happily gave Seagull my second-to-last silver *denarius* from my father's old moneybag. A silver *denarius* was usually considered the payment for a full day's labor for perhaps ten hours' work. Doing only one hour's work for valuable information seemed to me worth a day's wage, if not more. I know today my giving the helmsman a silver *denarius* for one hour's work was beyond excellent pay, but I only had two silver *denarii* remaining and did not have much choice in quibbling on the man's wages.

After I had handed the thin man the coin that was the size of my thumbnail, I thought about the last remaining silver *denarius* in the moneybag. If I had not used most of the remaining silver coins for my final year of schooling, I would not be financially embarrassed at this critical time. He eyed the silver coin and said he had not seen an Augustan-headed *denarius* in years. "All the *denarii* these days have Tiberius's or Sejanus's profile on them." I just smiled as I let him have the steering oars.

I found a place on the port side of the stern to rest and ate the remainder of the fruit from the red woolen bag and drank the last of the wine. I could not believe the trip from Piraeus had so far only taken two days and a night. The slaves below never stopped pulling at their oars except when they had a complement change. This occurred every six hours when 100 slaves would replace the same number giving a needed six-hour rest to the relieved unit of slaves. Six hours later the rested group returned to their benches relieving a third team of 100 who had been rowing for 12 hours. Each newly dismissed group of 100 was placed deep below deck, under where the rowing benches were located. There were a dozen or so extras for replacements when someone became too sick to row or died during the trip. The only time the galley slaves ate, from what I could tell was on their 6-hour break. Each man was given a bowl of fish soup, which was consumed very quickly because this was also the only time they had to sleep. I remembered they did have a cooked meal of lamb before leaving *Hellas* at the Saronic Gulf. Besides fish soup and dog bread, they were continuously given water while at the oars. Through the air slits, I could see a man could take a drink and never miss a stroke. A young slave boy about the age I was when I left Rome moved up and down the two levels of slaves carrying a bucket giving a sizeable sip of water with a gourd. The young boy was skilled at holding the handle attached to the gourd and placing the edge to the mouth of each slave. This little slave boy appeared to be the best-loved person on the ship. Each man nodded and thanked the little boy after each drink. Strangely, I envied the little slave boy for all the love he received. I had never received that kind of attention in my short life. I wondered what it would feel like, and I became slightly jealous for the first time in my life. I did not begrudge the boy as much as I admired him. But the slaves below unashamedly loved that faithful water boy.

By afternoon we were still moving at an incredible speed. It was a marvel to think the bireme was under human muscle strength as well as being driven by wind power. When late afternoon arrived, so did the wind. It came at us in a gale force blowing hard at our backs. From noon until now, the galley slaves had been using a gentle but straightforward oar-dipping motion. Prior to that, the slaves had been rowing at ramming speed. It was tormenting to my mind when I contemplated their lives of monotony and torment. The slaves did get some relief when the wind came at our rear with such force the oars were rendered ineffectual. If a fast-moving white cap didn't catch a pole, the other paddles would drag in the water slowing down the vessel. I heard a command from below and noticed that the slaves had been commanded to pull in their poles inside the ship. Looking through the air slits, I could see that the entire complement of 100 rowers had their heads and arms over the withdrawn poles and were already fast asleep, right at their benches. I assumed they would remain there until their rotation period was finished. Looking up at the stretched red sail, I felt the ship was now moving at double its speed with the tailwind pushing us forward.

Besides thinking about the slaves and staying away from Demos and his father, I spent much of the two days and one night at sea trying to harden my heart for what I had to do once I reached Rome. I felt like a baby bird who had been abruptly booted out of its nest, and it was now fly or die. I believed the indifference that Stoicism taught would be the only way to accomplish the task awaiting me in the Imperial City. Nevertheless, the hardening of one's own heart is not an easy task; and I learned later that it would not lead to personal deliverance as Stoicism proclaimed. However, this was the avenue of Stoicism I tried to practice since each must live by some belief system. There were only three main schools of Stoicism, and I chose at this time to embrace the classical school or original Stoicism as taught by its Athenian founder sometimes from the porch of the *Painted Stoa*. This I believe is where the term Stoicism originated. Since the ancient teacher named Zeno, who lived shortly after the time of Aristotle, did not have a school building to lecture from such as the Lyceum or Academy, he did his teaching in the *stoa* areas in Athens' many public buildings in the *Agora;* and thus, the word Stoicism.

With or without Stoicism to guide me, I believed I had all the tools to survive but realized my future was dark and might be very short. How could a person enter into the home of one of the most powerful men alive; murder him; and expect to live, let alone escape? Knowing he also had a small army of soldiers and *lictors* made it almost impossible to fathom. Add to that, I was going to try to rescue Eli while a Roman Praetorian officer was shadowing my every move. I had no plan except to go to Esquiline Hill and work as fast as I could in finding Eli if he were there and still alive. If I did not accomplish my task within 24 hours of my arrival, Senator Treverorum and Demos would, indeed, begin to complicate everything.

I had finished all I had to eat or drink shortly after the island of Capri disappeared out of sight. It was then I finally found sleep as I rolled up on deck in my new Spartan cloak. I knew I was going to need as much rest as possible for my task ahead in Rome. I awoke in the afternoon just as the gale winds started to blow and a mighty storm appeared on the horizon to the south moving across the sea northwards. This was the point when the galley slaves pulled in their oars and the ship flew across the waves by just the power of the high winds. The sailors were saying this was very unusual for this time of year, but they were also somewhat jubilant watching the winds filling the blood-red sail. I noticed with delight that the fat senator, Demos, and the three soldiers were all leaning over the rail in the front of the ship heaving whatever was in their stomachs as the bow jumped up and down in the swells. I was glad they were upwind protecting everyone else from being sprayed by their stomachs' contents. When I was a fisherman, this nausea was what the old salts called "feeding the fish." I must admit I had a good laugh to myself at their miserable condition.

Taking my eyes off them, I kept looking back towards the black, foul line of hammerhead clouds quickly marching towards us with dark black fingers that looked like it was clawing its way towards us. I had never seen anything as mesmerizing as this dark line of clouds towering high up towards the heavens. In the blink of an eye, lightning would rip a white line from inside the hammerhead clouds. After each blast of light, a thunderous boom reached us after a count of ten. I placed the storm out on the horizon to be about ten miles behind us because of my counting trick, which I learned from the old anglers I worked with for six summers. Each time I saw a flash I would count, "one pomegranate, two pomegranates, three pomegranates." The only comfort, based on my counting, was the ship was maintaining the same speed as the storm. When I repeated my count an hour later, from flash to boom, it was still ten pomegranates. Looking forward towards the bow, I saw one of the Roman *lictors* lose his grip when hanging his head over the rail. He flipped over and out into the sea, never to be seen again. About ten minutes later, the second *lictor* fell similarly into the sea. The rest of Demos's group stopped hanging over the rail to vomit but, instead, sat and vomited on the deck even though the contents fell upon some of the galley slaves below them. I was personally glad the wind was blowing all their smells away. I did not have any feelings for the two lost *lictors*, but I had hoped it had been Demos or his fat father who had fallen overboard.

The jubilant spirit, which the southwestern gale force wind had first provided, now left after everyone topside witnessed the two *lictors* fall overboard. How could anyone not think that, at any moment, all our lives could be taken from us? This wind and the storm coming at us from behind had become quite the object lesson. Now that everyone was silent, we all could hear every board creak and shake at each crash into a wave and drop down into a deep swell. Breaking out of each swell, a massive wall of water flew from the bow drenching the Praetorians and everyone else up front. No one tried to run back to where I was for fear of ending up like the two *lictors;* besides, Senator Fatman would not allow any from his group to come back near me.

The constant booms from the line of clouds from behind began to sound like a marching army of giants trying to gain on us. I was hoping the enormous red sail did not rip. If I had been the captain, I would have ordered the sail lowered before the sail tore or the mast broke. I would then drop both our anchors to drag behind the ship to slow it down and steady the ride. I knew this was not going to happen since the Roman commander of the ship was under orders to arrive at Rome as fast as possible; and as long as we were out in front of this storm, he was not going to drop the sail or anchors. Maybe he knew the hull would not split from the punishing it was taking as the ship cut a path through the high-rolling water, with whitecaps traveling in the same direction we were moving. I just settled down and held on knowing this was going to be a bumpy ride all the way to Ostia.

Each time I looked through the slats on the floorboards I could see the galley slaves still slumped over their retracted wooden poles, all fast asleep despite the coming storm. I judged that, because of the whitecaps racing past our ship, we were going faster than any human had ever traveled. It is true that all adventures are never fun while they are happening, but this was one time that adage actually applied.

Just before sunset, the bireme was still ahead of the storm. The skinny pilot at the two rudder oars yelled out pointing with his chin towards Ostia. The entire crew looked out towards the starboard side. There was the sprawling dockyard of Rome quietly sitting on the flat coastline of *Italia*. It did not look familiar to me; but the last time I was here was in the middle of the night almost ten years previous. Now I was surprised at how big Ostia was and how it fanned out for miles along the coast. I am sure it had also grown during my absence, but it was much larger than what I remembered.

"We are running with the tide!" called out the helmsman to the commander of the vessel who had a huge smile on his face.

"This is good news. The wind is still at our back," the commander called back to the Seagull. The old sea captain turned to me and yelled over the roar of the wind, "Ole' Neptune, brother of Jupiter and Pluto, must be on your side; and he wants to get you to Rome in a hurry!" I nodded to affirm his comment but then wondered why I agreed with him when I did not believe in any of the gods. I didn't even believe in the wind, which was a mighty force unto itself. The old naval veteran looked like he had been in many engagements, and today was something new he had never experienced. After my nod, the commander moved to the center of the ship and stood next to the single mast. From the heart of the ship, he seemed to be enjoying this wild ride even more than when he was at the stern. I just smiled back at him when the commander gestured to me with his eyes and a nod. He had his back to the mast and his legs spread wide looking now at the massive line of clouds coming towards us. I assumed he had just acknowledged to me that he knew I was not unfamiliar with the sea and was thanking me in his own way for helping for a peaceful trip up to this point.

When Ostia grew closer to our starboard side, the ole' war commander ordered the helmsman to head towards the mouth of the Tiber. Other commands were given to the officers below deck, and out came the long poles with the broad blades. Finally, the order came to lower the red sail. After it dropped and was secured, the helmsman turned the ship; and we made for the coast fighting the wind that was now hitting us broadside. Ostia expanded closer and closer as we still raced with wantonness towards the great and sprawling port of the Roman Empire.

I looked for the alley where Messina's father was killed by my father but could not identify the spot. I then watched the city pass as the ship slowed before cutting into the Tiber River's main channel. The slaves below were working rhythmically pulling at their oars as the little vessel skirted Ostia off to our right. The city limits ended as the river took a hairpin turn to the left, and we meandered back and forth until we could smell Rome long before we actually saw her. The smell brought back the memory of the alleys of the tenement houses in the valleys of the Seven Hills, especially the lanes of the *Urbs* and *Subura*. The sun was below the horizon once we reached Ostia, and the darkness was swallowing us up by the time we made the last turn in the river coming into sight of the capital city. Torches and oil lamps were burning from street corners and just about every window that could be seen. The city seemed very festive, something I had forgotten. An hour after dark in Athens everyone was home getting ready for bed. Not so in Rome – it was just coming alive. Wagons that were not allowed in the narrow streets during the day were just crossing the bridges and entering the city when we rowed past the Emporium District. Here were the large warehouses at the *Forum Boarium* that contained the *Porticus Aemilia*. When the bireme passed these docks, I noticed slaves, grain, amphorae of perfumes, rolls of silk, boxes of jade, spices, and other imports along with wild creatures in cages for the amphitheaters. These commodities generally arrived from Ostia by barges and not seagoing galleys, for the river was not deep enough for the larger sea-going ships. I could see activity galore where these barges were being unloaded; bags and wooden boxes were being carried by hundreds of slaves into the many warehouses. It looked as if Rome never slept. From what I could see was that night in Rome was a wild, noisy, and busy time.

The bireme ended its journey by mooring at a small but impressive-looking dock area right before the *Pons Sublicius*, the old timber footbridge that was the oldest bridge crossing the Tiber. I remembered this bridge but not the waterfront the night Eli, Zeno, and I passed this spot in our escape by foot from Rome to Ostia. Standing majestically was the Circus Maximus with the Imperial Palace standing high on Palatine Hill. People and curious lookers were crowding around the wharves looking to see what dignitaries were arriving. The wind was still blowing with a new, muscular strength from the south; and the black lines of hammerheads looked like they had turned and were targeting the city. Counting the seconds from flashes, I calculated the storm would be on top of the city within an hour. Not all the slaves and citizens on shore seemed concerned about the coming storm, but they would within an hour. Instead, most people appeared to be filled with the anticipation of a warm blowing wind that was bringing new thrills to this city. I judged everyone around the wharves to be curious sightseers or animated spectators from the afternoon games. I based this conclusion from the many individuals waving ribbons of various colors identifying themselves with their favorite charioteers or gladiators.

"You can tell it is Venus Day (Friday)," said Seagull. "The mob's excitement is never like this except the night before the Day of Rest, Saturn's Day (Saturday), which has become a holiday for most of the city, thanks to the Jews who refuse to work on Saturn's Day." The thin helmsman shook his head as if he hated the Jews, but why would he if Rome received a day off every seventh day? During the old Republic, citizens only got a rest day every tenth day. I believe the people under the Han Dynasty also rested every tenth day. "What god tells his people to take a day off before he lays down the law? Only the Jewish God – that's who," scorned Seagull with a hacked laugh.

When I learned that Seagull remained on the ship while it was in Rome as the only guard, I asked if he could watch my flop hat and red bag. I told him I would be back for them before sunrise. I did not want to be hindered with my hat and an empty bag in my hand. I had taken the black egg out of its small box filled with straw and placed it behind my back and wide belt that also held my two bronze daggers, one on each side. I also put the three star-daggers together into the top of my right boot. After thanking the helmsman and the captain, I was the first off the gangplank with my scarlet-purple cloak draped over my shoulders. I moved quickly through the crowds with both arms free just in case I needed to throw my two bronze daggers. I figured at least one of Senator Treverorum's ruffian soldiers would be following me, so I did not even look back but moved in the direction of Esquiline Hill; passing through a long tunnel that ran under the southern edge of Palatine Hill. After emerging out the other end of the dark tunnel, I noticed the streets were jammed with people and torches and lamps everywhere. There seemed to be a cheerful viciousness in the sea of flesh. I suppose spending all day watching men and beasts killing and maiming each other would lead to this condition. I wondered about Marius the gladiator and his fate since he won the wooden sword. I could have asked Demos back at the Lyceum, but I did not want to give him any hint at that time of who I might be. Besides, back in Athens, I did not care about Rome as I tried to bury all my memories of this city. Now that I had returned my Athens' life was over and all the old, repressed memories along with intimate thoughts being triggered by old smells and sounds were unearthing themselves as if they had only been hidden by a handful of dirt.

Noticing an alley full of garbage, I forced my mind back to my present problems and desired destination. Deciding to follow the less-traveled avenues, I turned onto a less-traveled and darker side street. Before I entered the street, I did look back; there sticking out like an injured thumb was one of the soldiers wearing his long, red cloak tied at the throat with a silver clasp. Once I rounded Palatine Hill, I passed through the heart of the city, the great forum where Julius Caesar's temple stood along with the Senate House. Passing through the most magnificent buildings in the world, I found myself soon entering into the slums of Rome's *Urbs*. Looming up on both sides of me were thousands of multi-story tenement houses or *insula* with sewage still piled high in the side alleys. Once again, the horrible memories of that last day in Rome came to visit as if it were yesterday. If I wanted to lose the soldier behind me, I could use that old trick; but it was not necessary. Besides, he knew where I was headed. My thinking turned to a more urgent, immediate problem – that of my guts.

My stomach was cramping with unbelievable pain. I had not been able to relieve myself in the past two days at sea. When I spotted a public latrine, one of the more than a hundred scattered around Rome, I hoped I could make it in time. There was an old woman at the entrance collecting the small copper coin for entry, and I only had the last silver *denarius* in my father's lonely leather moneybag tied behind my belt. I did not have time to make change. So, when I got near the entrance, the woman turned to collect a coin from someone else; and she did not see me slip past her. This was not my plan; but I was going in no matter what, or this was going to turn into a major drama, beyond what the god Dionysus's bowels did in the underworld in Aristophanes's comedy *The Frogs*. Inside there were over a hundred marble seats along a long wall. There were only about ten men and one old woman sitting away from each other doing their thing. I grabbed a stick out of a stone water trough with a large, wet sponge attached to the end. A little slave boy was picking up used sticks that were scattered over the floor in front of the many seats. He would then clean them in the open water drain that flowed in front of the seats and would then replace them back into the front stone trough of water to wait for the next person. I found an empty space at the very end of the long, narrow room that was mostly dark with light coming only from one torch over the front water trough. My visit was almost over when the Roman soldier in the red cloak entered the stinking, smelly room. He came right up to me, pulled off his cloak, pulled up his tunic, and sat next to me.

"So, you are following me," I said more as a statement than as a question.

"Those are my orders. But, between you and me, I think they smell like these sticks," the Praetorian said holding up one of the dripping sponge sticks with his left hand.

"Your orders are to follow me to Esquiline Hill and report back to Imperial Fat-one and his crowing son? Or are your orders to kill me?"

"I would not be as vulgar as you, but something like that."

"Why not make life simple? Let us go to a tavern after we finish here, and I will buy you a beer and some bread. Then you can report back I got to my father's villa, and all of us are happy."

"Are you really who they say you are?"

"I am Venustus Vetallus, but I have not had the privileged life the last ten years as Demos living off the largess of a wealthy father."

"You definitely do not dress like a rich senator's son; I will say that. Actually, you look more like a Spartan mercenary if you do not mind me saying so. Besides, the way you disarmed that spoiled... Well, now I am talking vulgar; and I should not talk against the one who pays me."

"Talk all you want; I agree with you. Demos and his kind are the ones destroying this Empire and its entire system. His kind breeds decadence, selfishness, and greed. Children like Demos are simply the foul seed of the future."

"You sound like a Stoic. Maybe you can tell me about it over that beer. But do you have the money? I did see you slither into this *lavo* without paying."

"It was an emergency, and I did not have time to hassle with the old woman at the door. Besides, my business today has nothing to do with latrines and old women." We both laughed as I stood to leave. The soldier, who was a good 15 years older than I, got up as well and told me his name was Felix.

"Call me Venu."

"Let's go to *Subura*," said Felix. "You do remember the valley between Viminal and Esquiline Hills. That district is notorious for its shady morality, which should be an excellent place for a Stoic to reveal his philosophy. Actually, there is a phenomenal tavern not far from Julius Caesar's old townhouse villa. Did you know Caesar lived in *Subura* just to appear like the rest of Rome's *thags*?"

"No, I did not. But it sounds like a plan; and, when we are done, I will just climb the hill for home."

"And I will report back to the senator and his *deva* son."

"It's a deal," I said throwing the dirty end of my stick-sponge into the channel of water flowing in front of the marble seats.

199

CHAPTER NINE

Rome – *The 15th year of Tiberius in the first week of the month of Junis, on Venus Day.* *(29 AD)*

Ten soldiers wisely led will beat a hundred without a head.   Euripides

Felix led the way through the crowded streets with the *Forum Romanum* behind us and Esquiline Hill to our right. When we reached the *Forum Transitorium* and then the *Argiletum*, *Subura* opened out into the bottom valley between Viminal and Esquiline Hills. We were indeed in the part of Rome that was famous for manufacturing trades along with the not-so-reputable businesses. "Shady morality" was the proverb spoken most often by anyone going into *Subura*. By the time we reached deep into the broad valley of *Subura*, both Felix and I could hear the roar of the wind buffeting around the tall, shabbily built buildings. I kept one eye on Felix and the other on the recognizable sights familiar to me as a boy. The multi-level *insulae* rising up on both sides of the street seemed to be swaying in the wind. Their high presence darkened the already-dark narrow streets, and we had to dart quickly out of the way of a couple of horse-driven wagons. The torches and lamps that were not yet extinguished by the wind cast eerie shadows against the red brick walls. It looked like tortured demons dancing on the sides of the tall buildings. Erected by speculator builders, these unsound structures brought quick profits from the tens of thousands of peasants displaced from the countryside by the hordes of slaves working the vast *latifundium* (or farm estates) now going on centuries back in Rome's past. Down into this murky valley of squalor that smelled of rotting garbage and human sewage, I understood why the aristocratic minority had the better homes on or around the Seven Hills of Rome. Living up higher was a simple environmental separation from the lower classes as well as a quest for fresh air. I believe it was also a statement of superiority, and this could have been why Julius Caesar chose to live in *Subura.* When Felix pointed out Caesar's townhouse, I realized this home was part of his genius to identify himself with the common man. Perhaps that is why, even today, he is considered the father of his country. It just goes to show the winners write the histories. For instance, Julius Caesar is not only deemed a god by the average Roman; but, when he was alive and living in Rome, he scripted himself as a humble citizen choosing to live with the lower plebeians in *Subura.*

Open to any seeing eye from *Subura,* the grand government buildings of the *Forum Romanum,* Imperial palaces, the amphitheaters, temples, basilicas, aqueducts, bathhouses, and triumphal arches were only a false front to Rome's real inner wretchedness. The whole, unplanned, grand-accident design of this supposed majestic center of the world turned my stomach as I followed next to the soldier in the red cloak. I took a quick look up towards the sky. Gray, ominous clouds were now skirting over the city; and I realized the ugly, black ones were not far off. I grimaced when I realized a mighty wind would hit first before the rain. I was sure, by the time we came out of the eating establishment, the storm would be pouring forth its fury.

"There is the tavern," pointed Felix with a charming grin. He seemed almost too friendly, and I put my right hand under my scarlet-purple Spartan cloak and felt for one of my throwing knives in my belt. My Spartan scarlet-purple was much more of a cape or even a long coat. All Spartan *chlamys* were made from lamb's wool, which made it soft to the touch with a spectacular dyed color that only was indistinguishable as the color of a Spartan mercenary. The coat could be used as a blanket since it was large enough to wrap around the entire body. When more temperate conditions necessitated, the *chlamys* could be folded in half and worn like the Praetorian's cloak but much thicker looking. I remembered Grillius telling me one night in the death-house that he never wore his cloak in a tavern because he had too many problems with men wanting to fight him for no reason other than he was a Spartan. For that reason, I decided to remove the *chlamys* and roll it up. As soon as I removed my cloak, I noticed Felix doing the same with his red Praetorian cape. I did not ask him why he removed his Praetorian cloak, and I followed Felix into the *popina* with our cloaks rolled and under our left arms. I had my hand on a bronze dagger hidden inside the rolled-up coat, which gave me a sense of safety.

"Come on inside before you both get wet," said the man guarding the door to the tavern and holding it open for the both of us. Why a tavern needed a guard was a mystery to me. We found an empty table along a sidewall inside the main room, which was the bottom floor of a ten-tier tenement house. An attractive slave girl, a few years older than I, came over to serve us. I was hoping the wind that was sure to be coming would not collapse this building down upon us.

"What will you have, Praetorian?" asked the slave girl as if she owned the place.

"Beer. Bring a cold jug," answered Felix, still sounding too friendly.

"Domestic or Egyptian? And you know all our beer is warm."

"Egyptian... he is paying, and make it cold," Felix said pointing to me with a quick flick of his left finger. I then noticed he had his right hand under the table resting on his lap.

"And you, Greek mercenary, what will you have?"

I wondered why she thought I was a mercenary, and then I remembered my boots. "*Garum* and a loaf of cheap dog bread," I said feeling hungrier than thirsty.

"Oh, no! Not that smelly fish sauce on bread!" cried Felix making a sour face. "You eat that in front of me, and I will start turning green all over again."

"Bring the bread and one bowl of *garum* and a jug of Egyptian beer as well," I ordered hoping the soldier would get sick over the *garum*. The slave girl turned after she beamed a beautiful smile at me and not at Felix. All her teeth were present and somewhat white and beautiful.

"So the young woman finds you to her liking," declared Felix.

"I would not know. I have not had much experience with the opposite sex. I have been too busy the last nine and a half years with school and work."

"Are you serious? No time for females? Not even a quick romp with a slave woman?"

"I'm telling you the truth. I've been too preoccupied to waste my time playing the *eros* game."

"You are an odd one. That is what the senator's son said for the past two days. He even said maybe you liked boys, but there was no proof of that either. But you did make a lasting impression upon him with that hand maneuver on the first morning out of Piraeus."

"That arrogant *deva*-demon's opinion has the worth of what's in the alleys of *Subura*."

"Magnificent! We have reached our only common ground so far except you were going to instruct me on Stoicism. That is what you are, is it not? A Stoic?"

"I would not call myself a Stoic. I agree with much of Stoics' philosophy, but there seems to be an element missing that makes the belief system fallacious. The whole idea of being indifferent to external influences so you can be free seems too academic. The Stoic's idea that all things are fixed by a higher power is also hard to accept. The question is, if we are powerless to alter our lives contrary to some plan preconceived by a higher power, how is that being free? Instead, the Stoics claim we are all chained like those galley slaves on the bireme to our destinies. That does not sound like freedom to me."

The slave girl returned with a clay jug of beer, two clay cups, and a round loaf of bread along with a bowl of *garum*. The smell of the fish sauce was atrocious if you were not accustomed to it. I handed her my last coin trying not to look at her, for I really did not know how to act around females. She said she would make change and return. I grabbed for the bread with my left hand when Felix placed his left hand on my wrist. My other hand, still holding my knife in the rolled-up cloak on my lap, was moving when Felix must have realized I was getting the wrong message and released his grip. "We have not asked the blessing for the food," he declared with great seriousness. "I did not mean any harm to you."

"Blessing? What blessing?" I blurted out, a little agitated.

"A well-schooled fellow knows nothing about blessing one's food?'

"What god do you wish to invoke?"

"There is only one, the Creator of all things. I'm not a Stoic, but I do believe in a higher power who has all things fixed even though I believe we do have a free choice in life and are also held accountable for all our options."

"Are you a Jew?" I asked remembering Anab talking almost the same way just a few nights ago in Athens. Anab had also bowed his head and asked some kind of blessing after Hector put the stew on the table. That was the only time I had seen anyone pray a blessing before eating. Hector never prayed to Athena or Nike; and my father, Gaius Vetallus, never prayed that I could remember. Maybe I had been living a sheltered life and knew little of what actually went on beyond my limited experiences.

"No, I am a Gentile like you; but I did convert to something a few months ago when I was in Judaea."

Now I became concerned, and I slowly pulled my right hand to the top of the table with the bronze throwing dagger showing.

"What is that for?" asked Felix with concern in his voice.

"To cut the bread after you pray."

"That would be very appropriate," exclaimed Felix as he lowered his head. "God of the Universe, Creator of all things, bless this food; and protect Venu tonight. Amen."

I kept my eyes on Felix the entire time of his prayer, and now I pointed the knife towards him to make my point clear. "Tell me what you know, and do not play any tricks; or this knife will be placed in your left eye."

"Well, Venu! I believe you could put that knife into my eye but not before I seriously injured you with my gladius." Under the table, the tip of what felt like a sword was slightly touching the area between my legs making a clear statement. I slowly lowered the knife, and he pulled back his sword. He must have drawn it from its scabbard before we came into the tavern and hid it under his red cloak, which he had carried into this drinking and eating *popina*.

"As sparks fly upward, a man is born for trouble," said Felix in an amiable tone. "I will answer all your questions; but first, let us eat and drink."

I was not happy with this eccentric stranger as I cut the round loaf of dog's bread into two equal parts and offered one section to Felix with the knife sticking into the extended section. While I was cutting the bread, Felix was pouring each of us a beer. After he had taken his portion of the cooked dough, I placed the knife on top of the table; and we each drank from our own glazed cups, which sweated slightly from the cold liquid inside. Somehow, the slave girl had produced cold beer. I ripped a smaller section of the bread with my hands and dipped the bread into the awful smelling fish sauce hoping again that Felix would be sickened by it. *Garum* was made from taking the cast-off parts of fish and letting them rot in the sun for several days. When it was nothing but paste, it was mixed with other things I really did not want to know. However, *garum* was a favorite of the plebeians, slaves, and freedmen. It could be smelled on a person's breath even if he or she were not close. A patrician would never touch *garum* as a matter of pride. Many things separated the classes in Roman society, and *garum* was just one of them. By my eating this poor man's fare, I was letting this soldier know what I thought about Rome's social levels. I had first learned of *garum* from the other older men I fished with out in the *Mare Aegaeum*. After I had washed down the bread and *garum* with a gulp of beer, the slave-girl returned and placed three large bronze *sestertii* on the wooden table that separated Felix and me. These coins were much bigger than the silver *denarius*, almost four times its size and weight. I understood that four bronze *sestertii* equaled one little silver *denarius*. However, I was shocked by the price this meal was costing me. Just four of those coins were a standard wage for a full day's work of hard labor for a freedman, soldier, or fisherman. One million *sestertii* qualified one as a member of the senatorial class. Fewer than half a million would allow membership into the equestrian class. The number of coins one possessed measured everything in Rome. My personal outrage subsided when the slave girl returned and placed a handful of smaller copper coins on top the three bronzes. Now I understood this meal was not that expensive, and my outrage was decreased. I also was relieved to see both of the Praetorian Guard's hands were on top of the table just like mine.

"Are the beers and bread to your liking?" the girl asked with a broad smile.

"Very much," replied Felix beaming back with his biggest grin.

"Good. If you want anything more, let me know," the girl said to Felix. She then turned to me and said with an all-encompassing smile, "Anything at all."

As she sauntered to another table, Felix said, "See, she wants the young fisherman/student. You must realize you are a temptation to women."

"You are not that old, Felix," I replied. "Besides, this girl is too old for me."

"Not true. But that slave might be too young for me. I will turn 36 next week, the same age as the Baptist. The girl is closer to your age."

"And what is your rule on age?" I asked.

"You take your age, cut it in half, and add seven. That girl is most likely 20 years old."

"So, using your rule then, she is five years too young for you. Is that right?"

"That is how my rule works. Any more questions?"

"You mentioned the Baptist. Were you referring to John the Baptizer from Judaea?" I asked remembering Anab's story and wanting to change the subject from females and my love matters.

Felix's eyes grew wide, and he put down his clay cup. "You have heard of the Baptist?" he asked leaning forward with genuine interest. I said nothing but only glared at Felix. Realizing he was too close to my space, he slowly sat up straight with a glint crossing over his eyes. "Now I need to tell you the truth before you decide to stick me with your bronze throwing knife. I only guess you were the one who met the old Jew on the Acropolis the night before the *Achilles* left Piraeus. It was dark, and you were dressed differently than now; but it was you, am I right?" The statement was more of an assertion than a question. "I know what you are thinking, and you are wrong. I did not follow the Jew from Judaea. But we were together on the same ship out of Joppa, which docked at Piraeus."

"Why were you in Judaea, and how much do you know about me?"

"The old Jew talked about the Baptist, did he not?" Felix asked with an incredulous eye apparently changing the subject, which was my trick.

"First, answer my questions; or I will kill you before you are able to reach for your sword. And I do not even need to use the knife."

Felix pursed his lips while he digested my words with a strange, defeated look. I waited. Maybe he believed I could kill him without the knife, but I could see he was trying to figure if he had enough time to use his gladius before I did whatever. He slowly grinned at me just as he did to the girl; then he began speaking. "I know of no connection between you and Judaea. I served under the governor of Judaea for the past year. That would be Governor Pontius, who is called the 'Pilate Man' or just Pontius Pilate. Actually, I spy for Sejanus, the Praetorian *Prefect* here in Rome. I have been a Praetorian soldier for the past 16 years. When I turn 36 next week, I will be able to leave and get a small pension. My assignment in Judaea was to observe Pontius Pilate and report back just before my 16th year of service expired. With Tiberius spending his time on Capri, Sejanus is really the acting emperor in everything except a title."

"I might be the son of a very powerful senator, but I know nothing of Rome's politics; nor do I really care."

"Allow me to instruct you. I came from the Order of Knights, but I rarely claim my title. My Equestrian Order comes from here at Rome. I am not a foreign *decurion* like many of the new aristocracies these days. My father served as an officer for 16 years in the Praetorians under Augustus. I was born into the Order of Knights. My father was able to get me a commission when I was about your age shortly before Augustus died. My father told me being in the Praetorians was much better than serving in the legions, which, for starters, mandates 20 years of your life, not 16, like in the Praetorians. In the legions, you sleep in tents out on the frontiers the entire time. Nonetheless, in the Praetorians, you sleep in barracks; and there is no problem with heat, freezing cold, bugs, and disease along with combat with the Barbarians. In addition, the pay in the legions is much lower compared with the Praetorians. The shorter service, the higher pay, and all the pleasures to be had in Rome – there is no comparison. This is why there is great enmity between legionaries and Praetorian Guards if you did not know. That is why I removed my Praetorian red cloak before entering this eating establishment. I am sure there might be at least one ex-legionary in this tavern."

"This is all news to me," I confessed. "All I know is Tiberius upped the number from 6,000 to 9,000 Praetorian Guards and relocated them to the city rather than outside the walls and down the road like Augustus had it."

Felix had taken another sip of beer before he continued. "You are observant and brilliant, my young friend; however, a little slow on being followed. But we will talk about that later. My orders from Sejanus were to report to Senator Treverorum in Athens on the day after his son's finals concluded at the Lyceum. I was to return to Rome on the dispatch bireme along with two other Praetorian officers who would be serving Senator Treverorum along with two *lictors*. Treverorum was recently elected as *aedile* with *imperium* power. That was the first time I had ever seen the senator or his *deva*-son. All I know about you is what Deva-Demos said over the past two days. My only instructions from Treverorum was to follow you to Esquiline Hill; but that part about killing you if you did not go the right way is not correct. Treverorum told the ship rudder-man what to say to you after you paid him to spy. I am afraid Rudder Man robbed you of a silver *denarius* for the highest bidder and gave you spurious information."

"The ship pilot? He lied to me? That is hard to believe, for I helped steer the rudders to give him many hours of rest in the night."

"Yes, the helmsman of the *Achilles* who came back to gather information for the silver *denarius* you gave him. He is not your friend; and in a way, he is worse than I am. You see, I am sorry to snitch on him to you. Nevertheless, I am telling you the truth only because I like you; and I do not like Demos or his plump father."

"How do you know all this?"

"Treverorum gave the pilot two silver *denarii* to tell you what he wanted you to hear. I am giving you all this information for just free beer and bread. Think of it as a gift to square the time you did steering the ship. Actually, when you were at the helm, my seasickness was abated because you kept the boat on a calm, steady course compared with that skinny malefactor of a rudder holder. However, I should lie to you because you sit there eating your *garum*, and make me sick all over again," Felix said showing some visible angst.

"I guess I am the fool here. Perhaps I should accept your words as truth. My apologies."

"No, Treverorum and his self-important son are the fools. But they do not know it yet, and most likely the both of them will go to their graves never knowing the truth. That is what is sad about this world, Master *Lao Tzu* Stoic."

I let out a jovial chuckle for the first time since leaving Athens. "You misuse the language of Serica. What you said was 'Master Master Stoic.' You should have said, 'Venustus *Lao Tzu* Stoic' if you wanted to correctly say 'Venustus the Master Stoic.' For instance, the father of Confucianism was *Chiu Kung* or, as his students called him, *Kung Fu Tzu*."

"You are telling me that *Fu Tzu* means the master?"

"Now you are learning. You could have said Stoic *Lao Tzu* or Stoic Venustus *Lao Tzu*. However, I am curious; where did you hear the word *Lao Tzu*?"

"I was born at night, but it was not last night," he said with a grin.

Once again, I let out a hearty laugh that caused several customers at other tables to look our way. Realizing my behavior might be dangerous by calling attention to us, I decided to sit up straight and change the subject. I also began to wonder whether the beer, which I had never consumed before, was having this jovial effect upon me. "Are you telling me the truth about your orders not to kill me?"

"That part was only to panic you to go nowhere but Esquiline Hill."

"And you followed the Jew from Judaea to Athens but not before you boarded the ship at Joppa?" Felix nodded yes with both of his hands folded under his chin and his elbows on the table. "Perhaps you are actually working for my father. I am sure he has a bounty out for my capture. Knowing my father, I believe there could be some serious money to be had for my capture."

Felix placed his hands on the table and also straightened up on his stool. "No, I work for Sejanus, not your father. And the bounty for your capture does not exist, at least not yet. By tomorrow, there might be a huge amount for your head. Actually, I have never met nor seen your *patra* even if he were sitting over there at that table," Felix said pointing with his cup of beer. "Believe me, I would not know him. But do not get me wrong; the entire Roman world has heard of your father and will soon know of you."

"Then why were you following the old Jew to Athens? And why were you spying on him up at the Acropolis that night he spoke with me?"

"I am a spy, and the rest of what I do is my business. An old, nervous Jew traveling alone does raise a few suspicions, especially when he climbs all those stairs to the top of the most pagan location outside of Egypt's Luxor and Karnak complex, which is also called Thebes. I am telling you the truth; I was only a passenger on the ship from Joppa to Piraeus. Remember that I told you I was only in Joppa to get a ride to Piraeus to meet the *Achilles* and Senator Treverorum. The ship from Judaea arrived in Piraeus a day early, so I had time to follow the Jew thinking I might make some extra money on the information. I assumed it was you he was talking with at the little temple with the shields around it, but the comment about the Baptist confirmed it. The old Jewish pottery man on the ship out of Joppa spoke of the Baptist for one entire day. He and I were of a kindred spirit since he believed this desert preacher was a prophet like Elijah of old. I would bet the gold in my teeth that Ole' Clay Man told you about John the Baptist when you escorted him to that little stone house at the base of the Acropolis. Am I correct?"

This soldier was more than a soldier; and he did confess he was a spy, a good one at that. I did not see anything that night I met Anab, but I did sense a presence. "Why are you telling me all this?"

"I told you I like you. Maybe you remind me of myself 15 or 16 years ago. There could be some money involved in the information I could get from you, not as much as your capture. Besides, it is hard to enjoy blood money when you know the person. I have changed my ways since I started following the teachings of that wilderness prophet in Judaea. That being said, I now must initiate my new avenue for money. Thus, a few questions for me that could make some money that would not be blood money but only if you helped me. As strange as it may sound, I want something that would take years to learn and cost me more than money. I believe that you, young Venustus *Lao Tzu,* are a real Master Scholar of religion and philosophies – that is, if Demos can be believed. Besides, what you already told me about Stoicism was actually fascinating."

"Why are you talking to me if Senator Treverorum said to just follow me?"

"I told you I do not work for Senator Treverorum, at least not directly. My orders are from Sejanus; and, after next week, I do not answer to him either. That is why I am talking to you. Think of me as a slave getting his freedom after many years of faithful service to this Empire. Once I get my freedom, I want to learn to spread my new wings. As strange as it might sound, you are worth more to me alive than dead. If it is true that you are the long-lost son of Vetallus, then there will soon be an enormous bounty on your head! But, by befriending you, I am actually protecting my own interests."

Looking at this man smile and noticing some gold in his teeth, I was not confident I could completely trust him. He was a professional snitch but a likable informer with possibly some new found morals, values, and ethics. If he did sit under John the Baptist, the man Anab spoke of before I left Athens, then perhaps Felix had changed his course of life now that he was about to leave the Praetorians. On the other hand, he was a crafty character when I considered that sword business under the table. Grillius would be upset with me if he were here and saw what happened. And that part about being tracked or followed were lessons Grillius never taught me. I now realized I had a lot to learn and was still between hay and grass. It was more than just letting down my guard. Felix was good at what he did. I felt shame as I eyed the soldier across the table. Now I knew the cold truth about myself unlike what Grillius told me just a few days ago out in the courtyard of the Lyceum. Here I was wearing a new tan *chiton,* and the Praetorian was dressed in a purple tunic that was faded just right to show who he was.

Felix was not a handsome nor ugly man. His short-cropped hair and beardless face needed a shave and a swim at a bathhouse. He was a man nearing the end of his prime just before middle age begins to overtake a man with a widening girth. Beneath his thick brows and a typical, long Roman nose, he had honest eyes. There was no mistaking him for anything other than a soldier; every few seconds he unpretentiously scanned the room looking at every person who came and went. He was like a feral cat in the wild watching for danger and, yet, appearing relaxed and under no strain.

"Do you believe I am Venustus Vetallus? And do you know why I have been missing for over nine years?"

"I do believe you are Venustus, and so does Senator Treverorum. I would also say without a doubt that is the same opinion of that over-indulged, coddled, decaying son of one well-fed senator. While you were missing for almost ten years now, you grew into a man, a hard-working man, which is rare these days for the son of a senator. Demos, the opposite of you and growing up during the same time period, became a spoiled imp who has now turned into a dangerous ruin, all by just being the product of a damaged class called senators of the patricians. I would guess about 800 senators are living in this city as I speak. Out of that number sits 300 in the Senate House when they are in session. Most of the young males of this class are just as diseased as your Deva; and when I am old, I will not wish to live in this city under their rule, especially with Sejanus as emperor. If Sejanus does not become the next emperor, I am guessing the future ruler will be on the same level of stock as Demos Treverorum. Too bad you will not be able to sit in the Senate House in the future. Now, on the subject of guessing, guess what the discussion at the bow of the *Achilles* for the past two days encompassed? Yes, it is a rhetorical question, which I will answer. It was all about you. That is right. Old Treverorum and his sick son could not believe you were alive. They minced, ground, shredded, and chopped every thought regarding you that came into their little, unimaginative, pathetic minds. It was all I could do not to kill both of them and throw them off the ship. After the two *lictors* had gone overboard, I did give it some thought. You have no idea what I had to endure the past two days and night. And that was beside the sickness from the sea, which only added to my misery. All I wanted to do during the voyage was to come over to you and learn that hand trick you used on that son of a shredded, botched senator. Now that I am talking with you, I realize my folly for not pushing both over the side of the ship, especially after the two *lictors* went over. I believe I could have done it, and all would have thought it was an accident. By then it was too late in the trip. Instead, I had to sit with two pitiful worms crawling around in the dirt and dripping their vomit on those poor slaves below us."

"A cheery metaphor if I have ever heard one," I said with a little chuckle.

"Your presence on the ship consumed them. What galled the senator was your ability to disarm that *thag* of a son without any empathy and toss that priceless dagger into the sea! That little maneuver still baffles even me, and I have given it a great deal of thought." Felix wagged his head in disbelief while he scanned the room again for possible danger. After feeling safe, he turned his eyes back to me and began reminiscing. "I remember the day almost ten years ago when Senator Carnalus was murdered. It was a hot, stormy day. Marius the Gladiator killed 40 men and won the wooden sword, a day most Romans alive on that day will never forget. I did not witness the combat in the arena because I was on duty at the Praetorian Barracks. That would have been about four years before Sejanus built the massive wall around the barracks connecting the barracks to the city wall; and since then, it has forever been called *Castrum Praetorium*. However, I distinctly remember that an old slave, as Senator Treverorum and Demos claim, did report the murder of Senator Carnalus. However, there was no report that Senator Vetallus's ten-year-old son was a suicide. I also remember the news of the death of the slaves on Esquiline Hill at the Vetallus villa. That story was brought by a *thag* named Lentulus, who I'm sure you know."

"I know Lentulus, and I'm surprised you know what a *thag* is."

"No, that is one of my questions for you," he said smiling. "Just to learn what that word means is worth more to me right now than your bounty, whatever it might be. Besides, I do not forget when someone calls me a name; and what eats at me is not knowing what a word means."

A warm feeling came over me as I contemplated explaining to this soldier the origin of the word *thag*. Perhaps it is prideful to know the answer to someone's question, which makes one look intelligent. This weakness of mine is clearly a sin, and I never did completely eradicate it from my long life. You might now understand why I babble on about everything I know. Perhaps it is my sin. But the only comfort I have today is knowing what is essential in your heart and not in your head. Knowledge will never get someone into the Kingdom of God. What is important to understand is, on the Day of Judgment, the Creator will evaluate everything including words as well as deeds; but the secrets of a man's heart are the focus of that eternal assessment. Just because a person feels clean in his or her own heart does not make it so. There is only one judge; and that is the one who owns the *cosmic latifundium* or, shall I say, the universe, which would include this little world where we live out our lives. Still, all the knowledge I have gathered in the many years I have been alive should be shared before I die tomorrow. It will not get me into Paradise but may help people understand their own lives, especially when they learn the little details that could and most likely will be lost in the future. I realize my mind is like a stream of consciousness weaving and flowing like a river headed to the sea. I feel as if someone needs my water before it becomes too salty in the ocean where it is headed.

"A *thag* is an old Sanskrit term from India. It is slang for a professional robber who strangles those he robs. A *thag* is a cold-blooded thief who leaves no witnesses to his crimes."

Felix leaned back with a broad smile. "I like it; and I will use it when appropriate in the future, which I think I already have."

"Yes, you already have used it appropriately."

"You might be right, and let us consider it my gratuity for not impaling you with my gladius."

"Gratuity? You mean money for a service?"

He nodded.

"I accept. However, that one word cost you a considerable fortune; that is, if you do not turn on me and try to collect my bounty."

"There will be a few more questions that I have that will replace my losses, which should be satisfactory to me. Now, tell me about that scar on your arm – is that what Demos claims to have done?"

"Yes, but I'm sure he did not tell the truth about how it happened. But, first, finish about Lentulus."

"I thought I was asking the questions?"

"Do not forget, I am paying for your cold beer and bread."

"That means I owe you something? I think I am going to spare your life and allow you to do what you came to Rome to do," said Felix with his teeth showing in a warm grin. "Now the question is how are you going to pay me for my answers to your questions? And my answers are costlier than beer and bread."

"If you wish, I will later show you how to disarm a *thag* with one hand."

"That sounds like a deal," said Felix as he let out a loud laugh. Realizing he was now causing others to look our way, he became serious and leaned towards me. "Beware of cold beer. It loosens the tongue of a man because it is easier to drink more of it over hot beer. Now, the last time I saw Lentulus was in Jerusalem maybe three months ago. He was with Marius the Gladiator."

"Marius the Gladiator? The one who won the wooden sword ten years ago?"

"Apparently your Jewish slave friend, who was captured in Jerusalem a few weeks back, had been hiding very effectively for the past ten years," explained Felix with a touch of mirth in his voice. "Here is a flash of news for you since you have been away from Rome's information stream going on now for almost a *deka*. Should I enlighten you?"

"I guess that will cost me the second trick with the hand that put Deva to his knees."

"You have a deal."

"Splendid. Also, tell me why you just said Lentulus arrested the slave in Jerusalem a few weeks back. I thought it was less than that. The Jewish clay thrower said he left Joppa as soon as possible after Lentulus apprehended him."

A smiling Felix nodded and said, "Since we now have a double deal, I will give you all the details. After Marius had won the wooden sword for the third time, he received an incredible amount of gold from Tiberius and other admirers. Within a year, he was bankrupt due to living a wild life of parties and unbridled debauchery. Your father came to the rescue and recruited Marius as his personal bodyguard in addition to Lentulus. It is rumored that Marius is also your father's personal assassin." Felix kept his eyes on me while he took a piece of bread not dipping it in the fish sauce and washed it down with more beer. I kept my eyes on him while I tried to absorb the enormity of what I was hearing. "I bet you are wondering why Marius and Mayus were in Judaea. You are possibly wondering if your father was also in that hostile, dried-up land the Jews call the Promised Land. That was also my concern. What I learned while in *Palestina* will pay me well from Sejanus. Here is what I know. After asking a few questions from the right sources, I discovered your *patra* rarely leaves Rome these days. His two shields against his enemies are the ex-gladiator and the ex-Praetorian, Marius and Lentulus. Therefore, I am guessing something imperative caused Ole' Senator *Patra* to send those two to the Promised Land looking for something without his presence. Are you following my logic?"

"Your logic is without blemish; please continue," I said hoping to learn more. If this man before me was telling the truth, I just might have a valuable ally-collaborator on my side, who also had the ear of Sejanus and maybe even that of Tiberius.

"When I first spotted Marius and Mayus, I said to myself, something strange must be happening if those two *thags* are in Jerusalem without your father. Now, this is one of my questions for you. The answer should give me some extra coins from Sejanus. I told you I work for Sejanus, not the Senate of Rome nor your father nor the senator with that *thag* son."

"I am afraid you must stop your narrative. I know nothing of this Sejanus person you keep mentioning. Who is Sejanus, and why do you work for him?"

"Fair enough. Sejanus's father was Praetorian *Prefect* years ago before the Guards were camped outside Rome. After Father Sejanus was appointed by Tiberius to be *Prefect* of Egypt, his son, Lucius Aelius Sejanus, became the *prefect* of the expanded Praetorian Guards here in Rome. That was when the *Castrum Praetorium* became a fort outside the northwestern walls of the city. I know this is hard to understand; but the Sejanus family now controls more than your father, which is saying a great deal. Sejanus has more power than any clan in Rome, and this rubs the 800 senators raw. For a pedigree, Lucius Aelius Sejanus does have a noble bloodline but only through his mother's side. Through his paternal side, he still is of the equestrian order, not the senatorial class. There lies the problem. Father and son are not completely from the senatorial class; yet, they control more power than any senator in Rome, including both your rich father and Senator Treverorum. Think about it. The father is *prefect* of the richest province in the Empire, and his son controls the only army inside the gates of Rome and on the soil of *Italia*. This is something to never forget. It was around the 54th Actium year when Sejanus, as *prefect* of the Praetorian Guards, and not Tiberius was the one who first quartered the Guards in Rome near the *Porta Viminalis* not hours away from Rome like during Augustus's rule. I am talking about the entire force, not just the few who stayed on Palatine Hill ten years ago or when I was stationed where the *Castrum Praetorium* now stands. Sejanus can truly be the founder of the Praetorian Guards because of his sole control that allowed him to move these cohorts to Rome as his personal army. Sejanus's justification for the entire force to be located in Rome is the argument that there is a need for more firefighters, police at night, and crowd control at the circus tracks and amphitheaters. To screen this obscene annexation of power came the treason trials. Since most senators secretly despise both father and son, those who openly voiced dissension ended up on the dockets before Tiberius. There have been thousands of treason trials, all orchestrated by none other than Lucius Aelius Sejanus, the *prefect* of the Praetorian Guards. He alone has silenced all antagonists. These trials all have been concealed as cases of disloyalty against Tiberius, but they are really aimed at the enemies of Sejanus. Most of those put on trial have not only lost much of their vast estates but their lives. This has been going on for years, all in the name of Tiberius, the Emperor of Rome. The senatorial ranks as I said are now around 800, not in the thousands when Tiberius first became pseudo-god of Rome."

"What is your role in these trials?" I asked wondering whether I was going to be one of Sejanus's victims.

"Anything that is out of the ordinary is worth money, and I am about to retire and could use a large payout. Yes, money makes this ugly world interesting. Over the years, I have been guilty of providing information that has led to many deaths. Those days are now over, thanks to my visit with the Baptist. He showed me the Way. When I asked him what I should do as a soldier, he instructed me personally to just do my duty and not lie and steal. He said soldiers are not to provide false information that could be used for someone's death. How John knew about my sins – only God could have told him. I repented right then, and he baptized me."

"Do you really believe this god of the Jews forgives when someone confesses his or her evil deeds?"

"Repentance means to turn around and go a different way – to change your mind. I will never sell anyone to Sejanus. However, all the information in the past that did lead to death did have more truth than falsehood; but I know God has forgiven me. You see, I have never falsified anything; but still I have blood on my hands. I sincerely repented before the Baptist. He would not put me under the waters of the Jordan River unless I had. How he knew I do not know, but he knew I was repentant. Now I want to spend the rest of my life rectifying my errors."

"It sounds like you are being honest with me. You have convinced me you have changed even though I never knew you until an hour ago."

"Now you can answer my question, which is why would Mayus and Marius be in Judaea without the richest man in the world, your father, Gaius Vetallus Crassus?"

If Felix were telling me the truth, I was not Sejanus's target; but maybe my father was. Why not give my father to Sejanus, and let Sejanus do my dirty work for me? With that in my mind, I began to test the waters. "All I can help you with is this: my father has been looking for me, and the reason for those two *thags* being in Judaea had to do with locating me. That old clay-throwing Jew on the ship leaving Joppa was coming to me to ask for help with his nephew, who knows where I have been the last nine and half years. That Jew on the ship out of Joppa did find me and told me his nephew was being taken to Rome. I believe Lentulus, Marius, and my old childhood friend are still on their way here considering how fast our bireme moved."

"I am sorry to inform you, but your friend and those two *thags* are most assuredly already in Rome. Actually, they all arrived here in Rome one week ago."

I just sat there with my mouth hanging open. How did this man know this?

"The ship I took out of Joppa with the boy's Jewish uncle put in at Rhodes for a good week. The main mast was cracked and had to be replaced. Did the uncle tell you that?"

"No, he said he came to Athens as fast as he could. Was there no other ship leaving Rhodes during the delay?"

"No. We all had to wait for the repairs before heading towards Athens. Normally, I would not tell you this; but I checked with the commander at Zea as soon as I arrived from Rhodes. I wanted to know if Senator Treverorum sailed on last week's vessel. He said no, Treverorum was scheduled for this week. While the commander was looking at his logbook, I saw the names Marius, Lentulus, and a prisoner on last week's bireme. The three of them left on last weeks' bireme. I am afraid you might be too late."

I must have looked like a chariot driver who came in last or crashed his chariot in the first turn. I wondered how long Eli could hold out under any type of torture. Everyone talks eventually according to Grillius, who spoke to me about such things. He said some men he knew held out for a week but talked in the end. Torture had been going on for eons because it works. Looking back at Felix, I asked, "Why are you telling me this?"

"I told you I like you. And maybe I am trying to change my ways. I will go one further with you. I will wait until tomorrow morning to report all of this to Sejanus. That gives you only tonight to do whatever it is you have to do. Since you most likely are too late to save your friend, Sejanus would pay a good price to learn of an assassination upon Senator Vetallus and why. By morning, you better be long gone from Rome." I just sat stunned by this new revelation. "What I want in return is why does your *patra* want you captured? He apparently needs you alive, not dead."

"This I cannot tell you."

"You cannot, or you will not tell me?"

"The latter."

"Like I just said, I am betting you are here to kill him tonight. Am I right?"

Now I was genuinely concerned, and I pushed away from the table very slowly while placing my throwing knife back into place at my right side.

"Look, Venu! I do not care if you kill him. I am sure you have your reasons. If I had those two *thags* looking for me, I would go to the snake and crush its head. Remember one thing: if you just cut off a snake's head, the head can still strike you with his fangs. You must crush its head before or after you cut it off. Do you understand what I am trying to tell you?"

I realized I had to give this man something that was truthful or I was going to be dragged before Sejanus tonight. "I will crush my father's head and be done with this foul business before morning." After I spoke, I just sat staring at Felix using the old Spartan tactic.

"Well, I think I just got my answer. Thanks. But the joke is on Vetallus and those two *thags*. All this time they thought you were in Judaea. Now you are here, and you are going to try to crush the snake before Marius and Lentulus *veto* you. This is all your business, not mine. But it all makes sense. I still do not know your motive, and I will not ask any further; but I will now change the subject. What does your term *veto* mean? Is *veto* a slang word here in Rome? This term I also picked up from your friend Demos. Apparently it is some slang you boys used at the Lyceum. Am I correct?"

"Deva is not my friend; and, yes, it is a word we used at the Lyceum."

With a broad smile on the soldier's face, he stated, "Veto means to kill. Now I have it. Another question you can answer. What does *deva* mean? Demos himself is willing to pay one gold *aureus* for this information."

I did not see any harm in this; and, actually, it would be fun for Demos to learn about the name Grillius used as his title. I moved closer to the table; and with both hands on top, I whispered, "*Deva* is another Sanskrit term for a demon, a fallen god, or an evil spirit."

"That makes sense. The Arabs I ran into while in Judaea used the word *jinn*. That is their word for a fallen angel or a dead person's evil spirit who cannot find a home and tries to possess people. A *jinn* must be similar to *deva*. Venu, you just made me a gold coin; I now owe you," he said still smiling and appearing almost too relaxed.

"If you owe me, then do not tell Senator Treverorum what I am doing here in Rome."

"Oh, he's already deduced that. My job was to make sure you got to Esquiline Hill safely tonight so you could *veto* Vetallus. That is what the term *veto* means? Am I correct?"

I nodded so slightly that, if Felix had not been watching, he would have missed it. "Treverorum and Vetallus are archenemies; and, if Vetallus were to die, I believe Treverorum could reap some of your father's assets, especially if Treverorum knew when Vetallus was going to be *vetoed*. But it might not be so easy with Mayus and Marius now back in Rome. I am not sure your hand tricks can defeat the both of them. What are you planning? Besides, that villa of your *Patra* is a regular fortress. Guards are protecting the outside and inside at all hours. Your father must have some serious enemies, and not just Sejanus."

"Do you think I am that transparent?"

"Come on, a schoolboy wearing the clothing of a Spartan mercenary is like a criminal carrying a *titulus* to his crucifixion. Nevertheless, if you have returned to Rome to kill your father, I would advise against it. That is between you and me and this table," he said thumping the wood with his knuckles.

"And if that is the reason for my coming to Rome, why would you advise against it?"

Felix leaned back on the stool and crossed his arms to show me he was not holding any weapon under the table. His gladius was probably leaning against his leg or resting on his lap, but he was disarming himself and openly showing me. "My reply to that is based on my real reason for entering the latrine and inviting you here."

Now I was confused; and, while I pondered different scenarios, the main door of the tavern blew open from a gust of wind rushing down the street. I concluded this was the prelude to the storm about to hit the city. The roomful of people all stopped to look at the open door as debris from the street skittered along the floor, and a slave boy ran to pick up the trash; and the outside guard closed the door. There was a strange silence; but the moment passed, and the crowd turned back to their conversations as if nothing had happened. I kept my eyes on the door and noticed the guard from outside stay inside. He stood awkwardly for a moment and then went and grabbed a stool and sat next to the door. I guessed he did not want to be out when it started to storm.

With my eyes fixed on Felix, I said with sincerity, "What do you think I have to offer you other than the meanings of *deva, veto,* and *thag*? Yet, I do appreciate the information concerning the return of Lentulus and Marius."

"Those three definitions are most valuable to me, but there is another reason for keeping you here for the moment. Now I will open my soul to you just a little. I envy you. Yes, as odd as that sounds, I do. For I wasted the past 16 years as a soldier and spy. I could have been studying and gathering knowledge, just like you. Knowledge is what I now wish to pursue. I once knew a very wealthy businessman, a *decurion* from Carthage, dying from a strange disease. He told me he once lived first for his work, second for his personal exercise, and last for his family. After the disease was taking its course, he said labor and training had been taken from him; but he still had his family, and he had realized family was the most priceless of all three. He had wasted his life with wrong views. In a week, I will have nothing, not even a family I can call my own. I want to find a wife and spend the rest of my life gaining the knowledge you have already taken the time to possess. You see, I am like the man with the disease. When I was in Judaea, I went out into the desert to spy on the man called John the Baptist. I found not a wild man but a powerful Jewish prophet commanding people to turn their thoughts and deeds in a new direction. Never have I witnessed a Roman general as powerful a speaker as this hairy, desert man wearing only camel skins and eating bugs. He claimed the Kingdom of God was near. As I have already told you, I asked him how a soldier could be allowed into the Kingdom of God. He said to follow orders, to not cheat and steal, and to not use my power to hurt others. I kid you not; it was as if he could read my thoughts. 'Soldiers are servants of the government, and all governments are agents of God even evil governments.' Those were his exact words. He told me to repent, change my thinking, and submit to what he called the washing of repentance. I did what he asked. I walked into the Jordan River; and with John's help, I went down into the water; and, when I came up, I was different. How do I explain it? I cannot. I stayed with John and his followers for a few days and learned a great deal. I learned of the prophecies of the Jews concerning their coming Redeemer-Messiah. I asked John if he were the Messiah, and he said no; but the Messiah was alive and coming soon. A myth you might ask? I do not think so. Have you heard about this Messiah?"

"I first learned about this person from my mother before she was killed on the 50th anniversary of Actium, the day Marius won the wooden sword for the third time."

Felix nodded, showing respect for my pain and then continued. "On my last day with John, a strange man about my age came walking out of the desert. He wished to be baptized, and John refused at first but finally agreed. What happened next is astounding, but I know what I saw and heard. It was as if the heavens opened, and I saw what John later said he saw. It was the Spirit of God descending like a dove, and it came upon this stranger. I did hear a voice that some said was thunder, but it was not thunder nor human. It clearly was a voice. It said, 'This is my beloved Son in whom I am well pleased.' Everyone present was stunned including John. What was very strange was I heard the words in Latin; and when I asked those around me, they all said the voice had spoken the very same words in Hebrew. That falls into the category of being a miracle. Later, after the stranger walked off by himself into the desert, John began to say this was the sign and this was the one. John said, 'I have beheld the Spirit descending as a dove out of heaven, and he remained upon him. He is the one who baptizes in the Holy Spirit. I have seen and have borne witness that this is the Son of God.' Those were the exact words of John. I am not sure why, but I must report this to Sejanus. It might cause other questions such as issues of my loyalty. My truthful answers might prove dangerous for me. My hope is he will accept my motives as pure, for I will not sell this information. I would like to retain my pension and my head. You see how valuable you are? Just by listening to me, I am able to work out a knotty problem."

"My mother on that last day of her life spoke of this Redeemer-Messiah. She told me to find him, but I always considered it just a woman's myth."

"No myth, I am sure of that. I asked about the stranger's name and learned he was a cousin of John. His name was Joshua or Yeshua. He is from the Galilee town of Nazareth. After I had learned where he was from, I knew then I had to investigate him."

"Would you say this man's Greek name is Jesos, or would it be Jesus in Latin?"

"That I would not know. But your being the scholar would know. I like the sound of Jesus over Yeshua."

"Tell me about this town in Galilee."

"I learned that the distance to Nazareth from where I was down on the Jordan to be a two-day walk. I came to John riding a horse but dressed as a peasant. John saw through my disguise. Jews, on the whole, do not ride horses; so that may have been the tip-off. I started out for Nazareth before sunrise and made it by the next morning. Yes, I traveled all day and through the night; but I was on horseback. When I arrived, I quickly learned that Jesus was not there. No one would speak to me, even his family. I met the mother, a couple of younger brothers, and one sister. I learned that a second sister was away in another town preparing for her wedding that would soon take place before the coming Passover Festival. The entire family was very humble but reluctant to share what Jesus was doing. No one would give me any details about Jesus until I had irritated them with questions for two long days. I assured them I was not leaving until I learned something about Jesus. The brother named James finally conceded. He said he would tell me one story on the condition that I leave after hearing it. I agreed."

"Do you still remember the story?" I asked now drawn into his strange tale.

"Of course! It cost me two whole days of waiting. How could I forget it?" Felix took another bite of dog bread and a swig of beer to soften it. After he had swallowed, he wiped his mouth with the back of his hand and was ready to tell the story that was told to him by the brother named James.

"This story happened in the fifth year of Tiberius Caesar when Valerius Gratus was governor of Judaea. The story occurred in the late summer around the same time Marius won the wooden sword here in Rome."

"That would have been about ten years ago, the time I left Rome."

"That is right, almost ten years ago. The story was about one day in the life of Jesus, which began before sunrise when James's father, Joseph ben Jacob, was on his way to find work in Sepphoris, a neighboring pagan town not far from Nazareth. Herod Antipas, the tetrarch of Galilee, was rapidly turning the town into a political and military stronghold. A famous builder from Syria named Jabin had used Joseph ben Jacob in the last several years for special projects such as elaborate doors, ceiling beams, and windowsills. You see, this Joseph ben Jacob was a master wood and stone worker. James was very clear in telling me that Joseph was his father but not the father of Jesus. However, Jesus was his brother through his mother. I never learned anything about the father of Jesus."

"Is Jesus a bastard?"

"It turns out this Jesus or Yeshua did have an unusual birth. The rumor was he was virgin born. I did ask his mother, but she would not respond; and James did not say 'yes' or 'no' to my question on this subject. Well, anyway, this Jesus does look like his mother in the eyes and in the shape of her face when I saw him at the Jordan River. I can tell you this: Jesus is not a handsome man, but neither is he a pretty boy or soft-looking man. Don't get me wrong; Jesus is not ugly but just ordinary. He does have a pronounced beaked nose almost eagle-like and is as tall as you, which, I might add, is taller than most men even though you are really still a boy and maybe still growing. Perhaps tonight that might change," he said with a grin. "But let's hope you survive the night."

"I guess," I said not knowing when a person stopped growing or what he meant about not surviving the night. Why was he grinning? I knew a great deal of history, philosophy, and medicine; but each day I always discovered many more questions than answers.

"Jesus being illegitimate is not a problem when it comes to God according to James. He mentioned a man who was a bastard in the Jewish Scriptures. This man was a judge whose mother was a prostitute, and God still used him to free the Israelites from foreign invasion. I had to laugh when James said that God could use anyone since God also used a talking donkey to deal with a wayward prophet named Baal."

"Go on with your story. Why was the step-father of Jesus traveling alone on this road to a pagan town so early in the morning?"

"You, my new friend, would make a good interrogator. You see, I asked the same question. James told me that lately only the younger and stronger stonemasons and woodworkers were getting the trade work and the senior master artisans were sitting idly by. Jabin, the famous builder from Syria, would select his craftsmen at the beginning of each day. Frequently the work was given to those younger men who were first in line, and that was one reason Joseph was on the road so early this particular morning."

"I assume pride is a driving force in most of us humans, especially when we gain some years in the harsh, old world."

"James told me his father, Joseph ben Jacob, was now in his late sixties. He was considered the best craftsman in his trade in all of Galilee, not just Nazareth. I think your assumption would be correct. Joseph must have known his most productive years were gone, and pride is a driving force. He had five sons, all trained by him in both trades, stone and woodworking. They all helped Joseph on many larger jobs. That day he had decided not to bring any of his sons along because Joseph feared that the Syrian builder would choose them because of their youth, thus hurting his position as the patriarch of his family."

"Sounds like pride to me."

"Perhaps, but, we should not judge so harshly until we reach that age. I can assure you that, for a man in his late 60s, it takes lots of fortitude to walk such a distance, work all day, and then walk home in the dark. I walked my horse to Sepphoris after I heard this story, and it took me a good two hours. Now for the truth – Joseph later confessed to his sons that it was evil pride, which led him down that road so early. He said he stopped to rest on a flat rock repenting to his Creator for his pride when he heard in the distance the steady thuds of horse hooves hitting the well-trodden road. When the rider finally reached him, Joseph realized it was a hired mercenary of Herod, not a Roman soldier. This was good news; for the Romans, in general, are hated and feared by all Jews. Most of the mercenaries for Herod Antipas are not Jews but hard men from lands faraway. Hard men frequently come from humble beginnings. Most have some sympathy toward the poor locals."

"'Peace and good morning to you, old man,' called out the soldier in a deep, husky voice in fluent Aramaic as he reined in his mount near Joseph."

"'A little early in the morning to be heading this way,' replied Joseph."

"'I have to find a certain carpenter in Nazareth.'"

"'And what carpenter might that be?'"

"'Joseph ben Jacob,' answered the soldier."

"Surprised and intrigued, he said, 'Go no further; I am Joseph, the son of Jacob.'"

"'Your God does work in mysterious ways. This is good news. Now I do not have to add any more miles to my trip, and neither do you. Jabin, the Syrian builder, has asked for you specifically. He needs three sandalwood beams for Herod Antipas's new bathhouse. They have to be 10 cubits by 1 cubit square. They must be delivered before your Sabbath begins at sunset today.'"

"'A difficult task,' stated Joseph. 'The almug tree is an import from the Far East. King Solomon tried to raise a forest of them down on the Plain of Jezreel a thousand years ago, but not many of them are left.'"

"The mercenary retorted impatiently from atop his fidgeting mount, 'Jabin wants sandalwood beams, and he wants them tonight. He wants Joseph ben Jacob to deliver. I am not interested in discussing the history of the almug tree. There will be three silver *denarii* for each beam produced; and, if they do not arrive on time, I will be paying you an exclusive second visit,' said the soldier as he slapped his sword."

"'The beams will be delivered as Jabin wishes.'"

"'Excellent,' the soldier stated as he turned his horse back toward the direction he had come. After the horse's dust had settled, Joseph became jubilant and gave a blessing to the Creator of the Universe for the work and future money."

"When Joseph returned to Nazareth, the morning glow was opening up a new day. Joseph quickly went to his two-room house at the end of a narrow street near the brow of the hill where Nazareth stands. As he entered the living quarters, he saw his wife and daughters still asleep on their floor mats. Joseph quietly went to the food shelf, poured a cup of watered wine, and drank the lukewarm liquid quenching his dry throat. After placing the clay vessel back on the shelf, he returned outside and climbed the wooden ladder to the flat roof of his stone house. Stepping from the ladder, the carpenter saw the empty blanket of his eldest son. Jude, James, Joseph, and Simon were still asleep; but where was Jesus? Joseph thought he might know. He climbed down and walked toward the brow of the hill. There was his son kneeling next to a large rock with his palms turned up in prayer and his head covered with the hood of a large, loose-fitting mantle called a *simlah*."

Felix stopped to eat more bread and drink. After he brushed his tunic sleeve against his mouth, he asked, "Do you want me to continue?"

"Yes, finish the story," I urged realizing Felix was a good storyteller; and I liked it when a fish swallowed the hook and could not let it go. His story had a hook, and I had taken it deeply. The slave girl appeared again next to our table leaving another loaf of bread and a second bowl of *garum*. She then picked up a couple of the smaller copper coins still resting on top of the table. After she had left, I put the remaining coins into my moneybag to prevent that from happening again. Perhaps the girl was being kind, but I felt like I was just robbed. Felix pulled out a large *sestertii* and left it on top of the table for the girl for some reason. I had never been to a tavern before and did not know the rules. What I liked was the beer but felt nervous about all the people sitting around laughing and the slaves moving from table to table.

"Well, back to the story," said Felix with a smile. "Joseph waited until his son was finished praying before he told him he had met a man on the road to Sepphoris before sunrise. 'This man was coming to find me to tell me Jabin needs three sandalwood beams 10 cubits long and 1 cubit square. The beams must be delivered in Sepphoris before the Sabbath begins at sunset tonight.'"

"Jesus said, 'The remains of King Solomon's sandalwood forest on the Plain of Jezreel are the only sandalwood trees that are not imported. Besides, there are not many of Solomon's trees left. What the climate has not killed, the box trees have choked out. I do know where there are still some standing.'"

"'There will be much work, but it must be done today,' said Joseph."

"'I will go wake Jude and James, and we will be on our way.'"

"'Good, and I will sharpen the ax and get things ready with Simon,' Joseph said as the two, one bent with age and the other tall and straight with youth, walked together toward the house."

Felix stopped his narration again for a moment to eat and wash down the bread. He was acting as if he had all the time in the world to tell this tale. "Jesus at that point would have been in his mid-to-late-twenties, the eldest of all the children. By the time Jude and James were ready to travel down to the Jezreel Valley, the old man had sharpened their only ax."

"'We have Samson ready and plenty of ropes,' said Jesus, looking at Joseph." Samson was the name of the family donkey."

"I wonder if Samson could talk?" I said trying to be funny. Felix looked at me with a peculiar squint in his eyes apparently finding no humor in my question. I waved him on to finish.

"Now, James told me while relaying this story that, on this morning, he was in a foul mood. He confessed to me he had stayed up late the night before with some village friends drinking uncut wine. This was something he did about once a week, the evening before the Sabbath. He told me he did this without his parents' knowledge."

"How old was James?" I asked.

"Younger than Jesus, maybe early twenties."

"Wasn't he old enough to drink without his parents' permission?" I queried.

"You have a point. I believe you are out drinking beer without your parents' permission, and you are younger than James. But remember this was a small village and a different culture. I cannot answer your question concerning manhood and such things regarding all Jewish customs."

"Continue. You left off with James nursing the aftermath of too much wine."

"Right you are... James said he remembered Jude was chewing on a piece of dried bread when Joseph's wife appeared and wanted to know if she should fix a lunch for the boys to take with them. 'No,' said Joseph. 'The boys will have to be back at noon with three trees.'"

"Jesus took the ax; his two younger brothers; and Samson, the large-boned donkey. They all headed towards the road that led down towards the Plain of Jezreel. Within an hour, the three boys found the ancient almug forest and selected three sandalwood trees to bring down. They all stripped to their waists, and sweat began to glisten as they took turns with the only ax. Cracking and breaking echoed through the dense forest of the box, algum, and almug trees as the freshly cut timbers fell giving off a sweet scent. After the third tree had thundered against the ground, Jesus handed James the ax to begin removing the limbs and told how King Solomon's builders selected these trees for the pillars and steps in the first temple."

"'Now, how do you know that?' asked James, who confessed to me he had always been jealous of his brother's intelligence and natural wisdom."

"'And that strong fragrance kept insects off Solomon's orchards,' added Jesus with a kind grin as he gently touched his brother's sweaty shoulder and relieved his brother of the ax."

"Nothing more was said that morning as they stripped the trees of limbs and cut the trunks to approximate lengths. The three timbers were finally lashed together and tied behind Samson. Jude led the animal up the steep road back to Nazareth while James and Jesus pulled on ropes attached to the dragging logs to help Samson."

"By high noon, the sun was blazing in the last days of summer when the exhausted brothers reached Nazareth. Laughing children played in the streets, and a few women carried large clay jugs of swishing water from the town well. A group of old men and young boys sat in the shade of an old sycamore tree next to the entrance of the synagogue, the largest building in Nazareth. One of the old men saw Jesus and called out to him to help with a difficult passage from one of the psalms of David. James told me that Jesus was well known in Nazareth for his understanding of the Scriptures."

"'Jesus, you should not go over there,' yelped James very sternly in response to the beckoning old man. Jesus touched James on the shoulder for the second time that day and said, 'It will only be a moment.'"

"'There is still a lot of work to do,' retorted James."

"'You speak honestly, but there is more work than you imagine.' Jesus turned and walked over to the synagogue and squatted with the group in the shade. James said he dropped his rope and followed to hear the question."

"'What is the passage that bothers your understanding?' asked Jesus very kindly."

"The old man who had called Jesus over said, 'It is the passage where David, inspired by the Spirit, calls his son 'Lord' saying, *'The Lord said to my Lord, sit at my right hand until I put your enemies under your feet.'*'"

"Jesus smiled, and his face beamed as he asked the group: 'The question is, if King David calls him Lord, how is he the son?'"

"No one understood except the old man. He was pushed back by astonishment; his mouth had opened in awe before he blurted out, 'His son is God but in the flesh. How did you know this?' queried the old man."

"'It is just as the Scriptures prophesied; and, if you look carefully, you will see it hidden throughout the Scriptures. Do not be overwhelmed if I tell you the Scriptures do not give you eternal life; but, instead, the Scriptures are all about the Messiah.'"

"'Would you say that this is a mystery?' inquired the old man."

"'It is a mystery to those who think they can see. You, however, see; and no longer is it a mystery to you,' said Jesus as he stood and left. The group continued to stare as he walked away. A little girl ran up to Jesus in the middle of the street, and his hand went to her head. He squatted down to her eye level and said something to her, and she smiled before running off to play."

"At the carpenter's house, the other sons helped James and Jude pull the timbers up onto wooden benches. Jesus helped snap chalk lines along the lengths of the trees marking their four corners. The wife of Joseph poured cups of lukewarm water and served figs rolled in bread to the boys who had returned with the trees. They gave a blessing for the food and then ate as they worked with the adz, a tool with a curved blade at right angles to the handle. It was used to strip, trim, and smooth away the bark leaving only the black skin of the trees. The sweet scent filled everyone's nostrils, and the ruby-red interior of the trees was moist and wet in the noon sun."

"A few hours before sunset the trees had been polished and transformed into three magnificent beams. They were tied to Samson once again, but this time the load was much lighter than earlier. Joseph had constructed a drag sled for the beams to lie on insulating them from damage and for easier transport. As Jude, James, and Jesus left, Joseph called out, 'Make sure you receive nine silver *denarii*, and hurry back before the Sabbath begins.' The three knew very well they would not be back before the Sabbath began, for it always commenced at sunset; but off they went."

"Just as the sun was dropping near the horizon, they arrived at Sepphoris and found Jabin, the builder, yapping out orders sprinkled with Aramaic profanity to a group of nearly naked slaves who were struggling with pulleys lifting an enormous stone to the top of Herod Antipas's bathhouse."

"'We are the sons of Joseph ben Jacob, and we have the beams you ordered,' said James to Jabin. Jabin's eyes opened wide in the faint light of the dusty sunset. The Syrian ran his expert eyes over the ruby beams inspecting their smooth texture. He then put his right hand on the wood and smelled the sweet smell while feeling the smooth texture. He was a man who knew his craft."

"'Splendid work. My quartermaster will pay you,' said Jabin; and he ordered a slave to take the youngest to be paid. Jesus and James stayed with Samson untying the ropes. James said he spotted the first star, which signaled the Sabbath was about to begin; but the inky-blue sky was some ways off, and they still had some light left. 'The Sabbath is about to begin, and we still have to journey home. What are we to do?' asked James of his older brother."

"Jesus chuckled and warmheartedly patted James on the shoulder for the third time that day. 'The scribes and their innumerable legal restrictions have become a burden to my little brother. The Sabbath was meant to be a day of blessing, not imprisonment! Now hurry, and untie these beams before a scribe attacks you with stones for untying knots on the Sabbath! I'll get water for our friend Samson.'"

"James did as his brother instructed but also watched as Jesus walked over to the city well only a few paces from the bathhouse. An old Jewish woman was leaning over the edge of the well trying to pull up a bucket of water. Jesus noticed that the rope was lying next to the well and the woman was using her girth-belt to pull up the pail."

"'Woman, why do you not use the rope?' asked a polite Jesus."

"She looked up, surprised a man was speaking to her; but she answered, 'I paid a scribe-lawyer years ago at the Temple who told me that I could draw water with my clothing as a rope on the Sabbath, and I would not be breaking the law. I have to come to the well late because the other women chased me away because I am a sinner.' She pulled faster and got the wooden pail up. She poured the contents of the bucket into a clay pot and then ran away with her head down carrying the jug and her clothing belt in her hands."

"Jesus fastened the rope back to the bucket and dropped the pail to the bottom of the well. After he had pulled the bucket up with water, he untied the rope and carried the wooden bucket to the thirsty donkey. Jesus then took a large cloth and poured water onto it for the beast. Samson made loud sucking noises as he drank up the liquid refreshment from the soaked cloth."

"'I have the money,' called out Jude running down the street. Jesus returned the empty bucket tying the rope back to it before they all left for home."

"Does that end the story?" I asked hoping for more.

"That is the end of the story, and I left James and the little family. However, I did ask about old Joseph; for I did not see him at all those two days, I was in Nazareth. The family told me he had died the year before as he was trying to lift a large stone by himself. James said he had collapsed backward with the rock crushing his chest. I was told it was a very quick and a painless death even though it was quite violent."

We both sat in silence as Felix finished his beer and the last piece of bread from the second loaf. My bread was already consumed as the door blew open for the second time that night. The slave boy ran again to pick up some trash that blew in, and the guard stood from his stool and shut the door. Felix said, "It is time to part. I will go see Senator *Patra Deva* and his son and collect that gold coin, and you can go and do whatever you feel you must do up on Esquiline Hill. I might add, Senator Treverorum said yesterday on the *Achilles* that there is talk that Sejanus has your father on a list for arrest or assassination. If you do kill him tonight, there will be no government action against you if you are able to escape. Just do not kill anyone else besides Senator Vetallus."

"I am curious. To get the gold coin, you will have to tell Fat Senator you sat and had a beer with me. How will Corpulent Treverorum react to that?"

"Do not worry about me. You have bigger fish to haul into your boat, Fisherman," he said with a broad smile as he stood holding his gladius. He placed it back into its scabbard, and I stood to leave wondering how he knew I had been a fisherman.

"Demos told me, and I heard the word fisherman mentioned after you put Demos on his back."

"After I threw his graduation knife into the sea."

Felix got a good laugh from my comment on our way to the door. Before we went outside, Felix turned and asked, "One last question? Have you ever heard of the *Eumenides*?"

"Has not everyone? They are the ugly and angry women called the *Furies*. They believe that spilled blood cries out for vengeance and that no one escapes their wrath. I believe that is the origin of justice."

"Well stated, scholar-soldier. I think justice will be served tonight even if the *Eumenides* are a false story of the Greeks."

I said nothing but just stared at him without a smile trying to understand if he were a friend or a foe.

CHAPTER TEN

Rome – The night of Venus in the month of Junis, the 15th year of Tiberius, and the 1st year of Jesus's public ministry in Palestina, which began about two and a half months earlier with the first Temple cleansing in Jerusalem at Passover. Approximately, two months earlier, Jesus of Nazareth was baptized in the Jordan River by John the Baptist. (29 AD)

"Death does not concern us because, as long as we exist, death is not here. And when it does come, we no longer exist." Epicurus (Father of Epicurism)

Felix the Praetorian and I, the ex-student-fisherman, left the Roman *popina* and stepped into the fiercest windstorm I had ever experienced. The wind gusts came rushing down the street at speeds that would be two times faster than a four-horse chariot could move. Felix's blood-red cape and my scarlet-purple *chlamys* whipped in the wild wind's torrent. I tried to wrap mine around me, to no avail. Finally, I took off my cloak and attempted to ball it up under my arm. That made things worse because the temperature was dropping dramatically, so I wrapped myself again in my cloak to keep warm as Felix and I walked together through the now empty streets. Most of the lamps and torches had been extinguished by the wind, and it was relatively dark. By the time our eyes had adjusted, Felix had pointed out the lane that led up Esquiline Hill; and I recognized it as the same corner where Claudia's litter bearers had attacked me on my way past here years earlier. I swallowed the bile taste in my throat as I acutely recalled that event that seemed as if it had just occurred. I felt an inner coldness looming above me that had nothing to do with the wind or darkness. Felix put his head near my ear and told me he was going to leave for Quirinal Hill, and I wondered again if he was really an ally or adversary. I could not figure him out or his story of the Jewish carpenter and his sons. What was that all about? Yet, there was something likable about Felix. I thanked him with my head, eyes, and a smile.

I watched Felix disappear around a corner and stepped up next to what had been the bakery building years ago. Leaning into the brick wall, I was attempting to remain still and wait to see if Felix would double back and follow me before I proceeded up the darkened lane to my father's villa. After a considerable time of waiting and watching, I tried to come up with a plan to get into my father's villa. Nothing came to mind, and I just looked around trying to move only my eyes. Everything seemed familiar except the trees and bushes that were on both sides of the lane twisting up towards Esquiline Hill looked much larger than I remembered even as they were bending in the wind. My mind launched into many schemes to gain entry into my father's villa; but all seemed fruitless, especially if guards were patrolling the premises. I was not certain on exactly what to do once I reached my father's villa. In an uncharacteristic act, I found myself asking Anab's God for help. It was either that or pray to the Unknown God since I was utterly void of religious faith of any kind. After I had whispered a short prayer, I wondered why I had done that and remembered Felix had also prayed for me before we shared our bread and beer. I wondered about all that Felix had told me. Was he now a Jew since he had submitted to baptism? Who was Felix? My mind was working like an abacus in the hands of Zeno, who could throw beads so fast the eye could not keep up. I had many questions and very few answers. Everything was twisting in my thinking just as the wind was pulling at the trees and bushes. A large piece of garbage flew down the street; and I wondered, if I were struck by anything heavy, could it kill me before I made it to my father's villa. I decided that Felix was not following me and stepped away from the bakery wall. Right at the moment a red roof tile went flying near my head did my life became much more complicated than I could have ever imagined. The roof tile stopped me out in the middle of the street, and then I heard a familiar voice call out from the dark shadows behind the bushes where the lane split off towards Esquiline Hill.

"Well, if it isn't Grillius Junior!" came the familiar shout, a second time.

I stepped towards the voice with both bronzes hidden at my sides but inside the flapping folds of my scarlet-purple cloak. After crossing the street, I brought out my right hand with the hilt of the dagger resting on the tips of my fingers concealing the blade behind my hand and wrist. From this position,

I could flick my hand straight out with an underhanded throw, and place the dagger on any target I wanted without anyone knowing I held a knife. Coming out of the bushes were Demos and five other dangerous-looking men. Had I not stopped to watch for Felix to return, I would have walked into a trap with three adversaries on each side encircling me. As it stood now, I had all six spread out in a line blocking the lane in front of me. I wondered how long they had been there. I decided to retreat a few steps to give myself more fighting room. Moving backward ever so slightly, I stepped out in the center of the intersection of the street and the lane going up towards my father's villa. All I had to do now was wait for someone to make the first move. There was some light coming from a wall to my left that had a few lamps still burning in wall niches. These lamps were like ship lights with thin transparent mica sheets forming a cover around the flames. While I waited, I recognized the two soldiers from the bireme; but they were now out of uniform, both having exchanged their red cloaks for dark gray ones. Everyone was dressed about the same with their heads covered with rags or caps like brigands or sailors. One man wore the signature red cap of a Roman freedman. The whole bunch was a tough-looking lot – Praetorians out of uniform or Rome's famous street fighters, the thags Demos used to talk about when we boys sat in hipbaths back at the Lyceum. I remembered the many stories Demos recited during his bragging sessions in the bathhouse. Apparently, he was not fabricating about gangs attacking people in the darkened streets of Rome and killing them for sport. Some of these men might be the very ruffians that roamed the streets killing and robbing anyone who ventured out without bodyguards. Even the wagon drivers, limited to be on Roman streets only at night, were in peril from these groups of *thags*. Most wagoners formed into small caravans armed with men clutching swords and spears for their own protection from the theft of their cargos or the possibility of being murdered just for fun.

"It must be the fate of Mars our meeting you, Venustus, out here in the dark on Venus Night!" yelled out Demos in a loud, sarcastic pitch, to be heard over the blowing wind. "We were coming to your father's villa to get the money for my dagger you tossed into the sea when we spotted you with Felix. That is a pity he left you since he knew we were waiting here at this corner. Having you eat with him at a tavern was to give me time to round up a few friends. You remember my telling you how dangerous the streets of Rome were at night, especially, a dark, windy night like this one?"

I felt like a fool regarding Felix. Now I took him as an enemy. I absently looked down the street where he had gone and saw no sign of him. Looking back towards Demos, I yelled back over the wind, "I told you I would bring it to you tomorrow!" I needed time to look for the type of weapons each man was carrying, but all were hiding their hands under their dark cloaks as they slowly tried to circle around me. I backed up some more until my left heel bumped into a stone curb. The six men had now formed a semicircle around me cutting off any escape. I was not worried, for I did not plan on running away from any fight. I was going to battle or die; but, hopefully, I would only have to take on one at a time.

Once I had assessed each man, I began to experience an elevated rush, a feeling of excitement that displaces the danger with a mighty boldness. This was an eerier and somewhat extraordinary stimulus building up as if I had the upper hand even though it was six against one. I began to feel an eagerness over what was about to happen, and fear became a faithful associate. A stratagem developed in my mind while I further assessed each man's particular movement. Several had old wounds that caused them to favor one leg over another or an arm that did not hang just right. These were all weaknesses to exploit once the fighting began. Grillius had taught me well, and I smiled to myself.

"So, where is your *Pater*? Isn't he here to rescue you, Deva?" I yelled across the wind stepping away from the curb making my final observations.

"Stop calling me that, or I will cut your tongue out!" he bellowed as he produced a new dagger from his cloak; this *cultellus* was not as bejeweled as the last one but was just as deadly.

Everything Grillius taught me began to race through my mind: Never tongue-lash; do not use your hands if there is a weapon nearby; study everyone; and take out the most dangerous threat first, not necessarily the one you want. I was never good with rule number one.

"One more step towards me, and I will *veto* you!" I called out very calmly buying more time to study my surroundings in the dark, windy lane with the light of only a few lights in the mica casings. Everyone stopped positioning possibly wondering how I was going to harm anyone.

"*Veto*? *Veto*?" Demos laughed. "These men do not know what you mean!"

"True!" said the meanest and ugliest of the six, the one wearing a red cap with the long end blowing out over the man's left ear. He took a step out of the line of six and said, "What? I forbid? Isn't that what *veto* means?" He snarled turning his head to see if anyone was laughing. When he looked back, the lamplight reflected two white scars paralleling his face from eye to chin, most likely received in some previous knife or sword fight. After he had perceived what he wanted from his friends, he pulled an enormous falcata out of a scabbard hidden under his cloak. I had seen this cruel-looking sword only once before. That was the one Grillius owned, and he had told me it was his primary weapon when he was a mercenary. Its origin was commonly believed to have been that of the Barbarians from *Hispania* known as the Lusitanians. The Lusitanians may have had this sword introduced to them by the Celts, or the Etruscans, or maybe earlier Greek colonizers into this land west of *Italia*. These Lusitanians were a proud people with a kingdom that occupied most of the western side of *Iberia*. Their last great leader was Viriathus, who eventually lost Lusitanian to Rome almost two hundred years ago. This was during the Roman Republic when the Senate sent *Praetor* Servius Galba to subdue these peaceful people. Galba was, in time, victorious after using unspeakable tactics, which led to the submission of the Lusitanians and their later demise into the Empire.

What is also well known about this Spanish sword was its presence decades before Viriathus and Galba when it appeared in the hands of most of the troops under the Carthaginian commander Hannibal Barca, son of Hamilcar Barca. During what Rome called the Second Punic War, Hannibal had attacked *Italia* from the north, first crossing the *Iberia Peninsula* before crossing the Alps. Not only was this an unbelievable feat, it was accomplished during winter; and Hannibal also brought some elephants with him across the Alps. Just a handful of Hannibal's troops carried another famous sword from *Hispania*. This second sword was called a gladius. In time this became the sword Rome adopted over the Greek *xiphos* or the falcata as its primary fighting weapon for the legions. The falcata, a single-edged sword, was not double-edged like the gladius but was about the same length or a little longer than its cousin. The falcata was more of a slashing and cutting sword over the gladius, which was primarily a thrusting weapon to be used with a simple underhand stroke. Unlike the gladius, the falcata had a long, enclosed handguard that enabled the user to twirl it into a stabbing or thrusting weapon; rotate it again, and it became an overhand slashing sword. The front half of the falcata blade from the tip to the middle was wider than near the handle. Grillius told me he felt it was exotic looking with its curved blade, which gave the weapon an erotic look. Grillius always said he liked the falcata because he felt it gave its owner a slight inner-emotional edge over any opponent, all because of its terrifying look, especially if an adversary had never seen one before. The sword was slightly heavier than the traditional gladius, and he warned me that this could become a disadvantage to its wielder if it were used like a gladius against a gladius. To use this sword correctly required hours of practice and powerful arms and fingers. This unique-looking, single-edged blade slopes forward toward the point. Near the hilt, the blade dips in; but near the point, it is bowed or arched out. I believe, but cannot swear to it, that its name originates from an ancient Greek-Thracian word for *sickle*. The word falcata certainly has a Greek feminine ending. If the word were Latin, it would be called falcatus or Falcataus, with a masculine ending like in the word gladius. No Roman I know would use a feminine name for his sword; only a masculine title would be acceptable. The Romans are just like every culture of which I am aware: the greatest curse from any god is for a man is to die at the hands of a woman. I personally see this strange sword with the curves of a woman deserves the name it has.

"When fighting someone with a falcata," Grillius instructed, "never allow your opponent to attack with the blade over his shoulder because the shape of this sword puts the weight at the end when delivered, which has the power of an ax along with a long cutting edge. I am sorry to tell you this, lad; there's simply no way to defend against this sword without a shield. You can try to roll away at the precise moment the swing is in motion; but, still, you better be ready for a counter move if the sword misses."

My thoughts were running through my mind as quickly as the wind was blowing. Red Cap apparently knew how to use his falcata, demonstrating as he twirled it twice above his head before settling it on his shoulder for a classic overhand, downward slash. I waited until he was two quick steps away from using this devastating blade. I made no move, showing Red Cap I was helpless to prevent either his blade from cleaving my head in half or chopping off one of my arms. Demos and the others grinned and seemed to relax slightly, indicating to me that they believed in the skill and strength behind Falcata Man.

"Never tongue-lash" was Grillius's rule number one, and now I knew why. Action or death was the only option in most cases. Red Cap started his attack by lifting his right foot; but, before his booted foot touched the ground out in front of him, he began an ungraceful fall backward with a bronze throwing knife sticking out of his right eye socket. There had only been an upward twitch of my right hand and a swish sound of the knife flicking up from my underhand throw. Now there was only a dull thud of the Falcata Man hitting the stone pavement with his mighty sword bouncing off the paving stones out in the center of the street. It was just like the story of David and that Philistine that Anab described in Hector's house just two nights ago. Even though this happened in a matter of moments, it was all that was needed to stop the others; and it was as if I had all the time I needed to think and react to the next attack.

"You are next, Deva!" I spat the words loudly over the wind. In my right hand, I was now holding my second and last bronze knife in the throwing position with the handle touching my right earlobe and the blade tip between my thumb and first finger when I realized I had again violated Grillius's first rule. The dense wood handle gave the knife equal weight to the blade. I should have already downed Demos before Falcata Man hit the pavement. What was wrong with me? Why had I hesitated? This may have been one of the greatest errors of my life. My mouth had overridden my training. Now I realized this scar-faced Falcata Man was not yet dead but was lying on his back with the handle of my knife sticking out of his right eye as he mumbled incoherently for help, which seemed to unnerve the other men with Demos. My plan had always been to put my last throwing knife into Demos and then go for the falcata that had been forgotten on the pavement one step away at the foot of the quivering, scar-faced street fighter. This I realized must be a touch of what war must be like with fear filling the air along with confusion and chaos.

"Back away, Galeno!" roared a deep, booming voice before a blur came out of the shadows. It was Felix bellowing before he lowered his shoulder into the back of someone who was now sprawled out on the street face first. The downed man could not get up because Felix's had placed his sword tip to his neck. "And what are you doing here, Dulius?" Felix asked loudly over the wind, looking towards another man. I now recognized Dulius as the other soldier on the bireme who was also out of uniform.

The man said nothing with his head lowered in shame. Felix then looked over to Demos and said, "Senator Treverorum clearly said Venustus had until tomorrow, and I alone was to follow him to his father's house. I am afraid I will have to help your school friend get home as ordered even if I have to kill Galeno and you, Dulius. And perhaps you, *Deva,* should tell your old school friend there was no plan for me to eat with him while you gathered your *thags*!"

I kept the knife ready but was becoming confused with what was the truth. I realized that it must be Galeno on the ground with Felix's sword at his neck, and Galeno was also no longer wearing his Praetorian uniform. Dulius slowly put away his sword and said something to Felix, which I could not hear because of the wind. The words had been some kind of threat aimed at Felix, but it must have been some sort of bravado to save face before Dulius left the circle. Felix allowed Galeno to stand; and he, too, followed Dulius down the street and into the dark with his gray cloak flapping in the wind. Falcata Man, with my dagger still protruding from his eye, stopped moving; but I did not lower my blade that was still aimed at Demos.

Felix figured what would happen next after Falcata Man stopped writhing on the ground. "Demos, let's be smart and go home; or Venustus will put his knife into your eye like this *thag* on the ground!"

"Father will deal with you, Felix!" hissed Demos probably wondering how Felix knew the word "*thag.*"

"I am only following his wishes as you well know. There will be no trouble if you extricate yourself now!"

Demos had been humiliated in my presence twice in the past two days. This time Felix most definitely had saved his life, and Demos was too stupid to understand he was seconds from having my dagger in his eye like Falcata Man. With a sour-looking face, he put away his cruel-looking knife and followed Galeno. Felix turned to the other two men still holding their ground; and in a deep, booming voice, he gave them an ultimatum to go or be *vetoed*. They now understood the meaning of the word "*veto*" and elected to leave. I noted Felix's tone considering it potentially useful in the future as a form of control. It was something Grillius never taught me because Grillius would never use his voice as a weapon, but it worked if you had the hardware to back it up. An ancient Spartan phalanx was well known for their silence when charging another phalanx. Evidently other armies using the phalanx tactic would scream like lions to build up their courage. The Spartans were trained to be silent. Their quiet discipline was maintained to hear the horns and flute orders blown by their commanders during a battle. Besides, the Spartans were already feared because of their unbeatable reputation for being the world's finest warriors trained from age seven to withstand any type of punishment in silence. In time, I, too, became more like Grillius enduring unbearable pain silently; I learned and discovered that silence does unnerve your opponent as much as a hard stare.

Felix went over to Falcata Man once everyone had gone and pulled out my dagger from his right eye in a quick, smooth motion. He then cleaned the blade on the man's tunic before handing it back to me. "I believe this ugly brute has a reward on him. A profitable day indeed! I will take him to the Praetorian barracks and see if I can collect. Do not worry about his death. You will be cleared on self-defense. I will make certain of that."

Do not worry about his death? I had never killed a man before, and then my right hand began to shake. Felix did not notice but instead scavenged the dead man's clothing. Pulling a moneybag from the man's belt, he tossed it to me. Surprisingly, I caught it in midair without any problem. After snatching the bag in mid-flight, the tremors had suddenly stopped when my fingers closed around the unexpected treasure. The moneybag was the size of my fist and full of heavy coins.

"Keep it. *Thag* will not need those worldly coins, and I do not want you arrested for sneaking into any more latrines," laughed Felix. Now he was making jokes with the dead. Grillius did not teach these things to me, and I felt unprepared for this kind of life. I still had a great deal to learn.

"You keep it," I said thinking it blood money.

"You *vetoed* him. That's why it's called 'war booty,'" Felix said as he removed the bronze-and-wood scabbard that was covered in a dyed-red leather. Stepping over the sword on the pavement, Felix placed the falcata back into the long, open-necked sheath. "This is not the best falcata I have ever seen, but it is dark out tonight. This sword could be worth more than the reward or maybe not. If I believed in the *Fates*, or as the Romans call the *Parcae*, I would say those three goddesses are watching out for you tonight."

"I will take his cloak as well," I said after I looked at the hooligan's scabbard and sword in my hands.

"Now that is the spirit," commented Felix who showed no hesitation as he completed stripping the body. It looked as if he had done this many times before. There was not any blood on the cloak of gray wool, and I wrapped it around the scabbarded falcata.

"How far is your father's villa?"

"It is just up the lane, not far from here," I shouted with my free hand cupped around my mouth to make sure he understood my words.

"I will go with you and then return to carry this *thag* across the city," he yelled close to my ear. "I like that term '*thag*,' and I did not realize I would be able to use it so many times in one day." We both laughed as we headed up the steep lane together.

"Thank you, Felix; you most indisputably saved my life tonight."

"Indisputably? Someday I shall talk like you. Now, about saving your life, that is not the way I see it. I saved Deva's life. I did not realize the Lyceum was a military school. If I ever have a son, I will send him there for his schooling."

"It is not a military school!" I said trying to defend its intellectual reputation.

"Someone trained you? You did not learn that hand trick on your own, nor how to throw daggers."

I did not answer remembering Grillius's code of silence.

"Well, Venustus, I am a good spy; and somebody trained you. That fellow is someone I would not want to meet out on a dark lane in Rome during an approaching storm. I will put that dead *thag's* moneybag on a certain Spartan mercenary named Grillius. And do not look surprised. Demos, or Deva as you call him, has a big mouth; and I had to listen to him brag and dribble on and on during the entire voyage here."

We both laughed again as the long-awaited rain began to fall from the sky as the wind increased to a steady gale force. Treetops bent completely over in the slashing, horizontal rain; and we were now shouting next to each other's ear to be heard. There were cracking sounds like bones breaking as branches tore away and flew to the ground. Some of the bigger trees actually uprooted and crashed to the ground with tremendous and terrifying force. Up ahead on the steep lane, an enormous tree came down in front of us blocking our way. We began to laugh since it did not hit us. Once the sudden, violent disturbance passed, Felix took my arm in the military shake with hand to elbow; and I did the same. It was a soldier's special ritual after combat to celebrate life and friendship, something Grillius did teach me. This was the first time I had shared this moment with another man beside Grillius, but there would be many other occasions in my life that this kind of moment would come and go. I am not sure what women do with each other in such cases, if anything; but men do bond differently than females, especially after they have shared a dangerous situation and survived.

After climbing through the downed tree, we soon stood soaking wet in the circular, paved entrance to my father's famous villa. The huge fountain and the carvings of stone figures in the center of the pavement were still the same. Wind and rain had extinguished any torches or lanterns on the walls near the entrance making everything blacker than if I had been in a cave without a torch. All seemed quiet inside the villa as we stood together near the front *ostium,* which guarded the villa with a heavy bolt on the inside of the massive, double wooden doors. I wondered where the guards were, but I guessed they thought no one in their right mind would attempt to attack this villa in a storm like this.

"This is where we part. My job with you is now over. I promise I will not follow you again, at least not tonight. I will go and carry Scar-Face, or shall we call him Falcata-Man, back and collect his indisputable fee. I am sure he is the *Cretan* I think he is; there is a bounty for his hide. I will also report to Senator Treverorum and get my version of the story on the record."

"I do actually owe you my life. I have a feeling we will meet again, and I will pay you back someday," I said realizing it was a stupid thing to say; for how would I ever find him again? "What is your family name should I need to find you someday?"

"I believe we will cross paths again, but it will be God who will direct us. You have the spirit of a Spartan. My father years ago taught me to be aware of Spartans. He taught me to tell a Spartan just by the way he walked with his nose up in the air. You have that air about you."

With that statement, my eyes grew wide; for I knew now I had seen Felix before. He was the vagrant, or pretending to be a vagrant, at the *Painted Stoa*.

"It took you a while to recognize me, didn't it?"

"The man at the *Painted Stoa* dressed in rags. What was that all about?"

"I had to confirm who you were after the old Jew and you entered that little, stone house in Athens. I waited until early in the morning until you left. I followed you into the *Agora*. While you were putting on your Spartan outfit, I paid a poor man I had passed in the streets for his rags only for a short time. When I talked to you, I put some of the puzzle together. I realized you had to be Venustus, the long-lost son of Senator Vetallus. I was thinking of capturing you; but after I saw you in that Spartan outfit, I thought maybe you could handle yourself. Now I know what you did to that *thag* with your knife and after I saw what you did to Deva on the ship... which reminds me, you still didn't show me your hand trick you used on Demos-Deva."

I held out my hand, and Felix gave his. In a split second, I had him on his knees. "Do you think you can practice that move?"

When I released him, he smiled and said, "I will practice. That is quite a trick."

"One question. How did you know I practiced throwing daggers out in the grove of cedars?"

"I told you I am a spy. When I returned wearing the rags, I saw the wooden target in your open storage room. Before I revealed myself, I walked out into the grove and figured out from the footprints in the grove of trees what you were doing with the target."

"You are telling me you figured all that by looking at the ground out in the cedar grove?"

"I told you I am good at what I do. Now, my family name is Cornelius if you require finding me. Ask for Scipios Cornelius Felix. Felix is my nickname or designate since my early military days. I will surely wager that our paths will cross again; I can feel it in my bones," he said with a genuine smile. "Remember our lives are in reverse. I will become like you now learning while you will spend many years in combat."

It was a strange prophecy given to me as if he were speaking for God. I accepted it as truth; and it did come to pass just as he said, but it would not be for many years later.

I will consider, if, for some reason, I survive tomorrow's ordeal at the *Colosseum*, to record the rest of my life's story and tell about Felix Cornelius, whom I did save from death after a battle with the Celts up in Gaul. That is a good tale if I do say so myself. Unfortunately, it will be lost to history after the sun sets tomorrow.

Now, standing in the rain in front of my father's villa, I finally concluded Felix was an ally. With his right fist clenched and touching his heart, the Roman ceremonial gesture of friendship or submission to another is not something Praetorians normally would do to another. It was more of a legionary gesture, and I returned the signal much in the same way Grillius and Felix had grabbed my arm to shake farewell. After Felix had thumped his chest, he turned in a smart military spin with his feet together and disappeared into the dark curtain of rain. I stood there wondering about this strange man until I remembered where I was and why. I put my hand on the falcata hidden by the wet gray cloak and walked up to Senator Gaius Vetallus Crassus's front door or *ostium*. Using my left hand, I rapped twice with the bronze knocker. I waited as the wind and rain seemed to slacken a bit. Bolts of lightning began their march for the city from the south striking here and there with loud cracks, and I quietly counted three pomegranates. Finally, one of the heavy wooden doors opened part way; and standing in the gap with light pouring out behind was the most beautiful woman I had ever seen. She was standing there in a simple white *stola* that went to her ankles, and she was holding a small clay palm lamp in her left hand. Her beauty struck all other thoughts from my mind; and, when recognition began to grow, my heart seemed to jump in my chest. Her simple, dimpled smile and the expression in her translucent blue eyes confirmed my suspicion that I knew her. It was the little girl from ten years ago in Ostia, now all grown up. Her olive complexion appeared almost perfect when a lightning bolt lit the entrance like the middle of the day. I think I was just standing there with my mouth hanging open in surprise when she spoke first. "Is that you, Venu?" she asked with the most pleasant questioning voice I had ever heard.

"Messina?" After I had asked, I thought of the small sea town out on the distant point of *Sicilia* when the Seagull pointed it out to me. I believe she said she was named after Messini, the city-state in the Peloponnese of Greece, not far from Sparta. I began to wonder if the town in *Sicilia* started as a colony of the *Hellas* city-state called Messenia.

My thoughts were vanquished when she nodded, and she looked as if she wanted to hug me; and here I was wet as a dog after a swim in a river holding a concealed weapon in my hands. She then looked over her shoulder apparently hearing something. Turning back to me, she quickly whispered in a voice loud enough for me to hear but not for who was coming. "Eli is in the atrium. I think I know why you are here. Everyone is looking for you and some scroll. I want to help, but someone is coming."

"Meet me at the back wall in the garden at the other end of the villa," I quickly instructed.

She nodded as a brick of a man in a short, green tunic pulled back the heavy wooden door in Messina's right hand revealing the marble entranceway that I knew very well. "Who is this?" croaked the ugly man like a frog filling the empty area where the door had just been. I at once recognized him from the arena also ten years earlier, and he had not changed much in all that time. I realized he was now in his late twenties, not that much older than Messina and I. There were many scars on his face, arms, and legs; and he was one of the scariest creatures I have ever seen. This still holds true today, even at my old age of 90. This had to be Marius. Besides his arms, legs, and face being marked with multiple purple-and-white scars, this man had an acid attitude that had to be Marius, winner of the wooden sword three times. He had no left ear, and even a side section of his front scalp was missing a clump of hair where he must have been cut by a sword at one time. Without a doubt, his appearance alone was unnerving even if someone did not know his reputation.

"Who is this?" Marius rasped looking straight at me with his dark-yellow, narrow, and little rat-like eyes.

"I am Falcataus from *Iberia* looking for the villa of Senator Longus." This was all I could think up hoping Senator Longus still lived next door. I noticed Messina, who was now a step behind Marius, smiling at my quick response. I wondered if Marius was going to purchase my story considering I had a hidden falcata in my hands and the sword originated from *Iberia*.

"Falcataus from *Iberia*? You look more like you are from Sparta, and that is on the opposite side of the Empire."

I stared at him as a true Spartan would do without any rebuttal. After a few moments, Marius finally replied to my question. "The villa you want is over that way," he spoke in his raspy voice as he pointed with his scarred hand. His voice sounded like gravel being grated over broken glass. There was a long white scar running across his throat, so the sound was most likely due to an injury to his vocal cords. I had learned about these small, stringy looking bands, which Grillius pointed out during one of our death-house visits. How these little strands or cords in the throat make sound was a mystery to me.

"My apologies for disturbing you people on such a wicked night," I said as gracefully as I could and gave a slight bow. Turning away with my head down, I left Messina and the green-tunic monster staring after me as I walked out into the driving rain. It must have been a sight with my hair plastered to my head, and three days' stubble on my face, and my wearing a soaking-wet scarlet-purple Spartan *chlamys* along with military-type boots poking out from beneath it looking for some senator at night on the stormiest night on record. I had not put a bronze razor to my face since I left Hector's house to take my finals at the Lyceum; and I must have looked eccentric, to say the least, holding a wet gray cloak, which was apparently hiding something substantial in my hands. I am sure Marius recognized the shape was not that of a baby in my hands but more like a sword under the wet cloak. I wished I had my gray flop hat, but I had left it on the bireme thinking it was only going to be in my way. It would have been valuable now shielding me from this rain as well as hiding my face from Marius; yet, it would have been in my way when I encountered Deva and his friends down the hill and whatever else I had to do tonight.

Once out of sight, I made my way around to the back wall of my father's villa. I was hoping Messina was not going to get involved in this; yet, what was she doing at my father's dwelling? Was she living with the man who had murdered her own father in Ostia almost a *deka* ago? Once I reached the back of my father's *domus*, I noticed the wall was much higher than I remembered. A bolt of lightning, now high above me, streaked across the sky providing me enough illumination to see something projecting from along the wall's top edge. Clearly the height of the wall had doubled since I climbed it escaping Claudia as a little boy, and it looked like sharp glass or metal objects had been cemented into the top to prevent any unwanted intruders such as I was tonight. I went to a tall, skinny cypress tree that was higher than the wall. I took the falcata; and, with several swift strokes using both hands and counting the seconds after each flash of lightning, I was able to chop down the tree under the sound of several cracking booms. The tree was also bending down in the wind making it easy to cut. While swinging the falcata, I recalled again the story Felix had told earlier of Jesus and his brothers chopping down sandalwood trees in the almug forest. I still could not understand why he told me that story. It was entertaining and full of little details of this Jesus character. Yet, it had to be an important story in some way if Jesus had gone to see the Baptist and this desert preacher had made such a mighty declaration concerning his cousin once he came out of the water.

After the tree had fallen to the ground, I dragged the cypress over to the wall and leaned it bottom up so I could use the branches like a ladder. I sheathed the falcata and wrapped it again in the gray cloak but decided to leave it at the base of the wall. I quickly climbed to the top of the wall; sure enough, I did discover bits of glass and iron shards embedded into the plaster-cement to prevent anyone from scaling over it. I realized again that my father inevitably strengthened the weakness of his fortress after I escaped Claudia by going over this wall. I climbed back down and searched for a fist-sized rock that could serve as a hammer. After I had found one, I returned to the top of the wall. I was soaked to the bone, but I tried to dismiss my miserable condition. Using the cover of the thunder and rain, I pounded with the rock smashing down an area large enough to cross without being slashed to shreds. When the area was finally cleared, I left the rock resting on the top as a marker of the cleared area. In the rainy dark, I pulled myself up and over the wall. My purple cloak was thoroughly wet and clinging to me once I was on the other side of the wall. Being wet lamb's wool, it was now too heavy and rendering itself useless and even a hindrance in what I had to do. I was in the process of removing it when Messina came out of the darkness.

"Venu, is that you?"

"Yes, over here," I beckoned her to the wall with my voice.

She ran to me and embraced me burying her head into my wet chest. "Oh, Venu, I knew you would return someday. I have been waiting a long time."

I did not know what to say, especially to a female. I just held Messina for what seemed like a long time but perhaps was only a few moments. I finally asked, feeling like a cold fish out of water, "Messina, where is Eli?"

She did not answer but, instead, started to shake. I kept my arms around this beautiful creature who really cared for me. She was little and petite, not more than 5 feet 2 inches tall, with a weight of a little over a hundred pounds. I felt like a giant holding a flower. No one had shown me such open affection like this except perhaps my mother years ago.

"I knew you would come. I have prayed that you would come. That is why I have stayed at your father's house waiting for you. I did not know what else to do." Releasing her, I asked again about Eli. She looked up at me as she was more than a head shorter than I was. When I was holding her, the top of her head had come up to my upper chest. "Eli is tied up between two pillars at the far side of the garden. They are killing him," she said with a sad sigh.

I left her side stepping carefully into the center of the garden and looked towards the brightly lit atrium that had several braziers burning that were sheltered from the wind and rain. I could see there was someone tied up between two pillars with arms outstretched while people moved around him. Messina came up to me out in the garden and held my hand. "What are you going to do?"

It was difficult talking in this driving rain, so I took Messina by the hand and made my way to my old room off to the side of the garden. There was the familiar door, and Messina said it was a garden storage room. Looking inside, I could not see anything because of the dark; but at least we were out of the rain. The room smelled of manure and wet dirt; yet, it brought back memories of my mother and feelings of safety. In the darkness, I turned to Messina while she was still holding my hand. I felt a hot rush course through my body; and I took her into my arms, and our mouths met. I had never experienced such warmth and security that was sweeping through my entire being. I could not believe how wonderful this felt. It was more intense than when Messina was a little girl and she kissed me in the warehouse in Ostia on another dark, dangerous night. I realized I could not stay here even though I wanted to hold onto this feeling forever. As soon as I tried to enjoy this sweet sensation, it fled like a butterfly taking flight from one's hand, never to return anytime soon. I gently released Messina feeling her body slightly tremble, and I realized she would let me do anything to her that was in my mind or heart. This was the most incredible feeling of power that I had ever had. A wrong decision and I could conquer her and possibly injure her in some irreparable way. How and why I arrived at this understanding I had no idea. Holding her away from me with my hands on her shoulders, I had to change the subject. "Messina, tell me quickly. How did you come to be here in my father's house?"

She hesitated and then in a whisper said, "Zeno told me what to do if something happened to him, and it did. I just did what Zeno said. A man named Lentulus captured Zeno and me only a few days after you and Eli left Ostia. For my own protection, Zeno never told me where your two ships went, but that wicked, vicious man tried to get Zeno to talk. Unfortunately, before Zeno died, he did reveal where your friend had gone but not you."

"Lentulus being the man who tortured Zeno?" I asked.

"That is correct – Mayus Lentulus and his ex-soldiers. They did to Zeno what they are now doing to Eli. They tied Zeno up to the columns of the atrium and used a whip on him for two days. Then they cut him with a knife and pulled out his insides while he was still alive. Can you imagine such evil? Lentulus then placed your teacher's innards on a table in front of his eyes and started smashing them with a rod. It was then that Zeno began talking. He just wanted them to stop. He told them he sent Eli to Jerusalem in *Palestina*, but that was all he said before he fell asleep and never woke up. They killed him, Venu, because they wanted you and some scroll. It took Lentulus and Marius years to find Eli, but all of them arrived about a week ago. Marius was that horrible man at the door."

244

"Marius the gladiator," I said more as a statement than a question.

"Yes, you know him?"

"I know of him. I've seen him in action in the arena."

"Venu, both Lentulus, and Marius are very dangerous! How are you going to save Eli? I heard them say they were going to cut him up as they did Zeno. I think they are going to do it tonight. They have already flogged him for six or seven days. This is just like they did to that poor old man, but Eli is lasting much longer."

"They will not cut open Eli because I am going out there, and I will save him or die trying."

Messina moved away from me in the dark room possibly fearing the latter. "I do not think Eli will survive. I thought that you had come to save me."

I could not believe what I was hearing. Run away with Messina? Of course, I wanted to; but, to save myself by sacrificing Eli, I would lose myself. I could never lift my head again if I abandoned Eli. I looked at Messina in the dark seeing her now that my eyes had adjusted to the darkness. Standing before me was the loveliest creature I had ever seen. "Did my father make you a slave?"

"I am not a slave, but I do not have my freedom either. After Zeno had been captured, I was confined with him. Your father recognized me as the daughter of Flavius, his old partner from Ephesus. I confirmed this when I was asked. To protect myself, I told your father robbers or assassins in Ostia murdered my *patros*. Naturally, I did not reveal that he was the one who killed my *patros* – him and Lentulus."

"You did the right thing," I said trying to comfort her by taking her back into my arms after a massive boom of lightning seemed to shake the room and Messina jumped at the incredibly loud noise.

Messina gave a little giggle at what just happened; and I still could not believe someone this beautiful could like, let alone love, me. Messina wanted to talk, and I relaxed my arms from around her. "But your *patra* actually has been very kind and has treated me like a daughter. At first, I thought he might make me a concubine as I got older; but Claudia told him, if she found out that he deflowered me, she would kill him in his sleep. She is the only reason I am still a virgin at the age of 22. I do not think there is a girl in Rome my age who is still a virgin other than the 35 Vestal Virgins. And I have heard rumors that they are not virgins. Your father also promised me that, on the day I wished to leave with a husband, I would be a wealthy woman as the only inheritor of all the riches in my father's estate. If I do not marry, I get nothing. I decided to stay here thinking this is where you would return someday." She turned away in the darkness, but I clearly heard what she said next. "I have rejected many offers of marriage."

I gently turned her towards me and kissed her again on the mouth. In what seemed like an eternity was only a short, brief moment. All I could think of saying was, "Thank you."

"Now you are here; may the Creator of the Universe be praised. I can now be free of this monster and his wicked wife and those two evil men who guard both of them."

I thoroughly understood her sentiments, but I also was baffled by that phrase of praising the Creator of the Universe. "Are you a Jew?" I asked in a non-intimidating tone.

"I told you years ago my mother was a Jewess; and, therefore, that makes me a Jew. My father was a Greek just like your *mater*. Remember my telling you this in the warehouse at Ostia?"

"Yes, I remember," I replied but was not sure what I did or did not remember. A great deal had happened since then. I had stuffed my mind with knowledge and hard work, and the last nine months were consumed with learning the art of war. Another bolt of lightning lit up the little room, and I could clearly see her olive-colored skin and those soft blue eyes. The seconds between booms and light were now on top of each other. There was not much time left. "I must act quickly, but I want you to keep this for me," and I handed her the wet, scarlet-purple, Spartan, lamb's wool *chlamys*. "Please keep this, and I will come back for it and you. I, too, am a virgin, which is rare these days. I have had no desire for any other woman because of your kisses that night in the warehouse at Ostia."

She took the cloak with a sweet smile at my confession. She carefully folded the wet garment and then held it to her chest before she buried her face into the wet wool as she began to cry. I asked, "What is wrong?" I had no understanding of the behavior of women and their quick-changing emotions.

She looked up at me and said in a sweet, pleading voice, "Venu, I will guard it with my life. I have been selfish, and you have to go and try to save Eli before I change my mind."

Change her mind about what? Once again, I did not understand the thinking of the female sex. I kissed her forehead, which is something I would do to my mother before bedtime. "Messina, there will be only one way to contact me"; and I told her of Grillius at the Lyceum in Athens. "Write or go to him; he will know how to find me."

"Grillius at the Lyceum in Athens. Yes, thank you, Venu. We will be together again, and I will pray every night after you leave with or without Eli."

"And pray to your God for me as well. I need help from this God of yours."

"Yes, now go; or I will never let you leave this room."

"Messina, one more thing; and this is crucial. I need for you to send a letter to Grillius tomorrow. You must tell him all you know and for him to warn a man who was like a father to me in Athens. His life is not safe. After tonight, it will not take Lentulus long to discover how and where I came from. I lived with this man for the past nine and a half years, and he will have to leave his work and move to a different city. Lentulus or some other dangerous men will soon be coming to kill him if he stays in Athens. This will happen if I am successful or not tonight."

"I will send this letter tomorrow, and you will succeed. May God Yahweh go with you. I will go to my knees and pray towards Jerusalem after you leave. Yahweh will answer my prayers. I know He loves me."

"Write it tonight. You do know how to write?" I asked, not trying to insult her.

"Yes, I know how to write, read, and count," she said with a little hurt pride in her voice. I could not tell if she was smiling or not in the darkness.

"Take it personally to the imperial wharfs near the *Sublicius Bridge* near the Circus Maximus. A bireme will be returning to Piraeus on Sun Day, which is the day after tomorrow. Find the helmsman-pilot, a tall, skinny fellow on the ship. He will get the letter to Grillius at the Lyceum if you tell him I know he cheated me with the silver *denarius*. Make sure you say what I just said. I know he cheated me; and if he does this, I will not visit any harm upon him. Make sure you say, 'silver *denarius* for information.'"

"What is a bireme?" she asked innocently.

"A bireme is a long, narrow ship with two banks of oar holes on the side and a single mast with a blood-red sail. The sail may be rolled up, and you will not see that it is red; but look for the name of the ship. The name of the vessel, I believe, is *Achilles*. I am certain now. It is called *Achilles*, like Achilles' heel in the *Iliad*."

"Yes, I have read Homer. His nymph mother tried to make Achilles immortal by dipping the newborn baby into the Hades River Styx. In doing so, she held his heel producing a weak spot that Paris of Troy found with his poisoned arrow."

"Impressive," I said thinking she was a well-read and smart girl. I would have loved nothing better than to stay and discuss literature as well as hold and kiss her.

"I will do this. And Venu, always remember, I do love you. But you will have to give up *garum* when we are together again."

I felt embarrassed that I ate that smelly, gooey stuff just to offend Felix; and now she would always remember me whenever she smelled that awful fish sauce on someone's breath. "I will give up *garum* for you, and I love you as well," I found myself saying. A bolt of light lit the room again, I think it was the third time, and I saw her beautiful smile and those deep dimples on both sides of her mouth. I remembered being in this very room and not telling my mother I loved her on her last day in this world. Yet, I was back; and I did say that little word to Messina. My confession to Messina made me feel warm inside; and it was a healing moment in a strange, mysterious way, which prompted me to repeat it. "I do love you, Messina; and I have loved no other."

She was silent after my declaration; yet, I knew she did not reject what I said. Finally, she broke our awkward silence by saying, "May God, whose name is Yahweh, go with you. He will also protect you because Eli is one of His chosen ones." I nodded at this revelation before releasing her hands. Saying no more to Messina other than asking her to stay put and pray fervently, I turned to the door and the driving rain.

Back out into the garden and the pouring deluge, I felt like turning around and returning to my old room. I just wanted to go back and ask Messina to place her hands on my shoulders and pray for me aloud, but I did not. This became apparent to me later that I should have. Instead, I trusted my own abilities; and the events that were about to unfold still haunt me to some extent even now, some seventy years later. I would like to think I was young, inexperienced, and naïve; and maybe there is some truth to that. However, I made the mistake of my life when I chose to live by my own abilities and not trust in the Creator of the Universe that dark stormy night. Clearly, I did not know who the Creator was; but I do not think anyone, especially at the age of 19, is without some inner knowledge that there is a Supreme Maker of all things. Even pagans all pick one of their many deities to be assigned with the role of creation. I never met a human, man or woman, who told me to my face that there was not a creator. On this dark, stormy night, the only god I would turn to was the Unknown God, whose altar I cleaned just two days ago. I stood thinking about all that had transpired since I washed the blood off the stones on that altar upon the Acropolis.

Another bolt of light caught me by surprise while I was standing out in the garden. Had anyone been looking, he or she would have seen me. I decided I had to get low and move quickly, or someone would spot me. I felt like my emotions were dancing on a bronze razor's edge. Driving forward with my legs bent putting me into a crouched position, I began to shiver from the cold, wet rain. I had to be careful with a wrong step, which could send me spinning to the ground. Like a metaphor, being careful was more than taking proper steps. I had to be aware of all my physical and mental actions tonight, for anything could cause me to fall into an eternity of the underworld. Getting closer to the atrium, I slowed my movement and began doing an inventory of events since I stepped off the bireme back into Rome. I believed this would help to calm my mind and nerves.

First, the man named Felix appeared and introduced himself while sitting next to me on a public *lavo*. I paid for an enjoyable dinner of *garum* in a *popina* (or eating house), which was now going to give Messina horrible, lasting memories of me and probably her last. Second, after parting ways with Scipios Cornelius Felix at the corner to Esquiline Hill, he returned and most certainly saved my life from Demos and his gang. After his farewell at the front of my father's villa, my third astonishing event for tonight occurred. I rediscovered my lost love, who just vanished again, almost exactly as it happened when I was a child in the warehouse of Ostia. Number four capped my emotional crisis: I realized I was standing in the middle of a thunderstorm at about the same spot my mother had died at the hands of Claudia. With the violent storm passing over me, I could easily die in this same place by a bolt of light. But, for some strange reason, I did not fear this because I genuinely felt the power of Messina praying to her God, Yahweh. But, still, I should have gone back to her and had her place her hands on my shoulders or the top of my head and pray for me like Felix prayed at the *popina* before we ate and like Eli's uncle prayed before we ate in Athens at Hector's house.

I placed my mind back on task. I had promised Claudia to return to kill her and not my father. Inexplicably I wanted to kill Claudia more than my father. Yet, Gaius Vetallus was not what I thought he was when I was a child. I watched him kill Messina's father, and now he was in effect acting as if he were the father of the daughter of the dead man he had murdered. What insanity was this? She, in essence, was his prisoner with the likes of Marius and Lentulus living with her as she now was entering womanhood. I also confirmed that Messina was a good two years older than I was, but that did not seem to be a problem. The problem was my father. He was a wild beast that lusted for the reigns of this world, and he needed to be put down like a vicious dog with a frothing disease. If my father were to take control of the Roman world, what evil suffering would the rest of the tens of millions experience? Oddly enough, in a strange way, I had received a blessing from a Tiberian Praetorian officer, the policing authority in Rome, to kill him.

"One way or the other, this will all end tonight," I said to myself. Nevertheless, I was completely wrong. It was going to be the beginning of a life of troubles with no foreseeable end. It is strange how we think we know something only to discover that later we humans are entirely deceived. Whatever logic I was using could not justify the moral error of my actions. I know now, as an old man, all I had to do was go back to Messina and ask her to pray to her God for help; and that night might have unfolded in some other way. However, on that night I did not understand the power of faith in the unseen Creator. I could not conceive of any other action other than to become a beast to destroy a monster. I actually had to become even more vicious than the creatures before me, or I would die tonight. One of those vile creatures won the wooden sword three times for killing over forty men. I began to feel weak and lost. If a flower bud had feelings, I am sure this was the state it would be before the bud bloomed into a flower. I was still just a boy, not really a man yet. It is an extraordinary place to be as I look back on it. However, my decision was made; and I justified all my actions that night to save a childhood friend, who was really a stranger to me at this time in my life. I also felt my threat to Claudia, even though I made it as a child, had to be fulfilled tonight. Now, as I was thinking upon all these reflections out in the rain that was blowing sideways and standing at the very spot where my mother took her last breath in this world, everything became frozen and surreal. Nothing in my life would ever be the same again, and my decision that night could not have changed. Even today, decades later, I still cannot think of any other outcome I could have made under the circumstances. I could have chosen the coward's way, but that decision was also no longer an option once I stepped onto the bireme in Piraeus. Down in the streets of the Urbs, I had just killed my first man; and death is something that does not usually reverse itself. My only error that night, once again, was not asking Messina to lay her hands on me and pray to her God, Yahweh. However, the last words of Messina to me before I left my old room were "Yahweh will go with you because I will ask Him to do this for me. I know He loves me." How or why her God would give her some favorable answer did not make any sense to me. This was a foreign concept as I stood crouched out in the rain in the middle of my father's vast garden. Besides, how could I get this God to love me as he loved Messina? I knew nothing of this God of Messina or Anab. Perhaps this was the same God Felix now followed. Why did I not question Felix about his understanding about this God of John the Baptist?

"Do the right thing" was the primary tenet of my Stoic thinking, pounding away in my deepest parts while I pondered this maxim. Hundreds of scenarios raced through my mind. How do I rescue Eli and still deal with Claudia and my father? To be brutally honest, I did not entirely trust in Messina's God.

Stoicism was the only moral system I knew and had at my disposal at age 19. Honestly, I must say my decision that night did set the course of my life in this world. If it had not been for a supernatural "mercy" later in my life given to me by the Creator Himself, I would have never learned that "mercy always triumphs over judgment." What I did learn that dark night and still believe is all our actions are either monuments or ash in eternity. What this means, even when this world is no more, is our actions today truthfully determine our eternity. Moment by moment – man in his present condition – does not have the tools to be logical. We are all spiritually dead walking around thinking we are alive. No quick fixes can help; and life is truly a mystery to be lived, not a problem to be solved. Life is also what happens to us after we make our plans, and the results are never what we plan. If I could have only understood and comprehended the beauty of any flower in my father's garden that was being beaten down by the driving rain, maybe I would have appreciated that we humans are more spectacular beyond imagination than any flower. Then, based on this conclusion, surely the Creator of all things cares more about a human over a mere flower. I would later learn that all humans are made in the image of God; and we humans are phenomenally crucial to God, more so than we will ever know in this life. Unfortunately, none of these observations crossed my mind on this stormy night.

Inching closer to the atrium, I could now see Eli sagging between two rose-colored pillars at the edge of the *vestibulum* much like a horse in a stall cross-tied by a groom. The dice had been thrown, and they would not stop until it was over. I crouched lower and removed the box containing the black egg from the back of my belt. I carefully removed the protecting box and straw. Discarding the box and straw, I secured the egg into the top of my left boot by wedging it in between my leg and the soft leather top that reached almost to my left knee. The throwing stars were still in the top of the other boot. I was ready after I had my two throwing knives out, one in each hand; I got to my stomach and crawled the rest of the way to the atrium stone patio. By the time I reached the marble benches, the front of my tan tunic was completely muddy. I was now only five running steps from Eli. With his face towards me, I could see his head slumped down; and his naked body was crusted with dried blood from head to toe. The sight of him made me sorrowful and angry at the same time. The rain was washing most of the blood down the white marble steps revealing white ribs exposed by the cuts from leather whip straps. He hung from the ropes like a crucified criminal. Had his feet not been touching the ground, he surely would be crucified. At a closer examination, I noticed his feet were crumpled under him onto the pavement with the ropes holding his weight. He seemed to be alone in the atrium. All I had to do was dash five steps, cut him down, and drag him out through the garden to the back wall under cover of rain and thunder. I could not believe my fortune. I was about to make my move but stopped when I heard voices to my right and from the rear of the *vestibulum*. In both locations were male slaves holding lanterns and torches. They placed the large lamps on tables and the torches into holders attached to walls. Once they were finished, the slaves quickly left the open room because something caused them to all leave the atrium. I moved my position to the opposite side of the bench to see what made the slaves exit so swiftly; and there they were, Claudia and Senator Gaius Vetallus. Both were off to my left at the back side of the *vestibulum*. I stared at my famous senator father as he stood next to a new acquisition of decadent art. It was a delicately crafted, life-size bronze statue of a nymph and a human male in an embrace of intimacy. I thought of the mother of Achilles being ravished by Zeus, and I felt disgusted because something that private should not be displayed in the open for all to see. My father was holding a wineskin bottle in his hand; he pulled out the stopper and took an enormous gulp. It was just like in the litter, and nothing had changed in almost ten years. He appeared drugged by this opium mix of wine that was his object of worship. He was still bowing to the poppy flower drink. All that was different was his face, which was now covered with fat and age. He had three chins just like Demos's father, Senator Treverorum; and his stomach protruded under his toga, which gave him the appearance of being pregnant. His gray, thinning hair also evidenced his age. It looked like he was now combing his hair over from the sides and back, which fooled no one. On his head was a laurel wreath of gold showing some military victory I knew nothing about but perhaps was also a cover for his thinning hair.

Claudia, on the other hand, had not aged that noticeably. She was standing only a few arm lengths from him in front of the mosaic wall depicting the fierce battle on the Jhelum River between Alexander and King Porus of the Punjab. Elephants were charging the Greek ranks of sarissa spears, and archers were shooting from the massive beasts' backs. Men were stabbing and gouging each other in this incredibly realistic scene. I took my eyes off the mosaic and studied Claudia. Despite her physical beauty, I noticed a look, especially around her eyes, which revealed a fierceness that was colder and more frightening than the melee of warriors in the life-size mosaic behind her. Her long gown of white silk was extraordinarily impressive but was in such contrast to her dark heart that almost caused me to openly laugh. Who was she fooling? Then more slaves began coming and going, all carrying trays of fruit and other foods to the back tables. It looked as if they were getting ready for a dinner party until I realized it was Venus Evening, the night of their weekly orgy. My father called out to one slave to get others to stretch out the *velarium* over the seating area of the atrium, the area where I was hiding. The slave quickly ran off to find more help.

My father, not caring if slaves were watching or not, pointed his finger at Claudia and began yelling something that was lost in a thunderclap. She started to hurl curses back at him. My father retaliated again with his own volley spraying forth white spittle with every word. The entire scene in the atrium made me want to vomit, which I found myself doing in disbelief. I bent over; and out of my mouth came my stomach's content of beer, bread, and *garum*. Just seeing these two evil creatures yelling at one another triggered this physical sickness. I tried to breathe slowly and deeply to gather myself for what I had to do. Grillius always said, "Smell the flowers; blow out the flame." This was the order of clearing one's head without breathing too rapidly to the point of losing something in your blood that kept you focused. "Breathe in through the nose, and blow out through the mouth: smell the roses; blow out the flame." Here I was in my father's garden on my hands and knees behind a marble bench, sick and wet, breathing like a Hindu *yogi*. I began wondering how things could get even worse than this. Yet, things were about to climax into chaos when I gathered myself to complete the purpose of my presence. I again looked around the side of the stone bench, and their current behavior began to revive my desire for revenge. These two hateful people deserved whatever they were going to get. The two objects of all my hate were standing a little further than my dagger-throwing distance but unaware of their danger as they hurled threats at one another.

I saw a flash in the distance and began counting the seconds to calculate when the boom would hit. The boom crashed before I could say, "one pomegranate." At the next flash, I just moved the five steps I needed to take. I was at a rose-colored column next to Eli long after the flash and boom had passed. It worked, for no one spotted me in my dash to the pillar. Looking up I could see the cord tied above my head, which was attached to Eli's right wrist. It was good to be out of the horizontal rain, and I could clearly hear everyone's words.

Claudia was still standing under the mosaic yelling her demands at Gaius. "I say we crucify him tonight for entertainment after we have dinner with our guests!"

"Listen, woman! This Jew has not told us where we can find Venustus!" screamed my father in return.

"Crucify him during dinner; and after desserts, cut him down, and ask him very nicely where Venustus is! The fear of being re-crucified again will loosen his tongue!" Screeched Claudia.

"Never! This Jew is like all the rest of that breed – haters of our gods with a spirit no human can break!"

"Let us see! Why not scourge him again and then do to him like we did to Zeno as we have already agreed."

"So you want to cut out his innards and beat them on a table in front of all our dinner guests?"

"It made Zeno chirp like a songbird. But let's do it right now before our guests arrive. I am tired of waiting!" screeched Claudia. I had moved my head slightly around the column I was hiding behind and saw Claudia clearly by the light of a brazier burning brightly not far from her. The tip of her red tongue did something strange, which I assumed was her licking her red-painted lips. On second thought, it looked more like Claudia was tasting the air over licking her upper lip. As soon as her tongue went back into her mouth, her right hand came up with her first finger pointing to my father's face. She then bellowed as loud as a woman could scream and still maintain authority, "We do it now!"

The Senator turned and said something over his shoulder near the nymph sculpture, and I recognized Lentulus in the room with them. "Go fetch the whip! Let's get this over with. Now!"

When Lentulus turned and left the rear of the atrium's *vestibulum*, I decided to make my move before he returned. I swiveled my head around and looked over to see if Eli was conscious. "Eli! Eli! Can you hear me? It is Venustus."

To my surprise, Eli turned his face towards me; and he smiled as if to ask why I was late. His face was swollen and distorted along with the rest of his body that appeared cut to ribbons.

"Venu, is that you?" he asked hoarsely. "I thought it was over; I did not believe you'd come in time."

"I am going to cut you down, but you will have to help get yourself over to the wall at the back of the garden."

"Do it, Venu. Do not fret about me. I will get over any wall if you cut me down."

After replacing my dagger in my left hand back into my belt, I quickly cut the rope to his right wrist while holding his hand up with my left until another flash of light. When it came, I released his hand and moved to the opposite pillar and began cutting the other rope. Eli crumpled down making a thudding noise between two more thunderclaps. I realized I forgot to time the booms to cover the sound of Eli falling to the stone floor.

"Look!" yelled Claudia as she saw me after Eli hit the floor.

"Who are you?" ordered my father with a tone that he expected would paralyze anyone below senatorial rank.

Everything began to happen very quickly. Eli was looking lifeless on the atrium floor in his own blood and filth. I stood soaking wet with only a dagger in my right hand. When it registered in Claudia's and my father's minds who I was, I decided to violate Grillius's number one rule once again. "I am Venustus, and I've come to square accounts with Claudia regarding my mother!" I roared with a deep, booming, Felix-type voice, which was even more commanding than my father's tone. I could not believe I successfully duplicated the exact intonation Felix Cornelius used on the two Praetorian *thugs* out in the lane. To my surprise, it worked freezing Claudia and my father from any quick action along with shutting their mouths.

I turned the knife over in my right hand positioning the tip of the blade between my thumb and pointing finger mentally marking my target in my mind's eye. Just when the thick wooden handle touched my right ear, Claudia stepped back realizing what was about to happen. She had stepped backward, bumping into the wall with the colorful mosaic. When I knew she would be stationary for the time it took the knife to twirl towards her, I snapped my wrist releasing the hurtling blade. It was a good 40 feet away across the open room. My target was further than what I had practiced, but the dagger hit squarely to the right of her chest with a thud exactly where Claudia placed the yellow bone-handled knife into my mother nine-plus years ago. Claudia opened her mouth without a sound, and she seemed pinned to the mosaic of war. Her painted eyes widened before she lowered her head to see the handle sticking out of her chest. What was only a few seconds seemed like a long moment of silence. Realizing her wages of evil, Claudia Varus let out the most hideous-sounding scream. Blood began changing her white silk garment red, and then she became deathly silent slowly sliding down to the floor into a sitting position with her mouth agape and her eyes now staring at me as if she were trying to understand something. The minimal thud sound of the dagger hitting its mark still resonates in my ears. I am not sure I actually heard it or if it was only in my mind; but at that moment the knife struck, it was the most self-satisfying sound I ever remembered. I just stood frozen with the knowledge I just brought down the evil witch of Rome. It is amazing how fast the mind works at times of crisis making time appear to crawl. I felt as if

I had all the time in the world to do whatever I had to do. There was no more fear, only excitement, which is rarely duplicated in any other activity.

Down at my feet, Eli was trying to get to his knees when Marius, in his classic green tunic, came running from the direction of the vomitorium charging us both without a weapon. Since he was unarmed, I made the fateful decision to use my last dagger on my father, who stood frozen near Claudia's dying form. Once her head dropped in death, he turned to me and yelled with the most menacing voice I have ever heard, "May the gods curse you, evil son of mine!"

I could not believe my ears. Here was my father thinking he alone was clean in all his thoughts and actions; thus, he was able to command even the gods. The truth was so disturbing when I considered my father actually thought everyone else besides him was corrupt. Does this man really think he is righteous and does not deserve the judgment that was about to come? I could not fathom what god he thought would listen to him. Even Mars, the war god, would be disgusted by my father's thoughts and actions in life. I had only a split-second left to deliver the dagger before Marius was on top of me, so I pulled back not replying to my father except with the dagger. I arrogantly decided to place the knife into his right eye just like *Thag* Man in the lane below this villa. It was a mistake on my part. I should have put it in his chest just as I did to Claudia. I was an expert at 25 feet, not 40. As I threw it, my father watched the knife leave my hand and twirl towards his face. I had forgotten he had been a soldier once and frequented thousands of gladiatorial matches. He, too, understood time slows down at these instances; and, at the last moment, my father jerked his head to the side as any experienced soldier would do. The blade missed the eye but cut into the flesh, glancing off bone and cutting along the side of his face taking off half of his left ear. It was a risky, foolhardy throw; but it was too late. Before the golden laurel wreath hit the floor, I realized my error.

In the meantime, out of the corner of my eye, I saw Eli driving his right shoulder level into the charging legs of Marius knocking them both down into a heap in front of me. Eli had grown since I last saw him, and he had become a stout young man but not strong enough to keep this bull of a man down. I stood there in stunned shock realizing I missed my target concerning my father and that a dangerous ex-gladiator was going to be attacking me as soon as he was back on his feet. The collision between Marius and Eli only slowed the Gladiator a few seconds as I watched him roll away from the weak arms of the downed Eli and then expertly flip back to his feet. It was like looking at a famous acrobat. It was exactly the strange flip I saw after the collision with the Nubian gladiator nine and a half years ago. I could have panicked; but my Lyceum training came back, and I began to assess all my options. I was out of knives, so I went for the star daggers in my boot. Once I had all three in my right hand, I threw all of them underhanded at Marius as he was getting ready to charge me. The shock of being struck by star daggers stopped him in his attack. One entered his left shoulder, and the other two were sticking out of his upper chest. The blades were not long, and there was only surprise in Marius's eyes; but the star daggers had only stopped him instead of putting him down. I did not have time to get the black egg out of the other boot, so I concluded I was going to have to use my hands and feet on the famous gladiator who killed over forty men in one afternoon. We both locked eyes, and I remember looking at his nostrils flaring wider than I have ever seen on a human before. Due to the damage to his vocal cords, he sounded like a blown horse after a long race. He was obviously older than he was in the arena but still dangerous even if he was sucking in air from his short run and collision with Eli, and having three star daggers sticking into his shoulder and chest.

"Go, Eli! The wall!" I commanded like a general ordering a phalanx to wheel left in the middle of a battle.

My voice apparently resonated in Marius's puny mind. Instead of trying to tackle me, he just stood and looked at me blinking his eyes open and shut. Finally, he asked, "Falcataus? You are the one at the door! Where is your outrageous robe?" Marius asked almost conversationally with his gravelly voice. At the very moment he was asking me about my Spartan *chlamys*, Lentulus came into the atrium clutching a whip at his side. Eli was now trying to get back on his feet, and I told him again to go. Once he was standing, he just stood his ground. It was a strange scene with Eli standing next to me naked and bloodied looking at Marius in a crouched fighting position with his shredded back arched. Nothing happened until Lentulus came up beside Marius with his eyes wide and mouth open in surprise.

"Mayus, do you know this *chit*?" hissed Marius almost unintelligible because of his voice and panting for air.

Mayus Lentulus first looked over at Claudia sitting on the floor with my father slumped over her lap dazed from the wound to his head. Turning back to me, he realized who I was. "Is that Venustus all grown up?" asked Lentulus with a fiendish smile as if it were a typical day at the bathhouse. "Marius, look at this wet, muddy rat. The gods have finally blessed us. All those years of our lives wasted looking for this mongrel in that dried-up Hades of *Palestina*. We looked and looked, and now he comes to us. This grown-up *chit* is mine. You can finish the Jew."

These two *thags* acted as if they had all day wanting to travel down all their old memories together in Judaea. Marius started pulling out the star daggers as if they were thorns and dropped each with a cling onto the stone flagstone floor. Marius examined the last star dagger and said with a laugh, "No wonder we could not find him; he was hiding in the land of Chin."

That statement reminded me of my black egg. I slowly reached down pulling out the black egg out with my left hand. I had to act fast, or I was going to end up like Claudia. Since Lentulus held the only weapon, I threw the egg with my left hand in a side-handed throw similar to throwing a rock into a lake and trying to make it skip on top of the water. The black egg struck Lentulus above his left eye bone, and a white cloud of powered glass erupted. Lentulus foolishly began scrubbing at his left eye doing irreparable damage not knowing he was driving shards of powdered glass deeper into his eye. He roared like a mortally wounded bull after he realized what he was doing. I moved my attention quickly to Marius, being the younger and stronger of the two and by far the more dangerous. Like a striking cat, I moved towards Marius before he moved on me. I remembered his own tactic I had observed as a little boy. Strike first and quickly. I took two steps; and with my last step and all my weight on my right leg, I deliver the hardest blow possible with my right fist's middle knuckle sticking out like a spike. I drove it deep into the center of his massive barrel chest just below the ribs. Grillius had shown me that one of the weakest parts of the human anatomy is the thin layer of flesh just below the lungs and above the intestines. He said, "If you hit this spot just at the end of the long, flat chest bone that joins the two sets of ribs, it is possible to rupture that membrane dropping the lungs and causing them to spasm. A man must breathe if he is going to be able to fight you," echoed the words of Grillius in my mind. "Stop his breathing even for a few seconds, and you bought some valuable time. Strike a man in that spot, and he will either be dead in two to three minutes or incapacitated for the same amount of time."

I knew my punch connected at the right spot, but this man had more muscle in his chest than I could have ever imagined. He was short and stocky and built like a tree stump. His muscle mass had prevented me from rupturing that membrane, but he did go down like a grain bag being dropped onto a quay from a grain galley at the wharves of Ostia. He was sucking wind from a fetal position when Lentulus's whip connected across my left arm and cut into my shoulder along my back. He was wild with rage at me for throwing whatever blinded his left eye. The whip stung and burned as if a hot rod had been placed against my skin. I knew at once that my left arm was shortly going to be useless leaving me only my right and I quickly grabbed the leather whip thongs with my right hand before he could pull them back for a second strike. It was as if I were dealing with a blind cobra with the power of a bull. Lentulus pulled as hard as he could with the short, wooden handle to get the leather bands out of my hand. I stepped back holding the half-dozen straps and pulling Lentulus towards me putting all my weight back on my left leg so I could transfer all my energy into my booted right foot at the strategic moment. When I finally felt that he was briefly off balance and Lentulus was close enough for me to kick, I released the leather straps. His momentum caused him to fly backward, precisely what I had hoped would happen; and I pushed off my left leg placing my right boot heel on the outside of his left knee. With his blinded eye on the same side, he did not see it coming. At the same moment my foot connected, a loud clap of thunder boomed through the *vestibulum*. Even though I could not hear how much damage had occurred to his knee, I could feel my foot following through telling me I had broken the ball joint in his knee. Lentulus continued backward screaming like a slaughtered pig at a Zeus sacrifice grabbing at his awkwardly angled knee.

I looked over to my father who was reviving and focusing his gaze on me and then back to Claudia. He wiped the blood from his eyes with his toga to improve what he was seeing. I wanted to go for my knife that had to be somewhere over there, but Eli's hand pulled me out into the rain.

"Come on, we have to go!" he yelled.

"No!" I screamed back. "I have to finish him!"

"Come on!" he howled; and I noticed other men rushing from the back of the atrium, soldier guards of some kind, maybe my father's *lictors*, and others carrying long spears. Hector had instructed me to save Eli first before revenge, and I did complete the job on Claudia that I had promised over nine years ago. I could clearly see that she was dead with my knife sticking out of her chest. Grillius had taught me exactly where the human heart was located, and that was where my dagger handle was. I had felt a human heart at the death-house, and it is no bigger than a closed fist; but a blade through it was fatal. There was the handle of my dagger sticking out a little to the right of her cleavage just where the heart rests inside a woman's chest. I turned and half-carried Eli into the darkness of the garden. A bolt of lightning flashed above us illuminating the wall. The booms were now more than a second apart meaning the center of the storm was moving away from the city. I ran towards the dark object on the top of the wall that marked the spot where we could safely cross over.

"I will lift you!" I screamed on the run and in the roar of the rain as the wind had abated considerably. "Once you are on the top, reach down and pull me over!"

"Just cup your hands together at the wall, and we are out of here!" screamed Eli in agony from all the pain he had suffered in previous days before I arrived.

Reaching the wall without looking to see if anyone was behind us, I cupped my hands where Eli put his foot. Using my knees and legs, I heaved him up as a horse groom would aid someone mounting a horse; but at the last moment, I lost my footing. We both fell into the mud with Eli on top of me. I pushed him off me and yelled, "Again!" This time I looked into the darkness of the garden, and shadows were coming in our direction. The second time was the winner, and Eli made it. His fingertips grasped the edge of the ten-foot wall; and he stepped on my shoulders and head before he was able to pull his naked, bleeding body to the top.

"Hurry; give me your hand!" I yelled as another lightning flash revealed the barrel-chested gladiator running through the garden holding a spear he must have taken from one of the soldiers. I jumped and caught Eli's hand that was stretching down for me. With surprising strength from a man who had been flogged for days, he pulled me to the top. I touched the rock that marked the cleared spot, and I took the heavy object and threw it blindly into the darkness at the form running towards the wall. It hit something solid, and I saw someone who must have been Marius go down with a groan that did not even sound human. The noise reminded me of a horse suffering from snots disease or a very sick man with some kind of severe nasal-mucus condition. When a flash of light revealed Marius trying to stand and not using his acrobatic flip technique, I turned towards Eli, who was struggling down the tree ladder, descending the outside of the wall. I pivoted my body to get my feet directed to go down the tree ladder when a hand grabbed my tunic sleeve. I looked back and saw Marius's squinty eyes looking into mine. How he was able to jump up a 10-foot wall as short as he was and grab the sleeve of my tunic was beyond me. A bolt of lightning flashed showing more details of his ugly, mutilated face for a brief moment. The rock must have hit him in the center of his nose as I briefly noticed his nose plastered to the side of his face and blood pouring out his nose like a spit squirting water at a forum fountain. I yelled over my shoulder to Eli, 'Throw me the bundle at the base of the wall!"

Eli grabbed the whole thing and tossed it up to me. I caught it as Marius's weight was pulling me back over the top of the wall. I couldn't believe this squatty man outweighed me. I yanked out the falcata from its red leather scabbard and twirled it once in the air to position the blade just right. I then brought the sword down on Marius's left hand that was holding onto the top of the wall for stability while he was dragging me back over into the garden with his right hand. The blade cut clean between the second and third fingers of his left hand. The force of the cut split the entire hand into two halves. This much was clear from another flash of a distant bolt of light coming from a lightning strike near Augustus's mausoleum on the edge of the Campus Martius. Another flash turned night into day as another bolt struck on the opposite side of the city near the Ostia Gate. Marius let out a horrible screech with his damaged vocal cords and fell back into the darkness after my tan tunic sleeve ripped in his right hand. I heard him thump at the bottom of the wall, and I realized I had made a mistake. I should have aimed for his head instead of his hand, and this was a strategic error that would cause me a multitude of problems in the future. Two spears from soldiers following Marius came flying by my head. I dropped the falcata and cloak down towards Eli before I scrambled down the tree ladder.

Once at the bottom, I knocked the tree off the wall and sheathed the sword into its red scabbard. Eli was looking at me crazed and naked with rivulets of water running down his bloody chest. "What is your next trick?" he asked making the whole scene seem peculiar and absurd. I tossed him the wet gray cloak that had been Falcata Man's coat and told him to cover up. We both laughed as he wrapped himself with the soaking wet *chlamys*. Not wanting to be here when the soldiers came around from the front, we turned and trotted in the driving rain down the lane that led to the bowels of the Imperial capital of the world.

CHAPTER ELEVEN

Rome – The 15th year of Tiberius and the 1st year of Jesus's public ministry in Palestina, which began about two and a half months earlier during the Feast of Passover in Jerusalem, marking the first event prophetically described in the Book of Malachi as the Temple cleansing. (29 AD)

A great city is not to be confounded with a populous one. Aristotle

The rain ceased as suddenly as it had started; but lightning continued to flash against a dark, foreboding sky with peals of distant thunder following. A peculiarly sacred sensation came over me as Eli, and I moved quickly through the darkened streets of Rome. It was very strange and, yet, remarkably real. I had the anomalous sensation that the throne of God was passing over the city of Rome, perhaps a long-awaited visit to confirm some angelic report concerning its wickedness. It was not just one of the many gods of Rome, but the one true God named either Yahweh or the Unknown God of Athens. With this monotheistic thought crossing my mind, I looked over to Eli and felt just as dirty and filthy as the rest of this horde of humanity that made up the Imperial capital. My deeds this night were more than questionable, to say the least. Did I have to commit murder? Could I have been more patient and just rescued Eli without all the violence? I did not know the answer. I had studied and searched for knowledge in Athens, and still, I did not know how to find the answer to life. Humans knew how to mine into the ground to incredible depths and extract iron, copper, silver, and gold; and, yet, who knew where the place of understanding resides? I concluded it was unreachable, no matter where it lived.

The Circus Maximus, in all its grand majesty, loomed up before Eli and me as we struggled in our escape. I knew exactly where we were, for the Circus lies in the Murcia Valley between the Palatine and Aventine Hills. The Circus Maximus was the most famous chariot track in the world. It was a gigantic, arrow-shaped structure, constructed out of wood-and-stone. We were skirting past it to our left, and the white stone wall gave the appearance of a massive vertical cliff stretching out for over a half mile. There must have been several barge loads of iron pins, holding the stacked stones together that stood to the height of a six-story tenement house. There was perhaps enough iron dispersed in the stones to make swords for Varus's three lost legions.

Over three hundred thousand people could gather inside the Circus Maximus on race day if they all stood. That meant one-third of the entire population of the city of Rome at one place at one moment in time. The Circus operated almost daily with death occurring in nearly every race. The incredible speeds caused horrific crashes – where human and animal flesh was torn apart for the enjoyment of the screaming spectators. Not only was there the excitement of the races for the spectators, but there was also the potential for substantial wealth by a single bet on the right team. Chariot racing was by far the most addictive activity in the city as well as the Empire, intoxicating three-fourths of the population of Rome on a good day if one counted the spectators in the other circuses that were scattered around the city of Rome. However, the Circus Maximus was the grandfather of racetracks in the world.

A traditional race consisted of four teams: red, white, green, and blue. Each color fielded three teams of four horses with one driver for each team. At the start of each race, 12 chariot drivers controlled 48 horses, all trying to complete seven circuits of the circus track with each circuit measuring out to be one mile or half a mile from end to end. Many horses died from exhaustion during each race, for a strong horse could only run maybe two miles at full gallop. A driver had to pace his teams at full speed along the sides, those being the half-mile stretches, and slow them down around each turn. Only a few drivers possessed this skill to complete a race without killing one or more horses in the grueling seven circuits. The most spectacular crashes occurred at the two corner turns. The standard strategy was for each color group of three to work together trying to block and interfere, so at least one member of their color won. This sport of chariot racing for both horse and man was, indeed, a very bloody and cruel game.

With the Circus Maximus on our left, we also passed on our right something even mightier in its sheer monstrosity over the considerable racetrack. It was the array of opulent buildings up on Palatine Hill, looking like a cliff of white marble. There were many large porches, protruding out over the white cliffs. From any porch on Palatine Hill allowed anyone from the Imperial Palaces to watch the all-day spectacles, whenever it pleased him or her. Here rested the center of the greatest political machine to have ever existed in human history. The palaces stood above Eli and me, gleaming like a marble hill with trees and flowering plants dispersed at different levels, making the polished cliff appear like the now-extinct Tower of Babylon. The Tower of Babylon, from what I read, was a giant, stepped ziggurat built of mud bricks with gardens of trees and flowers, climbing up like a fabricated mountain that stood in the center of ancient Babylon. Nevertheless, here was the tower's white, gleaming equal.

I stopped to give Eli a rest. We just stood in the dark between the world's most magnificent entertainment structure and the hub of the most potent, political, and mighty contrivance imaginable. It was at this extraordinary moment, I perceived the throne of God passing overhead, revealing its majestic power and putting to shame these manufactured systems of sticks and stones for entertainment and diplomacy. Then all of a sudden, a quiet realization came to me that the solution was straightforward. The answer to life was not in this world, not in this substantial entertaining monstrosity to my left, nor in the world's most powerful government to my right. Even if both held life and death in their hands, the answer was not to be found to either my left or my right. The answer to life was straight above. I honestly believed it was on this night, I started believing in the one and only Creator, whom Anab and Messina called, Yahweh. No longer would I think of the Creator as the Unknown God, honored upon the Athenian Acropolis. For the answer was simple: all one had to do was give reverence to the Creator and depart from evil, for only then would one have a hope of finding wisdom and understanding. The truth was not buried deep below my feet but was beyond the stars that I could now see as the clouds scudded above the breaks above my head, showing the glory of the heavens. This conclusion, as I stood next to my childhood friend, shaking from exhaustion and shock, was unmistakable to my mind, soul, and spirit. There was surely a God; and He knew me personally, for He knew everyone personally. No, He was not a God who made a visit to this world every thousand years, but He was present in every activity. If this were true, why would He not guide me? Perhaps I had not allowed Him to do so. I began to laugh aloud at the thought of people who had little statues of household gods in small niches on walls in their homes, and the idea that people prayed to nymphs of glens and springs, hoping for blessings and fresh water, was now complete foolishness to my exhausted mind. In addition, what folly it was for all the rituals and incantations people uttered in fear of these vainly perceived, pernicious, sentient beings. I, for the first time, could see the world was under the control of only one, all-knowing being, not thousands of nymphs and fairies, along with dozens of capricious nature gods. If these little gods did exist, they were in rebellion with the one true Creator, and were just fallen, defiant creatures parading their lies and deceptions to us lower fallen humans.

I had no idea how I would learn about this one Creator. Nevertheless, I can honestly say my life began to change forever, while Eli and I stood in the Murcia Valley, between the Aventine and Palatine Hills. I was going to pursue this hope, no matter how distant it might be. Was it my imagination that the throne of God was passing above me, or was it the eerie time of night that was challenging my Stoic opinions? Maybe it was the shock of combat wearing off that was causing my acuteness of the invisible. My favorite truism from the *Dialogues* of Plato was, '*The things which are seen are temporal, but the things that are not seen are eternal.*' Whatever bit of truth for any human to understand, was that. Unfortunately, I did not know anyone who lived for the world of unseen things, but like my father, we all lived to one degree or another for only what we could see and the pleasures we could feel. I finally realized this world was nothing but a petty, vain, empty shell of madness and insanity created in a fallen image of man. I decided at this point I was going to spend the rest of my life pursuing a quest to find the answer to life and to answer the next subsequent question: what was after this experience? Moreover, if it meant spitting into the eye of fear and the one evil *Deva* of this world, so be it.

"What are we going to do?" whimpered Eli interrupting my unfathomable but quiet contemplations.

"Tell me, Eli; if there is design in the world, then does it not stand to reason there must be a designer?"

"What are we going to do?" moaned Eli again apparently in pain and frustration.

I stared at Eli, who was not looking at me. His head was down, and blood was coming out of his ears and nose. He did not look good; instead, he was decomposing before my very eyes. Maybe he was dying. Grillius often spoke of shock that could kill as quickly as an arrow through the heart. To treat this condition, one must lie down and lift their feet slightly above the heart. The patient also should be kept warm and full of fluids if possible.

"We are leaving this diseased city. We will cross the Tiber by the *Sublicus* Bridge and hide in the 14ᵗʰ District, where Augustus placed most of the Jews before we were born," I said. "But first, you are going to lie down once we get to the river."

"Do you not think that will be the first place they will look?"

"What? The river?"

"No! The 14ᵗʰ District."

I did not respond, for he was right. I instead half-carried Eli around the long racetrack and on towards the Tiber. Once we reached the old, wooden footbridge, I noticed Eli was beyond exhaustion. I let him lie down near the bridge behind some bushes on the wet grass. I placed his feet upon a rock, and the color in his face began to improve. "You stay here and rest, and I will be right back," I instructed. The rain had stopped entirely, and a refreshing wind was slightly blowing from the direction of Ostia.

"Where are you going?"

"To fetch my hat and that red bag Zeno gave me years ago on the night we both left Ostia."

"What are you talking about?" he asked, but I left without answering. I walked towards the unguarded imperial wharves. The only noise was the gentle bumping of the biremes against the docks. I found the bireme that had brought me back to Rome; and upon the bow was the name carved into the side, *Achilles*. I would not have known its name except for Felix, who kept calling it in the tavern in *Subura*. I walked up the gangplank unchallenged by the absence of any guards and noticed the hold was empty of all the slaves. They all must have been taken somewhere to rest and recuperate. The only person I could see on the upper deck was my so-called friend, the helmsman-pilot, sleeping under the tarp at the bow. I walked up, put the tip of the falcata to his throat, and pushed it until he came awake with wide eyes.

"What are you doing? Are you possessed?" he squawked sounding just like a seagull.

"You stole a silver *denarius* by taking two from that fat senator, you stinking, deceitful, fabricating seabird."

"How do you know that?"

"Is it true, you thieving bird?"

He did not answer until I pushed the tip into his flesh drawing a drop of blood. "Yes, it is true. I will give it back," Seagull offered.

"No, you are going to keep it; and this time, you will earn it."

"What?"

I removed my sword from his neck and allowed him to sit up. "Is this ship returning to Piraeus?"

"Yes."

"When does it leave?"

"First light on Moon or Diana Day."

"I want you to deliver a letter to the school called the Lyceum in Athens."

"Deliver a message; that is all?"

"That is all. A letter will be brought to you here on this ship tomorrow, and I want it delivered by you personally to the Lyceum. Do you know the school?"

"Yes, Aristotle's school, clear on the other side of Athens from Piraeus, just outside the city walls. At one time the school must have been a gymnasium. I know it."

"I'm sure the letter will be delivered here before noon tomorrow. Do not leave this ship until it arrives, just in case it is late. If I hear that you have opened it or not delivered it, you will pay more than a *denarius*"; and I pointed the falcata back at Seagull's face.

"No trouble, I will do it."

"Now, where is my *petasos*; or did you sell it?"

He pointed to where I left it. I walked to the back of the ship and picked it up keeping my eyes on the helmsman the entire time. I also grabbed the red bag that was now empty but sitting next to my flop hat.

Back near *Pons Sublicus*, I found Eli asleep. He looked peaceful, and I was tempted to just give him more time to rest; but the hunt for us would be organized by now, and we had no time to lose. I noticed more breaks in the black clouds as they passed over the city revealing hundreds of stars twinkling in the heavens between the breaks. The rumbling thunder had now moved off and could barely be heard sounding like a steady, far-off drumbeat of an angelic army, marching away to the north.

I tapped Eli awake, and he rose very stiffly from all his injuries. "Come on. We have to get over the bridge." I half-carried the limping Eli as we crossed the sewage-smelling Tiber that was not as bad as normal because of all the clean runoff from the rain that temporarily washed the city. Once across the bridge, we entered the special quarter Augustus had assigned to the Jews during his reign, a part of Rome I had never been in before. Down a street not far from the Tiber, I pointed out a large synagogue that had four huge trees surrounding it. It was too dark to identify what kind of trees they were.

"We can find refuge in there," I said gasping for air.

"Not at all, Venu; this will be the first place they will look. Remember, I am a Jew."

"I cannot argue with your logic. Let's go to a place where a Jew would never go."

"And that would be what, a pig-pen?"

"Something better, the temple of Janus. It is where no Jew would ever go. That would be the most pagan of all pagan temples."

"That means walking back into the city to the *Forum*."

"I'm thinking of that old Janus temple not far from here at the bend of the river across from Mars Field, the one standing on Vaticanus Hill."

Eli stood there with a smile realizing the wisdom in my plan. We started moving with the Tiber to our right. I still had to half-carry the hobbling and shaking Eli towards the Place of Divination, or in Latin, Vaticanus Hill. This was the hill of soothsaying and witchcraft with an unauthorized racetrack located between the hill and the river. Vaticanus Hill sometimes was referred to as the eighth hill of Rome, located outside the ancient walls and not part of the original Seven Hills on the other side of the Tiber.

These days the vast, open area in front of the Temple of Janus is known as the Circus Vaticanus, where some of the deadliest chariot races in the Roman world are staged. There is no seating, just an open racetrack with a long *spina* containing two Egyptian obelisks at each end of the *spina*, which runs down the center of the course where the chariots run always turning left at the two obelisks pillars making the traditional seven laps. These are the "unauthorized" races, where drivers gather at midnight when there is a full moon. These races are against opponents of their own choosing. These are races until death with no rules and are somewhat spontaneously organized. Sometimes rich aristocrats duel to the death from two chariots to settle some grievance. Lovers and other revelers come at night to the open area before Vaticanus Hill hoping to see one of these legendary races usually staged 12 to 13 times a year generally on the nights of full moons. I was hoping no one would be out and about tonight due to the nature of the violent storm that struck the city and because the moon would not be full for another 12 days. My hopes were realized. Everything was quiet as Eli and I crossed the empty, stark racing circus with two stolen Egyptian obelisks marking the ends of the center spine. We headed up the slightly sloping hill to reach the old, black-stone temple of Janus. It was defiantly ugly and uninviting, the perfect place for two fugitives to hide. The hour must have been about midnight, the holiest time to Janus worshipers. Eli and I found cover in some bushes to watch the closed doors indicating the Empire was at peace. Had the doors been open, Rome would have been at war. Some old traditions never die.

The entire area of Vaticanus Hill, besides the chariot track, was planted with shrubs and trees that the emperors maintained as an imperial garden for the public's use. The truth is this park area is mostly used for the rendezvous of the most immoral and reprehensible kind. Again, the hard rains had discouraged even these people to stay away tonight. Eli was resting next to me on an out-of-place marble bed while I watched the temple. It was not long before the doors of the Janus Temple opened; and a dozen or so people, both men and women, came vomiting out in a state of exhaustion. They also appeared and acted as if they were intoxicated. Watching carefully, I noticed some were actually unclothed and moved without any embarrassment of their condition. One beautiful woman, who was clothed dressed like a queen from a foreign country, was walking next to a rugged-looking man who acted more like a bodyguard. He appeared to be acutely aware, and his head was moving around cat-like, similar to Felix's behavior earlier in the *popina*.

I waited and watched while Eli slept. About an hour later, I decided it was safe to reconnoiter the building. Leaving Eli alone, I walked up and opened the door. I discovered a few torches still burning inside revealing a chaotic scene of depravity and nefarious activities. This dovetails very well to another name of Janus: the god of Chaos. Possibly an orgy of some sort was part of the worship of Janus and his cohort, Hora. I could smell the faint odor stink of animal hormone scent. There were many articles of clothing strewn around the sanctuary area in front of the altar and a statue of the two-headed god. I gathered up a lovely tunic for Eli along with a pair of sandals. I could not find a pair for myself but did find a gray *himation* to replace my Spartan mantle that I had given to Messina. I figured it would be best to exchange my military-type boots as soon as possible. I am sure Marius would have reported a man in a purple cloak wearing military boots as the one memory he had of the one at the door looking for some neighbor senator on a rainy night. Not finding any replacements that fit, I decided to keep the boots.

After finding Eli asleep on the misplaced marble bed, I helped dress him in his new tunic and coat. After placing his liberated sandals on his feet, we left for the temple. Back inside the vaulted sanctuary of this pagan temple, Eli began going into great distress; but I was not troubled in any measure until I looked upon the statue of Janus, which did give me the snakes. I am sure working with Hector all those years at the Athena Nike must have forged my current attitude of ambivalence to pagan temples. However, this place was beyond unnerving to Eli. At the foot of this massive statue, carved out of one huge tree trunk and painted with bright colors, was a bowl of cooked goat meat. The figure was about three times the size of a human man except this ugly, bearded god had two faces: one on the backside of his head, and the other looking in the opposite direction looking forward. In his right hand was a massive club. Scanning the semi-dark room, I noticed something on the altar not far from the statue and located between the two-headed god and the front door. On top of the altar were a loaf of bread and plenty of wine for both of us to get drunk if we felt the urge. I did not tell Eli where I found the food and drink, and he did not ask. We sat behind the altar and feasted keeping a sharp eye on the closed doors. I noticed Eli was having trouble chewing. With the swollen cheeks on both sides of his face, I guessed he had taken a massive beating in the face during the past week. When Eli had all he could consume, I instructed him to get some sleep behind the bulky altar. Eli looked up and thanked me for saving him from my father and those other two Creatins.

"You should have let me finish my father," I proclaimed after Eli found a spot between the statue and the altar.

"Are you not prudent? We almost did not get out when we did. Was that not Marius the gladiator I tried to tackle and you put down with one punch?"

"Yes, it was; and he was trying to pull me over the wall before you threw me the sword in your gray cloak. Now he is nursing a sore hand after I gave him my falcata," I boasted with false bravado. I became quiet after the comment thinking now I had a serious enemy after me for the rest of my life, someone who would never rest until I was painfully slain. Once again, I cursed myself for not splitting open his head instead of his hand.

Eli finally said, "This is madness; I can't believe I am hiding in a pagan temple, especially a Janus temple on the Hill of Witchcraft."

"What in the *cosmos* are you talking about? We are safe here."

"I am talking about hiding behind the throne of Satan himself – that is what I am speaking about. The living God of Israel will protect us if we just trust Him, not Janus, the god of confusion. This is madness; I'm sorry I agreed to come here."

I was at the end of my rope considering everything I had been through since I met Anab two night ago, which seemed like an eternity. I began counting the many times I had been bombarded by this God of the Jews in the same period. I felt like this deity was hunting me, and maybe this was a good thing to be pursued by this God; but I had to change the subject, or I would lose control over my emotions. "Aren't you going to ask how I happened to show up to save you?"

"I know how – I prayed, and Yahweh sent you."

"Your uncle Anab found me in Athens."

"Good for him. He's a good man."

"That is all you have to say?"

"Sure, except praise to the Living God of Israel for sending you."

"Look, I'll worship your God if He is any more of a reality than this Janus."

"Venu, there is only one God, not dozens like Rome believes and what the rest of the world thinks. The God of the Jews is the only one and true God, and the Jews are His Chosen People."

"You say this like you know Him personally," I jested sarcastically with a sting in my tone.

"There is only one true God!" said Eli passionately. "And I think He is weary of the way the world is progressing. I predict, without any hesitation, Yahweh, the name of the only true God, is going to do some mighty things soon."

"Why do you think that?" I asked.

"There is a prophet in Judaea named John the Baptist, who proclaims that God's Kingdom is about to come. I personally heard him say as much."

Eli aroused my curiosity. He mentioned the same character Anab and Felix spoke about. Now I wanted to know more about this so-called prophet of water. "Did you talk to this John the Baptizer?"

"I listened to him speak out in the wilderness of Judaea near the Jordan River after he baptized me. He affects people as no man you have ever seen. If he is not a prophet, then there never was one. He is like the return of Elijah, the prophet who never died. Nevertheless, John was asked this question repeatedly; and he always answered that he was not Elijah nor the Messiah. Maybe you and I can get back to Judaea, and I will take you to him. He will convince you that there is only one God, and His name is Yahweh as given to Moses at Mount Horeb when he spoke with the burning bush."

I said nothing to that with words, but my silence was like the voices of a thousand souls screaming at me to listen. Of course, aside from the "convince me of God" idea, it was a brilliant plan. Escape to *Palestina*, no better place than at the end of the Roman Empire to hide. I was confident Marius and Lentulus did not want to return there anytime soon based on their strange conversation in the atrium tonight. There also had to be enough money from Falcata Man's moneybag to pay our way. I unconsciously touched the heavy leather bag tied to my tunic belt. I looked over to Eli and realized he was fast asleep. I left him to his rest thinking he was in a good spot that was out of sight being behind the altar. I went to the doors to keep watch through the center crack of the two closed doors. I untied the moneybag and counted what was in it. A smile came to me when I realized there was enough for passage for the

Blood Of Empires

both of us to *Palestina*. Demos must have paid a considerable sum to have me killed out in the streets of the *Urbs,* or Falcata Man must have robbed some wealthy man before the storm began.

When the sun finally began to rise the next morning, its radiance poured in through the seams of the doors. In the city of Rome across the river, the sun's rays were now striking the temple of Jupiter upon Capitoline Hill. I left my post to check on Eli. When I saw my long lost friend, he did not look too healthy. After I poked him to see if he was still breathing, he hoarsely said he had to relieve himself. He did not look like he could make it outside on his own, so I told him I would get him to his knees and he could water down Janus.

"Are you serious?"

"You think he is Satan. Why not make a statement? Your Yahweh might get a good laugh out of it."

"You are a sick animal that needs to be put down," he laughed hoarsely.

I did not respond as I went behind him to lift him to his knees by putting my hands under his armpits. Once he was on his knees, he started moving a few paces towards the wooden statue of the club-carrying, black-bearded giant. I returned to the doors while I heard a strange giggle coming from behind the altar. I guess he took my suggestion to heart.

After he had finished his desecration of Janus, he stumbled more than walked over to me at the door holding a silver bowl in his hands. "Look what I found at the foot of Beelzebub."

I looked at the contents of the bowl, and it smelled like fresh blood. I put my finger into the thick liquid, and it came out red. "I guess it must be goat's blood for Janus."

He put it down and then asked, "Have you been up all night guarding the doors?"

"Yes."

He motioned with his head back to the rear of the temple. "You get some sleep, and I will watch."

"Just make sure the doors stay closed, and keep an eye near the center crack so you can see if someone is coming." I handed him the falcata and curled up in the same spot Eli had slept. It was still warm, and I fell into a delicious sleep quickly forgetting about the urine smell.

Around the middle of the day, Eli violently shook me awake. "Be quiet. Someone is coming."

We both moved behind the tall statue, and in came an old man stooped over from either injury or just age. He started cleaning up the mess from last

272

night's Janus worshipers. Then out of the old man came a horrific scream, and he turned and ran out of the temple. After it had appeared like he wasn't coming back soon, I went over to where he had screeched; and there was a young, naked woman about my age with a white bone-handled dagger sticking out of her chest along with a slit throat. The old man apparently was a slave who was there to clean up and discovered the girl when he uncovered her. The garment he had peeled off her lay next to her naked body.

"What is this?" asked Eli horrified to the same degree as the old man who went running out of the temple.

"Some kind of ritualistic sacrifice to this god of gates. I bet the Furies are not happy about this."

"Who in the Hades is the Furies? Never mind, I told you this is the temple of devils."

"Eli, get your cloak! We are leaving now!" I commanded while I covered the poor girl again realizing she was the third woman and fourth person I had seen killed with a knife wound to the chest. The first was my mother, the second was the Ethiopian gladiator killed by Marius in the arena, and thirdly was Claudia. Now, this unknown blond Barbarian girl made the forth. I ought to mention Messina's father killed by Lentulus and my father, but he was not stabbed with a knife to the heart; but both Messina's father and this girl had their throats cut. The whole idea of killing a human for a two-headed, wood painted god made me sick. Bile was rising up into my throat, but I swallowed it down. Eli returned holding my sword and scabbard looking as blanched-white as a new wool toga even though his face was lividly bruised and lacerated. I swallowed hard again to keep everything down as I helped Eli stagger out of the temple. Out in the light, I could barely look at Eli; for he was almost monstrous looking with his cut and swollen face.

"Venu, do you think that was human blood I found in the bowl in front of that demon god?"

I did not answer, but we both jumped in our skin when we heard the heavy temple door slam closed behind us. Eli was the first to speak. "Maybe Janus is mad because he knows we are never coming back." I did not comment but did smile as I guided Eli to the nearest bushes. The sun was high in a blue, cloudless sky. Having been in the dark temple, my eyes were still adjusting to the brightness of the middle of the day. I realized we should have eaten something before we left or at least drank some fluids. But there was no way we were going back inside that beastly temple. From the protection of the bush overgrowth, I spotted a few people on this side of the Tiber. When my eyes had been fully restored, I looked down the gentle-sloping hill to the river.

All I could see were a few lovers walking down at the other end of the open-air racetrack. On the track itself were a few exercise boys, slowly walking horses, one horse jumping around the walker, most likely happy to be out of his stall.

"Do you see anything?" asked Eli with his strained voice.

"Just some hot walkers around the Circus Vaticanus, but no one else appears in sight except a couple that darted into some bushes on the other side of the racetrack. I think we should get some distance from the Temple of Deva before anyone shows up looking in these bushes," I stated with my hand outstretched for Eli to take hold of my arm. We slowly walked towards the Tiber looking a little like male lovers out on a stroll. I really did not care what we looked like knowing we had to be somewhere else when the old slave returned with someone in authority, most assuredly a Praetorian Guard. I glanced over at Eli; and he was still looking feeble with sweat pouring from his cut, doughy, puffy face. One eye was completely swollen shut, and he looked as if an angry horse had trapped him in the back of a stall and kicked him in the head a few times. I suggested we go to the river and hide in the bushes down where it was cooler. My plan was to stay hidden until dark, and then we would make a plan for tonight.

"So we go here; we go there – but you are in charge, Venu. Let me tell you one thing – I am not feeling well. Perhaps you should just leave me in a bush and make a break out of the city. But, if you decide to stay with me, I will not spend one more night in a demon house, especially one who craves human blood."

"You are right about that – no more nights in a Janus temple."

At the river's edge, we found a private spot with another marble bed in a grove of bushes; and there we stayed all afternoon with Eli sleeping on the stone bed. I hated the place because it reminded me of the afternoon I hid naked in the bushes on Tiberius Island while Marius was winning his third wooden sword. I looked, and there was the little island of the god Aesculapius; and across the river to the left was the *Statilius Taurus Amphitheater*. I could see people going and coming from the various tunnels at ground level. A gladiatorial game must be in action at the amphitheater. I turned my attention back to what some called Tiberius Island, the only island in the Tiber. The island was partially blocked by the curve of the river, but I could see the rear of the ugly temple of Aesculapius. Yes, this was the river island where I waited for Zeno all those years ago naked in the bushes. Now, almost ten years later, I was hiding in more bushes on a hot afternoon next to the putrid-smelling Tiber.

A READING GIVEN AT THE GREAT LIBRARY OF ALEXANDRIA BY EPAPHRODITUS

Given in the year of the four emperors. During this year of civil war, the great fire broke out on Capitoline Hill, destroying much of Rome's archives.   *69 AD*

THE ORIGINS OF ROME
JANUS AND MARS

The first Roman wall was constructed after the tattooed, naked Celts conquered Rome in the early years of the Republic. Eventually, these Barbarians had abandoned the city due to a strange fever, which drove these foreigners entirely out of Italia. Afterward, the early leaders decided to build the first wall around the Seven Hills. At that first stage of Rome's history, Janus was the principal patron god of Romulus and Remus, the reputed founders of the city who became rich and powerful by preying off the salt traders crossing the river at the ford between Vaticanus Hill and Mars Field. Romulus and Remus were supposedly the sons of Mars born to a human mother, Rhea Silvia. The vast, open area near the west bend of the Tiber known as the Campus Martius or Mars Field was the location where a she-wolf found and suckled the two baby brothers. The ancient story stated the she-wolf found the babies floating down the Tiber in a basket placed in the river to die by Rhea Silvia's father, all because of the twins evil parentage with Mars.

Another story says a shepherd, not a she-wolf, discovered the basket of babies in the river at this spot. The shepherd's wife, unfortunately, had pursued questionable activities and, therefore, was called a lupa or prostitute. The Latin word lupa also meant she-wolf. Either way, the she-wolf became one of Rome's primary symbols of its power. I believe the latter story as closer to the truth if one considers Rome turning into the world's lupa, but my opinion is shaded by my feelings.

The actual story of Rome's beginnings depends on who is telling Rome's history. Zeno, my first boyhood teacher in Rome, once told me the story of the wooden horse given to Troy by the retreating Greeks as recorded in the Iliad. Zeno always said it was not a myth but the story was based on truth. Once Troy was subdued by the Greeks, some of the fleeing Trojans relocated to the Tiber and founded a new Troy but called it Rome. If this version is correct, then the Trojan Wars led to the founding of Rome 1,000 years ago. If the story of Romulus killing his brother and becoming its first Rex, then the city of Rome only reaches back 800 years. I have discovered that traditions, whether based on fact or fiction, become very powerful over time. For example, every five years all Roman citizens gather on Mars Field for purification by the Marmar priests called the salii. An enormous altar to Mars still stands on Campus Martius across the river from Vaticanus Hill. This "cleansing" is not a law or something written on the 12 bronze tables in the Romanum Forum but just something people do. The people of Rome love traditions even if they have forgotten the origins of the particular ritual. Mars Field in the old days of the Republic was also where the legions gathered before marching off to defend the city. This area later became their encampment. This was before the civil wars when generals used their armies on the Roman citizenry and which led to the famous Senatorial Laws that forbade any Roman soldier to step onto Italia proper. Still today, as I speak to this distinguished audience of Alexandria, the Praetorian Guards are the only troops allowed in Italia. Due to the fear of soldiers in uniform on the streets of Rome, the Praetorian Guards do not wear an official uniform but a short toga to deceive the people an army actually controls the city. The Praetorians' encampment is not located in Mars Field but is on the other side of the city inside its own walled cam near Viminal Hill. Without the Praetorian Guards, neither Augustus nor Tiberius nor any Caesars in the last 80 years would have been able to maintain dictatorial control.

Initially, the god Mars was a fertility god and was only much later associated with bloodletting in battle. Since early Romans prayed to him for protection for their farms against weather, insects, and armies, my thinking is Mars eventually developed into the god of war. Back when Mars was the god of fertility and agriculture, springtime was his time of celebration. The Romans turned these simple Mars gatherings into eating, drinking, and sexual events out on Mars Field, especially in the springtime. Ironically, at the start of spring, the Babylonians' temple prostitutes offered their services during the famous Ishtar Festival.

Mars's name means The Rebel. However, Romulus is the ultimate rebel since he murdered his brother Remus and then called the Seven-Hill region after his own name. Today Rome is accurately called the home of the Rebellious Ones. Once again, the truth depends on who is telling the story. I see a merging and mixing of ideas between Mars and Janus. For example, Janus is the god of beginnings; and the origins of Rome start at the first bend of the river between Mars Field and Vaticanus Hill with the Janus temple upon the summit of the eighth hill, facing the walled Seven Hills. Once again, this is my opinion; but I think my theory is sound. Many may not see the connections between Mars and Janus; and perhaps this is due to a vast, open flat area that separates the Tiber from the base of Vaticanus Hill putting the slightly sloping hill of Vaticanus a distance from the river. If the Temple of Janus were on the bank of the Tiber, precisely across from the altar of Mars, the connection to the two might be more obvious.

Janus and his wife Hora had been the principal deities over the life of the Republic, but now just about any god is allowed in Rome, except Jesus Christos. What should be clear to all who live in Alexandria is that the emperors have adopted the status of all the pharaohs of Egypt from Augustus to even the legates battling for supremacy of the Empire. Why is it all these legates are trying to claim to be gods? The crisis the Empire is facing is the same crisis Egypt faced for 3,000 years: bloodlines of divinity. Is this why Jesus of Nazareth is not recognized in Rome? Is only the bloodline of Caesar legitimate? Unfortunately, with the death of Emperor Nero, who murdered himself a few months past, there appear no more bloodline claims to Julius Caesar, the god of Rome.

All the Greek gods, as well as those from Egypt and elsewhere, have been adopted into the Roman pantheon. For example, the Greek god Zeus has become Rome's Jupiter. Zeus's wife Hera is now Juno to the Romans and mother of Mars, who formerly had been Aries. Isis is currently Venus or Asherah, Semiramis, Diana of Ephesus, or Aphrodite. The most supreme temple in Rome, visible to almost every quarter of the city, is not the Temple of Janus; but, instead, the temple to Jupiter Optimus Maximus located on Capitoline Hill. This is the most significant hill in Rome, adjacent to Palatine Hill, where the emperors live. Yet, mysteriously, only the god Apollo is allowed a temple on Palatine Hill because of Augustus's belief that he was the son of Apollo. Only Apollo could live with the living gods or emperors of Rome. Apollo is the god of light and insight, and perhaps this is why Apollo's name does not change from Greek to Latin. These days Olé Janus does have a small, modest temple in the Romanum Forum near Julius Caesar's temple; and both temples are about the size of the little temple of Athena Nike in Athens upon the Acropolis. However, the main Janus temple in Rome is relegated to the other side of the Tiber. The doors of all Janus temples are to be kept closed during peacetime and opened during war. During Augustus's reign, the temple doors were shut three times symbolizing a new state of peace. Before the rule of Augustus, for hundreds of years, the doors were only closed twice. Today the Empire is at war with itself, and the Janus temples have their doors wide open. This door policy is a metaphor to Rome's sickness. Shouldn't the temple doors be closed during a war – why open? Does anyone else see this as odd and eccentric?

All the rules and rituals of the different religions in Rome could drive any scholar mad. Remember, Rome was famous for the introduction of new gods, especially if any Barbarians beat the Romans in battle. Ironically, Rome would even build a temple to its enemy's god and sacrifice a human, usually a Vestal Virgin, who would be buried alive after an accusation was given of her unchaste behavior, which meant she had broken her vows. This is why Rome has more temples and religions than any city in the world. It should be understood that all the emperors of Rome were very superstitious. Now it might make sense to understand why Janus has his main temple outside the walls of Rome. He has been pushed aside because he is the god of confusion but is still in sight of the palaces on top of Palatine Hill, especially Capitoline Hill. To most Romans, Janus is the custodian of the cosmos and father of all the gods. Janus still secretly carries a great deal of weight, but few openly pay much attention to his deity. He is called a contradiction in the hall of gods. Not only is he the god of confusion, but he is the guardian of gates and the two-faced god. Janus is considered to be very arrogant demanding that his name appears first on any Roman god lists giving the Romans January as the first month on their calendars. Being the god of confusion has also contributed, in my opinion, to the misunderstanding about him, which, in a twisted way, gives him the power he desires. His consort Hora is the goddess of fertility, and now we are back to the connection with Mars across the river.

There are also many parallel ideas between Hora and the four Greek goddesses of the seasons: Winter, Spring, Summer, and Fall. They are the Hourais, and this is where the Latin and Greek word hour comes from. The rituals of Hora and Janus are considered dark and mysterious, perhaps even more ominous than the practices of the mystery cults of Bacchus, Isis, or even Cybele. The Greek word orgia (or ecstasy) is closely associated with Janus and Hora. The way this word is used is very similar to the 'orgia' of the Dionysus or Bacchus cult.

CHAPTER TWELVE

Rome – The 15th year of Tiberius and the 1st year of Jesus's public ministry in Palestina, which began about two and a half months earlier during the Feast of Passover in Jerusalem, marking the event that is known as the first Temple cleansing. (29 AD)

The longest part of the journey is said to be the passing of the gate. Blessed is the one whose transgression is forgiven, whose sin is covered.
Marcus Terentius Varro

By nightfall Eli was delirious with a scalding fever, and his breathing was very shallow. This was reminiscent of Grillius when he had his fever about a year ago out in the exercise yard of the Lyceum. I knew, if I did not get some help soon, Eli would surely die. Before I could find some help, I decided to try to lower Eli's temperature. I went down to the river and soaked his wool cloak, the one taken from Falcata Man, and covered Eli with it. About every half hour, I went and dipped the coat and repeated this trick, which seemed to help. When the waxing moon began to appear, I decided to take Eli somewhere for help. It had to have been about the middle of the night, and there was plenty of light from the moon to move about but not enough to expose us if we needed to hide. I woke Eli and told him we had to go. His fever still seethed, and he moaned incoherently; but it was not as bad as it had been. I decided he was not going to be able to walk. I placed him on my shoulder and tried carrying his dead weight. Eli had grown larger than I since I last saw him here in Rome. I knew I wasn't going very far doing this. When I reached some humble mud-and-stick homes, I put Eli down and hunted for a handcar. When I finally found what I was looking for in someone's side yard, I liberated it. Dogs started to bark when I left, but I moved quickly away pushing the one-wheeled cart. I eventually reached Eli with the handcart, and off we went down the road by moonlight. I retraced our path from the night before and returned to the 14th District, where I found myself back at the synagogue with the four trees. I left the cart in an alley and carried Eli into the synagogue where I put him down on the floor between two wooden benches in the main room. I was utterly exhausted, but I had to get rid of the handcart. Back out in the bluish light of the moon, I pushed the cart down to the Tiber and watched it float away. When I returned to the synagogue, Eli was fast asleep but still burning with a fever. Not knowing what to do, I just prayed to Eli's God and then lowered my body down next to him and fell fast asleep from exhaustion.

During what seemed like a death sleep, I was unaware of the house-to-house search that was going on in the 14th District. There were hundreds of Praetorian Guards involved in the search including other police units and firefighting bands. The open story on the streets was, "two professional assassins had killed the wife of Senator Gaius Vetallus, who had been the widow of Publius Quinctilius Varus. The Fates had finally paid justice to Varus's loss of Augustus's three eagles." I learned all of this the next morning from Rabbi Issachar, who discovered us asleep in his synagogue. When this rabbi spoke about Varus losing the three eagles, I asked him if he knew this was the same Varus who ordered the death of about two thousand Jews after Herod the Great died when he was the *legate* of Syria. I did not think the 14th District was being singled out because of professional killers being Jewish, for I knew the Praetorians were here searching for me because my father knew Eli was Jewish and this would be the most logical place to hide. My father was not the wealthiest man in the world because he was stupid.

Sitting on the synagogue floor as Rabbi Issachar told me what was happening around us, I became concerned he was going to turn us over to the Romans. I studied this old, wrinkled, dark-skinned Jew and believed he was thinking what I was thinking. I later learned Rabbi Issachar was a member of the Pharisaic sect and head overseer of this synagogue. Without asking who we were, the old rabbi ordered us to quickly hide under a concealed door built into the floor that led to a series of tunnels and underground crypts. I learned later that night, if Rabbi Issachar had not discovered us when he did, we would have been captured. All these narrow escapes and events began to have an impact on my belief in the God of Eli, Anab, Felix, Messina, and now Rabbi Issachar.

It was after the sun had set when Rabbi Issachar came and told me to carry Eli to his home, which was the house next to the synagogue. His wife was waiting with cold towels and everything else needed to nurse my Jewish friend with a fever and multiple wounds. Cooked meat and wine were sitting on the table when I carried Eli into a side bedroom carrying him like a sick baby lamb. Before even questioning me, Eli said a short prayer after I placed him on a wood-framed bed. After his prayer, Eli started to go in and out of consciousness. I was ordered to the other room and to eat while the rabbi's wife stripped Eli in a side room and began anointing his wounds with oil and spices. While I ate, Rabbi Issachar joined me at the table after his wife ordered him out of the room where she was working on Eli.

"That woman has a mind that is stubborn more than an old donkey," he said with more affection than frustration. I had a lot to learn about the dynamics of men and women, and I began fantasizing this might be possible for me in a few years with Messina. On the other hand, in all reality, that was a fool's dream; and I blocked such notions.

"We both appreciate all your help, and we will pay you," I said hoping not to insult his kindness.

"Do you wish for me to lose my reward?"

"You are going to put us in the hands of the authority?" I asked.

"May the mountains cry out if I do! I will never do such a thing! My reward is in the next life," cackled Issachar, who spoke Latin to me as if it were his birth language.

"I apologize if I misspoke."

"In truth, young man, I was close this morning to giving the Praetorians their prey when I found you two sleeping. I came here and told my wife what I found and what I planned on doing. She wagged her bony finger at me and said, 'May the Creator forbid; and you better learn to manage your thoughts, old *abba*. Truth be told, I have heard stories about Senator Vetallus and his wife. Those two are evil to the core and haters of the Jews.' I told her that was the point. 'If we turn those boys over to the Romans, the Romans might later remember the favor. Sacrifice two young killers, and save the entire Jewish population in Rome.' So my wife says, 'So you would sell yourself to the leeches of this world for the souls of two boys you know nothing about?'"

I finally interrupted, "Your wife actually said all of that?"

"You read the end of the Proverbs of Solomon in the Jewish Scriptures, and it describes my wife perfectly. She is an excellent woman. I must confess I did argue with her, which is a foolish problem I have had all these years. I said, 'They are murderers, cold-blooded killers.' She said, 'You do not know that.

The Romans lie to us all the time. When there is a plague in the city, whom do they persecute?' Then she used a Scripture story on me. Teach a woman to read, and this is what you get."

"What story did she use? I only know one story in your Scriptures, and that is the one about David and the giant Philistine."

"Oh, you know that story?" he asked with genuine interest.

"That is all, but I would be interested in learning more. What story did your wife use?"

"She said, 'So you turn the lads over to the Romans, and what happens? A new Pharaoh in the land does not remember Joseph or his deeds.' That is a story from the end of the first book in the *Torah*, the words of Moses. There is no greater prophet than Moses, my lad. Now I have a question for you. Did you and your friend kill the senator's wife?" Rabbi Issachar's eyes were level with mine as he asked the question. I hung my head in shame and confessed it was true, but I felt the urge to justify my actions.

"Tell me your side of the story, and leave nothing out," he said as if reading my mind.

I began telling of the events ten years earlier; and at one point Rabbi Issachar said, "Yes, I remember that day. There were many reports of many killings along with the news of the champion gladiator and his unbelievable survival of the *munera sine missione*, the game of gladiatorial elimination, from which there could be only one survivor."

I continued about my escape to Athens and my education at the Academy. I lied about the name of the school to protect Grillius and Hector. I was also careful not to use any names such as Hector or Grillius. As I told my life's story, it was as if I were talking about someone else. I had become detached from who I was, and retelling my life up to this present moment was a release yielding up a strange healing. I began to step away and see that I was filled with anger and guilt. I was torn by my feeble attempts to live the supposed life of a Stoic. When I finished, the kind rabbi patted my shoulder as he poured more wine into my clay cup. I was reminded of the story Felix told about the carpenter's son patting his brother on the shoulder three different times. I now understood that a touch was just a kind gesture. I wondered if it was a Jewish tradition.

"A most fascinating tale, young man," he said as he removed his hand from my shoulder. "It sounds like the Creator has a purpose for you since you have survived so many vexations. I expect you are now in my life for me to instruct you on the story of God, and maybe He has ordained for you to become one of His Chosen People."

"Yes, I would want to learn. Please tell me," I found myself asking as if I were a little boy asking for sweet bread pudding.

A smile crossed his face, and he searched his mind for where he should begin. After taking a sip of wine, he started. "The Creator of the Universe appeared many years ago to a man named Abraham, who first lived in Mesopotamia in the ancient city of Ur. That was perhaps 2,000 years ago when the Hamites of Ur, the descendants of Ham, one of the sons of Noah, who survived the flood, foolishly worshiped the moon as their creator. To show the world and their god was the moon, these Urites wore gold or silver crescent moons around their necks as well as around the necks of their camels. God told Abraham to depart from this country and go to the land that the Creator would show him. Abraham, being a descendant of Shem, the second son of Noah, obeyed and left Ur. Abraham later had many sons with three different women, but only the son by his first wife Sarah was the Chosen One who would bring forth the Messiah. That son was Isaac; the name means laughter in Hebrew. Abraham and his first wife Sarah, who were both in their 90s, laughed when they learned from God himself, in a human body, as He told Abraham and his wife they would have a son before the year was out. Nevertheless, one year later, Sarah gave birth to a son; and they called him Laughter or Isaac in Hebrew."

I did not understand his word usage; so I interrupted, "What do you mean Chosen One? Is the Chosen One the same as the Messiah?"

"Well, that actually goes back to the Garden of Eden when the first two people failed to be obedient to the commands of God. Their punishment has put all of us into this evil world we live in today – a fallen world of pain and suffering. Adam and Eve and their children became dead spiritually and later physically died. All children today are born into this broken world, both spiritually dead and destined to die someday physically and then destined for Hell. That would be you and I as children of fallen Adam. However, here is the good news: God gave Adam and Eve, the two humans in the Garden of Eden, a promise that God Himself would fix this spiritual and physical problem of death. Yes, you heard me correctly. God Himself promised to give eternal life to anyone, by faith, anyone who believes in the coming virgin born, Chosen One. Later the Chosen One was called the Messiah by the prophet Daniel. It is all directly based on trust and faith in the coming Seed of the Woman. I know that was a long-winded answer to your simple question, but both Chosen One and Messiah are the same."

"Who is this Promised One, this seed of the woman? When will he come? And is he also called the Redeemer?"

"All those names would fit, and no one knows unless you understand the prophecy of the prophet Daniel. He tells us that archangel Gabriel explained to him about the arrival of the Messiah. This promised one would come to receive his throne in Jerusalem as the King of Kings. What is frightening is there are those who believe it could be at any time. I am one of those who thinks that we are in the last days according to the Scriptures and that the Messiah could be alive in Judaea right now. That is how I understand the promises of His coming as I believe it is stated in the Holy Words of the Scriptures."

"What are some of the signs?" I asked wanting to know more. Actually, everything that I had studied and learned up to this point seemed unimportant details compared with this kind of knowledge if it were true. "There are many promises to look for as stated in the Holy Scriptures. Actually, there are hundreds of signs. Some are very general while others are most specific."

"Give me a specific one."

"Well, the Messiah or Anointed One, the Greek word is *Christos* or Christ, will be born into the family of Abraham, Isaac, Jacob, and Judah. Later the Scriptures say that the Anointed One will come through King David, the second king of Israel-Judah after it became a monarchy. That was a thousand years ago. Before David was the king, he was the one you mentioned who killed the giant. This future son of King David will be from the village of David, the town of Bethlehem, that is about seven miles south of Jerusalem. He will come into Jerusalem riding on the colt of a donkey. He will enter His Temple and rebuke the priesthood, the sons of Levi. And he will be born only of a woman, the seed of a woman."

"You mean he will be virgin born?"

"That is the only way to read the Scriptures."

"What about all the virgin born claims in history?" I asked.

Rabbi Issachar looked at me with a questioning stare and asked, "What are you talking about? The Promised One has not been born unless you count the claim of this Jesus or Yeshua, cousin of some desert Essene named Yochannan the Baptizer."

"What about the Persians who claim Zurathushtra, the founder of the Ahura Mazda worshipers, who listen to the Magi priests from their fire temples? The Persians claim his birth was from a radiantly wonderful virgin mother some six hundred years ago. Then, what about the followers of Siddhartha Gautama from around the Ganga River on the other side of the Hindu Kush Mountains, who call him the Buddha or *Tathagata*: the one who came, left, and then came back? Their *Sanskrit* and *Pali* texts say he was virgin born about five hundred years ago. And do not forget Alexander the Invincible or the Great, who conquered Persia over three centuries ago. He claimed to be virgin born. Also, here in Rome, Romulus and Remus would qualify as being virgin born by a human mother with the help of the god Mars. And, of course, there are stories of Caius Julius Caesar claiming to be virgin born. Augustus is now considered virgin born by Apollo."

"This is all news to me, young man, all except Augustus being the son of Apollo. That myth I have heard out in the streets of the *Urbs*. However, remember Lucifer the Devil, also known as Satan, is the evil chief leader of the fallen angels and other fallen spiritual beings. Satan, Foe to God and Tempter of all humans, is always trying to thwart the truth. He is the father of lies, and he is attempting to copy what the Creator has promised. If there really are all these claims in history, it does not surprise me in the least. Moses warned of the coming of many false prophets 1,500 years ago in the *Torah*. Moses clearly states and warns about men who would come, lie, and distort the Word of God. Now I am curious; do you believe that any of these people you named are truly virgin born?"

"I never heard of this Devil character," I stated hoping I was not rude by not answering his question. Actually, I did know *deva* was a *Sanskrit* word; but I knew nothing of the name Devil, just demons as fallen angels.

"Satan is one of the most beautiful and most powerful creatures God created in Heaven, a son of God created before humans. He rebelled and took perhaps a third of all the many angels with him in his war against the Creator. His name was Lucifer before his fall, but now he is called the Dragon."

"Dragon?"

"Yes, a creature that looks like a snake but with legs. Now, do you believe any of these men you named are, indeed, born without the help of a man's seed?"

"Honestly, all I can remember from my personal studies is that Zurathushtra and Siddhartha never claimed to be virgin born. These stories began after their deaths, and their followers and devotees started those rumors. However, Alexander the Great did openly declare he was virgin born after his visit to a pagan priest in the desert of Egypt. He even minted thousands of silver coins with his horns of godhood for the world to believe his own self-serving, twisted narrative."

"Now you are teaching the teacher. This is the first time I have heard Alexander the Macedonian ever thought of himself as being virgin born."

"He did make the claim from that Egypt visit until shortly before his death, but I doubt he was virgin born. Once, when living in Greece, I had access to some old coins from Alexander's time. I looked at the image of Alexander on an old silver *tetradrachm* coin and compared his profile to his father, Phillip the II of Macedonia, on an old gold *stater*. Both profiles were almost identical. I am sure you have seen many sons who do look like their fathers."

After the rabbi had nodded his head to affirm my observation, I continued. "Therefore, I do not think Alexander was virgin born since he looked too much like his father, Phillip. Now it is my turn to ask you a question."

Issachar again nodded after taking another sip of wine to wet his mouth.

"You mentioned a fellow named Jesus. Who is he?"

"I will answer your question in a roundabout fashion. The Romans rudely call my land *Palestina* after the ancient pagans called Philistines. These ancient Philistines worshiped a fish-looking god named Dagon; and one of these Philistines was this Goliath of the city of Gath, whom David slew with a stone from his shepherd's sling. This you told me was the only story you know concerning the holy writings of the Jews. Many of these Philistines were giant men, but there are no more Philistines alive today that I am aware. No, I take that back. On one visit to my homeland, I did meet a man from Sidon who had six fingers and six toes. He was not that tall, but he was four times the width of you or me. I would say he weighed well over three hundred pounds. You see, Goliath had six toes and six fingers. Truth be told, the Philistines still have some of their people mixed with other pagans in God's Holy Land. Now the term *Palestina* angers my Hebrew brothers and sisters when the Romans call them by this pagan name. Therefore, *Palestina* is a crude Roman epithet of my homeland we Jews call the Promised Land or Holy Land. Sometimes we call it the Land of Abraham, Isaac, and Jacob. Since Jacob had a name change late in his life, some of my fellow Jews call our land Israel, the new name of Jacob. No matter the name, it is the land promised to Abraham, Isaac, and Jacob two millennia ago by the God of Heaven, the God of the Hebrews. Now to your question. Ironically, living in the Promised Land right now is a mere teacher the Romans call Jesus of Nazareth. His Hebrew name is Yeshua. He is apparently performing some spectacular miracles and speaking with high authority. This is most interesting since he never went to the academies in Jerusalem. He is not a priest or a son of the Levites, not that a prophet has to be a son of Levi. However, he is from the house of David; and there are rumors that he was virgin born. He is most definitely a fascinating character to keep your eyes on. Some say that the Prophet Daniel predicted that this is the time of the Son of Man to reveal himself. But I'm sure the Romans or even the Jews will kill him before too long if he, indeed, makes any such claim as being the promised Messiah or the Son of Man."

"Your people will kill him? Why? And what does the term Son of Man mean?"

"Moses warned of false prophets; and all false prophets must be put to death to protect the Chosen People, which is another name for the Jews. I personally do not think this man will survive very long. There are very strict rules that have been established down through the ages to test prophets."

This sounded a little extreme to me, but I desired to know something else that I had to ask. "Did you say that Jesus is his given name?"

"Oh no! As I have said, that is his Latin name. Yeshua would be his Hebrew name."

"Well, I can then tell you on good authority that this Jesus from Nazareth is not virgin born."

"What do you mean? Have you been to my homeland?"

"Never, but I have heard stories about this Jesus and his cousin John, who baptizes at the Jordan River. I am just saying this Jesus sounds like the son of a carpenter-stonemason from Galilee."

"Yes, he is from Nazareth, which is north of Judaea and part of Galilee. However, the story is he is not the carpenter's son but the stonemason adopted him as his son after his birth. That is what I heard if this is the same man. What story did you hear?"

I retold the story that Felix had told me of Joseph ben Jacob and his sons cutting down the sandalwood trees, the story told by the brother named James. Issachar found the part about Jesus explaining the Psalm of David to the old man in Nazareth most intriguing. To me, understanding the hymns, called the Book of Psalms in the Jewish Scriptures, was like swimming in a fast-moving river with many sharp rocks sticking up in the current. I still wanted to know what Son of Man meant.

Issachar was mulling over this concept when his wife emerged from the side room and told us Eli was sleeping and we, too, should also try to get some rest. I did not argue and took my falcata and scabbard into the room with Eli and fell asleep on the floor next to his cot. I covered up with my newly liberated, gray *himation*, the one I had found on the floor in the temple of Janus. The *himation* I had found was a very expensive cloak; and, before I fell asleep, I wondered why the owner had left it.

I awoke the next day, Moon Day, when Eli jostled me and requested I get him a chamber pot.

"Do I look like your nurse? Maybe your savior, but not your nurse."

"I thought we were friends," he said trying to smile.

"You are no friend of mine, and I will tell that to the next stranger I see," I said in jest; but, unfortunately, it sounded too sincere for Eli, who was in no mood for this kind of humor.

Defusing my tone, Eli tried to neutralize his abruptness by replying, "Then tell that stranger I need a chamber pot." Now we both began to laugh, and then it dawned on me that Eli was not going to die.

The rabbi's wife was delighted to see the improvement in Eli since his fever had broken sometime in the night. She said the color of his face looked much better. I just saw black and blue bruises with his one eye still swollen shut, so I did not know what she was talking about.

Issachar was gone when I came out of the room looking for a chamber pot. A little before the noon meal, Issachar returned. His wife served a simple midday meal of bread and *garum* at his arrival. Eating the *garum* caused me to think of Felix and Messina. Afterward, Issachar asked me to join him in his garden courtyard. It was secluded by high walls and covered by grape vines that hung from overhanging trestles with substantial grape leaves and little, tiny clusters of green grapes growing in bunches along the walls and above us. Within a few months, these grapes would be ready to harvest. We sat on wooden benches, ate figs, and drank more Judaean wine that I was beginning to enjoy, especially its sharp, sweet taste. This was one of those moments when life seemed to be beautiful and would last forever. Unfortunately, these moments are far and few between.

Rabbi Issachar wanted to speak first, but I had a curious question to ask. I wanted to know why no one was in the Synagogue yesterday since it was the Jewish Sabbath. The old rabbi told me that his congregation had an unwritten rule that no one would come to the synagogue on a Sabbath if the Romans were searching the 14th District. They did not want to all be trapped in a building just in case the Romans tried to block the doors and burn them all alive. He told me it had happened in other cities when there were plagues or other troubles where the Jews became the mark of people's fears. I nodded my head that I understood. After he had shared this information, I motioned for him to return to whatever he wanted to say.

Rabbi Issachar bobbed his head and began speaking. "I wanted to tell you privately what I heard from reliable sources this morning. Senator Vetallus's wife is dead, and the senator is going to survive his wounds. Apparently, the famous gladiator from the *munera sine missione* had his left hand maimed; and it quickly became infected. In order to save his life, physicians removed his hand and the lower arm just below the elbow."

I wanted to smile at this report, but I could not since I should have killed both men. "How much of a bounty is being offered?"

"Two hundred thousand *sestertii*. It is the highest reward anyone has ever heard of. That is more than a wealthy merchant can earn in eight to ten years. You, young man, are very famous and valuable."

"Why not turn us both in? My calculation tells me it would take a Roman soldier 160 years to equal what the bounty is for the two of us. Or is it just for me?"

"Just you, but still, with that much money being offered, it could make your grandmother a snitch. What is it that your father thinks you have that is worth that much money besides the fact you killed his wife?"

"The question is do I have to worry about you?"

"I would turn you in with little regret; but I love my wife more than money, so I would say you are safe."

"And what about the God of Abraham? What would He say if you turned me over to the Romans?"

"Yes, I do fear my God. For now, you and your friend are both safe," he said with a sly grin that did not give me great comfort.

"Are the soldiers still searching the 14th District?"

"They have moved on, but they will be back. This is a big city with more than one million souls. After the soldiers search the other districts, they will return and tear this one apart. It has happened before. They will first seal off all exits around the 14th District and spend weeks going from house to house destroying walls and floors. I am afraid it will be a painful ordeal for everyone in the 14th District."

I took a big swallow of wine. It started to get cold in the grape arbor courtyard, and I tightened the *himaton* string around the throat area. Issachar looked relaxed and comfortable. "Could you tell me more about Abraham's son Isaac?" Once again, changing the subject was a ploy I have always used to redirect someone away from a negative issue that disturbed me.

Issachar smiled for a moment as he mused. "Remember I said Isaac means laughter. Do you remember why?"

I nodded and repeated how God appeared to Abraham when he was nearing the old age of 100 years and told him he was going to have a son through his wife Sarah, who was also beyond the age of bearing children. "Both of them laughed when they first heard the prediction; but it came to pass a year later and, thus, the name Isaac."

"You have an excellent memory. I can see you were tutored well in Athens, but the story on the street is that it was the Lyceum and not the Academy you attended. Did you lie to me?"

I confessed and told him why. I did promise not to lie anymore, and he forgave me with a smile and an understanding twinkle in his eyes.

"Now will you continue?"

"Later Isaac produced twins. The second born was Jacob, which means the grabber because he was holding onto his brother Esau's ankle when Esau was coming forth from his mother's womb. The elder twin was named Esau, which means red. Esau had red hair, you see. Many years later, after Jacob had fathered all his children, God changed his name to 'Israel,' which means 'Prince of God.' According to the rule of the eldest son, Esau was the holder of the firstborn birthright. Oddly, Esau sold his birthright to Jacob for red stew; and, therefore, God said, "I have loved Jacob, but I have hated Esau.""

"God hates some people?" I asked.

"Hate is a harsh word, but God is injured when He gives something special to someone and that person, to whom it was given, spits upon it. For example, does your father, Senator Vetallus, hate you?"

"Two hundred thousand *sestertii* does not sound like love to me, but my father is not God even though he acts like it. He called me his 'evil son' last time he said anything to me. Actually, those were his last words to me after I killed his wife; yet, the words still sting even when I consider their source."

Rabbi Issachar had a sad look in his eyes when he said, "I apologize for bringing up your father, but permit me to continue."

I dropped my head in understanding, and he spent the afternoon telling about his people's history until he came upon the man named Moses. I became troubled and doubted the validity of Issachar's stories after I listened to the life and times of Moses. I finally had to express my discomfort and apprehensions. "That's impossible. A sea cannot open to allow over a million people to cross on dry ground at night. And then the waters come back together and destroy an entire army of chariots. That would be like the whole population of Rome vacating the city in one night. And what about the Nile turning into blood? I cannot believe that either! Then you add in an Angel of Death killing only first-born males in homes without the blood of lambs on the doors? This is all too bizarre!"

Rabbi Issachar had looked at me for a long time before he continued in a soft, soothing voice. "My young friend, you have an adamant mind. However, tell me, how can the obstinate mind of man understand the ways of the One who created that man? Can you understand how your own unbending

290

mind works or your own heart within your chest, which moves the blood throughout your body every day year after year? In addition, how is it your fingers can hold a sword or a woman as well as grasp a little needle to sew? What about your eyes that are never filled and, yet, never stop seeing? Can you explain any of this? Understand what I am saying, and you will have wisdom. The fear of God is the beginning of wisdom. That is what the Scriptures say. God is invisible except we see His personality through all the things of His creation. The heavens, plants, animals, and even you declare His glory. Yet, we still would not know His inner thoughts unless He spoke to us in our own language. True? And why is it only humans are the only creatures in this world who have language, and why is it most of the nations of people we know have invented writing? Isn't writing man's greatest invention? By written form, a man can preserve his ideas and transmit his ideas to future generations long after he is dead. That would be man's greatest invention."

I yielded this point by moving my head in agreement hoping this old man would continue and not think of me as unyielding in my thoughts.

"But God did choose to reveal Himself to man in words so men could know God's heart. He had to start with someone, and this was the man Abraham. However, it was not until Moses about six hundred years after Abraham, when God gave us Hebrew people His Holy Law. It is true; the commandments of God written on stone tablets are very negative. The Law is negative and cannot save anyone. Only faith in the coming Messiah is where salvation lies. The Law only defines what sin is; and, therefore, sin is negative. Yet, the Law is a kind of grace since we humans are unworthy to have fellowship with the One and Only Creator. The Law gives us humans a way to come before the Great God of the *Cosmos*."

Rabbi Issachar stood from his bench and went into his house returning after a short while with several papyrus scrolls. He also had a cloak draped over his shoulders. After covering his head with his cloak, he unrolled one of the scrolls. In respect, I also lifted up the hood of my cloak to cover my head.

Finally, Rabbi Issachar found what he was looking for and began speaking in Greek, not Hebrew. I just sat there listening to this man read as he stood in front of me. *"And the Lord spoke all these words saying, 'I Am the Lord your God, who brought you out of the land of Egypt, out of the house of bondage.'"*

"'You shall have no other gods beside Me.'"

"'You shall not make to yourself an idol, nor likeness of anything, whatever things are in the heaven above, and whatever is in the earth beneath, and whatever is in the waters under the earth.'"

"You shall not bow down to them nor serve them; for I am the Lord your God, a jealous God, recompensing the sins of the fathers upon the children to the third and fourth generation to them that hate me and bestowing mercy on them that love me to thousands of them, and on them that keep my commandments.'"

"'You shall not take the name of the Lord your God in vain, for the Lord your God will not leave him unpunished who takes His name in vain.'"

"Remember the Sabbath day to keep it holy. Six days you shall labor and shall perform all your work. But the seventh day is the Sabbath of the Lord your God; on it you shall not do any work, you nor your son or your daughter, your male or female servant, nor your ox or your donkey, nor any cattle of yours, nor the stranger that sojourns with you. For in six days the Lord made the heaven, the earth, the sea, and all things in them and rested on the seventh day; therefore, the Lord blessed the seventh day and made it holy.'"

"Honor your father and your mother that it may be well with you and that you may live long on the good land, which the Lord your God gives to you.'"

"'You shall not murder.'"

"'You shall not commit adultery.'"

"'You shall not steal.'"

"'You shall not bear false witness against your neighbor.'"

"'You shall not covet your neighbor's wife; you shall not covet your neighbor's house, nor his field, nor his servant, nor his maid, nor his ox, nor his donkey, nor any of his cattle, nor whatever belongs to your neighbor.'"

Rabbi Issachar rolled up the scroll after he finished reading. Still standing next to the bench, he looked up into the heavens and said in a loud voice, "Thus says the Lord!"

I was deeply moved by all that Rabbi Issachar had read. Never before had I felt this way; neither had I heard such bold power in something read aloud. Was it possible that there was only one true God? What was I to think? Was I better than the man next to me or the one next to the other? It was as if an internal washing was occurring. Was this the opening of the gates by the Creator to my "city of rebellion" that had been running free for so long? It was as if God was holding a falcata, sharper than any blade made by human hands, and was cleaving at my heart. I felt as if a bright light was striking the dam of my inner being and all the floodwaters of my internal illness were going to be released from the lake of my inner being. I had been holding back a wall of vile water that somehow had to be released before I could be washed by new waters from heaven. It was as if the City of God was marching over my puny existence and I needed to surrender and submit to the One and Only God.

"I understand only one thing," I finally confessed to Issachar, who now was sitting on his bench across from mine. "I see a God that you Jews worship, who is not an extension of man's own mind."

"I do not understand everything of what you just said," exclaimed Issachar appearing mystified but visibly pleased by the strange power working in me.

"The gods of Rome are the same gods of the Greeks or other lost people. The names are just changed. Zeus is Jupiter; Ares is Mars. Isis, Ishtar, Artemis, Aphrodite, and Venus are all the same but with different names. The people of Rome also worship the gods of the superstitious Barbarians; all are honored except the God of the Jews. Is not Mercury Day also Woden Day? Then comes Thor Day, which is followed by Frigg or Freya Day. These are Barbarian names. Why do you think Augustus put all the Jews in the 14th District? He did not separate any other religious group from each other. Why? To separate the truth from all the lies? The fact is this: the respective elements of all the gods and religions of Rome have nothing in common with your God and your beliefs. The truth is blinding to what is false; and it has to be located across the river from the lies, which is the foundation of the Seven Hills. Yet, the darkest of all the gods has his temple next to the 14th District and not on the Seven Hills; and that is Janus. Why is that? Is Janus really your Lucifer trying to emulate the truth that stands outside of Rome?"

"What about Janus?" asked the old rabbi. "I agree; this temple is located outside the gated city on this side of the river. For what reason I have no answer."

"Janus is the greatest lie of all. Don't you see? His temple is located next to the 14th District. Satan and the Jews are the same to the Romans. Alternatively, Janus is just the god of confusion, and so is the God of the Jews to the Romans. I mean no disrespect. It is just an observation."

"Perhaps you are right. Satan is the father of lies. But I'm still not sure what you are trying to say," said the old Jew apologetically.

He was right about this; no one could understand my mind except God. To change the subject, I said, "It is simple. You Jews did not make up your God. Your God is not human or animal like all the other gods, which is absurd if you only ponder it a moment. Did not your God say not to do exactly what the world has done? Is not the world worshiping and making idols of everything above and over the Creator including one another? It is almost laughable when you think of Janus with two faces looking in opposite directions and going nowhere. When there is peace, his gates are closed; but his gates are open when there is war. What logic is this, other than twisted reasoning? Should not the gates be open or closed in the opposite situation? It was as if Janus welcomes death and destruction of humans upon humans but demands his gates be closed when peace reigns. This is so obvious; it is hard to see."

The rabbi just sat there thinking. I wanted the truth, and it was not anything Rome had discovered. The only thing that made sense was relegated out of the city into this district. "If there really were a creator, He would not be like the creatures He has made. He would be far above His creation, and your God is the only God I have heard about who is not man or beast or a combination of both. He is far above this physical world. He is spirit and truth and light and life itself."

"Then what does this mean to you?" asked the rabbi.

"I am cursed because I was born a Roman. I do not see any hope for myself," I said hanging my head.

"Not true!" declared Rabbi Issachar as he fumbled for the second scroll he had brought out with him. He opened it and finally found what he was searching. "Here read this," he said pointing to a passage.

"I am sorry, but I cannot read Hebrew," I declared.

"This is in Greek. Surely, you can read Greek."

"Your Holy words are in Greek?" I declared in astonishment. Had he read the law of his God in Greek? Here I was thinking this man was translating from Hebrew into Greek, just for me. "Do you think it is acceptable to have God's Words translated into another language? Wouldn't there be the concern about mistranslation problems?"

"If God is the one who confused the language in the first place, don't you think God would reverse that problem when it came to His Word? Do you think God's holy language in heaven is Hebrew? I doubt it. God's Word can be written in any language and make sense to any human. That is what I believe."

"You make a good argument. Tell me more about this Greek translation of God's Word, and is the Hebrew translated into any other language?"

"Only into Greek. Around three hundred years ago in the Egyptian city of Alexandria, the son of Alexander's general named Ptolemy was establishing the greatest library in the world. This Ptolemy II wanted his Great Library to contain all the books in the world. He also wanted all books and scrolls translated into one language – Greek. The answer to your other question is I believe the Samaritans have a Greek translation of the *Torah*."

"Who are the Samaritans?"

"Never mind for now. Maybe later I will explain and also tell you about the angels, the good and the fallen messengers of God."

Maybe I should for once in my life stay on subject. "I am familiar with the Great Library of Alexandria," I said. "As I understand, some great scholars worked at the Great Library of Alexandria: Eratosthenes; Aristophanes of Byzantium; and Aristarchus, who said the world circles the sun and the earth is not the center of the *cosmos*."

"Even if Aristarchus is correct, the sun, earth, and the rest of the planets that we know might be in the center of this vast *cosmos*. But, putting that thought aside, let us just consider the Great Library of Alexandria. It was Callimachus who was chief director of the librarians when he drew up all its contents saying that perhaps there were as many as one hundred thousand scrolls, but a great deal was destroyed by fiery arrows fired from ships out in the bay when Julius Caesar besieged Alexandria to help Cleopatra against her younger king-husband-brother and his army."

"You are somewhat correct; yet, some of my Lyceum teachers maintain that the library did not completely burn to the ground. Most of the damage was the adjacent warehouses, but still an important repository of thousands of minor scrolls was lost to history forever."

"And don't forget there is still a smaller library outside of Alexandria's city limits located at the Temple of the Serapeum. This library is hated by the Jews of Alexandria because of its pagan scrolls and false explanation of the origin of the world."

"Someday I would love to visit Alexandria, and I shall investigate both libraries. But tell me now why you, a Jew, live here in Rome and not in the Promised Land or at least in Alexandria?"

"My story is very long. But the short of it is because of the burning of the library by Caesar in Alexandria. Caesar apparently had some guilt because his naval force was responsible for the fire and destruction of irreplaceable books and scrolls. Julius Caesar wanted to make up for his folly and started a library here in Rome after he returned. My favorite non-Jewish writer, Marcus Terentius Varro, was placed in charge of Caesar's dream. Unfortunately, it never became what Caesar wanted. A portion of the library was destroyed by the radicals, the same group which agreed with Caesar's assassination in *Pompey's Theater*. But it was Varro, the lone reason why I came to Rome. When I first learned of Varro's encyclopedia, I had to come here to read it. It is true I, a Jew, wanted to read and understand Varro's nine books on *grammatical, dialectica, rhetorica, geometria, arithmetica, astrologia, musica, medicina,* and *architectura,* which were only here in Rome. Those works are why I ended up in this unscrupulous city."

"Did you read Varro's encyclopedia?"

"That I did, and still I prefer the Septuagint over what man understands regarding his world. Don't get me wrong, Varro is a brilliant man, but how can a human compare to the Spirit of God."

"What is the Septuagint?"

"Now we are back at the Great Library of Alexandria. Its founder, King of Egypt Ptolemy II Philadelphus, had his librarian, Demetrius of Phalerum, almost three hundred years ago invite 70 to 72 Jewish scholars to come and translate the Holy Scriptures from Hebrew into Greek. They came and completed the project in 70 or 72 days on the island of Pharos, where the Great Lighthouse stands. The Roman number 70, or LXX, is sometimes given as the abbreviation of this work. I have a complete copy of the LXX right here in my home."

"Ptolemy II hired 70 Jewish scholars to come and translate the Jewish Holy Scriptures, which they did? Or was it 72?"

"That is the story. And the number 70 is significant because there were 70 men in 70 days, and that is the origin of the name *Septuagint*. Yet, that story might be a myth; and the number 72 is used because the translators were taken from Israel's 12 tribes, 6 translators from each tribe. I have been reading a Greek translation for you to understand since you know Greek. Remember one thing: someone years ago had to have translated the entire Scriptures from Hebrew into Greek."

I took the scroll from his hands and found where I thought his finger had pointed. "Should I cover my head?" I asked trying to show respect forgetting it was already covered. He nodded, and we both laughed when I discovered I already had my gray hood over my head. After I had stopped laughing at myself, I asked, "What am I going to read?"

"A Psalm of King David from whose loins will come the Messiah."

"David was a poet as well as a warrior?"

"Yes, I guess you could say that."

Now I had a new growing respect for this David character. I looked at the Greek text that had been carefully copied on a new-looking papyrus scroll. *"Bless the Lord, O my soul. Oh, Lord, my God, You are very great; You have clothed Yourself with praise and honor, who robes Thyself with light as with a garment spreading out the heaven as a curtain, who covers His chambers with waters, who makes the clouds his chariot, who walks on the wings of the wind, who makes His angels spirits and his ministers a flaming fire, who establishes the earth on her sure foundation; it shall not be moved forever. The deep, as it were a garment, is His covering; the waters shall stand above the hills. At Your rebuke they shall flee; at the voice of the thunder, they shall be alarmed. They go*

up to the mountains and down to the plains to the place, which You have found
for them. You have set a boundary which they shall not pass; neither shall they
turn again to cover the earth."

"No! No!" said Rabbi Issachar. "You are reading the wrong one. Read the
psalm before that one."

Maybe he thought it was the wrong one, but it was not to me. Here was a
picture of my thoughts as Eli and I crossed between the Circus Maximus and
the Imperial Palaces, two nights ago, the night we escaped over my father's
wall. I felt an electric tingle running up my spine. I rolled the scroll back; and
Issachar pointed to the spot he first wanted me to read saying, "This is the
psalm I want you to read."

I smiled at his frustration, but he did not know there was a higher power
than him in this grape arbor. It was one of those rare moments when the
Creator lets you know He is right at your elbow. I looked down and again
began to read. *"Bless the Lord, O my soul; and all that is within me, bless his*
holy name. Bless the Lord, O my soul; and forget not all His praises: who forgives
all your transgressions, who heals all your diseases, who redeems your life from
corruption, who satisfies your desire with good things so that your youth shall be
renewed like that of the eagle. The Lord executes mercy and judgment for all that
are injured. He made known His ways to Moses, His will to the children of Israel.
The Lord is compassionate and gracious, long-suffering, and full of mercy. He will
not always be angry; neither will He be wrathful forever. He has not dealt with
us according to our sins nor recompensed us according to our iniquities. For as
the heaven is high above the earth, the Lord has so increased His mercy toward
them that fear Him. As far as the east is from the west, so far has He removed our
transgressions from us. As a father pities his children, the Lord pities them that
fear Him. For He knows our frame and remembers that we are dust."

I was stunned and could not finish. "Certainly, this God is kind and
forgiving. But will He forgive a Roman-Greek Gentile?"

"Perhaps you now see the true God in a different light. Did not the
Scriptures say the Lord pities them who fear Him? That could be you."

"He has to be the true God, and all the others are false gods. I see and
understand that now. I want to follow and worship your God."

Rabbi Issachar grabbed my hands, and his eyes looked moist. "My boy, the
Creator has opened your eyes. What are you thinking at this very moment?"

Once again, darkness began to drop over me; I knew I had to confess what
the old rabbi knew. "I murdered my father's wife. I have done an evil thing,
and the Creator must be angry with me."

"I know, and God knows you killed the senator's wife. However, you have other iniquities besides murder. You are Roman and a pagan. To be aligned with God's Chosen People, you must first become a Jew; and next, you must go to Jerusalem and offer a sin sacrifice at the Temple of God. Are you willing to do this?"

"I can become a Jew? How is this possible?"

"A proselytized Jew. Are you willing to do this?"

"Yes, I will do anything for His service," I found myself saying without much thought.

"You are willing to comply with the Mosaic Law?"

"Yes, for it is what God demands of us all. And it does make perfect sense."

"Then you must first be circumcised; and then after recovery, you will be immediately immersed in water. And then you will make a pilgrimage to God's Temple on Mount Moriah in Jerusalem."

I nodded in agreement even though I understood very little of what he was saying. Within that very hour, Rabbi Issachar took me into the room where Eli slept. He took a flint knife and ordered me to lift my tunic. The circumcision was over in a moment, but a painful moment it was. I did not make a sound not wanting to wake Eli. I was bandaged and told to stay in the room with Eli until I healed. I remained there on the floor thinking about what I had done. Yet, if this is what the Creator wanted, then it was a small price to pay to be obedient. Soon I would be going to Judaea to the Great Temple of this God of the Jews, and the thought of this was overwhelming to my imagination. The Temple in Jerusalem was the largest and grandest structure made by man if one does not count the three great pyramids located south of the delta region in Egypt. The Egyptian temples at Thebes might be more extensive but not as magnificent in situation. I could not believe I was going to see Herod's Temple with my own eyes. Maybe I could even meet John the Baptist and the tree-cutter Jesus. I closed my eyes feeling an enormous weight being lifted off me, and I fell into a profound and long sleep.

JOHN LAWRENCE BURKS

WHAT ARE WE SUPPOSE TO DO NOW?

PART FOUR

ITALIA

IN THE TIMES OF JESUS OF NAZARETH

GAUL

PANONIA

ALPS

MACEDONIA

ARNO R.

RUBICON R.

MARE ADRIATICA

TYBER R.

ITALIA

CORSICA

MARE TYRRHENUM

SARDINNIA

ROME

OSTIA

APPIAN WAY (VIA APPIA)

CAPUA

BRUNDISIUM

CUMAE

MT. VESUVIUS

TARANTUM

POMPEI

(VIA MINUCIA)

CAPRI

MESSINA

SICILIA

SYRACUSE

CARTHAGE

AFRICA

© 2015 Vidvertise.com

MARE INTERUM
(MEDITERRANEAN SEA)

CHAPTER THIRTEEN

Rome – 15th year of Tiberius, 59 years since Actium, and the 1st year of Jesus of Nazareth's public ministry.   *(29 AD)*

Repent, for the kingdom of heaven has come near.   John the Baptist

The night after my circumcision Rabbi Issachar came and told Eli and me that the 14th District was being searched again. He led us to the synagogue surrounded by the four big trees. Inside we found the trap door; and with the aid of palm lamps, Eli and I were back underground in the tunnels and crypts of the 14th District. Here we stayed for two long months. Rabbi Issachar came once a day to deliver food and drink. He kept telling us it was too dangerous for us to come out: homes were being torn apart, and some people had been severely beaten. The rabbi assured us we were safe and not to leave the tunnels unless he opened the secret door. He had devised a secret knock, and we were not to open the hatch unless we heard the knock.

At the end of the two long months, Eli and I desperately wanted out of our dark and damp dungeon. We had not talked much during our stay underground believing sound travels further than one thinks. When awake, I kept repeatedly thinking that God's Word was God's mind. To meditate and muse on God's Word was to know God's thoughts. It seemed very simple; yet, sardonically, to perceive God with only our human minds hinged on understanding how far the east is to the west. There had to be some kind of supernatural way for God to renew our minds to fathom just a pinch of His brilliance and love. This seemed the missing element in what was happening in my new conversion to Judaism. It all appeared to be an outward transformation of a man's will. My heart or inner being was still dirty and filled with filth.

Tonight, dictating my story after all these long years of my life, this is all I remember as being the consumption of my thinking during those two long months living underground besides spending lots of time sleeping. The long slumbers did help both of us heal our wounds. When Rabbi Issachar came at the beginning of the third month, he made his special knock on the trapdoor; and I opened it. We saw Rabbi Issachar holding a palm lamp. He told us to get our things and follow him. Obeying his commands, we found ourselves out on the empty street in front of the synagogue. It was incredibly liberating to be out of those cold, damp tunnels. Only someone trapped underground for months can truly appreciate the joy of our new awakening, being released into the fresh air. Eli and I just smiled at each other looking like criminals freed from a sentence of death.

Rabbi Issachar pointed down the street and commanded us to follow him. It looked like the middle of the night with a clear sky and no moon, but it had to be close to dawn. The stars above were brilliant. Soon the sunrise would quietly awaken Rome, but the coming sun had yet to brighten the edges of the night sky; and we still had a good hour before the darkest hour started. With the only light coming from the stars, we walked in silence until we reached the Tiber River. Issachar stopped and looked at me intently and said, "Well, young Roman, do you still want to become a Jew?"

His behavior was entirely different from what I remembered over two months ago, and I did not know if he were angry or just scared. "Yes," I said wondering what he meant. After all, did I not let him circumcise me? Was I not already a Jew?

"Do as I say, and you will forever be a Jew. First, you will wade out into the Tiber until you are about waist deep. Forget that it is filled with sewage; it is still water and more clean than dirty on this side of the Tiber River. Second, lift your hands up to heaven; and tell the God of Abraham, Isaac, and Jacob that you want Him to become your God. Then squat down until you are totally under water. That is all there is to it."

"What?" said Eli looking a little confused.

"Troubled are you, Eli?" asked Issachar still acting somewhat roiled.

"He can baptize himself?"

"Yes! Why do you ask?"

"When I was baptized by John the Baptist, he laid me backward into the water. I did not do it myself."

"You were baptized by the Baptist?" he snapped indignantly.

"Yes, before I was captured and brought here as a prisoner."

"Why did you do that? You are already a Jew!" said Issachar; his wrinkly forehead furrowed in confusion and disgust. "Why him? You being a learned Jew should have an aversion to John the Baptist. Many false prophets have come and gone. How do you know he is not a false prophet?"

"Nearly everyone I saw at the Jordan River was a Jew. Only Jews were going down into the water. A few Gentiles were watching and laughing, but only Jews were submitting to his baptism. And when he dipped me, he laid me backward into the water as if I was being buried in the water; I did not squat on my own."

"The prescribed procedure from ancient times is to dip yourself if you wish to convert to Judaism. It does not require anyone else but the convert, may it be a man or woman. Now we must hurry, for it is not safe for you two to be out here together. And I do not want to lose my life because of you arguing with me on the procedure of baptism of a convert, which I do not think God really cares about," he said apparently flustered.

I looked intently at Eli. "I will do it myself. Rabbi Issachar is right. We must hurry," I said thinking the old man was scared and perhaps a little angry at being in this position. Possibly, he was still considering turning us in. My reward must be close to a million *sestertii* by now, and perhaps some of his congregation had been beaten because of us or even worse. I hoped no one had died, but the Praetorians looking for us now going on over two months could have led to violence. I climbed down the bank and removed my boots. I also left my falcata on the shore before I entered the putrid-smelling river. There was a lot of green plant growth from the shore into the river. I waded through the thick water growth before I was waist deep and had enough water to squat down and go underwater. Most of the sewage in the river was being dumped from the sewer outlets on the far side. I glanced up to both Eli and the rabbi noticing Issachar looking around like a scared bird. Ignoring his behavior, I did as I had been instructed. When I came out of the water, I felt different in a strange but pleasant way. I cannot really describe it other than I felt part of or connected to something bigger than myself. It was as if I stepped upon a stage that transcends understanding. One holds this holy stimulus when one realizes that the value of a gift just received was far greater than ever imagined. I felt happy to be alive and began smelling the air above the slow-moving river, and strangely I detected the aroma of freshly baked bread and not sewage. When I looked towards the end of the Circus Maximus and Palatine Hill, activities were already beginning for a new day in Rome. It was not the middle of the night as I first thought; it had to be closer to sunrise because the eastern sky was turning a light blue slightly.

Eli was at the water's edge when I returned to the bank. He gave me a hand pulling me up the steep incline. Rabbi Issachar was relaxed now filled with new-found courage that maybe God was pleased with him, and he put his right hand on my left shoulder once I reached the top of the river embankment. With his hand still on my shoulder, he asked, "Unto whom have you given yourself?"

"Unto the living God of Israel," I replied.

"Blessed are you, for you have given yourself to God. The world was created for the sake of Israel, and only Israelites are the Children of God. You will have much affliction, but your reward will be great in the end. You are not an Israelite, but you are now a *Yisrael*."

"I am unworthy to bear any afflictions for God, but what is a *Yisrael*?"

He smiled and removed his hand and said, "Excellent. It is important to remember many Jews will not receive Gentiles even after they become a proselyte Jew. That is what a *Yisrael* is, a convert to Judaism. Most Jews treat proselyte Jews or *Yisraels* with suspicion and somewhat as second-class believers. It is going to be a hard lot to plow, but you must not forsake the living God as the Hebrews did in the wilderness and during many other times in their history. Did you know many of those who followed Moses into the desert out of Egypt never forsook their idols? They kept them hidden in their tents and even took them into the Promised Land under Joshua, or Yeshua as it is pronounced in Hebrew."

At that moment, I did not understand a word he said; nor did I really care what he was trying to communicate. Later, however, it did make significant sense; and his words showed a legitimate concern for my future. Looking around in the sky, I was not able to spot the moon. Could this be a metaphor for my new second-class Jewish status in this world? Issachar told us, "It is about an hour before dawn. This is when the night becomes colder; and it takes on an eerie darkness, darker than any other time of the night." Was Issachar prophesying to me about the next few years of my life? If he were just speaking literally, it still stuck with me as a reminder of my present mood. During my summer months as a fisherman, I knew before sunrise the last hour was always darker than the entire night. But this morning was almost a forewarning of the troubles that lay ahead, perhaps because of my decision to become a Jew or more so a *Yisrael*. This was the last time I wanted to think about that word *Yisrael*. Why would fellow Jews want to be prejudicial towards converts to their religion? Over the new few years, *Yisrael* was to become a negative label that stigmatized or branded me as someone not born into Judaism. Unfortunately for me, after I baptized myself in the Tiber, I began to understand I was a second-class Jew or just a proselyte. Being a *Yisrael* was almost like having a contagious disease that other Jews wished to stay away from.

When we arrived back at the synagogue, the rabbi's wife was waiting with food and supplies for our journey to the Promised Land. Rabbi Issachar said we had to leave Rome now if we wanted to reach Jerusalem before the Day of Atonement. The rabbi's wife handed us two gray woolen bags and said, "You two are servants of the living God of Israel. May He bless you always, and may you both not leave the path of righteousness." With that, she then handed us each a fig cake, much like the one my mother gave me on her last morning a decade ago. We both thanked her and devoured the cakes ravenously after a quick blessing to the God of Abraham, Isaac, and Jacob.

"Everything you need is in these two bags," said Rabbi Issachar. I still had the old, red woolen bag along with the leather pouch with Falcata Man's coins; and I shoved them and the red bag into the newer gray bag. I also strapped on the red, scabbarded falcata over my shoulder allowing it to hang on my back and under the gray coat that I had found in the Janus sanctuary. The hood of the cloak fell back hiding the bulge of the handle up around my shoulders. I noticed the rabbi's wife had attached two short sticks to the neck of each bag so it would be easier to carry either with our hands or over a shoulder. This contraption of bag and stick was commonly called a "Mari Bag" after the famous Roman general, *consul*, and uncle of Julius Caesar, General Gaius Marius, who devised this stick and bag for his legions to carry during the last days of the Republic.

"You must leave the 14ᵗʰ District by going south," instructed Rabbi Issachar, who once again began to become extremely nervous. When you come to any tributary or river, do not use the bridges. You both will have to find a bend in the river and ford it. Spies are watching all bridges. In a day or two, start heading east. Stay off the main roads until you reach the mountains. After you cross the spine of *Italia*, turn south using only deer trails until you run into the *Via Latina*. Follow it carefully until you reach the *Via Minucia*, which will take you to Brundisium. Once you arrive at that great port city, you both will pose as Jewish pilgrims and find a ship going to Judaea. You are to tell anyone who asks that you are going to Jerusalem to celebrate the Day of Atonement. Remember you will have to move quickly in order not to miss it. There will be thousands of Jerusalem-bound pilgrims to mingle with who will be in Brundisium at this time looking for passage to celebrate the Day of Atonement. It will start in 64 days according to my calculations. If you do not slacken your pace, you both can arrive in Brundisium by the time of the Actium celebration or a few days before it begins. That will be in about 30 days. Hopefully, you will find an empty grain ship going to Joppa. Remember Joppa is not the only port but the closest to your final destination. Reach Joppa, and you both should be in Jerusalem by the time of the Feast of Trumpets or New Moon. About ten days later will be the Day of Atonement; this is more of a fast than a feast, and this is the day you do not want to miss. It is the exalted day when the high priest goes into the Holy of Holies and makes this year's confession for all the sins of the Children of God. This is the day God will show much mercy and favor. If you want forgiveness, this is the day you, Venustus, must sacrifice to the King of the Universe. Now, try not to take a ship heading to Egypt even if it leaves days before you find one going to Joppa. End up in Egypt, and you will discover it will be too far to travel by foot if you wish to reach Jerusalem by the Day of Atonement. If you have to, take a galley to Caesarea Maritima; or you might hear it called Sebaste, the name Herod the Great gave it when I was a little boy. Sebaste is the Greek rendering of Augustus and is where the word 'Samaria' originates. Venustus, do you remember when I mentioned the Samaritans? No matter, Eli will tell you who these people are; but this is the origin of their name. If you end up landing at Caesarea Maritima, you will see the largest temple ever built. It was constructed by Herod the Great as well as the temple to the Jews in Jerusalem. Both are beyond the grand scale and have to be seen to be appreciated. Ironically, the temple in Caesarea is dedicated to the first emperor of the Roman Empire." I noticed a sadness cross the old rabbi's eyes as he stood thinking about what he just said.

"Isn't the temple in the city of Ephesus the largest ever built?" I asked.

"You are thinking of the seven wonders' list compiled by Philo Mechanicus, and that was true back when he made his list at the time the Septuagint was being compiled. On that note, Philo Mechanicus lived most of his life in Alexandria and may have been aware of what was going on at Pharos with the 70 or 72 translators. There is the answer to your question. The Augustus structure in Caesarea was not yet standing; nor was the temple in Jerusalem, which today is known as Herod's Temple. It should be remembered that King Herod built both. That is what I call covering all the bets available in a chariot race. You will never lose, but you will."

Rabbi Issachar again looked to be slipping into a state of depression. I looked at his wife to see if she noticed. She was smiling at Eli who was smiling at her. Maybe they had developed a mother-son relationship before we went into the tunnels. When the moment passed, Rabbi Issachar looked to Eli and continued talking. "Just watch for any spies or bounty hunters here in *Italia* or *Palestina* who will be looking for two boys about your age. Try not to stand out. Blend in with all the other Jewish pilgrims." Both Eli and I lowered our heads in agreement. Rabbi Issachar touched Eli on the shoulder and not mine. I did not understand except I was beginning to understand a *Yisrael* was indeed a second-class person in the House of Israel.

I pulled out Falcata Man's moneybag to pay for our food and the Issachars' kind help. The rabbi's wife held up her hand and said they could not accept, but God would pay them much more than I could give them.

Rabbi Issachar said, "You will need all you have to get bread and secure passage to Joppa." He led us towards the synagogue door and looked out to see if all was safe in the street. "Excellent! The sun will be up by the time you are at the graves and catacombs on the outskirts of the city near the Tiber. Just follow the Tiber south, but leave it once it turns toward Ostia."

Eli embraced the woman and then the rabbi. I had never hugged anyone except my mother and Messina and stepped back during this show of affection. Zeno, Hector, and Grillius were not people who demonstrated emotion by touching one another. "I am still wet," I said giving my hand to Rabbi Issachar. He took it and pulled me to himself wrapping me in his arms. I tried to mimic Eli, but I am sure I was a little stiff. The rabbi's wife hugged me as well, cried, and mumbled that she loved us as the sons she never had.

"It is time," said Rabbi Issachar. "The morning star is up. That will be your new name, Son of the Morning Star," he said looking at me.

"Of course, the morning star is Venus," I agreed.

Rabbi Issachar stopped looking up at the eastern sky and had his head down like he was looking at his feet. It was as if he were thinking of something else. Eli and the woman were talking, and I waited for the rabbi to speak. When he saw that I was waiting, he said, "I have given you a present in the gray bag. You will find a scroll tube with the first 33 Psalms of King David written in Greek." Eli and the rabbi's wife were now listening as well. "This will be your first assignment. Read, and memorize every word. Eli will also help teach you our history as well as the 613 laws of the *Torah*. Now both of you must be on your way." This was the first I heard about other laws that would later cause me great dismay in my sentiments toward Judaism. I said nothing about this new revelation but thanked Issachar again and waved as we left the synagogue.

We left the 14th District and stayed away from the walled city with the Tiber to our left. Before the sun was up touching the top of trees with illumination, we were past the tombs that ran along both sides of the road as we left the *domus* part of the city. Off to our right were several high arched aqueducts stretching out across the plains to the mountains faraway. They looked like disciplined prehistoric creatures slowly inching towards the city. When we were away from the city, we began to feel free for the first time in months. Each day we walked as much as I judged Eli was able. We traveled mostly during the cold nights and slept in whatever shade or cover we could find during the day. On several nights when it rained, we holed up in pottery sheds that were out in the woods; but mostly we slept in bushes. We were living more like rabbits than humans. We "boxed" around most towns and villages to avoid any human contact. We covered perhaps twenty to thirty miles a day. A mile was a distance calculated by the Romans in foot and paces. A foot was divided into 12 inches. One hundred twenty-five paces equal one *stadia*, and one thousand paces were called a mile. It took us 30 days to reach Brundisium as Rabbi Issachar had suggested it might. We could have arrived at Brundisium much sooner had we not gone around towns and villages. Our travel was also slowed because of Eli's weakened condition including his insistence on us not traveling on the Sabbath.

Each Sabbath became a rest day; but, actually, these days turned out to be the most joyous days of our travels. We camped either near a lake or deep in a grove of cypress trees because of the pleasant smell the trees gave off. Each time we camped in a grove of cypress, I always thought of the Jewish tree-cutter and imagined what the pleasant aroma of sandalwood trees falling down in the box, algum, and almug forest in the valley of Jezreel might have been like. Those days were exquisite and precious times of just resting. It was during the Sabbath days I read the scroll Rabbi Issachar had given me. The words and concepts were unbelievable as I tried to memorize each word in the first 33 Psalms. I was discovering the flawless jewels of spiritual insight. The prosaic manner of the Greek translation was unequaled if not better than Homer's, Sophocles's, or Menander's prose. It was beyond doubt that these words captivated my mind and heart. I had no other explanation than to confess that these words spoken by King David were really inspiration from the Creator Himself. I began thirsting like a deer on a hot day for water to read all the other books that made up the Jewish Holy Scriptures. How I was going to do that I had no idea. Nevertheless, it was a goal I wanted to accomplish someday.

During our travel to Brundisium, I asked Eli if he could teach me to speak and write Hebrew. He smiled and bobbed his head up and down with excitement. From that day forward, Eli would point and name everything in Hebrew. He also threw in words and terms from Aramaic, which he told me was the universal language in his homeland used by most of the ordinary people. Aramaic was a hard language to pick up due to the numerous idioms used to make expressions. If one did not know the culture, then it was almost impossible to understand completely what a person was saying. For example, the phrase "beware of dogs" meant to stay away from gossips, not dogs. Eli explained the idiom was a picture of dogs eating something they could not digest and vomit it up. After a while, the dog would return to eat what was regurgitated. Once you understood the context, this specific idiom was a clever picture of the dangers of making a gossip your friend. As I have already stated, I personally have a deep affection for dogs more so than any other animal; thus, I never used this idiom. My only regret about dogs is they generally do not live more than a decade plus a few years beyond, and the grief of their passing is sometimes harder than one would envision. Perhaps the pain is due to their loyal nature to whomever they pick as their master, and it is loyalty beyond what a spouse can even render. Dogs are mysterious creatures that God has made for man's benefit.

I asked a thousand questions during our month-long journey to the other side of *Italia* and down to Brundisium. During this time, I worked hard at learning two new languages and how to read and write Hebrew. Learning all this and the history and culture of the Jews was like wading into deep waters that could drown anyone who got too far out from the shore. I discovered Hebrew was primarily used by the scholars in Jerusalem and was not commonly spoken except in the Temple area at Jerusalem and the synagogues in the little villages and towns that dotted the Holy Land and beyond. Only the priests, religious scribes, and lawyers used this ancient Semitic language; for it is the language of the Scriptures. However, some of the prophets chosen by Yahweh being ordinary men themselves spoke and wrote in Aramaic. This Semitic language of the Assyrians was meshed with Hebrew centuries earlier when King Sargon II of Nineveh defeated Israel's ten tribes in the north. After I had learned about the Assyrians and Jews, both being the descendants of Noah's second son, Shem, I could understand how two different Semitic languages could merge into one new language. The ten tribes of Israel were taken from the Promised Land by the Assyrians and became the lost tribes of Jacob or Israel. The tribes might be considered lost but not their new language nor members from each of the ten tribes, for I met men and women of all the tribes in *Palestina* once I arrived. This was always a mystery to me when I heard people say something about the lost tribes of Israel when I know for a fact there are people living today in *Palestina* from all the twelve tribes including the two sons of Joseph. How could their presence be lost if people from all the tribes still live today in the Promised Land? The reason why they were not wholly lost was that many families from each tribe returned to their homeland after the fall of the Assyrian Empire by Nebuchadnezzar even before the tribes of Judah and Benjamin were taken to Babylon. The complete dispersion of all the Hebrew tribes occurred after the destruction of Herod's Temple, but that is another story.

We had traveled a far distance considering Eli's physical condition, which by now was almost healed. He still had marks on his face, but both eyes looked somewhat healthy now. I did not think he was ever going to walk like an ordinary man again. He always walked with a wobble from side to side, much like an old man. The whippings and beatings he had received before I arrived must have been horrific. He did tell me there were several days when the beatings stopped because he was unconscious and could not be revived even with buckets of water. I always thought God was watching over him before I arrived that stormy night to free him from my father and Claudia.

When we reached Brundisium, I discovered it was a significant port city even grander than Ostia. I would compare the coastal port cities as two utterly different in many ways. Brundisium is a port as well as a city, while Ostia is a huge port facility for Rome. In Ostia, mostly warehouses and repair-supply buildings for ships occupy most of the structures hugging the coastline. Therefore, Ostia is not as picturesque as Brundisium, an ancient city that has been serving as a port for a good millennia. Both Eli and I appeared as a couple of poor Jews. Eli had a scraggly beard when I rescued him, but I had only a few days' growth when I arrived at my father's villa. Living underground for two months and now walking the length of *Italia* for a third month, I too, now had a Jewish-looking beard. My beard may not have been as magnificent as Eli's, but the two of us definitely looked Jewish. In the Roman Empire, only Greeks, Egyptians, and Romans were clean-shaven on a daily or bi-weekly basis. The rest of the Roman world fell under the label of Barbarians, who were all typically hairy-faced.

Rabbi Issachar had placed inside the gray bags a change of clothes and a pair of seedy Judaean garments that helped our disguises. I kept the falcata hidden under my gray *himation,* and I traded my *petasos* at a market in Brundisium for extra food the day before we left for our trip by sea. No Jew wore a *petasos* that I could tell, and I decided it was time to depart with my old flower hat. With the money for the hat, I was able to purchase whatever seasonal fruits were available. I also bought smoked fish and a pot of *liquamen,* a fish sauce similar to *garum* but not as smelly. *Liquamen* seemed to be the choice over *garum* on this side of *Italia*. Eli filled one gray bag with round loaves of cheap dog-bread, which we could dip into the fish sauce. Eli had no problem with the fish sludge, unlike the Praetorian Felix.

I put my expensive military boots in the old red bag and shoved the both of them into the gray bag with the fruits. I also carried one wineskin and a large clay jug of water, which had a rope handle. I could not find any sandals that would fit my feet, so I went barefoot. With both of us now wearing Jewish garments along with headgear that consisted of a piece of cloth wrapped around our heads, we not only looked like but also were a couple of pilgrims heading to the Holy City.

I bought passage for two on a 1,000-ton Alexandrian grain ship leaving us just a few coins still in the moneybag. No one carried documents of citizenship inside the vast Roman Empire. Travel authorization was money and nothing more. Even runaway slaves had no trouble getting on a ship if they had the required coins. I calculated that we probably had enough money for food to last a couple more weeks after we reached *Palestina*. Eli and I were the last of about three hundred passengers to board. We embarked separately thinking two young men together would attract unwanted attention. We did not discern any agents of my father, but I was confident they were in the shadows looking for Eli or me. Considering there was such a bounty on my head, there had to be some agents and others hunting us.

Once we boarded the enormous cargo-less grain ship, the crew unfurled the sail from the single mast. It unrolled quickly and filled with the morning wind like a huge frog blowing out its chest. The dirty, gray sail gently billowed out causing the ship to pull away from the mooring docks of Brundisium almost in slow motion. There was also the added aid of hundreds of slaves drawing at the same time with their oars inside two harbor triremes. If the harbor triremes had not been downwind, I am sure we would have been gagging from the stench of slave-sweat. I watched the oars on both trireme lift and drop like the wings of great birds. In the air drifting up and away from the two triremes were distinct drum beats keeping a steady rhythm. It reminded me of my quick trip to Rome on the dispatch bireme, the one shared with Demos and Felix when both remained at the bow for two and a half days. This trip would take weeks depending on the winds.

This time I looked for the name carved on the stern before I boarded. The vessel's name was the *Pericles*. This slow-moving, Greek-named ship was primarily filled with passengers who looked like us: a horde of Jews on their annual pilgrimage to Jerusalem for the triple feasts of Trumpets, Day of Atonement, and Tabernacles. Jews who were living outside of the Promised

Land were required to make one of the three festivals periods each year; that is, if they could afford the trip, which few could. The first festival time actually consisted of three feasts appearing as one. The three feasts were called Passover, Feast of Unleavened Bread, and First Fruits. All three are in the spring, and all occur within a one-week period making one big festival week frequently just referred to as the Feast of Unleavened Bread.

The second feast period is known as the Feast of Fifty, or Pentecost in Greek, or as some call it the Feast of Harvest. This was 50 days or literally 49 days after First Fruits and always occurs on the first day of the week, or Sun Day to the Romans, just as Sun Day is always the celebrated day of First Fruits. The Jews go by a lunar-solar calendar of 354 days based on 12 lunar rotations a year consisting of a seven-day week cycle. Once every three years an extra 30-day month is added to allow the harvest festival to fall at the appropriate time and to keep the calendar in sync with the sun. Thus, the Jews go by a lunar-solar calendar as the Romans only use a solar calendar. Some Barbarian cultures like the Sabians and Arab nomadic people go strictly by a lunar calendar. The Roman solar calendar controls the Empire of *Italia* and all their provinces. The dictator Julius Caesar influenced by his time in Egypt (people who are strictly sun-worshipers of the god Ra) first established the solar calendar, and this calendar today is called by its founder the Julian Calendar. Therefore, it is a strictly 365-days-a-year solar calendar. Before the Julian Calendar, the Romans' week consisted of eight days with the ninth as a market day. Rome later in its Republic changed to eight days a week, but Augustus Caesar modified the calendar into a seven-day week to accommodate the Jews. The Han Dynasty in the land of Chin had a market day every third day on a ten-day calendar. Based on the Jew's Holy Scriptures and the date of creation, the Hebrews were the only people who seemed fanatical about the number of days in a week. The only names for the days to a Jew was just a number like the first day or fourth day until the seventh or Saturn Day as the Romans call it. The seven planetary objects named after Greek and now Roman gods and goddesses supply their names; thus, Venus Day, Mars Day, Jupiter Day, and so on. The Romans believe each day is ruled by an individual god or goddess except the first two days of the week, which are Sun Day and Moon Day and somewhat secular. The Romans repeat these names after the seven have passed just as the Jews start over after the seventh day with their first day being theoretically the eighth day.

One of the most significant disputes and problems with the tens of millions of inhabitants of the Roman Empire was the confusion caused by the use of different calendars. The months in a Roman calendar are named after gods along with some secular terms such as February or *februum*, which means purification. The first month of the calendar is apparently named after the god of confusion, Janus, who always had to be at the top of any god list. When Julius Caesar created his calendar, in the same year he was assassinated, he started the beginning with the founding of Rome with Romulus. The old month of Quintilis was dropped by Caesar and renamed for himself, July. Since Caesar died on the *Ides* of March (the middle of the month), I doubt he was able to celebrate the month he named after himself. Three and a half decades after the death of Caesar, Augustus Caesar, not wanting to be denied a month (since he, too, was a god like his late granduncle), ordered the month Sextilis to be renamed as August in honor of himself. The major problem was Sextilis had only 29 days whereas July had 31 days. To rectify this issue, Augustus Caesar needed two more days to equal July; so he robbed two days from the secular month of February, which dropped February down to 28 days but no problem for Augustus since August equaled July with 31 days. Changing times and dates is one of history's most controversial acts, which only a mighty king or emperor can do. To keep the Roman Empire from internal rebellion over the change of time and dates, Rome allowed all its inhabitants to keep and use their own calendars; and there lies the confusion. The Roman solution for toleration and flexibility towards those under its yoke generally worked as long as taxes were paid and on time. Thus, the Julian Calendar is primarily used outside of Rome for taxation dates and the many different Roman holidays, especially the time of the Actium celebration.

One item to note: Rome could quickly become inflexible towards any group under its control such as the case regarding the Jews, whom Rome saw as not abiding by the Roman way of thinking. Rome's thought was to always force all its foreigners to assimilate to the ways of Rome, but this was never going to happen. Rome typically fell to the forms of those it conquered. When Rome tried to accommodate the Jews by changing their calendar to seven days, Rome discovered the Jews were still not happy. In the end, this became one of those breaking points that led to the Jewish Wars in the last years of the last Julio-Claudian emperors, specifically Emperor Nero. It could be correctly stated that Rome never understood the mind of the Jews. Here were a foreign but conquered people who would never mix paganism into their culture. This was one reason Augustus banished the Jews to the 14th District in Rome. If you do not become Roman, then you will be placed in your own ghetto.

One last point of contention between the Jews and Rome was the debate when a day started and ended. The Romans changed the day at midnight while the Jews amended the day at the sight of the third star shortly after sunset. I will talk more about this issue later, but first I should return to the Jewish feast days. But one crucial point that needs to be understood: Rome would never negotiate the start and end of a day. This was a clear line in the sand for Rome along with the Jewish practice of circumcision.

I now return to the Jewish feasts. The next festival after the three spring feasts, 50 days after First Fruits, is the Feast of Pentecost. This is the second significant festival period, which celebrates the anniversary of the giving of the Law by Moses when the greatest prophet of Judaism came down off the mountain with the ten laws on two stone tablets on which the finger of God had personally inscribed. These were the ten laws Rabbi Issachar read to me in his courtyard the day I decided to become a Jew.

The third and last festival period that was given by Moses occurred just before winter, and that was the one Eli and I needed to make. This final festival time is another set of three feasts all lumped together for the same reason the first three are combined – as one – because the three fall closely together making one extended festival period; this time spanning over several weeks. The day we wanted to celebrate was the Day of Atonement, which Eli was to explain to me once we were at sea.

Leaving the dockyards of Brundisium, the harbor triremes dropped their towlines; and a strong wind took hold of the *Pericles* driving it out to sea. I stood at the rail and watched the triremes return to port as the long oars pulled in perfect unison. Most of the passengers on the *Pericles* also watched the leaving of the two triremes. I stayed at the rail and observed smaller fishing vessels plowing by or being passed by our cargo ship of people. Looking around at those on deck, I recognized a few Roman military soldiers, tradesmen, and commercial dealers of all kinds along with slaves. There were very few females whom I saw on board the ship, and the ones I noticed were covered from head to toe hiding any form of their figures. It is hard to judge which passengers were slaves versus destitute freedmen. The city of Rome had a population that was split evenly between slaves and free people. The ratio of slaves to freedmen in the Empire may not have been as high as in the capital of Rome. Looking around and trying to figure out who was and who was not a slave was a difficult chore. Very few slaves these days wore a traditional single gold loop earring or anything else that marked them as free or under bondage. Nevertheless, a nobleman, politician, or a priest could easily be recognized by their clothing. The Roman Senate had debated for many years regarding *sumptuary laws,* statutes that required specific dress for slaves; but these laws were always voted down on the argument that, if all the slaves in Rome knew who they were and realized their enormous numbers, it would not be long before another Spartacus or Eunus would rise up and lead another slave revolt. Many slaves of rich masters actually dressed in clothes that were more expensive to poor free people. Again, an old saying rings true: "It is better to be a rich man's slave than a poor freedman."

A young slave on board the ship who worked the ropes of the single sail commented that the trip to Joppa would take up to two or perhaps three weeks depending on the weather and what ports the ship stopped at on its way. He told me it was the beginning of the fall season, and there was a rush to get across the *Mare Internum* and return before the arrival of winter. Once winter began around the early weeks of the month *Novem*, the *Mare Internum* would be considered closed. *Novem* was the ninth month from the month of Mars, and this was the time unexpected storms and violent weather became unpredictable until the early days of the month of Mars. Only foolhardy ship captains ventured out during the winter months searching for high profits. The city of Rome required at least 300,000 tons of grain a year to keep *status quo*. All of this had to be shipped to the port cities of *Italia* in the six months allowed by the government. One sailor speaking Hebrew commented to another passenger that the *Pericles* was to take on a load of copper and luxury items at Joppa brought there from as faraway as Chola, the southern lands of the Hindus. The *Pericles* was then going to sail on to Egypt, where the ship would load up on grain for its final return to *Italia*, where the *Pericles* would either hold up for the winter in Brundisium or Ostia depending on the direction of the winds.

I remained alone at the rail long after all the other passengers had retired to find shade for a nap, I just stared at where the coast of *Italia* had disappeared from sight. This was the first time since arriving in *Italia* I began to feel somewhat safe. The only enjoyable moments had been my evening with Felix at the tavern in *Subura*, my time conversing with Rabbi Issachar under his grape arbor, and the brief moments with Messina. I also should say I did not mind the last month with Eli walking and spending the Sabbaths resting on our way from Rome to Brundisium. Leaning at the rail, I began pondered my conversion to Judaism; and I was still pleased with my decision. For the first time in my life, I had a clear direction; and abiding by the Mosaic Laws was beyond being a Stoic. It seemed entirely logical to me: if everyone followed God's laws, then there would be peace and joy in the world. Jerusalem had to be a city of unbelievable peace, for it was there that the Almighty Creator accepts man through sacrifices. Besides, the word "*Jeru-salem*" was Hebrew meaning, "City of Peace." Little did I know then that Jerusalem was going to become a prodigious disappointment.

"The air is clear and sweet," commented Eli, who came and stood next to me at the rail. "Jerusalem is certainly a place you will not understand; be warned." I looked over at Eli wondering if he could read my mind. I did not comment on whatever he was trying to communicate to me but, instead, I changed the subject.

"Zeno warned me not to take revenge, or I would be hunted and followed for the rest of my life."

"Zeno was a dreamer. That is why he did not get out of Rome in time to save his own life. He should have left with us that night and taken the little girl."

"That little girl is no longer a little girl," I said feeling a fresh glow of joy.

"How do you know this?" Eli asked looking surprised at my response.

"I met her at my father's villa right before I cut your ropes free." He looked as if I had just slapped him when I told him about meeting Messina at the front door on that stormy night I rescued him. As I finished reminiscing, a stout wind gusted; and the ship's dirty, Indian-cotton canvas made a thunderous pop sound, stretching hold lines taut.

Eli said, "Let's find somewhere below we can call our own for the trip. We will take a nap, then we will begin your lessons on the law and the prophets." I slapped my companion on the back showing agreement, and we picked up our bags and went below. We were exhausted since we had been up most of the night making sure it was safe to board the grain ship in our escape out of *Italia*.

The days at sea passed quickly as the galley encountered good weather and calm seas. We harbored at Fair Havens on Crete for a day and then a day and night at Paphos on Cyprus before we resumed towards Joppa. During the voyage, Eli and I stayed together and tried to avoid other passengers without drawing suspicion. I would sit and listen to Eli as he tutored me in the stories of the Jewish prophets. I loved hearing about those fascinating men sent by God to warn the Jewish people of their wickedness but who were also hated and mistrusted by the Jewish rulers and organized religious groups. On our last day at sea, Eli began to quiz me on all that I had learned and what I had retained.

"Name the prophet who was thrown into the lion's den," quizzed Eli.

"Daniel – and the lions did not eat him," I answered.

"What does the Feast of First Fruits celebrate?"

"The day Noah landed on Mount Ararat and the day Moses and the Hebrews crossed the Red Sea. Moreover, it was also the day Joshua, 40 years later to the day of crossing the Red Sea, and the children of Israel crossed the Jordan River into the Promised Land. The crossing of the Jordan occurred shortly after Moses had died on Mount Nebo."

"And why was Moses on Mount Nebo?" asked Eli.

"God wished to show him a grand view of the Promised Land; perhaps it was a birthday present since it was exactly on the 120th anniversary of his birth that Moses died. Apparently, dates and anniversaries are important to Yahweh."

"Of course, dates and anniversaries are important. Now, name the feast that celebrates the departure of Jews from Egypt with Moses."

"Passover! And it is always on Nisan the 14th! It is called Passover because the Angel of Death passed over every home in Egypt that had lamb's blood painted on the door frames and lintels. Passover happened first, and Nisan 15 is always the start of the Feast of Unleavened Bread. This feast is always treated as a Sabbath Rest Day, no matter what day of the week it lands. Unleavened Bread is celebrated because the children of Israel had to depart Egypt so quickly they did not have time to leaven their bread."

"Now, what happened to those who did not have the blood of a lamb on their doors in Egypt during the Passover?" asked Eli.

"The Angel of Death killed all the firstborn males, humans or even animals. Come on; challenge me! You insult me with the simplicity of your questions," I chided.

"Oh, my friend is showing he is a bright student. Let me see now. Who is it that must return before the Messiah can come?"

"Elijah, the prophet who never died but was taken alive to heaven in a fiery chariot!" I answered with the manner of a vain boaster; but deep inside me, I realized I fathomed very little from all there was to know about Yahweh and His people's history. To stop my showing off, I changed the topic. "Now a question for you, Eli. Is this man named John who preaches in the Judaean desert Elijah?"

Eli scratched his bearded face and rocked his head in thought. "Well, John himself said he was not. So how could he be Elijah?"

"We will go and ask him ourselves. That is my plan after I sacrifice on the Day of Atonement."

Before Eli could respond to my declaration, we were interrupted by a Jew at the rail near us. He screamed out in a loud voice using Aramaic. "Look!

The land of our fathers!" Other Jews ran to the railing and yelled out with loud cheers of praises.

I, too, stood and made my way to the rail where I welcomed my first glimpse of *Palestina*. Seeing the Promised Land visibly touched me as well as the other Jewish passengers. I noticed many Roman soldiers on board turn their heads away from what they saw and spit and curse. "Oh, look!" said one soldier, "The land of prophets and seers! Let's bow and receive a blessing from the God without a statue of his image in his mighty temple!"

"What a wretched land!" said another soldier to his comrades. "The land of heat, insects, and foul tempers." He turned away openly displaying his hatred for this backwater realm of Rome. He completed his blasphemy by lifting up his tunic and making an obscene noise in the direction of the coastline.

Another in the group said in a sarcastic tone, "Everything that crawls is poisonous, everything that grows has thorns, and everything that can fly stings." His summary got a few lazy, scattered laughs from other Romans; but my eyes confirmed nothing of what he claimed.

Eli, at my elbow, stayed with me until Joppa came into view. I could tell it was an ancient seaport city of mud bricks and stone structures, a few simple-looking public buildings, and larger but newer stone-and-wood warehouses. The town was nestled in the sandy dunes and scrub of the lowlands on the Plains of Sharon. It looked to me that the long, hot summer had baked away all the green ground cover leaving only a burnt, brown landscape that stared at us as if giving a warning. "Perhaps when the winter rains come, the land might turn green again," I commented to an unspeaking Eli. He just seemed lost in his own thoughts.

Just after sunset, the *Pericles* moored at one of the many fabricated rock piers that reached out into deeper waters. Up close, I would say this ancient port was the most primitive-looking city I had ever seen. Most buildings were mud brick, and many of the sides of structures were freshly painted white, with some kind of a lead-base, lime substance. Many of the unassuming homes were flat-roofed dwellings, and many residents were eating their evening meals from their lofty perches as well as watching the passengers disembark from the huge grain galley. Once Eli and I left the stone pier, we discovered Joppa had mostly mud-hardened, rutted streets, which were foul from animal dung and odors permeating everything. Eli later told me the unusual smell was from sheep and camels. I was familiar with sheep, but the camel was a creature I had never seen until now; and many were to be seen in Joppa. Later I would learn to dislike these swaying, long-legged beasts. Riding one was not even close to the experience of riding a horse. Camels were not to my liking, and I disliked their strange grunting noises and spitting.

As we Moved away from the docks, the streets were illuminated by torches glistening light from bracket holders on the sides of buildings. Eli said, "This town is mostly Jewish, and we should find an inn to spend the night."

"We could walk out of the town for about an hour. That would put us closer to Jerusalem for our walk tomorrow. Besides, we don't have as much money as I thought. Shouldn't we just sleep out in the open tonight?" I asked.

"It could be dangerous. Thieves and robbers prey on pilgrims like us. Each one of us would have to stay up half the night guarding the other. Besides, an inn would be safer; and that way we both could get a good night's sleep and a good meal. Sleeping out in the open is something, I am sure, we will have to do once our money runs out."

I agreed only because a good meal was part of the price of a night at an inn in Judaea, and we had run low on food a few days out of Cyprus.

The next morning we awoke before the sun, and we felt well rested and still full from our evening meal. Eli told me he figured it was perhaps 35 to 40 miles to the City of Peace, and it would be a hard day's walk since it was all uphill; but we should try and reach the city in one day's hike.

"I agree," I commented. "We could be there by sunset since we are young and well rested,"

"Rested or not, we have been sitting around for the last couple of weeks; and it will take us some time to build up our wind," commented Eli with his chin slightly up in the air. I wondered if all the lessons he had given me, along with being back in his homeland, were having an effect on his attitude. I tried to dismiss my observations; but, as the days passed, Eli slowly became insufferable.

"We will make it or die trying," I said with conviction but added a little mirth in my voice. I wanted to reach this city I had been thinking about since Rabbi Issachar declared I had to go there and sacrifice, and by saying these words aloud was like branding it as fact. Eli gave me a nauseated look after I spoke. I wondered if it were my tone or words. If my tone were a little forward, the thought of Eli once being my slave might have existed in my mind without entering my awareness. Maybe I still treated him as my slave and not my equal. I have had many years to think about this moment in time along with my words and tone. All I can say is Eli's attitude that early morning was beginning to be repulsive to me in some odd way. I did not want to correct him and decided to place myself back under his instruction. Rabbi Issachar, before we left Rome, had declared that Eli was to teach me all there was to know about Judaism and the Holy Scriptures. "When does the Feast of Atonement begin?"

Eli was quiet for a moment before answering my question. "The innkeeper told me that the Day of Atonement will be in 10 days making the Feast of Tabernacles in 15 days. The Feast of Trumpets began yesterday and is already in progress ending tonight at sunset." From what I could tell, our slight rift was over.

On the ship, Eli had explained the significance of the Day of Atonement. God considered it a day of humiliation. The law said this day was to be in the Jewish month of Tishri, the seventh month of the Jewish calendar, on the tenth day; and on this day one should humble his or her soul and not do any work. It was also a day of fasting from any food or drink. This is a day of reconciliation with God and a day to cleanse one's self of all his or her unknown sins committed since the previous Day of Atonement.

I remembered Rabbi Issachar had insisted that this was to be the day I should make a sacrifice for my sins at God's Great Temple. This day was to start my obligations to the Law. It was a special and unique day because the high priest in Jerusalem went into the Great Temple and entered the back room called the Holy of Holies offering a blood sacrifice for all the sins of the Chosen People, specifically those sins of ignorance. That would be the sins the people knew nothing about. All the sins they knew they had committed were to be sacrificed personally whenever they occurred throughout the year but only at the Temple in Jerusalem. The high priest poured the sacrificed blood over the Mercy Seat, which was the golden cover on top of the Ark of the Covenant. Eli explained to me that God stands above the Mercy Seat and that we humans, in a mystical way, are inside the ark or box with the law given to Moses, the law written by the finger of God, showing all people that they are sinners. Without the blood of the sacrifice on the Mercy Seat, no human could have any relationship whatsoever, with the Creator. The only problem was, for centuries since the return of the Jews from Babylon, the Ark of the Covenant was missing from the Holy of Holies, and no one knew where it was. I had no idea if the high priest this year was going to place the blood of a bull on the floor in the Holy of Holies or what. This little detail I never learned.

Eli had continued to school me after we left the *Pericles* while we walked up through the Judaea hills towards Jerusalem. We left long before anyone else started out from the *Pericles* having the road to Jerusalem all to ourselves. Somewhere in the Judaean hills, Eli explained about the Ark and the Holy of Holies. "At the beginning of the First Temple built by King Solomon, the Ark of the Covenant stood in the Holy of Holies. It was a box or chest made of acacia wood and covered with gold, both inside and out. Two huge cherubim carved out of olive wood and also covered in gold stood guard at both ends of the Ark with their wings covering the Ark and the entire room. Inside the Ark were three items: the stone tablets that were given by God to Moses on Mount Horeb, Aaron's staff, and a pot of manna."

I later learned that the manna was a strange food God provided the children of Israel for the 40 years while they were in the Wilderness of Sin. It was said to be the same food that angels ate. It tasted, when unprepared, like honey and crackers but could be prepared in a number of other ways. It could be boiled, oven baked, or even roasted; and yet, the people got weary of this same food day after day. The children of Israel in the wilderness started to moan and complain. Eventually they were all came under punishment by poisonous snakes for their rebellion against the God of the Universe. Thus, the three items in the Ark of the Covenant were symbols of God taking care of his Chosen People as well as their rejection of His law, His spiritual leader, and His spiritual food. Why the Jews were continually disobeying Yahweh throughout their history was a profound mystery to me.

Eli had also told me many times in the past month that today there is no Ark of the Covenant in the Holy of Holies where the high priest enters once each year. "The Ark of the Covenant along with the two cherubim have been lost for many centuries," explained Eli. "This loss occurred before the destruction of the First Temple by the Babylonians under Nebuchadnezzar. Some Jewish scholars say a Pharaoh named Shishak came up to Jerusalem in the fifth year of King Rehoboam and took it back to Egypt, or one of the sons of Solomon ferreted it away to Ethiopia. I even heard a story that the Queen of Sheba stole it in the time of King Solomon. I personally believe, to prevent the Babylonians from stealing it, someone buried it in one of the tunnels under the Temple Mount of Mount Moriah in Jerusalem; and today no one knows which tunnel."

Eli and I struggled all day in the dry heat as we walked up and up with aching legs and knees climbing through the Judaean hills. Shortly before sunset, we heard the city of Jerusalem long before we actually saw it. What we heard came echoing down through the dry wadis and steep valleys that surround the city, which were the sounds of ram horns along with silver trumpets in honor of the Feast of Trumpets. These horns and trumpets had been sounding since morning, and Eli said they would end at the sight of the third star, which signified the end of the feast and the start of the civil year. This festival marked the time when the law had been read publicly after the

House of Judah had returned from their exile in Babylon. That would have been 400-plus years ago. It was also considered the anniversary date of the creation of the cosmos, and many Jewish scholars calculated a time period close to four thousand years ago since creation and time began. I know of no civilization or city older than that 3,000 years; and, if one were to add up all those living today from the Roman Empire, the people of the land of the Vedas, those alive in the Han Dynasty, plus those living on the Four Islands including all the Barbarians, the number would most reasonable reach way beyond 300 million souls. Four thousand years would be more than enough time for two people to bring about what is alive today. This would also include the factoring in life expectancy, wars, famines, and plagues.

By the time I spotted the walls of this mysterious hilltop city, I felt chills running the length of my back and neck. We circled around the outside of the looming, walled city turning at the northeast corner and walked past the famous Crucifixion Hill or Skull Hill located outside the Sheep Gate. Eli explained that this was also called the Bald Skull or Golgotha in Aramaic. There were several sycamore trees partially blocking the cave holes on the sheer eastern side of the knob of the hilltop, which did give the appearance of human skulls. These skull holes provided the name for this little knob of a hill standing alone outside the northern walls of Jerusalem. Eli told me this was actually the end of the ridge called Mount Moriah, and Golgotha was the highest spot on the ridge. Just as Rome existed on seven hills, Jerusalem also stood on top of seven hills surrounded by its walls. There was Scopus Hill to the northeast, Knob Hill in the center area behind the Temple, and Mount Moriah. The Roman fort called Antonia stood on Rock Hill, which was at the northwest portion of the Temple complex, a little hill behind Mount Moriah. There was Mount Zion, which was a small finger ridge that stood above the Tyropoeon Valley up to the Kidron Valley at the southeastern portion of the city adjacent to the Temple complex running in the same direction of Mount Moriah. Mount Zion was the location of King David's ancient city or sometimes just called the City of David or the Lower City because it was noticeably lower in elevation from Mount Moriah, the adjacent hill. At the extreme end of this hill was the famous Pool of Siloam built by King Hezekiah. The highest point west of Mount Zion or the City of David was called the Mount of Corruption or Mount of Offense. It stood next to the valley where the city's garbage burned day and night also known as Sheol by some or the valley of Hinnom. The last hill was called New Mount Zion, which was in the extreme southwest located at the far end of the Hinnom Valley with the Mount of Offense between it and Old Mount Zion or the City of David.

Eli and I walked through the ancient valley of Kidron passing outside and below the eastern walls that protected the Temple complex. Eli decided that we should not enter the city due to the late hour, and we had very few coins left in Falcata Man's moneybag. We, instead, walked along an old goat path meandering south and going down into the Kidron Valley. I noticed the hill outside of the city and to our left was the highest ridge of all the hills. This north-to-the-south hill with several bumps along the top was called Mount of Olives. Eli explained that halfway up this hill was a little garden, which would be the spot we would spend the night.

Before we began climbing up the Mount of Olives, I noticed a stream down in the bottom of the Kidron Valley, which was running with bright blood. Eli told me this was the life fluids of hundreds if not thousands of animals being sacrificed each day up above at the Temple. Lead pipes ran from the Great Altar in front of Yahweh's Temple and ended down here in this deep gully. Eli threw up his arms in exasperation maybe because of the look I was giving him while he was explaining the source of the blood. "Where do you think all that blood is going to go after thousands of animals and birds are sacrificed each day? The blood has to go somewhere."

"You mean all the excess blood is piped into this valley?" Eli did not answer me and started walking away. It was an unsettling sight for me to see a steady stream of bright, fresh blood gushing where water should typically be surging around rocks and roots. Looking to the direction of the flow of blood, I noticed a small gang of slaves throwing dirt onto the blood using tools just for this operation.

When Eli noticed I was watching the slaves, he called out, "The *Torah* requires that the blood of sacrifices be covered with earth!"

"Well, those slaves are not doing a thorough job from what I can observe! They are just throwing dirt into the air, and it looks like a pathetic ritualistic act."

Eli threw up his hands at my statement and left me watching the gang of slaves trying to cover the blood. One man was only making a blood dam causing the blood to back up. I decided to forget about all the blood and climbed the goat trail up the steep side of the Mount of Olives. Halfway up the steep hill, I found Eli sitting on a flat rock. Behind him was a six-foot wall made of stones encircling what looked like a grove of olive trees. I guessed this was the end of the road for this day. When Eli spotted me, he quietly stood and said, "We can sleep here tonight. This garden is a little-gated area of trees and grass. It is called the Garden of Gethsemane. The entrance is on the other side."

I followed Eli around and into the Garden of Gethsemane. Once inside, I discovered we were alone; and here stood a small grove of olive trees growing in neat rows with all kinds of wildflowers springing up everywhere. It was very peaceful and quiet compared to the cacophonous noise of horns and trumpets coming from the city.

"Come with me, and I will show you something while we eat our last meal." I looked to where Eli was pointing, and I smiled to show him I would follow. With his nose in the air, which I was sure Felix the spy would have commented on, I followed carrying my bag feeling as if I were the slave and Eli was my master. He led me back to the entrance, and together we climbed through some rocks to a spot above the garden. Finding an excellent flat rock on which to sit, I noticed Eli was out of breath, just like me. We both were drenched in our own sweat, and we both smelled pretty rank. I decided I smelled unpleasant, but Eli's aroma was beyond rancid. Truth be told, we never think we stink but are quick to assume everyone else smells even if we feel as if there is a dead animal inside our own clothes. First thing tomorrow, before we went to look at the Temple, we were going to a bathhouse. I did not care what it cost; we were going and also somehow washing our clothes. It had been over a month since either of us took a swim in a river or washed our clothes. I looked to where Eli was pointing, and out before us both was the ancient city of Jerusalem. Now I understood why he wanted to come up here to eat. I found myself looking across a vast chasm, which was the space created by the deep Kidron Valley that separated where Eli and I sat. The Temple of the Jews looked like an eagle's nest sitting all alone inside an enormous empty area that surrounded the tallest building I had ever seen. From where I was sitting, it looked to be taller than the most towering *insulae* in Rome. Here was the world's grandest structure, which would have been number one on Philo Mechanicus's list if Herod's Temple had been standing in his day. I would later learn this building built by Herod the Great had been standing only for the past 46 years, a short time compared with the pyramids of Egypt or the Parthenon in Athens. Taking my eyes off the Temple, I could see down into the vast Court of Gentiles that surrounded the Temple at lower levels; and hundreds of people all appearing like little ants were scurrying around.

The sun was dropping under the horizon of the western sky at the far edge of Jerusalem. I was mesmerized by the moment. All the little buildings and palaces were turning a pinkish color. It was a scene to remember for the rest of my life. There was a massive, formidable fortress way to the right of the open complex; and on the opposite side was a long, tall building facing from east to west. In the center, right in front of the Temple, was a lonely smoke pillar slowly drifting straight above the Temple from the burnt offerings of today's sacrifices. With my eyes fixed on the smoke column, I noticed the black and gray of the smoke turn to a mingled pink-and-orange hue from the setting sun. The Temple almost seemed to be at my fingertips and stood alone above the city like a diamond in a queen's ring. I could see the main entrance flanked by two tall square-looking pillars, each holding up the flat roof porch hovering above the tall doors. At that very moment, I could see the two doors being closed for the day; and it looked like perhaps twenty men in white robes struggling to shut the giant doors. The entire Temple and its buildings were ideally placed in the center of a vast, open courtyard, which I would later learn was the Courtyard of Gentiles. The Temple of Yahweh was the most captivating building I had ever seen – more magnificent and awe-inspiring with such grandeur over any structure seen on the Acropolis in Athens or at the *Forum*, the Capitoline, or on Palatine Hill in Rome. It was even more splendid and stunning than the lonely but sublime temple of Apollo high up on Cape Sounion that, as a fisherman in Greece leaving and returning from Phaleron, I would gaze upon during those long summer days. In my humble opinion, the Jewish Temple of Yahweh in its unique simplicity and setting was more exalted and noble than any structure ever created by man. It did not have a Greek or Roman appearance but something different, perhaps more oriental or even Egyptian with straight and straightforward lines. Maybe the Philistines had an influence in its simplicity since the Indo-European people of Crete were most likely the ones who sailed to this land 1,500 years ago establishing the people who are now long gone in history but were once known as the Philistines, Phoenicians, and Carthaginians. According to the Jewish Scriptures, the prophets Amos and Jeremiah referred to these people as originally coming from the island of *Caphtor*. I realize it is only a theory that *Caphtor* is an ancient name for Crete. The Greek LXX called the Philistines the *Cherethites*, which may mean Cretans. The ancient civilization of Crete still has buildings standing on the island of Crete with similar straight lines as the Jewish Temple. The other neighboring islands near Crete called Caria and Lycia were once part of this ancient maritime. It would be a logical guess to think *Caphtor* could have been the name of this maritime empire that colonized this region, which the Romans now call *Palestina*. The Scriptures of the Jews tells in its history books that King Solomon hired the king of Tyre, a Phoenician, to help build Israel's first temple almost a thousand years ago. I am sure that Phoenician influence carried on, and today this new temple with it two tall pillars standing guard holding the roof porch in front of a massive doorway of golden doors looked very Phoenician in origin. The building itself was fashioned with gleaming, white marble facing, and the porch of the Holy Place was inlaid with gold as well as the unique edging along its flat roof. While I stood with my unbelieving eyes, all the ear-piercing trumpets and horns became silent; for the Feast of Trumpets had now ended its second day. The whole city now stood in total silence, and I felt spiritually lifted and emotionally enraptured at the same moment the sun had set and the thunderous noise stopped. Everything seemed orchestrated just for me to form a perfect memory and an incredible sense of peace at the same moment. It was one of those rare times, which will never leave my mind's eye, leaving a lasting memory for all eternity. I just sat on the flat rock and swallowed in all that stood before me etching it into my memory. I felt forgiven, peaceful, fulfilled, and accepted by the Creator who had revealed Himself to me in Rome that night Eli and I escaped my father's villa standing between the Circus Maximus and Palatine Hill. I was satisfied that my spiritual quest was now over. Little did I know, starting tomorrow, after I first entered the Temple complex, my spiritual quest would end in a horrible twist. Starting tomorrow, a hideous crash – a monumental collision – was about to occur, something more heinous than any chariot smash-up at the Circus Maximus.

However, on this first night outside the holy city, I was at peace as Eli pulled out a loaf of bread and a wineskin that we had purchased earlier at Emmaus, a little Judaean town about halfway between Joppa and Jerusalem, right before the road began going up into the Judaean Hills. As I looked over at Eli, he just appeared hungry and did not seem to be sharing my sense of awe as he held out a piece of bread for me. After the sun was completely below the western horizon, the pink faded to an inexplicably dark purple. I thought nothing of it but would later think of it as an evil omen of the future. On this night, I just ate and drank; and we talked for the next several hours. While we spoke, I remembered the darkness covering the ancient sprawling city like a blanket being pulled over a cold child. That night on the hard, rocky ground with only our robes for protection, Eli and I slept under the stars in the Garden of Gethsemane.

In the middle of the night, I got up and exited the garden. For some reason, I climbed back up to the flat rock where we had our dinner. I stared up into the night sky looking at the stars that scattered across the heavens from one edge to the other. I noticed a long ribbon of white where many stars condensed together to form what appeared to be a long, narrow cloud of sparkling diamonds dipped in milk. One end of the ribbon of white stood over the Temple of Yahweh, and the other end went bending over my head and disappeared over the ridge of the Mount of Olives. I wondered about this; and, finding no answers, I actually became somewhat frightened. How many times had I looked up into the night sky and never really thought about the connection of the *cosmos* along with being alive at this stage in history? It was almost a scary moment of self-realization, which caused me to return to the garden and find sleep.

Still using my gray cloak as a blanket, I had a hard time finding sleep. Trying to divert my mind to find sleep, I began to ponder *Palestina* and my first impressions. This land was quite strange. Yet, it was not the land; it had to be the people; yes, the perplexing Jews who made it seem different. Their customs, manners, and whole aspect of existence were definitely distinct from the Roman or the Greek views I once embraced. I strangely felt somewhat alone although I had Eli with me. Judaea did not seem like my home, but where was my home? Was it Rome, or was it Athens? The only logic I could come up with was the fact that God, indeed, penetrated the daily life between one and another; and I was somewhere in the middle. A smile came to my face, and I gently closed down my thoughts as I understood it was possible that the one and true God had created the world for Israel. Yet, there still seemed to be an invisible piece missing from all that I comprehended. Israel did not actually love their Creator, no matter what the majority did or said. The oddity of it all was that they said all the right words, but there was this faith element that originates in the heart that seemed to be missing. In a curious way, these Jews were no different from Hector, a priest to Athena Nike. He looked and acted like he was devoted to Nike except he wasn't at all. The only difference was Hector, without any doubt, was honest about his doubts; and most Jews were not that honest. Maybe they were just deceiving themselves, or was it an arrogance of knowing the world was wrong and they were right? Still, having an intellectual knowledge you are right does not mean you have faith in why you are right.

I found myself talking to God quietly in my head discovering much later in life that He desires this act of communion between Himself and His creatures much more than we will ever know. To truly love God is to be known by God. "*Serve Yahweh with gladness*"; unfortunately, few discover this fundamental truth. Too many of us find the business of life more pressing over taking the time to quietly commune with a patiently waiting Creator. Moreover, here is the *nexus* of it all: two worlds intertwining, one being the world of facts overlapping the world of faith. Talking to God is a simple process of crossing the *nexus* of this world into the other. Yes, the kingdom of God and the kingdom of man are connected; and the Creator hears and sees all. The physical is in communion with the spiritual by just believing and quietly to the Creator. This mysterious God of the Jews hears all, even spoken words. The sincere reality I later discovered is prayer forms a ...ship with God, and it is not a ritualistic act of mantra-type words but just talking to the Creator in the same manner I would talk to Eli and Hector or even as I spoke with the Praetorian Guard, Scipios Cornelius Felix, that evening in the *popina*.

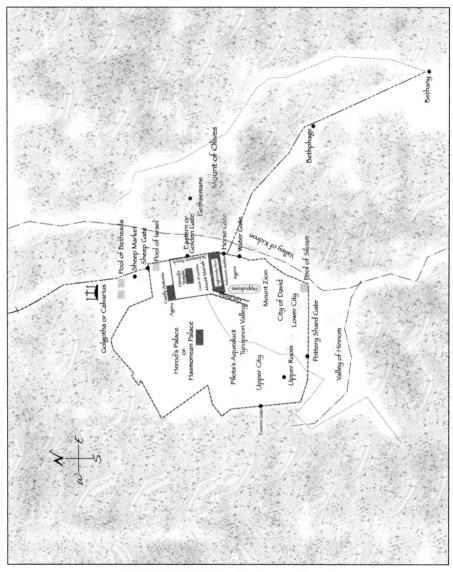

JERUSALEM (in the time of Jesus)

A READING GIVEN AT THE GREAT LIBRARY OF ALEXANDRIA BY EPAPHRODITUS

During the year of civil war between the four legates, a great fire broke out on Capitoline Hill destroying much of Rome's archives. Due to this loss, the scholars and librarians of Alexandria's Great Library requisitioned anyone with past knowledge to recreate the history of Rome and its Empire. Many scholars and others delivered many lectures on the afternoons of the seventh day of each week for about a year after the great fire. A generous fee of 25 denarii was paid to anyone who provided information that could replace any history of Rome. I decided to supplement my financial situation at this time by contributing several lectures. I have chosen a few excerpts from my lecture readings to coincide with this story. 69 AD

JULIUS CAESAR & POMPEY THE GREAT AND THE GREAT LIBRARY OF ALEXANDRIA

As a child in Rome, I had an excellent tutor named Zeno. It was from him I first learned about a famous Roman who marched his legions into Jerusalem about a hundred years ago capturing the holy city without much struggle. This Roman, General Gnaeus Pompeius Magnus, now known as Pompey the Great, may have been history's most celebrated man of hubris. Once Jerusalem had surrendered to Pompey, the general rode his horse up to Zerubbabel's Temple, the Second Temple built by funds given to the Jews by Cyrus the Great, the Persian general and king who liberated the Jews of Babylon after he captured Babylon in one night. When Pompey the Great dismounted and entered on foot into the Holy of Holies to see for himself the deity of the Jews, he discovered the last room behind the thick, purple-and-scarlet curtain, the Holy of Holies, was only a simple, empty, cube-spaced room. Pompey became enraged after discovering the room was void of the image of the God of the Jews. In his anger, he ordered dozens of the white-robed priests killed by Roman spears. Leaving Jerusalem, he marched to Egypt never getting the idea out of his head that the Jews were in a condition of insanity because they worshiped only one invisible God.

After reaching Alexandria, Pompey made a visit to the Great Library in the age of its apex. His confused self-esteem was revived when he viewed the body of Alexander the Great resting in death inside the Grand Antechamber of the Great Library's domed entrance hall. Legend states that Alexander could be visibly seen inside his sarcophagus, which was made of crystal, mixed with bits of clear mica forming a crystalline, translucent vault. His best armor was strapped over *his mummified body along with his helmet; and he was also covered by his royal, scarlet robe. Apparently, Rome's greatest general-admiral was utterly enamored by what he believed was a truly virgin born hero quietly entombed before him. The unusual sarcophagus was sitting on a high stone pedestal for Pompey or any other visitor to be enthralled. Pompey must have thought he was looking at a god worthy of worship and ordered his soldiers to remove Alexander's old and tattered cloak from his embalmed and mummified body. After his soldiers had adorned their own general with the faded scarlet-purple cloak, Pompey ordered that his own cloak be placed on the dead godman's mummified body. When Pompey returned to Rome, he appeared before the assembled Senate wearing the old, moth-eaten cloak of Alexander the Great. He forever from that point assumed the title "Pompey the Great." The vanity of a man at this level of power and height is something beyond my comprehension perhaps because I never had the opportunity to experience such authority.*

About fifteen years later while Julius Caesar was fighting the Barbarians in Gaul, the Roman Senate refused to allow Caesar to run for consul in that year forcing him to cross the river Rubicon; and the new general entered Italia with his legions. Thus began a civil war between Julius Caesar and the Roman Senate, which included Pompey the Great. The armed struggle ended a year later in Greece at the Battle of Pharsalus. Pompey lost about six thousand men, many being senators along with old veterans who had retired in Greece and had been gathered to fight Caesar's legions. This was the beginning of the end of the Republic. Within four years Caesar would be assassinated by members of the Roman Senate; and a new civil war would begin, which ended at Actium, leaving Octavius to become Rome's first emperor, Augustus Caesar.

After Pompey's loss at Pharsalus, Pompey fled back to Alexandria hoping to find sanctuary. Conceivably Pompey felt the dead god, Alexander the Great, would provide a safe haven for him. Apparently, taking something that does not belong to you might upset some people including the dead. Instead of finding refuge in Egypt, Pompey lost his life at the hands of the ministers of Ptolemy XIII, the younger brother, who was also the husband of Queen Cleopatra VII. If Pompey had not stolen Alexander's cloak, maybe he would have been more of a welcomed guest. I doubt it, but it is a thought. However, when Caesar finally reached Egypt, he received a simple wicker basket containing Pompey's head. Caesar apparently was a little perturbed at finding his old friend and son-in-law desecrated; and, besides, he wanted to kill Pompey himself. I ask the question: does no one ever learn from history? Did not Alexander the Great want to kill Darius III; and what did he do to Bessus, the Persian general who murdered Darius? History shows Alexander hunting down Bessus; and after he is apprehended, did he not die a horrible and slow death? The point is, Alexander and Caesar wanted to kill their enemies themselves.

Within a short period of time, Ptolemy XIII openly declared war against Caesar, and Caesar soon defeated this young boy's forces. All fighting ended after Ptolemy XIII was found floating face down in a tributary of the Nile. I should add it was this war between Ptolemy XIII and Caesar that resulted in the fire at the Great Library and its adjunct warehouses. One account that I have read at the Lyceum Library stated that flaming arrows shot from Caesar's ships in the harbor over-reached Ptolemy's palace and hit Caesar's transports' home setting them on fire. The flames spread from the port to the docks onto the overflow warehouses that belonged to the Great Library. Eventually some of the Great Library did sustain some minor damage from the fire. Either the Great Library was purposely set on fire, or the fire was an accident of war; either account led to the loss of immeasurable copies of tens of thousands of scrolls and books with no copies anywhere to replace them. Many inventions and cures to diseases were lost forever to humanity due to Caesar's fire. There were rumors of steam-powered projectiles invented by the Greeks that were lost and individual "hot stones" from Mesopotamia that cured some "incurable" ailments. I have also heard of a formula from the ancient Minoans that prevented obesity also being lost. Therefore, in one day, irreplaceable items vanished into smoke and ash a tragedy that will never be forgotten. The greatest collection of all human knowledge disappeared, and this marvelous library we are all presently occupying has become a proverb to man's folly of thinking. Why is it man always thinks knowledge will give him eternal life? The LXX, a product of this library, clearly states that the first lie of the Dragon presented to Eve in the Garden of Eden was the promise of eternal life through knowledge. The evil cosmic serpent said, "You will not surely die. For God knows that in the day you eat of the Tree of Knowledge your eyes will be opened, and you will be like God, knowing good and evil."

To continue looking at this theme in the Jewish Scriptures, does not this Great Library become a repeat of what happened shortly after the great flood of Noah? Did not the Tower of Babel suffer the same fate for the same reason? Man's combined intellectual search for truth always ends in disaster. Maybe there are many paths to the metaphorical temple of God; yet, there is only one entrance into the presence of this Mighty God. Men can try to scale the walls or tunnel under, but they will end up in the presence of the Holy God without the proper clothing; and then what? Having knowledge without faith in God is always a disaster. I know many listening to me are asking the question about me. "He does not look like a Jew. Why and how did he get to stand before us and lecture about this troublesome, monotheistic God?" Is not the Roman Empire destroying the

Promised Land as we listen to this lecture? Is not the city of Jerusalem surrounded, and the death of Jews now number close to a million dead? I am not a Jew, only a Yisrael at one time in the past. However, I was a youth in my early 20s when I began to see things in a different light. It became evident to me that man is born spiritually dead. We all start this walk of life as creatures born blind to the truth. Throughout history, the majority of humans foolishly look to knowledge as the means of salvation. The sad truth is that the quest for eternal life is not found in knowledge, at least not knowledge alone. It was in Jerusalem when I first began to comprehend that humans need to turn to the Creator, and this act alone has nothing to do with knowledge but is a simple faith move.

Julius Caesar undoubtedly did humanity a favor by accidentally burning down a good portion of the Great Library. That is because there was no knowledge in the Great Library to save man other than the LXX, which was not lost in the fires. Yet, the LXX does not provide salvation but only information concerning the Jewish Messiah from the House of Judah. Faith can never be destroyed as knowledge can; and, besides, false knowledge presented as truth is the greatest fallacy of humanity from the beginning of time. My understanding of all the ancient and even modern religions in the Roman Empire is nothing but vanity and fallacies. From beyond to the East of the Guptas, the Chola Empire, the Han Empire, and the people of the Four Islands all have one thing in common. They all offer a form of eternal life if the devotee or worshiper performs some work or purchases some kind of dispensation with much gold or silver.

I have learned that the winners write the history of what they want everyone to believe. Those who control the knowledge or information control the future. Herodotus, whom Cicero calls the Father of History, records in his Persian Wars only the point of view of the Greeks, not the Persians. What was the Persian point of view? The Persian assessment is lost to any humans looking for it today because the Persians were the losers in that war, especially when Alexander the Great burned the many libraries of the Persians at Persepolis. Even here in Egypt, what has happened to your Cleopatra VII? Is she not hated by Rome? In Rome today, all books and scrolls concerning your dead queen are anti-Cleopatra and anti-female rulers.

However, there is only one collection of books that are fair and balanced. I know of no other book other than the Hebrew Scriptures that tell all the iniquities, depravities, and immoralities of any of its main protagonists. The Jewish Scriptures do not hide Moses's anger problems that led to murder, and King David as a homicidal king who committed adultery with the wife of his most loyal soldier. David is guilty of lying along with all the consequences of those sins. Nevertheless; yet, that has to do with eternity and not necessarily here in this world. I can tell you, with my own experiences, we suffer the results of our sins in this world even if man or God forgives us. Two examples of repentant men are Hezekiah's son, Manasseh, who became king of Judah and Nebuchadnezzar, king of Babylon. Both caused a great deal of suffering to other humans. It is recorded that both men later repented, but still the damage spilled forth even after their deaths. Manasseh and Nebuchadnezzar both repented to the God of the Jews near the end of their lives: Manasseh after his captivity by the Assyrians and Nebuchadnezzar after seven years of crawling around his gardens eating grass thinking he was an ox.

My views are open for all to see; yet, I am not demanding anyone agree with me. My conclusions are not in the majority of many intellectual scholars; yet, I will go to my death proclaiming what I see as the truth. I shall give everyone one example. I personally accept Aristarchus's view of the Heliocentric Theory; yet, a great gathering of scholars at Alexandria hundreds of years ago voted on accepting Aristotle's Geocentric Theory as the truth of our universe. Today the Heliocentric Theory is still not the accepted explanation of our celestial mechanics. Yet, just one simple fallacy like this will retard humans for how long? Knowing what I know of most men, I believe this knowledge would have been used for significant harm and not good. I am personally grieved at the loss of the marvelous things described in the manuscripts that turned to ash in what had once been the most magnificent, intellectual repository of all times. Still, what would all that knowledge gain each one of us if eternal life is what we all seek?

After the civil war in Egypt that led to the destruction of many valuable manuscripts, Queen Cleopatra became the sole and last ruler of this land of sun worshipers. With Cleopatra and Egypt firmly in Rome's control, thanks to the help of Julius Caesar, the Roman Empire now had access to a land with at least three harvest cuttings a year and all the food to feed the Empire. There were also all the smooth, marble facing-stones from the pyramids that were eventually stripped away and taken to Rome for the Imperial city's new monuments and palaces. Dozens upon dozens of solid stone obelisks were also stolen and placed in the spines of the many circus tracks in Rome and elsewhere in the Empire.

To be somewhat fair towards Caesar, I note that he did return to Rome and tried to replace the vanished library by building a replacement in Rome; but it was never to be what it could have been because a few years later Caesar was assassinated.

Now, what is the truth regarding the death of Julius Caesar? Here is what I learned from secondary sources who learned from primary witnesses. At the time of Caesar's assassination, it was early spring; and the Senate House was being repaired due to damage sustained during previous riots. Rome's Senate sessions temporarily were being held in the Theater of Pompey out on the fields of Mars. Ironically, here is the truth as told to me. Caesar took his final breath in the Theater of Pompey. Death came to the great dictator by the hands of an unknown number of treacherous senators at the very foot of Pompey's statue in the main lobby of the Theater of Pompey. This lifeless figure remains to this day with unseeing eyes frozen on the spot where Caesar fell bleeding with over twenty knife wounds with his head covered in his purple cloak. The statue standing above Caesar's mortal, dying body was, ironically, a nude depiction of Pompey holding the round world in his right hand as a memorial to his mega-mental delusion of grandeur. The only clothing on this stone statue is a cloak draped over his shoulder and the arm holding the earth. Could this be Alexander the Great's cloak? I do not know the answer, but I suspect that it is. Yet, who knows the truth of Pompey, the killer of Jewish priests in Jerusalem because there was no statue of Yahweh in the Holy of Holies? Who also knows the truth about the stealing of Alexander's cloak off his mummified body? But all I can say is go to Pompey's Theater and see the statue for yourself. You, too, might conclude Pompey has only Alexander's cloak draped over his shoulder and the outstretched arm as his only covering. Is this not evidence of this man's passion for exaggerations masquerading as the reality of how he honestly saw himself? Still, Caesar was no better thinking he was a god before his death.

Zeno, my Greek didace when I was a boy in Rome, was alive when Caesar was assassinated and gathered all these details of his murder and related them to me as his student when I was still a child. What I am sharing is fourth-hand information; but I received some of this information third-hand from my didace, who claims his father was an actual witness to the assassination. Zeno always said a primary source was the best, that being his father as an eyewitness. Hearing the details from his father, Zeno became a secondary source to the assassination. If both were telling the truth, then both were good; yet, the primary is the best. I remember Zeno telling the story of Pompey and Caesar many times and then using his narration of Caesar's death to drill home an old adage: "Remember this, Venu; what you do today will come back to haunt you tomorrow. Even tyrants have to pay for their sins. Perhaps it is better to suffer in this world over forfeiting all in the next." It would appear Pompey and Caesar both suffered after it was too late since they both clearly died in their sins.

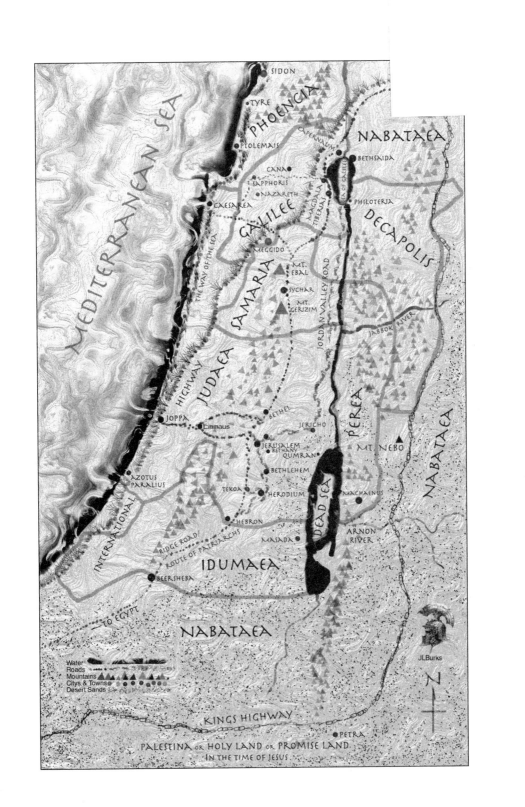

PALESTINA or HOLY LAND or PROMISE LAND
IN THE TIME OF JESUS

JLBurks

CHAPTER FOURTEEN

.{10}$Garden of Gethsemane – Tiberius's 16th year of sovereignty; 3rd year of the reign of Pontius Pilatus, Prefect of Judaea; and 60 years since Actium. Jesus of Nazareth's public ministry is now in its 6th month. Ten days before the Feast of Atonement.   (29 AD)

The Lord at thy right hand shall strike through kings in the day of his wrath. He shall judge among the heathen, he shall fill the places with the dead bodies; he shall wound the heads over many countries.   Psalm of King David of Jerusalem

"Wake up, Venu! You will want to see this," said Eli. Rolling over on the ground, I discovered I was stiff and tired. It was almost light, just before the rising of the sun. Trying to stand, I felt myself shaking. I had not slept well on the hard ground, and it had gotten cold in the night. Walking perhaps a 40-mile distance yesterday was a major feat for even a hardened soldier, and my inactivity from being at sea for almost a month did not help. Cold, frosty mornings and sleeping outdoors were not going to work. My only consolation was that the sun was about to rise, which would begin to warm this land up, along with my body. Stretching my arms and legs, I started looking for a big rock to sit on and wait for the sun to crest over the Mount of Olives and start to warm me. The sky was cloudless and turning a brilliant blue. I realized I was going to need more than one cloak or something heavier with winter coming. If it got this cold at night in the fall, what would winter be like?

Thinking I did not want to spend any more nights out in the open, I asked, "When are we going to look for work and lodging?" If it had rained in the night, we would have been in a mess."

"We could stay with some friends of mine tonight, but I do not think we should let anyone know we are in the city. We are fugitives, or have you forgotten?"

"We are victims of an insane system. And it would be wise to seek work somewhere besides pottery shops," I laughed trying to hide my discomfort.

"You remembered my uncle was a potter," he stated showing pleasure by the brightening of his eyes and the curving of the corners of his mouth. "Now come with me, and I will show you something," said Eli turning and walking towards the entrance of this quaint garden.

I followed stiffly still stretching my limbs. After we left the Garden of Gethsemane, I noticed Eli was heading for the spot where we had our supper last evening and I had revisited in the night. When he reached it, Eli sat on the same flat rock. He was facing west looking across the chasm, which he gave a new name. "The Kidron Valley is also called the Valley of Jehoshaphat."

"Why is it called the Valley of Jehoshaphat?"

"Because it is the Valley of Judgment. There is a prophecy that this valley will be filled with blood and judgment, which will occur sometime in the future."

"The blood we saw yesterday is not what the prophecy is talking about?"

"No, the blood will be as high as a horse's headgear."

I decided the name Valley of Jehoshaphat was something I did not want to think about, and I never used that term ever again. This deep crevasse would always be the Valley of Kidron. Both Eli and I sat in silence watching the effects of the sun peeking up behind us. Within a few minutes, both of us had to shield our eyes from the brilliant reflection from the gold on the Temple porch and roof as well as the golden grapevine over the gate leading into the courtyard that stood in front of the Temple. While we shielded our eyes, we heard a high-pitched blast from a silver trumpet; and afterward came loud clashing of cymbals that were followed by the voices of a dozen or so boys. The musical sounds drifted melodically across the valley.

"What are we hearing?" I questioned.

"The drink offering was just poured out ending the morning sacrifice," explained Eli. "It happens every morning, day in and day out. It is all part of the elaborate Temple rituals performed each day by the priests."

With my eyes still shielded, I looked away and noticed the red sky in the east spreading upward, which always spelled trouble before the day ended or the next one started. Reading the signs of the sky was the art of a fisherman that was always to be with me. I told Eli we were going to get wet tonight if we did not find shelter. "Come on, listen to the birds," was all Eli said unaware of what I was warning. I felt like Eli believed he was the teacher, and he could not learn anything from me being a *Yisrael*.

If we cannot learn the easy way, then we must learn the hard way. I turned my gaze back to the Temple, and it was a lovely sight. The Temple with its white marble looked like a snowfield on top of a mountain. The music from the courtyard made me feel something that was neither apparent to my senses nor evident to my intellect. It just seemed very mystical as the music from across the valley was harmonizing perfectly with the birds in the olive trees below us.

"After we eat, I'm going to show you the city and the Temple," declared Eli. "Then we will begin worrying about this rain you think is coming."

"First, we both visit a bathhouse; or we go nowhere."

Eli looked at me and then tried smelling himself. He nodded his head yes to my request, and it appeared Eli was now listening to me. I decided it would be best to now change the subject. "How tall is the Temple?"

"Perhaps 20 to 25 tall men standing on top of each other's head," he described for me to visualize.

"So it is about 150 feet tall?"

Eli looked at me with a funny expression and then said it was the tallest man-made structure not counting the Great Pyramids in Egypt.

"I have never seen the Temple of Ephesus, which has 60-foot pillars holding up a peaked roof," I interjected. "That could make the moon goddess Artemis's temple 80 to 90 feet tall. I do not know how tall the temple to Augustus at Caesarea Maritima stands."

Eli did not comment; and I, too, kept my mouth shut. I decided we might end up in another argument. It was at this moment I realized Eli had been my good friend as a child, but people change when they grow up. Besides his teaching me about Judaism, he was not someone I would today choose as a friend. But it was not Eli's fault considering I had no close friends for the past ten years. Maybe spending two months in a dark tunnel with him, not being able to talk, and then traveling with him and allowing him to make many of our decisions were grinding on me. I decided to try to be submissive, but it was all causing a mental strain on my part.

Later that morning when we entered the city by the gate leading into the section of Jerusalem called the Lower City, I noticed Eli was happy to be home. All the houses and buildings were built close together, and the streets were narrow and weaved around the different hills. Every street was paved with stones in the same fashion of all Roman roads. There were many bazaars and markets open for business. Eli looked at me smiling from ear to ear, and it was infectious.

This was when I learned the city rested on seven hills similar to Rome. Eli was quick to explain their names and locations. "And that bridge over there is where we are going to cross into the Temple compound. The bridge connects Mount Zion, which is also called the City of David, to Mount Moriah at the section of the Temple complex called the Royal Porch," explained Eli. I looked at where Eli was pointing; and there stood a colossal stone bridge with tall, immense arches that looked like long, narrow legs of some mythical creature. In some ways, it seemed like an over-built, double-the-size aqueduct except it transported people and not water. It was actually quite an image, an enormous, arched bridge in the center of a vast city. Eli explained that this was called Zion Bridge, and it spanned over the Tyropoeon Valley separating Mount Moriah from Mount Zion.

While I was still gazing at the impressive bridge, Eli wanted me to look over to our right at three massive arched entrances cut into a mountain of a wall. The three openings were at the top of a broad flight of stone steps and were the main entrance on the south side of the Temple compound.

"What are you pointing at?" I asked.

"The southern subterranean gates that lead to the Court of Gentiles on the far side of the Royal Porch. We, however, will use the Zion Bridge to enter the Temple complex; but you will understand why we must go through those gates."

I followed Eli through the Hulda Gates; and I instantly marveled at the huge, massive underground area of columns holding up dozens of arched ceilings. Scattered throughout the vast, underground open area were hundreds of terracotta tubs. Some people were sitting in the containers with their clothes on, and it looked like they were taking a bath as well as washing their clothes. "Did you not say we had to visit a bathhouse? Here is God's bathhouse. People are to purify themselves before going before Yahweh. Most people wash only their hands and feet; but, as you can see, there are people like us who need to go much further in their purification."

"Are you suggesting we sit in a tub and take a bath with our clothes on?"

"Isn't that what you suggested on the Mount of Olives?"

After a good cleaning, Eli and I were back out in the open Agora on the south end of the Temple complex allowing the sun to dry our clothes that were dripping wet. I had wet hair and clothes but felt clean for the first time since leaving *Italia*.

Still wet but not dripping water, we crossed the bridge. At the top I discovered we had a spectacular view of the city. Below us were winding streets and buildings meandering in a disorganized fashion but not depressing like the *Urbs* or *Subura* of Rome. From up here the city appeared old but spotless. It looked clean and smelled clean – free of the usual odors of a large city. The Jews apparently were sensitive to garbage and such, which was hauled daily to the far south of the Hill of Corruption and thrown down into the valley of Hinnom. Down in this valley, fires burned continuously consuming the waste and trash of over a hundred thousand people. I would later learn first-hand about this deep valley with burning trash heaps. The valley of Hinnom was commonly used as an illustration of Sheol or Hell, a place for the wicked after death. I stood for a moment and watched the people below wandering through the streets like little insects busy with work and other activities. All the sights around this strange city hypnotized me so that I did not want to leave.

"Come on, brother!" called out Eli.

"You called me brother," I said once I reached him. "Tell me, what was your purpose when we were boys in my father's house?"

"Are you joking?" asked Eli.

"I am serious. I know you were a slave, but what were your duties?"

"My duties? It was you! I was to be your companion and playmate. That was all."

"What? Are you teasing me?"

"It is true, Venu. I was purchased to be your companion when you were not at school or with your mother. I was put to work cleaning things or pulling weeds in the garden when you were at school, but my primary job was to be your friend."

"I did not know this. All the time until now I thought we were just friends because we liked each other."

"I did like you, and you are my friend! Your father bought me as a slave to be your playmate, but with you I was never a slave."

"And now?" I asked in all seriousness.

"In your father's eyes, I am a runaway slave, a fugitive, and your friend by choice. There is no compulsion here for me to be your slave. I am your friend, and that is what I am trying to say. Are you not my friend? Now let me show you the Temple," he said changing the subject in the same fashion I would do when something was uncomfortable. Looking at Eli walk ahead of me, I realized this was something a slave would never do to his master. A slave always walked 10 feet behind. Eli had made his last statement in a light-hearted way trying to put me at ease. I had attempted to smile when he asked if I were his friend before he changed the subject and led the way towards the Temple complex. This new revelation had taken me off guard. How does someone dismiss the idea after you learn your friend was purchased as a child to be a friend and playmate? I started following Eli; but, still, I grappled in my heart and mind regarding Eli as a playmate slave.

Near the end of the bridge, we took a right-hand turn into two large arched openings. There were mostly Jewish-priest-type men on the bridge and standing around the gate. When I asked Eli about this, he told me tradition stated this was the entrance into the complex for priests and other religious men while the common people came up the long flight of stairs from under the ritual bathing area on the south side.

"You mean the Hulda Gates were where we were supposed to enter?"

"It is not written anywhere, just tradition. Why should the priests get the good view of the city? We are just as important to Yahweh over any of these religious men. No?" asked Eli with a conspiratorial smile. I tried to smile back hoping my recent stressful feelings were now at rest.

Once I stepped through the gate into a massive arched area, Eli told me we were now in the Royal Porch section of the massive Temple complex. The enormity of my new insight concerning Eli prevented me from noticing everything my eyes were looking at. Why wasn't I able to vanquish the idea that Eli had been purchased by my father to be no more than a human pet. I could not believe the Roman world and its revolting ways. I believed Eli when he said he was my friend by choice, but was he still my slave? Of course not, I told myself realizing we were both fugitives. I asked myself if he would give his life for mine, which is the ultimate test of friendship. I risked my life when I rescued him from my father's villa, but I did not know if he would do the same for me. These thoughts bothered me. Besides, why was I thinking such thoughts? If I continued, they would ruin my first impressions of this spectacular edifice.

"Well, what do you think of the Temple?" asked Eli oblivious to my inner turmoil.

"I do not know," I said trying to turn my mind away from the dreadful subject of slavery.

Eli, with his infectious smile, waved his arms. "Ten years ago, when I first arrived here in Jerusalem, I came here before I found my uncle. I counted all the colonnades in this porch. There are 162, all with Corinthian capitals.

They are four deep making three aisles. The central cloister is twice as high with a cedar roof. This *stoa* is called the Royal Portico." Eli then walked out of the porch area and waved his arms to the north. I came up behind him and he said, "This area of terraced steps and pavement is called the Court of Gentiles. It girds the entire Temple, which you can see sits majestically there in the middle."

Now I saw it, and it hurt my neck to look at the top. The Temple was as big as Eli had said when the sun first rose upon it this morning. I could not comprehend where I was, and it put shivers down my shoulders and back. It was a magical moment just being this close to the Temple of Yahweh. It was hard to imagine that here was the meeting place between what I perceived to be the Creator of the universe and humans. All the other temples in the Empire were vain fakes of the real one. I could almost feel a holy presence in this place; but, as soon as I tried to enjoy the presence, it flew away like a darting flower bird. I felt a little sad but glad at the same time. After I had dismissed the thought, I fastened my attention on the heterogeneous gathering horde of people standing, sitting, talking, and praying in the Court of Gentiles. I wondered if anyone I was looking at felt as I did about the holy presence that mysteriously came and went. Most gathered along the edges of the enormous courtyard, which was about twice the size of Athen's entire *Agora* but closer to the area of the *Forum Romanum*. Taking my eyes off the people, I stared at the colonnaded outer perimeter, which formed more colossal *stoas* with stone columns reaching as high as 60 feet just as tall as the pillars holding up the Temple of Diana or Artemis at Ephesus. I remembered the unfinished temple of Zeus standing not far from the southeast corner of the Acropolis in Athens. If it were ever finished, it would be the largest temple in the world. Its front eight Corinthian-topped capitals had to be close to 60 feet high. Returning my mind back to Jerusalem, I gazed at the long rows of pillars. Some of these porches on the western side were multi-layered. I thought of the first psalm Rabbi Issachar asked me to memorize. It ended by saying, "*For Yahweh knows the way of the righteous: but the way of the ungodly shall perish.*" This entire area was only for the righteous, for why would an immoral person want to even visit this beautiful, sprawling edifice.

"Come!" said Eli pulling at my sleeve. "Does this not remind you of the psalm that begins '*As the deer pants after the water brooks, so my soul pants after you, Elohim.*'" He quoted the verse of a psalm I had never read or heard; it must have been beyond the psalms in the scroll Rabbi Issachar had given me. The syntax of God's word just amazed me. God was not only a splendid artist but also a poet and a watcher of men; and He loved each one of us and, yet, expected obedience. These were my thoughts as Eli led me through the crowded area out into the open courtyard on the southern side of the Court of Gentiles. I tried listening to my friend as a teacher, not my friend purchased by my father. There was only one thought at this time that disturbed me. I remembered the *Painted Stoa* in Athens remembering that last morning after retrieving my boots and Spartan cloak. There in my mind's eye was Felix Cornelius, the Praetorian following me but then disguised in rags coming out of the darkness and asking me if I were a Roman. He then told me about General Sulla filling the *Agora* in Athens with blood. I wondered how many times this area had been awash in human blood due to war and wickedness. The Roman, Pompey the Great, undoubtedly filled this courtyard with innocent human blood on the day he entered the Holy of Holies and found no statue of Yahweh. I was also sure the Babylonians, who destroyed Solomon's Temple, surely did the same.

My thoughts of blood were intruded when Eli began pointing out the different groups and what they represented. Actually, taking my imaginative mind off the sight of human blood was a good thing. Had I stayed on that thought, I would have begun to think of this entire area as Yahweh's altar of dead humans because of their unfaithfulness. Shifting away from those bloody thoughts, I listened to Eli elucidate about the differences in the speech and dress among a Galilean, a Judaean, and a Jerusalemite. He pointed out a group of men in white robes and puffy linen hats and said these men were the priests and Levites. They were the ones who carried out all the holy duties inside the Temple such as sacrifices and offerings. These must have been the ones I watched last evening close the temple doors, and they were the ones on the Zion Bridge.

"What about those men in the military uniforms?" I asked sensing the strangeness of soldiers in a place of worship. They were dressed in white tunics with silver and gold cuirasses. Each man held a tall spear tipped with a gleaming bronze point along with silver and bronze swords hanging at their sides in bejeweled scabbards.

"Those are the Temple soldiers. They are all Levites, and they keep the peace inside the Temple complex. At times, some troublemakers try to start riots here in these sacred grounds. This place can be an oven of bitter feelings. The Romans have a fort at the other end of the courtyard, and they will intervene if the temple soldiers are not able to maintain order. Over the years there has been much blood spilled right here on these hallowed grounds. There have been many Jewish uprisings as well as many nations battling right where we stand." This did not help my mind as considering I was trying to erase the image of bloodshed.

Eli was enjoying his role as teacher and guide, and I had learned a great deal from him since we began this journey from Rome. Eli led me towards the back side of the Temple where many beggars were pleading for alms. None of the vagrants approached us perhaps judging others more profitable over two young, ragged-looking Jews. Moving past the beggars, we came upon a group of well-dressed men with broad, light-blue borders at the bottom edges of their robes along with tassels at the four corners. They were vigorously debating one another while many young boys wearing traditional student robes and tunics sat at their feet listening intently.

"Eli, who are they? Those men with the long tassels at the edges of the blue trim on their robes?"

Eli looked over to where I pointed with my eyes, and he smiled. "Now this group is the most interesting of the Temple personalities," said Eli sarcastically. "Listen to them like their young disciples at their feet, and you will learn to hate your new religion."

"Who are they?" I asked not hiding my curiosity and ignoring his warning.

"They are the Pharisees, a sect that withdrew from another sect called the Sadducees about one hundred years after Alexander the Great and the descendants of his Greek army conquered this land. The Pharisees began as a group who struggled to establish purity in life and doctrine. They feared the new Hellenistic culture that was overtaking Jewish society at that time. Many Jews were accepting the Greek ways over the old Jewish traditions such as the gymnasiums and the nudity that went on in them. Many Jews even had their circumcisions surgically reversed just so they would not be laughed at when attending the bathhouses and gymnasiums, something that would have happened to us if we had gone to a bathhouse this morning instead of washing in the purification area beyond the Hulda Gates."

I remembered my own discomfort with nudity at the Lyceum and my battle over that issue. Maybe I would like the Pharisees, men who would not cave because of nudity rules. Why a Jew would embrace that form of dissipation I could not understand nor answer. How a Jew could be so weak to violate his ancient Abrahamic covenant was beyond me.

Eli interrupted my thoughts as he continued. "Today the Pharisees remain only as a legalistic and obstinate group with much power and influence over the entire population of Jews outside of Jerusalem and even to the far reaches of the Empire. They are the teachers and the controllers of the synagogues."

I thought of Rabbi Issachar. Did he not control the synagogue in Rome with the four big trees surrounding it? "Is Rabbi Issachar of this sect?"

"Yes, Rabbi Issachar is a Pharisee. Did he not read you the ten laws of the *Torah*, and did he not tell me to teach you the 613 laws?"

"But you did not teach me any of the laws. Why?"

"You will not become legalistic as long as I am your teacher and friend," explained Eli smiling to hide his seriousness. It was a disarming way of warning me of the trap of legalism. However, I was wearied of what I was hearing. What was all this talk of legalism? Did not God use Rabbi Issachar to lead me to Himself? Was this sect that wrong? What group did Eli identify with?

"Listen, Venu; we are not to judge men because of the way they dress. Rabbi Issachar was an exception to the mold. He is not a hard-core Pharisee as some here in *Palestina*, but do you remember his response to me when I told him I had been baptized by John? He was not happy to hear I was a disciple of the Baptist."

I looked away and noticed a well-dressed group of men in robes of purple and red. "Over there, the rich men," I pointed out trying to change the subject from Rabbi Issachar.

"They are the Sadducees, more of a political party than a religious sect such as the Pharisees. They consider themselves as an aristocratic priesthood functioning as the Temple administrators. Some are not religious at all and are called Herodians. Now remember this, Venu; you will never see these purple-robed men talking with the tassel-edged men. The Sadducees and the Pharisee dislike each other with a passion. Their hatred goes deeper than any fissure you could find on the earth."

"What is it that keeps them separated? Do they not worship the same God?"

"That is a fascinating question, and I am not sure what the answer is. All I know is this: to be a Sadducee, one must first belong to an aristocratic family here in Jerusalem. I think the real problem goes back to their different interpretations of the Scriptures. For instance, the Sadducees do not believe in angels, seraphim, cherubim, or any other spiritual beings while the Pharisees do. The Pharisees prided themselves on being very ritualistically strict in their actions while the Sadducees do not. The Sadducees believe a person has the freedom to do whatever whereas the Pharisees' thinking is somewhat archaic on this topic. Even so, Sadducees like to steer to the middle where most of the human events are already established and embrace the idea of free choice. Whatever you do, if you have a Pharisee and a Sadducee together, never bring up the afterlife. Sadducees think, when you die, that is it. The end of this life is just a long 'sleep in the dirt.' At least the Pharisees embrace the belief of a never-ending life with God."

All this was confusing; yet, I wanted to understand. "You mean the Sadducees do not believe in the resurrection at the end of time?"

"No life after death. What foolishness. All men, pagan and non-pagan, know in their inner being they will live forever, somewhere, in some fashion. The prophet Daniel in the last words of his book in the Scriptures is told this by God: *'But you, Daniel, wait until the end until you die, and then you will arise to your inheritance at the end of the days.'* Does that sound like there is no resurrection of the dead?"

I just smiled, and we continued looking around the back edges of the Court of Gentiles. I noticed other rich-looking men wearing crimson robes with matching headgear standing and sitting under the shade of the covered porches with groups of young, white-robed boys.

"Who are the ones in the crimson robes?"

"Those are the dangerous ones. They are called the Scribes, who are the doctors and lawyers of the law. They make the Pharisees look like children when it comes to legalism. Scribes are an intellectual class of Jews who devote their entire lives to the study of the law. But these religious men have been contaminated by Greek philosophy that has them entangled in their theology like being in a spider's web.

"That is interesting. The Greek philosopher Pythagoras said religion is derived from inner euphoria while faith and theology can be explained mathematically. My teachers at the Lyceum taught that most men were foolish creatures who cherish their own prejudices no matter what truth is shown to them."

Eli looked confused at my words before he returned to his own instructions. Did he forget I was tutored at the most prestigious school in the Empire? "The boys in white are the disciples of the doctors and lawyers of the law. Most of the boys' parents pay a high price to have their sons sit under the instructions of the Scribes, but the parents are wasting their riches. These viper-teachers are a remnant from Babylon who came out of the Jewish academies that had been established there during the exile under Nebuchadnezzar. The Scribes ravage the ordinary people who go to them with money to get a personal interpretation of the law. The peasants and ordinary people consider the Scribes a priestly group, but they are not. As far as I am concerned, they are billowed sails that never leave the harbor. There is also a deep fissure between this class of men and the Pharisees since the people consider the Pharisees as their teachers outside of Jerusalem. Remember the

Pharisees control all the synagogues, the worship centers outside of this place. Then there are the Essenes who reject the entire temple system and live down in the Dead Sea region all by their lonesome. There are also the Samaritans who are rejected by all Jews because they are only half-Jewish. They had their own temple on Mount Gerizim, which was destroyed by the Maccabees a couple of hundred years ago. The Samaritans still worship on the ruins of that temple and rarely come here."

"I do not understand. Why would someone pay to get an interpretation from the Scriptures?" I asked feeling somewhat disturbed by all I was discovering and wanting to understand more about the Scribes.

"Come, I will show you," remarked Eli leading me back to the southern side of the Courtyard of Gentiles near the Royal Porch. He pulled me until we stood next to an individual Scribe who sat at a little table with scrolls spread out on top. There was a line of about a dozen people waiting to speak with him. Eli got close enough to hear but not close enough to be noticed. Eli indicated with a head jester that we should just listen. A short, middle-aged man wearing a new robe was next in line. When his turn came, he stepped forward to the Scribe and his little table. "I have a serious problem, Doctor of the Law," said the man who had stepped out of line towards the small table.

"Let me hear your problem," said the Scribe.

"Tomorrow is the Sabbath, and I have to make a significant transaction with a particular Roman who will be leaving our country before the Sabbath is over. He refuses to see me until tomorrow afternoon. The Roman is a businessman staying in Jerusalem; and I live over the hill in Bethany, which is more than a Sabbath's walk away." The man waved his arm towards the east and the Mount of Olives apparently pointing in the direction of his village. "My family depends on me to feed them. How can I continue to feed my family and not violate the Law and the Sabbath, for I am a God-fearing man?"

The Scribe looked up at his customer and held out his hand with his palm up. The Jew put several silver coins into the open hand, and the Scribe pulled it back quickly just like the movement of a sea snake that hides in his hole under rocks below the surface of shallow reefs. When his empty hand returned from beneath his crimson robe, he spoke very softly; but Eli and I both heard.

"This is what you should do."

"Yes, what is it, Doctor?"

"The Law says you must remain near your property on the Sabbath."

"Yes, this is the problem."

"Tomorrow, around the middle of the day, go outside your house; and remove your sandal. Throw it down the road. Walk up to it, and you are still near your property. No?"

"Yes."

"Well, pick up your property; throw it down the road, and walk up to it."

"Yes, I understand. And once I am at the Roman's door, I might as well speak with him."

"True, but you must not enter the pagan's abode. He must come out to you." The Scribe sighed mournfully and continued. "Ah, but he is a Roman. He will probably refuse. Perhaps you have another *denarius* for me, and we can discuss how to further secure food for your hungry children."

"He will come out, I am sure. You have helped me tremendously. Thank you, wise one!" The little man hurried away smiling to himself.

I was ready to throw the Scribe off his wooden stool, but Eli pulled me away. "That is manipulation of Yahweh's words," I said once we were alone.

"Now you sound like a Pharisee."

I was bewildered by what I had witnessed, and I wanted nothing to do with any of it. I was also angry because Eli was now calling me a Pharisee. "What is your opinion of all the divisions among your fellow Jews?" I asked trying to curb my anger.

"I'm not sure. Being born as a slave in Rome, I do not know from what class my parents came, which would really determine what I would be today."

"What about your uncle? What group did he identify with?"

"He was a simple Jerusalemite pottery maker. He said he belonged only to the God of Abraham, Isaac, and Jacob. He studied the words of Moses once a week on his own at the *scriptorium* of the Synagogue of the Freedmen. That is a synagogue here in Jerusalem frequented mostly by proselyte Jews such as yourself. You and my uncle would get along grandly. He is the one who taught me to study and think for myself. I see the Pharisees as a group of overly zealous, self-righteous men who strut around as if they are holier than all others. They act as if they are blameless as sunlight and flawless as a gem in a king's crown because they follow all their fine details of the Law according to their own interpretations."

"Then you agree with the Scribe's interpreting for monetary gain?"

"We all have to make a living," he shrugged. "Obviously, what we just heard was an abuse of the Law for the sake of filthy mammon."

"Material wealth at God's expense!" I retorted angrily. "What about the Sadducees? What do you think of them?"

"The Sadducees? I personally hate the entire lot of them. You do not see them very often except here at the Temple. They busy themselves making sure the sacrifices are running smoothly and quickly, especially during feast days. At Passover, for example, there might be over two million pilgrims here in Jerusalem; and possibly 200,000 lambs will be slain just on that one day, which will make this event the largest gathering of humans at any one place. The Sadducees get their cut of the people's money through the sacrificial trade and the exchange of tithe money. Can you just imagine the money made by the Sadducees on a busy feast day? Nevertheless, I could not be a Sadducee anyway because I do not belong to an aristocratic family. They are a small but influential group. Annas and Caiaphas, who sometimes trade off the position of high priest each year, come from this sect along with the other men who control and run this city as well as all the activities here at the Temple. And they are all sharing the rule with the Roman invaders. But, of course, that is how Rome rules the Empire. Leave the kings in place along with all the religious rituals in the hope the tax collectors, or as the ordinary people called them tax-farmers, will collect a fortune for those in Rome without any trouble."

Knowing all of the strategies of rule by the Romans, I asked, "You still are not telling me what group you follow?"

"To tell you the truth, Venu, I haven't followed any group here in Jerusalem; but, instead, I embrace the teachings of John the Baptist. His father was a priest, but John will not have anything to do with the Temple. John will not even enter into this place. He is not an Essene, but he is closer to them than anyone is here before us. Sometimes you will see an Essene but not here at the Temple. They teach that this place is polluted just like the Tiber River. The Baptist lives out in the desert alone with his few disciples even away from the Essenes. He purposely preaches out in the wilderness and baptizes those who will change their ways and come out of the 'decadent system' as he calls it. I went to listen to him last summer as I already told you. He shouted over and over, 'Repent, for the Kingdom of Heaven is at hand!' I was moved by his words and submitted to his baptism; and now I wait for the Messiah, who is to come after him."

We both became silent after Eli had concluded his discourse on his own spiritual position. I watched Eli lower his head in thought and walk away from me heading west towards the rear wall of the massive white-and-gold Temple of Yahweh. I followed him through the crowds; and, once behind the Temple, we both wandered into the cool, shady area of the *stoa* on this side of the Court of Gentiles. It was at this point Eli and I noticed a curious-looking man sitting in the shadows of a cloister with a relatively large group perhaps numbering a score or more of young boys wearing both the white robes of the students of the Scribes and the familiar robes of the students of the Pharisees. None of the boys was older than Eli and I, and they were all gathered in a mesmerized state listening to this simple man. The teacher was dressed in a well-made, yet ordinary, faded, stone-white, Galilean homespun, which actually set him apart from all the other teachers. There was no pretense of this particular teacher flaunting his authority. He emanated a simple humility that was demonstrated by his quiet and amiable demeanor. He was tanned almost bronze from the sun, and his eyes were dark and penetrating but at times turned a blueish-green color. There was also something strange about the edges of the colored part of his eyes around the irises. He had a large, hawkish-beaked nose that gave him the look of a Bedouin chieftain. However, he did not have a look that was in any way violent; perhaps the nose was the result of his being beaten by robbers at one time, or he was born with the bump. The bump was perhaps more significant than any man's nose I had ever seen. His mouth was hidden somewhat by a full beard that was streaked with gray along with premature silver strands in his temples. His hair was curly and dark auburn swept back but hiding his ears. The length reminded me of the older men in Athens, who wore their hair long to their shoulders. The teacher looked to be in his late thirties or early forties but no older. He looked tall and well proportioned even though he was sitting. If one did not know him, one would not take a second glance. If one saw him again, one would not be able to place him or even remember where one last saw him. However, he was unusual in that there was a gleam in his eyes that was different from most men. He definitely had the eyes of someone who knew and believed in what he was saying. Other than his eyes, he was the same as any other Jew in *Palestina*.

"Let us go, and listen to this rabbi," suggested Eli. "He, for some reason, seems to be different from all the rest of the teachers."

I nodded sensing the same about him. We walked around the porch area and found a seat at the back of the group. The weathered teacher was speaking Hebrew with a strange accent that I later learned was Galilean. His words and voice, I quickly learned, were more convicting and piercing than his eyes.

"Remember also your Creator in the days of your youth. Do not the Scriptures say this? What does it mean?"

No one answered; all remained quiet for the teacher to explain his own questions even though the teacher had not framed the question as being explicitly rhetorical. "Understand this, and wisdom will fill you. There is a way in life that leads to vanity and death, this being the pursuits of pleasure through the love of the world and its systems; and this in itself leads to death. Do not misunderstand; we must live in this world, but that does not mean we must be part of the world system. Do the Scriptures teach otherwise? Remember your Creator in the days of your youth. Only by looking to the Giver of Life will you find true happiness and lasting peace. Always remember that life is a gift from the Creator. None of us chose to be born; yet, here we all sit. However, which one of you did not want to sit today and listen? Who or what was it that drew you to sit in this cool area and listen? That is how the Living God works. He loves those who seek Him, and He draws them to Himself. It is only faith in Him that brings the Creator of the *Cosmos* pleasure. Do not the Scriptures teach as much?"

The man stopped speaking to allow his words to seep into our inner beings. I was astonished by my feelings. They reminded me of the moment I came out of the water when I baptized myself in the Tiber. My heart burned as I listened to this man's simple, yet profound, words. He spoke in a well-organized, self-confident manner as he understood and believed everything he was saying. His comportment flowed with great kindness and gentleness to all who were listening. Sitting and listening, I felt as if time had been suspended; and the teacher was enjoying telling all who looked to him about whatever it was that was in his heart. The teacher did not smile as if he were happy, but I could tell he was enjoying the fact that there were people showing faith in God's words as he quoted the Scriptures.

"Now, while you are young, you will make many decisions that will set the pillars of your life – pillars that become rigid just like the ones some of you are leaning against." He stood, took several steps, and slapped one of the marble columns himself to show its permanence. After the example had been given, he returned to his sitting position with one knee bent up. The cold, snowy-white colonnades holding up the porch roof gave new insight to the young Temple students mentally weighing the lifeless permanence of the columns regarding the teacher's illustration. He was an excellent teacher, for he used examples and word pictures. Zeno had always said, "A good teacher makes learning a joy; an evil teacher sprouts rebellion. A good teacher will always tell interesting stories to illustrate his points." After this exceptional teacher had allowed us a moment to swallow and digest his words, he began again. He had incredible patience and a non-condescending air about him that welcomed any who would listen. Being with him made you want to make him your friend, and all else shrank in significance. I felt as if I could sit here for hours and it would only seem like a few moments.

Then this man began speaking as if he were reading my mind. "This world is passing away, and the young will soon turn old and decay. Nevertheless, true life in the Father will never fail even when you someday watch as the young ones eat and you are not able. Pains will come and stay with you; but, if you believe, you shall live. As it is written, '*Do homage to the Son lest he become angry, and you perish in the way; for his wrath may soon be kindled. How blessed are all who take refuge in him.*'"

I was amazed, for he was quoting the second psalm that Rabbi Issachar had given me on the scroll. He had quoted it exactly as it translated out in the Greek even though this man was speaking Hebrew minus the Greek word *cosmos*. Even at this time, I understood only a little of this ancient language; but now it was as if it were my native tongue. Here was someone who knew the Scriptures by heart, possibly in the Hebrew; yet, he quoted the standard Greek translation. This was a brilliant move on his part. Most people including these Jewish students would know the LXX, more so over the Hebrew Scriptures. These boys must have been students of other scholars; for this man did not appear to be a teacher by trade, especially when one looked at him and his clothing. All the teachers here at the Temple must have made a generous income; at least it appeared as much from the way they dressed.

"Look at what you cannot see, and you shall live. But all that you see will pass away," said the teacher spreading out his arms indicating all the magnificence of the Temple and other buildings. Everyone was now whispering, and I was amazed as I remembered these similar words written by Plato. This man was well tutored and possessed wisdom far beyond the casting of a sandal down the road. I wanted to hear more. My heart stirred as it never had. I did not want to leave, but this moment came crashing to a halt.

"Break it up! Break it up!" commanded a huge temple soldier standing in front of several Sadducees and a Scribe who had stealthily come up behind the teacher. "I'm informed that you are teaching without permission, and you will have to cease!"

The man in the white homespun looked up at the soldier. He stared for a moment as if he had all the time in the universe. Then he answered with a simple question in a soft voice. "Whose house is this?" There was no reply as if he knew there would be none, so he answered the question himself. "Is it not my Father's house? Is it not lawful to teach and speak in His house?"

"You have not been educated in the proper schools recognized by the respectable groups of this Temple. I'm sorry, but I'm just doing my duty in asking you to desist!" remarked the soldier in a tone short of a bite.

Eli leaned close to me and whispered, "This man is the Captain of the Temple. He is a very powerful and dangerous man, perhaps the most influential, just below the high priest."

One of the Sadducees standing with the captain eyed the group of young listeners and said, "If you listen to this man and his false words, it will be recorded and held against you. And I see that several of you hope to be graduating soon."

Some of the boys in white robes quickly stood and left with bowed heads. I, on the other hand, became enraged as I understood this threat and brusque interruption. I rose with my hand reaching into my cloak for the handle of the falcata, which was hidden at my left side. "You hypocrites are the false ones! There is no life in your words! You give threats to these boys because you know this man speaks the truth! Are you such strangers to the truth that you bully a simple man who has something worthwhile to say? Moreover, by bullying this man, you are bullying young students, who are innocent enough to hear the truth. What has this teacher said that is not in the Scriptures?"

Eli stood and pulled at my cloak to be quiet.

"Yes, stop your friend before he regrets what he says!" threatened the Captain of the Temple.

Eli released me and began trembling. I had never seen this before in Eli; he was frightened of this Jew in a uniform. Shame filled me to be standing next to a coward. Eli lowered his head, and I noticed a lonely tear running ever so slowly from his right eye. Eli turned and left me alone with the teacher and the Captain of the Temple and his religious cohorts. Most of the boys in white had gone just like Eli. Apparently, Eli's fear had spread to the few remaining students, who now began to silently stand and leave. Only the white-robed teacher remained sitting. Once all the students had gone, so did the Sadducees and the Scribe. All who were left were the soldier whose glare stayed on me and the teacher still sitting at his feet with his knee still bent up. My hand was resting on the hidden falcata's handle and could remove it and cut him down before he could pull his own long sword. I was fighting my anger like a charioteer holding back his team of four before a race.

"I suggest you leave, or there may be trouble," commanded the captain making his words sound more like a threat than a suggestion. "As for your pious teacher, this is not the first time we have had trouble with him. You tell him, if I catch him in here again doing anything other than offering a turtle dove, I will end his teaching career permanently." He smiled darkly at me and then down towards the rabbi who had his head down in a posture of prayer. After his slight glare, he turned on his right heel and strode away with a definite step of military authority.

Just as the Captain of the Temple Guards was lost in the crowd out beyond the *stoa* area, Eli appeared from wherever he had gone and was now back next to me. The teacher was now standing before the both of us, and he gently placed his right hand on Eli's shoulder. When Eli lifted his head, the teacher unashamedly used the back of his hand to brush away a tear that was hanging on the edge of Eli's cheek. The teacher then spoke in the most soothing manner in Aramaic as he looked Eli directly in the eyes. "You have been a good friend and teacher, but remember a good friend will lay down his life for his friend. I tell you now that your shame will be replaced by much courage. Be anxious for nothing; but just ask from above, and it will come upon you. The real struggle is not against flesh and blood but against spiritual wickedness from high places. Arm yourself with the weapons from above. Ask for this grace, and it will be given to you as well as the peace that will go beyond all understanding. Act upon the words that you heard the desert preacher teach you."

Then the teacher removed his right hand from Eli's shoulder, and I thought about the story Felix told me in Rome at the *popina*. I realized the man and I were about the same height. It was at this moment I looked directly into those strange but beautiful eyes. I definitely saw the remarkable flecks of rainbow colors around the iris of those penetrating eyes. While he stared at me, his eye color seemed to change dramatically from a dark brown to a bluish green. I had never seen such a thing other than the opposite when someone was angry, and his eyes turned from their normal color to darkness. This was very different, something I had never in my life seen before. His eyes seemed to match the soul behind them. For some strange reason, I did not want him to touch me as he had Eli. I had allowed only Messina to place her hands on me in an intimate way, and it was as if the teacher was reading my mind. At this point, his eyes turned to a darker brownish-green; before long they transformed into a darker blue and then reversed back to a lighter blue. His eyes not only showed his soul to me; I was confident he could read my heart as well as my mind. I understood that, when his eyes turned dark, they seemed to flash a fury because someone else other than he held my heart. I just stood there assuming that his eyes openly revealed a deep sorrow for me because I was like a lost lamb in a world of wolves. It had seemed like an eternity before he said any words, but volumes had been spoken to me with just his eyes in a few moments. This was beyond the way Messina used her eyes to talk to me when we were children in the Ostia warehouse. When he opened his mouth, time again stopped; and it seemed as if we had all the time in the world. "You must remember your Creator; and after you have come back, strengthen yourself." I just stood there astonished without a smile or any other facial expression. He understood I did not want him touching my shoulder as he had done to Eli.

"What is your name?" I asked.

In perfect Greek, he said, "You are Epaphroditus; and I am *Christos*, the one about whom your mother told you on her last morning." It was as if his reply had thrown me back and slammed me into one of those permeant pillars he had earlier touched. Not only did he speak in perfect Greek; but also he used the same dialect that my mother had from the area of Macedonia, which was where she was born. I received an answer, but why did I not have the faith to believe in the one who just spoke? What was stopping me from falling at his feet? Here was the virgin born one, the Son of God, who was coming to fix the issue of sin, which started in the beginning with Adam and Eve. This magnificent and noble man in all humbleness finally smiled at me as if to say he liked me or even more than that. It was a *philos* or brotherly type of love he was showing me mixed with a higher *agape* or a one-way love coming from him and not me. He then turned and walked towards a group of a dozen poorly dressed Galileans, who had just entered the compound from the direction of the Royal Porch. The group of men looked like older students who had great affection for their teacher-rabbi. They slapped and hugged their teacher and then began walking as a group back in the direction they had come. Here was something I had never seen before. Men who openly showed how much they loved one another. To me, it was an abnormal quaintness. How could they all be full of laughter and gaiety? Did they not realize how close their teacher had come to serious harm? I turned to Eli in amazed awe, and there he stood just as astonished as I. We both just stood and watched the white-robed man leave with his friends.

"Let's go and follow this man!" declared Eli suddenly.

"Let's leave and find a place to have a strong drink," I retorted with eyes not able to see anything. I just looked at the horde of people who seemed to have swallowed the teacher and his students.

"No, I am serious," declared Eli.

"Listen, Eli. First of all, we are fugitives. Second, we would only bring trouble to that good man. Besides, did you hear him ask us to come along? I would say no."

"But he knew intimate details of our lives. He knew your Greek name; he knew your mother – I think he knew her."

"I think, if he wanted us to follow him, he would have asked us to do just that. I believe he only told us to 'Remember our Creator.'"

"What do you mean he did not invite us? He is the Creator of the universe. What is there to ask? Why would we not follow him?"

"You heard what he said. You and I have some other task ahead of us, and following him at this time is not part of it. Now let's go *bacchus* at some tavern."

"Be serious, Venu. We only have a few coins left; besides, there is more to see before we leave – that is, if we do not follow him now while we can still find him."

"Trust me on this. Had he asked us to follow, we would give up all to do just that. However, he did not. On the question of this tour, I am not sure I can grasp any more of this odyssey. It is not even the middle of the day, and I am exhausted. Maybe a nap over in a cool corner would be in order."

"Who do you think he was, Venu?" Eli was now doing what I did best, changing the subject.

"Maybe he is your Messiah, who you think is coming or someone else from God. Yet, he thinks he is *Christos*. But I do not know what that means."

"It is Greek for Anointed One; Messiah, in Hebrew."

"On the other side of the coin, he could be just brilliantly crazy. I do not know which," I said without thinking.

"Venu, do not call him crazy. No! He is like a prophet of old, from the Scriptures. He actually is a lot like John, but he is not out in the wilderness. Did you hear his prophecies to us? Only a prophet could talk as he did. He has to be the Messiah, but I never realized the Messiah was also going to be God in a human body. Can you imagine that God knows us personally? He was aware that your Greek name is Epaphroditus. Remember as children when you were teaching me Greek? I called you by that name. Who told him that? Only God would know such information."

"You know Greek? You did not even know *patros* was Greek for father in the alley of Ostia before Messina discovered her father. Now, about prophecies. You said Elijah has to return before the Messiah is to appear. And the Messiah must come to his temple and cleanse the Levites before he reveals himself."

"Venu, this is very peculiar; and you are right. Maybe he is not the Messiah. But, it has been over four hundred years since a prophet has been sent to Israel; and I think we just saw and heard one. I think God has sent two prophets, and we must be in the last days."

"Why would a true prophet call himself *Cristos* if he is just a prophet? He is much more, but what I am not sure. It is almost as if this were God Himself standing in time talking to us."

"Well, John is a prophet; and we must go and find him. He will tell us who this teacher was. Do you think John is Elijah?"

"I thought you said John had answered that question with a 'no.'"

I shook my head trying to obstruct everything I had just witnessed. Maybe my heart was harder than a rock. All I remember next was walking in a daze heading aimlessly through the Court of Gentiles away from the direction of the Royal Porch. Eli just rambled on at my side trying to keep up with me. I stopped listening thinking he was too confused to think straight. My eyes fell upon a massive citadel that stood at the northwestern corner of the Temple compound. If it were a fort, it was a crude square affair that stood directly outside the Temple plaza walls with the southern wall of the fort being the Temple courtyard's northwestern wall. It consisted of four towers, one at each of its corners, looming almost as high as the roof of the Temple. I began thinking any observer could stand up on any corner and look down at us. Looking closer, I noticed observers looking down at us. I nodded to one who looked like a Roman legionary. He nodded back and then moved his eyes onto someone else.

"It is the Castle of Antonia," said Eli noticing I was staring at the impressive but ugly structure. "It is a harsh contrast to the Temple: one devoted to peace and union with God, and the other devoted to death and destruction. Pontius Pilate, the Roman *Procurator* of Judaea, stays there during festivals with an enlarged force of Roman soldiers and foreign allies brought in from Caesarea Maritima. The fort is connected to the Temple compound by tunnels." I looked to where Eli was pointing and saw two gaping holes in the compound floor. "Those holes are entrances to subterranean stairs and tunnels extending underneath the compound and then up again into the Castle of Antonia," explained Eli.

I looked away from the threatening citadel and stared at the Temple standing all alone in the vast Courtyard of the Gentiles. There was a high wall that surrounded the Temple, which jutted out in front of it hiding other buildings that stood in front of the high, two-room Temple. Dark, greasy, sacrificial smoke floated skyward from inside the inner Temple walls where the Great Altar must have stood located in front of the Temple. "I feel like a little child in an adult world. At first, I thought understanding God was straightforward and pure; but now, everything is growing complicated and dirty. I have an entirely different view of Judaism since that day Rabbi Issachar spoke to me in his courtyard arbor," I said to myself but loud enough for Eli to hear. Maybe I wanted Eli to understand what was in my heart.

"What are you saying?"

Now, I wanted Eli to know the burden of my thoughts. "What I have seen today is much different from what I understood when we studied history and the prophets on the grain galley. Did you know this was going to happen to me?"

"I'm sorry, but I am not going to listen to this; for what you are saying and thinking is on the edge of blasphemy," stated Eli before angrily walking away leaving me standing alone in the middle of the Court of Gentiles. I watched him storm away wondering if he were correct. I was just speaking my heart, but perhaps I had gone too far. Yet, should I lie about the rage smoldering just below the surface? I was about to go after Eli when a sharp blast of a trumpet came from the direction of the Castle of Antonia. I turned and saw temple soldiers emerging, marching two abreast, arising out of the nearest tunnel that led from the Roman fort. It was a spectacular theatrical sight of men appearing as coming out of a tomb in the middle of the Court of Gentiles. Afterward, a dozen or so white-clad priests appeared like magic also coming out of the ground traipsing behind the soldiers. The Jewish soldiers marched smartly, but the priests in the rear just followed like a bunch of sheep following a shepherd. However, it was an impressive little parade flowing towards me since I happened to be standing between them and the Temple. A swelling silence absorbed the voices of the bystanders nearest the priests. I noticed people near me falling to their knees or bending at the waist toward the blossoming of white robes. I stood frozen and watched. Eli came up from behind and told me to bow to the high priest. I looked to where he pointed and noticed an older man wearing an unfamiliar but astounding garment of a sky-blue color with white-and-purple piping. Little golden bells tinkled from the bottom hem of his garb along with miniature, golden pomegranates hanging from the edges appropriately spaced between the little bells. On his chest, he wore an unusual cuirass-breastplate of a dozen different stones in three rows of four, all embedded into gold fittings. It was quite a spectacular outfit topped off with a large, blue-and-white puffy head covering edged with gold stitching. I could not take my eyes off the breastplate of stones as the entourage got closer. Eli again implored me to bow as he went to his hands and knees. For some mysterious reason, I did not feel like bending to anyone; instead, I put my hand inside my cloak and rested my right hand on the handle of the falcata. The scabbard hung by a leather strap over my shoulder with the lower portion attached to a leather belt at my waist, all of this hidden from view by my gray cloak. If I were to pull the falcata, I would have to draw it straight up and then twirl the sword with a quick twist of my wrist to position it for a fight. The Jewish soldiers marching in front veered past me. The older man with the stones on his chest passed right next to me. Our eyes met, and he scowled bending an eyebrow up in disgust without losing his stride. The rest of his group moved in mass towards the Temple's northern gate.

I could not believe his arrogance, and I found myself wagging my head in disgust as I relaxed my grip on the falcata. I then brought my hand out from beneath my cloak while I watched his back. It was then I felt the hands of two men grabbing my arms from behind and pulling me off balance. I had been unprepared and tried to stay on my feet but to no avail. My back slammed into the stone pavement, and I attempted to release my breath just as I hit. This blowing-out-air technique managed to keep my ribs unbroken, and I was now gasping for air after I slammed onto the stone pavement. While I was trying to assess my situation, a third man stepped up and over me. I recognized him immediately as the Captain of the Temple, and I realized I was now in serious trouble.

"So we meet again and so soon!" he growled with a sneer. He then nodded to the two men who had thrown me down giving them some kind of prearranged signal. They now yanked me to my knees. From this position of prostration, I watched this arrogant man reach towards his belt and pull out a black leather glove that was missing the fingertips. He slowly pulled it onto his right hand flexing his fingers as he tightened the straps. At once, I realized what it was – a *cestus*. Gladiatorial boxers were the only people I knew who wore the *cestus*, which was a glove of leather straps weighted with heavy iron over the knuckles and the tops of the hand. I had never seen a *cestus* match but had seen a *cestus* when Grillius showed me a pair. He had warned me about fighting a man who used a *cestus*. Grillius once pointed to a man in the streets of Athens who had been severely disfigured; he was the survivor of a *cestus*-boxing match. The *cestus* could literally turn a man's face to a pulp with a few, well-aimed strikes. Such was the case with the unfortunate man in Athens who forever carried his grotesque deformities, which sickened most people who looked at him and forced them to turn their gaze from him and who would forever be a monstrous outcast.

The burly captain raised his gloved hand, and I felt a lonesome sadness pass over me at the realization he was going to hit me in the face with the *cestus*. It all seemed like a nightmare. I tried to stand and pull free, but a knee went into my back. It had to be a third person behind me. He pulled my headgear off and grabbed my hair forcing my head back so the captain would have a stationary target. The gloved hand came down swiftly and hard into my face. Its impact made a muted thump. Since the man behind me was holding my head, I was unable to allow my head to flow with the punch to prevent any facial bones from being broken. I wanted to scream, but Grillius taught me to be silent in my pain no matter what. "Never give your opponent the satisfaction of knowing he has injured you. Even if you have to die, do it in silence" were his very words. He said it was the code of a Spartan. More than once he told the story of the Spartan youth who stole a fox from a poor *helot* (a non-Spartan quasi-slave living in the Peloponnesus region of Greece hundreds of years ago); and, when an adult Spartan soldier stopped the boy on the road and spent a few minutes questioning him, the young lad kept the fox hidden in his cloak. All the while the fox was busy eating at the boy's stomach. The boy never revealed to the adult that there was anything wrong until the young boy collapsed and later died. Grillius drilled into me this Spartan way of silence during my private lessons at the Lyceum.

The two men released my arms after the captain's shattering blow with his black-gloved *cestus*. I felt like that Spartan boy as I fell face down with warm blood gushing from the dull wound from under my left eye. A booted foot caught me next in the ribs and then into my back as I barely heard the words: "Pretty Boy! That was the high priest who walked past you! Next time prostrate yourself when he is wearing the holy vestments! Oh, and no one will ever call you Pretty Boy ever again!" came the remark with a couple of dark laughs from those men who had been holding me like the cowards they were.

I must have lost consciousness; for all I remember next was sitting in the cool, shady side of the eastern *stoa* called Solomon's Porch. I recognized Eli and realized an old woman was tending to me. The woman was wiping blood and telling Eli to hold the lips of the torn skin together while she stitched the wound. I could feel the pinch of a needle, but the pain was nothing compared with the throbbing of my face and head. My eyes were watering from the pain, and I became angry with myself because of my vow never to cry, the promise that I made the day my mother died. I tried to stop the wet flow but realized it must have been a typical response to my injury and pain and not due to my emotional state.

"That will do," the old woman finally said. "And no! I will not take your money! It was worth it to see someone stand up to Gadreel Bully, who runs the Temple like it is just a facility and not the House of God."

"Who is Gadreel?" I asked weakly.

"He is an evil angelic 'watcher' named in the Book of Jubilees, who introduced weapons of war to mortals. The Book of Jubilees is not in the Scripture canon but is mentioned in the Book of Joshua." She patted my head. "Young man, you did what I would only dream of doing if I were a man. Thank you for your courage. Your scar will always be a reminder that a Jew does not have to bow to anyone but Yahweh. Never in my long life have I seen such courage. It was as if you know Yahweh personally and you will never bend a knee to anyone but Him. Come find me here on the Day of Atonement, and I will remove those stitches. I am always praying in these porches; just look for me. Ask for me. My name is Anna. My mother, whom I am named after, was a prophetess who lived here waiting for the Messiah before she died. She told me in her matured season of old age that she saw and prophesied over a child now 36 years ago. I, too, was alive but just a little girl. I was not with my mother on that day, but she was convinced with all her being that the child was the Messiah. Whoever that child was, He is alive and old enough to declare His kingdom. Maybe John out in the desert, the first prophet in 400 years, is the forerunning of the Messiah."

After the woman had left, Eli said, "That is just what you do not need to hear. A beautiful old lady telling you her mother was a prophetess, and you did the right thing. I told you to bow. That was Joseph Caiaphas, the high priest! Do you realize talk of this incident will ripple throughout the entire city?" rebuked Eli. "A couple of fugitives do not need that kind of renown! I would not be surprised this news even reaches the streets of Rome."

"I heard what the Captain of the Temple said!" I responded back in the same tone of voice. "Why does everyone have to bow to the high priest? The high priest is not God, is he? That old woman was right!"

"Even if she is correct, that is not the point. Bowing is proper and the expected protocol since Caiaphas or his father-in-law Annas ben Seth are the only men who enter the Holy of Holies once a year to offer a blood sacrifice on the Day of Atonement. He is also the head of the Sanhedrin, which is the highest Jewish court in the land. Plus, he was wearing the holy vestments kept by the Romans over in the Castle of Antonia."

"Is it written in the Scriptures that we bow to him?" I asked with an ultimatum in my voice.

"Of course not!"

After Eli's answer, I said no more. I gently probed the ugly, swollen wound on my face. My head, ribs, and back all hurt. I was now in a hot rage. I took the blood-soaked rag that was in my right hand and wadded it tightly. After it was a ball, I flung it towards the Temple and watched it sail up and fall harmlessly onto the paving stones out on the Courtyard of Gentiles. "There is my blood sacrifice, you wicked hypocrites!" I shouted to no one. There were a few stares from shocked worshipers and religious men, but I just glared at several in turn until they looked away.

Eli said no more and led me to the rag, which he retrieved. With the bloody cloth in his hand, Eli guided me across the courtyard and back to the Zion Bridge. From there we found our way out of the city and made our way down the steep path into the valley of the Kidron. Once at the bottom, we climbed a switchback trail halfway up the other side of the Kidron Valley until we reached the little garden of olive trees. My head was swimming in pain, and dizziness was now its companion. Eli said nothing realizing I was heading into a deep despair because of Judaism. I found a soft spot to rest under a shady olive tree. This day had started as a beautiful morning, progressed into a broiling bewilderment, and ended in a blistering disaster. My heart fractured as much as my face. I was regretting with every ounce of my being that I had chosen to embrace Judaism. Although this religion had once seemed the most influential of all faiths, I found myself seeking a way out. Was I stuck because I could not reverse my circumcision? I still could not shake the fact that this religion had a more considerable influence on people's lives than any other had; but, still, I wanted to run as faraway as I could get from Judaism. It now appeared to be just another cult like the ones in Rome and Athens, just more pervasive in a person's life.

The *Fratres Arvales* priests in Rome offered sacrifices to the goddess *Dia* to ensure the fertility of plowed fields. There were 12 *Arval* priests, all from patrician families, including the Emperor, who was one of the 12. Augustus and now Tiberius would dress up once a year in a gown-like ensemble to celebrate the *Ambarvalia*. The special clothes of Tiberius were very similar to the Jewish High Priest's outfit, minus the 12-stone chest plate that Caiaphas had on over his white robes. This I can attest to as an eyewitness. At the age of nine, Zeno introduced Decimus and me to the *Ambarvalia*. The very words of Zeno were "When you see Tiberius walk past us, you will bow or kneel before him. It does not matter that this year Tiberius will not be attending, but a substitute priest will be taking the emperor's place. Still, you still need to prostrate yourself when he passes."

The comparison was uncanny. I could not believe I thought Judaism was any different from the *Ambarvalia*, which was celebrated in a grove dedicated to *Dia* in the month of *Maius* according to the Roman calendar. The *Ambarvalia* was nothing but ritualistic hypocrisy heaped on top of empty emperor worship. The marching of the twelve *Fratres Arvales* priests and bowing of the people was precisely the same ritual as presented at the Jewish Temple. I still remember when Zeno instructed Decimus to bow when the *Fratres Arvales* high priest walked past us. Decimus went to his knees, but I did not. Zeno slapped the back of my head, and one of the priests smiled at

Zeno for his quick action against my sacrilegious behavior. Here I was almost eleven years later repeating the same action, but Zeno was not there to bop my head. Instead, the Captain of the Temple was there to teach me about the seriousness of sinful behavior at the Temple of God. The memory did flash through my mind moments before the Captain of the Temple struck me with his *cestus*. There I was kneeling before all these wicked men just before I was hit. When the booted feet began to connect with me, all I could think about was the similarity of the worship of *Dia* and Judaism. Now in the Garden of Gethsemane, all I could think of was the similarity of both religions and that both were just empty, phony, ritualistic exercises. Man's pride and vanity were behind both religious shows. And here I had been severely punished because I did not prostrate myself to the highest man in this Jewish ecclesiastical system. If I were willing not to bow before Tiberius, never would I grovel to this measly Jewish high priest. Maybe I would bow to the man calling himself *Christos,* but his comparison with anyone else was as far as the west was from the east.

Resting on my back under the cool shade of the olive trees, I believed this Gadreel Bully was nothing but a sadistic martinet; and I refused to be a sniveling sycophant to any human including Joseph Caiaphas. I did not share any more of my doubts with Eli, for I had hurt our friendship enough for one day. We had grown very close since I converted to Judaism, and he had been happy teaching me all he knew about his religion. I kept my pain to myself and nursed all the loss and loneliness that I had buried. The truth was I missed my evenings with Hector, my times with Grillius, and my bedtime stories from my mother. Mostly I missed Messina. I could have run away with her that night instead of saving Eli, and I would not be here under an olive tree feeling sorry for myself. Would I ever see any of them again? Would I ever see any of the people who at one time had been close to me? I even felt a loss for Zeno, who in a way gave up his life to save mine. Before I fell asleep that night, I thought perhaps this preacher in the desert named John was my last hope. Maybe I should go meet and talk to him before I totally rejected Judaism. Surely if anyone could salvage my faith in this one God of Israel, it would be he. I concluded that was what I was going to do before I threw it all away. Perhaps *Christos,* the eagle-beaked, white-robed man who put his hand on Eli and spoke those strange words to both of us, could possibly save me from my sinking spiral into the abyss. These two men were the only hope I seemed to have left spiritually.

The final insult occurred in the middle of the night: it began to rain. Eli and I had no shelter except to huddle together under the largest olive tree we could find. Sitting there in the rain, I remembered it was now the Sabbath; and we had nowhere to go and no food to eat. The only thing I could do was talk to God, which I did silently; and after a while, it helped. During the downpour and after I had prayed, I looked over at Eli who was wet but awake. I smiled up at him, and we both began to laugh and laugh. Neither one of us could stop the sudden hysteria. I had never laughed so hard in my life, and my sides as well as my face were killing me with each guffaw. Finally, after we were gasping for breath, we stopped, only to start again. It was an incredible release of all the caged emotions. After about an hour, we both fell fast asleep from pure exhaustion under the olive tree and in the mud.

CHAPTER FIFTEEN

Jerusalem ~ Day of Atonement ~ Tiberius's 16th year and Pontius Pilate's 3rd year as Prefect of Judaea; 46 years since the completion of Herod's Temple and 6 months into the first year of the public ministry of Jesus of Nazareth, whom the Jews refer to as Yeshua.   (29AD)

The school of hard knocks is an accelerated curriculum.   Menander, Athenian comic dramatist

I now possessed a nasty cut, which would leave a scar to remind me of my first visit to Herod's Temple. The Temple was actually the third permanent tabernacle to stand on Mount Moriah. Most Hebrews claim Mount Moriah as the same hill or ridge-line area Abraham had nearly sacrificed his son Isaac approximately two thousand years ago according to the first book of the *Torah*. A thousand years later, Ornan, the Jebusite prince called *Araunah*, used a flat plateau portion located at the center of this hill, which he owned, as a threshing floor. King David purchased Ornan's threshing floor after David's encounter with the angel of Yahweh during a plague punishment, which was halted by Yahweh when the angel of Yahweh was moving above the threshing floor with a sword pointed towards Jerusalem located on the next ridge over from Mount Moriah. This other hill was Mount Zion, and this lower area was where David's palace and the other buildings were built behind a stout wall. This was the original Jerusalem, the City of David, and the capital city of Judah. The plague had touched everyone in one way or another. It was a judgment sent in Yahweh's wrath because King David conducted a military census, which revealed pride in David's heart, as he had traded faith in Yahweh for soldiers of flesh. It was David's choice of judgment after he was confronted by Yahweh, and the result was the destroying angel inflicting a plague causing the death of about seventy thousand in David's kingdom. When the destroying angel was approaching Jerusalem moving southward over Mount Moriah heading towards Mount Zion, King David repented before Yahweh. This event occurred atop Mount Moriah, then known as Ornan's threshing floor. When the God of Israel heard David repenting, Yahweh ordered the destroying angel to halt. Once the plague stopped, King David purchased the threshing floor and was instructed by Yahweh through the prophet Gad to build an altar on the threshing floor to offer burnt offerings.

Years later King David erected a tent on the old threshing floor where he placed the Ark of the Covenant. The Ark had been lost after a battle with the Philistines during the theocracy rule in the days of the last judge, High Priest Eli, and his two wicked sons. Foolishly Eli's evil sons took the Ark into battle against the Philistines. The golden box was always to reside in the Holy of Holies, the back room inside the tabernacle that was standing in those days at Shiloh. This holy box was the ultimate symbol of Israel, a chest that was constructed in the wilderness under the direction of Moses. It always traveled before Israel in the desert for 40 years, and the children of Israel were never defeated in battle in a major way. After the death of Moses, the Ark led the way into the Promised Land under the leadership of Joshua. Just as the Levites carried the Ark on wooden poles into the Jordan River, the water receded allowing the Ark and the children of Israel to cross on dry ground. Once in the Holy Land, Joshua prayed before the Ark after the defeat at Ai and again after the victory over the city of Ai; and, according to the Scriptures, Joshua prayed before the Ark once again at Mount Ebal after the defeat of all the 31 city-states of the Canaanites and other peoples living in the land. According to the Scriptures, all of the area from the Euphrates River to the River in Egypt had been previously promised to Abraham, his son Isaac, his son Jacob, and all of Jacob's sons. For 400 years, the Israelites had departed from the Promised Land and had been living in Egypt due to a great famine.

Using human logic, Eli's sons thought that taking the Ark into battle might have made sense considering all the miraculous events surrounding the Ark of the Covenant as recorded in the Jewish Scriptures. However, Yahweh demands that His people have faith in His existence, not an object. Yahweh also demands obedience to His words. Yahweh never told High Priest Eli or his sons to do such a blasphemous thing. The result of such disobedience was that very day the Ark was captured by the Philistines, Eli and his two wicked sons died.

After a period of time, the Philistines returned the Ark of the Covenant back to Israel. The reason for its return was due to many plagues visited upon the five cities of the light-skinned people who had migrated from the sea to the west. It was finally King David who brought the Ark to Jerusalem for the first time. He had it placed on Mount Moriah at the flat part of the threshing floor, the very spot King David had purchased from Ornan, the Jebusite.

The Hebrew word for the Ark is *tevah*, which means a chest or a vessel that floats. Noah and his family were saved by placing themselves inside an ark or *tevah*; and Moses was saved as an infant in Egypt as he floated down the Nile in a basket of bulrushes, which was also called in Hebrew a *tevah* or ark. Today no one knows the location of Noah's seagoing ark, Moses's bulrush ark, or the Ark of the Covenant precisely. The Ark of the Covenant vanished mysteriously before the Babylonians destroyed the First Temple, which was also known as Solomon's Temple.

My understanding of Israel's history and knowing I received my facial wound at such a prominent location did not help in any way in my personal misery. I concluded I had been given a physical beating because of a violation on my part to a religious tradition, which smelled like the garbage pits of the Valley of Hinnom. I felt helpless not because of my permanent facial wound and broken ribs but the humiliation of having my arms held while the Temple Captain was able to take a free hit with a *cestus*. My wounded body and mind were screaming for revenge. If I killed Claudia for what she did to my mother, then this man deserved the same as Claudia. As far as I was concerned, this was also the final blow to my self-worth along with my faith in Judaism. I was no longer a helpless ten-year-old child. I was now dangerous and at the peak of a man's strength. I must also admit that my youthful vanity hated the fact I was now sentenced to live with a facial disfigurement for the rest of my life. I was only 20 years old and currently marked with a hideous facial scar. My 20th birthday occurred while Eli and I were on the grain galley coming to this city. Now, at this young age, I felt like the man in Athens whom Grillius had shown me, who was also disfigured because of a *cestus*. Of course, my one scar was not as bad as that of the man in Athens; but to me it was.

From that day forward, I looked at Eli with a different eye. I started to think of him as the man who shared his name in the Scriptures. Eli, my childhood friend, was also Eli the high priest who allowed his sons to take the Ark of the Covenant out of the tabernacle and into battle. I know this was not fair to my friend; but the mind is capable of some wicked thoughts, especially when a person begins to descend into a spiritual abyss. Strangely, I felt as lost as the Ark of the Covenant. My holy of holies was just as empty as Herod's

Temple. I refused to admit I was acting like Eli's sons, two wicked spiritual pretenders. Here was someone trying to appear spiritual to my friend; but, in truth, it was an imaginary shell of a deceiver. I was nothing more than a hypocrite in the eyes of God. I wanted nothing to do with this land or the Jew's construction of Yahweh. In many ways, I was no different from King David before the angel of destruction began killing the thousands through the plague. I knew I was a sinner like giant-slayer David; but, unlike him, I was unwilling to repent. In the Scriptures, King David most likely broke all Ten Commandments but was forgiven when he repented. I had no idea what it would take to bring me to repentance. Mysteriously "repentance" or *metaneon* in Greek was the only message John the Baptist was preaching on the Jordan River. *Metaneon* was a common and simple Greek word: change your mind. To go and find John the Baptist was my last hope according to my human logic. Yet, now some strange voice was telling me that John could not help me. "How can you repent of your sins? You are only a *Yisrael* and not even a Jew. Your only salvation would be to leave this city and land as fast as you can." Could this be the Evil One placing these thoughts in my mind? Did not the Dragon tempt Eve into sinning? Yet, if Adam and Eve fell to Satan's whims, what hope did a *Yisrael* have?

I was told by Eli that Herod's Temple was not as glorious as Solomon's Temple, but it should be noted that today no structure standing in the Empire or world is grander. It should also be understood that many of the prophecies concerning the coming Messiah in the Hebrew Scriptures demand that a temple must be standing in Jerusalem when the Anointed One appears to save the Jews as well as the world. One prophecy states the coming Messiah must walk through the Eastern Gate of the Temple complex to introduce Himself to the House of Israel. The Jews, therefore, intend, above all else, to ensure their hope for the coming Messiah by protecting the Temple with every ounce of their being. One of the last, great Messianic prophecies proclaimed by the prophet Malachi roughly four hundred years earlier announced the Messiah as God Himself coming to His Temple cleansing the priesthood and Levites as a sign he has arrived. Thus, the significant sign of the coming Messiah as the Scriptures declare in the last book of the Hebrew canon is *"God's cleansing of the Temple and its evil leadership."*

In the 15th year of Tiberius's rule and 46 years after Herod's Temple had been erected, Jesus of Nazareth had completed this very "cleansing." It had occurred unbeknownst to me on this date. But Jesus had cleansed the Temple of the moneychangers at the Temple during Passover a half year earlier before Eli and I arrived in Jerusalem. The Jews did not know what to do with this

Jesus or Yeshua, His Hebrew name, for He boldly and correctly turned over the tables of the moneychangers and drove out the livestock being sold in the Court of Gentiles. He never openly declared He was the Messiah except to one woman with whom I was later to become close friends. The only other person who was told by this Galilean rabbi concerning his title of *Christos* or Messiah was me. On the day he told me, it would be years later that I understood the two related events that happened on that day, both events taking place in less than an hour: Jesus telling me he was *Christos,* and my face being struck by the Captain of the Temple's *cestus.* The only information I knew at this time about the Messiah was what Eli had told me from the book of Daniel. The old prophet of Israel, who wrote while living in Babylon, stated that the Son of Man would come in the clouds at the judgment of the last days. Three and a half years in the future, this very passage would be quoted by Jesus to Caiaphas the High Priest; and those words would become the catalyst that led to the charge of blasphemy by the Sanhedrin, who then transferred Jesus to the governor of Rome demanding that Jesus be put to death.

A few months earlier before I arrived in *Palestina,* when Jesus had cleansed the Temple of the moneychangers and those selling sacrifices for unlawful gain, this unusual rabbi was asked by what authority he did such an act of turning over the moneychangers' tables and releasing the animals for sale. He replied, "Destroy this temple, and I will build it back in three days." He actually used the Greek word *naos,* which described the "Holy of Holies," where the Ark of the Covenant should have been located if it had not been lost. The Jewish religious leaders quickly replied that the structure about which he was talking had been standing for 46 years. They wanted to know how he could alone destroy such a well-proven structure and then erect it in three days? Was he speaking figuratively or literally?

Had I understood the words of the man claiming to be *Christos,* especially when, moments before, Jesus told the Captain of the Temple that this was His father's house, I'm sure my life would have gone in a different direction. I apparently was blinded to who Jesus claimed to be when he called himself *Christos.* Why I was faithless or ignorant at this point in my life is inexcusable. Had I only known then what I know today, it would have been as clear as the sun at noon on a cloudless day. Had I put into practice what this man had declared to all the students sitting in the *stoa* and politely listening, I would not have ended up in the pit I was now entering. I had no understanding that He was the true, promised Messiah. I just did not have any understanding and no faith in Jesus at all. The Scriptures say, "*Without knowledge, My people perish.*" I wish I had known this very Jesus had cleansed the Temple at Passover a few months earlier, during the springtime at Passover about the time I was traveling to Rome from Athens on the bireme to rescue Eli. My personal knowledge of Jesus cleansing the Temple at the start of his public ministry, would not be for several more years. When I did learn about Jesus entering the Temple compound and violently upended the tables of the moneychangers and merchandisers along with forcibly driving them out of the Temple area with a whip, I then understood it was the apparent fulfillment of the prophecy given by Malachi hundreds of years earlier. The words of Jesus, "*Take these things away; stop making My Father's house a house of merchandise,*" as told to me by an eyewitness later crushed me.

The morning after my first visit to the Temple, Eli and I slept until the hot sun dried the mud we found ourselves in during the night. When I finally opened my eyes, I discovered I could not move on my own power. I stayed where I was until early evening when a Jewish pilgrim and his wife had come into the garden to camp. This kind, elderly man came up to me and told me his wife was filled with a considerable worry. I looked around for Eli, but he was nowhere to be found. The elderly couple shared their food and their shelter of a goatskin tent, which was large enough for both of them as well as me. A few hours later Eli discovered me in the tent of the old people. They asked him to stay with me and share their tent. Eli had been looking for work and had not found any. Learning of this generous invitation gave Eli great joy. It was hard not to see that God was alive, and people who served Him were now helping two starving, young men. My heart was warmed by the kindness of these two godly people, and this was the only incident since I had arrived in this land that gave me any hope for the future.

The old man's wife found great purpose in tending to the grave cut under my left eye and declared it infected. She professed I was going to suffer several days of fever and much corruption around the wound while it drained before it would get better. By sunset the fever began as she predicted; and, with his humorous smile, Eli described my face as uglier than typical with a lot of redness and swelling around the wound. For nine days the fever and infection took its course, and I recall little except praying to survive. I did not want to die because a *cestus* had cut my face. At times I wondered whether the Captain of the Temple had soaked his *cestus* in some kind of filth to induce the fierce infection I was experiencing. I told the Master of the Universe that I would settle the matter with that "beast of a man" after I offered my sacrifice. Yet, I felt shame that I wanted revenge knowing vengeance should be given to the desires of the Creator, not us mere humans. However, my thinking was simple: the Creator knew my thoughts; why not be honest in your prayers?

Why lie to God? He already knew about my sacrifice I was going to offer on the Day of Atonement. He was aware that it was not coming from my heart but that I would do it because it meant something to Eli and Rabbi Issachar. I just did not have the heart to hurt either of them. I felt like the fraud that I was; however, my last hope was to be honest with God, which I was. During the long days in the black goatskin tent, I spoke to God privately for hours with great honesty.

Since I am on the subject of prayer, I have always talked to God more than prayed to Him. We have had some most interesting, one-sided conversations over these many years since I started talking to Him after my conversion in Rome in the presence of Rabbi Issachar. Today I consider God as my best friend, and why not speak to God as you would to your best friend? The only difference today is that my conversations with God are sometimes two-sided. I was to later learn that leaving a matter in the Almighty's hands was far more lethal to any enemy over trying to accomplish something on your own. Nevertheless, that knowledge of the Almighty came many years later after I came out of the school of rebellion – tutelage I chose to enter by my own foolishness after the Captain of the Temple struck me with his *cestus*.

My fever finally broke during the early morning of the Day of Atonement. When I was awake in the goatskin tent, the elderly woman informed me that I was going to live. I told her I did know I was not going to die. She smiled and said she was surprised I did survive, for she had her doubts during the past nine days. I did confess there were moments I did not think I was going to survive. "The Creator of the Universe must truly love you," she said after I had drunk a large cup of watered-down wine before the sun came up and the Day of Atonement fast began. "Now you can sacrifice on the most solemn day of the year. After the high priest offers the blood sacrifice in the Holy of Holies, we will also sacrifice and then leave for our home in Peraea."

I said my thanks and told them I would guard their tent if they returned before noon. "You are such a sweet boy. Oh, your friend told me when it was still dark that he was going into the city to find work."

Eli had been looking for work during the days I was sick but found nothing. He had earned a few coins doing odd jobs, but he had been in a disheartened and demoralized state. Now that the old couple was leaving, I was concerned about where we would stay tonight. If Eli had known the depths of my own inner rage, I am sure he would have lost all hope. Perhaps Eli did sense a little of my state but not the terrible despair I was genuinely suffering. I had tried to hide my sincere feelings, but how could I hide my feelings concerning the decadence of Judaism and its charlatan nature? My first and only visit to the Temple almost destroyed me. How could I accept all the contradictions within the different sects? All the various religious systems were just too straining on my mind to grapple with alone, but this is what occupied me during my convalescence for the past nine dark days. During those days, I was actually afraid of my own thoughts; and my future appeared bleak. The only bright spot was listening to *Christos* and thinking about him.

Before the old couple left to sacrifice, the old woman removed the stitches in my face. This was the advised day the daughter of Anna had suggested for the stitches to be removed. Soon after the couple had left for Jerusalem, I used the woman's bronze mirror and saw that the tissue under my left eye was an ugly red color with a long black scab running under my left eye up to my nose. I was sure it would leave an ugly scar that even Messina would abhor if she were ever again to lay eyes on me. Not only was it a jagged blemish, much different than a straight mark, which most warriors received from a sword cut to the face, but this scar twisted my appearance enough that anyone hunting for the son of Vetallus based on the description from my father and others would fail to recognize this new Venustus. If that was the purpose, then God does work in mysterious ways.

It took most of the morning dressing and getting ready to meet Eli. A few hours later the old couple returned, and I said my farewells. I had my falcata hidden under my cloak and wished I had my throwing knives. Although the day was going to be warm, I needed to wear the cloak if I wanted to carry my sword. I had on my military boots not having any sandals and had been barefoot since I left Rome; I believed that, since I was going before God to sacrifice, I needed to be the person I really was: not a fake, humble, proselyte Jew.

I decided to carry along my red bag with its only contents: the leather tube with the Psalms scroll. I felt that, if I left my red bag and the 33 Psalms in the garden, they might be stolen. I also had an odd feeling I was not coming back to this garden for a long time. Little did I know it would be over three long years before I would return to this quiet garden surrounded by its short stone wall. I had given the old couple the newer gray bag, which had been given to me by the rabbi's wife in Rome. I told them it was a gift for all their kindness and help. Honestly, it is better to give than to receive, even a woolen bag. The joy on their faces touched my heart when they accepted the simple woven bag.

Using the tie string on the red bag, I attached the leather Psalm scroll to the back of my sword sheath that went around my middle. The tube in the bag was hanging behind the sheath under my cloak but more like a short tail.

My falcata, boots, and scroll were now my only worldly possessions excluding my Jewish rags as clothes and gray cloak, which covered everything on this morning when I was going to sacrifice for murdering Claudia – a crime for which I was not sorry and, thus, not repentant.

The old woman had told me that Eli had instructed that I should meet him at noon around the Royal Porch near the tall bridge. This was going to be my first visit to the Temple since my encounter with the Captain of the Temple and High Priest Caiaphas. I later learned that afternoon that the high priest was to offer the blood sacrifice inside the Holy of Holies in the morning. This had to be the reason Eli wanted to meet me in the early afternoon.

As I walked alone towards Jerusalem, I had several questions: why was the Day of Atonement almost exactly half a year away from Passover? Why was there a scapegoat named after a fallen angel and released into the wilderness along with a second unfortunate goat sacrificed on the north side of the Great Altar at the Temple? These questions had significance, but I could not make any sense of it. Since I had no answers on this morning, my immediate intent was to make my sacrifice; and afterward, with Eli or not, I was going to find John the Baptist and ask him my hard questions. I wanted to know if he were the Messiah or if his cousin Yeshua were the Messiah. If I only knew who the Messiah was, then I would have all my questions answered and fulfill my mother's wishes. Yet, didn't I already have the answer to this question? If I could not find the desert preacher, I was going back to Athens to find Hector even if I had to walk the entire way. Perhaps Eli would choose to accompany me since his uncle might still be with Hector. That would be my argument if we did not find the Baptist. Those were my plans. However, what was to unfold this day at the Temple complex altered my life forever; and life is what happens to us after we make our plans.

I have always lived by two sayings: *Life is what befalls you after you make your own strategies*, and *Life is not an issue to be solved but an enigma that has to unfold in its own timing.* Yet, in retrospect, I am not sure events could have gone in any other direction on this infamous Day of Atonement. What did befall me resulted in a direction I would never have guessed in a myriad of years. I believe life is filled with inconsistencies that surprise us every waking day considering we are honest with ourselves; unfortunately, most people seem to live in a fog of deception. Maybe denial is a way of not taking responsibility for our actions. Perhaps our denial of truth is because many of our daily decisions harm others in some grand or minute way. Truth hurts; and we humans typically flee from any pain, especially the truth. I still could not get the idea out of my head concerning what the white-robed rabbi nine days earlier, had or had not done. He did not touch me but had placed his hand on Eli. Why? Besides, how did he know all those intimate details about both of us? Why did he not ask us to follow him? Was I correct in assuming it would cause trouble for him since we were both fugitives? I did not have any real answers.

Nine days after the second day of Trumpets (or ten days from the first Day of Trumpets), the Sadducees, who control the religious proceedings in Jerusalem, set all the religious dates for worship at the Temple. For the past nine days, I had been recuperating in the Garden of Gethsemane after my beating by the Captain of the Temple and his soldier priests. I had been resting and waiting for this particular holy of holy days. According to Rabbi Issachar, this was my final step in becoming a proselyte or convert to Judaism: circumcision, self-baptism, and now the offering of a sin sacrifice on the Day of Atonement.

Standing at the Royal Porch that noon, I was consigned in my mind to get this sacrifice over with. I stood in the shadows watching the faithful at the Temple coming and going across the high bridge that connected Mount Zion to Mount Moriah. There had to be over a hundred thousand people in the Temple compound at the time I was waiting for Eli to arrive. The crowd reminded me of the swollen masses who would fill the Circus Maximus on race days. With this many people moving past me, I realized waiting here in the Royal Portico was not a wise decision. Being a wanted man should have been my as well as Eli's concern. Yet, what I did notice was, when most people looked at me, they quickly looked away. Was it because of my facial wound that repulsed most people from staring at me? Whatever was the case, I decided to move further back into the periphery of the porch and found a fluted stone pillar to stand near and still watch every person crossing both directions on the bridge.

I waited for almost an hour before Eli finally appeared. Using Roman time, which counts the hours after the middle of the night, it was the 13th hour when I spotted Eli crossing the bridge. The accounting of hours by Jewish standards begins at sunrise making this the 7th hour.

Watching Eli crossing the Tyropeon Valley on the Zion Bridge, I noticed a peculiar expression etched upon Eli's dark, bronzed face. When he reached the massive opening of the Royal Portico, he passed me without looking; and I had to run after him. By the time I grabbed his shoulder, my face was throbbing in pain. We were out in the open at the southern end of the *stoa*, which was located next to the High Priestly Palace.

"Why are you late?" I asked holding him with both my hands. "Eli, what is wrong with you?"

"Never mind; I will tell you later," he said trying to jerk away from my grasp.

"Tell me now!" I demanded holding him even tighter.

"I cannot! First things first!" was all he said, and he pulled away from my grasp and headed in the direction of the High Priestly Palace. The palace of the priests stood behind the Royal Porch. The white stones of this structure were beautifully dressed giving the image of strength and stability to the building that served as the priesthood headquarters of both the Levites and Sadducees. The Sanhedrin also had some of their judicial courts in this building, which comprised of the entire southern end of the Temple complex. However, the Sanhedrin's main meeting chambers were in the area called the Courtyard of Women, which stood in front of the Great Altar to the east of the Temple located in the center of the Courtyard of Gentiles.

The High Priestly Palace was one multi-storied and long, narrow building with an open courtyard in the center of this rectangle complex. The primary function of this structure was to house the hundreds of priests who stayed in Jerusalem during their rotation service. There were thousands of male descendants of Aaron, the elder brother of Moses, who made up the priesthood residing throughout the land of *Palestina*. The priesthood of Levites was divided into 24 divisions of over eight hundred men in each group coming from villages and towns throughout *Palestina*. Each unit group served the Temple for one week, twice a year, making up a total of 14-days annual service period. When in Jerusalem, they stayed without charge in an apartment at the High Priestly Palace.

I followed behind Eli trying to understand his strange mood. I had never before seen him so perplexed and disturbed. He went up to a man sitting at a wooden table beside cages full of pigeons. Eli pulled two small copper coins from Falcata Man's moneybag, which I must have given him or he had taken it while I was asleep with my fever. He laid the coins on the rough-cut table. I never liked money and did not care that he was now carrying the moneybag. Besides, I was never comfortable in trying to make change and trying to figure out all the exchanges with the different bronze and copper coins below a *denarius* or *sestertius*. Now that I was in a foreign city, nothing made sense to me when it came to money. A second priest standing next to the one sitting reached into a cage and handed Eli two turtledoves. I began to wonder about my aversion to coins. Maybe because the first time I handled money was the coin to pay entrance into the *lavo* after running through the sewer-alleys of Rome. The next time I had a problem with a coin was when I was on the bireme and Seagull the helmsman cheated me on my silver *denarius*. Shortly after that, the slave girl in the tavern with Felix helped herself to my pile of change from my last remaining silver *denarius*.

I tried to dismiss my feelings about money and looked around at what was happening before my eyes. I noticed many other tables and cages with other worshipers standing in lines. It looked like all those in lines were having their lambs, sheep, goats, oxen, and pigeons examined as if this were the slave market on the island of Delos. Priests were charging fees for their inspections as well as selling their own supply of animals when a sacrifice was judged wanting for some obscure reason only the priest-inspector could see. Other groups and sects of Judaism sold their acceptable beasts and grain offerings they deemed blessed and acceptable for each appropriate sacrifice. I spotted moneychangers also sitting at long tables changing Roman currency into a money fit for worship; the point being, only a currency not bearing the image of Caesar imprinted on it was acceptable. Caesar worship was evidently considered idolatry and blasphemous to the Jews. The first two commandments that Yahweh gave to Moses were cited if anyone objected. I still could never figure out why, for instance, a silver shekel minted in Damascus or Tyre was exchanged for Roman coins considering these shekels normally had the image of some Greek god or goddess on one side. I walked closer to a moneychanger's table and noticed several silver shekels on top with the image of Heracles, a demi-god – so how was this acceptable? When I asked someone in line about my observation, I was given some strange and twisted answer.

The moneychangers feeding on the worshipers charged a hefty transaction fee. Why these simple Jews allowed this burden to extort them was beyond me. In the few moments of watching, I concluded this had to be one of the biggest money operations I had ever witnessed. I began to wonder why Eli did not show me this side of Judaism. Could it have been because of this duplicity Eli would think I would openly protest? Yet, to be fair with Eli, the Captain of the Temple and his *cestus* interrupted my tour of the Temple. Had that one event not occurred, I might have seen this side of the worship of Yahweh. Yet, what was disturbing to me was the priests were getting extra money beyond the tithes the ordinary people were bringing to Yahweh. My mind was now boiling at this moral abomination and open deceit that rivaled the market doings of the *Agora* in Athens or any of the forums in Rome. I became enraged to the point my vision was turning red. Could this be why there were so many guards standing around? Conceivably others felt as I did, and there was a need to protect the evil money men that functioned in the robes of religious legitimacy. Once again, to step outside of time, I should say I knew nothing of Jesus's actions towards these moneychangers on the previous Passover. However, whatever Jesus had done a few months previously did not have a lasting effect upon these false money-priests. They were back and apparently did not learn their lesson. I then noticed the temple soldiers and wondered whether they feared Jesus would return again and turn over their tables.

Eli broke my thoughts as he stood at my side holding two newly purchased birds. I blurted loud enough for several priests and guards to hear, "This is nothing but a religious front for financial gain!"

Eli gave me a glare that showed his disapproval of the remark. "What do you want me to do?" I retorted after reading my friend's glare. "I am not going to lie. I am speaking only the truth! All this merchandising is out of place! It cheapens the Temple! It makes a mockery of Yahweh and all that He stands for!"

Eli hissed at me like the snap of a whip. "Listen, Venustus; we have not entered this compound since the day you were struck by the Captain of the Temple! I suggest we avoid any more trouble! Please keep your thoughts to yourself, and do not again use the word 'Yahweh' for others to hear! Many sects think it is sacrilegious to use the personal name of God in public. Besides, I cannot believe that you are drawing attention to yourself after what happened just nine days ago!"

I turned to leave Judaism and the Temple forever, but Eli blocked my way. "Please, Venu; I'm sorry. I have not been acting myself today. I think it is because of the news I learned this morning."

"What news?" I asked seeing a shift in Eli's countenance. He was again trying to hide his previously perplexed expression.

"Let's go over where there are no listening ears, and I will tell you." We walked to the west side of the compound and found a quiet area to talk almost at the same spot where we had listened to the Galilean rabbi nine days earlier. I waited patiently for Eli to gather himself before he broke his news.

"While you were recovering from your injuries, I have been seeking work although unsuccessfully. This morning, to get money for your sacrifice, I went to an old friend who owns a pottery shop; and I earned wages for half a day of work. That was why I was late. After I had been paid, my friend asked whether I had heard the news about John the Baptist. He proceeded to tell me that John was arrested by Herod Antipas and is now in prison at Machaerus, which is a military stronghold out in the desert across from the Poison Sea on the other side of the Valley of Death."

My heart was gripped by this news as if a hard fist had just reached into my chest and squeezed with all its might. The pain surprisingly left as quickly as it came but, in its wake, a deep despair engulfed me. It felt as if a mountain glacier had just avalanched down a steep gorge scraping away any hope of ever seeing or speaking with the desert preacher. "Are you sure this news is reliable?" I blurted out realizing my voice was choked with emotion.

"Yes! And all the soldiers in the city have orders to deal sternly with any sign of trouble." With that pronouncement, Eli held out the two birds for me to take. "The offering of pigeons is the only sacrifice allowed for the poor, and you undoubtedly qualify for that status. Don't let the birds fly from your hands, for we haven't any more money to buy replacements."

I took the two frightened creatures into my cupped hands. I could feel their little hearts beating double-time, and I felt as trapped as these feathered creatures. Eli turned, and I followed him around the back of the Temple towards a long line that was formed at the north gate leading into the inner sanctuary where the Great Altar stood. Eli nodded towards the end of the line. "Get in line, and wait until it is your turn to enter the inner sanctuary. When you go in before the altar, hold the birds in your left hand; and lay your right hand on them. This is to identify the offering with you. At the side of the altar, you will be instructed to pull off the head of the first bird. Then give the bird's body to the priest who will collect a little of the blood in a silver bowl. After he has what he needs, he will move to the side of the altar and throw the blood onto its side below a red line that encircles the lower half of the Great Altar. Ring off the head on the second dove, which is your burnt offering. A second priest will take care of the rest. Now remember, if a priest should say anything to you, you are to repeat whatever he says using Hebrew. Then come out the southern gate, and you will find me praying on the eastern side of the Court of Gentiles somewhere in Solomon's Porch. I will be sitting in the same spot where that woman named Anna sewed up your face nine days ago."

I did not say a word as I was still numb by the news Eli had delivered. My friend again was acting distant and detached. He reached out and placed his own hands upon the birds in my hands and said, "May my sins also rest on these birds."

"Will you also pray for me while you are waiting?" I asked.

"I will pray that we both may dwell and meditate in the house of Yahweh forever as well as behold His beauty. Venu, remember an outward observance without any real inward meaning is only ceremony."

Eli touched my shoulder much the same as the man in the white robe had touched Eli's shoulder and indicated with a peculiar nod along with a sad smile as if he were saying goodbye. Before he had even walked a few paces away, I felt as if he were immeasurably far from me never to return in the same manner he just left. In a strange, dazed state, I turned and went to the end of the long line not knowing this was indeed the very last conversation I would ever have in this world with Eli. His words forever burned in my heart, and they still plague me even today, 70 years later: *"An outward observance without any real inward meaning is only ceremony."*

Once I entered the back of the line on this blistering, hot day, events began to unfold into unfaltering events that altered my life forever. If I could return to the past and take myself out of that line, I'm not sure anything would have been any different; but, of course, I would have tried. What was soon to transpire was an incident I wished never happened, but it did.

Standing in line became a picture of my life. I waited for hours in the heat, bored to madness. Life is like that. Many days and years are just slow periods of waiting. Then, when there is movement, it is almost terrifying to behold. The two birds acted like I felt, struggling to the best of their ability in my sweaty hands to flee. While I patiently stood in line, my thoughts were becoming belligerent towards me because my act of sacrificing was disgraceful and dishonoring to what was in my heart. To make things even worse, I remembered in my studies on the grain galley with Eli that this was the historical spot that the prophet Ezekiel received a vision of the statue of the naked goddess Ashtoreth. The idol and vision were now long gone, but whatever evil spirit encouraged its erection in the first place still thrived. I felt its slimy presence breathing down my neck and entangled in my hair. I was experiencing loneliness as never before. I looked over towards the east and spotted my friend walking in the same direction the prophet Ezekiel had seen the Spirit of God leave the Temple. Eli reached the *Portico of Solomon*, a stunning stone-pillared porch area. It was a magnificent-colonnaded, stoa-type structure with a long cedar roof supported by hundreds of white stone columns. Even though it was named after King Solomon, the ancient king did not build the present standing structure. For me, the *Portico of Solomon* was the most majestic section of the entire Temple complex not including the Temple. From this porch, the view across the Kidron Valley and up towards the Mount of Olives was breathtaking. King Solomon years ago sat at this location on a magnificent throne and dispensed justice. The Babylonian king Nebuchadnezzar destroyed Solomon's Temple about six hundred years ago including the original *Portico of Solomon*.

Nebuchadnezzar's only interest was the destruction of the Jewish religious center, that being the Temple. Ancient military writings teach that an empire must destroy its enemy's religion if it ever wants to dominate the newly conquered society. If the destruction of the gods, idols, and holy sites does not work, the only remaining alternatives are either to kill all the inhabitants or relocate the survivors as slaves throughout the conqueror's vast empire. When there are too many people to kill, then the latter is the only option; but so is the poison preserved. If these people are allowed to practice their religion, then in time the conquering nation ends up embracing the foreign religion as its own. This happened to Persia and now Rome. The very religion of their enemies now spreads its seeds for the conqueror's own demise. Historically, the practice of religious toleration does not work past a few hundred years. Cyrus the Great never lived to see whether his method worked, which it did not. Alexander the Great destroyed as much of Zoroastrianism as he could, the main religion of the Achaemenid Dynasty. Alexander tried his best to instill the worship of himself as a god minting coins showing his godhood with horns of divinity on the side of his head. In the end, Alexander worship died with Alexander.

Nebuchadnezzar the Babylonian destroyed the Temple thinking this would end Judaism and the worship of Yahweh. Those Jews he did not kill he relocated back to his capital city of Babylon and exposed them to his gods. Unfortunately, the Babylonian Empire did not survive past the reign of Nebuchadnezzar's son Belshazzar. The Babylonian Empire fell to the Medes and Persians, and the Babylonian culture was finally forever lost to the Greeks after Alexander the Great made the city of Babylon his capital. On the other hand, the Persians who replaced the Babylonians freed the displaced Jews allowing them to return to their Promised Land; and, as I said, King Cyrus paid for the reconstruction of their destroyed Temple in Jerusalem. Those who returned to Jerusalem discovered only an empty pile of rubble that had been dormant for 70 years. Those Jews under the leadership of Zerubbabel, a descendant of King David, cleared the pile of debris left by Nebuchadnezzar, the Babylonian ruler, and proceeded in the task of rebuilding their Temple. I am afraid the Romans may try to complete what Nebuchadnezzar did not finish, especially when Rome knows that Yahweh will not accept any other god or religion Rome embraces, including the worship of vile human emperors.

For over two hours, I stood in line and watched all the different activities of Jewish people waiting to confront their sins before their Creator at the Great Altar that stood in front of Herod's Temple. The birds in my hands had finally settled down or had accepted their fate. The practice of killing innocent animals and birds as a substitution for humans is a mystery to me. One of the great themes of the Scriptures is *"But without the shedding of blood, there is no forgiveness of sin."* Surely, repentance is the central theme of all the stories in the Word of God; but the killing of innocent animals in exchange for a man's life, how could this be a picture of a loving God? It would take a few years before I understood the profound picture of Yahweh's grace by taking something innocent and making it a substitutionary switch. Why the Creator gives us two-legged creatures a multitude of chances to change our ways goes beyond my understanding. Yet feasibly, the Almighty wishes to commune with us humans; and this is the only way to open that supernatural *nexus* door. Yahweh's Scriptures do allude to the fact we humans are His most significant creation even above all the different sentient, angelic sons of God. It is apparent humans today are not above angels but will judge them in the next life since Lucifer was correct in telling Eve she should not surely die. In the Garden of Eden, Lucifer just pointed Eve to the wrong tree to eat in his greatest deception of man. Knowledge will never save anyone. Interestingly enough, every religion I can recall has some kind of bloodletting. The picture of eating any fruit does cause the plant's ovary to release its life fluids. There is a new religion coming out of the land of the Parthians widespread among Rome's legionaries. This new belief is the worship of the god Mithras. In this faith, new initiates are baptized in blood rather than water. From my understanding of this ritual, a soldier stands in a pit with a bull above him standing on a metal grate. At the precise moment of the ceremony, the bull has his throat opened; and the beast is then gutted from throat to rectum above the soldier, who receives a blood shower or baptism. To me, this is a twisting of the greatest show of mercy to us humans perpetrated by the enemy of God in the highest spiritual realms. In the physical world, creation's lower domain, we do see virtual copies of everything in God's Word except they are always nothing more than deceptive counterfeits and twists to thwart the truth designed to cause confusion. Janus is a prime example, and he does not even hide his true nature wanting to be called the *god of confusion*. Was there not a bowl of human blood sitting on the floor before the statue of Janus, courtesy of the dead, blond slave girl?

The clear sky provided no clouds to shield anyone from the burning sun. Those of us in the slow-moving line on the north side of the Temple could hide from the sun's heat. If there had been a tarp awning for the long line of worshipers, it would have shown kindness to the innocent animals, who are the only ones who are going to lose their lives. Once the line snaked next to the high wall hiding the Temple from our view, only then did the wall's shadow provide any relief. At times I entertained the idea of removing my cloak; but my sword would be exposed for all to see, something a repentant worshiper should not be carrying into the presence of white-clad Levites and priests, not even counting the white-clad Temple priest-soldiers. I was tempted to draw out the scroll and read the Psalms, but I had no place to keep the birds and read at the same time. Putting the poor creatures into the hot, red wool bag would be cruel and might even kill them before I would be able to offer them as a living sacrifice.

As the third hour came and went, I found myself close to the entrance of the Temple. The fear of death was now passing from animal to animal as each got closer to the throat of the inner Temple compound known as the Courtyard of Priests. In this intimate courtyard stood the enormous, white Altar of Burnt Offerings. This was the place where all the sacrificing of animals took place. This altar stood in front of the Temple itself with a massive, stone bowl structure between the Altar and the Temple, which held water for the priests to wash their hands and bare feet before entering the Temple. It was called the Laver or the Sea; and in Solomon's day, it was supported on the backs of eight life-size bronze bulls. Presently the stone bath just sits on the ground.

Moving closer to the entrance, I noticed a stone plaque on the wall above the gate. Its words were in Greek capital letters and arranged in six lines. After reading it, I found the stone plate out of place here in the Jewish Temple. I quickly reread it: *No Gentile is to enter within the Temple and its enclosure. Whoever is caught will be responsible to himself for his death, which will ensue.*

I felt a bile taste rise to my mouth. I knew I was a proselyte Jew, but I was born a Gentile. Where was Eli? I needed to ask him about this sign. I looked over to *Solomon's Portico* and saw him with his head bent in either thought or prayer. Yelling would only draw attention to me, and my turn was coming up quickly. If I left the line to ask him about the sign, I would have to wait another three hours to sacrifice the two birds still huddled in fear in my sweaty hands.

The line moved, and there was only an elderly man in front of me holding a baby lamb in his arms. I noticed tears in the old man's eyes as he looked at his animal. Was it his pet he was offering? Standing next to the door was a group of four Pharisees all wearing the Pharisee garb of wide blue borders and tassels on the edges of their robes. They seemed to be privately laughing at the old man's grief. Why were they standing here anyway? They obviously were not going to sacrifice. They appeared to be displaying themselves as sinless, not needing to sacrifice, unlike the rest of us in line. The eldest of the group must have noticed my agitation as I looked at the sign and then towards the eastern porch. He stepped toward me and asked in fluent Greek, "You keep looking at the warning on the wall. Are you a Jew or maybe a Gentile?"

"Leave me alone!" was my response in Hebrew. It was more a nervous bark of anger that even surprised me. Apparently, a Gentile would not know Hebrew; and the man should have left me alone.

Disdainful of my response, he motioned his colleagues to join him. Once they were together, the eldest Pharisee asked in flawless Classical Greek, not the commonly spoken *Koine* Greek, "What is the offering you are making, young man?"

A priest from inside the Court of Priests waved the elderly man with the lamb to enter; and now it was only a matter of moments, and I would be done with this messy business. I tried to ignore the four Pharisees, but they clustered between me and the entrance.

"Well, what is the offering, son?" asked the same Pharisee now using the ancient Hebrew dialect. I looked at him with a Spartan stare and acted like I was memorizing his ugly appearance. He was not only old but had thick eyebrows that joined in the middle with the left brow crooked up in an arrogant arch.

Finally, I broke Grillius's number one rule. "My name is not 'son'; and it is a sin offering, something I'm sure you do not understand," I replied sarcastically in Hebrew.

"What is your sin?" Eyebrow insisted now with hard, beady eyes and his arms crossed over the chest. Despite his age, he was a big man about my size.

"What is the difference? Sin is sin." After I had spoken, I looked east again longing to see Eli hoping he would come to my aid.

"Not so! Sin is not just sin! Do you not know the law, son?" he snarled still blocking the entrance to the inner sanctuary.

"You are in my way," I said as a white-clad priest from the inner court waved for me to enter and sacrifice.

"No, I will not move until you tell us your sin!" Eyebrow demanded as the other three moved in closer, shoulder to shoulder.

I was sick of all this business, and I should have left the line. Why I stood my ground, I am not sure. Perhaps it was my wicked pride and lack of humility; but, over the years, I have looked back at this moment of decision wondering why I allowed it to alter my life. I remember especially the unbearable heat that reminded me of that fever-heat day ten years earlier in Rome as I walked towards the amphitheater where my father was watching the gladiators. Perhaps our past casts our present if we do not deal appropriately with the former. Whatever the answer, this one event became one of the colossal frustrations for the rest of my life. On top of the heat, I just could not fathom any longer all the sanctimoniousness that surrounded the stone hearts of the four Pharisees all cloaked in their plush robes. Everything was driving me over the edge. I stood trying to understand in my own power what action to take. Tonight, decades later in my prison cell in Rome, I realize I should have prayed for wisdom from above; but, instead, my seething thoughts were paralyzing me. I panicked and leaned on my own understanding, man's greatest weakness.

Strangely, something unexpectedly broke into my indecision. It was an unpredictable but familiar blast of a silver trumpet that signaled the entrance of the high priest to the Temple compound. Everything came to a halt; and, at first, I welcomed this interruption as a release to my current problem. Looking towards the commotion, I quickly realized I was now in a deeper pit. Coming up out of the far floor near the Castle of Antonia tunnel was the same entourage of Levites, priests, Sadducees, and soldier-priests who came out nine days ago. They were all marching towards this gate, but this time Caiaphas was out in front of the religious parade. He was wearing his magnificent and bejeweled high priestly garments. Apparently, it was true the high priest's attire was kept in the Roman fort when not in use. Evidently, Caiaphas had earlier this morning entered the Holy of Holies wearing only a simple white robe carrying a bowl of bull's blood. Since this was the Day of Atonement, Caiaphas was now allowed to wear his jeweled garments for all to see. My heart dropped when I noticed at the rear of the procession was the Captain of the Temple. In front of him were at least a score of white-clad priestly soldiers all marching by twos and carrying bronze swords in gold-and-silver scabbards along with long spears with bronze tips at both ends. I could not believe my eyes. This was the same ritual of nine days earlier except the soldiers, were at the rear, not the front. It was as if that day had been a rehearsal, and this was the real thing. I involuntarily lifted both hands to my cheek still holding the two birds and touched my unstitched wound with the back of my left hand. People near the trooping entourage obsequiously began to bow or prostrate themselves before High Priest Caiaphas. I looked once again towards the 60-foot columned porch, and there was Eli quietly staring at me. He understood exactly what my dilemma entailed. He first started to move his hands down below his waist indicating for me to bow. When he saw my head wag no to that request, he began waving me to get out of the line and come join him at *Solomon's Portico*. Everything that happened next was entirely my fault. My stubbornness cost me my childhood friend. Surely, if I had prostrated myself, I could have hidden my face with the ugly black scab running across my cheek. Yet, even if I had done this vile thing, I am not sure anything would have happened differently. Even if I had left the line with my two birds, the Pharisees might have followed and verbally caused a scene in front of the Captain of the Temple. Still, I have to take responsibility for my wrong actions.

The band of holy men along with Caiaphas marched right up to all those in line to sacrifice. To my dismay, the entire line of worshipers fell before Caiaphas like wheat being winnowed at harvest. I was not going to bow my knee to any man but God alone, and I was the only man in line not bowing. These hypocrites did not deserve one ounce of sacrosanct behavior; and, even if it meant my life, I would not commit this blatant sin. Behind me, the four Pharisees who had blocked my way moved away from the door and fell to their hands and knees when Caiaphas passed through into the Court of Priests. However, just before Caiaphas entered the open, double-door gate, he looked at me with the same sightless impudence that he directed at me nine days earlier. I did not stare back but instead looked towards the Captain of the Temple wanting to ascertain his reactions. He noticed me and was already giving orders to his soldiers, who began to lower their spears in one well-practiced motion. I knew I was in trouble when the four Pharisees jumped up after Caiaphas entered the Temple gate and grabbed me from behind, two on each arm.

In stepped the Temple Captain, a burly warrior and an ugly man, now that I had time to evaluate him. I looked at his hands, and he was not wearing the *cestus*. Bushy Brows spoke first and told the captain in Aramaic that I needed to declare my sin before they would let go of my arms.

"Tell us your sin, and maybe you might find some grace," said the military priest in a leveled but menacing tone along with a slimy sneer on his face.

"My sin is murder! Now let go of my arms!"

"Murder!" screamed Eyebrows. "You can't atone for murder with doves! The payment for death is your own life. Are you a Hebrew? You look Gentile to me. No Jew would wear soldiers' boots. And why are you dressed in a heavy cloak on such a hot day? What are you hiding?"

"Tell the rabbis how you got that cut on your face," the captain said in a wicked, depraved laugh and the look of murder in his eyes.

"I was born a Gentile, but I am a proselyte Jew. Now release me!" I ordered in weak and wearied bravado hoping my Hebrew would placate the situation.

"He is a Gentile!" yelled Bushy Brows. Swinging his right hand to point up at the stone sign above the door, he spat his words with great care. "The sign declares the death penalty for Gentiles entering the inner courtyard." The

Pharisees tightened their grips and pulled my cupped hands apart that had been holding the two birds for over three hours. A strange sadness filled me as I watched the two birds break and take flight together over the wall and wing westward towards the sea.

"Arrest this insolent pagan," screamed Eyebrows as the others tightened my arms behind me. I was not going down so easily as last time. If arrested, I knew I would stand before Caiaphas; and there would be no mercy. Admittedly, I would lose my life. I was not sure what to do until, out of the corner of my eye, I saw Eli running towards us at full speed. He was apparently coming to my rescue. What he was going to do was beyond me; but the surprise was going to be his only asset, for none of my antagonistic attendants had yet noticed his approach. The Captain of the Temple lifted his right arm and opened his mouth to give an order for his soldiers to grab me exactly when Eli drove his right shoulder straight into the legs of the burly commander. The impact of Eli into his legs prevented any words from leaving the muscular, military man's mouth. The collision was so violent that everyone including me stood in shock as both Eli and the captain struck the stone pavement with bone-crunching reverberation. I was stunned along with everyone else. The Temple Captain got to his knees choking for air and spitting blood from his mouth. I realized Eli was providing a diversion for me to escape. He did buy me a few moments as the score of white-clad soldiers turned from me to apprehend Eli, who was trying to stand and run for his life. He was not fast enough. The religious guards grabbed him from behind. Now standing, the burly captain was still gasping for air. He must have recognized Eli as my friend, for he looked to me and then to Eli. "Drag both outside, and execute these insurrectionists!" he ordered to his soldiers with white and bloody spittle flying out of his enraged mouth.

Eli was trying to break free, but to no avail. Four guards had dropped their spears, and each man had both hands on his arms. A fifth guard kicked Eli in the back while the other four forced him to his knees. Eli was in utter defiance, a state I had never seen in him before. He looked up at the Temple Captain and said, "You slithering worm, take me yourself." Eli's words apparently shocked everyone. The Temple Captain went for his long Syrian sword and pulled the long blade from its gold and silver scabbard. Thousands of onlookers watched the Captain of the Temple place the long, curved sword over his head with both hands gripping the hilt. After taking and holding a long, deep breath, the fifth soldier behind Eli put his knee into the center of his back. The other four pulled him down to all fours while maneuvering themselves away from Eli's head and torso. It was as if they had practiced this before; and, in a blink of an eye, the Temple Captain brought the sword down in a loud, swishing sound. The blade cut into Eli's head as he was getting ready to scream something else at the Captain of the Temple. The long Syrian sword cut deep into the top of Eli's head as if it were made of wet clay slicing all the way down to his breastbone.

I could not believe what I just witnessed with my own eyes. The religious captain began cursing because his sword was now stuck. Eli's body started gushing blood, slumping down, and pinning the blade even further. I put away the horror I just witnessed realizing I had to make my escape or die in the same fashion as my friend. Screams from bystanders erupted causing the contingent of guards coming for me to halt and turn towards the screams. What had been peaceful before the Pharisees had confronted me was quickly fading into riotous confusion. In the midst of all this bewildering horror, I violently stepped backward pushing my arms forward, which pulled all four Pharisees off balance including Eyebrows. This was not a hard maneuver since the soft religious men had just witnessed the most horrifying, monstrosity of their pathetic lives leaving them paralyzed to what I was doing to them. All four men had lost any conviction in holding a murderer and now found themselves being thrown as one towards the Temple Captain, who was still trying to extract his stuck sword. A stunned Eyebrows and the man next to him landed on top of Eli's twitching body. The other two took the legs out from under the captain, who fell on top of them. A feathery fountain of bright red blood shot out from Eli's final heartbeats spraying everyone on the ground. All four Pharisees screamed in horror as they realized what was happening to them and that human blood was making them all unclean. Eyebrows yelled the loudest, "I am now unclean! I am unclean! I am now unclean!"

Clarity of thought seemed to possess my mind after I tossed the four surprised Pharisees into Eli and his blood. My frustration was now being replaced with a new strength rising into my limbs replacing the dull confusion from moments earlier; I felt as if I had all the time in the world to defend myself. My own survival was no longer a concern. I removed my falcata surprising those who were brandishing bronze swords and spears. As the remaining guards were deciding their responses and the captain was still on the ground, I stepped forward executing two, quick sword swipes – one stroke down and the other up – literally disarming the two guards closest to me. With both sword strokes, I had cut two guards at the wrist severing their sword hands and adding to the bloody confusion. Two bronze swords went clanging across the stone floor singing only as bronze does, just audible above the screams of the Pharisees and the murmuring crowd. I raised my sword pointing the tip towards the others. Only one brave soul from my right came charging with his spear. I was barely able to sidestep in time. However, recovering quickly, I twirled my falcata in a complete circle and brought it downward onto his spear cutting the shaft in half as if it were a block of lard. From the corner of my eye, I saw another guard drop his spear and was going to pull his sword. In an upward swing, my falcata caught the guard in the face as he tried to bend backward knowing he was in trouble. He was not completely able to get out of the path of the tip of my falcata, which opened up the man's face from chin to forehead. He dropped his sword, and the others knew it would be foolish to attack a man with an iron sword when they only held bronze, ceremonial blades and wooden spears. The two guards with missing hands began bellowing in unison at the realization of what had just happened to them. The man with the bloody face tumbled backward in shocked dread falling on top of Eyebrows, who was still screaming and trying to disentangle himself from his colleagues.

The Temple Captain was now back on his feet but looking at me in what appeared like foreboding terror. I could have killed him, but he was defenseless; and, for some odd reason at that moment, I thought mercy meant something. Grillius would not have hesitated to gut-cut him, but I thought of my two birds and chose flight instead of fight. I turned and ran with frightening speed through the northern gate into the Court of Priests passing the carved stone sign forbidding Gentiles to enter.

Driving aimlessly forward, I noticed hundreds of white-clad men in their puffy hats around the Great Altar. Everyone was occupied doing various tasks. Blood was splattered around the lower half of the white stone altar, which stood the height of two men standing on each other's shoulders. On top, a massive fire was blazing away at the sacrificial carcasses. There were four corner horns smeared with ceremonial blood and blackened by fire. Thick, oily, black smoke from flesh and fat that was burning on the Great Altar rose gently into the clear blue sky. A great deal of greasy substance was also dripping down from the top mingling into the blood on the sides of the altar, all smeared below the red line in the middle of each side. Only a few priests looked at me running and holding my falcata at my side. Those who saw and were in my way moved quickly to allow me to escape out the southern gate. I emerged back into the crowded Court of Gentiles but now on the other side of the Temple. I quickly sheathed my sword as I sprinted towards the only outlet I knew: the Zion Bridge spanning the Tyropeon Valley.

CHAPTER SIXTEEN

Jerusalem – Day of Atonement – Tiberius's 16th year and Pontius Pilate's 3rd year as Prefect of Judaea; 46 years since the completion of Herod's Temple and 6 months into the first year of the public ministry of Jesus of Nazareth.   *(29AD)*

There is a way which seems right to a man, but its end is the way of death.   King Solomon, Proverbs

After crossing the Zion Bridge that spans across the Tyropeon Valley, I found myself on the western side of Jerusalem at the southern end of the Hippodrome Circus racetrack. It was a short ironic moment of my escaping once again beside a circus. The last time was in the middle of the night in Rome standing with Eli next to the Circus Maximus. Looking back one time, I could not see anyone following. I decided to make my way to the Lower City, the ancient City of David, built atop Mount Zion, a lower hilltop adjacent to Mount Moriah. I realized I had been darting down streets going downhill and then back up for some time. Mental flashes of fleeing Claudia's litter bearers at age ten crossed my memory along with passing over the Tiber into the 14th District. I slowed down to a determined walk realizing I was breathless. Turning south and then east and back south meandering through the narrow streets, I finally came to a dead end next to the city wall at the southern edge of Jerusalem. A cold sweat began to envelop me as I realized I could be trapped if I did not turn around. By reversing my movement back into the city, I realized that maybe I would fare better as the hunter than the hunted. My mind was numb with my foolish choice of routes. I began to feel the impoverishment of not having any food and fluids since the Day of Atonement was a day of fasting. Sweat was pouring from my brow; and I was still wearing the warm cloak, which was making my condition worse.

After removing it, I used it to conceal the falcata and its scabbard, along with the psalm tube. Now with the bundle under my left arm, I continued down a narrow street. When I passed an open doorway, I heard sounds of loose tongues and laxity. I stopped and realized this diminutive spot was just a wine shop that was strangely open for business even though it was the Day of Atonement. Considering I was finished with fasting and with Judaism, I entered and found a table. It was only after I sat on a wooden stool that thoughts of yet another wrong slapped me: the awareness I did not have any money. Eli had spent our last coins on the two turtledoves, the two most fortunate birds alive at this moment. I secretly wished I had wings to fly to the sea, but thoughts do not help when what is real is cruel. Scrutinizing my situation, I slowly gazed around the shop. Sitting next to me at the adjacent table was a soldier unashamedly staring at me while I slowly looked away. An elderly man who had to be the wine keeper approached me and asked, "Are you here to eat or just drink?"

I did not know what to say. I pretended to look for my moneybag before declaring I must have lost it or it had been stolen. I stood to leave, no longer feigning disappointment. The soldier, using his left foot, pushed a stool out at his table. Using broken Aramaic, he told more than asked for me to sit. Taking his eyes from mine, he looked at the wine keeper and ordered him to bring a cup and another jug of his cheap wine. I reluctantly sat down on the stool noticing that the stranger wore neither a priestly nor a Roman military uniform; yet, he was a soldier. On his chest was a well-worn leather breastplate blackened with age and shiny from wear. He also was wearing an old bronze helmet with a wicked point on top. At his side, he had an Iberian gladius in a leather scabbard that was also well worn and black. He must have been in his mid-thirties, which seemed old to me at the time. A week-old beard on his face could not hide a long, white scar running down from his left forehead over his deep-set left eye and continuing onto his cheek and jaw. The wound apparently had not injured his sight; for both dark, bug-like eyes looked menacingly at me. I thought of the priest-guard I had just cut with my falcata; perhaps this was how he was going to look in a few years.

"My name is Amcheck; I am the son of Parthian parents. I am a guard at the Palace of Herod here in Jerusalem and have been for the past six years. And we who wear the boots of a Spartan along with a scar on your arm and that fresh wound on your face makes us both soldiers. Am I correct?"

"I do not understand your question," I mumbled in Aramaic. Before he could respond, the wine keeper returned and poured a clay cup full of red Judaean wine. I took it and drained it in one gulp without taking my eyes off my new acquaintance.

"Thirsty are we? Have another," said Amcheck with a friendly laugh as he filled my cup with the new jug left by the old man.

"Perhaps I should not be rude. Thank you for your generosity."

"Oh, a polite fellow are we? So are we a mercenary or something like that?"

The wine was already subduing my anxious thoughts, and I drained the second cup before I answered the soldier who kept referring to me in the plural. "I am not a soldier. The only trade I possess is fishing."

"Those wounds look like you fish for monsters or maybe leviathans," laughed Amcheck at his own joke. "I suspect we have some kind of angry weapon wrapped up in that cloak that is resting on your lap," observed a smiling Amcheck.

I smiled back while my left hand rested on the hilt still hidden under the cloak.

"Look, if we are in trouble, do not worry about me. I will not turn us in. Have another drink. For some strange reason, we like you. It is always good to get legless with someone besides yourself. I have an idea. Why not ask me a few questions, and I will do the talking."

I was wondering why he spoke the way he did. Who were "us" and "we"? His Aramaic was also a little rough. I looked around the shop once again, and we were now the only ones sitting in the small room. The wine keeper was in the back cleaning cups and such. "Aramaic is not your native tongue. Am I correct?"

"That is right; but who knows Parthian in this wicked land, or for that matter who knows Akkadian these days? Akkadian is the common language from where I come from."

I nodded with a slight smile. I knew from my studies that, before Alexander the Great had conquered the Persian Empire, Akkadian had been the international trade and diplomatic language of the lands of Mesopotamia. Today, thanks to Alexander's successful conquests, Greek had replaced Persian, Akkadian, and in some places Aramaic. I asked if he knew Greek, and he nodded. I decided to speak Greek and see if he understood it better than his use of Aramaic. "You said you work for Herod Antipas," which was more of a statement on my part. "I believe he is the tetrarch over Galilee; yet, you said you work here in Jerusalem, which is in Judaea. Does Herod Antipas have jurisdiction here in Jerusalem?"

"I said I am a guard at the Palace of Herod. It is true that I do work for Herod Antipas. Herod Antipas has no real power in Judaea except the grounds of his one palace here in the city. That would be the largest palace located in the center of Jerusalem. Herod Antipas is somewhat unpopular, especially in Judaea. His biggest mistake was arresting a famous prophet, some desert preacher in Peraea. The Romans will not allow Herod, one of three tetrarchs in *Palestina*, to possess a substantial army. He can retain only a few hundred guards garrisoned at each of his city strongholds and palaces. These palaces were inherited from his father, Herod the Great." He moved closer to me and whispered, "If that is a sword under the table and you know how to use it, I can get you a posting here in Jerusalem with me. I believe you are in need of some money, and Herod is in need of a good soldier. Nothing to be ashamed about. I, too, have been financially embarrassed a time or two."

"It is true – I do need a job. When do I start?"

"Today if you're not too stewed by the time we get back to the palace."

After an hour of drinking plus eating dates and bread, Amcheck asked what happened to my face, and I trusted to share what happened nine days ago. When I told him about Eli getting the sword just an hour ago, he leaned closer and asked me to repeat what happened at the Temple only a few hours hence. Maybe this was to show me he was listening or maybe not. I repeated it; then he retold my story in his own words, more so to lock the story into his memory. "And this Eli was your only friend, and the Captain of the Temple killed him in front of thousands of onlookers this very afternoon? This I find hard to believe, for this is something even the Captain of the Temple Guards cannot get away with. You see, murder is one thing, but not with witnesses watching – and so many! Only Rome has the legal power to take life. Are you sure you are telling me the truth? This Captain of the Temple is hated and feared, but he is not stupid."

"I tell you the truth," I said with a slur realizing I had drunk too much.

"Maybe our story is true. Things at the Temple must have changed since I visited there six years ago," said Amcheck with a laugh and then slapped the table twice finding great humor in something he remembered in his past. "Now that was quite a story six years ago," he said with more laughter.

"Well, I shall never return; therefore, I hate this God of the Jews and His system. I cannot believe I even considered he was the one true God," I stated emphatically. Amcheck only laughed harder than before at my open blasphemy.

The wine keeper must have been a Jew even though he was doing business on the Day of Atonement; he approached us and gently asked us to leave his shop. Amcheck grabbed him by the throat without even leaving his stool. I persuaded Amcheck to release him after the wine keeper fell to his knees. Amcheck pushed him down, stood, and kicked an *amphora* of wine to the floor flooding the tiles with red liquid. I winced remembering the afternoon I accidentally broke a similar clay wine jar in one of the tunnels at the amphitheater in Rome. I wanted to run again, but Amcheck pulled the Jew to his feet and even apologized for his anger. It was as if this gruff man had some remorse that followed his hasty, volatile temper. I had never seen anyone swing from such extreme emotions on the flip of a coin. Did this man have some kind of problem with his mind? After the wine keeper had hung his head in disbelief, Amcheck placed enough coins on the table to pay the damages; then we left.

I noticed the sun was near the horizon once we were out on the street. Speaking in Aramaic, which Amcheck had used when helping the wine keeper to his feet, he said to me, "We have maybe an hour before dark. Come home with us, and we can arrange for you to be hired as a mercenary guard. What do we say?"

"What is this 'we' and 'us' stuff when you speak Aramaic? You talk as if you have a pet mouse in your moneybag maybe chewing away at your leg."

"What do we say? What is this pet you talk about?" asked Amcheck apparently not understanding my "mouse in the moneybag" statement.

"I will go with you if you allow me to teach you proper Aramaic and Greek." Amcheck smiled showing some missing teeth; and I realized I knew only a little Aramaic, let alone its many strange idioms, which rendered it a colorful but complicated language.

"Oh? We are a scholar-soldier-fisherman. Aye, it is a deal," he laughed.

I had neither money nor anywhere else to go. Even if I were to strike for Athens, I had no funds to make such a journey unless I considered thievery. The only other option was to go to work for Herod Antipas. When I had what I needed, I would return to Athens. As I left the wine shop, I at least had a plan; and it gave me some solace.

While we walked some ways down a narrow lane, a dirty-looking man called to Amcheck from the shadows of an alley. Amcheck seemed to recognize the voice and told me to wait for him. I watched Amcheck enter the narrow lane. I stepped into the dark passageway only to allow my eyes to adjust to the semi-darkness. It did not take long, and the man I saw in the shadows did not impress me. He had a narrow face with a long nose. I decided he was an egg-stealing weasel with a strange, straight grin when he was not talking. Soon the Weasel handed over a ratty-looking, frayed brown cloak, which Amcheck pulled over his uniform. Amcheck removed his helmet and gave it to the sneaky little man. In return, this wanton little creature gave a knife and a moneybag to Amcheck. After the exchange, the Weasel departed back down the dark throat of the alley disappearing as if he had never been there. My new-found friend returned to me looking no longer like a soldier except by his footwear. He instructed me to follow him. There was a new seriousness overtaking him as if his mind were scheming or calculating a problem. After a few turns down several streets, I found that he was heading towards the bridge over the Tyropeon Valley.

"Hold it! Is this some kind of jest? Where are we going?" I finally blurted out.

Amcheck stopped and turned to me looking long into my eyes before he spoke. "Is it all true what we told me about your friend getting the sword from the Captain of the Temple?"

Maybe I should have kept my mouth shut anticipating what was coming. After I had indicated yes, Amcheck pulled out a long, curved dagger and showed it to me. "Do you know what this is?"

"A fighting knife? For throwing, it is not worth a fig."

"Does the name *Scarius* mean anything to you?"

"It is the name of a dagger, but I have never seen one before."

"Now you have. This is a *sicarius*," said Amcheck tucking the long, curved blade back under his cloak. "*Sicarius* is also the name of a fanatical nationalistic group that is quite hostile towards Rome. They do not hesitate to use assassination on political opponents. Most commonly the *sicarius* dagger is used when the target is in large crowds; thus, the *Sicarius* organization and the tactic of assassination in crowds are the same." Amcheck never took his eyes off mine as he spoke, which was not the standard practice when one was talking. Apparently, he wanted to see my reaction to what he just said; and his Aramaic syntax now seemed different. Who was this Amcheck character? Based on his eyes staring at me, he must have liked what he saw; for he continued, and his speech construction began to again deteriorate. "I'm not a Jew as I told you. We are the son of a Parthian. I care nothing for politics either, but this group pays us 30 pieces of silver to do what submission to Roman law mandates they cannot. More so, we get 30 shekels when it is someone special."

"You are a specialist?"

"That is me – my unique name is *Sicarius,* and only those who know me use it."

I now understood correctly and spoke my mind. "What you are telling me is you are an assassin; and this man in the alley contracted you to kill someone, and this someone is in the Temple grounds."

"Very perceptive, and this particular person who will feel the *sicarius* is our Captain of the Temple. And we are right; he is still on Temple grounds."

"I want to help," I volunteered before realizing that I had committed myself. Delight overcame any fear I had when I learned who was to be killed.

"Good, because we could use your help," said Amcheck now back into his butchered Aramaic as he pulled out the moneybag Weasel had given him. Amcheck counted out 15 large silver coins to keep and then handed me the bag with the remaining 15. I took the bag as if it were a holy offering, and it had quite a heft to it. Amcheck put his share into his own moneybag tied to his waistband and shoved it under his leather chest protector. "You see, my new friend, Rome manipulates total control over the affairs of Judaea and the rest of the provinces it controls. The high priest is in Rome's moneybag just like those coins are in yours. The Captain of the Temple is a Levite and a member of the Sanhedrin. The Sanhedrin is the Jewish legal court in this province, and it is politically dependent on the Roman officials here in Judaea. I was sure what happened a few hours ago has since been gossiped over the entire city, and the group called the *Sicarius* are going to use it to their advantage. You see, this priest-captain does not have the authority to kill someone under Roman law. Besides, no one is to be killed on Temple grounds according to Sanhedrin Law; but that will change today. I suppose killing him will give the *Sicarius* prestige with the populace and solve a major problem for the Romans and even the Sanhedrin. One quick knife in the kidneys and everyone is happy including you. Besides, do we object to being a little richer?" laughed Amcheck for the first time since the visit with the Weasel.

I nodded with a false smile to show I understood all that he was saying. He then asked if I had any questions. I had only one. "Why the kidneys?"

Amcheck gave a broad grin, which contorted his scarred face. "If we hit the kidneys, the area low and to the side of the back produces so much pain and surprise that the victim is usually unable to scream. This makes our escape that much easier with our action going unnoticed in the crowded Temple area. Now, to earn your wages, all I need you to do is walk up to that beastly priest-captain. Let him see you. Turn and run into the crowd where I will be waiting. I will do the rest. Meet me here when it is all over, and I will take us to our new home."

After digesting his plan, I gave him a solemn nod that set one of those proverbial pillars that are hard to remove once erected. We crossed the Zion

Bridge going against the flow of people leaving the Temple because of the late hour. I did notice more priests in white moving over this bridge than worshipers. Once inside, it did not take long to locate the Captain of the Temple. He was standing in *Solomon's Portico* next to one of the forests of white columns standing all alone without his white-clad minions. I left Amcheck in a crowd out in the Court of Gentiles and boldly strode towards the wicked wretch whom others perceived as a sacred senior officer. I was surprised he stood alone. Perhaps he was preoccupied with other thoughts that kept him from seeing me even when I tapped his left shoulder from behind. "Looking for me?" I announced using a sarcastic tone.

He turned laggardly not recognizing my voice. When the old soldier identified me, his face quickly contorted into depravity and baseness. I spoke speedily but distinctly in Greek so he would understand exactly what I wanted him to hear. "You pompous coward! You stand alone after you have killed an unarmed man who was my best friend from childhood! Now you will pay the debt with the nefarious coin of your miserable life!"

He stood with a strange look trying to digest what I had said. It appeared as if he was deciding between either drawing his sword or merely blowing the silver whistle that was hanging on a silver chain around his neck. I thought, if I had a throwing dagger in my hand, he would have the handle sticking out of his eye just like the previous owner of my falcata. Perhaps I could kill him with my bare hands or with my falcata that was hanging under my cloak. But he was not destined to perish in my hands.

When he made his decision to go for the whistle, I took the moneybag with the 15 heavy silver coins that I held in my right hand and swung it with all my might into his lower jaw just below his bottom teeth. The crack of his jawbone was muffled by all the cacophony of activity around us. Seeing his jaw hanging slack at a strange angle, I knew I had done serious damage. The silver whistle had flown out of his mouth and was no longer hanging around his neck by the chain. Bizarrely, the Captain of the Temple put his hand back towards his mouth as if the whistle were still between his lips. It was odd watching him realize he could not blow air through his missing pipe even if it were still in his mouth. Then the captain stepped away in surprise trying to say something before noticing a tiny silver object from the corner of his eye skipping away from us along on the pavement stones of the Court of Gentiles. A weaker man would have been flat on his back with a hit like that, but he just looked back at me trying to refocus after we both realized the skipping object was his whistle.

I now acted quickly before he attacked. I put the right heel of my booted foot into the side of his left knee. The hit was not intended to break the knee but just injure the tendons that held it together. It wasn't until I saw his leg buckle that I realized I had hit too hard. I gave him an "I'm sorry look," and I turned and walked away as if I had just asked for directions. I was not going to run anymore. I would stand and fight to the death or just walk away. My running, I decided at that moment, was over. I listened for his steps behind me, and it sounded like he was hopping on one leg trying to catch up with me. When I did turn and look at him, I smiled at his pain. He was using his Syrian sword, which he had extracted from its sheath, as an aid to half walk and half hop. I kept up my leisurely pace passing Amcheck in a crowd of people who were busy in their own conversations or personal contemplations. No one seemed to notice this crazed man hopping on his right foot with his jaw and left leg hanging at strange angles. When the Captain of the Temple passed Amcheck, I distinctly heard a thud noise but no scream. I turned once again and observed Amcheck walking away in the opposite direction as the Captain of the Temple Guard was face down onto the ground with the *sicarius* sticking out of his lower back about the width of four fingers from his spine. The priestly soldier was clawing for the knife in his back and could not reach it. Our eyes met once more, and I noticed his flaring nostrils and profuse sweat pouring from his brow. I fixed my eyes on him uncaringly for a brief moment relishing the taste of revenge just as I had when I threw the knife into Claudia. I knew it was evil to entertain such thoughts; but it was such a sweet moment, which is precisely what sin delivers: a joyous, unbelievable, pleasure moment, right before the dread comes to rob the joy. Once the moment had flown away, I turned and calmly continued on my way thinking with a laugh that I was going to have to sacrifice more than turtledoves if I wanted to get right with Yahweh. It was as if I had cut down my spiritual tree; and each time I sinned, a forest fire burned the blackened stump into a harder blackened scar.

When I met Amcheck in the Lower City near the bridge and Jerusalem's Hippodrome, he asked in Greek, "Why did you not just kill him yourself?"

I answered, "That was not the plan." I did not tell Amcheck there would be a divine curse on anyone who killed one of God's anointed priests, which even the Captain of the Temple had to be. King Saul, the first Jewish king, had ordered the killing of Yahweh's priests who had aided David when he was fleeing from the same wicked king. King Saul's life from that point on was blighted with many execrable episodes, which I did not wish to add to my own postulated, detestable condition. This thought alone, not actually killing the Captain of the Temple by my own hands, was the only shred of hope that revealed itself to me that I had not entirely lost all faith in Yahweh.

"The plan!" Amcheck said throwing up his hands. "You crippled the man to the point I felt sorry for him when I stuck him. Besides, people were watching because of what you did to him. I am supposed to kill someone on the sly and not with the entire world watching!"

"You told me to lead him past you. You did not say what kind of condition he was to be. Besides, I checked; no one was watching. Everyone was busy doing other things. If anyone saw what happened, he was too faraway to see clearly who did what. I did not hear anyone yell at us as we left the assassination. Did you?"

Amcheck looked to see whether we were being followed and then finally laughed and reverted to his butchered Aramaic. "Next time I guess we will have to be more precise. I think me new-found friend will make quite a mercenary." Amcheck slapped my back in a gesture of friendship. The thought of Menander's admonition crossed my mind: *"Bad company leads to bad morals."* But what choices did I have?

We wandered down several streets of yellow-colored street stones dirtied with age and use. Amcheck kept turning to see if anyone was following. Just after it got dark, Amcheck took me to the Palace of Herod, which, true to his word, was located in the center of the city. Arriving at the back gate to the walled palace, he introduced me to the guard on duty. The next morning I stood before the Captain of the Guard, a man who only went by the name Saben, who agreed to hire me. I remembered this man from ten years ago as one of the guests of Tiberius at the amphitheater on the day Marius won the wooden sword. Thus, began my career as a mercenary.

CHAPTER SEVENTEEN

Jerusalem – A year and a half after the Day of Atonement and a week before Passover. Tiberius's 17th year as emperor of Rome and Pontius Pilate's 5th year as Prefect of Judaea. (31 AD)

'More law, less justice.'   Cicero of Rome

I became a mercenary guard for Herod Antipas primarily doing nothing more than guarding the rear gate of the enormous Palace of the Hasmonaeans also called Herod Antipas's Palace, which stood in the center of the walled city of Jerusalem west of the Temple Mount and Mount Zion. I had found a safe home in my new life: two meals a day, a dry bed, and intangibility – at least that is what I thought until the morning 19 lunar cycles after becoming a mercenary. The lunar cycle was approximately 29-½ days or 30 days making a 19 lunar cycle lasting about 560 days. A yearly solar cycle was 360 days. To measure the time since Eli's death and my becoming a mercenary guard by using a sun calendar, 18 solar months had passed. Using a Roman solar calendar, it had been about a year and a half. Whatever the length of time, I passed another birthday, now age 21; and I spent two cold and wet winters in Jerusalem. It was now the start of my second glorious springtime in Judaea, the best time of year in this part of the Roman Empire. Along with springtime came the Jewish Passover, the most festive and joyous of all the Jewish feasts. This was going to be my second Passover experience in Jerusalem when the crowds swelled the city to about two million people. The general population of Jerusalem was less than half of what lived in Rome, the largest *polis* in the Empire. On Passover, pilgrims from all over the Empire made up most of those in attendance. That huge number also brings possible trouble into the city.

Each morning at sunrise, no matter the season, all the guards assembled for roll call, drill, and marching rituals. Our force was perhaps 100 strong on this beautiful but fateful morning. I remember the early air was crisp, and the sky was a brilliant soft blue. Standing away from the other soldiers lining up in the courtyard of Herod's Palace, I could tell the last of the winter rains were now over and the spring season was finally upon the land of Judaea. Birds were flitting about, and their chirping reminded me this was my favorite time of year. Mornings were also my best hours of the day. I may have been alone with this belief since most of my compatriots passionately despised this early time of morning roll call, no matter the season. They cursed just about everything while they assembled for tally and drills. They found no appreciation for the simple things such as the fresh smell of flowers and new grass. I ignored their gripes while I genuinely filled my chest with the aroma of hope. I tried to follow the proverb *"Hope for the best, but prepare for the worst."* The last time I said this was to Eli's uncle in front of the temple of Athena Nike. This was just before I left for Rome to save Eli from death. Sadly, I failed in the end since I got him killed. It was my fault and all because of my pride. Not only was Eli now dead, but the inner light that had been provided by Eli and Rabbi Issachar was also almost out.

The triple festivals of Passover, Unleavened Bread, and First Fruits were less than a week away. These three celebration observances were the most festive of all the Jewish festivals. I assumed it was because it was springtime, the spirit of new beginnings, and the return to a life of all vegetation. That was why most Hebrews referred to these festivals as the beginning of harvest or "First Fruits." Winter was over, and life was restoring itself. In one week, the city would be spilling over with pilgrims coming from all parts of the known world. Both excitement and dread carried in the air. The biggest fear was the potential for dangerous agitation when scores of people congregated together in small places, which could easily overflow into trouble. It was also easy for spies of my father to hide in crowds as they hunted the world for the son of the richest man to be brought to justice.

During my year and a half as a soldier, I had become an accepted member of Herod's mercenary family. I was one of the youngest of the guards and knew my place in the pecking order. I befriended a few of the older guards who touched my thoughts with memories of Grillius. They lived by codes and ethics that only older soldiers would understand. It did not matter that Herod paid us; they knew that loyalty to a fellow soldier was higher than loyalty to officers or even Herod's coins. "Carry your own water" was the code of the old ones. Amcheck, one of the older ones, had taken me under his *aegis*, which helped the others to accept me as one of them.

During the first five months following Eli's death, searches for the son of Senator Vetallus or the killer of the Captain of the Temple were carried out by Herod's own guards. Looking for myself was almost comical, and I believed I had found the perfect hiding place. My appearance had altered drastically since the *cestus* treatment at the Temple. Below my left eye, a thin, purplish scar puckered out, which in time would turn flat and white. It would always pull the lower lid open enough to mark me as somewhat scabrous and definitely plebeian. Besides my shady fighter look, I kept myself well groomed. My mercenary uniform matched my new temperament: dark and black. I had not cut my hair nor shaved my face since I left Greece to find Eli, and my hair now fell over my shoulders and down my back; even when I wore my helmet, I did not tie my hair up, and it spilled out behind my neck onto my shoulders. My beard looked more Gentile than Jewish since I did trim the edges. I think in a way I was emulating the elite bodyguards of the warrior kings from that ancient Greek city-state of Sparta. At the Lyceum, I had read Herodotus's *Histories*, especially the section dealing with Greece's war with the Persian invasion of King Xerxes. The royal guards of King Leonidas and their last stand at the Battle of Thermopylae fascinated me. These guards, 300 in number, were called Sparta's *hippies*. These *hippies* all wore their hair long; some, down to their waist; and they would comb out their oiled locks before putting on their helmets as their last act before battle. No other Spartan soldier was allowed to have facial hair, let alone long hair, except the 300 *hippies* who were the most tenacious and fiercest of all the world's warriors. Unfortunately, all the *hippies* at the battle of Thermopylae along with King Leonidas perished by arrows once their phalanx had been compromised and surrounded by the invading Persian hordes. The *hippies* did fight valiantly for three days holding the strategic passage of Thermopylae that lies between the East and West Hot Gates near the waters of the Malian Gulf and the cliffs of Zastano, which is positioned across from the Euboean Channel.

I was not the only mercenary of Herod who had long hair. A handful of Indian soldiers from the Indus River area also had long hair. Some of them had hair that reached down to their waist. Howbeit, these men rarely showed their hair but, instead, tied their long locks in a topknot, which fit perfectly into the hollow part of the top of our bronze, pointy helmets. I remember Demos wearing his hair long and tying it in a knot like these Indus and Ganga warriors.

I believe I was the only one who wore long hair like Leonidas's *hippies* with the ends hanging out below my helmet and not tied up. Some guards shaved their faces, and some did not; but all of Herod's mercenaries wore the same bronze, spiked helmet. With these helmets on our heads, we were all feared and given room when we swaggered down any street or byway in Jerusalem. Even Roman legionaries left us alone, due to the many encounters in taverns and wine shops where blood sometimes spilled in response to rude insults made by boastful mercenaries or legionaries. Many of the men Herod hired were veterans from foreign wars in the East with the Parthians, the Arsacids, and the Bactrians. Herod Antipas, like his father, refused to hire any Jews as his mercenaries. A soldier far from home was considered more loyal than a local warrior. Some soldiers came as faraway as the Chera, Pandya, and Chola kingdoms; and these men were as dark in skin color as any Ethiopian mercenaries or *Burnt-Faced Men*, who were also soldiers among us. The only significant, physical difference between the men from the Land of Indra, the rain god, and the Ethiopians was their hair. The *Burnt-Faced Men* all had dark, wooly hair while the Indra men had dark, straight or slightly wavy hair. When helmets were in place, there was a tendency to confuse the two groups because their skin tones were identical. In addition, the men from Egypt or Ethiopia were taller and thinner than the men from the Far East, who were short but stocky.

Besides our helmets, the only other distinguishing marks of unity among Herod's mercenaries were the black leather cuirasses and the scarlet tunics protruding from underneath each leather cuirass. The bottom edge of the tunics reached down to our elbows and fell below our knees. That was the extent of our conformity. To show individuality, each man carried his own preferred style of a sword; most common was a simple Roma or Spanish gladius. I was the only one who carried a Carthaginian or Hispanic falcata, and my ability to handle it gave me respect from my older peers. The red leather cover on the scabbard contrasted well with the black and scarlet of our uniforms. Most did not like the falcata since it was a single-edged sword, not double-edged like the gladius. However, its peculiar broad curve at the end of the blade and narrow waist towards the handle made it a fierce-looking weapon. The falcata was a little longer than a gladius and slightly heavier in weight. I believe it was a better design from the standard sword of ancient times: the *sychar* or sickle sword. The sickle sword was a fearsome weapon with a curved blade extending from a short, straight shaft that was connected to the hilt. I believe the falcata rendered the sickle sword as obsolete. I have never read anything to prove my opinion on this matter, but it is just my observation.

Within a few months as a mercenary, I replaced my lost bronze throwing daggers, which I had to leave at my father's villa in Rome. Their replacements were now two iron daggers I had specially designed and made myself in a foundry on the northwest side of Jerusalem. These two heavier knives were kept concealed on the sides of my cuirass. I had rigged leather scabbards on the inside of the leather chest protector that held on each side the two knives upside down with the handles at my waist. After a while, their rubbing was not too noticeable, especially after I developed calluses where the handles rubbed on my hips. I practiced each day swiftly grabbing a knife and throwing it. I wanted the maneuver to be so swift I could disable an enemy before he had time to either notch an arrow or draw out a gladius. The heavier iron knives enabled me to throw them twice the distance of the bronze ones. I also worked on throwing overhand, side hand, and underhand from a more extended range. I religiously performed these exercises in private each morning alone in a long storeroom in the basement of the palace. Only Amcheck knew of my particular skill with the knives. He caught me early one morning practicing, and he seemed to be very impressed. Since Amcheck was a *sicarius* man, he finally understood my comment the first time he showed me a *sicarius* when I said, "It was not good for throwing." I asked him to keep my throwing ability a secret; and on this point, he proved to be a loyal friend.

Amcheck involved me on two occasions in the past year and a half for the group called the *Sicarius*, which I later learned was the militant arm of the Jewish Zealots in Jerusalem. The Zealots, an ultra-nationalistic political party formed during the early years of Augustus Caesar, used violence and assassination to force the withdrawal of Rome from *Palestina*. The Zealots had no problem killing Romans; but, when it came to assassinating one of their own brethren, their delicacies led them to contract a non-Jew such as Amcheck. On both occasions, Amcheck used me to bait the victims past him for the kill, similar to what I did to the Captain of the Temple but without breaking jaws and knees. Two wealthy Jews were the targets; both were sympathizers of Rome, who supplied Rome with valuable information that led to the death of their fellow Jews. Amcheck told me that the two were also vital assets who enabled Rome to further enslave the Jews of Judaea to the will of Rome. Both times Amcheck paid me half of his earnings, which I hid in a particular corner hole carved in our barrack room corner wall located in the lower quarters of Herod's Palace. This hiding spot was very similar to the one in Hector's house where the Carnalus scroll still remained hidden. Not only was the Psalm-tube concealed in the secret hold but also the red bag where I kept my wages along with the silver coins for the two assassinations and the killing of the Captain of the Temple. Since I just mentioned the Psalm scroll, I need to confess that my eyes had not seen any of the Psalms given to me by Rabbi Issachar since the day I was struck by the *cestus*.

I calculated that, when Passover was over, I would have more than enough money to travel to Athens by ship. I had 45 silver shekels along with about 300 silver *denarii*. Compared with most in the Roman Empire, I was a wealthy man owning no one any money; and I was coin-rich. My plan was to leave after the Passover-Unleavened Bread festivals and travel amidst thousands of Jews returning to Asia, Greece, or *Italia*. Amcheck knew nothing of my ideas. When the time came, I would only leave him a note. I suspected resistance from him since we had become close friends, and I was now someone he would not want to lose.

Most of my fellow mercenaries thought it strange I did not spend my earnings as they did on wine, women, or wantonness. Amcheck, like most soldiers, gambled and drank away all his seven *denarii* a week. We were always paid with silver or on occasions one bronze *denarius* for each day worked. Generally, Rome only allowed the provinces to mint coins in bronze or copper, not silver. I only knew of Syria as the only region authorized to use silver in coin creation. In contrast, Roman legionaries were paid one Rome-minted silver *denarius* a day but received only five in a week's time. The Roman silver *denarius* was worth quite a bit more than a local bronze *denarius* or even a silver *denarius* from Syria. Concerning the inequality of this matter, I did not care since I disliked the idea of money and never paid much attention to the value or its worth. My lack of interest in money did at times cause me to be cheated. I should also point out that all those who cheated me were severely punished one way or another. However, I always felt that money was only a tool and not something to covet.

Regarding money in Jerusalem, only silver shekels were accepted by the Sanhedrin for temple tithes and taxes. These coins were minted in the ancient cities of Damascus and Tyre; both cities were in the Roman province of Syria. To my knowledge, the silver Tyrian shekel was the only silver coin I knew that was minted outside of Rome. Most of the silver shekels coming out of Tyre had an eagle stamped on one side and were usually called Tyrian shekels or just *silver eagles*. The *silver eagle* was generally the only coin accepted for worship at the treasury room in the Courtyard of Women located in front of the Temple in Jerusalem. The shekels I saw the day Eli died at the Temple were *silver herculeans*. Moneychangers, sitting out in the Court of Gentiles, exchanged typical Roman coins for *silver eagles* or *silver herculeans*. The *eagles* were the preferred currency since they did not have an image of the emperor or a demi-god stamped onto one side.

Once again, Rome was the only mint allowed to cast and stamp silver and gold coins not counting Syria. I guess Rome felt this monopoly gave it control over the buying power of currencies. Interestingly enough, Rome allowed any province to coin its own money while coinage minted in Rome remained the standard. With Rome prevailing with what was the authoritative tradition of value, Rome never feared foreign coins being minted outside of Rome, mainly if they were not silver or gold. I think this was because the emperors and the Senate believed foreign-minted coins would eventually end up in the Imperial treasury in Rome. However, I noticed in my lifetime a form of destabilization occurring because of over minting of coins by both the provinces and Rome. Due to the overabundance of coins in circulation over the past 80 years, I have noticed that prices for goods and services have persistently increased throughout the Empire. I believe this over-minting of coins has steadily caused the value of coins to decrease. I guess, since I am not certain, this phenomenon was due to the ever-growing number of coins in circulation. I have also observed that Rome has continually increased taxes on all the inhabitants of the provinces. Did Rome believe this tactic would eat up the excess coins in circulation? Out of all the Roman emperors, I believe Tiberius was the only ruler who was aware of this problem. I know for a fact Tiberius purposely hoarded a vast number of bronze coins collected by taxes over the world and would not allow them back into circulation. During my lifetime, this one act maintained the only short stable period economically. If I am correct, Tiberius later ordered the bronze coins melted down and then gave the metal to commissioned artisans to sculpt statues, braziers, tables, bed frames, and other objects such as mirrors, hinges, locks, and even nails to be used in the construction of Imperial projects. What Rome never understood was that the local kings or governors in each province secretly minted more and more coins matching the increase of what Rome wanted in taxes. With more and more coins coming into circulation, Rome foolishly, but slowly, was falling under the burden of price increases leading to the devaluing of its own coinage system.

Another practice I found out about years later, most assuredly perpetrated by my father, was, when a provincial king discovered a new source of silver in his area of influence, the silver mines were quickly taken over by Rome and protected by Roman soldiers. Imperial slaves usually were brought in to work the confiscated silver or gold mines. I should also add, when individuals such as my father legally purchased a gold mine from some potentate in the Empire,

Rome still could take the mine from him whenever it decided. Foolishly, Rome thought gold and silver was its problem when it was copper and tin that habitually led to the inflation problem. I say copper and tin because bronze is the only metal that is man-made mixing mostly copper with a little tin when being produced in a foundry. Most coins in circulation around the Roman Empire were bronze and not silver. The intermediaries such as my father generally used gold and silver coins for more significant purchases whereas bronze was what the ordinary people used to buy their items for everyday use. With tens of millions of inhabitants using mostly bronze coins, there was the problem, especially when tin became more precious than gold.

While most soldiers drank together, Amcheck's favorite activity was drinking alone at the small wine shop in the Lower City where I first met him. Either he would go there alone; or, on some occasions, he would take me. No one else knew of the little "getaway" as Amcheck called it except his *Sicarius* contact, the Weasel. Amcheck was a very private man; yet, I became not only his roommate but also his only close friend. This was why I wished to conceal my plans before shortly disappearing over the wall some night.

My military Spartan boots were now well worn, and each guard wore different types of footgear. I found a sandal maker in the city and paid a week's worth of wages to have a new pair of Spartan boots made. The only difference is I had the new soles embedded with iron nail heads like the Roman military sandals. When I picked up my new boots, they looked like a Roman soldier's sandal except mine still had the high leg portion that laced up to my knees. After serving as a mercenary guard for a year and a half, I began to consider myself an old veteran despite my young age with no war experience. Strangely enough, most war veterans never spoke of any battles in which they had been participants. I would later learn this was partly due to the horrific and horrendous experiences they witnessed and wished to forget. I guess that my scarred appearance and my skill with the sword gave me some status; and, as far as anyone knew, I had some war experience since I never spoke about this subject. Actually, because of the *cestus* attack, my appearance had aged me by ten years according to those who did not know me and tried to surmise my age. According to them, a droopy eye was due to age.

With my falcata, I was as swift and deadly with either arm just as I was with throwing my daggers. I had entered into several fights with other soldiers on the drill grounds using wooden swords and once against a Roman legionary in a *popina* (or Roman tavern) with real swords. Each time I had disarmed my opponents before I had started to sweat. No one had died due to the tricks Grillius had taught me, for that was one of his rules: "Never kill unless there is no other choice." I was in my prime with strong muscles, good wind, and quick reflexes. I am sure, on this beautiful spring morning, most of the old veterans and young ones did not want to take me on after what was witnessed out in the drill yard of Herod's Palace.

In the streets of Jerusalem with the upcoming Passover, tempers were simmering just below the surface and were ready to erupt between Jews and Romans and between Jews Herod's dark uniformed mercenaries. The hatred against Herod Antipas was because of the arrest and jailing of the Baptist lingering in a pit at the desert stronghold on the far side of the Dead Sea in Peraea now going on for a year and a half. The hatred against the Romans focused more specifically towards the Roman governor, Pontius Pilate, and his legionaries stationed behind the Castle of Antonia on Rock Hill located at the northwest corner of the Temple complex. The governor of the province of Judaea was the *prefect* Pontius Pilate. He had earlier this year used money from the Temple Treasury to build an aqueduct into the city to provide more fresh water to the Temple and the Castle of Antonia thinking this would ingratiate him to the people. Instead, the common man perceived that Pilate had stolen what he needed from the Temple Treasury and was using the new source of water to fill lascivious bathhouses utilized by the Romans and Pilate's Hellenistic friends. With Pontius Pilate now in residence at the Castle of Antonia for the Passover, rumors of violence were blowing like a hot desert wind. His provincial capital was located north on the coast of the Great Sea at Caesarea far removed from the center of Judaism. Caesarea was strictly a Gentile city with an immense temple standing high in its center dedicated these days to all Caesars and their wives as gods. Only during the three yearly festival periods did Pontius Pilate move a large force of legionaries and auxiliaries into the Jewish capital since the city would swell to almost two million people by feast day. Due to the Romans' substantial showing of soldiers, the only recourse for the Jews was to stage a non-violent protest demanding the Roman governor give back the Temple funds. Pontius Pilate did not see it that way since the Temple would benefit by getting most of the badly needed water, to better keep the sacrificial area clean. At present, water had to be carried by hand into the Temple area from the Pool of Bethzeta or also called Bethesda that was located near the Sheep Gate north of the Temple complex and not far from the Castle of Antonia but outside the city walls.

I tried to deal with politics just as I did with money: ignore it. My justification was I was too busy waging my own war from within to have any impact of those bigger events around me. Whenever depression raised its ugly head, which was more often than not, I turned to using wine and gall to keep any angry moods at bay. This was becoming a dangerous practice, albeit I limited my fall-down-drunk days to the Jewish Sabbath when most of the city was quiet and many soldiers were given part of the day off to relax. On this pre-Sabbath morning a few days before Passover, I was eagerly anticipating getting drunk the next day. On top of drinking too much wine, I also was purposely depriving my mind of study whether it be scholarly study or spiritual meditation. I had never gone this long without reading or writing since I was a boy sitting under Zeno in Rome. I even found my speech and diction deteriorating. Instead of helping Amcheck with his Aramaic, he was corrupting my vocabulary. I was becoming fluent with filthy but colorful curses in several languages. I found it humorous to blaspheme all the Egyptian gods as well as the Greek and Roman deities. However, the one God I never cursed was Yahweh; for deep in my soul, I still feared He might be the one true God.

During the year and a half as a guard, I never wept over Eli's death nor allowed any emotions to overcome me concerning the loss of Messina. Whenever I thought of her, I barricaded away those memories, which was not hard since I had only spent a few moments on two different occasions with her. I told myself I did not really know her; yet, there seemed to be a strong connection that I could not shake. Maybe because of her, I had stayed away from the brothels, which most of the soldiers visited during their free time. Some soldiers called me a Spartan based on the ancient reputation that those soldiers were satisfied sexually by one another. I almost killed a fellow mercenary when I overheard an insult implicating Amcheck and me. I used only my hands and feet, and he was not breathing very well even a week later after his comment. I believe I had broken his windpipe with the heel of my hand, and it was a miracle he did not die. After that day in the dining hall, all such talk stopped. Yet, I wondered if some secretly questioned whether I was perhaps a eunuch, castrated after puberty. Amcheck put that rumor to rest after he and I had a drunken visit to a bathhouse for a late swim. He had told some gossiping soldiers that I was with all my parts. He just said I had no desire for women or men. He told them that I had a broken heart from a woman whom I could not get over. He was somewhat correct.

The real problem regarding my heart was its slow death of hardness. It had started to turn to stone, and I had become unfeeling about anything. I would later learn that a man is able to block his real feelings for only so long. Any structure man constructs, may it be physical or mental, will eventually rupture; and there will be an ugly crisis when the black waters come rushing forth. Friendship with Amcheck was the only outside force I allowed to enter into my well-guarded world; and, before this day ended, I was finally going to allow him to penetrate deeper into my darkest secrets.

It all began on that splendid spring morning in Herod's courtyard *tripedalis* or exercise yard in the center of Herod's Palace in Jerusalem. The entire cohort of 100 men stretched or engaged in their early sunrise routine. After smelling the air, I waited for Amcheck, who was usually last on the field of practice. When he finally arrived, he was stinking of wine and perfume. He had not been in his cot when I awoke, and I had no idea where he spent most of the nights when not on duty.

"Are we ready to be counted?" called out Amcheck to everyone as he entered the formation just moments before the captain of the Jerusalem mercenaries emerged from the far end of the *tripedalis*. As the Jerusalem captain approached, his century of men began to count off until we were all accounted. Saben was half Roman, and his name was slang for his lust of harlots. The word *saben* referred to the story of Romulus on the Tiber after he had murdered his brother Remus. Romulus had gathered a large band of villainous men on the Tiber River where Rome today stands. This criminal group of thieves and runaway slaves had no women to breed a future. To correct this problem, Romulus led a daring raid on a nearby city called Sabine. Romulus and his men captured and raped most of the neighboring *Sabine* women.

Regarding slang names, I should also mention that each Herodian mercenary was known only by a peculiar name. If anyone knew one's real name, he was a close friend. For instance, I was first called by the names Curus or Carius after the wild nature of a mongrel dog. I later was labeled as Leo or Leopard Man after I broke the soldier's windpipe. When I hit the man, I did it in such a quick motion that those who witnessed the attack said a jungle cat could not have moved as fast as I did. No one including Amcheck knew that my real name was Venustus. The last person I remember using my real name of Venustus or Venu was Eli the day he died. That was a year and a half back.

Amcheck was known as Sicarius because of the long knife he carried and the work he did on the side. Since I had helped Amcheck on two occasions, I also became Little Sicarius or Little Carius. Thus, Amcheck was Big Si; and I, Little Car. It became a big joke when soldiers at eating time would say, "Hey, Si–Car," and guffaw. Each man had to accept the names given, or it could result in a beating or even a knifing in one's sleep. I did not worry too much about the latter since Amcheck and I both shared a room, where we kept the door bolted when one or both were sleeping. We had developed a special knock to alert the other to open the door from the inside. Actually, it was the same knock Rabbi Issachar used when Eli and I were underground below the synagogue in the 14ᵗʰ District of Rome.

After the morning count had been completed, our fearless Captain Saben swaggered out in front of the formation. He was a squatty but stocky man with a full black beard cut in the corners and curled like his one Assyrian ancestor who was on his mother's side. His arm and leg muscles bulged from under his scarlet tunic; and he wore the only bronze cuirass at this post, which signified his rank as Captain of the Guard. His powerful legs and arms made his small stature dangerous. In some ways, he reminded me of Marius the gladiator. At his side, Saben held a short oak cane that was frequently used on the backs and necks of new recruits responding too slowly to his orders or too slowly to block his cane strikes during drills. This morning his dark and narrow-set, bug eyes roamed the compound looking for someone to humiliate. He walked up to a new soldier named Flatus, which was a name I knew nothing about; but most called him Puff or Pus. He was called Puff because he looked girlish with milky-white skin that was void of any facial hair. He was called Pus because he had a face with scabs and little pockets of infections that were full of yellowish-white fluid. His facial appearance was similar to that of Tiberius. Flatus/Puff/Pus was about my age but looked much younger due to his long eyelashes.

Saben ordered, "Pus, step out; and block my cane!" Flatus stepped out, and a wooden practice sword found itself in his hand placed there by Saben's lieutenant, a mean bear of a man known as Foul Breath or later as Monger. Pus took the sword and prepared himself to block Saben's cane. *Whack, whack, whack*! Pus went down to his knees with a loud moan and fell to his side clutching his stomach while rolling up into a ball. After a few moments, Pus lost his dinner from last night. Blood also began to trickle from his left ear as he heaved and rolled.

"Get up, woman! Learn to block the cane; or next time it could be a real sword, and you would be doing more than making an offering to Horus and his mother-wife Isis!" There was considerable laughter at Saben's remark, but it stopped when Saben turned and walked up and down the front row looking for someone else to fight. Finally, he called out for Leopard Man to step forward. Foul Breath took the wooden sword on the ground next to a moaning Pus and handed it to me. My stomach dropped, for this had happened to me only once before during my first week as a mercenary. I had been fortunate at that first encounter in defending myself, which was apparently a rare thing. Saben had said nothing since then, and neither had he rechallenged me until this morning. I sensed Saben disliked me for my small victory a year and a half earlier, and now he was going to try to shame me as he had Flatus. I heard other soldiers making wagers among themselves while I removed my falcata scabbard and handed it to Amcheck to hold. Then I limbered up my sword arm with a couple of swings of the wooden sword.

"Are you ready, boy?" hissed Saben like a river snake wrapped around a long, overhanging branch. I nodded and squared off in a crouched, cat-like position with my back slightly arched and the wooden blade ready for a thrust or parry. The captain came at me with great speed, and there were three loud whack sounds as wood connected to wood. Neither of us had been marked, and the captain came again.

Whack, whack, whack, whack, slap! I had marked Saben on the fifth hit, and a large welt reddened on his forearm where I had connected with the last blow. If I had been using a real sword, the captain would be one-armed forever. I waited for his next attack, but it did not come. He ordered Foul Breath to take my practice sword, and I returned to the line. I suppressed a smile as Amcheck handed over my falcata with a grin like a little boy who had just put a handful of hot sting ants down a little girl's tunic. Amcheck also won a small amount of money he had wagered on me.

"Where did you learn how to fight with a sword?" asked Saben rubbing his forearm.

"Sicarius taught me everything I know," I said with mock seriousness. The entire century of guards broke into laughter since everyone knew Amcheck could not fight his way out of Solomon's harem with two swords and a bag of rocks. He was only good at stabbing people in the back with his *sicarius,* and that was when they were not looking.

"Listen, you bunch of miserable *sirens*!" called out Saben after I had made my comment. "Tetrarch Herod might be coming to Jerusalem this Passover. He will be celebrating his birthday if he does. It always falls the day after Passover. His birthday celebration is a famous event that is more of a Roman orgy if you know what I mean. I am told by a dispatch that he will be traveling to Sepphoris in the Galilee after the Passover and then to his new capital that is named after the Roman Emperor Tiberius, which we all know is located on the Sea of Galilee or, as we are now ordered to call, the Sea of Tiberius."

"What about the Roman governor?" called out Amcheck.

"The Roman *prefect*, Pontius Pilate, is already in residence for Passover here in the city. He arrived in the middle of the night from Caesarea while most of you were sleeping your little hearts out. But word of his secret arrival has spread throughout the city. The rumor traveling about states that there is going to be a protest later today before the Sabbath begins by the inhabitants of this fine city and its neighboring districts. Passover this year will occur three days after the Jewish Sabbath ends, which starts at sunset tonight. For you Romanized thinkers, this will begin at sunset on Mars Day. It is important to understand that the protestors will be objecting to Pilate's recent use of Temple funds for the new Jerusalem aqueduct. In the same dispatch from Herod, he emphatically orders all of us to keep his palace in this city secure from the rabble. Therefore, there will be no venturing out of these walls in uniform this week or next unless it is for official business. You will wear non-military clothing when outside these walls during any free time for your own protection, and that will be until the Feast of First Fruits ends after next Sabbath."

One hundred men moaned under their breaths. We were proud of our black-and-scarlet uniforms and were not afraid of anyone, especially Jewish civilians.

"Now, before you are dismissed, we have some special guests from Rome who want to look at each one of you. Apparently, someone in Rome suspects one of you ruffians might be a murderer and is hiding among our ranks. Stand at attention in one long line as our guests come forward."

Out of a side court emerged three figures, two men and a woman. At first glance, the recognition caused my heart to lurch. I felt like I had been thrown from the pinnacle of the Temple, which was located at the southeastern corner of the Temple complex, which fell downward into the deep Kidron Ravine. It was the highest point of all the walls of this city. I stood like a stone-dead statue paralyzed as Lentulus, Marius, and Messina casually walked into the exercise yard or *tripedalis*. Lentulus was in the vanguard all the way to Saben's side with Marius behind and Messina coming last.

After all three stopped and faced the entire century of Herod's Palace, Saben pointed with his cane towards Lentulus and said, "Let me introduce these three distinguished guests. This man with the eye patch is Mayus Lentulus, the first agent of the well-known and opulent Roman Senator, Gaius Vetallus Crassus."

With sweat running in rivulets down my sides, I stood in a daze. It was like characters being introduced at some comedy production, but this was not funny.

"And this is Gladiator Marius, the triple recipient of freedom from the gladiatorial games in Rome, won each time from the hand of Tiberius himself. I actually was present at the final day he vanquished over forty men, one at a time, to win the 'wooden sword of freedom.'" It was at this moment I was certain I had placed Saben in Tiberius's box on that unforgettable day. My vision almost blurred thinking about that soldier sitting next to Tiberius's guests at the gladiatorial fight I attended more than eleven years earlier in Rome. Reality returned when a loud cheer went up for the "man of men" whom this group of soldiers all wanted to emulate.

"Saving the most beautiful for last," Saben said with a twisted grin, "I wish to introduce to you this lovely flower. She is none other than Messina Flavius Vetallus, heir and daughter of Epirus Flavius, the late financier of Ephesus and one-time partner of Senator Vetallus."

After the introduction of Messina, the nervousness in the ranks was palpable; everyone was reviewing his past for anything done that might make him the quarry of the distinguished guests. I did not have to speculate; I knew for sure why they were here. They were here for me. Nevertheless, I found myself not caring; for I could not take my eyes off Messina. She was dressed in a simple but elegant blue Egyptian linen *stola* that fell to her ankles. She also wore a *palla* of the same color draped over both shoulders. Her hair was pulled back in a long, cascading horsetail of auburn hair with flecks of red and gold tints tied by a long blue ribbon that matched her *stola*. The exquisite lines of her face were more precise than any Venus statue I had ever seen. She was utterly beyond beautiful, like sunlight on a lily flower at the edge of the Nile. I realized for the first time I had never seen her by daylight; and she was enchanting, much more than I ever imagined, with her wide-set eyes sparkling with the same matching color of her *stola* and *palla*. The outer edges of her eyes curved up almost cat-like. There was such a contrast from good to evil as she stood beside the two men who looked like hideous sea worms. The last time I saw her was the night Claudia died and I cut Marius's hand at the top of the wall. Thinking of that night, I immediately looked at Marius and saw his left forearm was, indeed, missing. Where his hand should have been was a leather device attached to the elbow and upper arm hiding the ugly stump the surgeons must have left him. He still looked menacing as he now sported a peculiar, barbarian, oriental hairstyle with most of his hair tied up on top of his head making his hair look like a head of grass in someone's hand. There he was with a high ponytail sticking straight up, his missing ear, and his missing hand along with all his scars on his face and legs and his infamous reputation, which made Marius the epitome of virility. His fame also matched his appearance and surprisingly was now legendary even at the far edge of the Roman Empire. This was quite a feat for anyone but especially someone who had not been in the arena for over a *deka*. My fellow soldiers, nervous as they were, also realized they were staring at not just one but three Roman legends.

I guessed maybe 2 or 3 out of the 100 had ever been this close in proximity to such celebrated personalities.

Lentulus, on the other hand, looked bored and tired; he was wearing his short Roman Praetorian toga. He had aged and reminded me of my father the morning my mother was murdered by Claudia. Perhaps this was because Lentulus was with my father in the atrium as he adjusted my father's toga, and now their ages had merged into the same time period. My mind shot forward ten years, and I remembered my kick to his knee that rainy night. It was at this moment I noticed his thick oak walking cane that had a bronze snakehead for its knob. Looking up at the left eye patch, I now concluded I must have blinded him that dark stormy night with the black egg. If Lentulus or Marius recognized me in the next few minutes, then I might be a dead man if I did not kill them first. I was not too concerned since I had both throwing knives at my sides.

Messina seemed embarrassed by all the staring eyes, and she lowered her head with it slightly tilted as if she were looking at our feet. When her eyes saw my boots, she looked up; and our eyes met. Neither of us smiled, and Messina moved her eyes away down the line looking again at everyone's feet.

What she was doing here with these two *thags* was beyond me until Saben announced the purpose of the visit after his introduction of the three from Rome. "Almost two years ago in Rome, Senator Gaius Vetallus's wife was murdered in her own villa. What we are going to do is allow these three to inspect each one of you to see if any of the three recognize the killer of Senator Vetallus's late wife. These three were all eyewitnesses when the wife of Senator Vetallus was murdered in Rome that night. Why they think one of you could be the killer is not our business," Saben said with a laugh. "So allow inspection; and, if they do not find the murderer, maybe Gladiator Marius will give us a demonstration of his famed swordsmanship."

There was a spontaneous cheer from many yelling, "Hail, Marius! Hail, Marius!" After the chant, Marius appeared to be relishing in the praise by waving his good arm in a salute.

I felt like running but knew this would not be wise. Besides, I had decided the day I broke the jaw of the Captain of the Temple in the Court of Gentiles that my running was over. My only option, if I were recognized, was to pull my knives and kill both Marius and Lentulus before being subdued by my fellow soldiers. If they failed to drag me down, then I would pull my falcata and see what might transpire. Saben ordered us to stand at attention in our long, single-file line. After we had straightened out our line, Lentulus started at the far end of the courtyard with Marius and Messina following. Now I realized why Messina was here. She had opened the door that night at my father's villa and had the best look at me. Marius had also seen me at the door but perhaps not as clearly as Messina. Although she accompanied them to help find Claudia's killer, she was my only hope. Lentulus surprisingly passed by me looking into my face for only a moment before moving to the next man. Perhaps all he remembered was a Venustus who was ten years old. On the night he last saw me, I was wet and did not have a long facial scar, long hair, or a beard. I was hoping he did not get a good look at me that night before I hit him with the black egg. Marius was a different story. When he reached me, he stopped and looked me over from top to bottom and then called Messina to his side.

"What do you think of this one?" he asked with a sly sneer. The moment Messina reached his side; she demurely raised her eyes to mine but gave no sign of recognition. She was being glacial and very calmly said, "No."

"Are you sure?" asked Marius.

"The man I remember did not have a scar running across his face, and this man is more muscled and taller."

"That could be because he is wearing a helmet," Marius said to Messina. He turned to me and in Latin demanded, "Where did you get that scar on your face, soldier?"

I said nothing but looked to Saben and shrugged my shoulders acting like I did not understand Latin.

From behind Marius, Saben explained, "Most of these men only speak Aramaic or Akkadian." Then Saben asked the same question to me in Aramaic.

"In Upper Egypt," I lied. "Ethiopian robbers set upon an Arab caravan I was guarding."

After Saben translated my words into Latin, Marius sarcastically commented looking deeply into my eyes. "You let a *Burnt-Face Man* cut your face?"

After Captain Saben had completed the translation, many of the mercenaries laughed except the few *burnt-faced* mercenaries in our ranks. During all of this, Marius never took his eyes off me. In mock seriousness, I asked Marius in Aramaic with a slight smirk in my tone, "Did a *Burnt-Face Man* cut off your hand, or did you trip over a sponge stick in a Rome *lavo*?"

The entire century let out uncontrollable explosive guffaws, this time at Marius's expense. Saben did not want to translate until Marius demanded to know precisely what "*burnt-faced man*" was in Aramaic. Apparently, the years he spent with Lentulus in this land, he had learned some Aramaic but not the word *burnt-face man*. When Saben failed to translate the comment about *lavo*, a word Marius apparently knew, Saben ended up explaining everything.

Once my comment was understood, Marius pointed the stub of his arm in my face and said, "The one we are looking for did this. When I find him, I will cut off both his arms before I begin with his feet!"

Saben translated to my expressionless face Marius's threat while Marius was trying to frighten me with his glare. I did not respond, and he finally moved on with Messina submissively following.

After each soldier had been stared into silence by Marius, Sabin lifted his hands into the air and said, "The inspection is now finished!" Everyone including me breathed deeply. Saben next asked if Marius was going to show us his swordsmanship. When Marius understood what Saben had asked, he walked back to me. I had a good idea why he did what he did. Glaring once again into my face, Saben laughed and said from over the gladiator's shoulder, "Are you sure you want to use this one for your demonstration?" Marius nodded as he took off his cloak leaving his familiar light green tunic tied at the waist with a green cord. The sun was just arching over the eastern palace wall; and it showed off the many scars on his legs, arms, and face. Hanging from his shoulder strap was a Roman gladius in a gold-and-silver scabbard that must have cost at least one gold *aureus*, the largest gold coin in the Roman monetary system. Marius removed the sword and scabbard handing it to Lentulus. Foul Breath gave him a wooden practice sword. I once again removed my falcata and placed it back into Amcheck's hands. Foul Breath–Monger gave me a matching practice sword.

My fellow soldiers began to make many wild wagers, mostly against me, while at the same time moving around to make a fighting circle. Amcheck again was taking on all bets on my behalf. I looked to see where Messina was, but she had disappeared as the men made the circle around Marius and me. No one wanted to miss this famous gladiator take on the one who just bested Saben in the arm. Perhaps they thought I was going to get what I deserved. I noticed Saben laughing at me while wagging his head in delight.

Marius loosened up his arms with a few thrusts and swings with his wooden sword. I did likewise and began to watch his movements. His rhythms and motions had not changed from that day I watched him kill the Nubian. That was my only advantage: I had seen him fight. Even though I was only ten at the time, that memory was still etched in my memory, especially the lunge of his sword into the black man's chest. I remembered he was a thruster more so than a real swordsman, and he always lifted his right foot seconds before each thrust. My guess was he would move in quickly and plunge for my throat. I doubted he would go for my chest since I wore a cuirass and he only had a wooden practice sword in his hand. I was surprised he did not demand I remove my leather cuirass.

Amcheck came up to me and whispered in my ear, "I know it will ruin us financially if we lose. If so, I hope we have enough silver to cover the wagers. On second thought, maybe we better let him win."

"Why?" I asked.

"We do not want this *thag* as an enemy for the rest of our lives. Just let Scar Bag win."

"Well, ole' friend, he's already an enemy for the rest of our lives. Do not worry; we are going to be rich in a few moments."

When Saben blew a wooden whistle, Marius did just as I figured. I was able to quickly sidestep his lightning-fast thrust. His right foot gave his move away and allowed me to move my body away from the tip of his weapon. His body momentum caused him to pass me and allowed for a hard whack to be placed on the upper part of his crippled arm. My wooden sword made a loud pop sound against the leather contraption straps on his arm. I did not think it hurt him other than his pride.

"That would not be a kill!" called out Saben. "So continue!" The *tripedalis* grew silent now that I had made the first strike and made it look easy.

Marius was a little more cautious; but, when he came at me, it was faster than any man I had ever fought. Without pulling his arm back before his thrust, his sword shot out like a rock from a shepherd's sling. The only warning was again his right foot lifting seconds before the tip came stabbing towards my throat. I almost was not able to knock his wooden blade away from my throat before he executed one quick overhand cut with a lower thrust on the follow-through. He repeated the same routine two more times. *Whack... whack, whack! Whack... whack, whack!* We both stepped back getting our wind without either gaining a strike on human flesh. Marius was better than I anticipated, but I am sure he felt the same about me. I was not going to win if I continued to just beat off his attacks. I had to do something to turn the tables. He circled around setting me up to look into the low-hanging sun, which just peeked over the roof tiles. When he got me in place and after I squinted my eyes, he expertly maneuvered a rounding swing against my left arm, which I did not see coming. I stepped back with an incredible burning pain that paralyzed my entire arm from the tip of my fingers to the top of my shoulder. He had not used the flat part of the blade but, instead, struck with the edge of the wooden sword. Now I knew what Saben must have felt earlier by my hit, and I wondered why he had not punished me for striking him like that in front of the soldiers.

"How does it feel?" called out Saben accompanied with a satisfied chuckle. "Do you want to quit, Leo?" yelled Saben, bringing forth snickers from many of the soldiers who had bet against me. Marius had more tricks and skill than I had at my young age. However, I had youth and speed to this somewhat older man even if he were only eight or nine years older than I was. I needed to keep him away from me for a few more minutes, and then he was mine. I did not answer Saben's question but circled back out of the sun and retreated a few steps back acting as if I were afraid of this man in green. Marius came at me lunging predictably, and I sidestepped his thrust. Now I could see that he was panting for air as his nostrils were flaring and his mouth was open trying to get air into his lungs.

It was now time, and I advanced using a trick Grillius had taught me in the training yard of the Lyceum. It was what I called the *bump and twirl*. After I had used it, I realized I should not have disclosed the technique because this was not a life-or-death situation. Had we been using real swords, then it would have been acceptable to use the *bump and twirl*. I also remembered Grillius saying to never show off what he taught, and I felt guilty the moment I did it. My justification was my hurting pride and anger after Marius had half-paralyzed my left arm. I also knew Messina was watching from somewhere, and I did not want her to think poorly of me. I knew this was my pride showing, but I did not care. The technique was a quick, double footstep that forced the opponent to block a thrust; but, instead, I pulled back opening myself up for an attack. As soon as my opponent moved with a predictable thrust for the neck, I turned sideways, lowered my shoulder and drove into the rushing Marius. When he tried to re-gather himself, I quickly spun in a full circle building up momentum for a backhand whack across his face raising a fat, worm-like welt in the same location of my scar; but it was on Marius's head, not mine. Unlike Marius, I used the flat part of the practice sword; but, still, the impact was devastating. Marius went down in a shameful heap with blood gushing from his broken nose. Tears were streaming down his face as he turned and threw his sword at me from his knees. I batted it harmlessly away; and he yelled in Latin, "You coward! What kind of a trick was that?" I said nothing to maintain I did not understand Latin.

"I am afraid that would be considered a kill," pronounced a newly impressed Saben. "Maybe we have a new gladiator champion here in Jerusalem!"

Marius stood holding his nose and said he would finish this later and left the courtyard with the help of Lentulus and his snake-head cane. Amcheck was busy collecting his bets while I had just gained a new standing with my fellow soldiers along with Captain Saben. I looked for Messina and finally saw her following behind Marius and Lentulus without looking back. My heart ached thinking I had lost her again. My fears were unfounded when Amcheck later gave me my falcata and said he had a message for me from the woman in blue.

"What message?" I asked.

"Not here, later," he murmured with a conspiratorial smile.

He turned away collecting more bets from soldiers who had to run to their rooms to get more coins. Most were not angry that they lost a week's worth of coins but, instead, were slapping me on the back. Some older veterans even apologized for betting against me. Saben declared that no longer was I to be called Leo, Leopard Man, Curus, or Carius; but, from this day forward, I was to be known as Falcata Man. Everyone began chanting my new name; however, it was later shortened to just Cata, which sounded like a name a child would call a pet dog. Yet, Cata was always said with respect; and it became my final mercenary name.

Later that morning when I was soaking my swollen arm in a terracotta tub, I began fearing it might be broken. Amcheck assured me it was not. "We would have heard the bone snap if it were broken. It is just a bad contusion. Besides, we hit that pompous, little gladiator harder in the face than he hit you on the arm. Just think about what he looks like when he gazes into a bronze mirror tomorrow morning," laughed Amcheck.

"You said you had a message from the woman in blue?"

"That is correct, but we will not give us this message unless we tell us all we know. Not a scrap of your past has you ever shared. We think it is now time to reveal who you are to our partner."

With that, Amcheck handed me a bulging leather bag of silver, bronze, and copper coins. "Your half of the winnings; but first we will go to the wine shop across town, and you will tell me your story over a jug of red Judaean wine."

He had me, and we both knew it. He would not say what Messina said unless I told him my story. I nodded yes as I wondered why I could not break him of his misuse of "we" and "us" when he spoke Aramaic, and now at times he had me talking that way. Later that afternoon after our duties were completed, we covered our uniforms in conventional cloaks and wrapped our heads in Arab fashion. We still looked like soldiers because of our boots and the way we walked with our swords hidden under our cloaks, but we had our orders. On our way to the Lower City, Amcheck wanted to go the long way and pass the Castle of Antonia near the western wall of the Temple complex. He wanted to see whether Saben had been telling the truth and see what Pontius Pilate was doing about the predicted protest.

When we arrived at the western side of the massive, formidable fortress with the four towers at each corner, we saw hundreds of Jews out in the small *agora* adjacent to the main entrance of the fort. The Jews protesting were numbered in the hundreds, all screaming with yells at the Roman soldiers atop an enormous stone staircase standing like an auspicious human wall.

"Saben was truthful this morning," said Amcheck. "These Jews are protesting the use of the temple money for that new aqueduct the Romans are building or maybe have now finished."

"What is that to us?" I said still eager to learn what Messina had told Amcheck.

"Something is going to happen; we can feel it. Let's get off the street," said Amcheck as he walked into a small yard and used a ladder to get to the owner's flat roof.

"What are you doing?" called out an old Jew who was on his roof watching the goings on in the area in front of his home.

"The same as you, old man," said Amcheck while he pulled back his cloak to show his *sicarius* and gladius hilt. The Jew stopped his complaining. I followed Amcheck onto the roof; and true to Amcheck's unstable nature, he pulled out a small silver *denarius* and handed it to the now-smiling man.

"Look, up there on the Castle of Antonia wall," said Amcheck. "The one in the white toga – that must be Pontius Pilate."

I looked to where Amcheck pointed; and, sure enough, a man was wearing a white toga with a thin purple border. He appeared past middle age and had a sour look on his face. He was not alone as other Roman soldiers and officials were standing with him; yet, he was alone by a few bodies from everyone else on the wall. It was at that moment I noticed the Roman *prefect* give a nod to some officer who, in turn, lifted a white cloth and then dropped it as if providing some kind of signal. Down in the street and out in the open *agora* area, the yells from the protestors turned to screams. The crowd, just moments before at a feverish pitch, had now turned quickly into panic once the white cloth floated slowly to the ground outside the tall wall of the Roman fort. Mingled within the protesters was a score of men in ordinary, homespun cloaks who had pulled knives and were now stabbing the defenseless Jews. These men must have been Roman soldiers in disguise and had dispersed themselves among the Jews. The signal from Pontius Pilate precipitated their bloody harvest as they decimated the crowd with quick, rapid unhanded thrusts.

"May Horus be a bloated swine!" called out Amcheck with a fiendish grin leaning forward upon the wall and enjoying what he was witnessing down below. "The Romans are using the Zealots' tactic on the Zealots themselves! Oh, how I love this!" I knew Amcheck was a debased man, but this was an aspect I had never seen before. It reminded me of all the people in the amphitheater in Rome when Marius had just killed the Nubian. The old Jew on the roof took his newly acquired *denarius*, gave it to me, and left his own roof in shock.

"Come on, let's get out of here," I said. "Remember what Saben warned us about this morning."

"Listening to you talk makes me think Hours and Hercules both wore a *stola*. Yet, you might be right. Follow me; I know a way around this." I left the coin on the top of the parapet hoping the owner of the house would find it later and climbed down after Amcheck while the screams below grew louder and more hysterical. I kept my hand inside my cloak on the hilt of my falcata while I followed Amcheck down a side street. Amcheck turned down a second street away from the screaming and all the madness, and the screams began to dissipate. By the time we started to sweat, we were at the wine shop; and it was as if we had never witnessed the massacre of the protestors.

We both toasted our clay cups full of red Judaean wine. I emptied my cup; and then I said with an ultimatum in my tone, "Now tell me what the girl said."

"First, we must tell us how you know this girl."

"It is a long story, and I need to know what she said."

"I will make you a deal. I will tell half of what she said for half of what you know."

"Then throw your dice," I said in Greek knowing he had me in a tight corner.

"She wants to meet you tomorrow," he replied in the common language of the Empire.

"Really? Where and when?"

"No, that is the other half. You now owe us a story, and make it the truth; or tomorrow you will be sent to the wrong side of the city," he said with a smile.

There was no sense arguing with Amcheck. I was touched and delighted to know she wanted to meet me. For the rest of the afternoon, I told him my life story. I started with the killings of my mother, Decimus, and Senator Carnalus. I explained how I first meet Messina after my father murdered Messina's *patra* in Ostia. Amcheck was intrigued, and I noticed he drank less than I had ever seen him drink. He just sat and seemed mesmerized by what I was telling him. To me, my life seemed somewhat dull or boring; but maybe that was because I had lived what I was describing. And to me, it seemed tedious and dreary in some strange way. I spoke of Athens leaving out the names of Hector and Grillius. I mentioned Eli's uncle without naming him either, all for their protection. When I told of my voyage back to Rome, the meeting with Deva, then with Felix in the public *lavo* and later in *Subura* at the *popina* and again in the darkened streets of Rome, Amcheck clapped his hands with delight. I left out the incident with Felix as a man in rags at the *Painted Stoa*. But I did tell how I acquired my falcata and knocking on my father's front door. When I described how I killed Claudia and chopped the hand of Marius with my newly acquired falcata, Amcheck roared with delighted laughter; and there were some teeth missing I had never seen before.

"Wow, you mean to tell us you are the one who cut off that green-tuniced gladiator's arm and had the gall to ask this morning how he lost his hand? Above the heavens, I declare... and you still live! Then we whacked him today across the same stub and then his face. I am sorry to inform you and me, but this stunted *lavo* sponge of Janus is going to kill us," bellowed Amcheck in what he saw as something hilarious.

"Clearly, he did not recognize me," I replied not really understanding why he did not know it was I he was hunting. Maybe he was blinded to who I really am; but Marius was my enemy for a new reason. I most likely was the only person to have defeated him with witnesses who will forever defend this truth.

"It does not matter. If Lavo Sponge were to come in here this very moment, we would have to fight; and it would not be with wooden practice swords or *lavo* sticks. And, should I add, it would be to the death."

"If he came in here, I would not fight him; I would put a knife in his eye before he could draw his sword," I muttered as if it were a completed act.

"Cata, you are one cold cloud for such a youngster. By the way, what is your real name?"

I guess it did not matter, for he knew who I was. "Venustus Vetallus; but, for my own protection, you must never use it."

"Listen, Venustus Vetallus; we will never betray us. Actually, we like you even if you are a patrician pretending to be a plebe," Amcheck said with great mirth entangled with some sincerity and what appeared to be genuine admiration. He finally took a long drink from his clay cup. After wiping his mouth, he said, "Remember also that we are partners in the knife business, and you could turn me in just as quickly as I you."

I acknowledged with a nod and took a long swallow.

"Now I want to hear the rest of your story."

"No more until you tell me where I am to meet Messina."

"Oh, yes! Messina is her name, the daughter of that rich but dead Flavius of Ephesus. So the bastard son of Vetallus is in love with Vetallus's partner's daughter, the partner whom Vetallus murdered along with the help of that old *thag* in his Praetorian finery. Oh, do not forget how Saben introduced Messina as the daughter of your father. If anyone knew – what a hoot."

"First of all, I am not a bastard. I was legally adopted, and that is why I had to be killed just like Herod the Great killed his two sons from Mariamne. And do not forget about Augustus's wife who most likely poisoned the two sons of Agrippa and Julia. One final note to never forget: that *thag* in the Praetorian toga might be more dangerous than Marius."

"You will have to tell me about him next because I think he also needs a knife in the back next time we see him. Maybe we can do Marius as well just as we did the Captain of the Temple. What do you say? I will do both free of charge just to show you I am your friend, and I don't mind if you break their jaws first."

"Where and when do I meet the girl?" I implored with frustration that I could no longer contain.

Amcheck knew I had waited long enough. Leaning back against a wall, he looked around the empty wine shop before speaking. "I assume the girl in blue came up to me because you handed me your sword before you fought Marius. There I was holding your sword after making wagers and foolishly told you to lose to that one-arm pygmy. Then Saben blew his whistle. I could not believe my eyes when you whacked Scar-bag on his short arm. Well, about then is when Blue Princess showed up standing next to me. She said, 'Tell Venu, the one whose sword you hold, to meet me at noon on the Sabbath at the Pool of Bethzatha, the one near the Sheep Gate.' That is all she said, and she slipped away. So Venu must be short for Venustus?"

I found myself beaming a huge smile at Amcheck. I could not believe it; we were going to meet tomorrow at noon. My chest was heaving as my heart was racing from sheer excitement. It felt as if I had run a mile in full armor, and here I was just sitting on a stool. I realized I loved this woman more than I had ever loved any human before. I filled my cup and drank without even tasting the bitter red liquid.

"You look as if your patron goddess Venus just had her son Cupid pierce your liver with an *eros* arrow!" laughed Amcheck. "You better watch yourself; you are now way over your head in love-water."

When we left the wine shop, we were singing arm in arm. Later in our room lying on our cots, Amcheck said he wanted all the details of my meeting the next day; or he would have to chaperone me if I refused. I warned him I would throw one of my throwing knives at him if I saw any part of his anatomy at the Pool of Bethzatha tomorrow.

"Do not worry, Cata; but you will give me all the juicy details since we are partners."

I did not answer acting as if I were asleep, but sleep was long coming because of the awful aching in my heart I had for my meeting tomorrow at noon. It was hard to believe that just in a few hours I was going to have an assignation with my long-lost love.

CHAPTER EIGHTEEN

Jerusalem ~ The Sabbath before the Feast of Passover in Tiberius's 17th year, 5th year of Pontius Pilate as Prefect of Judaea, 48 years since the completion of Herod's Temple. John the Baptist has been imprisoned by Herod Antipas for almost a year and a half, and Jesus of Nazareth was a few days from completing his second year of public ministry.   (31 AD)

In Your book were written all the days that were ordained for me, when as yet there was not one of them.   King David

The morning of the next day finally arrived, which was the Sabbath. Not since I was a young boy had I experienced such feelings of lightness and anticipation. Just knowing I was going to meet with Messina was the cause of these childlike emotions. Amcheck said I was smiling, which I rarely had done in the past year and a half. I noticed I was also dropping things, something I usually did not do. I concluded I was experiencing for the first time this emotion called love. I did not believe in Cupid's arrow, but it was more like being struck down by a battle-ax rather than a mere love-dart – if there were any truth to this myth.

Being the Sabbath, there was no muster of Herod's century; and most soldiers at the palace slept late unless one was slated for guard duty. I was the only soldier up before sunrise. Not being able to sleep any longer, I climbed to the top of the eastern wall of Herod's Palace to watch the sun come over the hills that could be seen over the walls of the Temple compound. After the sun's orb was completely visible, I began my unpretentious yet personal oblations to the Creator of the Universe. This was just a simple prayer of thanks and direction for the day. I was not praying to the sun but to the Creator of all things. I did not feel a need to bow or get on my knees. All that was necessary was to talk silently to Him in the same way I would speak to Amcheck minus the profanity. In the past year and a half, I would come up to this spot and have a one-sided conversation with the Creator confidently believing He understood my words and thoughts. I concluded I had not entirely rejected Yahweh – just the evil religious stratagems, which the false religious leaders had constructed in Yahweh's name. Judaism in every form had been corrupted into different fallen ecclesiastical organizations. The simplicity of Abraham's faith or even that of Moses was all I wanted. Why was it that people thought the truth was something in their moneybags, which they could pull out and use to the disadvantage of themselves and everyone else? On this Sabbath morning, I was going with my inner faith that had not entirely died regarding the reality of Yahweh, not my feelings; and that is all that appeared real to me on this lovely and joyful morning. Only a loving God could answer my prayer I had made regarding Messina. I had asked over a thousand times since I left Rome if I could just see and talk to her one more time. Now it had been arranged, something I thought in my mind would never happen. This had to be a God-thing. How could I explain this answered prayer of finally meeting this lovely flower whom I loved more than life? Now, what was also incredible was this beautiful woman wanted to meet me; and I had dreamed about her since I was ten years old. Actually, I had kept myself pure for her; and that was all I wanted to tell her. For some strange reason, this was imperative to communicate; and she needed to hear this confession.

Absently watching the sun peek over the high roof of the white and gold Temple, I counted the hours I would be free from any duties until midnight when I had night watch at an obscure back gate here at Herod's Palace. This gave me the entire afternoon and most of the evening with the girl I was confident I could not live without. This had to be the blooming of what the Greeks called *eros,* for I could not think of anything other than Messina. Nothing could be more exciting than meeting this lovely creature in just a few more hours. How much time I would have with her I had no idea. I realized the few hours before we met at noon would drag slowly; but, once we were together, time would melt away like wax on a hot rock.

"What are we going to do about our falcata?" asked Amcheck standing behind me at the parapet of the palace in the center of Jerusalem. He must have followed me up here this early morning.

"What do you mean? And what are you doing up here?" I asked being a little distraught, for I wanted this moment to last a bit longer.

"It is going to be a hot day and too hot to hide our sword under a cloak. Saben gave us strict orders when outside these walls not to look like soldiers. How then are you going to hide our sword?"

"I have not thought about it. What do you suggest? And it is 'my' sword, not 'our' sword. When are you going to learn to speak Aramaic correctly?"

"Bad habits are hard to break. Now back to important items. I would want our sword with us if that nasty, little brick-like Lavo Stick were looking for me. But, if you had your throwing knives, we should not worry."

"Good idea. I will have my two knives with me."

"How are you going to conceal two knives wearing only a tunic?"

"I do not know. I'll just take one and keep it hidden in my hand."

"Maybe we can rig a scabbard to your back; and all you would have to do is reach back, and you would have a dagger in hand."

"Maybe I don't need any weapons."

"We are in love," said Amcheck turning his head as he made retching noises. I punched him in the shoulder, but he only groaned louder in his uncouth and rude humor. I walked away from him to obtain some food before my noon meeting.

I had been right; the hours did drag painfully by. When I did leave the Hasmonaean Palace, the name Herod Antipas preferred over Herod's Palace because the former name gave more legitimacy to Herod, I still had some time to slay before the appointed hour neared. The Hasmonaean Palace was located in the center of the walled city directly behind the Temple complex and a little south of the Castle of Antonia. The Jewish Hasmonaean Dynasty had ruled all of *Palestina* mainly from this Jerusalem palace long before Antipas's father, Herod the Great, was even king. The political situation in Jerusalem, well known by the mercenaries and most Jerusalemites, was that Pontius Pilate and Herod Antipas were at enmity with each other. Herod Antipas's authority in Jerusalem was only at the behest of Rome. Peraea and Galilee were Herod Antipas's specific domains of rulership, not Jerusalem. If Herod had any power outside his lavish, palatial palace, then we mercenaries could roam the streets of Jerusalem openly in our uniforms. Having two powerful men in the same city was a problem. I guess that the Hasmonaean Palace was at the center of what antagonized the Roman governor of Judaea. Here was Herod, a pseudo-king with no power in a capital city; but, still, he controlled the largest estate in Jerusalem. Pilate, on the other hand, stayed in a fort; yet, his soldiers openly roamed the streets and guarded all the gates to the city, which revealed who had the real power in Jerusalem. Besides these humiliations heaped upon Herod by Pilate, the tetrarch had something

Pilate did not, that being Herodias. Herod's queen was a stunning beauty, and Herodias made all the necessary courtly decisions, which might not seem significant, but gave Herod Antipas the appearance of an established king. Pilate had a wife, but she was not the asset Herodias was to Herod. In all the little but essential ways, Herodias was an influential political strategist in the same way, Claudia had been for my father. Pilate's wife, also named Claudia, tried to help her husband only once that I am aware of. It pertained to Pilate's most important decision as a Roman governor, and he ignored her counsel. However, to be fair, Herod Antipas once listened to his wife; and it resulted in his most celebrated disaster.

After I had left Herod's Hasmonaean Palace, I strolled towards the Castle of Antonia, Pontius Pilate's Jerusalem fort-*domus*. Shortly before leaving Herod's Palace, I learned from Amcheck that Herod and Herodias were not coming to Jerusalem this Passover. With the absence of Herod in Jerusalem this Passover, there would not be any significant, antagonistic struggles between Rome and the mercenaries who guarded the Hasmonaean Palace. This one thought was on my mind as I noticed the tall western walls of the Temple area. I suddenly realized all the political doings in Jerusalem were nothing more than phlebotomy, the opening of a vein for medical reasons. Since I was out of uniform, I was able to wander slowly in the streets of Jerusalem without any open hostility from legionaries. I had decided to take only one throwing knife and had it tied to my waist open for view, but I really did not care who saw it. To any observer, it looked like a simple *pugio*, a small nonmilitary dagger. To look less military, I had borrowed a pair of sandals from a freedman who worked in the kitchen at Herod's Palace and had large feet. It wasn't until I reached the western walls of the Temple that I noticed my legs below the knee were actually whiter than my knees. I had not received any sun on my lower legs because of my boots. I always knew I had nice-looking calf muscles, but I was hoping that the no-sun-colored portion of my lower legs would not cause Messina to laugh at me. I also made sure I had not had any *garum* since yesterday morning. I had even rinsed my mouth with a little perfume I purchased yesterday just to be careful concerning my breath. After I had turned northward walking along with the high walls to my right, I thought I resembled a Greek more than any other nationality because of my clothing. I had on a newly purchased tan-colored tunic, which I bought yesterday after I left the wine shop with Amcheck. It was almost the same color I wore the last time I met Messina at my father's villa in Rome. Tied around my head holding back my long hair was a matching tan cloth. I ashamedly realized I looked like Demos on the morning I disarmed him of his dagger and threw it into the sea.

With that thought, I quickly removed the headband. Now, instead of looking like an Athenian, I appeared more like a Spartan *hippie* out of uniform with my long hair hanging over my shoulders and a trimmed beard. Actually, my beard was much shorter today than yesterday when I first saw Messina out in the exercise yard at the Hasmonaean Palace. The same freedman-cook, from whom I borrowed the sandals this morning, gave me a beard trim and did some cutting on my hair for one silver *denarius*. The cook used one of my daggers and layered my hair into different lengths, which the Freedman called "the feathered look." With the tan headband gone, my long, flowing hair fell cascading with various lengths, which I thought could someday become a new fashion in Rome. There was not much I could do to hide the swollen, black and blue bruise spreading from my left shoulder down to my elbow. I just let my arm hang stiffly at my side, for it was now almost useless. The only comfort it gave me was the knowledge that Marius's face had to look worse than my arm.

When I reached the open, square-shaped *agora* before the Roman fort, I noticed legionaries looking from the highest step on top of the wide stairs that led up to what had to be Rock Hill and the Castle of Antonia. Around my feet were dark stains on the pavement stones from yesterday's slaughter of several hundred defenseless Jews. I did not linger in this area but continued through the *agora* and circled north past the Roman fortress. I now moved quickly, not wanting to be attacked by any Jews thinking I was a Roman out of uniform. After I was out of the *agora*, I realized no Roman soldier would have long, feathered hair and a beard. To my delight, no one in the streets or the small *agora* in front of the Castle of Antonia had bothered me. Yet, I did notice from the corner towers beady-eyed soldiers looking down at everyone including me.

Not far past the Fort of Antonia, I spotted the Sheep Gate that led out of the city to the north. Several Roman legionaries were standing around its open throat in a relaxed state pretending they were guarding the Sheep Gate just because they were there. All of them eyed me as I passed through before snickering to one another. I am sure my clothing did not match with the rest of my looks. The soldiers' scrutiny of me confirmed I was not fooling anyone. It must have been obvious I was some kind of a foreign soldier out of uniform, most likely a mercenary working for Herod Antipas. The tunic could not hide the white legs, trimmed beard, long hair, a *pugio* in my belt, a sword scar on my right forearm, another scar under my left eye, and the swollen and bruised left arm. I wished I could have worn a long cloak, but I would have looked ridiculous wearing one on such a hot day.

Directly behind the Castle of Antonia and just outside the Sheep Gate was the Sheep Market containing thousands of sheep and lambs, all crowded in pens with buyers shouting out prices and pointing fingers to the ones they wanted to sacrifice. I wondered how this Jewish money operation was operating on a Sabbath until I realized religion can justify anything. With Nisan 14, the date of Passover, only a few days away, there was a need for thousands of people to obtain a lamb for sacrifice as well as for their Passover meal. Inspection and purchasing thousands of baby sheep could not be stopped even on the Sabbath. I dismissed this Jewish sham and placed my thoughts back onto Messina; but, still, I had to keep a sharp eye out for Lentulus or Marius just in case this was a trap. With that last thought, I began wishing I had both throwing knives instead of one.

Up ahead were the two pools of Bethesda, which were situated beyond the walls of Jerusalem towards the north. These ancient founts of water were not far from the Sheep Gate and the location of my meeting with Messina. The Jews referred to these two adjacent pools as the Bethesda Pools. The two reservoirs provided much-needed water for the city and were only a stone's throw from the Sheep Market. Another stone's throw from the pools and to the north was the last high up-crop where the Romans crucified their condemned men. There was no activity going on at what the locals called Golgotha since it was a Sabbath.

One pool was contained inside a building while the other was open to the elements. Both were called the pools of Bethzatha or Bethesda in Hebrew. When Messina spoke with Amcheck, she had given the Greek pronunciation *Bethzatha* for the two reservoirs but one name. Unlike pools in bathhouses, these reservoirs were not for swimming. These water-storage cisterns were for only drinking and washing purposes. All the land from Africa to Syria and on towards Babylon is dry and arid. Water is a precious commodity, and the pools of Bethesda were water-storage retainers for the people of Jerusalem. The Jerusalemites had several other water sources available to them located around the city including a couple of minor springs and rain-supplied pools. The main ones were the Israel Pool not far from these pools; and, on the other side of the city located in the City of David, was the famous Pool of Siloam. Actually, Amcheck and I passed the Pool of Siloam every time we went to our private wine shop. Since Jerusalem is a strategic city with tens of thousands of residents living in these Judaean Hills, it is understandable why Pontius Pilate wanted an aqueduct bringing in fresh water to the Temple and the Castle of Antonia. To a Roman, there never is enough water coming into a Roman city. Civilization meant there had to be an abundant supply of water. Regarding Pilate's aqueduct, I heard one of Herod's mercenaries eating with Amcheck and me this very morning who said years ago, when Pilate was a young man, he had been a *questor* in Rome. A *questor* was a one-year elected term, and Pilate's responsibility for that one year was the upkeep of all aqueducts and water supplies coming into the Imperial capital. Perhaps his desire to build an aqueduct into Jerusalem was not as sinister as many Jews believed but was a prudent project on his part. It should be understood that Rome wastes way over half of all the water piped into Rome by aqueducts. The overflow is believed to be necessary to keep the sewers flowing freely into the Tiber. I think it is a typical Roman attitude that one purpose of the Empire is to construct every city within its vast control into a mirror image of its capital: buildings of permanence, triumphal arches, fountains, bathhouses, circuses, and gladiatorial arenas. The more water a city wasted was a sign of its success. Only when there is more water than a town needs, then Rome is happy; and I am sure this is all part of the spirit of wastefulness that is synonymous with the mindset of most Romans. They waste food, money, human lives, and every luxury thinkable. Why the God of the Universe allows such wastefulness to continue is beyond my comprehension. Conceivably, there must be bigger issues on the Creator's plate than the wasting of water; and maybe the Romans understand this just like they do bloodletting.

The problem with the new aqueduct at Jerusalem was the Roman governor's creative and clever way of financing its construction. Unfortunately, the deaths of hundreds yesterday are part of the bloodletting that Rome thinks accompanies progress. Still, this phlebotomy of Pilate is just another mark against his unpopular acts as governor of Judaea and places a wedge between him and Herod Antipas, who really wants his domain of Judaea. Besides being a callous way of dealing with a problem, killing hundreds of taxpayers was not a brilliant tactic on any empire's agenda; and I wondered whether anyone besides me thought of Pilate's action yesterday in this light? Unfortunately, life is cheap in the Empire of Blood, especially if you are a non-citizen. In the end, once the aqueduct becomes operational, Jerusalem will have more water than it needs; and the people in the upcoming days will become thankful forgetting the protests and bloodshed. Jerusalemites in time will become like all inhabitants of the Blood of Empires; they will take their new water source for granted only because they will enjoy its benefits. Moreover, in a few years, all their protesting and loss of blood would have seemed pointless even though yesterday many more Jews were surely willing to sacrifice their lives for what they perceived to be an insult to their God. The character of a person usually can be observed by the fruits in his or her life. If these Jerusalemites standing up for Yahweh really understood who He is as revealed in His Word, they would not have protested the funding of this project with Temple funds. If they only spent a little time musing over the Scriptures, I am sure they would cease their complaining about water projects or the stealing from the Temple treasury. Why would the God of the Universe not want the people of His Temple-city to have water?

One final note concerning water in the Empire: The water carriers, those who transported water from fountains or pools to their homes and businesses, were primarily women. The long-standing tradition of water carrying was a woman's job. The female population fetched water using clay vessels and transported the water typically by supporting the clay pots on their heads. The water they carried was for their families' drinking needs, bathing, and other cleaning purposes. The only males seen in Jerusalem carrying water were slaves working for the Levites at the Temple, for the very wealthy, or at public facilities such as boarding houses. For a man other than a slave to carry water was a sign that man was somehow effeminate. Therefore, a male carrying a pot of water in Jerusalem was always assumed to be a slave working for the Sadducees or some wealthy slave owner. And it should be understood, until the Pilate aqueduct was completed, hundreds of male slaves were always moving in and out of the two pools of Bethesda because much water was needed to clean the bloody mess where sacrificing was occurring all day long seven days a week. When I approached the Pools of Bethesda, I did not see the familiar line of slaves or females transporting water to the Temple area. Perhaps the new aqueduct was now operational and a success that most Jerusalemites did not want to admit.

This noon was the first time I actually visited these pools. What I noticed was the two holding ponds were rectangular shapes that were cut from solid rock, apparently hundreds of years ago. In this Semitic world, any new change from the past was considered sinful. "What was good for the patriarchs is good for us" was the rationale before Rome arrived and tried to change the way things worked for centuries past. Looking at the one pool that stood outside without cover, I concluded it had to be a rain-filled cistern. The second pool that was covered with a roof and walls appeared to be spring fed because the color of the water was different from the open reservoir. The ceiling of the second pool had five stone masonry arches forming five corresponding porticoes. Several dozen stone pillars in the porch area held up the high arched roof with air and light vents at the top running along the four walls.

The rain-filled pool was fifty-some feet in length and maybe twelve feet in width. It was accessed by steep steps that proceeded one another in a serpentine fashion around the pool until the steps could not be seen because of the depth of the water. When there had been an abundance of rain during the winter, there would only be a few steps to be seen. During a long spell of dry weather, then one had to circle down to the lower water level by using over a dozen or so steps. When the water level was low, I concluded that it had to be a slow process with many waiting in line as each person had to circle down and then back up before another could take his or her place. I had noticed a few innovative foreigners using ropes and lowering wooden buckets down and pulling them up after they were filled. However, I did not see any females using the line method. I assume traditions are hard to break.

The covered, spring-fed pool was about the same width as the rain-filled pool but about ten feet longer with the water appearing cleaner and fresher. On this spring day, the spring-fed pool happened to be filled with twice the quantity of the open-air pool; and the water was near the edge of the flagstone patio area. Just this morning, Amcheck had shared an interesting story associated with the spring-fed pool. He said the pool was agitated at different times during uncertain seasons from deep underground; and, when this agitation occurred, it emitted a ruddy color that arose from below towards the surface. He saw it happen once years ago and offered his opinion that the Earth's blood was rising from the underworld when he witnessed the water turning a bloody color. The Jews, however, claimed an invisible being or perhaps the Angel of the Lord caused it. This red color, according to widespread belief, was blood; and, when it was stirred, any sick person could be healed if they directly entered into the water and baptized themselves. The story went that the healing occurred only for the first person who entered the water, and there was always a rush whenever the water appeared to be stirred and was turning red.

When I entered the covered area, true to Amcheck's description, I noticed dozens of disabled people lying on mats and stretchers along the four edges of the pool waiting for their chance to be healed. Now I had a story for Amcheck tonight when he wanted to know all the details about my visit with Messina. Strangely, it reminded me of Tiberius Island in the middle of the Tiber River dedicated to the healing god Aesculapius. I had a slight shiver run down my back as I reminisced about waiting for Zeno in the bushes and watching the sick, all waiting for some kind of restoration from their god of healing. For a brief moment, I stood trying to bury the vile feelings seeping back causing that old bile friend to rise up into my throat. The past always appears to be waiting in the wings to spring onto the stage in my life. It seems, whenever possible, these thoughts take on a life of their own to disturb my mind as well as my spirit. Since my past was mostly unpleasant, it did not take much to throw me into an agitated state and for me to retaliate by throwing verbal rocks from my proverbial "ugly bag" towards anyone in my presence. I had concluded that I was not a pleasant person to be around at those times, and perhaps this was why I did not have many friends. I began to worry I would fall into one of those phases today and drive Messina away if she witnessed me in such a state. I stood just a few steps into the enclosed pool area and lowered my head. I felt a burning need to have a quick personal talk with Yahweh. I silently spoke to the God of Israel asking for assistance. I also requested that I wouldn't drive Messina away by my unpredictable behavior. After I had lifted my head, I felt better and more at peace with myself. I knew this meant I still had faith in Yahweh. Why would I speak to the Creator unless I believed He would listen to my prayer? There was always another voice in my head telling me it was ridiculous to even think the Creator cared, let alone listened to my thoughts. That voice I always tried to ignore.

I continued in and started moving in between the sick and infirmed. Putting all these thoughts behind me, I scanned the area for Messina. Finally, I spotted a woman sitting alone on a stone bench in the far corner in the back looking at me. I had missed her at first because she was dressed like all the other women scurrying around drawing water. She was wearing simple peasant garb. I was expecting her to be wearing that tantalizing blue *stola* she had worn the previous day; that image was forever engraved in my mind. Her head and face were partially covered with a headscarf, and I realized she was in disguise more so than I was. She had the most radiant smile when our eyes met, and I could see only white teeth and the two deep dimples. At that instant, her face seemed haloed by a shaft of noon sunlight coming in from one of the vents in the ceiling. The light came and went because of a cloud that must have passed in front of the sun. To my eyes, she was breathtakingly beautiful even in her simple peasant clothing. I had searched again for any sign of danger before I rounded the spring-fed pool with the cripples lined up on all sides. Satisfied we were safe, I slowly walked towards her. She remained where she was patiently waiting for me. "Hello, Venu," she said with such a sweet voice once I reached her stone bench.

"Messina, it is wonderful to see you," I said almost shyly.

"Please sit with me," she said making it a gratifying command while she moved a little for me to sit beside her on the bench. After she had moved to her right, I wondered if it were so she would not have to look at my scar on the other side of my face. I did not know if that was why she moved to her right instead of her left, but I sat without question discarding that thought.

I am sure, if she did it for that reason, it was to be kind to me, not because it repulsed her. There was not much room when I sat, and our legs touched. I could smell her perfume, a faint, sweet fragrance that was imported from the lower tip of India known as the Kingdom of Chola; and the aroma was out of place for her disguise. I recognized it as one of the costliest fragrances in the world. It was then I remembered one of the richest women in the Empire was sitting next to me. She looked at me with a smile as I grinned like a foolish child. I wanted to touch her hand and feel her warmth, but I knew nothing about women and felt this would be too forward.

"How much time do we have?" I finally asked with my eyes once again scanning the pool area like Felix the Praetorian constantly did in the tavern in the *Urbs* of Rome.

"Not long, and I have a great deal to tell you."

"You begin, and I will hearken to every word," I said listening to her voice, which for some reason reminded me of a gentle stream gurgling melodically in a thick mountain forest in springtime.

"I want you to ask your questions first. I am sure you have many questions before I tell you what I must."

"I do have many questions. I will ask only one to start, for I do want to hear what you have to say."

"Splendid idea," she suggested glancing momentarily away looking like a bird that moves its head around scanning for danger before it pecks the ground for a bit of food. "We shall start with your question."

I realized that what we were doing, meeting in public like this, was very dangerous. "Did my letter reach Athens?"

"I sent it but not by the way you had intended."

"That vermin oarsman!" I hissed.

"No, Venu, it was not his fault."

"What do you mean it was not his fault? Maybe you should tell me everything since I last saw you in Rome."

She looked around again maybe fearing that maybe Lentulus or Marius had followed her. This time she took my hand and pulled it from my lap to rest between our touching legs. "Yes, I will tell you what happened once you and Eli escaped."

"Excellent point to start," I said gazing into her amazing azure eyes that astounded me whenever I stared deep into those pools of blue.

Sensing my long stare, she looked down; perhaps she was just thinking of that dark, rainy night. After a brief pause, she looked up and off at some invisible spot to her left. "Well, madness does not come close to describing what it was like – that is, once you and Eli escaped over the back wall. It was complete pandemonium."

I loved the way she spoke; her Greek was precise and showed a highly trained mind, something rare in a woman. She used the aorist tense, or as I called it the frozen-in-time tense, and then switched into the perfect tense focusing on the completion of the action as a certainty of the existing fact. When she used the indefinite pronoun when referring to me, she was calling attention to my actions as acceptable and not wrong in nature. Only a Greek scholar at the Lyceum or the Academy in Athens would understand her usage of Greek to communicate that there was no condemnation of anything I did to Claudia, my father, and Marius or of anything else that occurred almost two years ago in Rome, the last time I saw her prior to yesterday. I could have sat there and conversed with Messina for hours. Here was someone who could honestly use this complicated language, perhaps the most sophisticated and precise language any human had ever used to write and speak to its fullest. There was no misunderstanding of what she meant, and I realized she chose to converse in Classical Greek over the *Kione* perhaps knowing I had attended the Lyceum and would understand the many intricacies of this somewhat-dead use of Greek.

"A surgeon was called, and he said Marius had to have his lower arm amputated. Claudia lay dead in the atrium, and your father was enraged like a wild boar with a spear in its side. Vengeance was in the air, especially when Senator Treverorum arrived at the senator's door with his son Demos. Apparently, there had been another man found dead out in the lane up to Esquiline Hill, which added to the confusion. Before long, your father gathered all he needed to know from Senator Treverorum about your arrival from Athens on the *Achilles*. Later that night the oarsman of the *Achilles* was brought to the villa by one of Senator Treverorum's soldier-guards and eventually told everything including your escape with Eli across the *Pons Sublicius* into the 14th District. I realized then I could not send the letter by the quickest route; besides, Lentulus booked passage to Athens aboard the *Achilles* evidently arriving there before any message could reach your teacher at the Lyceum. Lentulus along with several soldiers and *lictors* belonging to your father accompanied him since he was blinded in his left eye and in great pain with his crippled leg. Once Lentulus arrived in Athens, he went straight to the Lyceum. Apparently, they teach more than intellectual subjects at the Lyceum to their students. At least that is what Lentulus reported on his return to Rome. Back in Athens, Lentulus directed a search for a man your schoolmate Demos called the Spartan. He was the teacher you wanted me to send the letter to. After Senator Treverorum and his son had been speaking to your wounded father, I learned about your dagger incident with Demos on the first day of your trip to Rome. I had to smile; you are a creative and bold individual."

I sensed something missing from what she was telling me. I did not like the way she kept repeating Demos's name, especially using the definite article in Greek each time she mentioned his name. When someone uses this grammatical device, apparently he or she wants to point out someone, similar to pointing your index finger at a person for emphasis, each time the name is mentioned. Messina was making it very clear to me that Demos was someone special in this story even beyond my role that night in saving Eli. By using the Greek article before his name, indirectly she was declaring she wanted to show honor to Demos. Why was Messina making it as clear as a mountain lake what she thought of Demos? I remained silent and listened but was utterly baffled considering there were many other grammatical means she could have used when speaking about Demos.

Somewhere in the middle of her narrating, she seemed to sense my thoughts. Messina paused for a moment; then, when she continued talking, she stopped using this intended syntax regarding Demos's name. I said nothing; but, with the nod of my head, I encouraged her to continue. Once again, she looked around the crowded pool area before proceeding. "Well, you were not found in the 14th District; and Lentulus returned a few weeks later from Athens with very little. His knee was still swollen twice its normal size, and he has since used a walking stick to get around. Lentulus always complained after his return from Athens that his leg might have healed properly had he not traveled to Athens so soon after it was injured. This I do not know; but he hates you, Venu."

"Tell me what he discovered after he returned from Athens."

"What he learned was that you did attend the Lyceum for some years and lived with a priest named Hector, who served Athena Nike up on the Acropolis. This priest was never found; and, in retaliation for his sudden disappearance, Lentulus had his soldiers torch his home with fire. I guess this Hector, as well as the Spartan teacher at the Lyceum, must have been warned somehow before Lentulus's arrival and had gone into hiding."

"Hector is a very perceptive man," I said to concur with her conclusion. Still, I was wondering if the Carnalus scroll survived the house burning. I was hoping it survived since it was in the bottom corner of my room surrounded by inflammable stones. "I am sure Hector left the city and is in hiding along with Eli's uncle. "What about the teacher Demos spoke of?"

"That I do not know. I believe your *didace*, too, was warned; and, as I said, he could not be found. Nevertheless, about four months after the return of Lentulus from Athens, a report arrived from Jerusalem about the death of Eli. One of your father's agents identified Eli after he was slain here at the Jewish Temple. I must warn you; many men are looking for you, besides Lentulus and Marius."

"My father has agents here in Jerusalem?" I asked with ignorance written on my face as well as my words; yet, I realized there had to be many looking for me.

"More agents than you would ever believe. By now thousands are looking for you all over the Empire. And now, more than ever. Most are converging here because of the discovery of Eli's death."

"Please finish your story," I said with some dread in my voice, which I could not hide.

"Your father ordered Marius and Lentulus back to Jerusalem believing the story Eli was with you when he was murdered. I was instructed by your father to accompany both men since I was the one who had the best look at you when I opened the door that stormy night."

"The night Claudia was killed," I mumbled.

"Yes. I agreed to accompany Marius and Mayus secretly thinking I might possibly protect you. Once we arrived here, Lentulus and Marius began searching all the Roman legionaries and axillaries located at Caesarea. Having no success, we moved on to the mercenaries of Herod; and that was the reason for being at the Hasmonaean Palace yesterday."

"Why search military installations?" I asked being somewhat confused.

"The day Eli was murdered near the Temple of Yahweh someone fitting your description was wearing military boots. That was also all that Marius remembered the night he saw you at the door of your father's villa. Even Lentulus remembered the boots when you kicked his knee out of its socket. I did not define your boots. All I remember you wearing was a wet purple lamb's wool cloak. I did not notice your footwear, but Marius and Mayus obviously did. There was also a story of the man who killed Eli being murdered the same day at the Temple complex by a man wearing high military boots."

"It is true. I was wearing military boots the night I rescued Eli."

"It looks as if you still wear high boots based on your lack of color on your legs."

Now I realized my mistake of just wearing the borrowed sandals. "What happened yesterday after the contest with Marius?"

"Yesterday was very close, but Lentulus and Marius believed me when I told them you were not the one. Tomorrow, before sunrise, we travel down towards the Poison Sea. After inspecting all the soldiers there, we will go to Jericho and then up to the Sea of Tiberius for more forts of Roman soldiers and Herod's mercenary guards. I will be gone for months, and I am not sure I will be back to Jerusalem."

This bit of information hit me like a collapsing wall. Messina was not going to be back. "This is not good news concerning you and me."

"This being the Sabbath I knew we would not be traveling. I risked all with the man holding your sword. My father always said, 'Only trust someone first before you let him hold your sword.' You must have trusted that man who held your sword. My intuition must have been correct because you are here, and I guess the man with the long scar on his face gave you my message." After Messina had mentioned the word "scar," she lowered her head in the way of shame.

"What is it, Messina; did I do something?"

"No, I'm sorry about the 'scar' comment," she said lightly touching her face under her own left eye. Now I understood why she moved to her right, and I looked away even though she could not actually see my scar under my left eye from where she was sitting.

"Please, Venu, your scar does not repulse me. It actually gives you character."

I looked back realizing I could not hide it, and I was going to have to live with it.

"If you did not have that scar, I believe Marius and Lentulus would have recognized you yesterday; and you most likely would be dead today. Maybe my God allowed it as a way of protecting you."

Feasibly she was right, but I could not say anything. The revelation that she was leaving Jerusalem to never return had sucked all my words and life out of me. I looked at her trying to memorize every line in her flawless face hoping I would not have an emotional breakdown in front of her or throw words at her from my ugly bag. Her eyes began to swim with compassion. "Venu, what is in your heart?" she finally asked sensing my lost and doomed state. The question demanded only the truth, and I gathered my thoughts before I spoke.

"I have missed you a long time; and this day is the happiest I have been in a long, long time." There was not much time, and I felt I had to throw all my "lots" by making my confession.

Messina turned away and lowered her eyes. I waited until she gazed back; and tears were pooling in her eyes, which prevented me from speaking. Finally, she spoke. "Venu, I can never see you again; that is why I wanted to meet you and tell you face to face."

"What are you talking about?" I demanded.

"Please! Keep your voice down," said Messina looking around to see if anyone was listening.

"What are you talking about?" I asked again but now in a quiet, controlled voice.

"I am engaged to be married when I return to Rome. I am not available for you. Besides, you are a wanted fugitive. You did... well, Claudia is dead; and there were witnesses."

"Who are you going to marry?" I said involuntarily releasing her hand and sliding slightly away from her on the bench. My heart crushed in upon itself, and the love that I had for her was now in jeopardy.

"Senator Treverorum's son."

"Demos? That slimy serpent? I will kill him!"

"No! Please do not talk like that Venu."

"Why him? Look at what he did to me," and I showed her the scar on my right arm and hand.

"And you did the same to Marius except you still have your arm and hand."

"What does that mean?" I demanded.

"Please, I did not come to argue. I really did not have to tell you, and I do not need your permission."

She stood to leave, but I took her slender arm. It was slight and delicate in my hand, and I tried not to hurt her. "You are right; but, before you leave my life, please tell me why you chose Demos?"

"Is it not obvious?"

"No, it is not obvious; it is the opposite!"

She sat back next to me leaning her back against the wall behind us realizing my ignorance.

"My father's inheritance will not transfer to me unless I am married. Your father controls it until then."

"This is all about money?"

"Do not be naive. Your father may be the richest man in the world, and my father was his partner in Asia. I cannot throw away my father's entire estate and his inheritance and just give it to your father."

"And you have chosen Demos?"

"He is not as bad as you think... but, yes, I have."

"Do you love him, Messina? Tell me the truth."

440

She lowered her head, began weeping into her hands, and said, "No, I love you, Venu."

"Then let us escape and get out of the Empire. We will go east as far as we can. We will be happy, maybe not rich; but we will be together."

"No, Venu, you will be hunted down; and I would only hasten the inevitable. The day Claudia died we both perished along with her. You just do not know it, but what I am saying is true. I am sorry; my mind is made up." She quickly left the bench and hurried out of the porch area and away from my life with no further words.

Messina's use of the grammatical article in front of Demos's name now came into focus, and I sat there dying from within. I could not have been more paralyzed if a viper had buried its poisoned fangs into my throat. I felt lonely and in a state of affliction beyond anything I had ever envisioned. In one moment of time, vexation in my heart totally engulfed me. My anguish seemed too much to bear. Every bone felt weak, and my strength drained as water evaporates in the heat of summer. I was like a piece of broken pottery, just an old, broken *ostracon* shard to be stepped on by anyone in any *agora* in any city in the *cosmos*. I slowly closed my eyes. I felt my heart pounding. The void I sensed was overwhelming. I desperately needed solace and relief from this disaster. I wanted to cry out for mercy to the One God, the Most High God of Israel; but I had no reason to have confidence any longer in Him. I knew instinctively I did not deserve any compassion even if the God of Israel were real. My transgressions and failings were too numerous. I felt unworthy. Mercy for me would forever remain a phantom into eternity. I absently stared at the pool thinking of stepping in and sinking while breathing water into my lungs as I dropped. I wanted to give up, and I distinctly heard an inner voice suggesting it would solve all my problems.

I was ready to do it when a hand rested on my shoulder. I looked up thinking maybe Marius or Lentulus had found me, but it was someone quite the opposite. It was the teacher from the Temple, the tall man with the skin of burnished bronze, wavy hair to his shoulders, and a hawkish-beaked nose. It was the kind man who had talked to Eli and me in the porch area behind Herod's Temple calling himself *Christos*. My thoughts changed instantly, and I felt a new tension that seemed to be palpably arising from somewhere deep within my being. I looked out towards all the sick and paralyzed in the covered portion of the pool area. They all seemed gripped by the same despairing needs I was just experiencing; yet, none of them was giving up like me. How could they endure their horrible physical needs for years and I could not bear my mental anguish for just a few moments? I desperately needed to be rescued, not from a physical problem, but a mental pit of thick darkness that had invaded and penetrated my soul and spirit, like drinking from a poisoned river.

"Do not choose the death of this world," the man said in Aramaic, with a Galilean twang in his inflection.

"What did you say?" I asked surprised by what I thought I heard.

Standing next to the teacher and also wearing a simple homespun robe was a young man about my age or younger. He stood a little behind and looked to be either a slave or a student. I figured the latter. The teacher's hand left my shoulder as I stood. The simple man picked up a carefully folded, purple-scarlet garment from the stone bench. Messina must have been sitting on it, for it was where she had been only moments ago.

He slowly faced me and then held the garment out in both of his hands for me to examine. "This is yours," he said without any doubt. I took it and studied the material. It had been two years now since I saw this cloak. I had given the scarlet-purple *chlamys* to Messina on the night I killed Claudia. She must have brought it to the pool to give it back to me.

"I do not want it; you can have it," I said handing it back to him after I realized it was mine.

His right hand stroked the top of the folded material, but he did not take it. A slight smile appeared; and he said, "A beautiful purple cloak fit for a king. The curtain that separates the Holy of Holies from the Holy Place in the Temple is the same hue as this cloak."

I thought this an odd thing to say since only the Levitical priests were allowed into the Temple, and this man undoubtedly was not a priest. Not wanting to argue, I repeated, "No, I do not deserve such a cloak; you take it. Perhaps you'll need it."

"I will borrow it later; you will keep it until that day," he said as he pulled his hand back from the folded cloak. I looked over the thick cloth in my hands remembering its familiar texture and smell. I looked up at this enigmatic man and asked, "Who are you? You seem to be much more than a teacher."

"I believe I have already told you. Who do you say that I am?"

I stood thinking for what seemed a long time before I answered with what was in my heart. My response was not diversionary even though I did not respond to what was precisely asked. "I wanted to find John the Baptist and ask him who he is, but now he is in prison. And now you are asking me who you are?"

"There is yet time to visit him. When you do, tell him something for me."

"How do you think I will visit him?" I asked somewhat confused, but he did not answer. I began to wonder if he knew I worked for the one who had imprisoned the Baptist. Yet, there he stood convinced I was going to converse with the desert preacher. I decided to humor him. "What do I say to him?"

He cocked his head slightly perhaps to tell me he knew I was not serious. Yet, he began to speak very earnestly. "Tell him the Kingdom of Heaven is being preached, and the sick are being healed; I raise the dead, the lepers are being cleansed, and demons are being cast out of the afflicted."

I hung my head as a great dread passed over me as I whispered, "The Kingdom of Heaven?"

"What is it that overwhelms you?"

"My wicked behavior from the past," I confessed. "I have lost everything because of my sins."

"A man can have remorse over his deeds and even destroy his own life over what he has done, but that is not true repentance. To turn away and sin no more – that is repentance. That is the message John preached, and that is what he will tell you when you visit him. Nevertheless, I tell you a day will come after the Son of Man has been lifted up and exalted; then you will understand true repentance. Then you will accept the forgiveness given freely from Heaven for all your sins."

"All my sins?" I asked secretly thinking this was incredible.

"All your sins – even if you were to strike the face of God."

"How can a man be forgiven for such a blasphemy even if it were possible?" I asked.

"What is impossible for man is possible for God. Now let me ask you a question."

I nodded as he gently waved for his lone disciple to come to the bench where I was standing. Looking back at me with the disciple next to him and not blocking my view of all the people around the pool waiting for the water to stir, he asked, "Is this the Sabbath?"

"Yes."

"What is the Sabbath?"

"The day God rested from all His creation work at the beginning of time."

He nodded slightly indicating I was correct. "What is wrong with the creation as we speak?"

"It is broken, ill, wounded. Evil permeates everything and spreads like a gangrene into all living flesh."

"Well spoken. Is it lawful under the law to work on the Sabbath?"

"No, it still is a day of rest."

"What do you see before you lined up around this pool?"

"Broken, sick, and wounded people waiting to be healed by the stirring of the water."

"But why are they here on the Sabbath if this is the day of rest? Would they not have to work to roll or step into the water if it were stirred?"

"I do not know; I guess you would have to ask them." It was no secret that this man before me had caused great debates with the Pharisees and others by openly and flagrantly performing healings and works on the Sabbath. This teacher perplexed me; and, yet, despite his complexities, he seemed to have a balance of character like no other man. Although this had to be the man who was accused of violating the Sabbath, he never apologized for anything. He never admitted a mistake or showed any type of remorse. He never exhibited any consciousness of guilt. People would discuss that he was a man of contrasts. He was severe with the Pharisees and Scribes and, yet, tender with the lowest classes of society. His teachings were profound and, yet, simple. Even small children were attracted to him. Those who knew him said he seemed meek and lowly and, yet, poised with confidence and intolerant of injustice. I struggled to understand, and I pondered what gave him the right to be the way he was.

"Why should I ask them?" he returned with my question back to me.

"Because they are the ones who believe getting into the water may heal them. Perhaps they believe in mercy even on the day of rest."

"And you, too, thought getting into the water would solve your problems."

How did he know what I had been thinking? No man knows another man's thoughts. This man was either from God or the kingdom of darkness. I needed to change the subject, or my mind would rip to shreds. "Do you remember me from the Temple?"

He nodded ever so slightly; his dark, penetrating eyes with the rainbow edging along the irises showed me he did remember.

"My friend is now dead, murdered at the north gate of the Temple, while I waited to sacrifice for my sins."

"I know; but he shall rise again, for he had faith in the coming Redeemer."

"He will what?" I asked not comprehending his statement because of his certainty of what he was saying.

"He who believes in me shall live even if he dies, and everyone who lives and believes in me shall never die. Do you believe this?"

"Who are you that I should believe?"

He did not answer but only turned away towards the pool. I just stood there holding the folded Spartan cloak. Watching him move to the edge of the water, I decided to follow. The Galilean began to speak perfect Hebrew to a man lying on a stretcher next to the water. "Do you wish to get well?"

The man on the pallet said, "Sir, I have no man to put me into the pool when the water is stirred up; but, while I am coming, another steps down before me."

"Arise, take up your pallet, and walk," ordered the teacher; and immediately the man obeyed. He stood as if he had been able to walk his entire life and had been faking illness all these years. The healed man was amazed as shown by the elated expression on his face. This was actually happening; I was witnessing a miracle. The man stood and bent down to pick up his pallet. Tucking it under his arm, he began walking away. One woman nearby started screaming that the man was healed. Others turned to see and gasped.

A Pharisee began to explode with a stream of vile words at the healed man telling him it was a sin to carry a pallet on the Sabbath. "Who do you think you are?" the Pharisee screamed at the top of his lungs.

I looked back at the teacher and his disciple, but they were nowhere to be seen. Both had slipped out of the pool area unnoticed. I wanted to find them; but, instead, I ran over to the man carrying the pallet.

"Sir, how long has your sickness been with you?"

He looked over at me and answered with a broad smile. "Thirty-eight years, and now I can walk. Do you see? Who was that man who healed me? You were talking to him before he healed me."

"How did you... well, become... 38 years ago?" I asked mumbling in Hebrew.

"It was shortly after I was born. I was pulled from my mother who told me soldiers of Herod the Great tried to kill all the infants and children under the age of two including me because Herod thought the Messiah had been born in Bethlehem. I am from the tribe of Judah from Bethlehem. I survived, but maybe twenty others were not as fortunate on that day. I have been crippled since the mercenary's sword entered my back. But now I can walk." He smiled, and it was beyond being ecstatic or even rapturous. "Do you know the man's name?"

"I do not know his name; but after today, I'm sure the entire city will know who he is. All I know is his title, which is *Christos*."

"*Christos*, is that not Greek for Messiah? Yes, in Hebrew the word is Messiah the same as the Greek word *Christos*. I cannot believe it. I have been crippled 38 years all because of the birth of the Messiah, and the Messiah just healed me – today on a Sabbath. Is that not amazing?" The man turned away with emotional excitement written on his face that was beyond a state of obliviousness while more Pharisees were yelling at him because he was still carrying his pallet on the Sabbath. I walked up to the first Pharisee who condemned the healed man and thought of Eyebrows. With a hard shove to the shoulder, the Pharisee almost fell into the pool. "Let the man alone! Do not spit on a work of God!"

I wandered out of the pool area walking back towards the Sheep Market. I began to wonder why the Pharisee wasn't yelling at the Levites for selling lambs and sheep on the Sabbath. I began to equate Pharisees with the word *hypocrite*, the Greek word for actor. That is what the entire bunch of them appeared to be. I turned away from the Sheep Gate and walked away from the city. I crossed down into the Kidron Valley and then climbed up to the quiet garden halfway up the Mount of Olives where Eli and I stayed when we first arrived here in Jerusalem. I was thoroughly baffled. I could not stop wondering if the Galilean just healed the man to show me who he was or whether there was more to the healing. I did not understand. I stayed until sunset, the time the Sabbath was officially over. Returning to the barracks, I put away the purple cloak into the red bag that was inside the secret hole that held the 33 Psalms and all my money. I then curled up on my cot and fell into a deep sleep.

Shortly before midnight, Amcheck shook me awake for guard duty. He wanted to know what happened, but I told him I could not talk about it except that it had not gone well with Messina. He seemed to understand and was about to leave the room when he stopped and turned back. "Did you hear about the healing of the lame man today at the pool of Bethzatha?"

"Yes, I was there and saw it. Does anyone know the healer's name?"

"The Romans are calling him Jesus, which means the one who saves. Jesus is Latin for Yeshua. Yeshua is the same as Joshua. Both share the same name. Joshua, you see, was the prophet of old after Moses, the one who led the Children of Israel into the Promised Land when they crossed the Jordan River. Maybe this Jesus thinks he is going to do the same except the Jews are already in the Promised Land. Maybe Jesus is going to force the Romans out and kill all of Herod's mercenaries."

I was not entirely listening to Amcheck but immediately recalled the story the Roman soldier Felix told me along with the one Anab, Eli's uncle, also related to me. Both talked about the Promised One. Could this Jesus be the one who cut down the sandalwood trees in Felix's story? Maybe he was the Promised One who my mother said was coming to save the world from its crippling ills. I began to repeat his words in my mind not wanting to forget. Even the pain of learning Messina was going to marry Demos began to fade as I spent time memorizing the words of Jesus. Later, I wrote them down on papyrus and kept them rolled up in the leather tube with the 33-Psalms scroll. As time went on, I added many other sheets of papyrus about the deeds of Jesus into the leather tube. I wrote all the stories I heard regarding this one who saves and placed all the stories in the scroll case until it was almost impossible to put any more in.

That night, guarding a back gate until morning drills, I memorized each word I had heard the man speak. Before roll call, I told Amcheck I needed to talk to Herod's prisoner, John the Baptist. Amcheck had the broadest smile and then said, "Ole' Sicarius had already arranged a visit."

"What do you mean?" I asked in astonishment. "Is Herod coming to Jerusalem for the Passover and bringing John the Baptist in a cage?"

"No. I told you yesterday that Herod Antipas is not coming to Jerusalem this Passover. He has to stay in Machaerus because he has serious problems with King Aretas, the king of the Nabataeans, who lives in the rock city of Petra. But here is the secret information: tomorrow you and I leave for Machaerus, and we are to get there before the Passover begins at sunset on Mars Day."

"The Passover begins... what, two days from today?"

"That should give us plenty of time since we are riding horses. I hope that expensive school in Athens taught you how to ride a horse. Saben told me before drill that I am to travel to Machaerus and take you along with a special dispatch for Herod Antipas. Yes, I am also to take you along with me. Herod wants to talk to an eyewitness, someone who actually saw one of Jesus's miracles! That would be you. Once we deliver the dispatch, I am sure you can have a few moments with this holy desert man before we return here to Jerusalem."

"You told Saben I was at the pool of Bethzatha?"

"Of course, it is going to help our situation. But do not worry; I did not say anything about the girl."

"But when word gets out to Lentulus and Marius I was at the pool at the same time Messina was there, do you not think they will put the pieces together? I cannot believe you compromised me like this!"

"Worry not! If need be, we will arrange for those two *thags* to have an accident. There is no need to fear; death solves all problems."

Amcheck spun and marched off after slapping me on the shoulder, the same shoulder Jesus had touched only yesterday; but the feeling was entirely different.

A READING GIVEN AT THE GREAT LIBRARY OF ALEXANDRIA BY EPAPHRODITUS

Given in the year of the four emperors. During this year of civil war, the great fire broke out on Capitoline Hill destroying much of Rome's archives. Due to this loss, the scholars of Alexandria's Great Library requisitioned anyone with past knowledge to recreate the history of Rome. These short lectures were delivered on the afternoons of the first day of the week for a fee of 25 denarii. I have incorporated several lecture readings that I personally gave during this pivotal year for Rome and its Empire.   *69 AD*

COSMOS, ANGELS, AND THE KINGDOM OF HEAVEN

Rabbi Issachar, the librarian of Julius Caesar's Library in Rome and the head scholar of the synagogue in Rome located in the 14ᵗʰ District, told me an interesting story when I was a young man. I remember sitting in his little courtyard at his home as he explained the realm and subject of angels for my evaluation. Whether everything he told me was just his preconceptions from his Pharisaic point of view or not, this I cannot say. What I can say is that the Sadducee sect of Judaism does not even believe in the resurrection of the dead nor the existence of angels. In my long lifetime, I have had several experiences with what I could only explain as angels; yet, my personal experiences have not contradicted the Scriptures concerning this subject. Rabbi Issachar explicitly told me that angels were messengers of God created in two groups: one for praising the Creator at the Throne of Glory, and the second for executing His behests. The number of the praising angels was 694,000 myriads. Since a myriad is an infinite number, exactly how many angels exist is something no human could comprehend. The number of the ministering angels went beyond the number of praising angels. When I first heard this story in the rabbi's courtyard, it sounded like some kind of wild, magical way of thinking. However, Rabbi Issachar was in a sound state of mind when he said that humans were created in God's image. At this time in existence, we are a little lower than angels; yet, at the resurrection, some humans will be lifted higher than the angels because we will be judging angels. I still cannot wrap my thoughts around this fascinating concept. To think that God's greatest creation are humans is beyond my understanding.

Equally impressive in consideration was how one-third of the countless angels, using their free will, were all involved in a premeditated defection against Yahweh under the leadership of a chief angel known as Sammael-Satan-Azazel. I later learned that Azazel was a different fallen angel and not Satan. Azazel

448

was the evil one who taught men to fashion swords and shields. Azazel also taught women to beautify their eyelids and other activities that involved illicit sexual practices. I did remember reading a biblios at the Lyceum Library on the subject of angels that was written in Greek by a Jewish rabbi. I did not share this information with Rabbi Issachar when he was instructing me. Honestly, I did not really understand that much at the time; but the subject was very similar to what Rabbi Issachar was saying. I remember the biblios at the Lyceum explaining how both men and women in Egypt painted their eyelids blue outlining them with black and using dark red for their lips and nails, both fingers and toes. Perhaps this is one explanation why Joseph's brothers in the Jewish Scriptures did not recognize him when they came to him for food in Egypt. I know of no other culture other than the Luna women around the entire Empire who use an abundance of colors to paint the "windows to the soul" along with their mouths.

To the Jews, Azazel is the scapegoat released on the Day of Atonement ceremony described in the Torah. Rabbi Issachar said this evil angel also goes by Apollyon in Greek and Abaddon in Hebrew. I later read in another biblios on the same subject when I first made a visit to this Great Library here at Alexandria. I am sure this biblios still can be found in this esteemed library. That book stated that Apollyon or Abaddon is someone else other than Azazel or Satan.

One crucial piece of information said to me by Rabbi Issachar, which I have never been able to discount, was the meaning of Sam-el. This root word means poison, and El is Hebrew for God or messenger. This super-powerful poison-messenger is also referred to as the "dragon" or that "old serpent," which is referenced in the Scriptures as Satan. The ancient Barbarians known as the Aryans used the word deva, which means devil-god in Sanskrit. These Sanskrit speakers invaded over the Khyber Pass in the Hindu Kush Mountains over a thousand years ago. Deva and dragon are synonymous; and, in every culture, a dragon is merely a snake with legs. Eve, in the Jewish Scriptures, was the first human to fall to the deception of the serpent-dragon. In enters Satan; and the result is God cursing all serpents to no longer have legs and to crawl on their bellies in the dust, the very substance God used to create Adam at the beginning of the sixth day of creation. This is mentioned in the first book of the Torah, the first five scrolls by Moses, as found here at the library, the LXX, the Torah translated out of Hebrew into Greek.

One-third of the angelic hosts defect from God and follow their own desires and that of Satan. The creation of God is now under attack by a very evil power that controls earth and hell, and they even have access to the third heaven where the Father's Temple on a mountain exists. These fallen angels are superior in power and knowledge over humans in our present form, and many are still in the presence of God in the third heaven knowing Him personally. Yet, they rebelled in the far past. This is difficult to comprehend.

Knowing what I now understand, I can have some empathy for Adam and Eve for listening and following the lies of the appealing serpent. However, Adam and Eve were able to talk with the Creator every afternoon in the Garden of Eden back in the far past, which makes it hard for me to understand why the father and mother of humans decided to rebel against Yahweh. According to Rabbi Issachar, all humans coming through the seed of Adam are born in rebellion against God. We humans know nothing but rebellion to the Creator. To complicate this world beyond any intellectual capacity of man is the question: why do these evil forces called fallen angels or demons even desire to fight us? The only logical conclusion is these fallen ones want to possess our souls and spirits. Perhaps it is the spirits of the dead children of humans and the sons of God who need a body to control until their judgment comes. Maybe these are the demons. I believe some people are senseless and irrational in their minds and behavior without the evil forces being the cause; but I have also seen people under control of evil demons, and there is no question or doubt about who lives inside those that are controlled by these evil forces. Usually when a person is rational at one moment and then switches into someone else at the speed of a cracking whip, this is one sign of a demon-possessed person. Queen Herodias, wife of Herod Antipas, along with Claudia Pulchra Vetallus Varus, the woman who murdered my mother in cold blood many years ago in Rome, are two examples of people who had submitted to the influence of evil spirits. Both women were not only controlled at times by evil spirits, but also both wanted to be under the influence of these evil fallen beings. Using this knowledge of faith, people must realize that we cannot fight these demons with our own power. We genuinely come upon and struggle at times personally with these unseen forces, which come at us from high and invisible places. Once again, it takes an undetectable ability to understand all I am saying. It takes faith to believe that the unseen is real because this subject cannot be determined true or false by any of our physical senses such as touch, taste, smell, hearing, or sight. Only our minds can think and accept or not accept this reality as true or false. Only by faith can we even begin to understand the spiritual war we are fighting each and every day. Every human will lose the war of eternity if what I am saying is rejected even by faith.

When I first learned about the spiritual war we humans have to experience, at first it plagued me for many months and even years. Even as I speak to all of you present today, I feel the presence of the evil ones; and I have now known about them for almost forty years. On a human level, there is no hope for any man or woman, great or small. This war can only be won by faith in Yahweh. This is *why the patriarch Abraham is called a man of faith. He believed in Yahweh not even knowing at that time that the Creator's personal name was Yahweh. As the prophet, Habakkuk said, "The righteous shall live by his faith." There were times when Abraham lacked faith, which resulted in the birth of Ishmael through the woman Hagar. It wasn't until a miracle took place with the birth of Isaac through Abraham's wife Sarah when were both in their nineties that their faiths began to grow. Two thousand years later the Messiah was born through a greater miracle when he came by a virgin girl.*

It wasn't until I learned about the power and authority God will give us weak humans if we ask that I understood how to be fruitful and victorious. The first step is to believe and ask for this conquering spiritual power and authority over these evil ones, but this can only happen after someone by faith accepts the promised Messiah. We humans have no power or authority to wage war against these evil ones except through God and His name. The exciting news is God will not turn away from any human who has a sincere heart and wishes to be victorious with Him in this struggle. The second step is the use of the Messiah's name, which all things have to obey. Otherwise, how could lowly humans be champions over these invisible evil beings other than with God's help?

Rabbi Issachar told me that Adam was created out of the very dust that serpents must spend their lives crawling through. This is poetic justice since both Adam and Sam-el are considered sons of God. If God creates a sentient being, then that living entity is regarded as a son of God, may it be Adam or angels. Humans today are not children of God but are sons and daughters of men or, specifically, of Adam. The first book of the Scriptures speaks of an attempt to change this before the great flood when sons of God came to the daughters of men.

I asked Rabbi Issachar why Satan hates man and God to the degree he does. He answered that the ancient rabbis in Babylon wrote about this very issue even though the Scriptures are silent on much of what I am talking about. Rabbi Issachar explained it all started with one event at the beginning of time. After Adam had been created out of dust, God allowed Adam to name all the animals that Yahweh had placed in the Garden of Eden. Since this task was given to Adam and not the angelic sons of God, the rebellion thus started in Heaven at the Throne of Yahweh in His Holy Temple. Such a seemingly little concern apparently led to the colossal revolution that still rages in all three heavens: the first heaven being this world and where the birds fly, the second heaven being the space where the stars exist, and the third heaven is beyond the second heaven. The third heaven is also beyond the waters that surround the universe as stated in Scriptures when the waters were separated. Beyond the final band of water is where the Throne of Yahweh exists on a grand mountain in a Holy of Holies

Heavenly Temple. *The Temple in Jerusalem is just a mere model or copy of the one in the third heaven. The throne of Yahweh has a Holy of Holies in Heaven, and it is there where God has a throne called the Mercy Seat, just like the gold lid on the Ark of the Covenant is called the Mercy Seat.*

For truth to be understood, the Kingdom of God or Kingdom of Heaven is anywhere God rules. That could actually be in a human's heart living in the first heaven as long as that heart has not been turned over to the control of the evil ones. If it has been turned over to the Evil One, the name of Jesus of Nazareth can break the chains of bondage allowing the freed person to freely choose a new way, in a matter of speaking. Jesus of Nazareth once said to a crowd of religious leaders who were accusing him of being able to cast out devils through the god Beelzebub that, if he with the finger of God casts out devils, no doubt the Kingdom of God has come upon that person. I can think of no greater promise for everyone than that statement. Yet, let this be understood: wherever God rules, there also is the Kingdom of God. Therefore, if a fallen human allows the Creator to rule his or her body, spirit, and soul, then the Kingdom of God is present in that person even if that human lives in the first heaven of this world, which is still fallen under the control of Sam-el. It is all a matter of submitting to Yahweh and not one's fallen desires. Believing and obeying the Word of God is the first step towards eternal life with God.

Rabbi Issachar told me after I was circumcised and later after I dipped myself in the Tiber River south of Tiberius Island that, after the humans had been cast out of the Garden of Eden, the wicked angels festered a plan of iniquity to corrupt all humanity. However, to be successful, the humans had to break back into the Garden of Eden and capture the Tree of Life, chop it down, and then burn its wood. If they had eaten the fruit of this tree, they would still be alive today in the state of fallenness for eternity. God prevented this by stationing at the entrance to the garden mighty cherubim with flaming swords. What they did not understand was God had a different and even better plan for man since the woman was deceived in her rebellion by eating from the Tree of Knowledge of Good and Evil. The simplicity of Adam's sin was he was not deceived like the woman but, instead, chose to worship the woman and not Yahweh soon after she ate from the forbidden tree. When he ate the fruit that Eve had eaten, thus began the new measurement of a spiritual war between humans and Sammael, the father of lies, murder, hate, fear, and every evil we humans can imagine.

Sammael's plan was the re-establishment of an image of supremacy over the creation he once possessed before man was given the task of naming the animals. The Scriptures speak about the two trees and explicitly that man was forbidden to eat from the Tree of Knowledge of Good and Evil. The Tree of Knowledge of Good and Evil was a beautiful tree that was a delight to the eyes with fruit tasteful to the tongue and the fruit if eaten would make one wise to what God possessed. After Eve had eaten, she did have knowledge that only God possessed. But the woman was tricked in every area of her being by the serpent: that being her body, soul, and spirit all turning against Yahweh. This knowledge, which is all the knowledge a human can conceive, is still what occupies a man to the extreme; but it will never lead to eternal life. Since we humans are made of matter that cannot be destroyed, (I am speaking of our soul and spirit; yet, our flesh does die) we live on for eternity but in a different form after death. Test your own heart, and tell me if you do not know that you will live forever.

I am sure you will also agree with me that something must have gone very wrong with Sammael or the Dragon's scheme. After the first man had fallen from his former position, God left Heaven and entered the first heaven to speak face to face with Adam. In history from time to time, God enters this realm of time and speaks to us humans just as the Scriptures record, God in a human form conversing with Abraham, Jacob, Moses, Joshua, and others, clearly showing these chosen men and women his intentions regarding mankind and the angelic watchers. Not only did God communicate with people, but He also did so personally by entering this decomposing world now ruled by Sammael-Satan-the Dragon. However, how could God do this if He were all purity and goodness? Also, why would He do this? Why would He choose to walk among corrupted humankind even when Moses and later Joshua had to remove their sandals because they were on holy ground when they were speaking with and talking to Yahweh in His various manifestations? It all points to the premise that God has a particular plan for mankind for whom He obviously has a deep love. This enigma of a one-way love for man when man does not love God but the Creator loves man explains His mystery of life to us in the Scriptures.

Repentance or "changing of man's mind" would be the message that the world was going to be given. If we individually and collectively changed our minds (changed our thinking), then the Creator would fight with us in all the physical and spiritual battles that we would ever face. The simple message of John the Baptist was the Creator was going to take this fallen world back from Satan. Over the many years of my thinking about this subject, why did John the Baptist have only one message? Day in and day out John called out for everyone to repent. The answer is so simple it is hard. This was the highest message any human has ever been given by God. John the Baptist was also the one who pointed to the Messiah and called Him the Lamb of God.

I also should say one thing. The day I spoke with John the Baptist I was 21 years old as one counts in the chronological events of a personal life. At that age,

I did not understand one iota of what I have just explained to all of you. All I knew at 21 was I had to talk to this man, John the Baptist; or I would die like any other dumb creature in this world. Jesus of Nazareth had told me just a few days earlier I would speak with the Desert Preacher, and I did just that.

At the age of 21, my faith was feeble. I cannot say I was strong enough to even believe in a Redeemer promised by God to Adam. This Seed of the Woman, who was somehow going to reconstruct the shattered relationship between man and God, would someday come and liberate this fallen world. Thousands of years after creating man, God gave His laws to Moses along with the design of the tabernacle, a mere replica of the Temple in Heaven. This must have been much harder for Sammael-Satan and his horde of followers to grasp if naming the animals was an insult. Here were fallen humans running around with a crude model of the Temple of Heaven but still a copy, nonetheless. Then God's providing information for Moses to produce a written book that explains these deep things must have been too much for the evil ones. As I speak today here in Alexandria, I am almost at the age of sixty and, still, do not understand half of what could be known. At the age of 21, I realized nothing close to what I know today. But, back then, all I wanted to do was just speak to the desert prophet even though he was in a prison.

The ancient rabbis in Babylon during the time of the 70 years of captivity taught that many angels opposed the creation of man from the beginning, and this was the reason God concealed from them that man would transgress; and this is because God is outside of time and knows what will happen. One must understand one premise: God is outside of time; and everything has already occurred not for us in time but it has for God in Heaven, who is outside of time.

Only God can read a man's mind, not a fallen angel. Sammael could guess what might be on a man's mind, and frequently he is correct. Therein lies the practice of divination, which is forbidden in the Torah, but practiced by humans from the beginning of time. Deep-seated envy intertwined with a burning jealousy of man must have been in the hearts of those rebellious angels and in their chief leader, Sammael-Satan. These harmful agents conspired to cause the fall of man; and, when it occurred, warfare spread further into the created cosmos and beyond.

When the Prophet Joshua took the Promised Land, every evil thing in the land of Canaan had to be destroyed; or it would infect God's Chosen People, who had already begun receiving God's spoken words. History tells us this cleansing of all the land was not accomplished, and now people who are not the Chosen Ones control the Promised Land. Evil spirits and fallen creatures infest the world we live in; yet, a monumental mystery continues: God still cares about man and his offspring; and He has saved them with the coming of the Son of the Blessed One or Messiah, Jesus of Nazareth.

CHAPTER NINETEEN

Jericho and Machaerus – Two days before the Day of Preparation or Passover. Tiberius's 17th year as Rome's emperor and Pontius Pilate's 5th year as Prefect of Judaea. Jesus of Nazareth ends his 2nd year of Public Ministry at the end of Passover. John the Baptist's last days of ministry after one-and-a-half years in prison at Machaerus in Peraea near the Dead Sea.   *Martius 26-27 (31 AD)*

'He has not dealt with us according to our sins, nor punished us according to our iniquities.'   King David

At the age of 21, I did not completely understand who Jesus was other than he told me his name was *Christos*. Could Yeshua-Jesus truly be the long-awaited Messiah? Was Jesus virgin born? I did not understand, nor was I asking the right questions. All I wanted was to speak with John the desert prophet. Maybe I could ask him these questions, and I knew he would tell me the truth. How Jesus was able to read my mind at the Pool of Bethesda was disturbing. Still, I believed only God can know a man's mind. Two days before Passover I was on my way to talk with John the Baptizer, literally two days after Jesus told me it would happen. How did Jesus know all this? My faith at this time was weak, but I perceived God loved me despite my doubts. What kind of a Creator would even care about humans? We are so small compared with the rest of the *cosmos*. Moreover, if God could and would do something like this, it would seem He could do just about anything. It is like trying to understand how many angels there are in the three heavens. Truly, our wisdom is only God's foolishness.

Before the middle of the day, about 38 hours after my meeting with Messina and Jesus, Amcheck and I ambled in tandem down the old Jericho Road on two beautiful mounts belonging to Herod Antipas. Earlier in the day, we picked our horses from many others that were kept at Solomon's Stables. The Romans as well as Antipas and other wealthy patricians along with hundreds of horses used at the Hippodrome were stabled under the southern half of the Temple complex. The main entrance to the stables was located outside the south wall below the Hulda Gates and under the High Priestly Palace that occupies the entire southern edge of the Temple compound. Solomon's Stables are named after Israel's third king, King Solomon, son of David. A thousand years earlier, Solomon had quarried a large number of stones for the first temple from this area. The result were vast open caverns and rooms deep below the compound, which made up the southern section of the Court of Gentiles. In those long-ago days in Jerusalem, Solomon actually kept thousands of horses in this area for his force of chariots that made him the super power of the world at that time in history. Massive sandstone blocks had been cut out of the interior of Mount Moriah, leaving perfect spaces that were divided up into stalls by wooden partitions and smaller stone blocks. Still, today, all of the long-legged creatures in Jerusalem are housed in Solomon's Stables, the area where many tunnels and caves are honeycombing beneath Mount Moriah in Upper Jerusalem. The Babylonians destroyed Solomon's Temple after it stood for almost four hundred years, but these caves and tunnels left from the old quarried stones still provide excellent stables.

It seemed very odd to me that a horse to a Jew was a beast not to eat or ride. Jews hate these fast, sleek creatures because horses pulled all the chariots driven by the army of Pharoah in Egypt when the Egyptians tried to exterminate all the Hebrews at the Red Sea. This was back when the Children of Israel were slaves in Egypt and under Moses's leadership when they escaped slavery. This was a more significant slave revolt than the ones led by Eunus or Spartacus, and the one under Moses was successful. When the Egyptians tried to exterminate all of them by using these beautiful creatures at the Red Sea, an unnatural hate developed against the horse. I believe the Jewish aversion towards horses also has to do with King Solomon multiplying horses and chariots in his days as King of Israel. God had forbidden this practice as stated in the Torah by Moses. It was a warning to the future kings after the Hebrews entered the Promised Land under Joshua. The future kings were also warned about multiplying wives, which King Solomon also violated by having over 600 wives. These were some of my thoughts as I rode behind Amcheck.

Personally, my love for these sleek animals is just behind my passion for dogs, which are also hated by Jews and other Semitic people. To be called a "dog" is one of the harshest insults a Jew can throw at someone.

While Amcheck and I were in Solomon's Stables choosing our horses for our journey to Machaerus, I experienced an incredible peace, not because of my love for these animals, but because of where we were. I began to ponder the idea that this place would make a safe haven in the event I needed somewhere to hide. I could not only flee here and cache myself if the need arose, but I might even pass myself off as a horse groom since very few would think to hunt for me down in these tunnels. I entombed this discernment away for a future time, which, in time, did save my life to tell this story.

Riding down the Jericho Road, Amcheck turned around on his horse and asked if I knew why Herod Antipas had imprisoned John the Baptist. When I fainted ignorance, he explained three motives, which were circulating among the population of Judaea. The first was John's public declaration of the marriage of Herod Antipas to his brother's wife. Herodias had been first married to Philip of Rome when Antipas stole her for himself. This was a forbidden practice according to the Law of Moses. Since Antipas was part Jewish, he was still under the precepts of the Jews given by Moses. To have a brother's wife while the other brother was still alive was unlawful and fell under the category of adultery with stoning as the consequences. If Antipas allowed the Baptist to publicly condemn him without any form of discipline against his accuser, this could lead his subjects to lose respect for their political leader.

Second, the tetrarch was afraid of the desert preacher's reputation even if John had never spoken publicly about Herodias and Antipas as perpetrators of adultery. If this popularity were left unchecked, according to Herod Antipas, a revolution could result with John leading the people against Herod's rule.

The third reason for John's imprisonment was the power and influence of the aristocratic priestly party in Jerusalem, the Sadducees. The Sadducees controlled most of the people's tithes given to Yahweh in Jerusalem, and this vast amount of wealth gave them enormous political power. I am sure the Pharisees also played a part in Herod's arrest of John since the Pharisee sect held most of the religious influence outside of Jerusalem, where John conducted his unique ministry. John spent his time on the side of the Jordan River controlled by the Romans but must have crossed the river from time to time into Peraea, Herod's domain, allowing himself to be arrested by Herod. "What do you think is the reason?" asked Amcheck.

"I think our leader arrested John the Baptist because of envy and jealousy. Are not the religious leaders of Israel also against John for the same reasons?"

"That would also include the Essenes down near where John had his ministry. But why would all the sects be against John?"

I did not say this to Amcheck, but my thinking was based on the uncanny parallel to Rabbi Issachar's view of the angels who were opposed to the creation of man – sons of fire having to bow down to sons of clay. No religious leaders who taught in the schools of Jerusalem were going to submit to John's baptism of repentance. Nor would they yield to the simple words of changing their minds about what the Scriptures said. They, out of everyone, did not need to repent. How could they? Why would they? They read and taught the Word of God to the people each day. The priests carried out the works they did at the Temple every day. "They think they are the children of Abraham, so why would they have to repent? That is why they are all against John."

I should express that there are good angels and evil angels, just like there are good religious leaders and bad ones. The good angels far outnumber the evil ones, which is perhaps the reason this world functions most of the time peacefully. Still, all that we see and cannot see appears locked in a colossal civil war; and everything converges on Israel with the religious leaders in constant tension with each other. They each want to prove their tenets as the correct path to Yahweh. Capping this pyramid of ecclesiastical tumult were the Greek philosophies, the mystery religions, and the whole menagerie of ancient cults that swirled around the rocks of life like a fast-moving river. These components rolled into a *cosmic* quarry destined to abscess the hearts and minds of all men. However, what a man or a woman chooses to accept secures his or her eternal destiny. That was the short of it. Life looked complicated, but it really was very simple: believe and obey Yahweh by faith. The quest of life is to discover this truth, which in the end is a faith move.

What I have witnessed in my long life is most humans could not care less about what I just said; they live their lives like my father following the teachings of Epicurus or throw their hands up and accept everything as a fabricated myth. Nevertheless, I was different. I wanted and needed to know the truth. I realized correct facts plus correct faith could be the only way to the truth; but I needed to make my choice soon before I died, which would seal my eternity. At this time in my life, I did not think I would see my 22nd birthday, which would come in the early fall. Time was of the essence regarding my eternal decision. Whatever the outcome, I was convinced John the Baptist was a beneficial participant on the gameboard of life; and I wondered whether he might be the first Jewish prophet to come to the Jews in over four hundred years; that is, if you do not count the woman's mother who sewed up my face after the Captain of the Temple hit me with his *cestus*. For some reason, I believed Anna when she told me her mother was a prophetess decades ago holding the Messiah in her arms when he was only a child.

My view of John represented a door opening and revealing a light that would drive away the darkness. Since darkness is not a color and is only the absence of light, John was a key to the mystery I was seeking. In some mysterious way, here I was on the edge of the Empire of Rome looking for the light that might drive away the darkness of shadowed humanity. Since John had been imprisoned for almost a year and a half, this narrow breach of light was not going to be available for much longer. Perhaps that was why my slave friend Eli, was profoundly disturbed when he learned of the Baptist's arrest on the day he was viciously murdered near the northern gate to the Temple. Ironically, the same spot where Eli died was the very place the glory of God left the Temple according to the prophet Ezekiel in his vision as recorded in the Scriptures. The leaving of the glory occurred in a time before the destruction of Solomon's Temple by the Babylonians. If the glory left, I began to wonder if it had ever returned. I decided the answer was no. Why? Because of what Pompey found in the Holy of Holies – nothing. That was the answer. No Ark of the Covenant in the Holy of Holies; no Glory – just an empty shell. If this had been a Greek tragedy performed in any amphitheater, John's scene would be almost at the end before the chorus of sirens begins singing a mournful lamentation. Thinking about John made me sad, and everything looked very tragic.

Who was John the Baptist? Was he the return of Enoch or Elijah, two ancient men in the Jewish Scriptures who never died? Certainly, the latter choice was the most attractive since Elijah had been prophesied to return and restore all things before the coming of the promised Messiah-Redeemer, the son of David. All of this was clearly stated in the last canonized book of the Scriptures by Prophet Malachi. On the other hand, was John the arrival of this promised son of David? I remembered this was the view Eli's uncle Anab entertained when he had spoken to Hector and me on my last night in Athens. Possibly John was the promised prophet whom Moses had revealed from the mountains of Horeb also called Mount Sinai, who declared someone would come to the House of Israel and be like Moses but greater. Others claimed John to be the virgin born one. This would be the anticipated "Seed of the Woman," the first prophecy recorded in the *Torah,* words given by God directly to Moses. The "Seed of the Woman" prophecy gave hope to humanity after the fall in the Garden of Eden if one had faith in this future-coming, virgin born Redeemer. My mother had faith in the coming of this Redeemer even believing he was alive 11 years ago. Why else would she have told me to hunt for him? In the Book of Job, a tormented, righteous man also had faith in the future Redeemer. The "Seed of the Woman" was coming to correct the corruption problem. Was this the reason this interloper rabbi from Galilee, the one I spoke to at the Pool of Bethesda, showed me how the world was broken and demonstrated to me how it was going to be fixed even on the day of rest? Rabbi Issachar's conviction was this future Messiah would remove death, the result of disobedience and transgression by all the children of Adam. Later, I sadly would wonder whether Rabbi Issachar really believed what he told me in Rome. Faith in God is best understood as a level of degrees. However, just a little faith can move armies that are standing against us. Even if this is a figurative statement, it is an astonishing reality to contemplate.

History chronicles many individuals proclaiming to be virgin born. The Persians, who embrace Zoroastrianism, declared Zurathrustra, the founder of their religion, as being virgin born. Even the name Zoroaster in Greek means the *seed of a woman* or *seed of a star.* In the Ganga River region of India, a religious leader named Siddartha Gautama, who founded Buddhism over five hundred years previously, was declared in the ancient *Pali Texts* to have been virgin born. More recently, the Macedonian, Alexander the Invincible, while in Egypt informed his troops he was virgin born. I do not suspect these similar stories are all by an unusual accident since history has been waiting for a virgin born savior since Adam. These virgin born tales have impregnated just about every culture. Therefore, the "Seed of the Woman" is history's only hope; and the exact identity of this "virgin born redeemer" surely is man's greatest quest and Satan's greatest deception. Cicero called Aristotle the Father of Logic. Based on Aristotle's system of logic, there was only one truth to any one question. Therefore, not every person claiming to be virgin born could be the true Redeemer – only one.

I was chewing over these thoughts as I rode behind Amcheck heading down a steep trail towards the ancient city of Jericho. When we encountered anyone coming up towards us, the travelers would move off the road giving our horses all the room they needed to pick their footing carefully. Choosing one's steps going down is harder than going up a steep trail. At times, the people had to climb high up and off the path to keep from falling to their deaths as our horses had the right to the roadway. Soldiers were never challenged on this question of who owned the road. In the entire Roman Empire, the Jericho Road was considered the most dangerous road to travel. Not only was it narrow and treacherous at places, but thieves were common;

and murderers launched assaults on many unwary travelers. These crimes were problematic and frequent. The opportunities for these *thags* were numerous because of the many Jewish travelers coming up from the Jordan River area to Jerusalem coming this way from Galilee. As I have already stated, Jews living in the northern regions such as Galileans chose this route not wanting to go the easy way through Samaria. On the Jericho Road, there were plenty of wadis and boulders shouldering the narrow roadway for any nefarious person to conceal himself on this last leg to Jerusalem. Of course, Amcheck and I being two well-armed soldiers on fast horses would never have any encounters with malicious robbers nor see any trouble being enacted upon others. The only problem we encountered was at what speed to travel on this Moon Day. We were to be at Machaerus before Passover, which would begin at sunset on *Dies Martis* or Day of Mars (Tuesday evening). That gave us about a day and a half to reach our destination that would begin on the Day of *Ides* (full moon).

Amcheck kept telling me there was plenty of time. "The Jewish Passover begins tomorrow at sunset, and we are only going to the ancient city of Jericho for the night. Tomorrow we would make it to Machaerus in plenty of time before the Jews begin observing Passover."

In all truthfulness, traveling down the old Jericho Road, we had no choice about the speed we were progressing. Descending through the Judean hills on this second day of the week or Moon Day was very slow even though we rode horses. This was due to the heavy traffic of pilgrims heading up towards Jerusalem trying to reach the Temple City before sunset tomorrow. Amcheck said we could actually reach Machaerus in one hard day by foot if necessary, but the Jewish festivals complicated our progress. This year Passover started at sunset on the third day of the Jewish week precisely at the sighting of the third star. This is according to the lunar-solar calendar used by most Jews in *Palestina*. Ironically, this year's Passover Day coincided with the meticulous Essenes' strictly solar calendar. The Essenes considered all other Jewish sects to be heresies placed in this world by Satan. Calendars and dates of Jewish festivals were the foremost theoretical and theological arguments that caused the most significant divisions in this land between the different sects or factions of Judaism. Calendar calculations were critical, and the people trusted the religious leaders to not lead them astray.

Amcheck said it would be best if we arrived at Machaerus by sunset the next day. He also said we could even arrive on Passover Day as long as we reached Machaerus by noon, the traditional time on Passover Day to have a cessation of work. Most sects believed all work must achieve cessation at noon on Passover Day. However, sunset tomorrow was the cutoff point that started the Feast of

Unleavened Bread or Preparation Day, which commenced first with the start of Passover on Mars Day stretching into Mercury or (Wednesday). At sunset on Mercury Day, the 14th day of Nisan turned into Nisan 15, the start of Unleavened Bread. The first day of Unleavened Bread was always considered a Sabbath, no matter that this year it fell in the middle of the week. A thousand and a half years ago, Moses had commanded that the Hebrews in Egypt slaughter their lambs before twilight on the 14th of Nisan and apply some of the lamb's blood on the doorposts and lintels of their houses; they were to eat the rest of the flesh of this sacrificed animal after roasting it. If there were no blood from a lamb on the doorpost and lintel during the night of that first Passover into the start of Unleavened Bread, the Angel of Death would not pass over, but kill the first-born males whether human or beast. After this event in Egypt, Nisan 14 became a memorial to be maintained each year throughout their generations.

Over the years because of the hundreds of thousands of pilgrims coming to Jerusalem celebrating this meal, the entire population of Jerusalem could not all arrange to sacrifice a lamb and roast it at the same time. Therefore, some ate their meals at the start of Passover or had the meal at the ending of Passover. If some chose to eat their Passover meal near the end of Nisan 14, it would be acceptable if the meal began on the 14th and ended on Nisan 15. Nevertheless, once Nisan the 15th started, there was no eating of leaven bread for a week; and Nisan 15, sunset to sunset, was a day of rest. Unleavened bread or bread without yeast appears flat because it is the yeast or leaven that causes the dough to rise while it is cooked. Therefore, the 15th of Nisan would be a strict Sabbath since it was the first Day of Unleavened Bread celebrating the day the Children of Israel left Egypt because the ten plagues under Moses forced Pharaoh to send them away. Once again, this would be a Sabbath no matter on what weekday it landed; and all Jewish groups agreed on this point. Interpretation of the Scriptures was not an easy job, and many have died over such arguments even at the hands of their fellow Jews.

As we traveled to Jericho on this Nisan the 12th, we passed some large groups of Jews on their way to Jerusalem hoping to arrive before the evening stars appeared over the City of Peace.

When we finally reached Jericho well before sunset, we entered the ancient Hasmonaean Palace on the outskirts of this ancient of cities. The palace was also referred to as Archelaus's Palace since Archelaus, son of Herod the Great and brother to Herod Antipas, had lavishly rebuilt it. It now belonged to any Herod who wished to use it; and this was true of the palace in Jerusalem that was built by Herod the Great, who made a claim to be a Hasmonaean by marriage. Once again, this is shades of bloodlines comparable to Tiberius through his mother, Livia. The same can be said about Herod the Great killing his two sons by Mariamne, the last Hasmonaean princess. After these two boys were dead and Mariamne was put to death by Herod the Great, there were no more Hasmonaean bloodlines to contest a true dynastic inheritance to the throne of *Palestina* or the land of the Jews. Foolishly, Herod the Great thought death solved all problems. I am sure this maxim was on the mind of Herod Antipas when he later decided to execute John the Baptist and when Pontius Pilate allowed the death of Jesus of Nazareth.

When we rode our horses through the Hasmonaean gate, Amcheck declared we would spend the night at this winter palace of Antipas even though it maintained a despicable legacy. According to Amcheck, before the place was rebuilt, Simon ben Mattathias, also known as the Hammer and the greatest liberator and High Priest-King of the Jews, had been murdered in this very palace as were the two sons of Simon ben Mattathias, Judas and Mattathias. The slaying of the Hammer occurred at a grand banquet given by one of the Ptolemies of Egypt long before Cleopatra VII's time. It was Simon's daughter and her husband, the Hammer's grandson, who were the first to reconstruct this palace along with the palace at Machaerus, where John the Baptist was now imprisoned. Amcheck stated that this cursed castle was also the location of where Herod the Great took his last breath in this world. I might add he died a very horrible and painful death at this fertile area in an arid region.

If there were an unnerving place to spend the night, it was this palace in Jericho. Archelaus's Palace actually stood outside of Jericho proper but close enough to the Jericho destroyed by Yahweh in the days of Joshua and the Children of Israel. Jericho was the first Canaanite city built by the Hamathites, who started the families of the Canaanites. Jericho was the first city attacked by Joshua and the Children of Israel after they entered the Promised Land. This happened after 40 years of wandering in the wilderness once the Jewish slaves exited out of Egypt under the leadership of Moses. The remains of that old city of Jericho could still be detected next to where we spent the night. I did walk over to those ancient ruins in the last light on this Moon Day; and my fertile imagination imagined what happened long ago when Joshua had all the horns blown and the walls fell down flat, which allowed the Israelites to enter the city and put it to the sword. I could still see an ancient portion of a wall down below many levels of cities that might have confirmed the Scripture story. It was a broad area that had been dug out by someone, perhaps looking for gold and jewelry; and, down at the bottom of the trench, the wall stones did appear to have fallen outward. I am testifying to what I witnessed, but trying to find the city level that stood over fourteen hundred years ago would almost be impossible. How would anyone know which section of the wall was the one during the time of Joshua? This would be a problem because of the many times over the years this city was destroyed and rebuilt on top of each previous town.

On my way back to this infamous Palace of Archelaus, I spotted the famous Jericho Hippodrome used only for chariot races. Its reputation for death and brutality during races was well known even in Rome. The new Hippodrome in Jerusalem did not, yet, have the status of Jericho's famous circus. I had a desire to visit a racing venue; but it was quiet today, and I knew we would be leaving early the next day. I must confess that my stay at this famous city and immoral palace did not live up to it malevolent past. I had a splendid evening that night in this ancient oasis city perhaps because it was pleasantly cool at night and located in the middle of nowhere. We ate and drank with mercenary friends of Amcheck, who reminisced in their quarters about many stories of everyone who still was or had been soldiers for other kings. No one spoke of all the deaths that occurred in this palace but instead we drank, ate, and laughed. Before the evening ended, we all sang many bawdy songs.

Due to our late celebration into the early hours at Jericho, Amcheck and I left Jericho almost near midday. Still, it was the third day of the week, Mars Day or Preparation Day for the Passover. The Jewish calendar would not begin Nisan 14 until the third star was spotted this evening, which would still give us plenty of time to reach the palace and stronghold of Machaerus. By the time we reached the Jordan River, it was the hottest time of day; and there were no other travelers in any direction along the old Roman road to Machaerus or going towards Jerusalem. Near the Jordan River, Amcheck pointed out the city of Qumran from behind us and to our right. This was the old Essenes' separatist community of a couple hundred men. Members of this sect were the only humans we saw after leaving Jericho. We spotted about ten men relieving themselves in the shade of some bushes down from the rickety wooden bridge at the Jericho River. After Amcheck had stopped laughing, he explained that these were Essenes who were violating their stringent rules about where and what direction they could do their business. Evidently, Essenes could not use toilets in any city or town but had to go a certain distance to the west of any city they found themselves in when they had to relieve themselves. This explained why in Jerusalem the Essenes Gate was pointing west of the city when usually a gate was named for the destination of the road that passed through the gate. The only city occupied by Essenes around Jerusalem was to the east, not the west. Now I understood why the Essenes Gate in Jerusalem was in the west. That was the direction of the Essenes' *lavos*, where they would go and do whatever bodily function of excrement that had to be done while they were in Jerusalem.

"Why are these Essenes doing their business to the east of Qumran and not the west?" I asked.

"These men will not be allowed to have a bowel movement on the Passover or the first day of Unleavened Bread. You see that would be considered working on the Sabbath. Therefore, we men down near the water have to be relaxed and try and empty everything today. I am sure the shade of those trees down by the river is the most relaxing spot within miles," explained Amcheck with great laughter coming up deeply from his lower belly, all at their expense.

When he stopped his laughing, I asked, "How far does an Essene have to go outside his city to use a *lavo*?"

"All latrines have to be just past a Sabbath's walk from Qumran or any other city the Essenes may find themselves in. A Sabbath's walk is the distance from the Temple to the top of the Mount of Olives. I guess that would be less than a mile."

Whatever the reason, it was funny to Amcheck watching these men squatting in the bushes east and not west of their city. I was just trying to understand or comprehend why people lived out their lives according to their own personal interpretations of whatever religion or holy books in which they placed their faith. These Jews were the strictest I knew of any religion having the most stringent rules and interpretations of the Law of Moses. The commands they placed themselves under, especially concerning the Sabbath, put even the Pharisees to shame. Still, why would someone violate one rule for another? Using the *lavo* towards the east and not the west was beyond me.

"See how carefully they prepare even though they are on the wrong side of the town down there," he laughed again.

Using the old, rickety wooden bridge, we crossed the Jordan River now swollen from the headwaters originating in the hills north in Ituraea and Abilene. Once on the other side, Amcheck pointed out Mount Nebo rising to the east of Jericho and the Jordan Valley from the first wadi north of Lake Asphaltitus. Amcheck told me that up on that ridge to the east was supposedly the spot the Hebrew God had taken the prophet Moses to display the Promised Land to him before Moses died.

"So that is where Moses died?" I repeated. I was filled with extraordinary awe. Looking up at where the most famous personality in the Jewish Scriptures viewed this land chosen for God's Chosen People was extraordinary, to say the least. Mount Nebo, I remembered was the last location of Moses before he died on his 120th birthdate. I began to wonder if this was Yahweh's idea of a birthday present. Amcheck asked why I was laughing. After I had told him, a smile appeared on his face; and he asked me whether this was true. I joked and said, "No, I was just making it up." Amcheck did not know whether I was telling the truth. He finally turned his horse putting his heels gently into his mount's sides.

When we reached the first wadi to our left, Amcheck circled back towards Lake Asphaltitus to go around the steep, dried-up streambed. The heat was atrocious, and it was hard to breathe maybe because it was the middle of the day and we were at the lowest known spot in the Empire. Heat waves distorted the distant views across this dead sea valley; thus, the origin of its most common name, the Dead Sea. Moving closer towards the lake, Amcheck picked a circuitous path precisely to avoid the nearly poisonous stench that the stagnant water emitted. The sulfuric smell, combined with the surrounding cliff-like walls, made this dead-end lake feel like a place of death.

I called out to Amcheck, "This hellhole only lacks smoke and fire pits to be a perfect location for Hades."

Amcheck answered back, "Drinking water down here is worth more than gold. If anyone spends much time down here, the sun will strip any color from their clothing and even turn our hair blond if we keep our head uncovered."

Once we were near this mammoth lake, which has no outlet, it was quite picturesque in a depressed kind of way. It possessed a turquoise color and looked inviting to a thirsty man; yet, to drink the water would be lethal. Amcheck suggested that I take a swim to cool myself. Before we started up towards Machaerus, I accepted Amcheck's offer. After stripping, I walked out into the buoyant-feeling water until I was deep enough to swim. I found the water strangely cool and realized this lake had to be very deep. I discovered that I kept popping up on top of the water like a cork because of its density of salts and minerals. I tried only once to open my eyes under water, which almost blinded me. With my eyes burning, I came out and redressed. Amcheck laughed when he learned about my opening my eyes under water. "All the other soldier-boys at Jerusalem are going to get a good hoot out of that when we tell them once we return." I gave him a dirty look, but it was not necessary; for he never told anyone to my knowledge. It would be many weeks before we returned to Jerusalem, and by then Amcheck had better stories to tell his audiences.

When I was back on my mount, we continued towards Machaerus; but now I had a sulfur smell sticking to me that I hoped would burn off in the heat. Riding late in the afternoon and crossing over the eastern side of this curious lake, Amcheck related a fascinating tale of why this body of water was so foul.

"Two thousand years ago this was a lush and beautiful valley. Unfortunately, the God of the Jews turned it into the Hades we have today."

"Should I ask you if you are joking?" I said in jest.

"On the contrary. This place is God's greatest object lesson. The problem is the world does not listen to most of Yahweh's lessons including this one. During the time the patriarch Abraham lived in this land along with his nephew Lot, this was a pleasant location to raise sheep and grow crops. Lot decided to leave Abraham in the higher hills and live down at the other end of this body of water. Remember it was not a dead lake back then. It was green from the rains, and the temperature was consistently comfortable. Many cities were situated here because of its beautiful and abundant setting. In those days, people even called it the Valley of Eden or the Valley of Siddim. However, this Yahweh God destroyed the ancient cities of Sodom, Gomorrah, Admah, and Zeboiim, the cities once occupying the southern area that was lush and fertile. I believe there was a fifth town, but I cannot remember its name right now. The story goes that two angels arrived at Sodom to rescue Lot, his wife, and his two daughters. Yahweh had decided it was time to destroy Sodom because of the licentious behavior and extreme selfishness of these people, who refused to repent of their evil deeds. The story goes that, since there were fewer than ten righteous people in this entire valley, the cities became slated by God for punishment and destruction."

After hearing this story and seeing this dead valley, I wondered about Rome. What would happen if tomorrow all the righteous people were to walk out of the city of Rome? Would God destroy Rome like these cities of the plain? I concluded that would be the only way to destroy the city of Rome: convince the righteous to leave on the same day. I snickered at my own fantasy of how to destroy the city I loathed. The Lake of Death is now a monument and reminder that it is far better to repent than to be destroyed. The prophet Ezekiel said, "*Sodom and her daughters had pride and arrogance, abundant food, pleasure, and careless ease; but they did not help the poor and needy. Thus, their ample leisure led to a shared haughtiness and all kinds of acts of abominations before Yahweh; the results were what happens to dastards.*" This became one of my favorite stories in the Scriptures because God sent two visible angels to rescue Lot and his family, and then the cities were no more. Stories of angels have always intrigued me. The two heavenly messengers were so handsome that the evil men of Lot's town wanted to rape and ravish them. This was not to be because the two angels stretched out their hands, and all those wicked men lost their sight before the city was destroyed by fire and brimstone. This happened on the next day, and Sodom vanished from the annals of history.

We continued south around the Dead Sea until we reached the Wadi Nahalie near the town of Callirrhoe. Here we began an uphill traverse into the wilderness of Peraea before entering the famous mountain fortress and citadel that held the Baptist as a prisoner of Herod Antipas. I had been paid by Herod Antipas for over the last year and a half and never saw the man who was my employer. Still, going to Machaerus did not mean I was going to meet this notorious man, let alone see him. I had eyed him from across the arena the day Marius won the wooden sword for his final time; but that was over eleven years ago, and I was only a child at the time. When I did see Herod and Herodias sitting next to Tiberius, I did not even know at the time he was the man I would be working for later in life. Life seems to have many of these strange twists and turns as we go through it.

Riding into this fortress was a riveting experience. Before we even reached the citadel, we had to pass between high walls and towers that protected a remote little town that guarded the entrance to Machaerus. After passing the entrance a mile further from Callirrhoe and more deep, dark valleys, we finally came upon Machaerus. The main fortress stood as a stronghold on the southernmost boundary of Peraea. It was an impregnable structure chiseled a hundred years earlier by the Jewish priest-king Alexander Jannaeus, the grandson of Simon, the priest-king murdered at Jericho. The stronghold was a bulwark of freedom after the Jewish people had fought under the leadership of the sons of Maccabeus or the Hammer and gained temporary independence from the Syrian-Greek rulers. These Syrian-Greek rulers were the descendants of Seleucus I Nicator, one of the generals of Alexander the Great from Macedonia, who borrowed the same idea from Alexander, that being he was also virgin born. Seleucus I Nicator propagated the narrative that he was the son of Apollo, and this was centuries before Augustus made the same claim.

Though Alexander Jannaeus originally built Machaerus, Herod the Great enlarged the complex adding perhaps the most celebrated defensive innovations known to man. There were towers and walls 150 yards high if one included the sheer cliffs with walls on top. On the vertical rocks, the fortress stood standing almost four thousand feet above the floor of the Dead Sea region. Within the walls stood a modern and magnificent palace containing many cisterns, storehouses, and weapon arsenals to endure any long siege. As we rode in on horses, I wondered whether Rome could conquer Machaerus; but, given what I know of Rome, the answer is Machaerus would eventually fall as it did under Pompey. Still, it would be a significant feat since deep, unassailable valleys bordered three sides of the fortress. The only access was from the east where the walls butted up against a mountain. Here the Romans could erect siege craft and lob catapulted devastation at Machaerus over its walls. At the present, it was not Rome Antipas worried about but the Arab Nabataeans centered at the city of Petra.

The current Nabataean unrest was because of Herod Antipas's marriage to Herodias, the woman who was the cause of John the Baptist's arrest and imprisonment. South of Machaerus spreads the dominion of King Aretas, Herod's ex-father-in-law. Aretas, king of the Nabataeans, a proud people of traders and warriors, inhabit the amazing and atypical city of Petra. Antipas feared Aretas might come for revenge with an army of Nabataeans and mercenaries to punish him for the insult to Aretas's daughter since Herod replaced her with Herodias as his wife. Aretas's daughter was Herod Antipas's first wife, but she escaped from Machaerus when she learned of the marriage betrayal in Rome over a decade past. She returned to her father in the Arnon Valley taking refuge in Petra, the capital city in a hidden gorge about twelve miles to the south of Machaerus. Due to the possibility of a frontier war, Herod Antipas embedded himself at Machaerus to direct his forces in a defensive position if war came. I remembered, on the day I fought Marius, our Captain of Herod's Palace in Jerusalem, Saben, suggested this might be the reason why Herod Antipas was not coming to Jerusalem for Passover this year.

The fortress at Machaerus, as I have described, is atop a conical hill with the palace at the center. From the highest tower of Machaerus, one could easily see on a cloudless day the oasis of Jericho, the wilderness of Judaea, and the hills of Jerusalem. As one looks out past Jericho at the northern end of the Dead Sea, the Jordan River appears as a thin, silvery wire meandering into the distance into the fresh, blue lake of Galilee. Perhaps the view looking westward from Machaerus would be almost comparable to what Moses had from Mount Nebo on the last day of his life. Much later in my life, I investigated the life of Moses. I discovered why he was not allowed to enter the Promised Land, and I learned Moses and I were alike. We both had an anger problem. To be obedient to God's Word is essential even for a famous prophet like Moses. Striking an Egyptian to death who was beating on a Hebrew slave shows a lack of restraint. Later in life, when Moses hit a particular rock, this was the reason he was not allowed to enter the Promised

Land. I know that hitting a rock with your staff may not seem like a dangerous act, but it is if God has explicitly stated what He wants you to do with a specific rock. In Moses's case, he was to hit the rock with his staff the first time to produce water; then 40 years later he was instructed to merely speak to the rock in order to get water to come forth.

After we had turned our horses over to the head groom at Machaerus, Amcheck delivered our dispatch to a surly man who was the Captain of the Guard at this palace fortress. The captain told us we could not leave until Antipas himself had spoken with us, and that would not be until sometime tomorrow on Passover Day. Amcheck explained to me that this meant we had to stay the next two days or more, which we had to anyway because it would be unwise to travel on the Passover and the first day of Unleavened Bread if we were to leave immediately. Amcheck asked me if we should spend the next Sabbath in Jericho or here at Machaerus. I wanted to see John the Baptist, but I also wanted to watch a chariot race or two at Jericho. I told Amcheck my desires, and he said he would work on both.

Since we had no guard duties at Machaerus, it was as if we were on holiday even if we were in a hot, depressive, barren place. We could drink and stay up late and sleep in if our hearts so desired. After learning we were going to be isolated here at Machaerus for the next few days, we went to the western wall to watch the sun descend over the mountainous horizon. Both Amcheck and I enjoyed a spectacular, emblazoning treat of a fiery-red sky at sunset. With a red sky at night, I knew tomorrow would be a delight. Those Jews who were living and working at the complex of Machaerus all began private celebrations of their Passover meals in their own quarters. All of Herod's mercenaries at Machaerus were non-Jewish, and Amcheck and I found them drinking and celebrating something that looked closer to a Bacchus ritual.

Just as the sun set and before the drinking to Bacchus got out of hand, Amcheck led me to the lowest level of the palace, where we found two deep pits being utilized as dungeons. One of the pits held John the Baptist, and Amcheck had no problem arranging for me to see the desert prophet. Only one guard was on duty, and Amcheck knew him from years ago during the Parthian Wars. The man was minus his right hand removed by Parthians after his capture. I later learned it was Amcheck who had been ordered to remove the man's hand and was his guard before the one-handed man turned his allegiance to the Parthian army. I never did learn what people the left-handed man came from. Being friends with the man who cut off my hand would be hard for me to accept. It would even be hard if it were the other way around. Yet, I witnessed both men slapping each other on the back and calling each different rude names with great delight and laughter. Amcheck had brought a jug of Judean wine for his friend while I was allowed to visit with the Baptist.

After watching these two unlikely men reacquainting themselves, I noticed the two pits in the floor that dropped about twenty feet below the stone floor. The entire room stank of human excrement and sweat. Ventilation was negligible making the air almost impossible to breathe. I had to burn my red tunic the next day and scrub my leather cuirass serval times to remove the stench. I still do not understand how someone could stay alive for any length of time in what was little more than a sewer. However, this was the home of John the Baptist for the last year and a half. Now that I was finally here, nothing was going to keep me from meeting the desert preacher, now that he was only 20 feet below me. I had come too far to stop because of unpleasant smells. For nearly two years, I had wanted to meet this man. I first learned of him in Athens from Eli's uncle, again in Rome from Felix the Praetorian Guard, and finally in the Temple of Janus from Eli. I had traveled from *Hellas* to *Italia* and now to *Palestina* to see this man. The desert prophet had already been somewhat woven into the fabric of my life even before I learned of his imprisonment a year and a half ago on the day I witnessed the brutal murder of my childhood friend Eli. I also could not believe Yeshua told me just a couple of days ago at the Pool of Bethesda I was going to be speaking with John, and here I was just as Yeshua-Jesus had predicted.

I asked the one-handed man which dungeon held John; and after he pointed with his stump, I stared down into its stifling gloom seeing some movement at the bottom. The guard dragged a one-pole ladder; and I realized, if John decided to attack me once I was beside him, rescue could not come quick enough. Nevertheless, I had no fear of meeting this man; and, almost seventy years later, I hold the unbelievable memory of what happened that evening as one of the grandest and momentous moments of my life.

"I am a soldier of Herod!" I called down in Aramaic. "Do you object to speaking with me?"

"No, but come down if you wish to talk with me!" echoed a deep voice from below also speaking in Aramaic.

"I have a Passover meal that a Jewess provides for you," I called down.

"Praise Yahweh! Come down with your meal, and I will not harm you!" called back the likable-sounding desert preacher.

A READING GIVEN AT THE GREAT LIBRARY OF ALEXANDRIA BY EPAPHRODITUS

Given in the year of the four emperors. During this year of civil war, the great fire broke out on Capitoline Hill destroying much of Rome's archives. Due to this loss, the scholars of Alexandria's Great Library requisitioned anyone with past knowledge to recreate the history of Rome. These short lectures were delivered on the afternoons of the first day of the week for a fee of 25 denarii. I have incorporated several lecture readings that I read during this pivotal year for Rome and its Empire.　　　　　　　　　　　　　　　　　*69 AD*

THE MACCABEES–HASMONAEANS AND THE STRONGHOLD OF MACHAERUS

Alexander Jannaeus was the third priest-king of the Maccabees or Hasmonaeans. Maccabee is Greek for hammer, the title given to Mattathias and his sons who hammered their enemies to gain their freedom from the Seleucus rulers. Hasmonaeans in Greek means pious ones. The pious hammers or Hasmonaean Maccabees are today only terms of identifying this somewhat-dead regime because the Roman occupation pushed them aside; and the Rome puppet king, Herod the Great, killed the rest. Rome did allow a fraction of what used to be their kingdom to remain after the death of Herod the Great, but Herod Antipas did not want to accept this as status quo. Rome always breaks up territories it controls leaving the local kings in place only if the broken-up dynasty pays taxes to Rome. Alexander Jannaeus, who had come to the throne after the death of his elder sibling Aristobulus about one hundred seventy years ago, built the formidable structure in Peraea named Machaerus to be the last stand if necessary against Rome.

Aristobulus's widow, Salome Alexandra, released Jannaeus from prison where his brother had kept him captive while he was alive and after Machaerus was completed as an elegant stronghold. She then married Jannaeus, thus elevating Alexander Jannaeus as the next priest-king of Israel. Alexander Jannaeus waged war against Egypt and extended his territory to what it was during the reigns of King David and King Solomon 1,000 years earlier. Alexander Jannaeus began minting his own coins and constructing a fleet of ships hoping to make Israel a great maritime power as it had been under Solomon.

During that time of great dreams of world control, the Sadducees and Pharisees erected their impervious barriers upon the people constructing these two dominant religious groups that confuse and enslave most of the Chosen

People of God. This was when all the lands under Alexander Jannaeus's control became entangled and were compelled to conform to the teachings and decrees of the Sadducees or Pharisees. Even the Edomites, the children of Isaac's son Esau coexisting in Jannaeus's realm, were forced to be circumcised and to accept one of these brands of Judaism. The only people able to resist the Sadducee or Pharisee influence were those living in Galilee and Samaria. Today Samaria is still in revolt against the rule of any Jewish group, but Galilee has fallen under the influence of the Pharisee sect. The people in the Samarian region are today called Samaritans and are mostly a mixed blood of Jews and Assyrians. However, I would like to stress my view on this practice of mixing cultures. Most empires in history, starting with the Persians, merely destroy a group's religion by eclectically mixing together people of different beliefs, but this practice bewilders all the people since all faiths are allowed to co-exist. This is why I believe someday Rome will implode because of the spiritual confusion and befuddlement caused by religious toleration promoted by the emperors and the Senate before them. Alexander Jannaeus in his day magnified the rift between the Sadducees and the Pharisees, which was started by the Hasmonaean ruler, John Hyrcanus. This practice of religious toleration never works in the long stretch of an empire or kingdom. Political leaders only have two options when conquering the world: First, tolerate religion; or second, allow just one religion and persecute all the others with death or deportation. The former will work for a few hundred years but will eventually destroy the society with confusion and the new religion that will rise up, which I call secular politicisms. Since humans get their values, morals, and ethics from religion, all faiths begin to breed a form of spiritual warfare in any society practicing religious toleration. Having only one religion drives all the others underground, and that actually makes the outlawed religions stronger than the one state religion: the one religion the political powers try to establish above all others.

Long ago Priest-king Jannaeus during a Feast of Tabernacles poured a libation on the ground at his feet instead of on the altar in Jerusalem as prescribed by a Pharisaic ritual command. Open rebellion erupted. Many Pharisees were carrying citron melons for the feast, and they used these fruits as flying weapons to strike the heretic Jannaeus. After being hit, he ordered his foreign mercenaries to maintain order. Six thousand people were killed, and civil war seethed and bubbled lasting for the next six years. Its culmination solidified the deep hatred shared between the Pharisees and the Sadducees because of an obscure break of protocol. I still remember the "protocol" rift between a Jewish childhood friend of mine and a Pharisaic rabbi on the morning I baptized myself in the Tiber River becoming a Yisrael. Should I have baptized myself, or should the rabbi have joined me in the water laying me back as if I were being buried in a watery grave? I thoroughly understand that the little things grow into massive disputes, but I think you know my point.

Jannaeus captured 800 of the leaders of the Pharisees. At the end of a very intoxicating dinner feast given in honor of his Sadducees supporters, Jannaeus ordered the 800 Pharisees to watch the slaughter of their family members. Afterward, the 800 Pharisees were crucified.

Jews killing Jews seemed a common practice when no other threats were pressing upon them. We have seen this very practice in Palestina over the past few years. However, the warfare and cruelty visited by Alexander Jannaeus grew into a pastime activity. The Pharisees and even the Essenes from that time declared the vile ruler Jannaeus as the Wicked Priest, who persecuted the Teacher of Righteousness. After Jannaeus's death, his wife, Salome Alexandra, took control through her offspring. Her two sons ruled the land of Palestina until one was poisoned and the other was executed. This coincided with the Roman arrival under Cneius Pompeius Magnus or, later as he wanted to be called, Pompey the Great. It was this Roman general who made this Promised Land part of the Roman Empire. Political power and the bestowal of the office of high priest went to the highest bidder submitting himself to Rome. Today money and corruption are primary in deciding the appointment of who gets to be the high priest of Israel. Personal piety has nothing to do with who enters the Holy of Holies once a year on the Day of Atonement to offer bull and goat blood for the sins of the Jews.

Corruption in the Promised Land slowly and progressively intensified until the time Herod the Great married the granddaughter of Alexander Jannaeus, the daughter of the High Priest Hyrcanus II, whom Herod the Great killed in order to get rid of the last member of the Maccabean family. Herod the Great's irrational suspicions controlled him when he murdered this daughter of Hyrcanus, his favorite wife (some reports say by drowning her in her own bathwater); and many years later with Roman's imperial permission, he killed his two sons he had sired by her. This woman, known merely as Mariamne, was the last queen-princess of the Hasmonaeans. As I am sure all present understand, Roman law requires a father to obtain public permission before he can kill his own children. Herod the Great received an imperial sanction for his crimes, and I ask you what has happened to our world under the wings of Rome?

The pious Hammer House Dynasty was no more, just like Egypt after Cleopatra, daughter of Ptolemy XI, murdered herself and Augustus ordered the murder of her son with Caesar, which ended that dynasty and possible god-bloodline of Caesar.

Honestly, when King Solomon said, "There was nothing new under the sun," he was correct in his observations upon life. Please understand I am sharing all of this somewhat-confusing history to show how the minds of most rulers work. They all seem to believe in the power of the bloodlines of divinity, and this faulty thinking always leads to horrible results on people's lives including mine. Yes, even I am a victim of this power lust and how it led to the death of my mother, my childhood friend, his father, and later my teacher. Also, over three hundred slaves in the home of my father, Senator Gaius Vetallus, all lost their lives on a hot September day 50 years after Actium.

CHAPTER TWENTY

Machaerus in the Peraea Desert of Ancient Moab – The beginning of Passover and the start of Jesus of Nazareth's third year of public ministry.   *Nisan 14 (31 AD)*

And in that day shall the deaf hear the words of the book, and the eyes of the blind shall see out of obscurity, and out of darkness.

The Prophet Isaiah

The voice of him that crieth in the wilderness, "Prepare you the way of Yahweh, make straight in the desert a highway for our God."

The Prophet Isaiah

Amcheck helped his friend, the one-handed guard, slip the pole ladder down into the deep shaft so I could join the voice in the shadows down below. Going down the ladder, I had the handle of the basket with the Passover meal cradled over my elbow along with a palm oil light. At the base of the pit, I stepped off the ladder; and the pole was quickly drawn up. This I assumed was a precaution in case the prisoner tried to escape up the ladder. I could tell Amcheck and his friend were not interested in me as I could hear their voices fade as they walked away reminiscing. Had this madman from the desert tried to kill me, I do not think even my friend Amcheck at this time would have cared. I should point out that Amcheck's behavior of late was beginning to concern me. It started when he told Saben about my witnessing a miracle at the Pool of Bethesda without my permission. But, if he had not shared this information, I would not presently be in this pit visiting with John the Baptist.

From the light of the small clay lamp, I recognized the clothing of John to be of camel hair. His hair was long, greasy, and tangled. Everything about him matched the appearance of his wild look. He had a massive wooly beard, which he kept stroking as we talked. He was about my size wearing no sandals and his camel-hair tunic; he had a thin, moth-eaten woolen blanket draped over his shoulders; the blanket was more rag than cover.

After I had lifted the lamp, I was able to see into his eyes from the dancing light. I looked beyond the smells and outward grime peering deeply into those warm, brown pools. He seemed delighted that he was going to have a Passover meal. I felt no fear as I stared into his formidable, staid look. Deep lines were etched around the corners of his eyes caused by his grateful expression confirming to me that such delights as a Passover meal were rare these days in his life. It was almost the same look many galley slaves had when they received a cup of water from the water boy knowing that they were destined to occupy the oar benches of Rome's war galleys until death. Aside from his grave, consigned look, he seemed harmless as a gentle, old guard dog that was all bark and no bite. His forehead and cheeks were sallow, likely the result of living underground for a year and a half. He must have been twice the size when he was baptizing down on the Jordan a year and a half ago. When Eli and I were living in the caves below the synagogue in the 14th District of Rome for almost two months, I, too, began to lose muscle strength. I thought two months was a long time, but I could not fathom living in this hole for a year and a half. If he were a prophet of Yahweh, why would the God of the Universe allow such abuse upon a faithful servant? Yet, I told myself the ways of God are beyond the ways of my understanding.

"Who are you?" he asked in Aramaic without any anger or malice.

"My name is Venustus Vetallus. Does that name mean anything to you?"

"Should it?"

"I am what some would call an *opprobrium* fugitive wanted at the highest levels in Rome."

"What kind of a fugitive?"

"*Opprobrium* is Latin for someone who brings disgrace to his father and the Senate System of Rome."

He seemed to think about that for a moment before he said, "Is that why you share this hole with me?"

"I am here to offer you freedom."

"How can you do that?" he asked in a gentle, questing tone.

"It is simple. You trade the information I have just given you for your own freedom."

Now I had his attention; and he moved back a little from me, which was only one step before he bumped into the smooth rock wall. "What exactly is your crime, and what was your name again?"

"Venustus Vetallus. I committed murder almost two years ago in Rome – the grandniece of the Princeps Augustus. The entire Roman Empire has been marshaled for my capture. I am presently hiding in the service of Herod Antipas as a mercenary as you can see by my uniform. I am the one who belongs here in this hole, not you. You have not committed any crime, especially one punishable by death. To be brutally honest with you, I am weary of running and living a lie."

"Is that why you came down here – to submit yourself to death?"

"I do not wish to die, and neither do you," I replied. This desert preacher did not seem to believe me by the way he wagged his head. The man before me was perhaps the most astonishing or arguably the bravest individual I had ever met. He did not seem to care whether he lived or died. Yet, he did not seem suicidal; it appeared to not matter what would happen to him. He seemed resigned to any fate that awaited him as the will of God.

After his head had stopped its wagging, he said, "If you are who you claim, then surrender yourself on your own. Living a lie is not freedom, no matter what you have done."

"That would not help you," I said. "What I am offering you is permission to trade places with me – my enslavement for your freedom."

John put out his hand as if to push me away. "Are you the Poison Messenger disguised as a soldier, coming here to tempt me?" He turned away slightly and said with disappointment in his voice, "I thought you were sent to me by my Lord."

"Never! I am not the Devil even though I am sure his finger impressions and smell are all over me." I found my words about smell a little ironic and almost laughable considering what this man before me smelled like. John gently touched my left shoulder before he slid down the smooth wall into a sitting position with his knees up under his chin. I squatted with my back against the opposite damp wall and placed the palm lamp on the floor between us. For what seemed like a long time, we both just looked at each other in the flickering, lambent light.

The Baptist eyed me as time appeared to dilate. Finally, John took a deep breath and a sigh before he finally answered. "I am sure you are sincere. However, I am closer to the Kingdom of Yahweh if I stay right here. Yahweh is sovereign, and nothing happens in life unless He allows it. Our task is to remain in the boat of life and not jump out when the seas begin to stir. Do you understand what I am saying?"

"No, not really," I said even though I liked the boat metaphor. "I began to search for you when I first learned of you two years ago in Athens. I heard of you again in Rome. Still, it was about two years ago. I heard how you baptized repentant Jews and a few Gentiles. A Roman soldier who you baptized saved my life because of you. At first, this Roman was setting me up to be murdered by stalling me in a tavern in the heart of Rome. He apparently changed his mind after he spoke to me of you and how you were instrumental in changing the direction of his choices. Maybe you do not know it, but you are famous in the Empire. I have sought you since I learned of you. I was hoping you might give me answers. But now it seems all I can do is offer my freedom for yours."

"Enslavement to God is not bondage as the world sees it. I am perhaps the most liberated man in the *cosmos*." He waved his right hand as he spoke drawing a flicker from the palm lamp when the wind caused by his hand passed gently above the wick. "I spend my days quoting Scriptures to myself, those passages I have long committed to memory. They feed me and give me refreshment. The Word of God is like water that makes you thirsty for more truth. Do you know any of the Scriptures?

"I became a proselyte Jew almost two years now but have since rejected Judaism as a false ecclesiastical system. This happened after I witnessed what occurs at the Temple on a daily basis, the deceitfulness of all the different sects of Judaism."

"The Scriptures are not the same as the rituals you must have observed and performed by the leaders in Jerusalem. Your observations were correct to a point. Many religious leaders are snakes and wolves in sheep's clothing. Why do you think I preached out in the desert away from all that filth? You must have seen in your heart all the darkness that is dressed in robes of light."

"Then you understand what I am saying?"

"In this darkness of this hole, I walk closer to my Creator than I ever did in the vast, empty, sun-baked desert. Now all of my life is removed, save this pit; and Yahweh sits with me day and night. Would you rob me of this particular blessing by trading places?" After he had said this, he smiled with a new life now coming from his brooding eyes. It almost startled me as I realized he was telling me the truth as he believed it. This man understood my very own feelings. What a delightful confirmation to my troubled spirit.

I finally had a memory I desperately wanted to share with this man I perceived to be a great prophet of the Creator. "My mother told me something on the day she died over a decade ago in Rome. When she was a little girl in Greece, she heard about a Redeemer born in Judaea 30 or even 40 years ago." Now I wanted to ask what everyone wanted to know. "Are you this person born to correct the world's problems?"

The light quickly vanished from his eyes, and he turned his head as if he had been asked this question far too often. "No!" he finally snapped.

"Do you know who it is?"

He turned back; a smile formed, and the inner light came back into his eyes. "Yes," he gently answered.

I also asked in a gentle voice, "The teacher from Galilee, the one they are now calling Jesus?"

"Yeshua is my cousin. Yes, he is the one about whom you ask; at least I hope he is the Expected One."

"You are not certain?"

"Death to the body, doubt to the soul – that is what is wrong with this world. We all doubt. All of us are born in darkness, except Yeshua. He was virgin born and not subject to the fallen nature of you and me. He does not come through the loins of Adam except by his mother, who is a long descendant of Adam's rib. He is the Son of God as well as the Son of Man but not contaminated by Adam and his sin. You and I are only sons of Adam; Yeshua is not. We children of Adam are like sheep destined for slaughter. But Yeshua, or Jesus as the Romans like to call him, has come to save the world just as his name suggests."

"How will he do this?"

"By doing what you have just tried to do – taking our place and giving up his precious life for ours. If we accept that sacrifice, we will be free forever. That is the only way into the Kingdom of God. He is the only way to truth and life. All the prophets spoke about it; yet, it remains a mystery to how it will finish. Seven hundred years back from where we are today the prophet Isaiah spoke of it, and it has not changed. '*But He was wounded on account of our transgressions. He was crushed for our iniquities; the chastisement of our peace was upon him; and by his scourging, we were healed. All of us like sheep have gone astray; each of us has turned to his own way, but Yahweh gave him up for our iniquities.*'"

His words did not make any sense to me as I listened to what he seemed to be quoting from memory. Years later those words would mean everything a human needs to know to enter into Yahweh's Kingdom after death, and this is all that is necessary to become a child of God even before our physical death. A faith operation takes place in each person's heart, not the mind or even in one's soul. Faith comes from one's spirit, and that is the key to eternal life. It is a spiritual operation only God can perform, but each human must request the Living Creator to perform it. It is entirely a new birth, not a reformation; a new beginning from a new foundation, not a remodeling. It is something one undergoes and not something one produces in his or her own power. The mentioning of pain and suffering led me back to one of his first questions. I picked up the lamp because I wanted to see his eyes better when I asked my next question. "You asked me if I came down here to contemplate death; why such a question?"

"Do you try to deflect the very Word of God, or do you so little understand what I just quoted?"

He was right. His insight had just pulled my covers away. Here was a man who was, indeed, being controlled by the Spirit of God. I realized I could not trick God nor this man. The only simple solution was to tell the truth and stick to the subject God wanted us to stay upon. The thought about the passage he had quoted was where I had to return. After a few moments of reviewing his words in my mind, I answered, "It sounds like the prophet Isaiah is saying pain leads to death. The Greeks, the Romans, and even the Jews say life is in the blood. All peoples over the ages have sacrificed to offer the life that is in the blood. I assume Isaiah is talking about the Chosen One being put to death, but what you quoted was in the past tense as if it has already happened; yet, you did say it was spoken 700 years ago. Perhaps it has already occurred, and we missed it."

"No, it has not taken place, but soon."

"Yet you quoted the passage in the past tense. Am I correct?"

"Exquisite observation! I believe God gave you that understanding and will supply the answer in time. Now, respond to this question for me. Have you contemplated death recently before you came down here?"

"How did you know? Just last Sabbath I considered jumping into the Pool of Bethesda and breathing in water." My mind began flowing with everything I had ever learned, but I made the mistake of answering him as if he were a teacher at the Lyceum and not a man of God. "I was taught as a boy that the Greeks and the Romans think one crosses the River Styx with Mercury's aid and goes before the three judges at the Gates of Hades, who weigh each individual's life. There will be a three-headed dog there as well to keep anyone from escaping the fiery underworld. The Egyptians believe that Thoth, the god of the moon and writing, escorts the dead to the Trial of Maat, where one's heart is weighed on a scale against a feather. If your heart is lighter than a feather, then Osiris will allow you to enter a beautiful place.

The Zoroastrians say one cross on a razor-sharp wire over the pits of Hell; and, if you are righteous enough, you will make it across into *Paradesa* or Paradise; otherwise, you fall into the fiery pits."

John threw up his hands as if tired of what I was saying. "I do not think you believe any of those stories, so why even mention them? What do you really think?"

His perceptions were correct. I had no confidence in anything the Romans, Greeks, Egyptians, or any other culture put forth. I thought for a moment on what I considered my deepest conviction regarding the subject. "Death resembles a deep sleep, for the dead bodies I have seen appear peaceful once the life has made its *exodus* from the flesh." I looked at John but could not interpret his blank expression. "What do you say?"

He finally smiled again, and a twinkle in his eyes showed me he was patiently waiting for that question. "At death, your soul and spirit leave the body and go to be with Abraham in the underworld to await the resurrection. At the resurrection, every human who has ever been will get a new body – even the wicked – because of what the Chosen One is going to do. Our spirit and soul will have a home that will never die, and we will be higher than the angels. But what determines our destination from that day forth will be what we held to be true in our hearts in this life along with our actions towards God and our fellow man determining our station for eternity. If we have believed and trusted the Chosen One, our names will be written in the Book of Life; and we will be able to enter into Yahweh's eternal presence and pleasure. You see, this life is only a place before eternity. We are here just for a short time in order to make the right faith decision. Only that decision determines which way you go on the Judgment Day. Now, the mystery is repentance. Repentance must precede that choice. True repentance is the only evidence you have made the right decision. No one can cheat his or her way into the Creator's presence without changing the way he or she presently think. The word 'sin' in the Greek language only means the distance from one point to another. We all have missed the target, and each one of us has sinned. The range of each person's sin is not a factor; but the realization that we all have sinned, great or small, that is the factor. One little sin will send you to the Lake of Fire just as quickly as a million great sins. Repentance is the key; it is the key. I tell you again, it is the key to open our way to God's presence. Remember it is because of sin that we must ask forgiveness from Yahweh, who is the one who placed us in this world.

"You seem very confident of this."

"The Redeemer, the one your mother told you about, did she not tell you to listen to His words?"

"Yes, how did you know she said that?"

"The Holy Spirit that was given to me before birth is speaking to you, not this dirty, starving man. I was born under particular circumstances as was Yeshua. Nevertheless, my purpose was to be the voice of the one crying in the wilderness to make ready the way of Yahweh to make His paths straight. *Every ravine shall be filled up, and every mountain and hill shall be brought low; and the crooked shall become straight; and the rough roads, smooth; and all flesh shall see the salvation of Yahweh.* Understand what I just said; and you will repent and trust your body, soul, and spirit to Yahweh."

John then gave me a look of great pleasure. He excitedly explained further. "On the day Moses spoke with the 'burning bush' on Mount Sinai, he asked God for His personal name since no one knew it in those days. The 'burning bush' replied, 'I Am who I Am.' You see, God's name is a verb. 'I Am' Hebrew is Yahweh. The name was rarely used after Moses's day because of the third commandment, which dictated no one should use Yahweh's name in vain. Over the years, many Jewish leaders even forbade anyone to say 'Yahweh' for fear of breaking the third commandment. Yet, when you read the Scriptures, the word Yahweh is everywhere. I would not be surprised if the name 'Yahweh' is mentioned as many as 7,000 times in the Scriptures. Many of the leaders in Israel today will actually accuse a person of blasphemy if he or she used the name Yahweh openly and publicly. They think the only time the name Yahweh is to be used is by the high priest when he is in the Holy of Holies on the Day of Atonement. Priests today privately use the word *Jehovah*, a corruption of the words Yahweh and *Adonai* woven together. You see, *Adonai* is the Hebrew word for Lord, which was the common name used for God before Moses. The two terms meshed together and produced the combined name *Jehovah*. Many think this made-up name will protect anyone from blasphemy – so they think. Yet, it seems to me, when you call the Holy One by an invented name, how can that please God? Now I would say using the name *Jehovah* would be considered blasphemy. Therefore, understand that Yahweh is God's personal name, not *Jehovah;* and Yahweh or YHWH is how it is written in the Scriptures. Should I not show honor to *Adonai* by using His personal name Yahweh as it is employed in heaven?"

I found that explanation most interesting even though I had not encountered the word *Jehovah* but would listen more carefully in the future. I decided it was now time to deliver the message from Jesus. "There is a second reason why I came to see you. I have a message for you from your cousin Yeshua."

John grabbed my shoulders and told me not to amuse myself at his expense.

"I am not making sport of you," I said. "I spoke with your cousin in Jerusalem on the past Sabbath, which was just a few days ago. He said I would be speaking with you and to tell you something. I did not think it would be so soon."

"You exchanged words with him this past Sabbath in Jerusalem?"

"Yes, at the Pool of Bethesda, right after I was thinking of ending my life. Did you not ask me if I recently thought of death? Actually, your cousin interrupted those thoughts. Then I watched him heal a man who'd been on a stretcher for 38 years."

"Glory to Yahweh! Thirty-eight years you say. That was about the time he and I were born. Was the man he healed one of the children from Bethlehem?"

"You are a prophet!" I said with astonishment excitement. "Only Yahweh would have revealed that to you!"

"Now I see that *Adonai* did send you to me, not the Devil!" He lifted his hands up as if pointing to the top of the pit. I noticed his eyes were closed, and his lips were silently moving. When he stopped, I told the story of the healing after Messina had left the pool hoping to understand something that was bothering me since I witnessed the miracle. What was troubling me was whether angels employed their powers for Yeshua when he told the man to arise. I could not say why this was an essential question for me, but at the time it was.

"What is your answer?"

Without hesitation and with utter assurance, he said, "Yeshua bypassed the stirring of the waters when the man said he had no one to help him." If John was right, Yeshua was working a new thing because he did it on the traditional day God rested. Why else would Yeshua heal on the Sabbath unless God were now creating something new? Some of the religious leaders were claiming Yeshua did the miracle in the power of the prince of the fallen angels. They based their accusations on the fact Yeshua violated the Sabbath by working on the day of rest. If the Pharisee at the Pool of Bethesda was correct, there was no hope for humankind as promised by God to Adam concerning a coming Redeemer. The rebellion that had started before the creation of man and shortly after seemed to be coming to a climax, and I desperately needed to know the truth. Did John have the truth? I had to ask this man a strange question. "You said you were Yeshua's cousin; yet, you speak as if you did not know him very well."

"That is correct; I did not know him until recently. We are related through our mothers. In the Hebrew culture, a man only comes together with the male family members, not the females. A woman when she marries leaves her family behind even though it should be the other way around. A man should leave his family when he takes a wife, but that is another subject. The way it is today, unless you live in the same village or city, you might see your maternal relatives only on a few festival days in Jerusalem. Yeshua lived in Nazareth most of his life and worked as a stonemason to support his family, especially after his adopting father died. You see, Yeshua had no human father but was raised by the carpenter-stonemason named Joseph ben Jacob."

"And you believe this?"

"Of course. My mother, who never made up stories, said Yeshua's mother Mariam came to her after Mariam's encounter with the archangel Gabriel. My father also met the same angel in the Holy Place of the Temple six months earlier who told him about my upcoming, miraculous birth. You see, my father was a Levite and a priest. I rejected the traditional work as a priest, for Yahweh had other plans for my life. It is important to remember my mother was like Abraham's wife Sarah. Both were old and barren. My mother told me many times growing up as a little boy how she prayed to be like Sarah. Finally, after my father Zacharias had his encounter with Gabriel, she conceived with my *Abba;* and I was the result. I was born six months before my cousin Yeshua. Mariam, Yeshua's mother spent perhaps three months with my mother, following her angelic visitation. This was while I was still in the womb. Once I was born, Mariam returned to Joseph ben Jacob, the man who had paid the bridal fee for Mariam as his young wife. The marriage had not been consummated because Mariam had not entered into puberty when Joseph had paid the bridal payment to Mariam's father, Heli of Nazareth."

"There is a story in Roman legend that a vestal virgin was raped by the god Mars and gave birth to Romulus and Remus. Understand I believe this story to be a myth. But the story goes that she was to be buried alive, the penalty according to Roman law when a vestal virgin has had carnal knowledge. The Babylonians believed that Tammuz was conjured by the priestess Semiramis by a sunbeam. The Assyrians have a story that King Sennacherib's mother was a virgin. There are dozens of such stories, but the most recent would be Alexander the Macedonian who said Zeus impregnated his mother Olympias through a snake. Is it possible your mother's cousin made up the virgin birth story just to protect herself from being stoned to death? Does not the *Torah* state that a girl who has a child with another man other than her husband or husband-to-be is to be stoned to death."

"Satan has lied about the virgin birth throughout history just as you have quoted. He hates the truth. He is the father of lies and has counterfeited many prophecies in the Scriptures. Why is it that Moses warns in the *Torah* about false prophets and teachers? Many will come to deceive the multitudes. Did I not tell you that what a person believes will determine their eternity? The war against the truth has been waged by the Dragon since the Garden of Eden. That is why my message was only for people to change their minds or repent, for the Kingdom of God is at hand. If a person believes a lie, then they first need to change their mind or repent. The truth is Yeshua is the one and only virgin born Redeemer, not Alexander, Tammuz, Sennacherib, nor any others in the past. Do you not understand Satan, the old dragon, would know about the very first prophecy Yahweh gave to Adam and Eve? Yes, the virgin birth was the first prophecy given after the fall when Adam and Eve disobeyed Yahweh in the Garden of Eden. That prophecy was a promise made that a 'seed of a woman' would come and bring the remedy for the sin dilemma. There are many prophecies throughout the Scriptures as a sign of the Righteous One, the coming Messiah; but the very first prophecy is the most powerful of them all. Even the Prophet Isaiah spoke concerning a virgin giving birth to a son and his name would be *Emmanuel* or God with us. Yeshua is Yahweh in a human body. How profound is that? Now, what was His message to me?"

John, or his Hebrew name Yochannan, was so wholly relaxed with who he believed Yeshua to be that it made my visit seem like an irrational dream. I still recalled Yeshua's words and remembered him smiling simply after he told me I would soon visit the Baptist. Jesus never revealed an ounce of doubt in who Yochannan was. Yochannan now had the same firm conviction of himself as Jesus showed me at the Pool of Bethesda. I decided to delay no longer in the message I was sent to deliver.

"It was a straightforward message. He said to tell you the Kingdom of Heaven is being preached, and he heals the sick and casts out demons. Also, he said, 'I raise the dead and cleanse the lepers.'"

John smiled behind his matted beard and repeatedly bobbed his head up and down indicating that he understood. He seemed so excited that he felt he had to get to his feet.

"Is that all he said?" asked John stroking his beard and looking down at me.

I, too, stood and asked, "Yes, what does it mean to you?"

"It confirms my question that I sent to him, which he has not even received. I sent a message by my disciples just yesterday. I am looking for that very answer. It means a lot to me. I am sure my own disciples will return soon with the same message, but thank you for your faithfulness anyway," said John. "Now I will ask you a question."

I leaned against the cold, smooth wall now holding the palm light in my left hand. I noticed that I had not used my left hand or arm since Marius had injured it with his wooden sword. I took the lamp into my right hand and used it to inspect my left arm. There were no bruises, and it felt normal. All the swelling was gone that had been there when I had held the Passover basket coming down the ladder. It was a miracle, or did it just heal on its own? I did not know when it happened, but it was completely recovered. It was just like the red rash leaving Hector's arm when we spoke of John the Baptist in Hector's stone house. John was watching me without any expression on his face. I smiled a little and said, "Ask what you will."

"Did you actually commit the crime of murder?"

"Yes."

"Why?"

"Revenge. The one I killed murdered my mother."

"And she died on the same day she told you about the Redeemer?"

I nodded my head and ended by looking down at the darkness by my feet.

"An eye for an eye and a blood grudge I am guessing," he concluded. "But the Scriptures say only a king or the government has the right to capital punishment and not the individual. 'Vengeance is mine, says Yahweh.' He takes care of all the injustices for us if we just let it be. Seeking revenge is like drinking poison. You think you are hurting the one you hate, but it is you who actually suffers."

"Well, I did not drink poison; but I understand your metaphor. I will be captured sooner than later. I think you should take your freedom from me; and, besides, how do you know this is not God's plan? You still have many years left to declare the message of repentance."

"It is tempting, young man; but it would be wrong. You are the only one who can take care of the task of declaring repentance. You are the one who will live a long life. Soon you will begin to live for what cannot be seen over living for what can be seen, that being this world. Understand this, and then you shall begin to live. Regarding your offer, I could not live with myself if I allowed you to take my place down here. I now know that you have a good heart, but I will accept whatever sacrifice Yeshua makes. You see, Yeshua has already declared that I must decrease while He increases. Yeshua's ministry still has some time left to lead the nation of God's Chosen People back to repentance. Repentance is what will save me and you, thus says Yahweh. Because you have a good heart, He wants me to tell you that the arm you keep looking at was healed by the Spirit of Yahweh. He wants me to also tell you that the power of His Spirit passed from me to heal your arm earlier when I placed my hand on your shoulder."

"When did that happen?"

"When you convinced me you were not an agent of the dragon, and I touched your shoulder before I sat. It was then I felt the Spirit jump from me to heal your arm. I believe the arm was injured by an evil force that you have been battling since your mother went to wait with the others for the resurrection of the dead."

This God of the Jews had to be the Creator. I now began to relax and felt myself returning to the mindset I had when talking to Rabbi Issachar in his grape arbor at the back of his house in the 14th District. It was then I felt a horrible dread come over me, and I said something that came from deep within me. "Herod is going to kill you!" I said this with conviction, and he looked as if my words came from the lips of God. "Are you sure you do not want to leave now and allow me to take your place?"

"Whatever happens is God's will."

"Don't we have the freedom to choose?"

"I spent half my life in the *scriptorium* of my village. During those days, I memorized the Law, the Prophets, and the Psalms. My father, a Levite, served as a priest in Jerusalem during his twice-yearly rotation; and I was to assume his place once I reached the age of 30. As I grew older, I knew what I had to do; and it did not mean going to the Temple schools in Jerusalem. I was to be the *voice in the wilderness making straight the paths.* My purpose was to introduce the Lamb of God to the world and then decrease. I have known my place in Yahweh's plan for as far back as I can remember. I am now satisfied that I have completed my journey, and it is almost over. There might have been more to my purpose had the people accepted their Messiah, but they have rejected him. I also know that could change, but it is very remote." John became silent for a moment and then smiled the biggest smile since I entered his dark world. "But I was permitted to see what all the other prophets longed to see. Yes, the time has come for me to decrease; and Yeshua is to increase. My favorite psalm that sustains me above all others I will give to you. Listen, and tell me what is important to Yahweh. For some reason, I learned only this one psalm in the Greek from the Septuagint. I will quote it to you in Greek. I never knew why I memorized it in Greek until this moment. It is for you to hear in your native tongue and understand."

He gazed towards his feet as he drew the psalm from his memory. When it seemed to have arrived, he lifted his eyes up with a slight smile in the lamplight. The vacant look turned into a brilliant, faraway acknowledgment of recognition of something extraordinary far in the distance. In a haunting voice, he began quoting the psalm in Common Attic or *Koine* Greek using the Alexandrian dialect of a Hellenistic Jew. The Alexandrian dialect was something I learned when I was questioned by an instructor at the Lyceum, who was using the same vernacular on the last day of my final exams, the very day I met Eli's uncle on the Acropolis in Athens.

"*Bless Yahweh, O my soul; and all that is in me, bless His holy name! Bless Yahweh, O my soul; and forget not all His kindnesses in forgiving all our offenses, in curing all our diseases, in redeeming our life from the pit, in crowning us with mercy and compassion, who satisfies our desires with good things, in renewing our youth like that of the eagle. Yahweh executes mercy and judgments for all that are oppressed. He made known His ways to Moses, His acts to the children of Israel. Yahweh is compassionate and kind, long-suffering, and full of mercy. He will not always be angry; neither will He be wrathful forever. Yahweh had not dealt with us according to our sins nor rewarded us, according to our iniquities. For as the heaven is high above the earth, so is the greatness of His love for those who fear Him. As far as the east is from the west, so far has our transgressions been removed by Him. Just as a father has compassion on his children, so Yahweh has compassion on those who fear Him. He knows our bodies; He is mindful that we are but dust. As for man, his days are like grass; as a flower of the field, so he flourishes. When the wind has passed over it, it is no more; and its place acknowledges it no longer. But the loving kindness of Yahweh is from everlasting to everlasting on those who fear, like His goodness to their children's children, as long as they keep His covenant and remember to obey His precepts. Yahweh has fixed His throne in the heavens; His Empire is overall. Bless Yahweh, all His angels, mighty in strength, performing His bidding, attentive to His word of command. Bless Yahweh, all His angelic armies, servants to enforce His will. Bless Yahweh, all His creatures in every part of His Empire! Bless Yahweh, O my soul.*"

John now looked inquiringly at me to see whether I understood. He waited very patiently for my response. Zeno would have swatted my hands for being this slow. But this man was less volatile. Finally, I realized what he wanted to hear.

"The Psalmist talks about remembering and obeying. But I see the essential element is in the words 'those who fear Him.'"

"Splendid! Those who fear Him obviously have faith in Him, but to fear requires us to first repent. Is not fearing Him the first step of us creatures in these frail bodies? We must also act on that faith, and our reward will be everlasting life with Him. Do you see and understand that without faith you cannot please Him? It is all about faith in who He is. He is loving but also can be longsuffering like allowing me to languish here in this hole for almost a year and a half. There is a judgment that comes but not until there has been time for repentance. That was my job, to proclaim repentance and to prepare oneself for the coming of the Lord God Yahweh. That is the message of the Kingdom of Yahweh. You, Venustus Vetallus, must repent and turn your life towards Him. Remember it is only Yahweh who can put you into the Lake of Fire for eternity. No one else has that power, not Satan nor man nor the man who had me placed in this pit. Fear and give reverence to the one who made you and has a purpose for your life. Fear only Him, and you will fear nothing else as long as you live."

"Yeshua said you would tell me that."

"What?"

"That I should repent."

"I am unsurprised He shared such a thing. A blind man can sense your problem. Your bondage is by your own iniquity. Turn to Yahweh, and pray for repentance! He will hear you; He will heal you but only on that day when this repentance comes from your heart. Then will His healing hand come upon you, and He will drain the poison of bitterness consuming you. Do you have anything else for me?"

"Yes. Why did one-third of the angels in heaven rebel?"

"You gave me the answer just a moment ago."

I thought over my words and then answered, "Fear – it has to do with fear? The angels stopped fearing Yahweh?"

"Only the Spirit of God could have shared that with you. That is the correct answer. The demon world seeks to achieve what Yahweh desired us humans to hold at the beginning of time. Extinguish the fear of God from the hearts of men, and they will worship the fallen ones. You see, that is all this struggle we call life is about. Do you fear Yahweh, Venustus Vetallus?"

I kept silent not wanting to speak and reveal the terror and pain his words had wrenched from the very center of my being. The truth was I did not fear God, and I believed John knew this.

"Then there is no more to say. I am now to partake my Passover meal alone. The *maror* (or bitter herbs) means a great deal to me this night. Maybe I will see you again in this world. I am sure of it if there is collective repentance by the Chosen Ones regarding Yeshua."

"I would like that very much," I said; and my voice sounded normal considering what I was thinking. Only my throat was parched, which was a result of what I took to be a dread of my realization. The simple truth I just learned was I was no different than the band of angels that did not fear their Creator. I lacked the underlying fear of Yahweh. Perhaps all those years at the Lyceum had corrupted that little spark even children have regarding the Creator. The lies of the Evil Deva had filled my mind with myths and rubbish. Even the histories I had learned were all one sided and slanted. I needed to wash in the Word of God. I could see that John had cleaned himself over the years by just memorizing one psalm. Why was I so stubborn? Why would I not return to Yahweh after all that I had witnessed? The state I was in must have something to do with the lack of repentance on my part. My heart was as hard as flint and the conviction of a lie. That lie was Yahweh would not forgive me. It was a lie from the halls of Hell, but it was a stronghold that I could not shake at this time. I may have had one foot in the Kingdom of God, but God wanted me in all the way. To do this required a form of death to this world, not a physical death but a spiritual death to the things and lies of this fallen world. Years later I would learn something that would mean a great deal to me. *'Love not this world, he who loves this world system does not have the love of the Father in him.'*

John nodded as if reading my mind. He then covered his head with his blanket and began to pray over his meal still wrapped in the basket I had brought down. I noticed he was not facing towards the direction of Jerusalem. I did not ask him why, and this one departure from a ritualistic act gave me great hope. My guess was I was looking at the only spiritual light left in this world, and his cousin was possibly the real Redeemer my mother told me about on the day she died.

Thus ended my first and last visit to John. There never was a collective repentance by the Chosen Children of Israel; and, therefore, I never saw John again in this world. I would have enjoyed knowing him better and longer. His words seemed to give purpose beyond himself. His manner was friendly with an unfathomable concern that his listeners understood the complexities of God in the simplest terms. In just a few moments, he gave me enough to carry for years or, for that matter, eternity. I did not know all that he was saying about "fear only God," but it often sustained me years later as did his lecture on repentance. I wanted to repent immediately, but it would still be some years before I was finally broken. For before honor is humility, and that frequently comes with great pain. Yeshua had been correct when he told me at the Pool of Bethesda: "After the son of man has been lifted up and exalted, then you will understand true repentance." All I could understand in that dark, smelly hole was a fraction of what I had heard. That night I did write down all Yochannan the Baptist said. I always returned to his words for the remainder of my life. I kept this sheet of papyrus, which held John's words, between my heart and my cuirass. All the other sheets I maintained in the leather tube hidden in the barracks wall in Jerusalem, but not this page.

It was not long before I was out of the pit. When I called to Amcheck, the pole ladder appeared in the hole. I said no more to John, nor did he say anything more to me. After I was out, both Amcheck and his one-handed friend both laughed when I said I enjoyed the visit. They began calling me "Little Yoc." I frowned but inwardly took the name as a compliment.

Amcheck and I left the dungeons, and together we burned my tunic as well as scrubbed the stink from my black leather cuirass. Amcheck found a new red tunic in a storeroom, and I put it on after I placed my cuirass next to my cot in the soldiers' barracks for it to dry. Before sleep that night, I used some ink I found and a sheet of papyrus along with a palm lamp and recorded all that I could remember. It was late when I finally found sleep, which ended one of the most remarkable days of my life.

TO BE CONTINUED IN VOLUME II